THE UNDYING LIGHT

THE
UNDYING LIGHT

STEPHEN ZIMMER

SEVENTH STAR PRESS

Cover art and illustrations: Matthew Perry
Cover art in this book copyright © 2014 Matthew Perry & Seventh Star
Press, LLC.

Editor: Amanda DeBord

Published by Seventh Star Press, LLC.

ISBN Number: 978-1-941706-08-4

Seventh Star Press
www.seventhstarpress.com
info@seventhstarpress.com

Publisher's Note:
The Undying Light is a work of fiction. All names, characters, and places
are the product of the author's imagination, used in fictitious manner.
Any resemblances to actual persons, places, locales, events, etc. are purely
coincidental.

Printed in the United States of America

First Edition

DEDICATION

.

To the Author of my own life's story. I may find it very difficult to travel the road at times and weather the storms, but my hope is that the story You have in store for me is a neverending one that takes an upswing in a much better place, one where I rejoin the rest of the many loveable and good-hearted characters who have had such an amazing part to play in this Tale of Life

To my mother and my father, the greatest gifts I've ever received. You may be gone from this world, but you are a major part of me always and forever. I love you more every day.

To my sister, for continuing to move forward.

ACKNOWLEDGEMENTS

The road to the release of *The Undying Light* has been the most difficult period of my life to date. I must first acknowledge my beloved mother, who passed from this world in June of 2013. I would not be who I am without her. Her strength, faith, and heart inspire me to keep moving forward, onward and upward. I can never heal within this world from the loss of those I love, but I can try to honor them. This is the case with my mother, who along with my father's passing represent the two heaviest blows I've suffered. Though I may stumble and fall at times I can strive to become the person she saw within me

I would like to thank Amanda DeBord, my editor for this series, and Matthew Perry, who has done the cover art and illustration for this series, for keeping our Rising Dawn Saga team intact. The work you have done is deeply appreciated and I hope we are able to continue forward to the grand finale!

I would like to extend a special thank you to Susan Roddey and Terry Bentley. In the darkness, I've found myself drifting far, and the both of you gave me tethers to hang onto. Susan, you encouraged me to get back to writing full force, which has given me a refuge in the midst of an ongoing storm. You were the one person who understood what I have been missing and what mattered so much to me, and bothered to tune in and stay on me to get going again with new writing Terry, the photo session meant so much to me and I am still amazed when I think about the song that played while we were doing the shoot. I won't forget it. It mattered more than you might ever realize.

Thank you to Jennifer Hendren for letting me keep my home at Joseph Beth Booksellers of Lexington. Such a wonderful tradition continues, one that includes Brooke Raby, Michael Cruikshank, and now you. It is a true honor to have Joseph Beth as my bookstore home.

As always, I thank my reader-friends. Without readers, an author isn't much and you make all the difference in keeping the fire burning to go forward. I will always give you my best effort in all I do. I hope I can both entertain you and provide you with some light for the tougher times in this world. This is not an easy journey and I thank you for being a part of mine.

"Courage is not simply one of the virtues, but the form of every virtue at the testing point."
-C. S. Lewis

"Sometimes the heart sees what is invisible to the eye."
-H. Jackson Brown, Jr.

"Where there is love there is life."
-Mahatma Gandhi

"Those who make peaceful revolution impossible will make violent revolution inevitable."
-John F. Kennedy

"Government is not reason; it is not eloquent; it is force. Like fire, it is a dangerous servant and a fearful master."
-George Washington

"We are fast approaching the stage of the ultimate inversion: the stage where the government is free to do anything it pleases, while the citizens may act only by permission; which is the stage of the darkest periods of human history, the stage of rule by brute force."
-Ayn Rand

"Only those who will risk going too far can possibly find out how far one can go."
-T. S. Eliot

"Only a real risk tests the reality of a belief."
-C.S. Lewis

"Courage is being scared to death... and saddling up anyway."
-John Wayne

SECTION I

SECTION 1

GREGORY

A sprawling forest of concrete and steel loomed across the river from Gregory Andreas. An eerie pall shrouded the urban metropolis once home to well over two million people. Lavish football and baseball stadiums once filled with the roars of many thousands now lay silent as mausoleums.

Losantiville was a prime gateway into the north from the border of Venorterra. The Adena river marked the boundary line between two contrasting provinces; one held by rebel forces, and the other still firmly in the clutches of the UCAS government.

No traffic crossed the great river anymore. All of the bridges in the vicinity had been knocked out by the retreating UCAS forces, consolidating their positions after insurrection swept like a brushfire through the south and midwest. What remained of the bridges made it look as if some giant of legend had ripped the crossings right out.

Gregory peered across the water from a well-concealed position. The caution was necessary, as the city was far from unoccupied. Large numbers of well-equipped UCAS troops were dug in on the opposite side. Though no major battles had occurred yet, there had already been a few casualties as snipers from both sides exacted bloody tolls.

The UCAS had tried bringing a few drones close during the first days of the tense standoff, but several were shot out of the sky in short order. Advanced, portable, and shoulder-fired, the surface-to-air missiles allocated by General Robert Jackson for the border areas proved more than capable deterrents to drone activity. Most of the latest model missiles were in the hands of military forces from the south, but a few had been given over to highly-organized militias and carefully chosen irregulars, to assist in the ongoing fight.

To Gregory, General Jackson was a realist. The existing southern military forces could not adequately watch and defend the lengthy borders of the breakaway provinces such as Venorterra. The irregulars and militias were serving a crucial role in a precarious time, when an active state of war existed.

The general was wise enough to take advantage of the large

numbers of volunteers available in the region, a great number of whom were ex-military like Gregory. Volunteers were expected to fend for themselves for quartering and food. Though the general did what he could to get some additional supplies to them, the militias and irregulars did not put undue pressure on already strained resources available to the military.

Heightening Gregory's wariness was the hard fact that anything could happen at any moment, whether a raid, an air strike, or a full-scale invasion. For the first time in a long, long while, the government of the UCAS had made a formal declaration of war.

Not even invasions and occupations of several foreign nations over the past few decades had spurred the UCAS government to adhere to the Grand Charter in that regard. In a twist of strange irony, the withdrawal of consent to UCAS authority by the cluster of southern and midwestern provinces had evidently inspired the UCAS to follow, even if for just a moment, the provisions of the Grand Charter regarding war declarations.

In Gregory's eyes, that declaration was far more a function of political theater for UCAS audiences than it was any heartfelt sign of change or repentance regarding the government's persistent loathing for the Grand Charter. The freedoms embraced by the founding document were still being shredded and trampled each and every day in the UCAS, with its martial law, massive surveillance, and the imposition of the entrapping, shackling Living ID.

Those grievous violations of rights had been stopped and rolled back all across the southern provinces by the will of the people living there. Like so many of the irregulars, Gregory held a firm conviction of what he was fighting for.

Gregory would resist the former regime and the evils it had insidiously cultivated to his dying breath. The authorities in control of the UCAS had betrayed everything that he embraced and took an oath for, when he had first become a marine so many years before. His conscience held no misgivings. It was the breakaway provinces that were the defenders of freedom and the principles underlying the Grand Charter.

The sharp crackle of gunfire sounded in the deepening night.

The tone of it told Gregory that the weapon was a 30-06 rifle, most likely someone in one of the militias taking a potshot at some military target across the river.

"Ready to go?"

Gregory turned his head at the voice, and saw the stocky, thick-bearded man that he had been expecting to see. He grinned at Jack Morgan. "You are later than I expected. Are the Iron Grizzlies in hibernation?"

Jack smirked at Gregory's remark. "Had to rouse up all the boys and girls goin' on this little foray here," he replied in a deep, gravely voice. "A few of them strayed, waitin' for the rain to fall."

"Got everyone together then?" Gregory asked.

Jack nodded.

"Cloud cover and rain?" Gregory countered, raising an eyebrow.

"All good," Jack replied.

"Then I say let's get you across the water," Gregory said, walking away from his observation point.

They left the room and continued through the building to the outside, exiting at the rear. Lights were being kept to a minimum, so the streets were draped in dense shadows that made it seem as if the town was in a deep slumber.

Few civilians remained in the area. There had been no mandatory evacuations. Each homeowner made their own personal choice of whether to leave the area or not. Most had chosen to go live elscwhere, or take up a place in one of the temporary refugee camps that had cropped up a little farther south.

After a ten-minute walk, Gregory and Jack came to a large open space being used as a staging area. Within it were a few flatbed trailers pulled by truck cabs. Rows of motorcycles were arrayed on the trailers, about thirty in all, beads of water glistening in the touch of the light rain that was falling.

The bikers to whom the motorcycles belonged were milling all about the area. They were a tough-looking assemblage of men and women, all of them armed with an assortment of semi-automatic and automatic rifles.

"See you in a few, I need to go check on a couple of things with the boys," Jack remarked. He strode over towards the trucks, leaving Gregory standing at the edge of the clear ground.

"Hey Gregory! I got one!" a younger-sounding voice with a thick southern accent called out to him.

Turning his head, Gregory saw Jameson walking up briskly, with a proud expression lighting up his face. In his right hand, the blond-haired twenty-year-old carried his .308 caliber semi-automatic rifle, with a scope mounted on top.

His left hand held onto what looked like a small robotic toy. It was anything but a child's plaything, as Gregory knew from his first glance at the metallic object.

"The sensor y'all gave us worked just great," Jameson said, eyeing the small drone. "This little son of a bitch stood out big time in the night. No worries, I put an end to its visit pretty quick."

"You'll be collecting some bounty on that one for sure. Cost the UCAS a pretty penny too. Those are pricey devices. How many shots did it take to disable it?" Gregory asked.

"Just one," the youth replied with a grin. "But ya know what? I had almost given up on finding one tonight."

"They're out there, believe me," Gregory said. "In the air, and on the ground. We just need to get as many of them as we can. You and the others are doing a great job."

At his words of commendation, the young man straightened up a little higher, and his smile spread a little wider. When such comments came from Gregory, everyone knew they were not idle praise.

Jameson and a slew of other younger men from the rural areas of Venorterra, used to shooting and hunting on a regular basis, served a definite purpose in taking out enemy drones wherever they could be found. A concentrated watch and lookout was kept up, wherever there were concentrations of rebel military forces, such as in the town of Taylorsville.

"Thank you sir," Jameson said. "Just doin' our best to contribute and all."

"And you are all doing a great job," Gregory replied firmly.

"Think you can bring us along on some missions, or patrols?" Jameson asked, a little hesitantly.

Gregory could hear the eagerness in the youth's voice. He knew Jameson wanted to go along on the patrols ranging across the countryside, but those forays held the most danger by far. Enemy probes and incursions of operatives had lethal results for both sides whenever the militia patrols came across them.

Nevertheless, Jameson had showed good discipline on a consistent basis, and he had to get experience at some point. "I'll get you out with us shortly. Don't be in such a hurry; it isn't all it's cracked up to be," Gregory chuckled, though his words were only partly in jest. Jameson truly had no idea just how ugly war could get.

"Thank you, thank you very much sir," Jameson replied quickly, with a spark of excitement in his eyes.

"Well, you'd better get going, and claim your bounty, Jameson. I've got some business tonight to focus on," Gregory said, shaking his head, and giving the youth a firm pat on the shoulder.

"Yes sir!" the young man replied, his voice running with zeal as he nodded to Gregory and headed onward.

Gregory could not stifle the small grin that lingered on his face at seeing the young fellow's enthusiasm, even if there was a bittersweet aspect to it. He had once been much more like Jameson himself, before overseas tours had brought him face to face with a much greater darkness.

Though he doubted it possible, he hoped Jameson's eyes would not behold the same awful things that Gregory's had. There were some scars that ran far too deep to heal.

The grin fading, Gregory looked around and saw that the raiding party was fully assembled. He started across the ground, making his way to the trucks.

"It's time, Jack," Gregory commented, interrupting a conversation the other man was having with one of the drivers.

"Alright, let's get this show on the road," Jack replied.

Together, Jack and Gregory signaled the truck drivers to fire up their engines. As the air filled with the deep rumbles of truck motors, the men and women gathered climbed aboard the trailers to ride along with their bikes.

Gregory rode in the cab of the lead truck. Its lights remained off, like the others in the convoy, as the drivers were wearing sets of night-vision goggles.

Despite the rain and thick clouds, no chances could be taken in regards to enemy drones. Sensors could pick up flashlights from a great distance, and vehicles going down a road stood out glaringly in the darkness. Thermal sensors would detect the small convoy no matter what, but it was a good practice to conceal themselves as much as they could.

The trucks lumbered down the road paralleling the course of the river, and Gregory became lost in his thoughts. So much had happened over the last few months.

A nascent resistance had been empowered by the defections of many military units, including several entire divisions. Gregory had experienced that unexpected boon himself when he and other irregulars had been besieging a federal detainment camp. General Jackson had showed up with a huge armored column, and pledged support in liberating the detainment facility, the vanguard rocks of a huge avalanche that followed swiftly.

A swathe of provinces, while not yet joined together as a new nation, had seceded from the UCAS. While the breakaway provinces did not harbor as much military strength as the UCAS still held, there was more than enough strength in the defections to give the old regime pause.

Following the liberation of the detainment camp, and after meeting General Jackson, Gregory and his brother Benjamin had headed north with a large movement of volunteers. They made their way to the most fragile zone; the border area between the breakaway provinces and the reduced territory of the UCAS.

Thankfully, the full fury of the UCAS had not yet been unleashed, as the regime had to lick its own wounds and take account of unexpected losses. Both sides entrenched, and began engaging in low-level skirmishing and raiding.

Gregory knew in his gut that a much larger hammer would fall from the UCAS at some point. But for the time being, the southern military, allied militias, and irregulars had to do everything possible to disrupt their enemy and gain information.

He was glad his brother had chosen to come north with him. New police forces had quickly formed up in Venorterra, but Benjamin wanted to be with his brother during the turmoil.

With the relative autonomy granted to the militias and irregulars by those such as General Jackson, Gregory and Benjamin were able to put their skills and ideas to good use. The approaching raid Gregory was helping facilitate was one such example.

There was no mistaking that the UCAS would be well aware of any concentration of heavy military equipment on the part of the rebels, but a small contingent of motorcycles was not likely to attract too much attention. Yet anyone familiar with special forces and guerilla tactics knew that low numbers could still wreak a lot of havoc on an unsuspecting enemy.

"Here's the rendezvous point," the driver remarked, breaking Gregory's train of thought, and slowing the truck down before pulling off to the side.

It took some time to offload all the bikes. The men and women who would be riding them checked their gear and weapons one more time. Gregory saw them donning cloaks, and knew they were not just for protection from the elements. The anti-thermal material of the helped them evade.

Gregory searched out his newer friend among them. He located the gruff leader of the bikers right where he expected him to be; at his bike.

"There you are," Gregory said, walking up. "Ready for our kind of biker rally?"

"We're ready. Just don't expect us to look as impressive as the bike rallies you remember. Covering up the chrome wasn't a small sacrifice, you know," Jack remarked with a chuckle, looking up at Gregory.

Once bright and shiny, and prepped to gleam radiantly in the sunlight, all of the bikes had been well-masked for their new purpose. Their riders did not dress much differently, but they were not about to head into enemy territory with highly reflective surfaces, in a climate where such a thing could mean the different between dying or surviving.

"No, I know it wasn't," Gregory acknowledged. "And when you

can get them all shiny and polished again, I think I'm going to get one myself. I've put off having a bike for far too long."

"It would be great to go riding with you, marine," Jack replied, with a grin.

Gregory clasped the strong, callused hand of the biker, and looked him in the eyes. He expressed the wish of one soldier to another. "Be seeing you soon enough, Jack."

"You got it, and we'll drink a few beers together when I return," the other man replied with a smirk, though the look in his eyes reflected the same earnest sentiments as Gregory. "Don't need shiny bikes to do that."

"Looking forward to it already," Gregory replied.

Letting Jack focus on his final preparations, he strode away from the biker. He made his way over to where some other vehicles, which had not been part of the convoy, were parked in the darkness a short distance from the trucks. The side door of an SUV was open, revealing the conspicuous form of Chuck inside with his ham radio gear.

Standing outside the SUV were Consuela Gonzalez and Dante Johnson. The two were sharp contrasts in appearance. Consuela was a fairly attractive Hispanic woman of shorter stature, while Dante was a muscular, broad-shouldered black man that towered over her. Of the group who had come north with Gregory and Benjamin, Consuela and Dante had consistently proved to be two of his best and most dependable.

"Good evening to the two of you. I figure things are pretty quiet on this side of the river," Gregory greeted the pair.

"Nice and relaxed, just the way we like it," Consuela replied with a smile. "Chuck's gotten reports in from all up and down the river."

"That big militia out of Franklin Province is taking part," Dante said. "Over a thousand of them. Helping watch the waterfront."

"We've probably got more irregulars up here than what General Jackson has deployed in military assets," Gregory remarked, smiling as he thought of the ironies inherent in the situation.

The UCAS had always worked relentlessly to recruit, dangling large enlistment bonuses in front of young men and women from poorer areas with few job prospects. Now, with no offers of money involved, the mere idea of defending freedom had men and women flocking from near and far to risk their lives.

Gregory walked over, and leaned into the open door of the SUV. He grinned at Chuck, who had his usual nervous expression and display of fidgetiness.

"How's it goin' in here, Chuck?" Gregory asked. "Everything okay?"

"Oh … real good Gregory … really good," Chuck replied with a polite smile.

In his way, the man had even more to overcome than most people, especially with the extreme anxiety he incessantly contended with. Gregory had to admit he had come to really like the guy, and his expertise in ham radio operation and electronics in general had been invaluable to the irregulars.

"Consuela says we've got extensive participation up and down the river," Gregory asked.

"All over," Chuck replied, with an excited gleam in his eyes. "They've all checked in … using the code of course. All up and down the water. Very strong militia presence."

"Good, then our people providing the cover will have a little extra protection," Gregory said. "Which, by the way, should be taking place pretty shortly."

"Just a couple more minutes," Chuck responded with a hesitant edge. He quickly added, "According to my time."

"Are you having fun yet?" Gregory grinned, patting Chuck on the back. "That's the main thing, you know."

"Oh … yeah," Chuck replied, though it was clear he did not really know what to say in response.

Gregory chuckled, but the mirth faded as his voice took on a serious tone. "You are a good man, Chuck. Keep up the excellent work. We need guys like you to win the day," He patted Chuck on the back one more time.

"Thank you … sir," Chuck replied, his eyes sparkling a little brighter.

Every word Gregory spoke was true, as it took all kinds of individuals to prevail in a modern war. Gregory also knew that individuals like Chuck needed a little extra reassurance from time to time, and he could see the anxiety ebbing in the man in the aftermath of his praise.

Leaving Chuck with his beloved electronics, Gregory walked back over towards Dante and Consuela. They eyed him expectantly. "Time to get this show on the road," Dante remarked.

Gregory glanced down at his watch, which now read twenty-one hundred hours. "Yes it certainly is. In fact, it looks like it is time to start things right now."

They waited a few more minutes, until the first signs of the next phase of the operation unfurled. Up and down the riverbank, large volumes of smoke were released. In minutes, it was as if a thick fog had settled over many sections of the river for several miles in either direction. The smoke would help obfuscate the movements of the rebels, and make it harder to identify the true crossing point for the raid.

Large pontoon boats were slid down into the water from where they had been concealed along the river bank. Special platforms, designed to hold two bikes each, end to end, were accessible by ramps that could be pulled onto the modified boats.

Gregory watched the riders and their bikes as they were loaded up and then ferried across the river, through the thick layers of smoke. A grin sprouted upon his face, as it was more than a little amusing seeing all of the riders wearing night-vision goggles and the thermal-resistant cloaks, the latter draped over backs bulging with packs filled with materials for the ongoing mission.

For so many individuals who were fiercely independent in nature, the unanimity on display was undeniably humorous. Yet even the bikers were not so foolhardy in their zeal to increase the risks of being detected and targeted by lethal drones. The sound of their engines would not be stifled, but no headlights would announce their approach.

The raid itself would be like several others before it. Destroying bridges, attacking small checkpoints, and blowing up power stations, the bikers had spread considerable mayhem behind enemy lines. Moving fast, they hit designated targets, and then got out before the enemy had much of a chance to organize and engage them.

Over the past few months, the bikers had become a dedicated guerilla force, and the damage they inflicted on the enemy was effective. Jack Morgan's force had quickly become one that General Jackson was more than happy to oblige with intelligence and extra material support.

The seceded provinces were still working out ways to coordinate military efforts with each other. As things stood, the rebel military forces were spread thin across a border that was impossible to ward entirely.

Incursions from both sides were a foregone conclusion. But when raids and strikes could be conducted by irregulars, whether militias or groups like the bikers under Jack Morgan, it meant that General Jackson's troops could concentrate more of their focus on monitoring and defending the boundaries.

Jack Morgan's bikers also deployed small drones for the rebel military, another strategic benefit of the punitive raids. Every edge that could be gained in intelligence gathering was potentially the difference in whether the UCAS could be fended off or not.

The present evening's raid would be focused on deploying a few of those drones, as well as blowing up a coal-fired power plant that was not actively in operation. A fair amount of explosive material had been gathered and would be put to quick purpose when the bikers arrived on the site. Their departure after setting the charges would be followed by a parade of detonations that no person in the area would overlook.

The site was likely unprotected, but the choice of target was not frivolous. Though the UCAS's environmental and energy policies had resulted in droves of coal-fired power plants being shut down prior to the outbreak of hostilities, everyone knew it was only a matter of time before the UCAS began making use of them again. A pre-emptive strike to reduce one of the power plants to rubble would take yet another useful asset away from the UCAS.

Gregory took a deep breath, and stared into the fog covering the river, the light patter of rain falling on his camouflage-pattern jacket. Suddenly, a sense of loneliness overcame him.

There was nothing to do now but wait, and be prepared to assist if there was any kind of hot pursuit when the bikers came back, if they came back at all. That was the hard reality about conducting various missions and fighting wars. There was no guaranteeing that anyone would be coming back alive.

In a couple of hours, Gregory would know one way or another what kind of night it would be. He just hoped that the later stages of the night would see him sharing a cold beer or two with Jack Morgan, with the two men talking about a successful incursion with zero casualties.

FRIEDRICH

Standing on one of the small islands dotting the vast expanse, Friedrich gazed in tranquil wonder upon the glassy, sparkling surface of a cerulean sea. The calm waters gleamed with a luminous quality that did not exist in his former world.

Reaching the island was easy enough. The waters were warm and soothing. Crystal clear, they contained a host of incredible sights just beneath the surface.

Sea grasses glowed with celestial light from within, swaying elegantly, as if responding to some music that only they were attuned to. Spectacular reef-like structures appearing to be fashioned of a spectrum of gemstones dazzled any soul who looked upon them.

Moving through the grasses and reefs were an array of exotic-looking fish and other creatures. Conspicuously, there was not even a hint of the violence permeating the oceans and waters of the material world.

The sea dwellers around Friedrich were not engaged in a furious struggle for survival, but rather a harmonious celebration of life. There was no longer any need for the larger to consume the smaller, as all the creatures were sustained perpetually by the Great Throne's Light.

The nature of the sea's inhabitants was one that gave the Exiles in the Middle Lands a hint of the wonders that lay ahead for all of them, beyond the gates of the White City.

As Friedrich and his companions had discovered long before, the inhabitants of the waters were playful and without fear. Everything from sea horses to dolphins approached and interacted with those swimming through the waters.

On his swim out to the islands, one of the dolphins had deftly maneuvered beneath him. The creature had gotten him to hold onto its fins. Pulling him swiftly through the water, the dolphin had taken him most of the way out to the first island.

The ride had been exhilarating, and Friedrich laughed as he saw the creature break the surface a short distance away. Spiraling upward, it lifted completely out of the water before landing back down in a great splash. Every movement of the creature exuded a feeling of joy.

"I've often wondered what the seas beyond the White City are like, as beautiful as this place is," Friedrich commented to Asa'an, who hovered nearby, staring out across the water with him.

"Like nothing you or I can imagine," she replied, looking over, and giving him a sprite grin.

"Someday we will see for ourselves, together," he replied with an encouraging smile, looking upon the fairy-like being who had become such a dear friend to him.

She smiled joyously at his words, and he knew the reminder was needed from time to time. While she had always been a creature of spirit, Asa'an was as much of an exile as he was, though for very different reasons.

One having a celestial origin, and another with a worldly one, their paths had come together in the Middle Lands. Bonds of the deepest friendship had since been forged. She had gone into the depths of the Abyss with him, even into the Ten-Fold Kingdom itself, and the Void.

The experience had been harrowing. All of those who had gone into the dark depths needed a little extended recovery, now that everyone was safely back within the Middle Lands.

Spirited laughter drew Friedrich's eyes out to where Valaris and

Maroboduus were being pulled rapidly along the surface. Both held onto the fins of other dolphins, both of which were swimming in an upside-down manner to give the two human souls purchase.

It looked as if the pair were racing each other. Valaris would draw ahead, only to be outpaced by Maroboduus. The two souls yelled with exuberance, caught up in the thrill of the experience.

"Look above," Asa'an remarked.

Friedrich followed her eyes upward. Falling like large snowflakes, the bread-like substance called Manna descended. An abundance of it fell in a slow cascade from the shimmering sky, alighting gently upon the land and water.

He caught a piece of Manna in his palm before it landed on the ground. Friedrich drew the light substance of pure white up to his lips, catching its sweet scent before putting it into his mouth.

The effect was immediate, as feelings of renewed energy and strength flowed throughout his spirit body. He gave a silent thanksgiving to Adonai for the grace of the celestial sustenance. As much as the Manna had restorative properties, it was also a vivid reminder to all the souls dwelling in the Middle Lands that they were never forgotten.

Asa'an was standing on the ground eating another piece, though she had to hold it with two hands due to her diminutive size. The Peri's body had already brightened, her wings taking on a radiant sheen. Out in the water, Friedrich's friends and the creatures of the sea were feeding on the bounty.

"The bread reminds us of the One who is the sustenance of our very existence."

The melodiously layered feminine voice prompted Friedrich to turn around. Behind him stood a tall, dark-haired woman of incredible beauty. She exhibited the same form she had been in when Enki, Friedrich, and all of the others had accompanied her back from **Manzazu,** the shadowy realm of Erishkegal.

"Inanna," Friedrich replied in a reverent voice. His manner was formal, as he did not feel the same sense of familiarity with Inanna as he did with Enki.

"I came to look in upon you, to see how you and your friends are faring since your return from below," Inanna said to him.

"We are doing well, recovering and resting," Friedrich responded.

"I thank you again for what you did for me, and for Enki and Erishkegal. You, and those with you, did not have to take the risks that you did," Inanna said with an air of solemnity, looking from Friedrich down to where Asa'an stood quietly. "I have told many of what a small group of souls in the Middle Lands chose to brave."

He did not have to ask her to know that she was referring to others beyond the White City. Inanna was a powerful Avatar, and it was humbling to take in her words of praise. He could feel her gratitude in the essence of his soul.

"How could I do anything else?" he finally responded. "There was only one right choice to make, for all of us."

"You will know the realms beyond the White City ... you and all of your friends," Inanna replied with a gentle smile.

"It is what we all seek, those who dwell in these lands," Friedrich replied.

"The infinite realms are the only realms where true life can be known," Inanna said. "So much sorrow, and so much pain in the realms outside. Even Erishkegal suffers greatly dwelling outside the White City."

Friedrich thought back to the powerful Avatar whose human-like guise echoed that of Inanna. Among people, the two Avatars would pass easily for sisters.

Erishkegal had appeared so intense, even angry, when Friedrich and his group had encountered her. He could recall the unease he felt inside when they had gone to Egalkurzagin, her lofty, palatial dwelling atop the immense plateau.

The audience that came later before the Tribunal of the Anunnaki had been no easier to endure. But he had come to learn of the tremendous strain she endured in maintaining the realm that harbored so many outcasts from his own world.

The darkness found within Manzazu was not of the same nature as that filling the Ten-Fold Kingdom. Its origin was not the result of wickedness. Rather, the gloom was born of toil, hardship, and sacrifice, all accepted willingly to provide a merciful refuge for the most desperate.

There was little doubt that the tortured-looking souls washing up on the shores of Manzazu an outgrowth of Erishkegal's beneficence, even if she did not understand the phenomenon herself. Truly, Erishkegal was a light in the darkness.

"Will we return to her?" Friedrich asked, feeling a surge of compassion for the embattled Avatar, who remained with her growing flock of Anunnaki in the Abyss.

"I do not think so," Inanna replied, with a tinge of melancholy. "She carries her burden onward, and our place is here."

Friedrich was moved by the deep sadness in Inanna's voice, wishing he could think of a way to console her. She had gone so far to find Eriskhegal, who was, in the way Friedrich saw it, like a sister to her in the way that Enki was a brother to them both.

It was difficult for Friedrich to imagine how powerful such connections might be. While he had grown deep affinities for others in a mere handful of years, the Avatars had known each other since before the beginning of time itself.

"Do not feel sorrow, Friedrich," Inanna said. "Eriskhegal takes a path of mercy, though it is one not easily walked. We must turn our hearts towards another time, when hardship is cast aside and we are all brought together once more."

The longing in her voice was unmistakable. Her human form was unable to mask the fact that she missed Erishkegal greatly. The Avatars loyal to Adonai might have had a place before the Great Throne throughout all of their existence, but since the beginning they had come to know the pain and sense of loss that so often shadowed a genuine friendship.

"I have always found it difficult to control the way I feel," Friedrich said.

"As have I," Inanna replied, and her eyes held Friedrich's gaze for a moment.

Looking into her eyes, he knew what had driven Inanna to seek out Erishkegal on her own. Two powerful forces, her own separation from Erishkegal, and the pain she felt over Enki's long suffering, had compelled her to search through the darkness.

She had found what she had sought, but had ended up at the brink of the Void. Not even Erishkegal's great power could have staved off Inanna's slide into the unconscious state of the Void for much longer.

Enki's foresight and the aid of two mystical creatures he had brought along with him allowed Inanna's spirit to be restored to fullness. Friedrich had learned little of what had transpired, for the exiles had not witnessed what the strange little creatures had done. But there was no question Inanna's spirit was strong and vibrant when they left Manzazu behind and ascended back to the Middle Lands.

"We can only react to the things set before us," Friedrich replied, after a long pause. "I have learned not to have expectations about what those things might be."

A bemused smile crossed Inanna's lips. "Or you have come to expect the unexpected."

Friedrich chuckled. "I suppose you could say that. I have certainly given up predicting anything."

"An Avatar is sometimes given foresight into what will come, but only Adonai knows everything that lies ahead," Inanna responded. "There are mysteries that even the greatest of my kind do not fathom."

"I have to admit, there are cases where a glimpse of what is ahead would be helpful," Friedrich stated with a laugh, thinking about the battle he and his companions had survived against Beleth's legions, and the abyssal quest they had undertaken, with all of its hazards.

"Then I will give you such a glimpse, to the best of my ability," Inanna said.

The response took Friedrich by surprise, and he was puzzled at her words. He made no reply, and waited for the Avatar to continue.

"One who braves the depths of the Abyss, who goes into the Void itself, and who treads the Ten-Fold Kingdom, where even my kind fear to tread, is a soul capable of much in a time of great need," Inanna replied. "Gird yourself, and stay watchful, for you will be called in the service of the Great Throne to step forward at an appointed hour. The days grow short. It will not be long."

"What ... hour?" Friedrich asked, hesitantly.

"It is not for me to know this hour, but keep your spirit in a state

17

of readiness," Inanna replied. "The day approaches."

Her references to time-based measurements were perplexing, as time did not govern the realms of spirit. The structure of minutes, hours, days, and weeks held no dominion. Day and night did not exist in Purgatarion. The only places where those things mattered were in the realms he had passed beyond, and left far behind.

Friedrich nodded slowly, doing his best to stifle his apprehension. "I will be prepared."

Inanna smiled. "Do not fear or be troubled, Friedrich, for Adonai's Light is within you."

The human form before him condensed into a sphere of light, the brilliance of which forced him to squint. When he was able to open his eyes wide again, she was gone.

"What did she say?"

Friedrich looked over at Maroboduus, who had just emerged from the crystalline sea. Sparkling drops tumbled from his long dark locks of hair and thick beard. Behind him, Valaris was striding from the water, which still reached up to his waist.

"I don't really know what to make of it," Friedrich said, conceding the confusion he had at her words.

"Avatars are rarely idle, or so I've observed," Maroboduus said. "And I've been here a lot longer than you have Friedrich."

Reaching forward, the tall, brawny figure tousled his hair, eliciting a laugh from Friedrich. "What does time really matter in the face of infinity?"

"There is that, Friedrich, but I think you think too much," Maroboduus retorted amiably, with a broad grin.

"Yes, you definitely think way too much Friedrich," Valaris said, joining them in time for Maroboduus' comment. "So what are you all talking about?"

Asa'an, Friedrich, and Maroboduus laughed. "Speaking before you know what is being discussed is not the wisest course," Asa'an chided.

He laughed and shrugged. "I only heard Maroboduus say that Friedrich thinks too much, which is true enough!"

"Yes, I will admit that too," Asa'an said, with a merry laugh.

"Why do I suddenly have the feeling I am under siege?" Friedrich countered.

"If you are, here comes more reinforcements for us, you might as well surrender," Maroboduus said, looking out into the waters.

Hans, Ulrich, Stefan, Dietrich, and Heinrich were among a larger throng of male and female spirits standing atop the back of an enormous whale that was approaching the island. Silas emerged into sight a moment later, working his way through the mass of figures to stand with the others.

"Want to get a ride?" Stefan called out. "We're getting ready to go back to the shoreline. This friendly big fellow is willing to carry us all the way there."

Friedrich smiled at his friends, thinking of Inanna's comments about expecting the unexpected. In the Middle Lands, such words could serve as a constant truism.

"Why not?" he called back, heading towards the water. "We can't fly!"

"Speak for yourself!" Asa'an chided playfully, causing those on the island all break into laughter.

Valaris and Maroboduus entered the water behind Friedrich, and the three swam out towards the whale. Skimming just above the waterline, Asa'an kept pace with the trio.

Friedrich enjoyed the excursion to the oceanic realm immensely, but he was returning with much to ponder. He was glad he had seen Inanna, but she had not come to him for just a friendly visit. She was preparing him for something, though what it might involve he had no idea.

Reaching the whale, he accepted the assistance of his friends to pull up onto its sprawling back. Pushing conjectures aside, he chose to enjoy the ride back in the company of his friends. What would come, would come, and it was best to savor the moment at hand.

FATHER BRUNNER

A terrible nightmare engulfed Troy. Elites controlled the levers of government and dwelled within small, heavily fortified sections of the city. Gangs ruled the streets, having emerged in great numbers, thousands upon thousands, after the great upheaval struck the UCAS.

People just wanting to live their lives and raise families were caught squarely in the middle. Job prospects were few and far between, as the employed clung tenaciously to what they had. Inflation had inflicted hardship on everyone, and weighed more heavily with the passing of every day.

Those who had foreseen such hardship and prepared far in advance were not spared either. Under the powers of Executive Order 2015, also called the National Security Resource Efficiency executive order, the CSD and military was empowered to confiscate anything deemed to have been stored by an individual in excess, such as food or medical supplies, equipment, and much more. Sizeable bounties were paid to those who alerted authorities about individuals concealing large stocks of foodstuffs and other items, deepening a growing air of mistrust.

The atmosphere was growing ever more tense and cold. Goodwill between neighbors continued to decay, and desperation spurred behaviors deemed unthinkable during other times.

Father Brunner rubbed his forehead slowly, trying unsuccessfully to ease the sizeable headache that had plagued him all morning. A short distance away, a large mass of people were gathering; men and women, young and old alike.

Many wore masks and other forms of facial concealment. Though Father Brunner did not hide his face, he shared one thing in common with most of those who were hiding their identities.

The majority of the masked figures were likely holdouts who still refused to accept the mandate of Living ID. It was rapidly becoming impossible to function without Living ID, and Father Brunner knew he was on borrowed time.

A monumental decision approached in his life. Yet until that day of reckoning arrived, he intended to do everything that he could for the beleaguered and increasingly oppressed people of Troy. Fatigue, headaches, and the like had to be shoved aside with the force of will, as the darkness choking the city was unrelenting.

Far above, Father Brunner could see the conspicuous form of a drone slowly crossing the skies. The aerial devices were a regular presence over Troy nowadays, especially as citizens and gangs alike had turned angrily on the network of installed cameras in the streets. Many streets were littered with shattered lenses and casings where individuals had taken their frustrations out on the ubiquitous electronic eyes watching them around the clock.

Many good people had died during such riots, as the UCAS government had shown no reservations about using weaponized drones. The idea that the government would use armed drones against civilians was once deemed preposterous, and openly scoffed at by political and media elites. Now, the practice was commonplace, but those who had denied the potential so vehemently during former times said nothing.

"Going along with them?" a gentle voice interjected.

Father Wilson Rader continued to remain at Saint Bosco with Father Brunner. The pastor had refused to leave the city, which was effectively being transformed into a prison for the individuals inhabiting it.

"I am," Father Brunner responded, shaking his head ruefully. He rubbed his wrist, in one of the areas where the implants were usually placed on individuals. Nothing had been embedded under his skin, and his position on Living ID was resolute. Catching Father Rader eyeing his activity, he commented, "As long as blood flows in these veins, it won't be placed in me."

"What have things come to?" Father Rader asked, turning his gaze toward the crowd and shaking his head. "A perpetual war on terror, leading to a perpetual state of emergency...and all with the markings of a deeper plan."

A tall man with a megaphone began addressing the crowd. He spoke in a loud and confident manner, and Father Brunner knew he was the sort of individual that any undercover law enforcement agents present would be taking careful note of.

Raucous cheers met many of his bold statements as the man exhorted the crowd. Minutes later there was a surge of humanity, as several thousand people began marching forward.

Father Brunner had no doubts they would head towards **City Hall.** It was the likeliest place within walking distance suitable for holding a massive demonstration.

"Looks like it's time for me to go and join them," Father Brunner observed, looking upon the sea of people flowing onward. "That's my cue."

"I should be with you," Father Rader said. The steely look in the other priest's eyes showed that the words were not idly spoken.

"No, you should not. It would be the worst folly if both of us were put at risk. This church is one of the few havens left in this city," Father Brunner replied firmly, looking to Father Rader. For just a moment, the hierarchy between the two men appeared to switch, as the pastor of St. Bosco was admonished by his subordinate. "If both of us were swept up and detained, so many people would be left without a sanctuary, both physically and spiritually. That can't be allowed to happen. I'm going, and you need to stay here. Too much is put at risk otherwise."

"I can't argue with you. May Adonai's Grace go with you, and all of the people in this protest march. Keep safe, and return as soon as you are able," Father Rader said, an edge of anxiety within his voice. "Our doors will be open for any who need refuge after this."

Father Brunner nodded, and then chuckled, breaking the building tension. "You really didn't know what you were getting into when I came to this church, did you?"

Father Radar smiled. "No, I didn't. But I'm glad you were assigned to St. Bosco. You are a blessing to this community."

"This community has been a blessing for me," Father Brunner replied. He gave the other man a firm pat on the upper part of his left arm, and turned towards the crowd. "I'll see you in a little while."

Father Brunner walked forward, and fell in alongside a teenage boy and a middle-aged woman. Their appearances echoed the rough times that everyone was experiencing, but there was a spark of fierce determination in their eyes. They exemplified a crowd harboring a simmering. The grievances carried within the huge crowd were many.

An electric energy ran through the air as the heavy tramp of thousands of footsteps accompanied the river of people approaching City Hall. A phalanx of militarized police in riot gear barred the end of the street. A couple of drones hovered in the sky far above.

Several armored vehicles were in place. A couple featured black, circular objects of about three feet in diameter raised above the vehicles on metal poles and oriented towards the oncoming crowd.

Father Brunner knew what they were. He had seen their effect before. They were sound cannons, capable of spreading pain, nausea and fainting by channeling over a hundred and fifty decibels across a distance of nearly two thousand feet. Used regularly by the police force, the officers would not be hesitant to unleash the power of the devices.

A chant began rippling through the crowd, swelling fast as people vented their fury. "We the people! We are the government! We demand that you listen! We the people! We are the government! We demand that you listen!"

The chant thundered as the forefront of the multitude came to a halt a short distance from the police line. Father Brunner suspected that more than a few of the faces hidden behind the dark visors of the police officers' helmets appeared nervous as the chant took on the tenor of a lion's roar.

A voice suddenly boomed over the loudspeakers set up beyond the wall of riot shields. "Citizens of the UCAS, this is an illegal assembly. We order you to stop this unlawful assembly immediately, or you risk being detained under the provisions of martial law!"

For a few minutes, there was an eerie contest as the roaring voice of the people contended with the voice of the spokesman for the government authorities. Father Brunner knew that the patience of the authorities would not last for long, and it became apparent the crowd would not disperse so easily.

"Here we go," said one of the nearby protestors, his face obscured with a black ski mask. He then shouted out, with an air of urgency, "Get ready everyone! They're about to hit us!"

He proved to be correct. The government response was ferocious and concentrated.

The majority of the crowd was soon running back the way they came, overcome with waves of sound from the cannons, canisters of tear gas, and a barrage of rubber bullets. The unified chant of the people was replaced with a chaotic host of screams, cries, and shouts.

The shield-bearing ranks of police then marched steadily forward, approaching the edge of the crowd that remained. Some of the more reckless and enraged in the crowd beat against the shields, while more calculating individuals farther back lit up vessels filled with flammable liquid, and hurled them at the line of shields.

Father Brunner's heart sank as he watched men and women being knocked to the ground and beaten savagely. Several were being dragged and shoved towards the open bays at the rear of waiting trucks. A terrible feeling of dread came over him.

Rumors of internment camps had taken firm root after footage of a purported detainment camp was aired by a rebel element that had briefly taken over a television station in downtown Troy.

The government had claimed that the camp t was not what it was said to be, and that the footage was the work of terrorist agitators. But nobody with any sense believed the regime or its puppet media outlets.

Father Brunner feared the worst for those who were being swept up by the security forces. The government's definition an "enemy combatant" broad and encompassing, those detained were said to have no recourse and no rights, left to the total mercy of a regime that could do anything it wanted with them.

Father Brunner was not yet counted among the beaten or the apprehended, and nor did he flee the area. The reason that brought him along with the protestors now compelled action, to help the people however he could.

He knelt down by the side of a young woman whose face exhibited a grievous injury from a rubber bullet. Her nose was bent at an awkward angle, clearly broken. She was shaking, and her expression showed that she was still stunned in the aftermath of getting hit.

"Shhhh … keep calm. I'm going to get you out of here," Father

Brunner said gently.

Blinking back tears sprung by pain and frustration, she nodded to him. Father Brunner was relieved to see that she would cooperate, and that she was not too dazed from the head trauma she had undoubtedly suffered.

Glancing back up, he saw the wall of government troopers pushing steadily forward. In no time the phalanx would roll right over the area where he was tending the injured woman.

No consideration would be given to what he was doing, or even to the fact that he wore a priest's collar. If anything, especially in light of the current age, the outward marks of a priest would invite an even harsher response from some within the oncoming ranks.

With a grunt of exertion, he hoisted the young woman over his back and trudged away from the mayhem. Blocking out everything else from his mind, he narrowed his thoughts to taking one step at a time. His shoes planted heavily into the concrete and his legs braced stiffly with every stride, but he made steady progress.

Behind him the troopers kept pressing forward. Many demonstrators were pummeled and apprehended, and farther away the rear holds of the police trucks were filling up with new occupants.

His face ran with sweat that trickled into his eyes, stinging them. Blinking, and holding his eyes shut for brief moments, he did his best to clear them as he peered ahead.

People raced past him as the demonstration turned into a desperate retreat. When he had gone another block, he turned to the right and kept going.

There was little use in pausing and looking back. He was not going to abandon the woman, and if the troopers were about to catch him then there was nothing else he could do.

The Knights of the Order and the Shield Maidens maintained some clandestine relief centers to assist the beleaguered citizenry of Troy as often as possible. The locations shifted periodically, as surveillance was everywhere. Yet everything possible was being done to help anyone who did not wish to have Living ID forced upon them; as even the most routine visit to any city hospital would result in.

At the moment, one such emergency center was located in the

basement of an abandoned retail store less than a block and a half from the church. Saying a silent prayer to Adonai in thanksgiving for making it safely to the entrance, Father Brunner mustered a smile for the tall, broad-shouldered figure who greeted him there.

"From the protest?" the man asked, looking at the woman carried by the priest.

"Yes, Diego," Father Brunner replied. "And she's going to need some help right away. She's taken a hard hit to the head from a rubber bullet."

"We'll get right on it," Diego replied, before turning and calling out for some assistance.

A couple of other men stepped forward, and assisted Father Brunner with the young woman. Bracing her, they led the woman away to get some treatment.

"Mass arrests again?" Diego asked, when the others were gone from sight.

"A great many today. They had vehicles at the ready," Father Brunner replied grimly. "Sound cannons, tear gas, rubber bullets, everything was in place."

"We don't know where they are being taken, but everything we know says there are camps not too far from the outskirts of Troy," Diego said. "The video captures by those kids down south has helped to get people talking more. That footage is getting spread all over the UCAS."

"Word needs to get out, and I don't doubt there are camps relatively close by," Father Brunner responded. "Some people from my own parish have been arrested and taken away. We've tried to do everything we could to learn their location, but there's no indication that they're being held anywhere within the city's confines."

Diego's toned changed, growing more somber. "The woman you brought back was extremely lucky. And you are taking a terrible risk, Father."

The hint of admonishment lingered in the air between the two men. Father Brunner was not about to apologize for trying to help where he could, but neither could he deny Diego's logic. Nevertheless, he was not about to change course.

"Let's just say I couldn't sleep very well at night, if I didn't go," Father Brunner said finally, breaking the impasse. Changing the subject, he asked, "How is the Order faring?"

"It's becoming nearly impossible to get in or out of the city," Diego replied. "Doing what we can on the ground here. But in some sections of the city, the gangs have asserted full control."

"They were bad enough before martial law was declared," Father Brunner replied. "Now, I'm sure in some areas they have virtually free reign."

"That's true. They are without restraint. The only thing that holds them back a little is the constant infighting," Diego said. "We have reports of a ferocious power struggle going on between the stronger gangs.

"Some stories have killings being done that have all the marks of those creatures that helped get Juan Delgado back into the city, to air the broadcast. Many leading elements in several gangs have been slain in brutal ways."

Father Brunner had harbored Juan for a time when he had defected from Babylon Technologies, where he was one of the higher-ranking figures in the world-renowned company. The Order and the Shield Maidens had used a clever ruse involving the kind of make-up techniques employed in professional movie-making to get Juan out of the city.

An extensive operation coordinated by the Knights and Shield Maidens had then been conducted to bring him back into Troy; where he had taken to the airwaves with a dire warning about the nature of Living ID. Father Brunner had heard the fantastical stories reporting towering, wolf-headed creatures ripping through the government troopers manning the bridge Juan had been brought through.

Even now, Father Brunner could not believe the ubiquitous accounts were real. In his eyes the stories were a new urban legend.

A part of him expected another explanation to emerge regarding specialized body suits, at the very least. But members of the Order and the Shield Maidens who had been involved in the mission that day were convinced of what they saw.

"Do you think these stories have something to do with the

Order?" Father Brunner asked, studying the other man's face closely for his reaction.

Diego shook his head emphatically. "No, this is all coming from somewhere else. We don't know much about what's behind it, but I can say it has absolutely nothing to do with anything that the Order or the Shield Maidens are involved in."

"It sounds like the situation will need close watching," Father Brunner said firmly, feeling strongly that the other man was not holding anything back.

"We've got eyes and ears wherever we can get them," Diego said.

"I hope you learn something soon about what's happening with the gangs," Father Brunner stated, suspecting something of a very dark nature at the heart of the reports.

"We'll do everything we can," Diego responded. "And what we can't do we'll have to remember always to keep our faith in Adonai, Most High."

Father Brunner smiled at Diego's words. "Yes, we will, Diego. I think that just about sums things up for both of us these days."

"Yes, it sure does," Diego agreed.

Father Brunner reached forward and patted the other man on the shoulder. "Well, my work here looks done ... so I'd best be getting back to the church. No telling what Father Rader has gotten himself into since I left. See you this Sunday, at the Sacrifice?"

Diego nodded. "Unless I have to do something on behalf of the Order, you can count on it."

"I'll be looking out for you," Father Brunner replied. "Take care of yourself, and may Adonai protect and guide you."

"You too, Father," Diego said, lowering his head as the priest gave him a short blessing.

Father Brunner turned and exited the building. His mind was heavily weighed down, filled with foreboding thoughts as he made the short walk back to St. Bosco. The streets were all but vacated, creating an unsettling contrast to the recent protest.

The world was breaking down all around him, crumbling at its foundations. The worst thing about it was that the decay and decline were all the result of design and effort. Diabolos had the world bound in chains, and was securing the final locks.

There really was nowhere to run to, and Father Brunner knew the worst was still coming. The Sacred Writings had been very clear in that regard.

He could only hope that he was able to stay in the fight, and be in the right places so that he could pick up a few more battered souls from the ground, just like he had that day. When an even darker day arrived, as he knew it inevitably would, he prayed he could meet it with the kind of courage and conviction he witnessed each and every day out on the streets of Troy.

From a young, defiant man staring down a phalanx of shield-bearing riot troopers, to a single mother working herself to exhaustion, scraping up just enough to provide for and protect her children, an inspiring toughness and resilience was being demonstrated again and again. Those displays were rays of light cutting through the darkness. They were beacons that Father Brunner had to look to, lest he despair in the face of all the wickedness and cruelty encompassing him.

Adonai was present in every word of encouragement and act of compassion. The thought emboldened Father Brunner, right as the finial atop St. Bosco drew into sight.

As always, the Rising Dawn symbol stood bold and strong amid the cold gusts buffeting the streets. Father Brunner's gait was slower as he approached the church, as fatigue was catching up fast with him, but he felt much better within his heart when he finally reached the rectory door. After taking a moment to locate the right key among the cluster tethered to his key chain, he unlocked the door and entered.

A smile burst onto his face as Athanasius pressed forward to greet him. The big, enthusiastic mastiff almost pushed him right back through the doorway.

Laughing, Father Brunner ruffled the top of the dog's broad head. "So are you going to let me in, big fellow?"

The dog, as if responding to his words, shuffled backwards on the tile floor. A few paces beyond him, Simeon sauntered into view, glancing up towards Father Brunner with an expression that looked inquisitive.

"Ah yes, it was a long day, and it is really good to see you guys again," Father Brunner said to the cat, like he was responding to an unspoken question. "And if you want to hear about the day I had, I'm going to fix myself some dinner and go to the living room. I'm sure I can scrounge up a few treats for the two of you."

Simeon stood still as Father Brunner worked his way past Athanasius. Leaning over, he stroked the cat's fur from the back of the creature's head down to the base of his tail. Simeon responded with a motor-like purr, before stepping forward and rubbing his head against the priest's leg.

"You and Athanasius follow me to the kitchen now, and I'll get everything taken care of for the three of us," Father Brunner said, straightening back up after a few more seconds of stroking the cat's soft fur.

His footsteps accompanied by the patter of paws both large and small, Father Brunner continued on towards the kitchen. He clicked the light on as he entered the room, and took a deep, relaxing breath, simply glad to be home again.

Father Brunner had not gone out of the city when he had the chance. But he had no regrets about his decision to stay behind when the large group of people was ferried out of the tent-city of Paladin's Light.

He knew he was right where he needed to be. From Simeon and Athanasius, to Father Wilson Rader and Francis Drummond, the older lady who was the caretaker of the rectory, to the members of St. Bosco and the people of the surrounding neighborhood, Father Brunner had an immediate family to care for.

He thought of the girl he had carried from further harm. Pausing, he thanked Adonai for helping him get her to a place where she could be cared for. What Father Brunner had done for the girl, Adonai did for the state of his soul, something he could never forget.

With a smile and feeling of peace in his heart, he opened a cupboard and got a couple bags of treats out. He was more than happy to take care of his dear, four-legged friends first, before he saw to his own dinner.

JOVAN

A magnificent edifice set against a large hillside loomed within the midst of a vast wooded acreage owned by the UCAS government. The building was the core of a sprawling compound ranging from constructions intended for residential uses to others of more specialized purposes.

The semi-circular façade of the main structure was a triumph of architectural savvy. There was a slant to the windows on the multi-terraced structure, bestowing it with a modernistic feel while giving the impression the place was an outgrowth of the great hill it was set against.

On the highest level, a spectacular overlook was afforded to the two figures standing together in the moonlight. Kaira strode forward, to the edge of the balcony, quietly gazing out over the tree-blanketed valley unfurled before her in silvery luminescence.

"It is far too dangerous to remain in Yorvik. The unrest is unpredictable at the moment," Jovan commented, as the chilly touch of a night breeze brushed lightly across his face.

"Order will be restored soon enough," Kaira replied, matter-of-factly.

Jovan nodded. "It will be, Kaira, but everyone wants you to be able to carry out your work without distraction or threat. It's my job to help facilitate that, and we have this property available for your use. More remote, well-secured, and equipped with everything you need. The airfield will allow for anyone to come here to meet with you."

Kaira turned, and cast Jovan one of her broad smiles, an expression radiating with angelic grace. "And your dedication in all of this is very appreciated, Jovan. To think we were visiting at your beach house, drinking wine, and walking along the shore not all that long ago."

"It seems like an age ago," Jovan replied wistfully, recalling those magical walks in the embrace of moonlight.

If he closed his eyes, he could recall the sounds of the waves rolling in and breaking upon the sand as he and Kaira talked and laughed together. At that time, Jovan had entertained thoughts of something more with her, but the nature of their relationship had seemed to change overnight.

He had once seen himself as kind of a mentor to Kaira, or at least a supportive friend, but now it felt like he was subordinate to her. Jovan's focus when it came to her had undeniably shifted. Where he had once offered friendly advice and conducted periodic favors on her behalf, he was now prioritizing her every wish and need, even above his own affairs.

Yet he did not mind the change at all. If anything, he had never felt stronger in his affinity and loyalty. She was blossoming ever since circumstances involving the death of the previous head of the World Summit's Peace Commission had seen her thrust into the leadership spot.

She had taken right to the job, exhibiting a passion for it and wasting no time in implementing many of the ideas she had expressed during casual visits with Jovan in the past. The Peace Commission had very powerful mechanisms embedded within its structure, and Kaira was making use of all of them in addition to instituting some new expansions.

Kaira glanced back at Jovan with the deep, encompassing gaze that he always found so mesmerizing. "We will be able to visit again, when this world is brought back to full order. It is just that there is so much that needs to be done right now. There's just not enough time to spare."

"You won't find any arguments from me on that point," Jovan replied.

He almost sighed aloud, thinking of all the work he was embroiled with. Jovan's itinerary was constantly filled, from business concerns, to facilitating everything Kaira needed, to carrying out various tasks for the Convergence and the Order of the Red Shield.

He did not want to think of how thin and precarious the line was between being completely overwhelmed and keeping up with his responsibilities. Sleep was now a precious commodity, and skipping meals had become a regular practice. The days were largely a blur as he went from one thing to another, trying not to look at the entirety of what he was expected to do.

At the very least, his primary assistant, Julianna Pullman, had been relocated to the woodland compound. Jovan was highly relieved to have her taken out of Yorvik, and removed from the dangerous threats cropping up all across the unstable city. She was indispensable to Jovan, and had even shown a fervor towards the things involving Kaira.

"Simpler times, Jovan," Kaira said, in a reflective tone. "Even Mandaria wasn't stirring quite so prominently then."

"Yes, there is that too," Jovan said.

The giant eastern nation had gone head to head against the might of the UCAS when it had resolved its longstanding intent to reintegrate the island of Taiyoan. Unveiling new military capabilities, and executing previously demonstrated ones very well, Mandaria had crippled the UCAS' satellite grid in a daring, pre-emptive strike.

The brief war that had broken out in the aftermath had resulted in large casualties incurred on both sides, and the world's economies had been shaken to the core. Yet Mandaria emerged intact, and even highly respected in political circles, when Kaira had so deftly negotiated the end to hostilities at the World Summit.

Now that the UCAS had been plunged into the depths of severe internal problems, Mandaria was asserting its hold over the Southern Sea. Disputed island territories and the vast resources lying beneath the sea floor were now effectively Mandaria's. None of the neighboring countries could even hope to confront the economic and military giant without the aid of the UCAS.

"At the very least, there is no significant military conflict to address in that region," Kaira said.

"And I doubt there will be," Jovan said. "Kyotowa is probably the strongest country in the immediate area, and they are in no position to challenge Mandaria without UCAS assistance. I think everyone's economic interests will hold hostilities back, even if most are very disgruntled."

"What are your thoughts on the Central East?" Kaira asked.

"A little easier for us to deal with in its current state, than when they had secularist dictators," Jovan observed.

The current climate of the Central East was one of the biggest achievements of the Convergence. A parade of rebellions presented to the world as the people speaking their voice were all carefully nurtured and supported.

The UCAS, Western Nations, and a few key oil-rich allies in the region had patiently, and carefully, lent assistance to each rebellion as one regime after another toppled over. When they needed to play both sides of the same coin, they did so without hesitation.

A group purported to be an enemy at one point was provided with arms and resources at another. To the public, it often looked perplexing and contradictory, but there was a solid reason behind every move that took things one step closer to the goal.

Each of the nations now existed in name only. Those coming into power in every instance were connected to one another by common ideologies and purpose, rendering geographical boundaries irrelevant.

"I don't foresee any problems in the Central East either," Kaira stated. "I know many will be seeking to attain their long-sought prize at some point, but that can be dealt with when the time comes."

The stalwart Davidian nation holding out against all odds was the greatest of jewels desired by the new leaders who had taken power in the region. To the new powers, the seizing of those storied lands and its legendary capital, which prominently factored in three of the world's largest religions, would culminate their victory in the region.

"Hopefully that time will be later. We certainly have our hands full right now," Jovan commented.

"We do have more than enough to keep us quite busy," Kaira agreed. Turning, she grew silent, and stared out over the quiet forest.

"So, is there anything else you want to talk with me about?" Jovan asked in a low voice, after a few minutes had passed. Every instinct in him said that Kaira wanted to be alone at the moment.

"No, we've covered everything," Kaira replied. "I think I'm going to wind down here by myself, and we can meet again in the early morning."

"Sounds like a plan," Jovan replied amiably.

In the past he would have given her an affectionate hug. Now, it was like he was a business associate being dismissed. Strangely, the fundamental change in that area did not bother him either. If anything, he felt a deep gratitude for the fact that he still got to meet with her privately.

Wishing her a good night, he left Kaira standing on the balcony edge. Heading inside the building, he walked through the spacious living quarters to the elevator at the back.

Hitting the lone button to the right of the frame, he knew that he was not quite ready to turn in for the night. There was more than enough to occupy his mind, and sleep would evade him even if he tried to get some rest.

After a couple moments, the lighted button dimmed and the elevator door slid open. Stepping into the compartment, he rode down to the ground level.

His primary obligations finished, Jovan strolled out of the building's main front entrance and headed away from the complex of structures. Without pausing, he strode across the wide lawn and out of the reach of the floodlights, entering the shadow-filled trees rising just beyond.

The woods presented no danger, filled as they were with dedicated guardians. Jovan had admittedly been rattled at his first sight of the unusual creatures brought in by the TTDF.

The great beasts were like nothing he had ever beheld in his life, prior to coming to the compound. Yet in time, his apprehensions had eased, as he came to understand their purpose. Continually patrolling the woods, the creatures warded the men and women residing at the compound.

Taking a deep breath, he loosed the air slowly from his lungs. It issued forth in a ghostly vapor, and he felt an icy touch coming over the air surrounding him. The sharp drop in temperature told him he was not alone.

"You are carrying out your tasks well, Jovan." The seductive, feminine voice emerged from the shadows to his left.

He turned to look, and could barely make out Lilith's form, which blended closely with the pooling darkness beneath the trees. With scrutiny, only the vague outline of a shapely woman in flowing garb could be seen, along with the reddish glint of two eyes.

"I do as I am asked. Have I not always?" Jovan countered, a little agitated at the interruption. All he wanted was a few moments of peace, and he could not even get that.

Yet he wondered what the incorporeal entity wanted, as Lilith never visited with idle purpose. Seeking out a few moments to diffuse his stress with a night walk through the woods, Jovan knew he was about to get even more tasks heaped onto him.

He was distracted momentarily by a number of small winged shapes that suddenly came into view and began gliding around him. Bone-chilling screeches emitted from the owl-sized forms, whose distorted, skeletal visages were a mockery of the natural world.

"What … are those?" Jovan asked, finding himself highly unnerved, watching the little winged horrors swirling around him.

"My children, who flourish abundantly within my realm … a realm not of this world," Lilith responded with a deeper lilt to her voice. "Many of my children help in the watch over the compound now, having eyes to see the things that the guardians cannot."

Her laughter carried through the cold air, as the eerie cries of the flying creatures faded along with their forms. Jovan's heart kept beating fast, and he hoped the bizarre things did not return.

"Do you find my children frightening?" Lilith asked him, with a hint of amusement in her voice.

"I just haven't seen anything like them before," Jovan said, not wanting to offend her. "Not used to them I guess."

"They are not the only ones you'll see clearly. Soon, you may even be seeing me in a more substantive appearance," Lilith declared.

As she spoke, her form solidified further and took on a silvery, moon-like hue. Jovan could not help but feel a wave of arousal building within him upon beholding the stunning, perfectly-shaped woman just a few paces before him.

A husky laugh came from her full lips, which were spread into an alluring grin. Her eyes appeared to gleam brighter. "I sense that would please you, Jovan."

Every part of her form appealed to his most primal instincts. He could not take his eyes off her, nor stymie the lusts that surged powerfully within. He simply could not resist what she was manifesting.

Her form then began fading back into the shadowy, vaporous appearance it held moments before, save for the glittering orbs of her eyes. "Desire is a very powerful force in this world. It can be useful in many ways. It can overcome even the strongest."

Jovan did not know how to respond, greatly embarrassed by his reaction. He looked down at the ground, keeping his eyes from meeting hers.

"The hungers of a man are nothing to apologize for," Lilith continued. "And your desires will be uninhibited in the age to come, Jovan. It will be an age of great reward for those who have served the Risen Throne well.

"But for now you must continue in your support of Kaira. The world must be drawn closer together, to address the ills that plague it. Kaira will soon invoke the powers of the Peace Commission in ways that have never been done before.

"You must be ready to help facilitate her initiatives. Wherever necessary, bring together every person of influence who is part of the Convergence to assist."

Jovan nodded, grateful that his natural urges were finally subsiding. Still, he felt a little defensive that Lilith would even question him regarding Kaira. There was nobody that he was more dedicated to than her.

"You know I will do as you ask," he said evenly. "There is no need to remind me."

"It is a critical time, Jovan," Lilith replied. "Everything the Convergence has worked towards is within grasp now, and those who are set against us will do everything they can to get at her. Never assume she is safe, not even for a moment."

Jovan felt instant rage at the mere thought that anyone would want to harm Kaira. The idea was incomprehensible, and his eyes narrowed with the anger he felt burning inside.

"I would die for her," he stated.

"If you have to, you will, without hesitation," Lilith responded.

The way she said the words left some ambiguity, of whether her statement was just an affirmation of his own or a command. It did not bother Jovan either way.

"Keep wary always, for the enemies of the Risen Throne have not yet been vanquished," Lilith continued, as she began receding into the shadows. "Kaira will overcome them in time, so serve her well with all your strength."

Her voice trailed off and there was no more sign of her. The chill left the air, and Jovan stood in place for a few moments, coming to terms with the brief encounter. Even after so many interactions, Lilith always had a profound effect upon him.

He had to admit that he looked forward to seeing her in full clarity. The hint of invitation she had left him with was tantalizing beyond measure.

He shook his head and laughed to himself. There was no time for prurient thoughts. Jovan had a task to carry out, and a goal sought for millennia was at the cusp of full realization. There would be time enough for personal indulgences once victory had been achieved.

For the present, he recognized that a little rest would be helpful, and decided to cut his walk through the woods short. The visit with Lilith had taken him well out of his earlier mindset.

Turning about, he headed back in the direction of the compound. A deep calm rested over the forest, and the only sounds in the air were those of his shoes snapping small twigs and crunching leaves littering the forest floor. Taking in the sharp scents of pine, he thought about what Lilith had told him.

She had not asked for more of him, like he had initially feared. Lilith had merely reinforced his current path, exhorting him to vigilance, and given him a hint of things to come.

He wondered what she knew about Kaira that he did not, especially in regards to invoking the power of the Peace Commission in new ways. He had the sense that Lilith expected something momentous to be occurring in the near future.

In some ways, her beseeching of him was redundant. Jovan had never had feelings for another person like he did for Kaira. There was no question he would do anything and everything that he possibly could to help her with any initiatives she put forth.

His recent feelings for her were so very strange to Jovan. They reflected a deeper kind of devotion, one that was fundamentally different from romantic affections, friendship, or the love of a family member.

Though it amused him immensely to deem them in such a way, his feelings for Kaira were similar to those of a dedicated adherent of a religion towards their faith. For a man who had shunned and despised things of a religious nature all throughout his life, it was a bizarre thing for him to admit.

Shaking his head, he laughed to himself about the odd notion. Yet he did not apologize for the unprecedented feelings he harbored.

He mused that if Kaira were truly some sort of goddess, then he would finally have a religion he could embrace wholeheartedly. In some ways, he hoped that he would discover that she was.

Stepping from the trees, he started across the open lawn towards the building where his personal quarters were. He looked forward to getting some rest, and already felt a little renewed gazing towards a future filled with tremendous possibilities.

BENEDICT

Benedict sipped carefully from a cup of hot coffee, looking around at the café filled with a diverse assortment of patrons. From the clean cut to the rough and tumble, spanning from youth to elderly, and including folks of many ethnic backgrounds, the group as a whole represented the fabric of the UCAS, though that cloth was now in a much more tattered, soiled state.

The nation was in the early phases of its second civil war. It was clear that most people were not listening to the mass media's portrayal of the rebel provinces. If one were to believe the broadcasts, the midwest and south had been overrun with insurgents, traitors, and terrorists, including the defections of significant portions of the UCAS military.

To those with any sense, the claims were laughable. Benedict had come to discover there were rampant sympathies in the UCAS populace for those in the breakaway provinces who had stepped up to throw off the yoke of an increasingly oppressive government.

After some initial chaos and strife, the conflict was settling down into a period of relative calm. There were still reports of skirmishes and exchanges of fire all along the new borderlines, and stories of small incursions from both sides, but no large scale battles had taken place as of yet.

Benedict knew hostilities of a much bigger nature would be coming soon enough. It was simply that the UCAS was consolidating and preparing for the next phase, after enduring the brushfire of rebellion and defections.

The defections were not limited to just the military. With the markets going haywire, the economy brittle, and martial law in place with no end in sight, a great many suffering in the UCAS provinces looked towards the south as a beacon of hope.

The rebel provinces made no promises other than committing to a steadfast return to the ideals of the Grand Charter. But that was all that many people residing in UCAS-controlled provinces wanted in the first place.

Though the UCAS was doing everything possible to seal off the borders to the southern provinces, the sheer length of the latter made for a porous environment; one that savvy opportunists began to heavily exploit. Taking payment in everything from silver and gold coins, to guns and other material assets, the guides led groups of men and women who wanted to live in the south and midwest through the border zones.

It was a dangerous risk to take for anyone seeking to go east or south. Some of the perceived guides were nothing more than thieves; and others were even worse. Mostly betrayed by the unscrupulous or outright government collaborators, there had already been many groups swept up by UCAS security forces and taken away to the increasingly feared detention camps.

For men and women wishing to relocate their families, agonizing decisions had to be weighed. Yet the beacon of freedom and self-reliance shining from the southern and midwestern provinces proved a worthy enough goal for many thousands crossing raw wilderness terrain in the dark of night.

A caravan of such defectors would be setting out on foot that very night, and Benedict intended to join them. Using a guide was his only real option of getting back into the free provinces.

The main roads, especially any which crossed into rebel-held territory, were not an option. Military checkpoints were everywhere, and Living ID was being imposed on all citizens of the UCAS.

Like Benedict, the defectors had no intentions of accepting Living ID on their bodies, under any circumstances. He had spoken to several of them during the hours he waited in the cafe for night to come, and their feelings on the matter were abundantly clear.

During the conversations, he had addressed many of his own curiosities. Above all, he had wanted to get a more comprehensive sense of the people who were among thousands upon thousands flocking towards the rebel provinces, seeking desperately to get out of the UCAS and its suffocating environment. As night loomed, he felt he had attained a much more solid grasp.

"Mind if I sit here?" interrupted a low voice.

A weathered-looking man stood to the left of Benedict, whose table had one of the few open spots available in the crowded café. The newcomer had narrow features and a lean build, with short gray hair, and nothing about the man set off any alarms in Benedict. The look in the man's eyes was direct and warm, and his tone polite.

"Not at all," Benedict replied amiably, offering a smile and gesturing to the seat across from him.

There was little doubt the man would be heading out that night, as the large backpack and duffel bag he carried attested. He set the backpack on the floor and let it lean against his right leg, and he stuffed the duffel bag underneath his seat.

He looked across at Benedict, and let out a long, sighing breath. An expression of relief rested on his face. "So nice to just sit down for a minute."

"Might as well take advantage of that while we still can," Benedict said. "Looks like you are going where I am, and I'm sure we'll be getting a lot of walking in later tonight."

"Yes, we certainly will," the man agreed, with a tone sounding less than enthusiastic. He then smiled, and extended his hand across the table. "Name's Royce ... Royce Brandenberg."

"I'm Benedict." He shook the other man's hand, opting to leave his last name out of the equation for the time being. Any recognition of who he was would bring no advantages.

"So, what's your story?" Royce asked him, folding his hands and resting them on the table surface.

"Not the usual one," Benedict replied, with a rueful chuckle.

"We've got plenty of time until the sun goes down," Royce commented.

"All I have to say is that I was locked up until recently," Benedict responded, with a bittersweet grin as he recalled his incarceration in the UCAS facility.

Royce laughed. "In this world turned upside down, about everyone's being locked up. Hard to believe this country was a symbol of freedom."

"They don't know the meaning of the word anymore," Benedict replied dourly. After a second, he added, "Few do anymore, I'm afraid. It's such a sad thing to admit, but that's what I see everywhere I go."

"I know what you mean, and I'll take my chances in the free provinces," Royce replied, with a look of determination. "So what did you do before all of this mess happened, and before you got locked up?"

"Worked in a radio station," Benedict answered. "Seems like ages ago, but that's what I did for a long time. Right up until everything unraveled. And you?"

"Construction," Royce answered. "I was lucky to get onto some larger commercial construction projects when the housing market went bust a few years back. Then everything went to hell." The man shook his head ruefully.

"A good, reliable trade to have. You shouldn't have any trouble finding work, wherever you go, once you are across the border," Benedict said, wanting to give the man some encouragement.

"I hope I don't have trouble, but we won't know what things are like until we get there," Royce said. "You can't trust the news on this side of the fence. They aren't going to tell us straight. Never really did before, you know."

"There is that," Benedict admitted.

"I just hope we make it there smoothly," Royce said. "Lots of drones in the area they say."

"They might love their drones, but they're spread very thin," Benedict said. "They can't cover every inch of the new borders. They couldn't cover the old ones, and those were much smaller. I'd say our chances are still good."

"At least our guide has a solid reputation," Royce said. "They say he used to help lots of people cross our old southern boundaries."

"That's what I've been hearing too," Benedict said, taking another sip of his coffee. "If he led groups across the border in the old days, then he has plenty of experience evading authorities. That's going to count in a big way with what we're doing tonight."

"So what are you going to do when we're across the border?" Royce asked. "Anything particular?"

"Just planning to reconnect with some family," Benedict said, thinking of his brother and his niece. "I'll still have a little way to go to reach them in Venorterra when we cross, but that's the goal."

He had no doubts they were worried sick about him, ever since the moment of his capture by the TTDF operatives. Benedict had thought of them both often during his incarceration, and longed to see all of them again as soon as possible.

"Venorterra? I know about that big horse race, some of my friends used to bet on it about every year," Royce responded, with a laugh. "I never was much of a bettin' man."

"Used to live in Troy, but my family is mainly in Venorterra now," Benedict said. "What about you? Any family to seek out?"

"I've got family in free provinces too, just a little more spread out," Royce said, though he grew quiet and did not offer anything more.

Benedict sensed it was not a topic to press. He then felt a light tap on his right shoulder. Turning, he saw a hispanic man of about forty years of age, with a short-cropped goatee.

"It is time to get going," the man announced in an accented

voice, looking purposefully to both Benedict and Royce. "Gather your things, and come outside."

"Thank you," Benedict replied. The man nodded and moved onward, giving the word to others seated around the café.

"Time to head 'em up, and move 'em out, as they say," Royce said in a spirited fashion, getting up and preparing to put on his pack. Once that was done, he leaned over and dug his duffel bag out from under the booth seat. "It was great meeting you Benedict, and I'm sure we'll get some more time to talk tonight."

"I'm looking forward to it," Benedict replied politely, shaking Royce's hand.

He turned his attention towards gathering up his possessions. Since his unlikely escape from the underground detention, Benedict had acquired few things, not enough to warrant anything more than a backpack he wore out of the café.

The man who summoned them led the group to a place where a pair of dark vans was parked. Benedict squeezed himself into a space on the middle bench seat of one of the vans, and held the backpack snug in his lap.

He looked around at the faces of the people surrounding him. Some looked nervous, and others appeared resolute, but he had little doubt that fears nagged at every last one of them.

Outside his window, he saw a couple children, of maybe ten or eleven years of age, getting aboard the second van with their parents. Sitting on the bench seat in front of Benedict was a young couple who looked to be in their mid-twenties.

Most of the rest were loners like Benedict and Royce, including some very hard-looking individuals that he was more than happy to have along for the trek. Capability was more important than sociability under the circumstances. If push came to shove it was nice to think there were some tough, potentially military-trained individuals included within their group.

The vans pulled out of the parking lot and proceeded far out from the small town, traveling along a lonely road. They encountered no traffic on the way out. Just after nightfall, the group was dropped off in what looked like the middle of nowhere.

Chilly winds swept through a dry, flat landscape pockmarked with hardy shrubs and other rugged plant growth suited for an arid environment. The uninviting, remote atmosphere was exactly what Benedict had expected.

Their guide, a lean, wiry man of about forty-five years of age, was waiting for the group. A couple of assistants, younger men wearing large hiking backpacks, were standing with him, one to each side.

After conducting a brief orientation, which was little more than making an announcement regarding who he was, the guide led the group off across the rough terrain. One of the guide's assistants stayed with him at the forefront, and the other kept to the rear of the column.

At first, everyone in the group kept to themselves. With nothing else to listen to, Benedict soon became acclimated to the sounds of shoes scraping against parched soil as they progressed forward.

After about three hours, the guide called for the human caravan to halt. The abrupt sound of his voice breaking the rhythmic monotony jarred Benedict out of his meandering thoughts.

Bottled water was passed out from the packs carried by the two assistants. Although Benedict was tempted to consume it all at once, he stretched the contents of his bottle throughout the break. Sitting by himself, he thought about his circumstances.

It was fortunate that he had done a lot of hiking since unexpectedly being freed from his imprisonment in the bowels of the huge military complex. Dropped off at the side of the road with nothing but barren wilderness in sight, Benedict had been left with no choice but to walk.

Occasionally, he was able to benefit from the generosity of passing truckers. Yet for the most part he had been left to his own devices, which involved many long treks on foot.

His endurance had improved considerably in the weeks and months that followed. Allowing a full beard to grow in, he had done everything he could do to avoid being identified. To his relief, there had not been one instance of recognition to disturb his travel.

Benedict had gradually worked his way south and east. The borders were said to be most porous there, and he had wanted to give himself the best possible chance of crossing back into the free provinces before the authorities could grab and confine him again.

Like many who refused Living ID, he was forced to live in the shadows. There was a lot of sympathy from many who had unhappily accepted the yoke of Living ID, fortunately, so food and shelter were never terribly far away.

With the outbreak of civil war, there was no chance of reaching anyone in the breakaway provinces by phones or online networks. Virtually all of the private communication links between the two territories had been severed.

Benedict knew he had to reach the rebel provinces and bring back the news of what he had seen deep in the chambers of the military complex. The unwelcome discovery had immense implications for the future.

It was daunting to think that the Nephilim were capable of reproducing. The images of the baby dragons he had witnessed in the underground chamber were still emblazoned upon his mind. Every time he recalled those moments he could feel the chill that had come over him when the huge female stepped aside to reveal the existence of several offspring.

The development did not surprise him. The Nephilim, while bearing a supernatural heritage, were ultimately creatures of flesh and blood.

Their wide variety of forms, and mostly monstrous natures, were due to the way that the supernatural heritage expressed itself within the parameters of a material world. The Nephilim were not creatures intended for Terra, and the fact that they could multiply in number boded grave ill for the future.

The Nephilim were dangerous killers, guided by spirits of darkness. Loosed into the chaos permeating the world, the beasts would be all but unstoppable.

Benedict glanced up at the shimmering constellations arrayed across the night sky, and sought to get his mind off such brooding thoughts. He wondered how Arianna was doing, and also how the An-Ki were faring.

The only stroke of good fortune he could see was that Venorterra, where the An-Ki dwelled, was firmly in rebel hands. That made it much harder for anything from the UCAS to get at the wolfish refugees from another time and place.

Still, Benedict could not forget that the UCAS had snagged him from the midst of his companions deep in rebel territory. Their reach was not limited to their own boundaries. There was no telling what the UCAS operatives were capable of when they had a firm target in mind.

The guide finally called for the hike to resume, bringing an end to the break. After standing and stretching for a few seconds, Benedict fell in with the others as they started forth again.

While in far better shape than he had been in during his incarceration, Benedict was gradually worn down on the extended hike. One of the older members of the group, he inherited a more difficult challenge in sustaining the brisk pace.

At first, he noticed his breathing getting more labored as aches grew in his lower back and knees, and his legs felt heavier. Increasingly, he had to call upon his willpower to keep from drifting farther back in the column.

When the sky had just begun to lighten on the eastern horizon, the guide brought the group to a stop. He gathered everyone together and announced that they were at the border.

There were no signs, fences, or anything else to reinforce his claim. The ground going forward looked the same as the land behind them, and to either side.

Everyone in the group was left with the choice of whether or not to trust the guide. Benedict, highly relieved to be afforded a respite from the hike, did not see any use in worrying about the reliability of their guide at that point.

The dice had long since been cast, and there was no turning back. Whatever would happen, would happen, no matter how much or little the members of the group worried about the situation.

The guide wished all of them well, and then gave the group a little information regarding the city of Coranado. It would be the first larger metropolis that they would encounter within rebel-held territory.

He advised them to avoid the city if at all possible. According to the guide, Coranado was plagued with all the same problems affecting the major population centers of the UCAS.

The information did not come as a surprise. He had anticipated such a climate. Crime, violence, and an eruption of gang-related activity were undoubtedly the norm for most large cities on both sides. Wherever government services had broken down, and restive, sizeable populaces struggled to deal with the harsher new realities, both the predatory and desperate began emerging from the shadows.

Though dispiriting, the truth was undeniable. Goodwill was short-lived within the hearts of most people during such a time of severe hardship. Neighbors who had once greeted each other politely soon preyed upon one another, as fading kindness was gradually replaced with a surge of barbaric cruelty.

He could only imagine how fertile the ground was for the well-armed gangs in cities all across the UCAS and breakaway provinces. If there ever was a golden age for the murderous and pitiless, then the modern age was gilded abundantly.

The guide bid the travelers well. Benedict did not doubt the sincerity reflected in the man's voice and face. He joined his voice to the others as they thanked him for his help.

Accompanied by his two assistants, the guide started back the way the group had come. Royce walked over to Benedict, just as the group of expatriates started forward again.

"Looks like we're on our own now," Royce commented.

"Indeed we are," Benedict agreed, glancing back and eyeing the forms of their guides blending into the deepening night. "Very clearly."

"Figured I'd come over and ask you, any advice to follow?" Royce queried. "About avoiding the cities? Is that a wise idea?"

"Without question," Benedict answered firmly. "But we can go around the outskirts of Coranado. Hopefully we can find someone who knows a little more about what's been happening around here."

"They've got to have some security in the area, I would think," Royce said. Then, as if forgetting to clarify, he quickly added, "The province, I mean."

"Coranado Province looks like it's split between the former UCAS and the free territories," Benedict replied. "But I'm sure the folks on this side of the border wouldn't want anything bad spreading, not when things are this fragile. I'd say we'll find some police or military from the province somewhere on the perimeter of the city."

"Kind of like a big time bomb, wasn't it?" Royce queried.

"What do you mean?" Benedict asked, not sure what Royce was getting at.

"The gangs. They sure didn't crop up overnight," Royce stated.

"No, they didn't," Benedict replied with a somber air. "And I've watched this problem growing for many years, right before everyone's eyes. When I lived in Troy, the most recent estimates had them well over a hundred thousand there alone, in terms of active members."

"That's an army," Royce said, with a noticeable lilt of surprise at the large figure.

"Yes, it is, and it's an army beholden to nobody," Benedict said. "It's ironic, in a dark way. Troy had some of the strictest gun laws in the entire country, yet it still had the highest number of murders. Want to know why? The overwhelming majority of killings were due to gang violence. The gun laws did as much good in stopping the gangs from arming as the drug laws did in stopping the flow of narcotics on the streets."

"Which means they were all armed to the teeth and overflowing with drugs," Royce responded, nodding. "It must be a nightmare to live in Troy now. The rotten times we're in probably have lots and lots of new members joining their ranks."

"It's hard to even think about it," Benedict said ruefully. "Those neighborhoods are probably like prisons for many good people, who are just sitting victims for those monsters. I hope the new governments across the south and midwest decide to clean house. Believe me, it could be done if there was a will to do it."

"Let's hope," Royce said. "After all, it's a new day in the free provinces."

"Yes, it certainly is," Benedict said, a brief smile coming to his face at the hopeful words.

" I'm looking forward to it," Royce said. "But I hope we have somewhere we can stop for a little rest before too much longer. No use in denying it, I'm wearing down."

"Tell me about it. You and me both," Benedict commiserated.

His legs were effectively wooden at the moment, and his feet inflicted with a growing soreness. Stiffness pervaded his lower back, and every step met with discomfort, but he could not afford to dwell upon the aches and weariness.

"I don't know how much longer the group will stick together, either," Royce said, his voice sounding laden with concern. He paused a moment before asking, in a lower, apprehensive tone, "Any chance I can tag along with you for awhile?"

"We can watch each other's backs," Benedict replied, mustering a grin. He found the idea very welcome, especially when he had no idea what they would come across as they passed near to Coranado.

Now solidly across the border, and without their guide, it was not much longer before the members of the group finally engaged in a little discussion. It swiftly became apparent that before long most of them would be going their separate ways.

A few elected to band together for security, but nobody wanted to chance the outskirts of Coranado, other than Benedict and Royce. Several of the others looked at Benedict like he was crazy, though nothing was said aloud.

Most of the group was still intact when the morning was in full bloom and the chill of night had been brushed away. With the sun attaining command of the clear skies, and loosing a growing heat across the landscape, it was decided together that everyone would take cover in some brush and rest for a few hours before continuing the trek.

Benedict could not remember the last time he had felt so relieved than when the long march was mercifully brought to a halt. Looking around at the exhausted faces on several of the others, he surmised many harbored similar feelings.

Nevertheless, a great weight was lifted off his shoulders. They were in rebel-controlled territory, and the specter of UCAS security forces did not loom quite as large anymore.

Benedict had lived for quite awhile with the threat of discovery lingering in his mind. That longstanding source of anxiety would not ebb overnight, but he welcomed the start of its decline.

The brush surrounding them could not provide comprehensive shade, but it would provide concealment from any aircraft flying over the area. After guzzling a full bottle of water, Benedict used his backpack as a makeshift pillow. Laying his head upon it, he eased his breathing and let his body begin to settle.

Royce plopped down a few paces away, but like Benedict, was far too tired for words. A hushed calm descended over the area as the entire group took to rest following a long night of exertion.

Lids feeling like anchors, Benedict could not keep his eyes open. His body demanded some time for recovery, and he did nothing to fight the pervading cloak of fatigue. In a moment, he was fast asleep.

URIA

Stinking of fear, the two men wearing blue head cloths ran frantically down the alleyway, clutching tightly onto their guns. Farther behind, but gaining fast, wolfish monstrosities raced through the dark streets after the terror-consumed pair.

So panicked were the two that they did not sense their grave peril until the last moment, when a couple of huge, thick-furred shapes towered over them out of the shadows. Fangs flashed and claws drove mercilessly into flesh. The two men were torn to shreds in moments. Neither was able to loose so much as a single scream, though their eyes were wide with shock when life fled their torn bodies.

Hot blood coating his muzzle, Uria peered down the alley as Nymagas and Ikassian finally came into sight. On four legs, the other two drew to a halt a few paces away, taking deferential postures.

"That is the last of them," Nymagas said in a low voice, keeping his bright yellow eyes from looking directly into Uria's gaze.

"Then the hunt this night is finished," Uria stated.

"It is as it should be. We are finally hunters of men," Zeyya remarked, with a fiery gaze enthroned within her eyes. Leaning over,

she casually tore off a chunk of meat from the arm of one of the dead gang members, gulping the flesh down her throat.

Zeyya had taken to the tasks given them with a frenzied enthusiasm. In the dark of night, like a great pack of hunters unleashed, Uria's clan had become instrumental in changing the order of things on the streets of Troy.

As Carlton had explained on more than one occasion, any authorities searching for large wolves would become confounded while Uria and his kind walked the streets undetectable in a human form. The An-Ki were the perfect assassins, as the trail of the beasts who were slaughtering humans vanished before the eyes of any would-be investigator. Without knowledge of the shape-shifting nature of the An-Ki, the authorities were ill-equipped to pursue their inquiries concerning the rash of blood-drenched murders that had been taking place lately.

Uria was pleased with their assignments from Carlton for other reasons. Zeyya finally had an outlet for her powerful urges. Yet as task after task was completed, it seemed impossible to slake her thirst for human blood.

He knew she had never harbored an affinity for humans, but he had been unaware of just how much she loathed the weaker creatures. Sometimes, she dragged the killings out, toying with her prey and savoring every last moment of their fear.

Uria thought back to the gang member she had cornered earlier that evening. Trapping the man at the end of an alley, her shadow appeared to engulf him as she slowly approached. Uria had held back, watching in fascination as Zeyya filled the alley with a rumbling growl.

The man had voided his bladder, shaking as she took one slow stride after another towards him. His screams were pitiful and shrill, and the knife he drew at the last instant to defend himself quickly lay on the ground, still gripped in the hand of the arm Zeyya ripped off a moment later.

The rest of the kill was anti-climactic, and Uria would not have been surprised if the man's heart had simply burst from fright by then. Like she tended to do with most of her kills, she had fed for a few moments upon the body. To Uria's eyes, her consumption of flesh from those she had slain had a ritualistic aspect to it.

Zeyya, like Uria, had discovered great power in the fear humans showed towards the An-Ki. It swiftly became obvious that most humans were in an extreme state of disbelief that Uria's kind even existed. He had few doubts that the terror the An-Ki caused had a lot to do with Carlton's reasons in utilizing them.

Uria had no misgivings whatsoever. The gangs were brutal and showed little care for life. They had no qualms about killing other humans, which was something Uria found very hard to understand.

An An-Ki slaying another An-Ki was the gravest of transgressions, unless it occurred as a result of a fight for leadership of a clan. In that instance, both combatants knew the risks involved, and accepted the possibility of death.

Even then, killings were rare. Most often, the one who lost a battle was able to recover quickly enough from the wounds suffered.

The low value humans placed on the lives of each other bolstered the growing sense of superiority that Uria, Zeyya, and many of his clan harbored. With each passing day, he became more incredulous about the leadership he had once accepted, and submitted to for far too long.

The old fool Sargor had always acted as if the An-Ki were secondary to the humans. He had avoided contact with them as much as possible. Content to let a few An-Ki slink in the shadows of the human world to gain information, he showed no inclination to gain influence or authority over the weak race.

Humans responded quickly to fear and strength, and Uria knew the An-Ki wielded both of those things in abundance. In his eyes, humans could be mastered, though he hid the provocative thought from Carlton.

For the time being, it was important to continue assisting their powerful benefactor. Carlton was clearly guiding the An-Ki along a path that taught them of their own strengths, and also the frailties of humans. Every one of the latter that Uria's clan discovered was another advantage for the An-Ki to wield in time.

Uria suspected there would be other significant revelations to come, and some patience would serve his clan well. Following his instincts brought all of his An-Ki a better level of assimilation with the modern world than any path Sargor had been guiding them on.

It was no time to change course. If anything, the progress that the clan was making called for his every effort.

He glanced towards Zeyya, and her eyes locked with his. Her loyalty and ferocity thrilled him to the depths of his being. Uria felt more conviction than ever before that she was the optimal female for him.

As the clan's leader, taking a Life Mate was nothing he could take lightly. The female he bonded with would have to reflect him, both in his strengths and vision of leadership for the clan.

Zeyya had supported his vision in every way, and she was unmatched among his clan's females in her physical capabilities. She was a lethal hunter and a tremendous fighter.

"What are you thinking, Uria?" she asked him in a low voice.

"The future, Zeyya," he replied, holding her gaze.

"Always the future, Uria," Zeyya replied, with a trace of amusement. "Do not overlook the present."

She held his eyes a moment longer, and then leaned over to take another chunk out of the dead human's body. He could not deny his belly was fairly empty, and the human corpses were prizes of a successful hunt.

Moving to her side, he joined her in the feast. Ikassian and Nymagas kept a few paces back. They would be able to feed shortly, once the strongest male and female in the clan had indulged their appetites a little further.

The practice was an older one that had fallen into disuse within Sargor's clan. Uria had restored it within his own, as reminders of the hierarchy in his clan instilled discipline in those who followed him.

He savored the taste of human flesh and blood within his jaws. No longer did humans need to be evaded when their meat was filling his stomach.

Uria glanced up as he took another tender bite. His eyes met with Zeyya's once again, where her muzzle was almost touching his own.

Feeling a fiery wave of heat ripple through his body, he held her eyes for several moments. Deep down, he knew it would not be much longer before he had a Life Mate; Zeyya was the one for him.

SETH

Dreaming of ethereal skies had become a regular occurrence for Seth, ever since he had transcended worlds. Desperation had compelled the powerful Watchers to take Seth, Jonathan, Annika, and Raymond across the Veil from the material plane, bringing the four into a realm of supernatural wonder.

Now that Seth had been returned to the world governed by time and space, he found that a small part of him yet lingered in thoughts of the incredible, breathtaking realities beyond. He knew he had still not fully come to grips with the life-changing journey he had undertaken.

It was irrefutable that other realms existed. Knowledge gained from personal experiencehad taken firm root within him.

There was no way he could suppress the spectacular memories. Colors of kinds he had never beheld in all his life, a lake whose surface sparkled with the brilliance of precious gemstones, and swaying grasses shining with light from within were just a few of the amazing visions he had encountered within Purgatarion.

By comparison, Seth's own world could be likened to a pale reflection of such vividness and clarity. But he would not have wanted it any other way. Thoughts of the awe-inspiring otherworld gave him a beacon to look towards, during all of the hardships and struggles surrounding him everywhere.

Video footage of the federal detention camp acquired by Seth and his friends had been taken onward. He could still remember the spellbinding, bright blue eyes of the Avatar Calliel on the night Seth handed over the pack containing the digital video files.

What had ultimately been done with the video footage Seth still did not know. He could only hope it had been used for a good, effective purpose, as it served as an unshakeable witness to a national atrocity.

Though nothing was the same as before, and a great deal of disruption had been loosed within his own life, Seth was glad that a massive rebellion was underway. A government that could build and operate such a loathsome thing as a mass detainment camp for its own citizens was something entirely alien and hostile to everything the country had once stood for.

Before, Seth had often wondered exactly what a domestic enemy was. Now, he understood the term completely. A noxious enemy had manifested from within, and now the people of many provinces were seeking to purge the malignant disease and restore freedom.

Nevertheless, an excruciating sense of idleness had settled in ever since Seth and the others had returned from their astonishing foray. The timing of the major outbreak of rebellion was most inopportune, occurring as it did with Seth and his friends far removed from their homes.

Like Jonathan, Annika, and Raymond, all he wanted to do now was go back home. Madison and all of Venorterra had been fully liberated from the draconian UCAS forces and their harshly imposed state of martial law.

Yet every time he or one of his friends inquired about returning, the answer was always the same. The journey back to Madison would be too hazardous at the present time.

While the land was nominally under the control of the breakaway provinces, stability had not yet been achieved. Roving enemy drones, UCAS agents, and a wide variety of other threats loomed, while the larger cities were anything but secure.

Swiftly forming security forces were doing their best to handle the situation, especially in the bigger urban centers. But the great upheaval had set off a firestorm of barbarity within the more densely populated areas.

All across the refugee camp, Seth had heard many tales of gangs asserting themselves at gunpoint in the aftermath of the UCAS' breakdown. They were heavily armed and strong in numbers, a longstanding time bomb whose moment of detonation had arrived.

Civilians were not being left helpless. The rebel provinces had facilitated the acquisition of firearms for personal defense in a move that Raymond said was unprecedented. People in the cities were being encouraged to defend themselves and fight back against rogue elements, while the provinces' security forces, police and military units alike, were working diligently to roll back the huge criminal tide.

Seth wondered how similar situations were being handled in the UCAS provinces. He doubted the methods were similar. He had experienced the UCAS' approach far too intimately, on the night his house had been ringed with TTDF troopers. Only the intervention of Watchers had saved him from being taken captive.

A restless, disgruntled feeling pervading him, Seth shifted off his sleeping bag and crawled out from the dome-like tent serving as his current home. Standing up and stretching his limbs slowly, he squinted in the light of the midday sun.

Looking around, he eyed the kaleidoscope of colors peppering the sprawling mass of tents, recreational vehicles, and trailers. It was a very large refugee camp, with most of the occupants facing similar situations to his own.

He could not see any immediate sign of Jonathan, Annika, or Raymond. His mobile device no longer functioned, so he could not call or text them to see where they were.

The habit of reaching for his mobile device had not subsided just yet. Getting used to a decidedly low-tech mode of daily existence was one of the most difficult adjustments for Seth, without question. At the least, a few of the faces he saw around in the camp were familiar ones. For a moment, he considered paying a visit to a few of them.

Rowan Forrester, the younger fellow from his high school, was staying with his family on the other side of the encampment. While he would not have minded a visit with Rowan, the long walk necessary to find him did not hold much appeal.

A lengthy trek to see Christa, the girl who had worked at the store near where Raymond's father had his lake house, would be a different story, if he were able to muster the nerves to go see her by himself. A dampening feeling of melancholy washed over him as he thought of the young lady.

58

Her long, toned legs, the sheen of her flowing auburn air, and the expressiveness of her light brown eyes were just a few of the many reasons Christa rendered Seth virtually mute every time he interacted with her. She had always been friendly enough with him, but he felt it had to be more out of a sense of compassion. He had no doubts he appeared gangly and awkward to her.

He was well aware she resided in the same camp as him, but despite all that had happened in the world, and within Seth's life, things had not gotten any easier for him when it came to her.

It was the same story each and every time. No matter how girded and prepared he thought himself to be, one look upon her melted his resolve.

With an extended sigh, and a bitter feeling of resignation, he turned his thoughts away from her. He knew it was no use torturing himself further by pondering his inadequacies.

Without a firm destination, he opted for the woods and a little more solitude. Walking briskly, he set out for the tree line. It took him about fifteen minutes to reach the western boundary of the encampment and edge of the hilly woodlands spreading far beyond.

There was not much for him to worry about in terms of security, as the Free Venorterra Militia roamed the hills to the west. Seth had seen well-armed groups of their members coming out of the woods often enough. The militia maintained a regular presence in the camp, and it was common knowledge that the hills were deemed to be clear of any significant threats.

The cool air wafting underneath the tree boughs began soothing his heated skin from their first gentle touch. The choice of getting away for awhile from the mass of humanity ensconced within the camp felt wiser with every stride he took under the lofty forest canopy.

The noise of the camp faded a little more with each step. Seth listened to the sounds of his shoes lightly crunching on the forest floor, birds chirping, and the low buzzing of insects; all formed an ambience welcome to his ears. He took long, slow, relaxing breaths, watching the sun's rays flickering as leaves swaying in the breezes scattered the daylight.

Seth had not gotten very far when he took sudden notice of a man and woman standing just a short distance ahead, in the shadows of a large tree. He immediately slowed his gait, but he was much too close to act as if he had not seen the silent pair. Anxiety pinched him, for there was no way to politely avoid interacting with the two. Seth felt increasingly jittery the closer he drew to them.

The woman was easily six-foot-four in height, or perhaps even six-five, with long, tumbling locks of raven black descending over a set of strong, athletic-looking shoulders. Her eyes were of a light blue shade, and the intensive gaze cradled within them was fixed solidly upon Seth.

The man with her was a hulk of a physical specimen. Over seven feet tall, thick-built, with broad shoulders and a bull neck, he was quite possibly the largest man Seth had ever set his eyes upon. A lengthy, dense beard covered much of his broad face, but his eyes unsettled Seth, giving off a decidedly reddish hue that he believed to be contacts, or a trick of the light.

Adding another exotic touch, the man's long hair was entirely of a silvery gray. The hair color seemed a premature characteristic, given the rest of his features, as the man's age could not have been much past his late twenties or early thirties. The silver locks hung loose and unkempt, lending the man's appearance a touch of the wild.

"Hi … how are you?" Seth greeted them, with noticeable hesitancy. His voice sounded thin and meek in their presence. "I … hope I didn't bother you."

The woman shook her head. Her voice had a lower pitch, one that echoed her robust appearance. "No. You not bother us."

Her words were stilted and thickly accented, though Seth could not place the origin of the latter. Troubling thoughts of incredible transformations began pulling at the edges of his mind.

A chilly tendril of fear crept up his spine while suspicions flowed swiftly to the forefront of his thoughts. Flashes of lengthy talons, muzzles lined with glistening fangs, and savage gazes interspersed with the disturbing notions gripping him, spreading the icy feeling all throughout him.

At the very least, both of the strangers were fully clothed. He recalled the pivotal time in the woods with Jonathan and Raymond, when the three witnessed two men shed their clothing and undergo stunning bodily transformations.

Skin pulsing, bones realigning, hair bristling, what Seth had thought were humans became massive wolves right before his eyes. The shock of that encounter still resonated within his mind, and was evoked vividly again as he looked to the two rugged, towering strangers.

"I'll ... I'll just head back that way ... I'm so sorry for interrupting you," Seth said apologetically, feeling increasingly awkward under the weighty stare coming from the huge man.

The others made no immediate reply, and continued gazing upon him. Seth could not deny he felt extremely intimidated, if not a little scared. Their mere presence unnerved him, and made him want to back away without taking his eyes off them.

Other, earlier memories also returned, of wolfish beings standing on two legs, with bodies covered in coarse fur. Seth could still recall the terror he had felt with his friends at the top of a ridge while three two-legged monsters hastened steadily towards them. Only the guns in the hands of Seth and his friends had prevented something horrific from happening to them that day.

He had no gun in his hand now, and nor were any of his friends at his side. Alone, and unnerved, Seth quickly strode back the way he had come.

He forced himself to take his eyes off them, but he still felt their iron-hard stares boring into his back. Nearing the edge of outright panic, it was all he could do not to break into a run.

Seth did not stop for a moment, even when a rather large dragonfly darted into view, slowing to a hover a short distance ahead and to his right. Something about its form begged his closer attention, but fear overpowered any shred of curiosity as he hastened onward. His senses were heightened, and Seth was poised to react to any movements in the underbrush, where every shadow conveyed menace.

Breaking out from the tree line and stepping into the embrace of the open sunlight, Seth continued into the camp. At a quick gait, he made his way towards the central area, where some food could be had.

He did not look back towards the woods, wanting to keep his

focus on the things ahead. Moving among the tents, and surrounded by fellow refugees, his heart rate began settling down into a more normal pace. The chill of fear ebbed and was replaced with the comfort of being back within familiar environs.

"Hey! Seth! There you are! Finally I found you!"

The exuberant voice brought him to a halt. Seth looked up to see Raymond trotting through the maze of tents towards him. A big grin was spread across his friend's face.

"I've got great news for you!" Raymond shouted, well before he had reached the place where Seth patiently awaited him. He pumped his right fist into the air excitedly, and declared in a boisterous tone, "It's what you've been wanting to hear! We're getting to go back home! Not a joke, I'm serious! We're finally heading home!"

The news scattered all thoughts of the two intimidating strangers in the woods, bringing along with it the promise of a large step back towards normalcy. There was nothing in Raymond's face to suggest he was kidding around.

He looked jubilant and energized as he strode quickly across the remaining distance to Seth. It had been a long time since Raymond had looked that happy and at ease.

"That's great!" Seth replied. He then asked, "What happened?"

"Large security convoy is going to be coming close to here," Raymond answered. "And it so happens they are willing to escort anyone wanting to return to a certain group of towns. Evidently, the towns are in a safer regional zone … and Madison happens to be one of the places they can help with!"

"This is fantastic!" Seth exclaimed. "I don't know if my parents will be there yet or not. But it would be great to just go back home again, and be in my own house."

"No kidding," Raymond agreed. "I know we all want to be in our houses again, but I want you to know that you can stay with me, if your folks aren't back just yet. That's no problem at all, man."

"I appreciate it, a lot," Seth said, grinning. "So when is this all taking place?"

"Later today, from what I know at the moment," Raymond said. "So we need to find Jonathan, Annika, and anyone else we know, pronto. You're the first I've found."

"Not giving us much notice, are they?" Seth responded, chuckling.

"No, but I'm not complaining," Raymond said, with a laugh. "I'll take what I can get these days."

"I'm not complaining either," Seth remarked. "And it won't take me long to pack, that's for sure."

"Just the thought of being in my own home again," Raymond said, wistfully. "Waking up in my room, in my own bed. Maybe playing some video games. All that kind of stuff. Man, I can't wait."

"Well, let's round everyone up, looks like we've all got something to look forward to!" Seth responded, giving his friend a vigorous fist bump and smiling broadly.

"And Christa? I think you should check in on her," Raymond said with a pronounced wink.

"Yeah, I should," Seth replied, with feigned confidence.

"News is traveling fast, but she'll appreciate that you made the effort to tell her. I'm telling you, you'll score some points for sure. Don't pass the chance up."

"I'm sure it will impress her," Seth retorted with thick sarcasm. He then added with sincerity, "But maybe you're right."

"Of course I'm right, and I'm not being cocky when I say I know women a lot better than you do. Let's compare records, shall we?" Raymond responded, lightly elbowing Seth's upper right arm.

"Let's not," Seth replied firmly, shaking his head. "I'll concede that point immediately."

"Go, shoo, get out of here!" Raymond said exuberantly, making large gestures to wave him off.

Grinning, Seth turned and strode in the direction where Christa and her family were staying.

Giddy, anxious, hopeful, and a little fearful all at once, he felt his heartbeat quickening as every step drew him closer. He sighed to himself and grinned, knowing there was nothing he could do about it.

All the same, he would follow Raymond's advice, and follow through with delivering the good tidings. Just seeing her would be rewarding enough.

ARIANNA

Benton Crandell stood at the back of the pickup truck. The vehicle's rear gate was down, and a number of small sacks were resting within the bed.

One of them had been opened. Arianna, Sarangar, and Quinn looked upon the mass of seeds.

"Common sense can finally return once more," Benton proudly exclaimed. The old man looked about fifty years younger in the glow of enthusiasm emanating from him. "The exile of reason is coming to an end, my young friends."

"What kind of seeds are those?" Arianna asked, having just joined the others gathered around Benton.

"Hemp. Wonderful, beneficial, bountiful, industrial hemp. This region is going to see its first full crops planted of hemp in quite some time," Benton replied. He glanced towards the others. "There was never any logical reason to ban it before. And now that stupid federal laws aren't choking off common sense anymore, everyone is going to see what damn fools they've all been for not demanding it before."

"I've always wondered what the big deal was," Arianna replied, looking to Benton. "From what I understood, it seemed really silly to keep it banned."

"And it was," Benton said, shaking his head. "Basically, it was another example of the cancer that big businesses and big government bring to a country when the two are in close cahoots. That's all it ever was about. Synthetic material industries had a whole lot to fear. And we all know how big industries played a big part in drafting UCAS legislation."

"With seeds like this, we can get it going again," Benton continued. "This new nation, or whatever it is going to be, will need to develop some trade and commerce fairly quick. This bunch of seeds right here can be a big part of the solution. It will grow like gangbusters in Venorterra. And it can be used for hundreds of products. You'll see what happens."

"Then those seeds, in the bags right there, represent a whole lot of hope, literally," Arianna said, looking upon the mass of seeds with a growing enthusiasm.

"That they do, young lady," Benton said with a grin. "A whole lot of hope is right. For you all, for me, for everyone. But I will need some help getting initial stocks of seed around to some of the farms in the area. We're all in for some lean and tough months … no doubt about that … but the return of a spirit of self-determination will see us through it."

"What kind of plant is this … hemp?" Sarangar asked, staring at the bags of seed.

"A plant you can make clothes from, fuel, rope, food, and hundreds of other things, like Benton said," Quinn responded.

"And it grows really, really well in the soil of Venorterra," Benton added. "We've got a prime climate for this plant."

"Was banned?" Sarangar asked slowly, with a perplexed expression. "You mean you could not grow this hemp? It sounds like good thing. Why not grow before?"

"It was always a great thing," Arianna replied to the younger An-Ki male. "But you have to understand the ways of humans often make little sense. Hopefully the free provinces will apply a little more reason and logic to how things are done from now on."

Sarangar nodded, though she could see he was still unclear about everything. She imagined it was a hard concept for him to digest.

"So, do you think you two strong young lads can help me unload these sacks, and get them over to the cellar for now?" Benton asked, looking towards Sarangar and Quinn.

"Sure, it's no problem at all," Quinn responded agreeably, grabbing up a couple of the sacks without hesitation.

Sarangar lifted four bags with no difficulty, two in each of his large hands, and followed Quinn away from the truck. They headed towards the side of the large cabin, where a set of double doors covered a series of steps leading down into an undercroft.

"Do you think the UCAS will leave the breakaway provinces alone?" Arianna asked Benton, a few moments after they were left to themselves. She had her own ideas regarding the matter, but was curious about what the old man thought.

"No, as they are all about control and power. Make no mistake about that," Benton stated flatly. "They won't rest until they get all of this back under the heel of their jackboot. Every last bit of it. But they are reeling at the moment, and there's instability all across the remaining provinces of the UCAS. It will take them some time to get things together."

"I suppose that's fortunate for us," Arianna said.

"It is. Very fortunate," Benton replied. His next words had a determined edge. "Gives us some time to get ready for the bastards."

Arianna grinned as Benton gave her a merry wink. She had come to love the old man's fiery nature. Even if time had worn his body down, his spirit still had plenty of fight left in it.

"Maybe we can show everyone there's a better way of doing things, in the time we've got," Arianna said. "Maybe word will spread to the places still under UCAS control."

Benton smiled, but there was something bittersweet about his expression. "Even if we do succeed beyond our wildest hopes, the kind of powerful folks we're contending with will make sure the people they have firmly under their boots will just see us as selfish and uncooperative. The UCAS media will cooperate fully with the authorities there to hammer that message home to the masses.

"They won't ask why they are struggling, and why we might be doing better. They'll say we are reckless, and ask why we don't conform to the ways everyone else have accepted. They will paint us as dangerous and radical. Mark my words."

"We still need to do things the way we choose to do them," Arianna said, with an undercurrent of defiance in her voice. "Not how others choose for us."

"It's what freedom and self-determination are all about," Benton replied, with a smile. "Even if we're the last bunch left on this world willing to champion it. Says a lot about the strength you have inside, if you are willing to stand alone for the right thing."

"I'm willing, believe me," Arianna said, looking straight into the old man's eyes.

"I know you are," he replied gently. "You've got a strong spirit in you, Arianna."

Looking up, Arianna took notice of Godral striding out of the woods, a little farther beyond the large barn. Wearing jeans, hiking boots, and a long-sleeved brown shirt, there was little indication he was anything other than a large man, and a very good-looking one at that.

She knew she had to speak with him, and there was no better time than the present. Arianna turned back to Benton. "If you'll excuse me, Benton, I need to catch up with Godral. I had something I've been wanting to talk to him about. I've really enjoyed talking with you, and I hope you don't mind."

"Not at all," Benton said. "I wouldn't get in the way of such a wonderful young lady as yourself."

She smiled at the old man, turned, and started off towards her An-Ki friend. "Godral!" she called out to the large figure, waving to him.

He slowed to a halt, and looked in her direction. "Arianna!"

She continued making her way towards him across the grass. "I need to speak with you for a moment."

Godral said nothing, and waited for her to reach him. Arianna found herself wondering for a brief moment what he would look like without his thick beard.

Even if he did shave once, she was curious whether the beard would return after a transformation, or whether the shaved hair would somehow be reflected in Godral's other forms. She could not deny that her speculation about the nature of shape-shifting was rather trivial, but it was intriguing nonetheless.

"How are you doing today?" she asked, slowing to a stop a couple paces before Godral.

"I am learning," he responded. "The men of the Order are teaching me how to use your weapons. The guns. They are very powerful weapons."

"Guns are powerful, but I'm glad you are learning how to use them," Arianna said. "They can help you defend yourselves even better."

"I believe that they will," Godral replied, nodding. "I believe they could kill a Night Hunter."

Arianna nodded. "I believe they could too."

"The guns will help us protect the clan," he stated. He then smiled, the look having a decided gentleness to it. "I speak too much. You wanted to ask me something?""

Arianna hesitated for a moment. "I wanted to talk with you today, because I have come to an important decision. I didn't want to act on it until I had let you know."

"What is this decision?" Godral asked her, his voice growing somber.

She had no doubts the sensitive being could perceive her unease. Arianna girded her resolve and prepared to openly voice the decision that she had wrestled with for days on end.

Taking a deep breath, Arianna gazed straight into Godral's golden eyes. She stated firmly, "I am leaving. I know it is a crazy thing to do, but I can't just sit around here. I have to go, for the sake of my uncle. I won't be going alone, though, as Quinn and Maureen will be traveling with me."

"Leaving?" Godral asked, his brow furrowing. There was no question he was bothered by the declaration. "Where are you going?"

"I'm going to try and find my Uncle Benedict," Arianna replied. "We know he is somewhere to the west. Even if I learn where he is being held, it is something.

"I believe the forces of the free provinces along the border with the UCAS provinces will know something about where people are being held or detained. We may find someone who knows a whole lot more. As much as the UCAS is spying on us, I'm sure our side has a few eyes among them."

"Many dangers," Godral remarked dourly, and she could see the deep concern reflected in his expression.

She sensed that her friend feared for her, as she had expected he would. The An-Ki had an inclination towards being protective of those of their clan, and she had watched that tendency expand to include their human friends.

"We have seen it is dangerous just to stay here, as my uncle learned," Arianna replied. "Our enemies can get to us if they want to.

You know what they are able to do."

"I will go with you," Godral stated firmly.

Caught off guard, Arianna cast him a look of incredulity. It was not the answer she had expected from him.

She was prepared to argue with him if he tried to send other An-Ki with her, but there was no question he was needed in his own clan. He was Sargor's greatest warrior, and provided invaluable leadership and guidance for the clan during its current time of trial.

"You want to go with me?" she asked, collecting her thoughts.

Peering down at her, Godral replied. "Yes. We must find Benedict. Will tell Vailia, Kantel, and Sarangar. They will want to go with you. You will not go without An-Ki friends."

His words were conveyed with the distinctive air of authority, as if she had become his subordinate for a moment. Arianna knew there would be no arguing with him. The look in his eyes reflected an unwavering conviction, and his stern tone demanded no attempt at disagreement.

Arianna could not deny that his response bolstered her spirits. The uncertainty regarding her uncle was threatening to consume her.

The Shield Maiden, Skylar, had been entirely confounded in the search for Benedict, and nobody knew the reason why. Laborious weeks had dragged on, and then months, with no sign of her uncle's precise whereabouts. Whatever early trail there had been had grown cold and faded.

More than a little guilt pervaded Arianna. It was long past the time to go on a search. She could no longer live with herself, sequestered in relative safety on Benton's land while her uncle was still missing.

Anything she did was a long shot that had the slimmest chance of accomplishing anything, but her troubled conscience could only be mitigated by action. She loved her uncle, and she had to try to the best of her ability.

"Thank you, Godral, but you do not have to do this," Arianna said. "Like I said, Quinn and Maureen will be going with me. I am not doing this alone."

"It was you and Benedict who helped the Messenger," Godral

said. "You faced danger for An-Ki."

"It would have been very wrong not to help you," Arianna replied. "You owe me and my uncle nothing. I know how hard it has been for the An-Ki. You have had to adjust to a whole new world. I've never had to do something like that."

"We will help you, Arianna," Godral said fixedly, and she knew he would listen to no further comments on the matter.

"Thank you, Godral," she said in a low voice, emotions rising within her. "I am so lucky, so blessed, to have friends like you."

"I shall gather the others," Godral told her.

"Sarangar was helping Quinn, up by the house," Arianna said.

"Send him to me, if you see him," Godral replied.

"I will," Arianna promised.

Godral nodded. "When will we begin our journey?" "Tomorrow, or maybe the day after," Arianna said.

"An-Ki will be ready."

"Thank you, Godral."

Stepping forward, she gave him a hug. He returned the affectionate embrace, and she could tell he was getting more comfortable with the human gesture.

Arianna had long observed that the An-Ki tended to tilt much more heavily towards their wolfish forms. Human-style embraces were not something commonly reflected, even when they took the forms of men and women, but Godral and many others were gradually assimilating several common human practices. It would not be too much longer before the An-Ki could move amongst the human populace without too much difficulty.

Arianna then took leave of Godral, and headed back towards the cabin. Other thoughts swirled within her as she reflected upon what he had just committed to.

Arianna knew Godral's Life Mate, Mariassa, was pregnant. She could remember how the female An-Ki's bright yellow eyes had shined when speaking with Arianna about the new life growing inside of her.

As a whole, even with their numbers divided among many physical locales, Sargor's clan had gone through their first period of Life Unions within the new age that they all now lived in. Many pairs of Life Mates, Godral and Mariassa included, were currently expecting new offspring. It was a development Godral had expressed great happiness and increased worry about, the latter largely because Sargor's clan was split up for the time being.

The forthcoming births represented a milestone, being the first wave of new An-Ki to arrive within the modern age. For Godral to commit to help her in finding Benedict during such a momentous time for the clan was a profoundly moving gesture.

Arianna walked up to the front of the cabin. Looking around, she did not see any sign of Sarangar, or even Quinn, for that matter. Benton's truck was gone too. After peering around for a few moments more, she continued up to the sheltered porch and proceeded through the door.

Once inside, she saw Quinn and Maureen cuddling together on the couch. The sight of her two close friends brought an instant smile to her face.

The two were so deeply into each other, which gave them added strength to rely on during all of the hardships everyone was enduring. There were a few moments when Arianna wished she had someone of her own, like Maureen did with Quinn.

Arianna was comfortable and quite secure with herself, but that did not mean she never harbored hopes of finding someone to share in her life's journey. She had walked alone for a long time, and a true companion would be more than welcome.

"You sure wasted no time taking a break," she said to Quinn, grinning. "Got all those bags of seeds put away already?"

"I'm very efficient," Quinn replied, with a laugh. "Get my work done, so I can spend more time in ways I like."

Maureen smiled at Quinn, and looked back to Arianna. "So when are we going on this big adventure to find your uncle? Quinn and I have been talking about it some more, and we want to be sure to plan for some sightseeing stops along the way."

Arianna knew her friend was not taking the situation lightly. Maureen was just putting a positive face to something that had all three of them extremely nervous.

"I'm sure we can work in a few extra stops," Arianna replied, chuckling. "Just budget for souvenirs."

"See, my love? I told you it would be a nice vacation," Maureen told Quinn, giving him a playful kiss on the cheek.

"I've been in need of one for a long time," Quinn remarked. He looked back to Arianna and his tone grew more serious. "I've got our packs pretty much ready. You said we'd leave in the next day or so?"

Arianna nodded. "And I have some news. Our group has gotten larger."

"No, he's not going, this may have too many physical demands," Maureen said immediately, in a sharper tone.

She knew instantly who Maureen was referencing. "No, no, Gerald's not going. I'm not giving way on that either," Arianna interjected quickly, watching the smiles and joviality fading from her friends' faces in the wake of her announcement.

Benedict's brother would have insisted on going, but there was no guarantee that physical hardships did not lie ahead on such an uncertain foray. Arianna and her two friends had made a solid pact not to tell Gerald about the excursion.

It had been difficult keeping the decision from her other uncle, but she knew that if things went badly awry his older body would not be able to hold up for long. She knew she would incur tremendous grief for the subterfuge in hiding the journey to find Benedict from him, but she saw no other way. She was not about to go searching for one uncle, and then lose the other.

"So who's going then?" Maureen asked, a little apprehensively.

"I just found out we are being joined by Godral, Vailia, Kantel, and Sarangar," Arianna replied. "We are going to have four of the An-Ki with us."

"I'm liking our chances much better now," Quinn said, visibly perking up. "How did you manage to convince them to do this?"

"I didn't," Arianna said. "I just wanted Godral to know where we were, and what I had decided to do. He insisted on accompanying us."

"I'm not objecting either," Maureen added. "If things get difficult, it will be great to have them with us."

"It means we might have to take a second vehicle along," Arianna said. "I have no idea what the fuel situation is out there."

"They aren't rationing, just the cost is sky high, from what I've been able to tell," Maureen said.

"Which means that there's probably gas to be found," Quinn said. "Just the high prices mean only those who absolutely have to get somewhere are buying it."

"And we have to get somewhere," Arianna said. "Possibly in two vehicles. So what do we have for barter?"

"I've got some cash, and we've got a little silver," Maureen said.

"The fellows from the Order said silver and gold can get you a lot right now, while all the currency issues are so shaky," Quinn said. "Even lighters and those small little bottles of alcohol work really good as currency, they say. Ammunition and firearms too."

"We probably don't have a lot of the last two to spare, though," Arianna replied.

"No, we don't," Quinn said, shaking his head. "So we'll have to hope for the best with the rest of it."

"Then we'll scrape up as much as we can," Arianna said, wishing she had bought herself some silver or gold before everything went so chaotic.

"I'll see if Benton might have a thing or two he can lend us," Quinn said. "I need to ask him about getting some extra ammo for the guns anyway, to bolster what we've got for our protection."

"Sounds good," Arianna said. "After we look into whatever we need to look into, I suggest we all get a good night's rest. If we end up going tomorrow, let's be ready for it."

"Agreed," Maureen said, nodding. She glanced at Quinn, and winked. "And that means rest, Quinn. Actual, genuine rest. No debates on that. No bending the rules."

"You are so cruel," Quinn replied, laughing, before giving her another kiss.

"What am I thinking? I must be crazy taking you two kids along with me on this trip!" Arianna exclaimed, laughing herself.

"I don't know what you were thinking. But I promise you'll have your hands full with us along," Maureen replied, grinning.

"Yes, I will, my dear friends," Arianna replied, shaking her head in amusement.

Maureen loosed a high pitched shriek from the sudden tickle given by her boyfriend. In moments, the two were wrestling playfully on the couch.

Arianna smiled and walked on through the living room, making her way to the quiet of her bedroom. She clicked on the lamp on the stand by the bed.

Kicking her shoes off, she lay down on her back and closed her eyes for a few seconds. She could still hear her friends giggling in the other room, but it was not enough to disturb the peaceful feeling that came over her.

Another journey was about to begin soon. She wished Calliel would make an appearance, as he had been absent for awhile. Advice from an Avatar would have been most welcome for the coming sojourn, but she was not going to wait around for anything.

Her uncle was somewhere out there, a victim of a hostile power. Arianna was determined to do everything she could to find out where he was; and if possible bring him back.

DAGIAN

Drifting about twenty feet above the ground, Dagian Underwood passed through the shadows beneath the boughs of lofty trees. Though the night was steeped in darkness, with thick cloudbanks obscuring the crescent moon, she could see clearly enough.

Amorphous shapes flitted amongst the branches to her left and right. They were not the movements of natural creatures, but rather part of the ethereal host drawn to the vast tract of forested land that Dagian now warded.

The compound served as the residence of Kaira Antipalos. The young woman headed the World Summit's Peace Commission, and was now the center of the Convergence's focus.

Dagian had enough concerns to occupy her full attention. Jibade, the only Walker of the Setian Path to fully master the ability of traveling out of body, was dead. Dagian knew his spirit was now answering for the man's failures in the depths of Set's realm. She avoided thinking of the nightmares Jibade's spirit now endured, a costly price paid in agonies indescribable.

Dagian, in the wake of Jibade's demise, had elevated her own abilities considerably. She had even absorbed some of the power given to the Setian, and now possessed an ability that she knew was of tremendous value to the Convergence.

She recalled her last mystical visit into the heart of Set's realm. There, she had encountered and spoken with one of the powerful Avatar's priests. Dagian could remember the tall being's face with vivid clarity, as she stood with the powerful entity beneath the Sky of Enduring Midnight.

Framed by the rectangular extensions dropping down from the headdress it wore, the visage of the broad-shouldered entity was bestial. From its erect, square-ended ears and down-curving, lengthy snout, to its radiant white eyes, the priest's appearance was one unique to Set's realm.

Only the priests among the Fallen Avatar's servants dwelling within the dark, ancient realm exhibited such a visage. As such, there had been no mistaking the realm where Dagian had traveled to. Nor was there any dispute regarding the figure's high authority.

In addition to warning her of the Enemy's warrior who had slain Jibade, the Setian priest had given her an unexpected message. He had instructed her to depart Troy, and help the One who held the direct favor of the Risen Throne.

There was no question Kaira was that designated individual, but exactly why she was so vitally important to the Convergence was still a great mystery to Dagian. It was something she pondered often, while applying her abilities in the service of the Abyss' eminent Lords.

A towering, dark form lumbered forward, just to Dagian's right. Turning her gaze, she beheld the huge shape of Helel, one of the many Erkorenen who had been transported by the TTDF to the compound site. Like Dagian and many others, they had been relocated to provide support and protection for Kaira.

The giant's dark eyes shifted in her direction, and it was clear that Helel sensed her presence. A low, rumbling growl welled up from his throat, a sound that brimmed with the creature's agitation and frustration at detecting an unseen entity.

Helel would have recognized Dagian immediately from back in the underground facility at Station Central, but there was no way for her to reveal herself to the brawny giant. The only things that could see her were the ubiquitous spirits gathered to help keep a constant vigil on the large compound.

Dagian drifted forward and left Helel among the trees behind, moving farther away from the compound. Acclimating to her woodland surroundings, she felt the other Erkorenen before she saw them. She across individuals of their kind in many various forms as she proceeded through the trees.

From the concentration of spirits, to the Erkorenen, to the large contingent of TTDF troopers who were all fanatical Initiates of the Faith, Dagian found it hard to believe that anything could reach Kaira when she was staying in the compound.

Yet despite the dense layers of security covering both physical and non-physical states, Dagian harbored some fears regarding the situation. They were far from frivolous concerns, having been generated by the enemy's own actions in the recent past.

A unique, powerful weapon had been used by the Enemy's warrior to slay Jibade while he had been in an out of body state. An image of both the weapon and enemy warrior who had wielded it had been given to Dagian by the Setian priest. Wreathed in flames, the black blade had been held firmly in the hands of a tall, blond-haired woman with an intensive, blue-eyed gaze.

There was no doubt in Dagian's mind that the image represented a mortal woman just like herself. But she was one who held a thorough command over her spiritual form, similar to Dagian.

Perhaps the enemy warrior knew even more about the disembodied state than Dagian. There was no room for ego-driven postures. Only analysis devoid of emotions would bear fruit. Underestimating the enemy warrior's capabilities was not a mistake

Dagian would make, as such an error could easily prove fatal.

The weapon that the woman had wielded vexed Dagian thoroughly. She could not ascertain whether the blade was a conjuration or something else entirely. The only thing she knew for sure was that she could not replicate something similar, which meant that she was vulnerable to the strange weapon.

Now, Dagian found herself filling the role that the dead Walker of the Setian path previously held. It meant that she could find herself confronted with the same enemy and weapon that had resulted in Jibade's death. She knew she had to find something to counter the weapon, even as she actively hunted for the enemy warrior.

Complicating the situation further, the Setian priest had intimated that an enemy Avatar had directly aided the enemy warrior. If the weapon was not a conjuration of the woman's, the involvement of an Avatar was the only conceivable way that the spectral blade could have been provided to the enemy warrior, when she was out of her physical body.

Yet even then, the nature of the weapon still eluded her. So much of it was a confounding, foreboding mystery. Despite scouring every reference she could, there were still no answers.

While in a non-physical state, the Enemy's servant clearly had a method of severing the connection between body and spirit. Dagian had not deemed such a thing remotely possible, but it had happened nonetheless.

Dagian could not relax her guard for even a single moment. She was not about to share the same terrible fate as Jibade.

If she were to die now, Dagian knew deep down that she would face an afterworld like Jibade was now experiencing. She had already been warned of that horrific fate in a vivid fashion, when she had been called before no less than Azazel and Mammon. That encounter had followed one of her greatest unveilings: the revelation of Living ID to a large gathering of the Convergence's global leadership.

An icy chill came over her every time she recalled that distressing night. She had soared to the heights of triumph, only to plunge minutes later into the depths of blackest despair.

Yet not everything was of a worrisome or threatening nature. At the moment, she was looking forward to the looming possibility of another significant opportunity to advance her mystical abilities.

Only a day prior, she had been informed that a delegation steeped in eastern arts involving the Craft was making its way to the UCAS. Even further, many Walkers of the Setian Path were accompanying the veteran practitioners.

The arrival of more Setians was expected. The otherworldly priest had promised they would come and be placed under her authority.

The news of the easterners had been a complete surprise to Dagian. It was a development rife with many intriguing potentialities.

All of them, easterners and Setians alike, would be landing via aircraft very soon on the grounds where she now resided. She looked forward to conferring with both the Setians and easterners about a number of topics.

The grace of Diabolos known as the Craft was a wide and diverse undertaking for any of its adherents. Early on their path, a practitioner of the Craft came to discover the immense value of delving into the mysteries revealed and practiced by various factions. The elite such as Dagian refined the blending of various influences and traditions, building a personal arsenal in their service of the Risen Throne.

Different arts carried their own strengths, and Dagian had long desired to explore more of the dark mysteries hailing from all across the lands of Asu. As had happened in Kemet, with the journey into the realm of Set, a leap in her own advancement could be attained if she could gain audience with one or more of the great Powers guiding the Ten-Fold Kingdom's human servants living in the east.

Since her visit to Set's realm, Dagian had unlocked so many insights, powers, and revelations that Anat had bestowed within her. Apep and Set had also empowered her further, adding to the incredible boon she had received in the infernal region.

Looking back on the recent past, the gifts that Dagian received from the infernal Avatars had undeniably enabled her to assume a role similar to what Jibade's had been. She was one of the only humans living in the entire world who could leave and return to a physical body while maintaining full retention of mental faculties and memories in both states of existence.

Her abilities coupled with the fact that she was one of the most powerful practitioners of the Craft in all the world had undoubtedly led to her relocation to the old forests north of Yorvik. Her political influence, wealth, and position as the CEO of a major, multi-national corporation were substantial assets to the Convergence, but there were many other elite men and women who possessed similar attributes. When it came to her mastery of the Craft, and newfound ability to navigate while being in an out of body state, Dagian was unique, and currently irreplaceable.

Dagian continued on her way around the outer boundaries of the sizeable acreage. To a degree, it was like taking a long walk through the woods. Afforded a clear, undistracted mind, while assessing the various levels of protection, she pondered many questions ranging from elements of the Craft to mundane business regarding Babylon Technologies.

She had many capable lieutenants to keep the multi-national firm on course. An array of innovative projects in various stages of development proceeded apace. Living ID, which had propelled her company and name to worldwide prominence, was poised for massive expansion.

The UCAS was just the first step of a planned worldwide implementation. Following closely would be the transition to entirely digital currency, the Nummus, which would be adopted soon enough by several other economic unions right alongside Living ID.

The final stage of the Convergence would see both Living ID and the Nummus become the standard for the first truly global order realized in all of human history. Sometimes it was hard for Dagian to believe she was going to both witness and play a major part in the attainment of such a worldwide, transformational goal, one that had been worked towards, and sacrificed for, by countless individuals over the span of millennia.

So many dedicated servants of the Shining One had gone to their graves knowing that the things they labored so arduously for would not be realized within their lifetimes. Sheer good fortune had been with Dagian, in terms of being born within the age when everything would finally be achieved.

Her thoughts returned back to Kaira, as they often did as of late. The head of the World Summit's Peace Commission was clearly going to perform a crucial function for the Convergence. Nothing else could explain the immense security put in place for her.

Even Aaliyah Satrinah had moved her center of operations to the compound, along with many more prominent figures. In some ways, the compound had swiftly evolved into a command center for several diverse aspects of the Convergence.

Of the circle involved with the Convergence that Dagian normally interacted with, only Xavier Gerard resided off site. The stalwart TTDF commander had his hands full with the instability across the UCAS.

He had come to the compound a few times, to confer with Aaliyah or one of the other higher governmental authorities in person. But for the most part he was somewhere else, dealing with the most pressing issues.

The TTDF had a very important role in regard to the compound. In addition to providing physical security for the site, the TTDF had been tasked with the transportation of the Erkorenen from their underground refuges to the large tract of woodland.

Dagian did not envy Xavier, who seemed indefatigable as he confronted all the problems plaguing the UCAS, and still saw to the essential needs of the compound. At the very least he was supported fervently. The contingent of TTDF troopers at the compound, every last one of them an Initiate of the Faith, was fiercely loyal to him.

The airstrip and helipads serving the compound were in regular use. From what Dagian had observed, the flow of prominent individuals in and out of the compound showed no signs of letting up anytime soon.

Captains of industry, political figures, and even celebrities were ushered in and out of the compound. Some stayed for as long as a week. Most of the prominent individuals met with Aaliyah and other Convergence leaders who had made the compound their dwelling. Yet there was no mistaking that everything about the place and its occupants hinged upon one person: Kaira Antipalos.

She was a beautiful young woman with great vision. Kaira was also one of those individuals whose path in life enjoyed harmony with timely opportunity. The death of David Sorath, the previous head of the World Summit Peace Commission, had paved the way for Kaira's meteoric rise within the international body.

Kaira had not been at the Peace Commission for very long when David's death had occurred, but she had already found great favor with him. She been designated his successor over several experienced individuals who had served at the commission for many years.

Interestingly, there was none of the usual backbiting and infighting so common to institutions filled with highly ambitious individuals. Not one shred of resistance to Kaira's rapid ascendancy manifested from within the long-established organization.

It was undeniable that Kaira had quickly made a name for herself amid all the global turmoil. The Peace Commission had been critical in seeing to the end of hostilities between Mandaria and the UCAS.

Stories abounded of how Kaira herself had navigated those precarious days, when the world had teetered on the brink of war. She had stared down hardened diplomats from the UCAS, Mandaria, and even Muscovy in the most tense of moments, and gotten them to cooperate with her vision.

It was just the first of a parade of instances showcasing Kaira's keen insights and wisdom regarding international affairs. Her relative youth was swiftly all but forgotten.

The Peace Commission was even playing a major role in the World Summit's response addressing the pandemic with the Thanatos Virus, known to the higher ranks of the Convergence as the Abundant Harvest Virus. Under Kaira's leadership, the Peace Commission was helping in the development of new protocols for quarantine areas and vaccine distribution.

Talk was also now swirling in higher circles about Kaira's next steps involving the Peace Commission. She was said to be very close to unveiling several unprecedented new initiatives, ones that would harness the full potential of the Peace Commission.

Dagian suspected that the forthcoming initiatives would give her a much better idea of the pivotal role that Kaira so evidently filled within the context of the Convergence. Yet she could not deny that both her mind and instincts were honing in fast upon one prominent conclusion. Increasingly drowning out all other speculations, the emerging answer set Dagian's mind to the brink of spinning.

Only one being in all of recorded history could perfectly embody the Will of the Risen Throne. Prophets and mystics all across the ages testified to the nature and mission of that expected individual.

A thread of consensus ran through all of their visions and accounts. Dreaded by those who served the Enemy, and longed for by those who served the Shining One, a spirit unrivaled would arise in the flesh to herald the last days of the current world; and proclaim a new world to follow.

The world's true savior, the manifestation of the incarnated spirit stood at the epicenter of a maelstrom of prophecy regarding the final age of the world. Visions of seers, mystics and prophets predicting all manner of ends were spread across the face of human history.

Dagian could only laugh at the prophecies put forth by the Saviorans, whose communities were being steadily whittled down and eradicated all across the world. The gates of the Nether Kingdom were prevailing spectacularly against the Saviorans, giving the lie to the claims of the Enemy's servants that their church would never fall to the Abyss' might. The prophecies of the Saviorans would prove false as well.

Soon enough, the full force of the emerging new order could be turned upon the last remaining strongholds of the Enemy in the world. The world would then be cleansed of the disease that had plagued it for so long.

Leading that force would be the purest servant of the Shining One to ever walk upon the surface of the world. Like the light of a new day, revealing things previously hidden in the dark of night, signs abounded that Kaira could possibly be that legendary, transformational figure.

If that turned out to be true, it meant that Dagian was closer to the Risen Throne than she had ever been in her life. Humbling, daunting, and inspiring, the notion spurred her to the highest levels of wariness and diligence in her tasks.

The choices she had made in her life, and the paths she had

pursued, had brought her to a place brimming with momentous implications. She could well be at the side of the imminent ruler of the entire world. Further, that glorious ruler would open the doors of a wondrous new age, the Remaking, when the Shining One's Light would illuminate all of creation.

For a woman who could just as easily have remained a slave to the faith her parents once sought to instill in her, Dagian's current position reflected outright triumph and vindication. She was no victim of fate. She had mastered it, far beyond her wildest expectations.

SKYLAR

Twilight filtered through the pines as Skylar slowly made her way to the top of a hill. The serenity of the view spreading out before her as she neared the summit did little to relieve the heaviness weighing down her lonely heart.

It was the quiet times when she was the most vulnerable, but she knew she had to come to terms with the terrible loss of her brother Matthias. The moments when Genevieve told her of the terrible news had been surreal to experience.

She knew Genevieve, her closest friend among the Shield Maidens, brought horrid tidings from the moment Skylar had looked into her eyes, glistening brightly with tears. Skylar had known in that instant what she was about to be told. Her breath had stilled inside her, her gut had clenched up, and a cold, dizzying feeling ran through her body.

Matthias had died during the mission to get Juan Delgado into Troy. He had been a key participant in the operation, conducted so that the defector from Babylon Technologies could deliver the truth of what was happening at the insidious company onto live television.

Government troopers storming the broadcast facility had shot Matthias multiple times in the aftermath of the presentation. The bullets they fired had been intended for Magdalene, whose exposed back was squarely in their sights as she and the others hurried to evacuate the rooftop of the building. She would never have made it alive out of the city if Matthias had not intentionally dived into the path of the gunfire at the last moment.

In the act of leaving by helicopter from the roof, they had been unable to take Matthias' body with them. Skylar understood why they had to leave her brother's body behind, but it was still something that haunted her days.

So many memories flowed through her mind. In a way, she was glad that her recollections would never include seeing a coffin or grave that contained him. Matthias had been so full of life and energy, and that was how she would always remember him. In some ways, the protection of his memory in the fullness of life was a small mercy and blessing.

At a young age her father had taken her to the Sister who had guided her in the direction of becoming a Shield Maiden. It had then been Skylar who had guided her brother, when he expressed a burning desire to protect the Savioran faith from the increasing onslaught against it.

As a Shield Maiden, she had known of the Order, and knew her brother had the intrinsic qualities to become one of the latter's vaunted Knights. Skylar had helped Matthias with the introduction that began his own path to becoming such a Knight.

Now, after he had died violently in the service of the Order, she felt a sharp stab of guilt. But she knew in her heart that he had lived the life he wanted. In giving his life to save another he had expressed the value he harbored within his fiery spirit for an irreplaceable soul.

She could see Matthias even now, speaking of how every single person who had ever existed was of inestimable value. As her brother explained it, very individual was a one-of-a-kind spirit who could never be replicated; not in all of eternity.

She smiled to herself, remembering how he would continue on at length about how each soul, unique and intrinsically individual, reflected the wonder and boundless Grace of Adonai. He even speculated that the Avatars serving Adonai could see this special nature of each soul clearly; and that they regarded every soul as a most precious creation.

It was such a beautiful understanding of souls. Deep in her heart, Skylar found that her spirit resonated with his insights.

"You had the eyes of an Avatar, my brother," Skylar whispered into the night air, as she took another laborious step up the hillside.

Matthias had demonstrated just how precious and valuable he esteemed each soul to be with the very last moments of his life. In her eyes, his life was a resounding triumph, and she knew she must never forget that, even if she was now shrouded in the darkness of sorrow.

Adding further to her grief was the stark absence of any kind of consolation. The lack of any sign at all from her brother since his death gnawed incessantly at her mourning spirit.

Skylar just wanted to know that he had made his way to Adonai's eternal realms. Even if Matthias had found his way to Purgatarion, that place of mercy allowed for those crossing the Veil who were not yet perfected enough to enter the heavenly realms, her heart could rest more easily.

After everything she had seen and experienced as a Shield Maiden, she found that she expected at least something regarding Matthias' place in the afterworld. All she needed was a single message, a brief vision that her brother had found his way to an eternal home.

Whenever she had been out of body since his passing, she found herself desiring to go looking for him. It was an urge that Magdalene sternly warned against. Such a quest could easily consume her, and lead her to incredibly dangerous places. Some boundaries were not to be crossed.

Coming to a standstill on the crown of the hill, Skylar loosed an extended sigh. The evening breezes flowed gently through her long, blond tresses. The sun was dipping beneath the rolling hills, as if tucking itself in for the night. Shadows were growing, and light was ebbing, much like the state of her heart.

"They say You are in the silence, the whisper of a breeze," she said in a low voice, gazing out over the beautiful vista. "Just let me know he is okay ... please, that is all I ask. Please, let him give me a message. Just one. I ask nothing more. I love him. I just want to know he made it to Your realms."

She spoke the words slowly and deferentially, but there were traces of desperation, and even despair, within her tone. Answers eluded her, and left her heart plagued with uncertainty.

Often she had counseled mourning friends to hold fast to their faith in the wake of personal loss. Now that she was in their position, she clung to it as tightly as she could.

Even so, she could find no comfort to pacify the gaping void inside her. The loss left her with a deep wound that would not heal.

The breezes washed against her face, soothing her tear-streaked skin, but she heard no voice. She stood upon the summit for a lengthy period of time, staring outward as the night unfurled a star-filled sky.

The deep silence persisted. No response was forthcoming.

Skylar peered into the hint of the infinite, gazing upward, as another tear trickled down her cheek. Her next words were intended more directly to the source of her abiding sorrow.

"Just something, Matthias. Anything. Anything at all. Let me know you are okay. I miss you so much."

Set free from her swollen eyes, a pair of tears accompanied her last words. As before, no response manifested. The stars seemed bitterly cold, and the depths of night an empty void.

Her pain unresolved, she finally turned away from the hilltop and made her way back down the slope. The moonlight bathing the forest gave her plenty enough luminance to watch her steps.

Thinking about the absence of any consolations, some other thoughts jogged loose within her. The lack of resolution tearing at her heart brought her an increased level of sympathy for the niece of Benedict Darwin.

Skylar had not gotten very acquainted with the young woman. But her inability to find Benedict's location caused Skylar additional suffering, especially in light her own inner burdens.

Turning her thoughts to the situation involving Benedict brought her no respite from sorrow. Yet at the very least it took her mind away from the agony of thinking about Matthias for a few moments, which was a small grace in and of itself.

There was simply no trace of Benedict, nothing that she could hone in upon when traveling in spirit. The complete absence of any hint of a trail to him occurred not long after the final visit from the Fallen Avatar.

She wondered what had happened to cause that, and continued to worry about the decision she had made to cooperate with the Fallen Avatar. The infernal spirit claimed to be repentant, even if the possibility of a Fallen Avatar coming back into Adonai's Grace was something deemed impossible by theologians.

There was no question the entity had guided her in the means of destroying one of the Enemy's most valuable weapons. If the Fallen Avatar was deceiving her, such pivotal assistance did not equate.

It was so very rare that a living being could go into spirit and return with a complete command of memory all throughout. To her knowledge, she was the only one of that kind serving Adonai, and it was highly possible that the Setian had been the only one available to the Enemy.

To help deliver such a heavy blow to the Convergence was not the act of a Fallen Avatar dutifully serving Diabolos. Rather, it was the act of a truly penitent spirit, desirous of proving its intent through bold action.

With the Setian gone, Skylar knew she gave the resistance to the Convergence a great advantage for the moment. Undoubtedly, the Enemy would move fast to try and address the shortcoming among their living servants, but there was a window of time that could probably be exploited to the advantage of the Shield Maidens, and all others fighting against Diabolos' forces.

Magdalene had counseled caution, but things in the world were moving so very fast, and not in a favorable direction. The breakaway provinces were highly vulnerable, as Skylar knew the regime governing the rest of the UCAS was not one to give up control so easily.

A malignant shadow was deepening all across the world. Living ID, the deadly Thanatos Virus outbreak, the wars in the east, and everything that had been happening were not mere coincidences. They were tools of a much grander, darker scheme, one that was on the cusp of realization.

That thought deeply unnerved her. If she was right, it meant that one of the most dangerous beings in all of recorded history, if not the most dangerous, was about to move to the center of the world stage.

In that regard, the Sacred Writings were not fully encouraging either. They spoke of a shadowy, eminently powerful figure gaining full dominion of the world, and wielding authority over all lands and nations. A terrible persecution would be levied against the followers of Adonai in an age of blood and fire.

As she walked beneath the boughs of the tall pines, her thoughts centered upon the fact that it had been TTDF forces that had killed her brother. She knew Whom they ultimately served, and they would have to answer for what they had done.

"I'll find a way to hurt you deeply," she growled, speaking into the darkness. Her eyes narrowed, and a fire churned within her heart. "If I have to cross the surface of the entire world, I'll find a way. You will answer for what you took from me."

The burning resolve flooding into her heart as she spoke the words did not erase the pain she felt, but it did numb it. If she could not rid herself of the inner sorrow, dulling it was the next best thing.

Her anger towards the TTDF served as a spark reminding her that she was still alive and had to apply herself to good purpose. Skylar could not waver from the path she was on, and she intended to follow it with as much dedication as ever.

With no sign of Benedict, she would likely have to search much more broadly if there was a clue to be found. Yet if a lead existed, she intended to find it. She would just have to cast her net wider.

She might not be able to end the uncertainty and sorrow afflicting her, but she might find a path to some answers for Benedict's niece. At the very least, she could bring the kind of comfort to another that she could not attain in her own life.

SECTION II

DAGIAN

Dagian quietly stood in the background, looking onward as Aaliyah concluded her video conference with the latest UCAS Senator to take up residence within Gaia City. She knew the underground metropolis near Larimer was massive, but the video gave a fuller sense of the incredible extent of the facility.

Behind the senator, through wall to ceiling windows, Dagian could see what looked to be a city street complete with storefronts, a movie theater, and everything else typically found along an average downtown street. There was even wheeled traffic moving along the thoroughfare in the forms of small, electric-powered vehicles.

Dagian knew well that those such as the senator could look forward to spacious personal accommodations, and many other amenities, including tennis courts and swimming pools. The enormous subterranean city was a far cry from the dingy confines of the average bunker. It offered all manner of luxuries and recreation to its prestigious inhabitants.

It was an architectural triumph carefully designed with longevity and comfort in mind, stocked with vast stores of food, medicine, and equipment. Bristling with security features, it was a veritable fortress as well.

Every consideration had been made with regard to the location of Gaia City. Accessed by a former international airport far removed from the city of Larimer itself, it was easy and safe to reach for those intending to stay there.

The refuge was not the only such underground facility within the UCAS. Many had been set up for the elite and those serving the Convergence to wait out the storms of upheaval sweeping across the globe.

A populace of moderate size could survive with miniscule hardship for a very long time within the facility, if need be. Dagian had a sizeable personal dwelling set aside for herself inside one of them, but she only intended to use it as an absolutely last resort.

"Has the Abundant Harvest Virus had the effect that you

projected?" the senator asked Aaliyah.

Behind the question, Dagian perceived more than a little unease in the older man. She wondered what he could possibly be afraid of, as all of the Convergence's elite had been given access to the vaccine immediately.

"Well over one billion deaths, and still mounting, the great majority occurring in the third world nations, just as we intended," Aaliyah replied evenly. "The goals of population reduction sought for the new age have still not been met. But we anticipate some of the forthcoming initiatives advanced by the Convergence will see us to more manageable levels of population."

"That is good to hear," the senator replied calmly, as if taking in the figures of a stock report. "From what I can follow, the outbreaks seem to have been effectively isolated in places such as the UCAS, Germania, and Angalaland."

"You are correct, and that is no coincidence," Aaliyah responded, though she did not offer the man any further explanations.

Dagian knew the primary focus of releasing Abundant Harvest had been to reduce the heavily-populated, underdeveloped nations of the third world to much more sustainable, manageable levels. Yet the virus could not be fully corralled, and had exacted a toll from all across the globe.

The vaccine, developed by the scientist who had engineered the virus itself, had aided the implementation of Living ID in the UCAS. Access to the treatment had been combined with receiving the nanoscale implants developed by Dagian's company.

Problems with supply and inefficiencies of distribution were cited publicly as the reasons for the vaccine's sparse dissemination within the third world. Yet any casual observer could see that the vaccine was prevalent in nations where it was vitally important to retain some degree of stability.

Of course, with the Convergence steering the discourse of the mainstream media, there was little worry of such an analysis gaining firm footing in the mass populace. Alternative media had been effectively muzzled with the lockdowns of digital networks. National security was easy enough to cite wherever censorship had to be employed, to silence anyone who tried straying too far from the official narrative.

Dagian was simply glad that the end of the old world was looming. The dawn of the new age was imminent, and she could not see it rise a moment too soon.

"What of the continued, untenable situation with gangs and crime so rampant in the cities of the UCAS?" the senator asked, a little more pointedly. "The insurgency in the south and midwest prevents us from being able to use all security assets. But we cannot shift resources being used along the new boundaries between the UCAS and rebel-held territory. The borders must be secured as tightly as possible."

"It is interesting to see your sudden dedication to border security, Senator," Aaliyah replied firmly. "But you need not worry yourself. The World Summit will play a part in that situation. I would not lose too much sleep about the matter, senator. You will understand soon enough."

"I'll take your word on that, Aaliyah. You have never given me bad counsel," the senator said, sitting back in his black leather chair. "It is just that there is so much chaos, it is hard for me to see how it can all be shepherded in the right directions. Everything seems to be fraying apart."

"It is well-managed chaos, I assure you," Aaliyah said. "Each crisis we engineer creates the opportunity for another step to be taken. Every brushfire lasts only as long as we wish to stoke the flames."

"Like I stated, it is hard for me to understand how it is all guided, but you know you have my support in all things," the senator said. "I will be working from here to facilitate any legislative support required."

"And I appreciate that, senator," Aaliyah said. "You will have a seat at the table in the new age. It will not be very much longer."

"That is the best news I have heard yet," the senator replied, with a winsome smile. "I will not take up any more of your time, Aaliyah. I just wanted to voice some concerns and let you to know I was settled here, and will be carrying out my administrative tasks from the refuge so generously provided for us."

"I appreciate the consideration," Aaliyah said. "I shall talk to you soon. Enjoy your accommodations and have a good day, Senator."

"And you have a good day, Aaliyah," Senator Reid Kerry replied amiably.

"Another one takes to the ground," Aaliyah remarked coolly, the monitor going dark. She turned towards Dagian. Her expression was humorless, and her gaze was like steel. "It seems many more of them have lost their backbone in recent weeks. I am not sure we should tolerate such weaklings having any place in the age to come."

"I share your sentiments," Dagian responded. "But they probably just want to be as secure as possible while they adjust to the currency transition and other elements happening at this time."

It had just been announced that the UCAS would be embracing the Nummus, as would the Europa Alliance. Dagian knew that in the long run it would become the currency of the forthcoming global order, but for the moment it was being sold as a way to help stabilize and manage the fragile economies.

"Most of them are just feckless in the presence of danger," Aaliyah stated with a biting air of derision. "Rats going to their holes, when enemies need to be confronted and overcome."

"Have you spoken to Xavier recently?" Dagian asked.

"There is one who does not shy from confrontation," Aaliyah said with approval. She nodded to Dagian, "Yes, I have spoken with him. He is doing everything he can at the moment, but his resources have been spread dangerously thin."

"When you spoke with the senator, you mentioned something about the World Summit playing a part in the security situation," Dagian said. "I was curious about that."

"An initiative is coming very shortly," Aaliyah said. Her eyes narrowed. "But do not worry yourself. Kaira Antipalos needs to be protected at all costs, and these grounds must be a safe haven for her. Nothing must get through. Do you understand?"

"I understand, and nothing is going to get near this building complex without being detected well in advance," Dagian assured Aaliyah.

"You had better be correct," Aaliyah responded tersely, and Dagian did not miss the coiling threat underlying her words.

"I will need some personal time with the arriving delegation from the east," Dagian said. She added quickly, not wanting to sound like she was making a demand. "If at all possible, that is."

"Understood," Aaliyah said flatly. After a short pause, she continued, "Your abilities have grown significantly since your trip to Kemet. That was a very advantageous journey."

Dagian nodded. "It was very beneficial. And I hope to grow my abilities much further."

"Do whatever it takes to defend against or hunt down this enemy assassin," Aaliyah said. "Adding to your abilities in the Craft can only help."

Dagian did not need to ask for any clarifications as to who it was that Aaliyah was speaking of. "She will be found, and she will be destroyed."

"You are responsible for warding the non-physical elements intertwining with this material plane," Aaliyah said. "As Xavier is a commander of forces in this world, you have authority over forces unseen to human eyes."

Dagian nodded. "And they will be well utilized. You can be sure of that."

"No Avatar of the Enemy will approach through this plane, as it would draw one of our own in response," Aaliyah proceeded. "Even if one of them were to enter this plane, it takes them a great expenditure of energy to conceal themselves. With a horde of lesser spirits from the Nether Kingdom gathered here, our enemy would not go undetected."

"And what of the large number of spirits here?" Dagian asked, seeing an opportunity to satisfy one concern she had. "Surely they draw some unwelcome attention to this place."

"As you know, Dagian, lesser spirits from the Nether Kingdom roam the world free," Aaliyah said. "It is well-known that they gather to draw strength from energies resonating with their essence."

"Which is why the large cities look to be shrouded in spirits from the Ten-Fold Kingdom these days," Dagian commented, with the faintest trace of a grin. "It is as if the cities have been claimed in full."

The sight of entire cities enveloped in hordes of dark wraiths always gave her pleasure. From the heights of the skyscraper housing Babylon Technologies' main offices, Dagian had often gazed out upon the living darkness infesting Troy.

If she were able to take the time to journey across the UCAS and open her special vision, Dagian had little doubt that all of the largest cities were in a similar state, appearing to be engulfed in perpetual shadow. The visions always bolstered her spirit and inspired her, giving strong evidence regarding the course of things. The energies of humanity itself were turning solidly towards harmony with the Nether Kingdom.

"The cities are becoming like temples to the Shining One. The energy I find in them now is invigorating," Aaliyah responded, with a ghost of a smile that echoed Dagian's own expression. It was clear Dagian was not the only one drawing pleasure from the current state of the nation's larger cities. "But a great cluster of spirits from the Nether Kingdom around a facility known to contain leading individuals in the Convergence is to be expected. Someday, you should view the darkness swirling about the White Pyramid in the capital. I could recommend a few other places, too."

"But the large number of spirits does mark this place as important and filled with energies aligned with the Nether Kingdom," Dagian stated.

"There is no avoiding that," Aaliyah replied.

"Which is why myself, and the memunim I am able to summon, must be very careful," Dagian said.

"You, and the more powerful spirits you command, bring a greater strength to the protection given to Kaira here," Aaliyah explained. "You give us the element of surprise over our enemies, and ward against a human using non-physical arts, such as this incorporeal assassin dwelling amongst them."

"I understand," Dagian said, nodding.

"I do not need to remind you of the consequences if you should fail to carry out your appointed tasks," Aaliyah said more sharply, with a colder glint in her eyes.

Dagian shook her head. "No, a reminder is unnecessary. I

understand the consequences very well."

"Good, then succeed, and your rewards will be unimaginable when the Remaking takes place," Aaliyah said. "That day when a new light shines across all the world, and everything beyond."

"A day we will all embrace," Dagian said, with a reverent bow of her head.

Dagian knew better than to speculate about that glorious day when the universe, and all planes of existence, would be remade in Diabolos' image. To be held in favor by the Shining One when that time arrived would make every hardship, sufferance, and sacrifice worth it.

"Just do not fail, we do not have much longer to go now," Aaliyah said, and though her tone did not change Dagian felt the words themselves exhorting her to vigilance.

"I will not waver, Aaliyah," Dagian responded, looking her in the eye. "I will use every art I know, every power I can call on, and all the strength I have within me."

"Then let your arts, powers, and strength continue to grow," Aaliyah said. "I will let you get back to your tasks now. The delegation from the east arrives soon enough. I have a few more video conferences to attend here."

Dagian nodded her head to Aaliyah, and departed the chamber. She always felt a little relief when dismissed by Aaliyah, as a little anxiety arose every time she was in her presence. It had been that way ever since the chastisements following the terrible debacle with the gate device.

Yet even though she was away from Aaliyah's presence, there was still a constant pressure bearing down upon her. Dagian occupied a pivotal role in more than one area, entailing both worldly affairs and matters of the spiritual. She had now been called upon to focus more heavily on the latter, in a situation she suspected was of far greater importance than she currently understood.

As much stress as she was contending with, she would have liked nothing more than to indulge in some pleasures of the flesh. There was nothing to stop her from bringing in a partner to be used for her carnal appetites.

She often had immersed in lusts back at her palatial estate near Troy. The call of the primal was always an inviting outlet to defuse from the pressures involved with matters of the ethereal. But she could not afford let her guard down in any way. A purity of darkness had to be steadfastly maintained.

It was not a matter of it being a difficult thing to do, as she had long subordinated personal urges to her unyielding discipline. But a dalliance of the flesh for a few hours would have been a welcome distraction, nonetheless.

Pushing the temptation aside, Dagian took the short walk back to her own quarters from the building that Aaliyah used as her center for CSD and Convergence matters. Soon she would be changed into loose-fitting clothing and lying flat upon her bed, as she went into spirit and detached from her flesh. There were wooded perimeters to inspect, and much to ruminate upon.

Dagian quickened her step and focused her mind, the hard soles of her calf-high black boots striking the paved walking path with a purposeful rhythm. She was going to do nothing less than execute her tasks to the fullest, and gain the favor of her Lord. There was only a little further to go until a radiant new dawn broke out over the entire world.

GREGORY

Gregory walked into the conference room. He looked into the large, unblinking eyes of the broad-shouldered figure seated at the far end of the room.

Flanking the general was no less than a colonel and a couple of other staff officers. All had the solemn, dutiful expressions of military men, holding solid posture where they stood around the general.

His instincts snapped to the fore. Standing to attention, Gregory rendered a formal salute to the dark-skinned general, a man who he was coming to admire more by the day.

"At ease, Gregory, you are not active duty," the general said, in his deep-toned voice. "But, like they say, once a marine, always a marine. That's one thing about you boys and girls I've always liked."

Gregory grinned. "It's just the way we're forged, general."

General Jackson smiled in return. "A good way to say it. I'll have to remember that."

Gregory thought of his first meeting with the general. The introduction had occurred following the successful assault on the federal detainment camp. A report had arrived when the glow of victory was still bright, that a massive UCAS military column was steadily approaching the battle site.

At first, the news had been dismaying, a kick to the stomach, as the fall of the camp had been so uplifting for Gregory and the rebel fighters looking to eradicate a cancer from the area. The fighting had not been easy.

An influx of rugged bikers, Jack Morgan at their lead, had come unexpectedly and provided the tilt in the battle. To find fortune so fickle, bringing a boon in one moment, and dread in the next, was greatly disheartening.

Yet Gregory had gone out to meet the general openly, with his head held high, and his heart full of conviction. He had been ready to deliver the message that he and the rebel forces would fight to the end, come whatever may. There would be no backing down when the alternative was subjugation to tyranny.

The general, standing between a colonel and a command sergeant major, had been the image of stoicism and authority. Backed by a massive force including Lafayette tanks and Devers Armored Fighting Vehicles, any officer would have looked strong in that moment. But General Robert Jackson gave off the distinctive air of a warrior and commander: resolute and determined.

The impression did not cause Gregory to second guess himself, or shy away from his own stance. Instead, he stood on his own two feet and looked the general eye to eye, as he explained his position and why he was fighting. He had spoken of the oath he had taken as a UCAS marine, and how there was no question in his mind that the federal elements he had been battling were domestic enemies.

Gregory would never forget the feeling that came over him when General Jackson had informed him that the huge column of armored vehicles and tanks were on his side. The response elicited the heights of both shock and elation in Gregory, though he had somehow maintained an outward image of solid composure.

Further, it turned out that the general had made his decision based upon the same principles that Gregory was honoring. To turn the military's guns on the people of the UCAS, when it was clear to anyone with eyes that egregious transgressions of the Grand Charter were being committed in abundance by a reckless, hostile government, was not a course that General Jackson was willing to live with.

As he had explained to Gregory then, he intended to stand with the people, not against them. He had taken the same oath that Gregory had, and he was also committed to honoring it in full.

The two had several more interactions as the detainment camp was taken over and General Jackson solidified his position in the region. Military assets had been deployed and defenses prepared, as remaining UCAS forces vacated Venorterra swiftly and retreated north.

As things had sorted out further in the ensuing weeks and months, and the front lines had been drawn between the breakaway provinces and the UCAS, General Jackson's position had been elevated. Through the consensus of the highest-ranking generals and officers to join the rebellion, he had been designated as the highest-ranking general of the armed forces defending the free provinces.

"So I suppose you are wondering why I'm here on the northern border of Venorterra, and wanted to meet with you personally," General Jackson said.

"I can't deny I'm a little curious about your visit, General," Gregory replied. "I know you have a lot more important things to do than meet with irregulars like myself."

"And that is where you are wrong," General Jackson stated. "I might be thinking along some lines that many would have found unorthodox before this conflict started … but then again, everything these days has an unorthodox flavor. The rules are different, and the wiser among us must accept that reality."

"I agree," Gregory said, his curiosity heightening.

In his experience, generals did not tend to depart from orthodoxy. Conforming to a doctrine was a hallmark of the upper ranks in the military. To say that he was intrigued by the general's comments was a great understatement.

"We want to establish better coordination with all the militias and irregulars," General Jackson said. "Of course, I want to make it clear we are not looking to take control of your activities as free citizens defending their homeland. That natural right is one of the things that compelled me to make the choice I did in standing with the seceding provinces.

The general paused for a moment, and looked purposefully to Gregory. "But I would like to have stronger channels established among the different forces. Better coordination and information sharing beyond what exits now. We can help each other in many ways, and reduce the possibility of tragic mistakes."

"That's something I've wanted much more of," Gregory said. "If only so we don't work at cross-purposes sometimes."

"I'm intending to extend special official ranks to you, and to others such as Jack Morgan and your brother, any who are helping to lead large groups of irregulars," General Jackson said. "Mainly, to help you interact more efficiently with our facilities and officers. It won't be a hard adjustment for those of you with solid military backgrounds, and I'm sure any others gifted in organization and leadership can acclimate soon enough."

Gregory kept his facial expression serious, but almost chuckled at the idea that his brother and Jack Morgan would be receiving official military ranks. His brother had never been in the military, and the highly-respected, grizzled biker Jack Morgan, who was a veteran from the hundred and first airborne, had made many colorful remarks to Gregory about military bureaucracy and the ineptness of officers. He hoped he would be able to see their faces when they first received the news.

"Your boys and girls and ours are crossing paths quite a bit these days," Gregory said. "Helped each other out on more than a few occasions."

"Yes, and yours are doing some incredible things," General

Jackson said. "The militias and irregulars have proven inventive, and very effective at asymmetrical warfare. I also think the efforts of the irregulars are a big part of the reason we haven't faced a formal offensive from the north or west just yet."

Gregory had no doubt things like supplies and power infrastructure had been effectively crippled in many areas of the UCAS along the boundaries of the territory they still held. It was as the general had said: asymmetrical warfare at its finest.

Such methods kept their enemies constantly off balance. But to hear it voiced from the supreme commander of the seceding provinces' military forces gave Gregory a feeling of pride in what he was involved in.

If the irregulars had helped delay a larger invasion and buy some more time for General Jackson, then even better. Yet as the general's words had intimated, it was only a matter of time before the UCAS military sought to regain control of the south and midwest.

"When do you think they'll be coming?" Gregory asked.

"They're spread a little too thin at the moment, from what our intelligence reports," General Jackson replied. "They're still dealing with pressure from Mandaria, even though formal hostilities have ceased. Mandaria is asserting itself over the Southern Sea, and taking formal control over some additional islands. Its neighbors do not have the strength to challenge these moves, and the UCAS can only take up a defensive posture alongside them.

"Domestically, things are an absolute mess for them right now. The borders are very porous. They are having to deploy many units to assist with operations taking place in every province. There are sporadic outbreaks of unrest, the cities are ablaze with gang violence, and the continued imposition of martial law drains them. They have proceeded to full gun confiscation in many provinces. Not an easy task in times like this, I can assure you."

"They're actively disarming the citizens up there even now?" Gregory asked, incredulous. There was no question that any person of good character living in the UCAS now was surrounded with threats amid all the instability and skyrocketing crime.

"It is a zero-risk initiative, as their leadership sees it," General

Jackson said. "As I see it, they want to be assured of having no threats at their back whenever they do make their big push."

"I got a lot of ribbing over the years for being from Venorterra," Gregory said. "But I'm so glad this province is my home. I can't imagine what it's like living in the north, or out on the west coast."

"Little more than prisoners these days, sadly," General Jackson said in a lower voice, and for a moment he turned his gaze from Gregory and stared quietly. "I would love nothing more than to liberate them, but my mandate is to protect the seceding provinces that chose to withdraw their consent from a voluntary union."

"It's hard to hear what is happening," Gregory said sympathetically, sensing a painful inner conflict within the general.

The general's dark brown eyes reverted back to Gregory, looking away from whatever distant scene they had been gazing upon. "The old serenity prayer was always a hard one for me. I am not the type to easily accept what I cannot change. We will just have to give it all we have towards the things that can be changed," General Jackson said, his voice regaining some vigor. "Won't we, Lieutenant Andreas?"

A smile spread slowly across Gregory's face. The last two words of the general sounded awkward to his ears, though he immediately understood what they implied.

"Thank you sir," Gregory said.

"We will have to get ahold of Jack Morgan, your brother, and a few others I have on a short list here," General Jackson said. "Would you like to assist?"

He smiled even broader. "Yes, sir, it would be an honor."

"Then let us not waste any time," General Jackson said, rising up from his seat. He extended Gregory a salute. "Lieutenant Andreas."

Gregory snapped back into a formal mode, returning the salute. The general strode down the length of the room, followed closely by the other officers. Gregory stepped aside, and then fell in with the others as they departed the room.

Though the general strode briskly by Gregory, he did not miss the small addition to the man's uniform that had never been a part of UCAS military attire. Located not too far from his elegant set of gold stars was a pin in the shape of a silver sword.

ARIANNA

Two vehicles sped down the highway, heading towards a destination that none of the passengers inside could envision or define. Arianna, Godral, Kantel, and Dedran were in the lead, while Quinn, Maureen, Vailia, and Sarangar brought up the rear.

They were traveling through lands still afflicted with the symptoms of great upheaval. There was no telling what kinds of dangers they might face on the open road. Having another An-Ki at her side was anything but a liability.

Gerald would remain behind, as Arianna intended it. A part of her felt deep guilt at her veiling of the journey, but Benton had promised to convey a note from Arianna explaining everything well after they were underway.

She knew her uncle would be extremely upset. But she hoped he would think upon the things she put into the letter, and ultimately see her rationale.

In addition to the fact that Gerald would not be up for extended physical hardships if things took a dire turn for the worse, it was good to have him there if Benedict were to somehow return while the rest were gone. The manner of Benedict's return, as long as he came back unharmed, was of no preference to Arianna.

The two vehicles were packed to the hilt with supplies. Everyone had weapons and ammunition. Some emergency fuel was carried along in five-gallon containers, and there was food enough to see them through to the border region. Godral had reassured Arianna that food would not become a concern, as the An-Ki were skilled hunters.

Seeing road signs and old billboards along the way, it was sometimes easy to forget just how much things had changed. Arianna wished she was simply on a road trip with friends, heading to some vacation site for some rest and relaxation, but reality could not be ignored.

Evidence of the new order of things could be seen all along the way. In better times, cars that had broken down could be occasionally seen pulled off by the side of the road. Now, there were many abandoned vehicles littering the sides of the highway.

Wrecked vehicles that would normally have been towed away were now discarded at the roadside. The crumpled vehicles had likely been shoved aside for the military traffic using the highway.

There was much more garbage and debris in evidence, both in the road and in the areas immediately adjacent. A few times they had to steer carefully to avoid some large chunks of tire from a blowout.

She doubted she would be seeing any cleanup crews, clad in their bright yellow vests, out walking the shoulders of the highway. Arianna hoped it would not be too much longer before things fully normalized, but it was sobering to see how fast things were changing in the wake of a breakdown of society. If left on its own for too much longer, the roadway could easily become impassible.

For the most part, they traveled without too much conversation. The three An-Ki males were content to listen to the rock music Arianna played.

It was like riding with three foreigners. There was no mistaking that the three loved the sounds, and were fascinated with the technology. Recorded music was yet another thing that she took for granted, realizing that it probably seemed magical to the An-Ki.

She had to laugh to herself about the fact that Godral and his two companions definitely looked the part for the style of music playing through the speakers. Exceedingly masculine, long-haired, and bearded, they would have fit in very well at any rock concert.

Yet Arianna also had to admit that they were grooming themselves quite well lately. Their long locks were brushed nicely, and their beards, though lengthy, looked well-kempt. The long-sleeved, collared shirts they wore were not rumpled, and their jeans were clean in appearance. Only their large size and striking eyes would have drawn any extra scrutiny within a crowd of people.

Without any impetus for stopping, they made great time as they headed southward. There were no speed limits to heed anymore, and Arianna took advantage by going a full fifteen miles an hour above the former maximum.

Driving an SUV, she did not feel comfortable going any faster than that. The last thing she wanted to have happen was to tempt fate by being reckless.

She also had to remind herself that there was not likely any significant road repair going on, and any breaks or holes in the road created since the upheaval were laying in ambush for the tires of a careless driver. They had spares in both vehicles, but nothing beyond that, and it was best to keep things as they were.

After a few hours of smooth travel, the pair of vehicles rolled to a halt, stopping a short distance before a high bridge crossing a river. The way onto the bridge was blocked, due to what appeared to be a recent wreck.

Two vehicles, their fronts showing significant damage, clogged the way forward. Broken glass littered the ground, and Arianna's breath caught in her throat as her eyes settled upon a pair of human bodies lying out in the road. A man and a woman, both were rigidly still, and she feared them dead.

Turning the music off, she gripped the steering wheel tight and took a deep breath. Glancing in the rear view mirror, she saw Quinn getting out of the other SUV. He hustled up to the driver's side, as she rolled down her window.

"Looks like it just happened, from what I can tell," Arianna said, eyeing the bodies.

"No way through, it doesn't seem," Quinn said, peering at the area ahead of them.

She looked at him, and said nothing for a moment. "And those people?"

"Be careful, Arianna," Quinn told her. "You know what we've been warned about."

"We can't just leave people injured in a wreck in the middle of the road," Arianna said firmly. "What if they are still alive? This just happened. Look at the glass all over the road."

"Anyone could have spread some glass," Quinn said.

Arianna saw one of the bodies move slightly. The female lifted her arm up weakly, before it flopped back down onto the hard surface. A sense of urgency filled Arianna at the pitiful sight.

"She's not dead," Arianna said. Turning her engine off, she got out of the car. She cast a brief glance to Quinn. "We need to do something to help her."

"What if it's not a wreck?" Quinn asked warily.

"I'd rather take that chance, and if we want to get through we'd have to go right over them," Arianna said. "I'm not going to just run over a badly injured lady. That's not who we are."

She heard the sound of footsteps approaching on the asphalt. Maureen walked up to them with a somber expression.

"They are staying back," Maureen said, glancing back towards the vehicles where the other An-Ki had remained. "What's going on here?"

Arianna and Quinn quickly explained the situation to her. A frown deepened on her face as she listened, and Arianna could tell that her friend did not trust the situation at all.

"I don't know what to say," she said, looking out towards the two figures lying on the ground.

"Hey, can anyone talk?" Arianna called out towards the two prone individuals.

"I'm ... injured. I can't ... get up!" the woman responded weakly, her voice sounding strained and desperate.

"We've got some first aid with us," Arianna shouted back.

"I ... I think my brother's dead," the woman replied, her tone even more feeble, almost too faint for Arianna to hear her.

Looking around, Arianna could see nothing amiss, though her heart beat a little faster. She knew she had to make a decision, and eyed the glass spread across the ground from the busted windshields of the wrecked cars.

"I can't just stand here," Arianna said to her two friends a moment later.

She drew out the gun holstered at her waist. Keeping a firm grip on the .45 caliber pistol, she took her first steps forward. A full seven round magazine was loaded and ready if anything went awry.

She moved forward cautiously, keeping her handgun up and continuing to look from side to side. As before, nothing seemed out of order as she reached the first of the crashed vehicles, a dark, four-door sedan. Warily, she took one step, and then another, finally reaching the figures lying in the road after a few more paces.

"I'm here," she said gently to the dark-haired woman, who had started to try and roll over slowly. "Don't move just yet. You've got help now. We'll take care of you."

Arianna flinched and her heart leapt as an authoritative voice shouted abruptly from the side of the road. "Don't move lady! We've got you and your friends in our sights! Keep really still, and don't try anything stupid."

Looking back down, she saw that both of the crash victims had rolled over, gripping pistols that were trained squarely on her. Both were alert and uninjured, having played their parts to perfection.

"Set the gun down, lady," the first speaker said, a heavy-set man who emerged slowly into her view, walking out from behind the second car. He was holding an A-15 rifle, and its barrel was leveled at her. "Do it slowly. Nothing funny."

In the background, she could hear other voices shouting forcefully to her friends, telling them to stay in place. Though her adrenaline was racing, she focused on her breath and strove to settle her mind. She had to keep her wits about her, and reminded herself that she was likely facing a group of thieves, not cold-blooded killers.

Following the large man's directive, Arianna crouched slowly and set her gun down on the ground. A couple of other men came to stand at the sides of the burly leader.

Both were armed with rifles, and she did not like the look in their eyes as they gazed upon her. One of them grinned, the expression decidedly salacious. Openly, and unashamedly, he looked her up and down.

"Just cooperate, and we'll be on our way," the woman told Arianna in a hard-edged tone, getting up from the ground and brushing a few pieces of glass off her clothes. Gone was the veneer of a wounded lady needing help, and underneath was the reality of a calculating predator.

Arianna said nothing to the woman, contending with some considerable fear and a simmering anger. Three guns were aimed at her, so she remained perfectly still, but a great bitterness welled up within. She chafed at the thought that the journey to find her uncle was going to come to an end in such an unceremonious way. Tears of frustration glistened upon her eyes, but she kept her head held high, and her posture remained straight and firm.

"Some of 'em are takin' cover behind the second vehicle! Two I think," one of the other voices called out in alarm. "What do we do?"

"They ain't armed," another said. "Some big fellows, but I got a good look at 'em. They got nothin'!"

"Your friends better not try anything funny," stated the heavy-set man who Arianna now deemed to be the group's primary leader. His voice was thick with irritation and warning. "We'll pull the triggers in a second, young lady, don't think we won't! No messin' around here."

Arianna clenched her jaws as the woman from the ground walked up to her, brought forth a long, plastic cable tie, and secured her hands firmly behind her. She winced as the plastic dug hard into her bare skin.

"Just a precaution," the woman said from behind, in a low voice. "We'll let you all go when were done. Don't get in our way and you'll be just fine."

Arianna could only hope the woman was telling the truth. She watched helplessly as the leader directed Quinn and Maureen to step away from the vehicles.

A few moments later, both of her friends were standing next to Arianna with their hands bound behind. All three were placed under the watch of the woman and man who had initially baited her into the trap.

The An-Ki in the second vehicle, Vailia and Sarangar, were still evidently behind the SUV, much to the agitation of the ambushing party. As far as the An-Ki from her vehicle, Arianna saw no sign of Godral, Kantel, or Dedran, and she certainly was not going to volunteer any information.

"Looks like the girl must've been alone in vehicle one, I don't see no one else here," a skinny male called loudly, edging closer to the two SUV's with his finger perched on the trigger of his semi-automatic rifle. Just behind him, a shorter man with a beard clutched his weapon.

"It's all secure here, no worries with these three," the heavy-set man pronounced casually, indicating the three bound captives. "Red, Dawson, you two get to searchin' those vehicles, once you flush the others out."

Arianna watched the two gunmen standing with the leader walk towards the SUV's with rising interest. She wondered what Godral and the others were planning.

They were far too big to hide effectively in the SUV. The three must have slipped out the other side quietly. Whatever it was that they were up to, she doubted it boded well for the highway robbers.

The gunmen called out several times for the An-Ki behind the second vehicle to come out, but there was no response there either. Arianna could hear the tension growing in the robbers' voices as their demands continued to go unanswered. After a few more minutes had gone by, the heavy-set man cursed angrily, and began making his way towards his nervous companions.

"Keep wide, and come 'round there, 'round the first SUV," he instructed the skinny man and his bearded companion. He looked to Red and Dawson. "You two got the second, incase they try to come 'round that way. Flank 'em. No way out for 'em now. Don't hesitate to shoot, if you think they got anythin' on them!"

The two gunmen stepped cautiously along a wide, arcing path, moving to the right with their rifles trained towards the second vehicle. Their trigger fingers were poised to fire in an instant, and all of their movements were deliberate and careful.

The other pair of men passed slowly in front of the first SUV. Mayhem erupted a second later. Just as one of the robbers reached the other side of the lead vehicle, he was engulfed in a huge mass of dark fur and muscle propelled on two legs. His companion barely got a cry out of his throat before he was barreled to the ground under another hulking, fur-covered form.

The killings were brutal and fast. Neither man got so much as a single shot off.

Red and Dawson had no time to respond to their comrades' plight. Two more large, four-legged forms, one covered in white fur, and the other with a silvery exterior, burst out at full speed from behind the second vehicle. Both of the men were slammed to the ground a moment later, where they flailed and cried pitifully out before going silent.

The silver An-Ki sprang forward, while the white-furred one

110

hurtled over Dawson's body and charged towards the heavy-set leader. The two An-Ki separated farther, positioning themselves to come at the man from two distinct angles.

The terrified man cried out, panicking in his confusion and spraying a few haphazard shots. His head turned to the right and left quickly, eyeing the beasts converging fast from two directions. He was caught in a pincer that was closing rapidly.

The body of the nearest An-Ki, the white-furred one, jerked for a moment as one of the bullets found purchase in An-Ki flesh. Arianna's world spun and her heart jumped as Sarangar loosed a guttural cry rife with pain.

Yet as tears of sorrow welled in her eyes, she saw that the shot did not stop him. Sarangar kept charging forward, reaching the man a few strides before Vailia.

Leaping onto the heavy figure and taking him to the ground, Sarangar's jaws spread wide and his fangs flashed. In an instant, the leader of the robbers was dying with his throat torn out.

The two An-Ki did not linger for even a moment. Both Vailia and Sarangar bounded towards the side of the road, as a few more bursts of gunfire sounded. Arianna saw where the shots struck the road surface, all of them well off the mark of the fast-moving targets.

One of the concealed shooters broke out from their cover, and tried to run towards the area where Arianna stood. Vailia ran him down in seconds, springing onto his back and bearing him down heavily. Her jaws clamped down on the back of his neck and ripped savagely.

With a soaring leap Sarangar dived into the brush and a raw scream broke out a second later. It ceased abruptly within the depths of the foliage.

"Call 'em off!" shrieked the woman holding Arianna, Maureen, and Quinn captive.. "Oh god, call 'em off. Please call 'em off."

"We didn't start this," Arianna responded icily, looking back to the now-terrified woman. The coldness of her tone came as a surprise, but it reflected the way she felt.

The simple fact was that the robbers were among the worst kind of human predators. They took advantage of compassion and a willingness to help others in dire need, two things that were in dwindling supply during times of severe hardship.

The An-Ki's fearsome response was not something that Arianna would have done, even if she possessed the ability, but the robbers had brought their doom upon themselves.

"We'll shoot ya, if ya don't!" the man with the dark-haired woman yelled, though the bravado of his words was rendered hollow by the shaking of his voice.

A throaty, resonant growl sounded behind all of them. Dedran was a stark image of primal fury, with a vicious-looking snarl revealing the lengthy, glistening canines within his shaggy muzzle.

During the outburst of violence, Dedran had circled around and come up behind the robbers holding Arianna and her friends. Though he was the smallest of the five, he was still much larger than the two robbers and his presence greatly intimidated them.

"Call 'em off!" cried the woman, desperation brimming in her tone. "My god! What the hell are they? Oh god, please, call 'em off. Oh god!"

Deep growls sounded from all around, filling the air with menace as the other four drew near to the last two robbers and their bound captives. Arianna could see the dark crimson marring the snow-white fur of Sarangar in the place where he had been struck by the bullet.

Baring his fangs, Sarangar slowly padded forward, and Arianna could feel the anger wafting from him as he eyed the two remaining robbers. There was no question he desired to tear right into them.

She could only hope the wound he had suffered was not serious, but there was a significant amount of blood matting his fur. Even if the outcome of the confrontation was not in doubt anymore, Arianna did not want him taking another bullet. In a last gasp, the robbers could decide to shoot at point-blank range.

There was no need for further bloodshed. She had to try to defuse the situation any way that she could.

"I wouldn't try anything if I were you," Arianna said, seeing the man and woman fingering their triggers nervously. She kept her voice calm, but firm. "Two of you. Five of them. You just saw what happened to your friends, and you know you aren't going to get them all. You can't outrun them either. So let's talk some sense now."

"What do you mean? What do you know about them? What are they?" the woman stammered in rapid succession, her body shaking like the man standing with her. Fearfully, she eyed the other An-Ki drawing closer, step by step.

Her companion's face looked ashen, the blood drained from his face. He stared forward, wide-eyed and in the clutches of a paralytic fear. A dark stain had formed around his crotch and was growing fast, the patter of urine accompanying the expanding puddle forming around his shoes.

"I suggest you two get out of here, right now," Arianna said evenly to the man and woman, glowering at them. "Just go, and thank Adonai you are alive. Or you can stay here and die for sure."

She did not even bother to ask them to free her. In their states of extreme fear, she did not want either of the two handling blades anywhere close to her wrists.

"How can we go? They'll just kill us!" the woman retorted after a moment, continuing to tremble from the terror rising in her.

"One of those cars work?" Arianna said, nodding towards the supposedly wrecked vehicles.

Now standing close enough to really scrutinize them, she saw that while the front grills were dented and smashed up, and the bodies of the cars exhibited all manner of damage and broken windows, the tires were in perfect shape.

The woman nodded, tears streaming down her cheeks. Then her eyes widened abruptly, as she replied, "But ... but the keys are with Orrin! Out there!" She pointed out towards the body of the heavy-set man.

Arianna looked towards Godral, whose golden eyes were pools of ferocity as he gazed down upon the robbers. She spoke to him calmly. "Can you bring me the vehicle keys that are in the pockets of that man?"

The tallest of the An-Ki looked back towards the dead body. After a moment, Godral turned his eyes back to her.

He answered curtly, "Yes."

"Wha ... what ... ?" the woman muttered as Godral strode away, heading towards the maimed corpse of the leader. "It … it spoke."

"He spoke, not it! Shut your mouth and count yourself lucky. You are going to live, if you don't try anything funny," Arianna snapped at the woman, giving some vent to the considerable ire swirling within. "And you'd better get it straight, because I don't have any patience left. Godral is a he, not an it, you moron!"

"Getting off way too easy," Maureen said to Arianna, her voice bristling with anger.

"I don't think they'll be ready anytime soon to try this kind of thing again," Arianna replied, keeping her heated gaze fixed on the woman.

Godral returned a moment later with a set of keys affixed to a metal ring. He extended them towards Arianna, and she saw that he had gotten some blood on the cluster of keys from his wetted claws.

"Toss them down in front of her, to the ground," Arianna directed Godral, nodding towards the woman.

Godral flung the keys towards the feet of the woman. They clattered on the road as they struck the ground. She bent over and picked them up, while keeping the gun aimed back at the An-Ki. The woman then maintained enough presence of mind to keep Arianna close, as she began moving towards one of the cars.

Mimicking the woman, the man shuffled close behind his comrade. Still trembling, he mumbled incoherently under his breath.

The man got into the car first, and the woman seated herself quickly on the driver's side. She wasted no time once she was in place, starting up the engine immediately as Arianna backed up several paces.

Tires squealing, the woman took off down the road, heading away from the bridge fast. Arianna stared after them, watching the car growing smaller in the distance.

"It's over, Arianna," Maureen said gently, a few moments later.

"It is over," Arianna replied in agreement.

With the An-Ki's assistance, a knife was found on the bodies of one of the dead robbers. They used the blade to free Arianna and her friends. Rubbing her wrists where the tightened plastic had bit harshly into her skin, Arianna took a deep breath and collected her thoughts together.

"I think it would be best to get back on the road and underway again," Quinn said, massaging his own wrists, graced temporarily with red-hued tracks from the cable ties.

"I'm with you," Arianna said. She felt a stab in her conscience, as she thought of what her friends had just been put through. With a contrite tone she continued, "And you were right. I am so, so sorry. I should have listened to you, Quinn. I shouldn't have fallen for that."

She looked around at the bodies of the robbers and the car left in the middle of the road. Arianna wondered how many people they had taken advantage of, before running into her group. The deception had been an elaborate one.

"Don't apologize, what you did is why I think the world of you, Arianna," Quinn said, smiling at her. "Because you are the kind of person who will take a risk to try to help someone like that. I wasn't any more clever just now. I didn't see any sign of a ruse. I'm just harder of heart than you are. And that's not a good thing, or something I'm proud of."

"Make that two of us," Maureen said, laying her arm gently around Arianna's shoulders and giving her a reassuring hug. She smiled, and continued, "That man and woman could just as easily have been two people injured and desperate for help. You are a light in a dark world, girl, and don't ever stop being that way. It gives the rest of us something to hold onto, when we think everything's gotten too ugly, and too cruel."

"Don't forget, Arianna, hindsight always looks so clear, long after the fact," Quinn added. "Like I said, I didn't see any sign of a deception, and neither did Maureen. I hope even this doesn't change you, Arianna.

"It might even be us someday. Our hope to live might rest entirely upon the chance of someone just like you coming along. So don't apologize, Arianna. Don't apologize for who you are."

"I just need to figure out a wiser approach to it, I guess," Arianna said, mustering a grin.

"Different tactics on the approach, perhaps," Quinn retorted, grinning, with a light laugh.

"Well, we're all okay this time. All of us are alive. Let's count our blessings, and get going on this mission," Maureen said amiably.

"Sounds good to me," Arianna said. "Once our friends are ready."

Godral and the other An-Ki were finishing the transitions back into their human forms. It would take a few minutes for the five of them to get their clothing back on. Arianna walked among them and approached Sarangar as his muzzle finished retracting, reforming into the handsome visage of a younger man.

The wound was still visible on his upper arm. As a precaution, Arianna and Maureen attended to him.

Fortunately, the projectile had not worked its way in too deep, and did not involve any extraordinary difficulties in extraction. Looking closely at the wound site, Arianna got the sense that Sarangar's body was slowly working to expel the foreign object.

Once the bandage was on, Maureen excused herself, and got up to go rejoin her boyfriend. From where she kneeled by Sarangar, Arianna saw that Quinn was busy collecting up pistols, rifles and ammunition from the dead men.

"I wanted to kill," Sarangar said with a grim expression, looking to Arianna when they were alone. "When they took my blood. When they used their weapon on me. I wanted to kill them."

"If I'd been shot, I'm sure I'd feel like I wanted to kill whoever shot me too," Arianna replied, in a spirit of solidarity.

"I had strong anger," Sarangar said. "Much anger. I wanted to kill the two humans who lived."

Listing to her friend, Arianna suspected he was rattled at the thought of losing control. He was the son of Sargor, an An-Ki who had proven to be strong of will and temperament during the most difficult of times for their kind.

"But you did not lose control, Sarangar," Arianna replied. She looked into his eyes. "It is natural to feel something like anger. I know your father has felt rage before too. But you mastered it just now. You did not attack the last two. Remember that, and don't doubt yourself."

Sarangar held her eyes for a moment, until the trace of a grin touched his lips. "Thank you, Arianna. You are right. I will remember that."

"And I need to thank you, Sarangar," she responded, seeing the surprise blooming in his eyes at her words.

"Why?" he asked, with a quizzical expression.

"You did what you did to protect me, Maureen, and Quinn," she said.

"You are friend, and you are like one of clan," Sarangar replied. "The clan fights for one, as one fights for clan."

"I'm honored to be your friend," Arianna said.

"Ready to go?" Maureen interrupted, approaching the two.

"Ready as I'll ever be," Arianna answered, looking up to her friend.

"Quinn's about wrapped up, I think," Maureen replied.

"Then let's get everyone together," Arianna said to Sarangar, as she got back up to her feet.

She accompanied Maureen, and the two walked over to where Quinn was packing some of the new acquisitions into the rear of the SUV he had been driving. As loaded up as the vehicle was, it did not look to be the easiest of tasks.

"So are we about ready?" Arianna asked him.

He looked towards the two women, and paused. "You know, the thought just occurred to me. We might as well gas up a bit before heading onward."

"Gas up a bit? What station?" Maureen asked, chuckling.

"There's still one of their vehicles left behind, and they were obviously functional," Quinn said. "Probably something left in the tank."

"Not a half-bad idea," Maureen replied approvingly. She looked to Arianna. "Can we delay just a little more?"

"Makes good sense to me," Arianna said, adding her consent.

Quinn took up the next several minutes siphoning gasoline from the remaining vehicle left in the road. While the gas was retrieved, Arianna and Maureen rummaged through the car. They found a few useful items inside of it, including another handgun in the glove compartment. Quinn then split what he had taken between the fuel tanks of their vehicles.

"All done!" he proclaimed in a sprite manner.

"Alright, let's head out," Arianna said, having grown very eager to be on her way again. There was no way of knowing whether the two they had let go free might return with an armed mob.

Everyone got back into the SUVs, and Arianna turned the engine on. After letting it warm up for a few seconds, she pulled forward slowly. Careful to avoid the main sprawl of glass on the road, she edged around the abandoned car and started across the bridge.

"If stop, let us search first," Godral told her as they accelerated to full speed, quickly reaching the end of the bridge. His voice was almost apologetic as he added, "I did not know what you wanted, when you stopped."

"Lesson learned," Arianna replied evenly, recalling Quinn's remark about using different tactics the next time. She stared ahead in heavy silence, watching the road rushing by as she drove onward.

Though acknowledging the risk she had taken in stopping, a part of her did not want to apologize for seeking to help injured people. Yet she knew their journey would have come to an abrupt end had it not been for the An-Ki's intervention.

Benedict had nobody searching for him, other than Arianna and the small group accompanying her. In the future, she knew she could not jeopardize her uncle's one slim chance of getting help.

In all likelihood, he was depending on Arianna and her companions. They were the only people actively looking to find him. That stark reality had to be balanced with all other considerations.

Taking a deep breath and loosing a heavy sigh, she pressed down on the accelerator pedaland increased the vehicle's speed another five miles an hour. A little time had to be made up.

XAVIER

"Let me ask you a question, Xavier, before you commence with the operation."

Xavier Gerard looked back to Samel Malkira and nodded, knowing it was not a request. He waited patiently for the enigmatic man to continue.

"If there are a hundred men and women of a heart like ours, should not this place be spared?" Samel asked him.

"If there were that many, I would try to get them out, at the least. But there aren't a hundred to be found, I can guarantee that," Xavier responded confidently.

"What about fifty? What if fifty allied to our cause could be found in the town?" Samel questioned.

Xavier did not know what the man was getting at. His face gave no hint of his purpose in regards to the strange questions, but there was no denying his great authority. The current operation, in fact, was at his direct behest, which made the unexpected queries all the stranger.

"I would try to get fifty of our people out, if I could find such," Xavier answered.

"How about ten?"

"No different," Xavier replied immediately. "I'd work to extract them first."

"Is there not one to be found in this place?" Samel asked. "One with the reason to understand the need for the new age that is coming. One who is enlightened enough not to be stuck in obsolete, fast-dying ways. I tell you, one would be enough to spare that place. If you believe there is one to be found here, we can halt this operation right now."

Xavier did not answer Samel at first, and a hint of nervousness played about his features. The stalwart commander of the Threat Tactical Defense Force was not sure what Samel was ultimately seeking. He found in that moment that he feared delivering the wrong answer to the mysterious, powerful figure.

"You can give me your answer with your choice of action," Samel stated casually, settling into the high-backed, dark leather chair with an icy smile on his face. Huge monitor screens filled the front of the spacious room, and a couple rows of headset-wearing operators and technicians sat alert at their stations, awaiting the final command. "You know the answer to that question, Xavier. Have conviction in your directive."

Xavier nodded one more time to Samel, before looking away. He knew where his conviction rested.

"Commence," he stated firmly, staring at the large video images.

The drones that had been circling the small town of Alesia, nestled to the northwest of Ponchartrain, were put into action. It took a few minutes for the operators to guide the unmanned aircraft near the outskirts of the town, which was fast becoming a hotbed of resistance within the remaining territory of the UCAS.

Though kept as much as possible from the media, there were pockets of insurgency spread all throughout the north, and even along the west coast. Some involved well-organized and heavily armed militias, such as the one in Alesia.

Many outbreaks of resistance were easy enough to tamp down. Yet some threatened to spread like wildfire through a restive populace. With an entire town under control, the militia in Alesia presented a serious threat.

The nature of the resistance also had to be put under scrutiny. Streams of people had been making their way southward in recent months, desiring to leave the UCAS and join the breakaway provinces. It was not a one-way flow, however, as many wanting to continue living in the UCAS had trekked north in the months following the emergence of new boundary lines.

The ones coming north always presented a serious concern to Xavier. Enemy operatives and the smuggling of weapons could stoke new fires of rebellion where there had been none before.

At least the insurgency Xavier now confronted on UCAS territory was native, and not due to those who recently migrated to the north. Everyone coming across the borders was immediately being given Living ID. Once they had the implants, their movements could be tracked.

The small brushfires of resistance across the north were, overwhelmingly, entirely homegrown in nature. Xavier knew many insurgents fancied seeing a replication of what had occurred in the south.

That would not happen anytime soon, as the military units in the north were solidly aligned with the federal authorities. Any commanders with suspect loyalties had been weeded out.

The smarter ones among the insurgents had taken to more remote areas, including the depths of hills and mountains. The more foolish had formed into larger concentrations. The town being confronted that day was one such instance, with a large militia force having rallied around a sheriff who defied the federal authority.

Now the people of the town were about to reap what they had sown, in the form of weaponry that had not yet been employed in the operations to suppress resistance. The firm that had developed the deadly weapon system about to be unleashed was one tied to Samel.

Xavier glanced over towards Samel, whose iron-hard eyes were locked to the images from the video transmission. There was no change in his rigid expression.

Xavier watched quietly, and for a couple of minutes nothing happened. Then, floating down like so many cottony seeds adrift on a summer breeze, a number of cylindrical objects suspended by parachutes descended into sight.

There was a surreal beauty inherent in the scene. The metallic containers glinted radiantly in the sunlight as if the downward-drifting array was a cluster of jewels being sprinkled across the town by some lofty benefactor.

The objects were anything but a grace to the occupants of the town. One by one, the containers came to rest on the ground. In many areas, a number of individuals from the town began to approach them, perhaps thinking them to be some kind of parachuted supplies blown off course.

A few moments later, all of the objects detonated in unison. Death swept through the town in pulses of high energy neutrons, claiming all visible life within Alesia. Surveillance images documented bodies lying out in the open, all over the town.

Property and buildings were left almost completely intact. It caused no significant physical damage. It simply cleansed a territory of the living inhabitants within it.

"Incredible," Xavier stated, amazed at the power and efficacy.

"It is a very evolved enhanced radiation weapons system," Samel commented. "A way has been discovered to minimize heat and blast effects, while retaining the lethality of a large neutron bomb. The distribution of the pods and coverage radius of each one ensures that the entire town is wiped out thoroughly, with virtually no damage to structures."

"Your demonstration appears to have worked perfectly," Xavier said. He gazed at the images of bodies lying in the streets. "We will send in troops to look for any survivors, but there's not a single person moving in the town."

"As you saw, this system works very effectively, and that is also how you deal with expendables, Xavier," Samel declared, his dark eyes cold and steely. "You have resistance breaking out? Smother it, with no hesitation. We are on the verge of final victory. There is no time to tolerate those who stand in the way. Remove all obstacles from our path."

"You will find no disagreement with me," Xavier replied. "I have no reservations about eradicating any opposition, wherever it is found."

"When you drive into the heart of the rebel provinces, remember that, Xavier," Samel told him. He paused, and stared into the TTDF commander's eyes, as if to imprint his instruction right into Xavier's brain. A moment later, Samel continued. "That time will come. In the meantime, do what needs to be done, to put out every last fire throughout the north."

Without another word, Samel rose from his seat. He turned and strode from the room, leaving Xavier behind in the control chamber.

Xavier had the distinct impression that he was being regarded like a young student before a master, left to ponder the essence and wisdom of the lesson just imparted. He was not offended in the least by Samel's mentor-like posture towards him.

Xavier sensed there was much to learn from the eminent man. There was no doubt Samel enjoyed the highest favor with Aaliyah.

Xavier gazed back at the monitor screens, taking in the video beamed back by the drones circling above the doomed town. He marveled at what he saw confirmed time and time again.

There was no disputing the effectiveness of the advanced weapons system Samel had brought to him. Xavier had already begun to think of ways to use it in other places, including the cities of the south.

As Samel had stated, the time would come soon to strike into the heart of the south. Xavier intended to be well-prepared to unleash a hellish storm on all who had dared to rebel against UCAS authority.

IAN

Ian watched the last of the former inmates shaking hands with Sheriff Chris Howard. Deputy Lucy Hammond stood to the back of Chris, a friendly expression on her face and a clipboard gripped in her hands.

As each man passed by the pair of officers, Lucy checked their names off a list affixed to the clipboard. One by one, a number of captives were being set free.

A federal detention facility loomed to the back of the men. Before each and every one of them, a chance for a fresh start beckoned. Free men once more, they had all been pardoned by the judges who had agreed to help facilitate the transition period involving the new provincial government.

The detention facility would still be kept in use, though it was no longer federal in nature. It was now under the full control of Venorterra authorities.

Violent offenders and the mentally ill were to be kept incarcerated for the time being, until a more thorough examination of their circumstances could be made. But most non-violent offenders were being set free of their extended confinements.

Eyeing the men shaking Chris' hand, Ian wondered at the thoughts passing through their minds. He could not imagine it would be easy for any of them in the days and weeks ahead. All of them had been suddenly liberated into a world that had changed dramatically from the one existing on the day they had been locked up.

Even a span of five years contained profound changes and evolutions, both in popular culture and technology. The fact that the UCAS no longer wielded authority, and a new nation was rising in its place, only added to the big challenges the newly-pardoned men would have to overcome.

Yet no matter what problems they would be dealing with soon, their faces all reflected the simple joy of being free again. A few had a giddy, almost child-like look about them. Ian suspected that for those individuals it all appeared to be a miracle.

The decision to empty out the prisons had been one that personally gladdened Ian. He knew enough of the old situation with federal detention centers, from many discussions with Chris over a few cold beers.

Prior to the rebellion, the UCAS had already become engorged and bloated with an overflowing level of incarcerations. It had reached the point that its jails and prisons held far more individuals than were locked up in Mandaria, a nation that had well more than four times the populace of the UCAS.

Another change Ian was pleased to hear announced was that the acting sheriffs and others forming the new ranks of law enforcement in Venorterra had been unified in their determination that no prison would ever harbor a profit incentive for incarcerations. Private companies had operated many prisons of the UCAS, and had benefited tremendously from high rates of incarceration.

Many of those being turned loose, while not without their flaws, could become very productive and motivated individuals if encouraged. The men were not objects to exploit for financial gain, and they represented no real threat to others. There were no compelling reasons to keep them locked up in cells behind bars.

"This is the right thing to do, yes it is," declared Rumble Dog, towering over Ian at his right side. The huge man looked almost emotional as he witnessed the ongoing liberation. "I know a couple of my guys are still in there, but I know there's reason for them to be."

"They're sorting everything out, but I'm very glad this is being done," Ian replied, glancing up to Rumble Dog. "Nobody coming out of there now is a threat to me or my family. Or anyone for that matter."

"Don't forget, our work's about done too. Just one more facility to check, and then we go back," Rumble Dog said. A mischievous grin spread through his thick-bearded face. "I'll tell you what, I'm really looking forward to gettin' scratched up real good by my hot little wildcat!"

He winked and his smile grew wider. As crass as Rumble Dog could sometimes be, there was no doubt the man loved his woman every bit as much as Ian did Alena.

"Just hope Raven's feeling a little better by now," Rumble Dog added in a lower voice, one that conveyed a deeper concern.

She was not that far away. Raven had ridden along in the column with Rumble Dog and opted to wait in their vehicle while the prisoners were loosed. Evidently, she had imbibed a little too much drink the previous night, and was contending with a bothersome headache that the bright sunlight exacerbated.

"You said she got the best of your guys last night," Ian remarked.

"Drank 'em all under the table," Rumble Dog stated proudly. "They're still not awake I'd bet. One thing's for sure. All of 'em know by now they can't keep up with her! That's my woman!"

"I'll concede right now to her, no need to have a contest," Ian replied, as the two men laughed together.

"Wise decision, Ian," Rumble Dog proclaimed, patting him on the shoulder. "You got a head on your shoulders."

"I would like to sit down with Alena, and just have a beer or two with her," Ian said wistfully. "That'd be good enough for me."

"I know you want to get back to your woman, and you got yourself a really good one there," Rumble Dog stated.

"Yes ... yes I do," Ian affirmed, with a broad smile. He was glad that Rumble Dog and Alena had taken a liking to each other upon meeting.

He had first worried a little about what Alena would think of the rough and tumble biker, but she had warmed to him quickly enough. Her comments to Ian later revealed that, like him, she saw through Rumble Dog's tough exterior to the big heart dwelling just underneath.

"Once you got a good one, you hold on to 'em," Rumble Dog stated, as if he were imparting a piece of sage wisdom to Ian. He looked back towards the freed men. "I bet some of these lads are gonna be lookin' up their women fast as they can. Ain't healthy to be kept from your woman for a long time. Not good for any man."

"After being cooped up in there for so long, I don't doubt it," Ian said, chuckling. "They'll be making a beeline for wives and girlfriends."

"I've been locked up before, never for too long," Rumble Dog commented. "Don't think I could stand bein' in there as long as some of these fellows have. It'd drive me crazy."

"You think they'll get along okay, the ones that are getting released now?" Ian asked, glancing back up to the big man.

"All depends on how each of these boys were treated in there," Rumble Dog answered. "If they were talked to and treated like men, then we're good. If they were harassed a lot by guards, or talked to like animals, then they'll want to settle a score or two. That's the way it goes."

"I wouldn't feel any different," Ian said.

"Me neither. And if I was messed with, the ones that did it would get a visit for sure," Rumble Dog said firmly, and a shadow of his more intimidating side passed across his face.

His mood changed abruptly, as he looked forward. Like the sun breaking out from behind a thundercloud, a beaming smile broke through his dense beard.

Rumble Dog yelled out, "Catfish Charlie! Ha! Thought that slick, whiskered bastard would be one of those stayin' locked up! This is a good day!"

He gave Ian a boisterous pat on the back, and then strode towards one of the last men to emerge from the front doors of the detention facility. The tough-looking man looked to be in his early fifties. He had a long, bushy gray beard that reached down to his mid-chest.

Seeing Rumble Dog approaching, he smiled, laughed, and came to a stop. The two men gave each other a big hug, the kind of embrace that spoke of a solid camaraderie existing between them.

Ian waited patiently while the sheriff finished speaking with the final men being released, including Catfish Charlie. Rumble Dog stayed with his gray-bearded friend all throughout. He talked further with the fellow, after the last of the freed prisoners had been checked off the list.

His task completed, the sheriff turned and headed towards Ian. Lucy followed a couple paces behind Chris, cradling the clipboard under her right arm.

"That about finishes it up here," Chris announced. He looked relieved to be done, but his mood was bright. "I have to admit, I enjoy these kinds of moments. Never did think so many deserved to be put behind bars. Kind of nice to be the guy that gets to let them out."

"What's happening here is a very good thing," Ian agreed, nodding.

"No rest for the weary though, we've got one more facility to go, before we head back," Chris said. He looked over towards Lucy. "How many at the next one?"

Lucy raised up her clipboard, peeled the top page back, and replied after perusing the page for a moment, "Looks like about two hundred. Smaller facility than this one."

"Won't be too long then," Chris said with a grin, looking back to Ian. "Take a look at their systems while I'm getting everyone checked out. We'll probably be ready to go by the time you get done with your inspection. You won't have to wait around like here."

"It's alright, Chris, it's what I signed up to help with," Ian replied amiably.

"You are a trooper, Ian," Chris replied.

Ian shrugged, and smiled. "Not nearly as bad as some of the older houses I've been in! These prisons are in pretty good shape."

"I just want to be sure we cover everything," Chris said. Ian could see the weight of responsibility in his friend's gaze.

The temporary authorities in Venorterra had chosen Chris to attend to the release of prisoners. Sheriffs, as elected law enforcement entities, were being relied heavily upon during the transition period. Many, like Chris, had seen their duties expand well beyond their original territories.

Ian wanted to do everything he could to help his best friend. Making sure the electrical systems in the facilities were working solidly was easy enough for him, and it served a valuable purpose for Chris.

For the most part, the systems were in good working order. The prisons had not suffered any damage during the upheaval in Venorterra.

"I'm glad you came along," Chris said a moment later. "Real glad you are okay with all this."

"Like they say, that's what friends are for," Ian said, laughing. "I can say I won't mind getting back home and seeing Alena, though."

"I'm looking forward to a little time off myself," Chris said. "Things have just been way too busy, and I don't want to burn out completely. A few cold beers, watching the sun go down, maybe doing some fishing ... just the simple stuff. That's what I really want, and kinda need, right about now."

"You can say that again," Lucy chimed in with an air of weariness to her tone.

"Sounds really good to me too," Ian said, before changing the subject. "So what's the itinerary we're looking at, specifically?"

"First, we're going on to the Davidson Federal Penitentiary," Chris stated. "And we'll do what we just did here, with one little difference, since this one's a facility for women. Then, since we have some heavier security assets, we are going to meet up with a big caravan of folks that have been wanting to return back to our area. A lot of folks from Madison and some of the other surrounding towns.

"They've been stranded in one of the makeshift camps that sprung up these past months. Been too dangerous for them to attempt to return on their own."

"Really were a lot of people displaced during the early chaos," Ian observed.

"Things are still chaotic, in many areas," Chris said grimly. "And I don't blame the people in the camps for staying put. Not safe to travel long distances.

"First of all, the roads themselves are still not fully secure. You've got some pro-UCAS elements still inside our territory, as well as incursions by the UCAS itself. Not to mention the criminal elements that came into the open when order broke down. More than a few bands of highway robbers these days. Then there's the gangs."

"That's mainly in the big cities though, right?" Ian asked, referring to the latter element. "I know that's where the gang activity is centered. But the UCAS sympathizers? The pro-UCAS elements?"

Godwinton, and even larger towns like Madison were largely peaceful at the moment. They were communities filled with a wonderful energy from what Ian had experienced. He knew things were different in Jeffersonville and other larger urban centers, but hoped the trouble spots were confined. Seeing Chris' expression gave root to doubts.

"You'd be surprised," Chris answered. "Our former masters want to disrupt us as much as they possibly can. As porous as the borders are between our provinces and theirs, and with sympathetic elements in the populace, they can stir up a whole lot of trouble for us. And believe me, they're doing just that."

"The UCAS will be coming in force, at some point, I don't doubt that," Ian said.

It was the one thing that everyone he knew saw as inevitable. The UCAS was not about to accept the withdrawal of consent by the people of the south and midwest. The former regime would come to impose their authority with force.

"They will, you can count on that," Chris replied evenly. "Which is why my job, and that of the new police force, is so much tougher. The military is deployed wherever large enemy forces are detected, which spreads things a little thin on the interior right now. It's why we're depending heavily on some citizen militias and the like to help out locally. We simply need everyone we can get to help."

"I think we should hit them hard, before they can build up," Ian said, with a harder edge. "If I was in charge, I sure would."

"I'm not privy to the planning by the generals, but I agree with you a hundred percent and then some," Chris said. "They've made it clear they have not relinquished claims on the breakaway provinces.

We've still got a state of war, declared by them, and they're going to try to get the provinces back."

"I can even see them going to the World Summit sometime soon for help," Lucy interjected dourly. "Getting some sort of resolution passed, to bless and ordain their assault on the free provinces."

"Yes, and we're not going to be called freedom fighters in any discussions there," Chris said, looking between Ian and Lucy. "There won't be any talk of the will of the people, or blathering about democracy when it comes to these provinces. We are going to be called insurgents at best, or, more likely, terrorists."

"I don't care what they call us, I don't need their approval for anything. I know what I am," Ian declared with an angry edge. "Just someone who wants to live free."

"That's the truth of it, for all of us," Lucy added.

"They can call us whatever they want to, we'll still give them hell when they come," Chris said, a steely glint in his eyes. He then looked up and around, and took a deep breath. "No sense getting too worked up now. They're not attacking in force yet, and it looks like everyone's about loaded up here."

"I'll let them know to get ready to pull out," Lucy stated.

Taking brisk strides, she started for the lengthy column of vehicles lining the road approaching the detention facility. Raising a handset to her lips, Lucy began speaking into the communication device.

The sounds of engines coming to life up and down the column filled the air a few moments later. Like a signal, the noise of the engines spurred others to quickly return to the vehicles.

"Let's get this show on the road," Chris said. "No sense waiting around here longer than we have to."

Ian walked with his friend towards the vehicles, which included a few armored ones with shielded, fifty caliber machine guns mounted on top. Ian eyed the military-style vehicles, and took consolation from the sheer size of the column.

The bandits conducting ambushes on the highways and other roads largely preyed upon single vehicles. Nothing would interfere with such an extensive force, and he knew he could start looking forward to seeing Alena again.

Thinking of her brought a feeling of peace to his heart, and a little impatience to get the day over with. In helping to stabilize what was essentially a new nation, he knew he was doing the right thing for his family, but nothing in the world replaced being with them.

Getting into the back seat of an SUV a short distance down from the column's front, he settled into his seat and waited for Chris to get in the driver's side. Lucy joined them a moment later, sitting in the vacant front passenger seat.

Minutes later, they were rolling forward as the column eased back onto the highway and started towards Davidson Federal Penitentiary. Ian reminded himself that a great many of the prisoners about to be freed at the next stop had husbands and children, family that they had been kept from for quite some time. The thought mitigated his restlessness to get back home.

He knew he could endure a little longer for the sake of such women, especially those who had been needlessly incarcerated. In that sense, very little separated some of them from Alena. Had she partied with her friends at a different place and time during the days of her youth, it could have well been her locked up.

The thought was sobering, and it was another reason Ian was glad that a new day had come. He just hoped it would not take too long for the processing of the prisoners, and the rendezvous with the refugee camp. Having Alena in his arms and looking into the depths of her loving gaze could not come a moment too soon.

BENEDICT

Benedict stared towards the far horizon. The darkness was broken up here and there by scattered lights, where a broad, continuous glow would have lit up the entire sky not so long ago. Like random crackles of thunder, gunfire rang out across the night, the outbursts coming from various points in the distant city.

If the city of Coranado were a living being, it was one assaulted with a deadly cancer. The struggle now taking place within the large metropolis was like a body's reaction to a malignant invader. The flicker of life was still present, but the outcome did not look good.

"Not very encouraging, is it?" Royce asked, from his side.

The two of them were alone. The rest of the group that had crossed the border with Benedict and Royce had split up and gone their own ways a short while before.

Benedict did not think much of the chances of the ones who had indicated they were going to head directly towards the city. He wondered what had gotten into their heads to decide on such a course.

"It's why we are keeping to the far outskirts," Benedict replied. "We go no closer than this. Not a step."

The sounds of gunfire from afar had accompanied their travel for quite some time now. From what Benedict could glean from the different tones, a variety of guns were being used. Further, there were no explosions like one might expect if military forces from the free provinces were involved.

The only conclusion he could draw was that the shooting involved criminal elements, civilians defending themselves, or a combination of both. He hoped that the former group was faring badly, though he doubted it. Predators tended to thrive in the wilderness when prey was abundant.

"Let's keep going," Benedict stated dourly, starting forward again.

"Alright, but I'm really getting tired," Royce said. "Can't we call it a night yet?"

"We haven't found a suitable hotel yet," Benedict replied, with a laugh.

Royce shared Benedict's levity, chuckling in a lighthearted fashion. "Oh, I'm sure we will find a nice four or five star establishment, in full operation. Hopefully one with a complimentary breakfast too. I could use a big omelet."

"One can hope," Benedict replied. The notion of a big omelet did sound appetizing. He looked up into the skies, and watched the drifting clouds outlined in moonlight for a few seconds. "Just be glad we don't have rain yet."

"That's the last thing we need right now," Royce said.

"And if it does ...."

"Don't take another step!" a voice with a thick southern accent shot out of the darkness from just ahead. "Get your hands into the air ... now! We've got our guns on you!"

Though Benedict could see nothing in the darkness, he chose to cooperate without hesitation or protest. Standing out in the open, and without a weapon in hand, there was not much he could hope to do if the speaker did have a gun.

Glancing out of the corner of his eye, he saw that Royce was also following the directive. That was a relief.

"More of you damned border crossers," the voice resumed, in a heavily-irritated tone. The dark shape of a man holding a rifle then emerged into Benedict's sight, framed within the light from the crescent moon above. "Keeping clear of the city, I bet, and you had to come right onto my property."

Benedict sensed the exasperation in the man's voice. He surmised that it was not the first time the other figure had dealt with unwelcome travelers.

Looking to the left and right, he saw that a couple of other individuals were approaching, with the distinctive outlines of rifles held within their hands. Whoever had stopped Benedict's night trek, there was no doubt they were well-armed. He just had to hope that they were not of criminal intent.

"Doesn't seem the city is a very good place to go at the moment," Benedict replied politely. As if to reinforce his words, another rattle of gunfire, from an automatic rifle, broke out far away. "We didn't want any part of that. We just wanted to be on our way. Avoid trouble. Definitely not wanting to stay around."

"No, the city's not a good place to be, and you're not dumb to be avoidin' it," the man replied evenly. He took another few steps forward, and drew to a halt, as did his quiet companions. "But what to do with ya? That's the real question. You're still on my land."

"Just show us a path around your property, and we'll be happy to keep going," Benedict said. "We're just trying to get back home. Not wanting to cause any trouble at all."

"It's no man's land for a good long way," the other man replied. "You would probably run into much worse than us. A lot of folks are shootin' first these days.."

"I thank you for not shooting right away," Benedict said, with no trace of jest in his words.

"I could tell you two weren't gang bangers," the man stated, matter-of-factly. "Would of dropped you right away if you were. Those scum you can't take any chances with."

" Just two guys trying to get home," Benedict replied. He then risked a question. "Who is in control of the city, overall?"

"The UCAS was driven out completely from the region, and the military of the new provinces hasn't been able to reach this area yet," the man replied. "I think they're coming, but they're slow. Too slow for my liking."

"So nobody's really in control of this region?" Benedict queried, a little dismayed at the notion.

"Gangs have a pretty good lockdown on the city itself. That's most of what you're hearing," the man said. "Their reign of terror, and maybe a few good folks standing up for themselves. But the good folks don't stand much of a chance. There's thousands of gang bangers running around the city, and they're armed to the teeth. With no law and order, they're runnin' amok."

"Surely they aren't cooperating with each other," Benedict said. "The gangs, I mean. There must be different ones. Fighting with each other over turf or things like that."

"That's the only thing goin' for the regular folk," the man responded. "Gangs are fightin' amongst each other. Don't want to think of how things would be if they worked together."

"I guess you can hope they kill each other off," Benedict said.

"Wish that was the case," the man replied, ruefully.

"Hey, it just hit me … I know your voice!" one of the man's companions interjected suddenly, with a deep, masculine voice. There was an excited undercurrent to his words, as if he had just made a big discovery. "You sound just like the radio guy. The late night fellow. I know your voice, I do! It's you, I know it."

A moment Benedict had anticipated occurring along his journey had finally manifested. A major decision loomed, and he had to make it fast. Taking a deep breath, he picked his course.

"If you are thinking of Benedict Darwin, that's me," Benedict replied with a calm tone, trusting his choice and hoping with all his heart that the armed figures in the night had a favorable impression of his show. "Sea to Shining Sea. I had to give way to Zeev Steiner, when some unavoidable things came up."

"Yeah, you just disappeared from the air," the second figure replied. A little skepticism crept into his next words. "But then, you could just sound like him. Let me ask you a few things about the show. If you're really him, you should know this stuff really easy."

The man proceeded to ask Benedict several questions related to the show, and some of the interviews he had hosted. Thankfully, Benedict recalled everything with perfect clarity, and responded flawlessly to the light interrogation.

"You're him, no doubt," the questioner stated finally. "You couldn't fake that if you weren't. No way. Don't even think you could if you were a big fan."

"I assure you, I am Benedict Darwin," Benedict said. "I don't have a driver's license with me anymore, unfortunately, or I could prove it further to you."

"Well, why didn't you just say you were him?" the second man replied, as if Benedict pronouncing himself as a celebrity was the most logical choice for making an introduction during a random encounter in the middle of the night. "Can't tell you how many nights you got me through a work shift. Really appreciated your show."

Benedict had never minded having a degree of celebrity, but now he was immensely grateful for it. He could feel the tension defusing swiftly from the air.

"I listened to your show a lot too," the first speaker said. "Liked it quite a bit. Really interesting stuff with the UFO's and all."

The leader started walking forward again. As if that were some sort of cue, the others with him also began approaching.

Walking out of the night was a tall, lean man with a scraggly beard, carrying a rifle fitted with a high-capacity magazine. To either side of him were women, also armed with rifles, one roughly his age, and another that Benedict estimated to be around twenty or so.

The older woman was a little heavyset, with a more rounded face, while the younger was a few inches taller, with narrower features. Stern-faced, they both had long hair, the locks flowing free on the older, and pulled back into a ponytail on the younger. It was clear from the look about them that neither woman was given to any sort of nonsense.

The second man who had proclaimed Benedict's identity turned out to be a big burly fellow with a long goatee. His broad head sported a baseball cap, and he grinned as he trudged up to Benedict.

"Name's Walton," he introduced himself in a casual manner. "Never thought I'd meet a real famous person like this."

"Can't say I ever thought I'd be sneaking across a border in the middle of the night," Benedict replied, with a chuckle.

"I'm Les," the leaner man announced. "And this is my wife Tonya, and our daughter Melanie."

"Nice to meet all of you," Benedict said, looking to each of the others.

"You can take your hands down, ya know," Walton told him, with a friendly laugh. "You're all good with us."

Benedict realized he still had his arms upraised, and slowly let his hands drop to his sides. He watched Walton for any indication he had misunderstood. As unpredictable as the world had become, he was not about to assume anything.

"So, who's your buddy?" Les asked, glancing over at Benedict's traveling companion. Royce remained quiet, keeping his own arms in the air as he watched the proceedings.

"This is Royce, who was part of the group that crossed the border area," Benedict answered. "We decided to stick together, and watch each other's backs."

Royce nodded. "Just wanted to make our way around the city. A few of the others in the group went right towards it."

All of the others frowned or shook their heads at the statement. The reaction brought Benedict a pang of sorrow.

"City's no man's land," Les said. "I'm not kiddin' when I say gangs run it. Take what they want from the people unlucky enough to be trapped there right now."

"It's why we're bein' careful here," Walton said. "No tellin' when they're wantin' to try and spread out."

"But if they do," Tonya interjected in a cool tone, raising up the rifle in her hands. "We'll be ready to greet 'em nicely. Give 'em a lead salute, if ya know what I mean."

"I'm glad we didn't go that way. Sounds like it's a total nightmare," Benedict said. He then ventured a question. "So, is this where you all lived, even prior to all the chaos?"

"Yep, didn't have to go anywhere. We've been gettin' ready for a long while," Les announced, with a tone of pride. "Some said we were nuts. Well, lots of folk, actually, even friends and kin. One thing's for sure. Nobody's laughin' at us now."

"We were ready as could be for all this," Walton said.

He looked over at Les, and the latter turned towards his wife. Not a word was spoken, but a consensus of some kind was reached as the three nodded intently to each other.

"We'll show ya," Les said, looking back to Benedict. "You and your buddy, come on."

"You can put your hands down too and relax," Walton told Royce. He chuckled as Benedict's companion eased his arms to his side. Looking to the duffel bag Royce had dropped at the outset of their encounter, he added, "Pick up your bag too."

Guiding Benedict and Royce in the dark, Les and the others led them towards a cluster of low structures. From what Benedict could tell on his first view of the silhouetted buildings, they involved a modest-sized home with some extensions built onto it.

"You had some folks just like us on your show once," Walton remarked as they neared. "Some call 'ins too. But we think our setup's one of the best around."

"We'll show you the main house in the morning, and the rest of this," Les said. "For now, we're goin' to our little underground refuge."

They continued around to the back of the above-ground structures, and continued walking for a few hundred paces across open ground until Les came to a stop. Leaning over, he pulled up what looked to be a generic manhole cover, hinged to one side.

"Alrighty, everyone down!" he exclaimed, a little boisterously.

Down the rabbit hole everyone went, with Benedict and Royce descending in the middle of the group. A light was turned on somewhere beneath when Benedict was midway down the ladder. Reaching the bottom, Benedict saw Walton, the last in their line, closing the hatch above and locking it from the inside.

Les, Tonya, and Melanie all had their eyes on the newcomers, though notably, they had set their rifles down. It was then that Benedict noticed they were still armed.

All three had short, curving dark sheaths at their waists. Eyeing the sizeable blades for a second, it was clear to him that they were individuals who kept up a constant state of readiness.

The group stood within a rectangular space, lined with shelves along the two longer sides. An open doorway at the far end led into another compartment of the underground bunker.

"You all certainly did make some preparations," Benedict commented appreciatively, looking around at an immense collection of well-ordered, cleanly-labeled jars, cans, and big plastic buckets topped with lids.

"Some pantry, ain't it?" Walton chuckled, though a clear undercurrent of pride girded the humor.

"This alone has us taken care of for pretty much a couple years," Les announced. He nodded towards the open door. "Come on. We're not done yet. There's plenty more in this little hidey-hole of ours."

While not bedrooms, alcoves had been fashioned with mattresses and curtains, offering a degree of privacy for sleeping. There was another larger space that had been set up like a living room, complete with couches and a flat screen television.

As Benedict eyed the television, and noted the electric lights providing the illumination in the rooms, Les explained that his group had all the power they needed in the bunker. He indicated that most of it came from a series of solar panels and solar-powered batteries.

There were a few doors that were left closed. Benedict had little doubt that one of them harbored an arsenal, based upon the weapons his new hosts had been carrying with them above ground.

Les and his group had even set up a small station where several cameras on the surface transmitted images to a cluster of small monitors below. Even when down in the bunker, they could keep an eye on what was happening around their property outside. A couple of the cameras were mounted at a higher angle, providing a broad view of the structures they had passed on their way in.

At the end of the informal tour, Benedict and Royce were invited to make themselves comfortable in the living room. Sitting down, he sighed as he eased back into the cushions. It felt so good to simply relax.

"Take a load off," Walton invited, amiably.

"You two boys drink?" Les asked.

Benedict and Royce nodded.

"Good to hear! You can try out some of our homemade wine then," Les announced with a grin.

"Good, good stuff," Walton said, nodding. "Really is."

Benedict had sampled home-brewed beers and the like before, and many were far less than exemplary. Doubts about their claims lingered as he was given a glass cup, full of a dark liquid.

The scent was not bad at all, and putting it to his lips, he tasted it. Raising his eyebrows and nodding, he said to James and Walton, "You are right. This is very good stuff."

"I like it too," Royce added, when he had taken his first sip.

"When there ain't much to do, you can hone your craft," Tonya commented from where she was seated to Benedict's left. "I've got this all pretty much figured out."

"She's got it down for sure, don't she?" Les said, evincing obvious pride in his wife.

Benedict had nothing but full agreement to offer, as the wine was indeed of excellent quality. Swirling his glass, and sniffing, he took another long sip. After the long night-time hike, he savored every last bit of the unexpected experience.

Walton and Melanie followed up shortly after with an ample portion of rice and fresh fish for each of their guests. From what they said, the fish was raised on the grounds above, in the area they had passed by.

Though basic in nature, the food proved to be a delectable feast to Benedict, as famished as he was. Walton got him another plate when he cleaned off the first.

When they were finally finished eating, everyone got refills of the sweet wine and continued to relax. The conversation soon turned towards events both current and of the recent past.

"You all really did see the storm coming," Benedict told his hosts in a complimentary manner. "I have to commend you. You got yourselves prepared very well. All of this is more impressive than any of the groups I ever had on my show."

"I just knew something big was coming," Les replied, with a hint of vindication in his voice. "Like I said earlier, lots of folks thought our type was paranoid, or plain crazy. But we weren't harmin' nobody, so we always wondered why they seemed to be so put off in the first place."

"Unfortunately, lots of people act strangely, or disapprovingly, of the things they can't relate to," Benedict said. "It's been my experience that there really are few who are live and let live types. If it's not something that kind agrees with, supports, or understands, they belittle it or mock it. Believe me, all of my guests, no matter what they were involved in, dealt with that kind of thing to some degree."

"So whatever happened to live and let live? Why so rare?" Walton asked. "You know what I mean?"

"Maybe we'll give that idea another shot in these freed provinces," Benedict remarked. "Hopefully we won't lose hold of it so fast this time."

"Let's hope so!" Tonya exclaimed. "The way things were didn't work out so well."

"So what do you all plan to do?" Royce asked Les. "Do you think things will get back to some kind of normal state?"

"Gonna ride this hellstorm out, first of all," Les declared. "We got enough down here to go for a long while, as you've seen."

"We've been developin' our own food sources too, for the longer term, but most of that's above ground," Walton added.

"We'll see what happens with the city, the gangs, and all that,"

Les stated. "If that mess gets sorted out, then maybe it can get back to normal."

"Is there a way you'll know what's happening in the area?" Royce asked. "Like what happens in the city?"

Les grinned, and pointed towards the far wall, where some electronic gear sat on a table. "We've got the TV, and we can pick up a little there. But as far as local news goes, that's the best means over there. Just a good, old-fashioned ham radio setup."

"You'd be surprised how many folks are using that nowadays," Walton added in. "All kinds of chatter going over the airwaves."

"We've reached a lot of people around this area," Les said. "Got a pretty good idea of what's goin' on. Even some direct reports out of the city itself."

"It's our very own news station, guess you could say," Walton said. "Airwaves are ours for now."

"And no commercials either," Tonya interjected, chuckling.

"Maybe I should give an impromptu show, right from the underground here," Benedict said, with a brief laugh. He then added, with a bolder tone that echoed his radio voice. "The civil war edition of Sea to Shining Sea. A broadcast from the bunker, with your guest host Benedict Darwin!"

Everyone in the room laughed at his pronouncement.

"We're gonna need to play that weird theme music you got to make it more official," Les said. He started humming out the distinctive tune.

"Wow, that'd be somethin', to host a show from right here," Walton said. "But probably our system don't reach quite as many folks as you're used to."

"Believe me, it'd be great to do any kind of show at all again," Benedict said, finding that he enjoyed hearing the theme music. It brought back a wave of good feelings and memories. "To tell you the truth, I'm about starved for something resembling normalcy."

"So what about you?" Tonya asked. "I guess the radio show's on hold for awhile. What are you lookin' to do, durin' all of this mess that's goin' on?"

"I'm just trying to get back to the territory held by province military or security forces, at the very least," Benedict replied. "Where I'm needing to go eventually is farther north, up to Venorterra. That's where my family members are right now."

"Oh yeah! That's bourbon country, ain't it?" Walton asked merrily. "Gotta be a good place."

Benedict smiled warmly. "Bourbon country it is, and hopefully that will be one thing kept over fully intact from the old days."

"Walton likes his bourbon and whiskey, that's for sure," Tonya said. She grinned, eyeing the big man. "We'll probably have to figure out how to make that too, if things don't get settled soon enough. He's goin' through his stash pretty quickly."

"Don't tease me, that's mean," Walton retorted, with a rumbling laugh. "If you can make good whiskey, means I can drink from my stash faster!"

"That's all we need," Tonya replied, rolling her eyes. "Maybe I won't try to make any at all then."

"You are bein' cruel now," Walton said, though his warm smile belied his accusation.

"You're a captive audience, Walton," Tonya riposted playfully. "Who else do I got to pick on?"

"Alright, I can't hold back no more. To my big question," Les interrupted, breaking into the banter. "What's a celebrity radio guy like you doin', walking around in this no-man's land?"

Ever since they had sat down to talk, Benedict had suspected the question would be forthcoming. He had thought it through, and was ready with a response.

He told Les and the others the bare minimum. He spoke of how he had crossed the government, been apprehended, had discovered intelligence of great value to the rebels, and then managed to escape his incarceration.

Left entirely out of his condensed account were his encounters with the Nephilim and the Fallen Avatar. He made no mention of the An-Ki, or anything else the others might find impossible to believe.

"We've heard lots of rumors, of camps and all," Les remarked dourly, when Benedict had concluded. "UCAS is detaining loads of folks, they say. Thousands and thousands if you believe what you hear. All herded up and kept in big camps."

"Wow, that's all just like some of the things you had on your show, but you lived 'em," Walton stated. "Can't dispute what you've seen and been through."

"Sounds pretty wild," Les said. "Can't say I envy you. Been good to stay safe and comfortable right here."

"Hey, I gotta root for you all the way," Walton said. "No love for the government here. They just wanted to leech off us all anyhow." He chuckled after a moment, shaking his head. "I always thought you would piss them off good someday. You were waking way too many people up for their liking. I was surprised you lasted as long as you did."

"Can't say I saw any of this coming, as clearly as you all did. But I keep my mind open to all possibilities nowadays, that's for sure," Benedict replied, thinking back on all the bizarre and unexpected things that had happened to him in recent months.

"Well, I just gotta say thanks," Walton said, voice becoming more serious. "Because without your show, I never would have thought about what might happen, and wonder if I was ready or not. In a lot of ways, it's what led me to meet Les, and eventually work with him and his family on this bunker here, and everything else above.

"When I think about it, in a lot of ways I'm alive today, probably, because of your show. So the least I can do is help you and your friend out a little, if we can do something."

Benedict smiled at Walton's sincere words, feeling an increasing drowsiness with his belly full and his body sunk back into the couch cushions. "Your hospitality has been far more than we could have hoped for."

"It has. Thank you all so much," Royce added.

"That's the least we could do, give ya a little food and shelter," Walton said. A thoughtful expression came to his face. "So, tell us, how we can give you some help for your journey back home."

Benedict looked at Walton, and then towards Les and the two women. "If you don't mind hearing me out, there are a couple of things we could use."

FATHER BRUNNER

A palpable sense of fear and anxiety pervaded the air as Father Brunner settled down into one of the few open seats left near the rear of the crowded hall. What few people still talked did so in hushed, pensive voices. Faces were somber and nervous, with not a trace of good humor to be found.

With his section of the city receiving no power at the moment, there was not much that Father Brunner could be doing back **at St. Bosco**. The outage was part of the rolling blackouts administered by the provincial authorities to ration energy use. At the very least, it was not the dead of winter, when such outages could be extremely dangerous for the sick and elderly.

Father Rader had opted to stay back at the church and do some reading with the use of a battery-powered lamp, but Father Brunner had grown curious about the town hall meeting being held on campus at Mary Riley College. The assembly's stated purpose was to explain several new government initiatives being set in place.

As always with such affairs, the event advertised the opportunity for discussion and input from the citizens. The invitation for public participation did not fool Father Brunner in the slightest.

He knew the opinions and desires of regular people were entirely irrelevant to the individuals hosting the gathering. It would be the same process as it had been for quite some time: the government officials would do whatever they planned to do, with or without the consent of the citizenry.

It was all just a grand display of theater, to give the people the illusion that they had some say in the process. Sadly, most of the people sitting in the hall would probably go home later that evening thinking they actually did have some influence.

Undoubtedly, more controls were coming, and whatever shreds of freedom still remained to the people were going to suffer another vigorous round of assaults. The whole thing was diabolical at its core, and Father Brunner found it increasingly harder to hide his disgust with all of it.

Yet there was a little of use to be extracted from the night's itinerary. Father Brunner wanted to see if he could read between the lines and get a better idea of the mechanisms the authorities would be using in the days to come. Figuring out what his community would be dealing with went along with the adage his father often told him when he was growing up; forewarned is fore-armed.

Being well-prepared for the sake of others was a mandate as Father Brunner saw it, in light of his responsibilities. Every day of his life was spent tending to all kinds of people. The government initiatives would be affecting them all, adding to their struggles and bearing down upon their worries.

To give wise counsel to others was to understand, as best as possible, what people were contending with in their day to day lives. Only in knowing the nature of those problems could he hope to render the kind of help that would truly address their concerns.

Some motion near the front of the hall attracted Father Brunner's attention. He sat up a little straighter as the whispers and low voices around him began to die down.

Narrow of face, with glasses and a receding hairline, the lean man striding to the podium looked about as non-threatening as a person could get. A friendly smile was exhibited on his face as he looked out over the attentive crowd, which had become pensively silent. All eyes were focused in his direction as the audience waited for him to speak.

"Good evening. My name is Warren Paulson, with Troy's Agency of Sustainable Advancement," the man introduced himself. "I want to thank all of you for coming to this town hall meeting being given to explain the Sustainable Health and Prosperity Initiative being activated in Troy and other urban centers of the UCAS.

"It is a program that will implement the foundations of a sustainable future, good for all, both here and throughout this trouble-filled world. With the integration of the new currency here in the UCAS, one we will soon be sharing with our brothers and sisters in the Europa Alliance, it is an opportune time for discussions of significant change."

Warren's voice reflected his appearance: calm, unremarkable, and devoid of intimidating qualities. Father Brunner mused that he was the perfect government official. Warren was the kind of person who could speak softly, and even amiably, about things that would soon be taking liberties and self-determination away from people, all the while convincing them that they had a genuine say in the course of things.

He would be like so many others of his kind. His voice would never rise in volume, nor carry any significant emotion. Warren's image was that of a secure individual, at ease with his surroundings, and imbued with reason and thoughtfulness.

Anger was something Father Brunner increasingly struggled to keep at bay, but it was hard not to be provoked by wickedness posing in such an innocuous guise. Warren Paulson knew exactly what he was doing. He was a true believer, advancing a devious agenda, and he was doing it exceedingly well.

"All of what I talk to you about tonight regarding the Sustainable Health and Prosperity Initiative will be integrated fully with Living ID," Warren continued. "For the few of you who still have not received Living ID, and if you have not, you have not gotten the vaccine for the Thanatos Virus yet, then I urge you to do so, as soon as you possibly can.

"I know there are many who are making all sorts of outlandish claims about Living ID. Unfounded statements and absurd conspiracy theories take deeper root in good people than they should. I find it unfortunate that they seek to play upon the fears of men and women during the very difficult times we are all facing together.

"Living ID is in your best interest, and Living ID was implemented for your security, and the security of your families and children. Living ID protects your identity and your money, and helps you avail yourself of all the benefits and support available to you from the UCAS during these deeply troubled times."

Father Brunner kept the rueful laugh he felt building inside from showing on his face or escaping his mouth. He suspected Warren Paulson had a much different definition of benefits and support than he did.

What the man really offered was outright subjugation, and a life of increasing subservience for everyone in the hall. Whether it leaned towards the form of a soft tyranny or hard tyranny, it was all still tyranny in essence.

"I hope we have some business owners with us in this audience tonight," Warren proceeded. "I know things have been disrupted extensively during all of the national turmoil, and the terrorist insurgency in the south and midwest. But I have some very good news for you as well, in the form of new, innovative programs of public-private partnerships.

"Everything from reduced liabilities, to tax benefits, to robust subsidies are available to those who choose to partner with the UCAS in a number of industries and sectors. Much of this predates the upheaval, and was already being integrated nationally, as some of you might be aware. But we are accelerating these partnerships across a broad spectrum to help stimulate the economy and create jobs."

Father Brunner clenched his jaw tight. He knew what was coming, and Warren Paulson did not fail to deliver it.

The priest's heart went out to those living in the rural areas, who were about to be hit with a swarm of new regulations regarding property development, land usage, and several other things that would interfere with their self-determination and property rights. Many would suddenly find their situation untenable and relocate to the bigger urban centers, which, Father Brunner could see right away, was precisely what men like Warren Paulson wanted.

It was the subtle nudge whereby the government controlled the choices available to the people. In turn, the people acted on the predetermined choices presented to them, falling right into the trap prepared by the Warren Paulsons of the world. No security forces would be needed to sweep out the rural areas when people packed themselves up.

Father Brunner had gotten into many debates with individuals, pastors, and even other priests that supported such initiatives. He could not let it pass when he heard someone claim it was all in line with the Sacred Writings and the Will of Adonai.

Father Brunner always challenged them to come up with the passages in the Sacred Writings where it called for Saviorans to seize governmental power to wield the force of human-made laws. Acts of charity and giving, and walking along the Savioran path, were based upon individuals exercising free will, not being coerced to do things by governmental authority. If anything, the words of the Liberator had made it abundantly clear that His Kingdom was an entirely separate entity from the worldly kingdoms and authorities.

Not once did He call for his followers to take over the realms of the world, and enforce anything He spoke of through wielding the power of human government. His was a path of volition, not one of coercion.

It merited a Savioran nothing to have money taxed from them and then given to someone in a government program. No matter what kind of endeavor it was, or how noble it appeared to be, it was not an act of free will.

As Father Brunner ultimately saw it, free will, and freedom itself, resonated with the dominion of Adonai. Control and coercion were the noxious air breathed within Diabolos' Nether Kingdom.

At the end of life, it was the individual who answered before the Great Throne, not a collective. Each and every person would be judged according to their own works and choices, not the works of others. As such, it was freely chosen actions that expressed the heart of a person and the state of their spirit with Adonai.

Ultimately, there was no mistaking the nature of what underlay the authority Warren Paulson represented. That was nothing Father Brunner could ever compromise with. He knew the only path he could live with in terms of his conscience was to resist in every way he could, as he helped the beleaguered people of Troy.

At the end of the presentation there were a number of questions allowed from the audience. Some were delivered with hostile tones, but Warren was unflappable and answered everything without the slightest trace of irritation.

He made it appear that he empathized with his audience, and held their concerns to heart. In a world where most people expected devils to have horns and pitchforks, men like Warren Paulson could thrive unabated.

Finally, when Father Brunner feared he could hold his tongue no longer, Warren Paulson concluded. "I know this might seem like a lot of change. I understand that concern. I want all of you to know it was our intention to bring these initiatives into place much more slowly, but the unique circumstances facing our nation have demanded swifter action.

"We do understand the challenges you are facing in raising your families, and the difficulties facing the job market. All of what we are doing is being done to ensure that each and every one of you can achieve harmony and prosperity with a sustainable world."

Warren's last words were accompanied with a congenial smile etched on his face. Father Brunner was probably one of the few in the room at the end who understood the amiable façade was only skin-deep. Peel that layer away, and a ravenous monster would be revealed just underneath.

When the address was concluded, Father Brunner got up and made his way through the crowd towards the exits at the back of the hall. He listened to any comments that he could, though many of them were disheartening. It was clear the people talking had been won over by Warren.

A sharp expletive broke out from a young man to the right. "Is everyone so damn stupid as to believe that liar?" he stated in a raised voice. A couple of his friends worked to calm the agitated fellow down. "These bastards got us here to begin with, and you all are actually buying this load of crap? What the hell is wrong with you all? Have you lost your minds? He's only going to make your lives worse than it is now!"

Pausing, and catching the young man's eyes, Father Brunner nodded towards him, and said. "I don't follow liars either. You've got it right."

"Thank you. I was worried I was the only one here with any sense," the young man replied in a lower voice after a couple of breaths, looking a little winded from his tirade.

His companions, still clutching onto their friend, shot the priest a few glares. They were clearly displeased with his unsolicited expression of solidarity.

"You aren't the only one, and there are many more out there, so don't give up," Father Brunner exhorted him, ignoring the hard looks from the others. "What that man represents is rotten to the core."

"I won't give up," the young man responded firmly, looking Father Brunner in the eye. "Not ever."

"C'mon man, let's go," one of his companions said, grabbing him by the upper arm and seeking to pull him away.

Father Brunner nodded once more to the young man, and then rejoined the flow of the crowd to the doors at the rear of the hall. The brisk air invigorated his senses as he walked out into the night.

Reaching the streets, he cast a glance around. Not far away was an armored police vehicle, attended by a few officers in military-style attire. With assault rifles, helmets, and body armor, they cast an intimidating presence over the men and women filing out into the city streets.

Beyond the law enforcement troopers, and set off to the side, a distinctive van sat idle. Father Brunner had seen them often enough rolling slowly through the streets.

It was a scanning vehicle, designed with backscatter x-ray technology and likely other advanced sensory devices. They were being used to scan residences for weapons and other contraband.

He could only imagine what effects the scanning vehicles had on the health of the populace they monitored constantly. Father Brunner had probably absorbed more radiation than he cared to know over the last few months. He was probably being irradiated even now.

Looking up, he saw a camera mounted on a streetlight, its eye unblinking as it stood witness to everything in its field of view. Even higher up, cruising slowly far overhead, was a surveillance drone. It was probably weaponized and ready to engage any perceived disruptions on the part of the crowd below.

Yet despite the immediate presence of cameras, drones, scanning vehicles, and troopers armed to the teeth, Father Brunner felt anything but safe. In truth, he had never felt more under a cloud of threat in all his life, as he started back towards St. Bosco.

A dark order was entrenched. Like a massive python coiled around its quivering prey, it was constricting bit by bit until its victim died.

BENEDICT

The morning greeted Benedict garbed in raiment of brilliant light when he, Royce, and Walton made their way up the ladder and exited the bunker. Squinting for a few moments, he adjusted to the sheer brightness of direct sunlight following the night spent in dimmer confines underground.

He had slept well and felt greatly refreshed. His body needed to limber up more, having stiffened up after the lengthy hike across the border, but for the most part he felt better than he had in quite some time.

Benedict joined Royce as Walton took them on a brief tour. Les, Tonya and Melanie were already engaged in various chores around the property, though none of them were in sight as the walkthrough got underway.

One of the main elements of the above-ground operation was a substantial series of solar panels mounted on the roof of the main structure. Walton showed them where batteries could be charged for storing up the energy collected by the solar panels.

He then took them to the far side of the main building to where the daylight revealed a couple of narrow monopole towers. Both of the towers were surmounted with small, three-tine wind turbines. There was little question the place had ample energy for its needs.

Moving onward from the wind generators, Walton took them into one of the extensions from the main building. It turned out to be long greenhouse, fashioned out of a framework of metal, the latter supporting a series of translucent, polycarbonate panels.

The interior space featured a series of water tanks with rectangular growing beds set above them. The steady sound of trickling water accompanied Walton's narrative as he proudly explained the aquaponic system that they had designed and built. Benedict imagined it would be quite peaceful tending to the greenhouse, with the sunlight beaming in and the gentle sounds of running water serving as a background.

"Like broccoli? Tomatoes?" Walton asked his two guests. "How about cucumbers, beans, lettuce, or carrots? Well, we got it all, and more, year round."

"Impressive," Benedict commented, looking at the rows of vibrant greenery filling the upper growing beds.

"Definitely," Royce concurred.

"And below, in the tanks we've got lots of tilapia," Walton continued. He pointed to a few tanks at the far end of the space. "And there, we've got catfish and bluegill in each of those tanks. Catfish take the bottom, bluegill stay above. They work good together."

"All self-contained," Benedict said appreciatively, remembering how good the fish had tasted the previous evening.

He looked at the pipes running between the water tanks and the grow beds. The whole system prompted him to think of Conrad Rudel. He speculated that the man would be very interested in the efficient setup within the greenhouse.

"All the fish and vegetables you can handle," Walton said.

"Just ingenious," Benedict complimented Walton. "Everything is so straightforward. There's a complete loop here."

"Yessir," Walton replied with a grin. "We run everything off 100 watt pumps. Power them off solar. Keeps the aeration going, moves the fish water above where it gets filtered in the grow beds, and then it returns back down to the fish tanks. Great system. Not much trouble at all."

"You all really did your homework," Royce commented.

"Really ain't that hard," Walton said. "Once you get it up and running."

"What do you feed the fish?" Royce asked.

"Duckweed, fly larva that we cultivate here, scraps," Walton replied. "We're covered there too."

"So what do you think of all this?" Les's voice sounded from behind.

Turning, Benedict saw Les entering the greenhouse. "You are well set for the future, it seems. It is really incredible."

Les grinned. "If all the fracas drags out that long, we're ready, but hopefully it won't. Still like being self-sufficient though. This whole experience has hammered that lesson home, believe me."

"I bet it has," Benedict replied. "I think I've learned a few things in the short time I've visited here."

"We like to help," Walton said.

"So you done with the tour Walton?" Les asked his friend.

"Just got done," Walton said.

"I'm ready for the parting gifts, be back in a second," Les announced, abruptly taking leave of the others. He turned about and exited the greenhouse.

"Looks like it's getting about time to leave," Benedict observed, looking after Les.

Walton led them out of the greenhouse, where the sunlight warmed Benedict's face out of a clear sky. He was glad to see that there were no signs of rain anytime soon.

"Good day to be heading out," Benedict observed.

"Weather is nice, and I hope it holds up for you," Walton said. He then chuckled. "If the weather gets bad and you need shelter, you know where you can go."

"I appreciate that," Benedict replied with a smile.

About that time, Melanie and Tonya walked into sight from around the building. They joined Benedict, Walton, and Royce.

"Wanted to be sure to say goodbye to you," Tonya announced.

"Me too," Melanie added.

"Thanks for coming to see us off," Benedict said.

"Wouldn't miss it," Tonya said. "We haven't known ya long, but we consider you friends now."

"Feeling is mutual. You all have been just incredible," Benedict said.

"You really have," Royce said. "We couldn't have hoped for more than what you gave us."

Tonya shrugged, and smiled. "Just glad we could be of some help."

"I want to wish the both of you the best of luck," Walton said, his expression growing more serious. "And Benedict, I wanted say a couple of last things to you before you go."

"Sure, Walton, I'm listening," Benedict replied, sensing the shift in the man's demeanor.

"You're a really good man, and I hope one day I can talk with you again," Walton said.

His rising dawn pendant gleamed in the sunlight as he looked to Tonya and Melanie, and then back towards Benedict. There was a trace of nervousness in his face as prepared to continue.

"I thought about it all again last night, and I'm sure of how I feel," Walton proceeded. "I never would have found my way here, if it wasn't for your show. Thank you, Benedict ... thank you for everything. You made a big different in my life, and I genuinely feel you saved it. I wouldn't be here with Les, Tonya, and Melanie if it weren't for your show. And they're my family now. I can't tell you how much that means to me."

Benedict thought he caught a glistening in the man's eyes as they shook hands. He had never thought of his radio show in the kind of light that Walton was revealing to him. The thought that his life's work had possibly saved lives and brought good people together was both humbling and incredible to ponder.

"If my show was of value to you, in some way, you are most welcome, Walton," Benedict replied. "That makes me so glad I did it ... more than anything."

"It was of a priceless value," Walton said, in a low voice, looking Benedict directly in the eyes. "It really made a difference."

"I got their presents," announced Les in a loud voice, cutting into the sentimental atmosphere with a jarring effect. He walked around the corner of the building and heading back towards them.

Walton's face erupted into a big grin. "Yep, we have some goin' away presents for ya Benedict!"

"Parting gifts, yes we do!" Les exclaimed. "I wasn't joking!"

In each hand, Les held a very recognizable type of rifle. The telltale wooden stocks, pistol-grips, curving magazines, and other features on the two rifles told Benedict immediately they were MKZs.

"Modified 'em a bit. You won't mind. They're full auto," Les said proudly, handing one of the rifles to Benedict, and the other to Royce. He laughed and exclaimed, "UCAS law doesn't count anymore, so you can't say they're illegal!"

"We wanted to do somethin' extra special for you guys," Walton said. "You said last night you could use some weapons. Believe me, these will do the job for you. They'll take care of business."

"I don't want to take away from your protection here at all," Benedict responded, surprised at the significant and unexpected gift.

When he had made the request for a weapon following the meal the previous night, he had imagined them having a spare pistol, or maybe an older bolt-action hunting rifle or shotgun. He had never expected to be given something of such quality and utility. Both powerful and dependable, MKZs were one of the best firearms ever made.

Les and Walton laughed heartily as they looked upon Benedict's amazed expression. Tonya and Melanie joined in their amusement a moment later.

"I think he likes it," Walton observed.

"I think he does too," Les concurred.

"You saw how much food we had," Tonya said to Benedict. "Well, we're pretty stocked up in other areas too. Trust us on that. Don't worry yourself at all about taking these two bad boys with you."

"Yeah, we've got maybe a few more of those set aside," Walton said, with a knowing wink. "One or two, at the least."

"Yeah, one or two," Tonya echoed, with a light chuckle.

"Brought you boys some extra mags, with their bellies all full," Les said. From a pouch at his side, he handed over two magazines to Benedict, and another pair to Royce. "Like the one already affixed, they're all thirty rounders. Should get you guys out of a fix or two, if things come to that. But ammunition goes quicker than you think, so use your best judgement."

"Thank you," Benedict said to Les. "Hopefully things won't come to needing to use these, but you just can't be sure anymore."

"And if you do need them, you'd better have them," Walton stated. "That's always been the truth about guns."

"No kidding," Benedict agreed, looking at his new weapon.

Benedict was surprised at the weight the magazines had as he held them in his hands. He took a moment to put them in his pack. It turned out that Royce was fairly experienced with guns. But Walton and Les still took a few minutes to show Benedict how to change out a magazine, and load the first round in the chamber. They also explained how to change the mode of the gun from fully automatic to semi-automatic.

They fired a couple of rounds off as well, letting Benedict test out the weapon in the semi-automatic mode so that he did not waste too much ammunition. He found that the rifle did not have as much recoil as he expected. He knew he could keep it under fairly good control, which bolstered his confidence with it.

"Kinda fun, ain't it?" Walton asked as Benedict squeezed off another round, the air cracking loudly.

"I can't deny it," Benedict chuckled, taking in a strong whiff of gunpowder.

"You're not too bad," Les said to Royce with an air of approval, as his bullet struck a small metal target set up a couple hundred yards out.

"This shoots real good. Thank you all for these," Royce replied with clear sincerity. "I'm really grateful."

"No problem, man," Walton responded. "Our pleasure."

"Sure you boys don't want to stay? We got room, plenty of food, and we'd sure love the company," Les said. "Don't get many visitors these days, if you know what I mean."

The temptation to take Les up on his offer pulled strongly at Benedict's will. Having a real dinner, and then breakfast, to start the day had been wonderful beyond measure. A night's rest, even a partial one, on a mattress with a clean, soft pillow had been immensely rejuvenating to his sorely-taxed body.

There was no doubt that another day or two spent like that would bring much more restoration to his depleted body. But he knew he had to reach the rebels, and warn them that deep in the UCAS strongholds there were monstrosities breeding at a rapid pace. Every single moment was of the essence.

"I'm so sorry, I really do have to get back," Benedict said. "If it wasn't so important to reach the province's military forces, I would take you up on the offer. You don't know how much I'd like to say yes."

Les and the others looked disappointed with the answer. "Well, you gotta do what you gotta do," Les finally said, plainly melancholic.

"If you're ever this way again, please look us up," Tonya said. "The both of ya are always welcome to stay with us."

"Definitely," Walton stated. "Anytime you're around."

"Hopefully everything will settle down and get back to something close to normal, and I can come back someday," Benedict answered.

The words were not just a matter of being polite. He found that he wanted to see his bunker-dwelling benefactors again someday, perhaps in a time where they could enjoy each other's company without the specter of danger looming so near.

Having more of Tonya's homemade wine was also something that Benedict had no objection to experiencing again. If she started making whiskey for Walton, then it would be all the better.

With all his heart, he hoped they made through safely to a better time. At the very least, there was no doubt that few people had prepared better than Les's group had for the dire times they were all enduring. If anyone could make it through the maelstrom, the two men and two women standing before Benedict were prime candidates.

"I'll be lookin' forward to it," Walton said. "You come back as soon as you can."

"Okay, let's go over things one more time," Les said, his voice reverting back to a serious tone as he changed the subject.

Les went back over the territory he had covered with Benedict and Royce earlier that morning down in the bunker. He described exactly where they were, and what lay in the path they sought to take.

A few suburbs, well beyond the reach of the gang menaces plaguing the city, were all that stood between Benedict and territory that was firmly under the control of the free province security forces. The biggest concern, in Les's eyes, were jumpy, frazzled locals in a highly defensive mode.

Scared people tended to be a little more trigger-happy. Even though they were a fair distance from the gang-controlled areas, the locals were probably not overly accommodating to armed strangers.

That was a chance Benedict would have to take, but there were some options for lessening the risk a little. Producing a small map, Les and Walton talked about how Benedict could largely navigate the perimeter of those suburbs, though that course would add a little more time and distance to their journey.

Committing details to memory, Benedict listened closely to the landmarks Les and Walton described. Royce kept busy scribbling notes down on a small pad he carried in his pack.

When everything had been covered thoroughly, Les folded the map up and tucked it away. "That about does it. I really wish y'all the best of luck. We'll all be praying for you."

In the past, Benedict would have taken his last words as a polite expression, one that had no real consequence. Suddenly, he found that those words meant something much more to him.

A momentary thought of Calliel flashed in his mind. This time, he did not receive the words in such a light fashion.

Benedict and Royce then said their final round of goodbyes to their hosts, thanking them again for their generosity. Setting out towards the east, there was a little more spring in Benedict's step, and not just because he had gotten a little food and rest.

The safe zone described by Les and Walton was not too much farther away. Before the sun completed its journey overhead, if they kept to a steady pace without too many stops for rest, he and Royce would reach their intended destination.

Once the warning was delivered to the free province military forces, he could make his way back to Venorterra. Seeing Arianna, Gerald, and the others again was the only desire he harbored within his weary heart.

SECTION III

Seth

Seth slumped back in the seat, idly staring out at the woods passing by as the convoy traveled down the highway. Annika, Raymond, and Jonathan were seated in the van with him. He knew that others like Rowan were in the lengthy column of vehicles taking hundreds from the refugee camp back to their homes.

It would be a few hours yet before they got back to Madison. There was plenty of time to reflect upon all the things parading through his mind.

There was little to worry about for the return journey. The lawless marauders said to be preying on single vehicles would not interfere with a heavily armed convoy like theirs. The highway was safely within Venorterra, and while it was one of the provinces bordering those still controlled by the UCAS, the front lines were still far away.

Going home was the first step. Getting his parents back, and their cat Niles, would be the next. At the very least, a concerted step towards a semblance of the life he knew before was being taken.

Everyone in the van were in good spirits, all of them excited to be leaving the camp and returning back to homes they were familiar with. Seth wondered how things would be in the days, weeks, and months to come, as the patterns of day to day life resumed.

Before all of the upheaval, he had been wondering whether or not he should go to college. Now, he could not say for certain whether college institutions would even be operating in the near future. That was just one of many disconcerting thoughts he had about the new realities.

He wondered about Guillermo and his old job. There was no telling how long it might be before places like the sub sandwich shop were operating in a manner resembling the old days. It was still a mystery as to what would be used for money.

From what Seth had gleaned during his time in the camp, all sorts of things were being utilized for trade, from objects of silver and gold, to straight bartering of goods and services. The old UCAS currency was still being used.

STEPHEN ZIMMER

Seth had to admit he was very curious to see what the new money would look like. All of his life, the only coins and bills he had known were UCAS currency, save for the few foreign coins he had come across in his change from time to time.

He also wondered what living in a new country would be like. All the talk around the camp indicated that the breakaway provinces were working out a structure for the future.

Seth did not know many of the details, but the rumors claimed it would not be much longer before a more formal organization of the provinces was established. He figured that would be a good thing, as he doubted the UCAS government was very pleased with being driven out so unceremoniously. He had a bad feeling that war would be coming to the breakaway provinces in the near future.

Even with the idea of a new country, the most basic things normally enjoyed by a teenaged male were still in question. From video games to movies and new music, pop culture itself had been turned upside down during the massive eruption of conflict.

The things Seth had taken for granted before, like a new movie coming to a theater, or a new song being released by a band he liked, might not happen again for quite awhile, if at all.

Glancing out the right side of the van, he saw that the column was about to pass by a large hillside. He eyed the layered facing of rock that had been cut through, to allow for the course of the highway, wondering how many years it had taken for each of the horizontal levels to transform from sediment to stone.

Suddenly, the van shook violently, as a deafening explosion rocked the vehicle. Tires squealed and Seth lurched forward as the driver slammed down on the brakes. Swerving, the van barely avoided the SUV screeching to a stop just in front of them.

Seth's eyes spread wide, his heartbeat soaring and adrenaline surging through his bloodstream. His hands remained tightly clenched on the back of the seat in front of him, where he had caught his forward momentum at the last instant.

"Get out, get out now! Make for the woods now and go far in!" the driver yelled urgently to his passengers. "Everyone! Hurry!"

Seth and his friends scrambled to exit, as Raymond slid the side

162

door open on the van. In his panic, Seth nearly tumbled to the ground when his shoes hit the gravel.

Seth's heart accelerated further, seeing Christa a short distance away, hurrying towards the woods to the other side of the road. In that instant, he forgot about his own plight entirely.

"Come on guys!" shouted Raymond, starting to run towards the opposite side of the road. "Drones! Get the hell out of the open!"

As he spoke, vehicles farther down the column exploded, sending a host of fragments soaring up within a huge, fiery burst. Another missile struck a second later, hitting near the rear of the column and rendering several more vehicles into shards. Seth could feel the powerful reverberations beneath the soles of his shoes.

The highway in both directions was now blocked with the burning wreckage of many vehicles. The rest of the column had nowhere that it could go. Seth did not want to think of the grisly fate that the people riding in the contorted, roasting husks suffered.

Seth felt helpless and exposed out in the open, as columns of black smoke began rising into the sky to his left and right. An acrid stench was filling the air. He nearly tripped over himself in his desperation to make the line of trees.

He could see Jonathan and Annika sprinting farther ahead of him, a few paces behind Raymond, who was the first of his group to make the boundary line of the woods.

Seth kept his mind fixed on running. He felt a deep sense of relief when the shadows beneath the tree canopy finally enveloped him.

The ground sloped upward, and underbrush ripped at his jeans, but he kept his legs pumping. When they finally slowed to a halt, his lungs were burning in his heaving chest. Leaning over and resting his hands on his knees, he took in large gulps of the cool, woodland air.

He looked around at Raymond, Annika, and Jonathan, all of whom looked winded and frightened. Looking back, through breaks in the trees, he could see columns of smoke ascending to the skies, like a surreal forest growing taller by the moment.

"What the hell just happened?" Seth asked the others.

"UCAS, no doubt," Raymond said. "Using drones."

"Why attack us?" Jonathan queried, with an incredulous look on his face. "Just a bunch of civilians, and some police. No military present. None at all."

"Maybe the few armored vehicles in the convoy fooled them?" Raymond shrugged. "Beats me."

"So what are we going to do now?" Annika asked. "The survivors are probably scattered all over the woods here."

"I wouldn't suggest going too far," Jonathan said. "Probably see if we can find the ones who organized the caravan."

Seth nodded. "They might figure out a way to get through the wreckage, at one of the ends. The vehicles in the middle are all intact, as far as I could see."

"Let's hope the drones don't return and hit those too," Raymond said dourly.

"Maybe we can find a way through, when the fires settle down," Annika suggested.

"Do we really want to take a vehicle down a highway that we know has just been hit by enemy drones?" Raymond asked. "Makes an easy target."

"There is that," Jonathan replied ruefully.

"You're right," Annika said, looking to Raymond. "They'll probably hit anything that tries to move out of the column."

"So we're pretty much screwed, is what we're all saying?" Seth asked, glancing at his friends.

"Yeah, I'd have to say so," Raymond said.

"Well, let's at least get moving soon, and see if we can find a town or community, or something," Annika said, looking to each of the others. "We can shadow the highway, use it as a guide, and maybe find something at an off ramp."

"I can't think of anything better, so let's do it," Raymond stated.

Seth found his thoughts drifting towards Christa, wondering where she was in the woods, and if she was safe. He saw that the others were looking at him, and hesitated for a moment.

"What is it Seth?" Jonathan asked. "Tell us. I know that look. Something is on your mind."

"What about the others, like Christa?" Seth asked, after a pause.

"I agree we should move, and try to find a place to get some help. But shouldn't we try to find some of the others first?"

He had initially thought of Christa, but there were so many more who had undoubtedly survived the attack. Some were probably still lingering around the area of the column itself, while others were probably coming to conclusions similar to Seth's group.

"We can try," Raymond said. "But we just have the clothes on our backs, and no food or water, or anything else."

"Do you think we can risk doing a search of some of the vehicles, at least?" Annika queried. She looked towards Raymond. "Would that be too much of a risk, as far as drones go?"

After a few moments, Raymond responded. "I don't think they'll go after a few scavengers. Driving away is one thing, but a couple people picking through the vehicles shouldn't be of much interest to them. I'm sure they expect some of that."

"Then maybe we can look out for others, while a couple of us see what we can find in the cars and trucks," Seth suggested. "Does that sound good?"

One by one, the others nodded, and full agreement was reached.

HADAR

While it was necessary that the population be culled significantly to protect the health of the world, Dr. Hadar Tricheur never envisioned that he would become the victim of his own devices. It was his mind that had conceived of an effective way to ease the burdens on a planet groaning under the onerous weight of an excessive human population.

Though he believed in no gods, he had thought good fortune would be with him as he addressed the world's dire population affliction. Evolution had produced a bold genius in Hadar Tricheur, a champion willing and able to fight for the planet. His current plight was the cruelest twist of fate he could envision.

The virus had apparently mutated, and even more incredibly it had infected him, despite all the layers of redundancy put in place to protect his team in the research facility. The abrupt turn in events both terrified and confounded him.

There was no mistaking the onset of symptoms. Hadar knew he did not have much time left. As he pushed himself to come up with something to save himself, his mind told him his chances were slim to none.

Answers evaded him, and his anxiety increased as his team succumbed swiftly to the virus. For whatever reason, life still clung to him, leaving him with a thinning shred of hope that he could find the elusive solution in time.

Hadar did not even bother to notice that the clock read a couple of minutes to midnight as he labored through yet another long, tedious night. Day and night were blurred together now, and every moment spent away from research was precious minutes wasted.

The door to the laboratory opened. Hadar looked up in surprise, as the facility was supposed to be locked down. As he was the only man left alive in the building, he had not been expecting any visitors.

His eyebrows raised as he saw Samel Malkira striding into the brightly-lit room. The man had an impassive countenance, as always, but on this particular night there seemed to be a markedly different air about him.

"You don't want to come near me," Hadar said at once.

"You are a sick man," Samel replied, calmly.

Hadar nodded. "Yes, something has gone terribly wrong. But I didn't mean for you or anyone to come here in person. The facility is supposed to be sealed and locked down completely right now, to contain the virus."

"I came to make sure everything is closed down here," Samel said. "It is time to tie all the loose ends up and finish this project."

Hadar found himself deeply unnerved by the iron hard gaze embedded within the other man's eyes. Samel Malkira was very matter-of-fact in nature, but the look on his face at the moment was something far more. There was a hint of expectancy, or anticipation.

"Closed down?" Hadar replied, confused at the statement.

"What do you mean?"

"The full team involved in developing the Abundant Harvest Virus has died, except for you, yes?" Samel asked him.

Hadar nodded, frowning. "Yes, the mutation took all of my team. I did not expect this new development. None of us did."

"So you think the variation of the virus you are now experiencing is just a random mutation?" Samel asked.

"Yes, that is precisely what it is," Hadar replied, with a little more surety in his voice. He had examined the problem thoroughly and there was no disputing what had happened. "We thought we had engineered safeguards, but this anomaly surfaced anyway. It is a mutation and nothing more."

"You have such a limited imagination, Hadar. In many ways, that is part of your undoing," Samel said.

"What do you mean?" Hadar replied, becoming increasingly bothered by the strange tone in the other man's voice.

"There is so much more to existence, the world, everything around you," Samel replied. "Your faith in science betrays you now. Did you ever think you could master something that operates beyond the rules of your science? Do you think that any of your instruments are capable of measuring or evaluating things non-physical in nature?"

Hadar had no response, and could make little sense out of what Samel was saying. He attributed his spiraling confusion to the sickness wracking his body.

"I think it is time for you to experience something that defies scientific explanation," Samel stated, and the faintest hint of a smile came to his lips.

Defying all logic, and every sliver of rational explanation, Hadar felt the symptoms of his infection advancing swiftly. Delirious, and seized in a new wave of agony, he fell heavily to the tiled floor.

An icy, suffocating feeling came over him as his eyesight dimmed. Finally, total darkness enveloped him. And then, a blinding, pure light.

Awareness flooded him, and he knew at once that he was not dreaming. He still existed, even though he was separated from his physical body.

The realization shocked him to the core. His very existence in a disembodied state contradicted everything he held fast to during his life.

What happened next brought Hadar a level of terror and desperation that he had never felt before. One who he had mocked and derided year after year now met him in person, face to face.

There was nowhere he could run to, and nothing he could hide. Every thought and action in his life was exposed, and he understood the vile nature of what he had engineered with the Thanatos Virus. He could not turn his eyes away as the faces of all those who had died from the virus were presented to him in perfect clarity.

Yet even in the clutches of overwhelming terror, he clung to hatred and resentment of the One who made him face the unobstructed reality of what he had done. A choice was made in the darkest depths of his soul, and he refused any thought of contrition, or seeking of forgiveness.

Hadar was then shown visions of places filled with astounding beauty, the likes of which he could never have imagined. Colors and radiance like nothing he had known were only a part of the wonders he gazed upon. No person living in the world had ever seen or heard of anything like the sights he was witnessing and had just rejected.

When the experience concluded, he found himself falling downward, plunging into a vast, yawning darkness. Hadar now had full cognizance of the evil that he had been engaged in. He also understood the nature of the realms that he could not enter, as well as the ones that were now laying claim to him.

Screaming, he felt a burning sensation come over whatever kind of body he now possessed. He could do nothing to mitigate the rising pain as he fell farther and farther into the darkness, part of a cascade of souls tumbling towards the center of an enormous, swirling vortex.

When he finally reached the outer rings of the vortex, Hadar's vision blurred, and was then obscured for a time. When his sight returned, he found himself floating in a reddish miasma. A cold, clammy feeling crept over him as he struggled in a state of severe disorientation.

He could not sense whether he was rising, falling, or drifting, and he lost all track of time. To a man used to being in command of his faculties, the inability to hold onto even the simplest of thoughts was among the worst afflictions of all.

After what could have been minutes or ages, he found himself facedown in muck and grime. A stronger sense of physicality returned to him, bringing with it the unwelcome feeling of tiny things crawling all over his bare skin.

He pawed and scratched feverishly, unable to bring himself any relief. To his further distress, he realized he was naked. He felt entirely physical again, as he sloshed and flopped about in an awkward effort to get to his feet.

Hadar was then seized by a violent series of coughs. Blood came from his mouth and spattered all over the front of his body. The reddish effluvium he had initially found himself floating within still surrounded him, though he was shin-deep in some kind of swampy morass.

Faint screeches and throaty cries carried through the air from all directions. Frozen with indecision, Hadar turned his head, peering into the dense mists.

"Haaaaadddaarrrrr!"

The breathy, sepulchral voice crept into Hadar's ears. Mind racing, he looked all around, but could still see nothing.

Vague forms then began taking shape within the reddish mists, becoming more substantial after a few moments. Hadar realized with dread that the figures were all approaching him. They shambled with awkward gaits, sloshes accompanying their every stride.

Some of the figures had mottled skin, others were covered in pus and tumors, while still others were emaciated, with skin drawn taught over bones. The disease-ridden figures had the look of death all about them, and the scent of rot and decay enveloped Hadar when the first of them drew close.

Gagging and nauseous, Hadar shifted one way, and then another, trying to find a path through the incoming throng. Anywhere he looked, his way was eventually blocked.

He turned around quickly, seeing a brighter light manifesting a short distance away, parting the mists. A towering, multi-winged figure took shape within the growing luminance.

Staring at the imposing figure, Hadar was fascinated. He saw that its body was composed of an uncountable number of small flames. Three pairs of fiery wings swept out from its back, and the being's blazing eyes fixed upon Hadar.

Strangely, the outline of its form was wreathed in a black, mist-like aura that exhibited a peculiar quality. The thin, flowing dark layer appeared to absorb light, rather than merely cloaking the entity.

Hadar had no idea of who or what the strange figure was, but its appearance stilled the approach of the diseased horde. For that factor alone, he was greatly relieved.

"How does it feel, Hadar, to know that you still exist, in a place far removed from the world you knew?" the entity asked him, its voice a harmony of many layers.

Cowed into silence at the being's awe-inspiring presence, Hadar stared without uttering a single word in reply. The appearance of the entity was both beautiful and frightening, and he struggled to come up with any sort of response. A man known for his sharp intellect, he was at a total loss for words.

"I ... I do not know where I am," Hadar finally replied to the figure.

"Where? It is more a question of your state of being," the entity said.

"I know nothing, of any of this," Hadar confessed. Every premise he embraced had been shattered with the simple cognizance that he still existed, while devoid of a physical body.

"This will be all you will know," the entity replied. There was no change in its tone, but the words carried a menacing air.

"What ... will happen to me?" Hadar said, fearing the answer as the words fled his lips.

"You belong to the Ten-Fold Kingdom," the entity replied. "As your service to the Convergence was to the Risen Throne, so shall your service be here."

The mention of the Convergence gave rise to a splinter of hope within him. "But ... but did not my work benefit the Convergence?" Hadar replied, his voice shaking.

"Your work was of great benefit to the Ten-Fold Kingdom, yet you never gave yourself openly to the Shining One," the entity replied. "How can you expect to be rewarded now? You mocked even the idea of the Master you were serving, as much as you mocked our Enemy.

"You went through life thinking there was nothing beyond the existence you knew. Now that you know otherwise, it is far too late. This is my dominion, one among many in the service of the Risen Throne. You will find no mercy in this place, or any other."

"No ... No ... " Hadar replied, shaking his head, the words sounding weary and resigned. There was only one path he could see out of his terrible predicament. He looked up and pleaded, the words born of desperation tumbling out quickly from his mouth, "Please, allow me to serve. Let me serve you."

"Shall I make an instrument of you, to serve the Will of the Shining One?" the entity asked.

"Please ... please," Hadar begged the powerful being. "Make me an instrument. I will serve willingly."

"It may be you will become what you most desired during your mortal life, when my power is wielded upon the world of matter," the entity replied. "When Abbadon opens the way, my weapons shall be set loose in the world."

Most of Hadar's energies had been spent in pursuing his work. He searched his mind to find the specific desire spoken of by the entity, and could only recall one thing.

It was a fanciful desire, something he had previously deemed to be impossible. Yet now he was experiencing a state that he never thought could exist. Perhaps all things were possible now.

Hadar looked back at the entity in amazement. "I ... I could become that?"

"The souls who find their way to me can become my weapons," the entity stated.

The still air was broken as Hadar felt a moist breeze against his face. The grating cries he had heard before returned, swelling in volume.

A terrifying visage appeared suddenly out of the mist, belonging to some manner of shade or phantom whose form was more than half-translucent. A skeletal, decaying torso trailing off into insubstantial

wisps floated in the air before Hadar as the bizarre apparition slowed to a halt.

The specter's features distorted, even as Hadar looked upon it with a feeling of fascination and horror. Chin elongating, forehead stretching wider, every aspect of its corrupted appearance was malleable.

The apparition loosed a piercing cry and reached towards Hadar. Bony fingers elongating as its hands drew nearer, the thing opened its mouth and expelled a noxious vapor directly into Hadar's face.

The entity's fingers wrapped around his arms like coiling snakes. Hadar tried to pull back and free himself at the clammy, ice cold touch upon his skin. Though translucent, the phantom felt substantial enough, its grip feeling as strong as steel as it held Hadar fast.

Where the apparition's hands wrapped around his arm, Hadar's skin began to corrupt and decay. He could feel the flesh and muscle underneath rotting to the bone, an unprecedented sensation that sent his mind spinning and terror spiking.

The fumes of the specter's breath seared the insides of Hadar's throat and chest. The poisonous, gaseous substance had him convulsing violently, and a terrible agony consumed him from the inside.

"So it would be for any living being in the world of matter that my weapons strike," the entity stated.

Blood poured from Hadar's mouth as he continued gagging and retching. The withering decay that the apparition's touch sprouted on his arms had already spread to the ends of his fingers, and also worked its way up close to his shoulders.

Hadar fell heavily to his knees, sending up a muddy splash, though he could not shake the phantom's hold. The shred of hope he had harbored when the winged being had mentioned the Convergence was extinguished. Overwhelmed, his spirit succumbed to hopelessness and despair.

He did nothing more to free himself from his ghostly tormentor, finding he no longer had the will to resist. Corruption was spreading throughout his body, and his insides burned without respite.

"Many who died because of you have found their way here," the entity said, when the weariness of surrender had filled Hadar. "I shall leave you now to those who died from your work, so that they can introduce you to your new existence."

The spectral creature finally loosed its hold upon Hadar, and drifted back into the red mist. The fiery sensation in his chest and throat began ebbing, but the other affliction remained in place. His withered arms were now little more than dry parchment stretched across bones, the appendages consumed by whatever power the apparition set free through its desiccating touch.

Exhausted, Hadar looked up and saw that the winged entity was disappearing. He had never felt more empty inside than he did while watching the fiery form of the being grow insubstantial, and then fade out entirely. Somehow he knew the entity was the only authority holding back the horde of revenants in the mists.

Hadar looked into the grisly faces around him as the brighter light receded and vanished, leaving him alone to face whatever horrid fate loomed. The feeling of terrible emptiness pervaded him, but there was no time to try to come to grips with what he had witnessed.

The diseased, gruesome figures were upon him. Somehow they had moved closer while he spoke with the winged entity and suffered the cruel torments of its horrific servant.

Jagged, elongated fingernails found purchase in Hadar's skin and started digging deeper. The pain was tremendous, and he loosed a guttural, primal scream.

It was a forlorn sound, utterly devoid of hope, and echoing the searing pain he was now suffering both inside and out. He knew the agony would be a constant in this new, terrible place that he could not escape.

SETH

Seth and his companions were not the only ones to return to the remains of the convoy. Several others had either lingered in the area or made their way back in the aftermath of the attack. Some were talking together in small groups, while others were rummaging through the vehicles, pulling packs and bags out.

"Let's get this started! I want to take some time to look for a few specific things, since we're likely to be spending the night outside, and we'll be going on foot," Raymond announced, starting towards an SUV with Annika and Jonathan close behind him.

Seth paused and looked up at the clear skies with a little trepidation. He wondered if something deadly was still lurking in the upper heights.

The sun was going down, but night brought no promises of safety. Blocking his fears out of his mind as best he could, Seth started after Raymond and the others.

Fortunately the SUV and the other vehicles they searched afterwards were unlocked. They proved to contain quite a bounty, their cargo areas stuffed with all kinds of practical items.

Seth found a plastic-wrapped case of bottled water in the trunk of a car. He lifted it out and set the case on the ground. He started to look for a backpack or duffel bag.

"Seth!"

He looked up and saw Rowan Forrester approaching him from farther up the column of vehicles. Seeing another familiar face who had survived the attack on the convoy brought a smile and feeling of relief to Seth.

"Hey man, good to see you're okay," Seth greeted Rowan as he neared, giving him a handshake. He pulled him in for a quick half-hug.

"You too," Rowan said. "We were just a few cars behind ones that got totally destroyed. My dad and some others are talking right now about getting some vehicles moving after a little while."

He looked over his shoulder, and Seth followed his glance. A little farther away, Seth saw where some men were looking over a large SUV, while a couple of others were busy changing a tire on it.

"You guys are going to risk the drones?" Seth asked. The mention of the death-bringing devices caused him to cast a brief, wary look towards the skies. "What if they come back? They incinerated the vehicles they hit."

"My dad and the others don't think they'll come back," Rowan answered. His eyes shifted towards the bottled water on the ground. "What are you all doing?"

"We're just gathering up some food and water," Seth replied. "Going to follow the road, but we're gonna stick to the trees, and travel by foot."

"It's still a long way back home," Rowan said.

"We're hoping to find a place to get some help, and maybe we'll try the road later," Seth replied. "Just don't wanna chance the highway so soon after the attack."

"I just want to get home, as soon as I can," Rowan said, a current of anxiety rising in his voice. "We lost my dog, Sunfire, just before the evacuations were getting underway. I hope he's okay."

"I understand," Seth replied, thinking of his cat. His only reassurance was that the lovable feline had been sent away in the care of his parents. "I know we're all eager to get back."

"Well, let me help you all for now. I'm just waiting around for my parents," Rowan offered. "Not doing anything else."

"Check with Raymond, he's kind of our quartermaster," Seth responded, chuckling.

Rowan nodded and grinned with the eagerness of a younger individual grateful to have a chance to ingratiate himself with an older set of peers. "You got it!" he exclaimed.

He turned and walked towards Raymond, who had worked his way closer to the van that Seth and his friends had ridden in. Seth turned his attention back to his immediate task. Finding a gym bag stuffed with clothing, Seth emptied it out. Ripping off the plastic sealing the case of water, he began transferring the individual bottles over. Once the bag was full, he carried the water over to where Raymond was collecting the things they planned to take onward.

Looking up, a smile jumped to his face as he saw a lone figure emerging from the trees.

"Christa!" he shouted out, before he even had a chance to get nervous. It was the boldest he had ever been when it came to her.

Seeing Seth, she broke into a jog and hurried over. Without

thinking, he spread his arms out to give her a hug. Christa walked right up to Seth and embraced him, holding him tightly for several moments.

She fit perfectly within his arms. He felt a little light-headed and giddy as he felt her embrace snugly around him.

"I'm so glad to see you guys," Christa said with a look of relief, when they disengaged. She glanced towards Raymond and the others. "Did you all find anything useful here?"

"We just got here a little bit ago," Seth replied. "How are your parents?"

"They're in the woods right now," Christa replied. "My mom sprained her ankle, hurrying to get away. My dad's staying with her at the moment. I came back to see if I could find some food, or water, maybe some jackets. Should be plenty in the packs and bags we took from the main camp."

"Let's get to work then," Seth said with enthusiasm. "I'll help you gather some things up for your folks."

"Thank you, Seth," Christa said, a warm, lively smile blossoming on her face.

Looking upon her beautiful face, Seth felt a little of the all-too-familiar nervousness returning. He would not have been surprised if his skin had reddened a little, as he thought about the full focus he was receiving from her.

"Let's check the car we were riding in," Christa said, leading him a little farther down the column.

"Sounds good," he replied, grateful for the distraction, which blunted his surging feeling of awkwardness.

After a short time had passed, Seth, Christa, and the others had gathered together a sizeable cluster of duffel bags, packs, and other portable storage containers carrying food, bottled water, and other supplies. There was more than enough for Christa and her parents, in addition to what Seth's group would take for their journey.

It was then decided that Seth's group would help Christa take a portion of the items back to her parents first, before beginning their own trek. Christa looked both grateful and relieved at the group's decision. By then, the sun had descended out of view, sinking behind the hills. Seth could not fault her for not wanting to walk back through the woods alone in the darkness.

It would not be much longer before the area was steeped in the fullness of night, and Seth hoped they got moving soon. "We do have some flashlights, I hope?" Seth asked.

"If we need them, yes we do," Raymond answered. "At least three, plus some extra batteries."

"Well, let's get all this stuff picked up, and let's get moving," Annika said, looking to be of the same mind as Seth. "We're going to be walking in the woods at night, so make sure all the flashlights are accessible."

"Not a worry," Raymond replied. He eyed the pile of supplies. "But it looks like we've got a lot of stuff to lug with us."

"Too much?" Jonathan asked, raising an eyebrow.

"It may be that we'll feel we didn't take enough," Raymond replied, grimly. "We don't know how long it might be 'til we find help."

"We'll have to take as much as we can," Annika said firmly. "I'd rather be tired and have supplies than be a little less weary and lacking food or water."

"I'll help carry the stuff to where Christa's parents are," Rowan interjected. "That'll give you all a little break. Just give me a minute to tell my parents. Shouldn't be any problem. We're not going for too long, are we?"

"We could use an extra hand," Raymond replied. He then added, with an air of impatience. "Just hurry it up."

Rowan jogged off to find his father, as the rest of the group waited. Seth looked around, and took assessment of his surroundings.

After such a harrowing day, the onset of evening felt so thoroughly peaceful. A gentle breeze ruffled his hair, conveying a cool, soft touch.

Seth loosed a wistful sigh, staring off down the highway. After being sequestered in the makeshift refugee camp for so long, they had been just a few hours from returning home and settling back into a familiar, comforting environment. The thought left him with a bitter feeling.

It was hard to believe their ill fortune, especially when it was said that the UCAS had found it difficult to violate the airspace of the breakaway provinces like Venorterra. Yet UCAS drones had pierced the airspace of the breakaway province, and of all the possible targets in the world they had selected the column of refugees on their way back home.

He felt a little unease when he saw Rowan returning with an older man at his side. He noticed that the man was carrying a set of crutches horizontally, gripping the two supports about midway down their length.

"Hey everyone, this is my dad," Rowan introduced the man when they reached Seth and the others, prompting a flurry of acknowledgements and greetings from the others.

"Your parents are still in the woods, as I understand it?" Rowan's father asked Christa, after the formalities were concluded. "And your mother's got an ankle sprain?"

She nodded. "They headed for the trees, to get out of the open, after the attack. My mom stumbled on something and hurt herself. We don't think anything's broken. Just looks like a sprain."

"Here, take these, then," Rowan's father said, handing over the set of crutches. "It won't be easy going on rough ground, but it might help her a little."

"Thank you, Mr. Forrester," Christa replied, looking surprised and appreciative as she accepted the set of crutches from Rowan's father.

"How far are they in?" Mr. Forrester asked. "Do you think they could make it back here before too long?"

"They're not too far. We could be back pretty soon," Christa said, casting the older man a curious expression. "Especially with the help of the crutches. I really don't think it would take too long at all."

"If nothing bad happens here, we're wanting to set out around midnight," Mr. Forrester replied. "All of you, and Christa's parents, can go along with us, I you want to. We'll make sure there's room for all of you."

"Thank you for the offer," Christa said politely.

Seth shared glances with Raymond, Annika, and Jonathan. He could sense they were opting for discretion about their plans to go on foot.

"So you think your parents would like to go with us?" Mr. Forrester asked Christa.

"I think they would, and I think it would be great to go with you all, Mr. Forrester," Christa said.

"Tough times, we need to stick together," Mr. Forrester said with a smile, though it did not cover the anxiety Seth saw within the man's face and eyes. The world was turned just as much upside down for parents as it had been for teenagers.

"So can I go with them Dad, to get Christa's parents?" Rowan asked his father.

Mr. Forrester nodded. "Just get back here as soon as you can."

"We will not take long," Christa said reassuringly to Mr. Forrester.

Glancing to each of the teenagers one more time, he ruffled Rowan's hair and turned back for the column. There was nothing left to do but start out for Christa's parents, even though Seth knew it meant going separate ways before the sun rose again.

DAGIAN

"I am quite glad to see you again, Dagian," Gordon Weatherford greeted in polite fashion, from where he was seated across from her. The two were inside her primary office on the grounds of the compound, with the door closed, engaging in a few moments of private conversation. "It would seem that many traditions are coming together in common cause during these final stages of the Convergence. Quite fascinating, if you ask me, and very beneficial to our cause."

"Every advantage must be gained, and each of us have our strengths," Dagian replied amiably to the High Priest, with the trace of a smile on her lips.

The last time she had seen Gordon, Dagian had been in the bosom of Kemet itself. The journey to the heart of ancient, sacred traditions had been a deeply profound experience.

Powerful rituals had transcended worlds, and Dagian had been taken before Set, beheld Apep, and been personally graced by Anat. Her own power had increased as a result of the audience, only to be augmented further when she inherited what was taken from Jibade when he had been severed from the mortal coil.

"I trust that things are going well here," Gordon stated. "I have seen a lot of activity in this place since arriving."

"All is going very well here. The troubles that beset the UCAS do not touch these grounds, I assure you," Dagian replied, folding her hands together and resting them on the desk surface before her. "We have several potent layers of security."

Holding Gordon's eyes, she let the implications sink into him. She could see in his eyes that he understood her meaning.

"That is wonderful to hear," Gordon said, nodding. "Troubles beset all parts of the world, as the final stage nears. The only grace in Kemet is that unity binds the region around it more than ever."

"It was no easy task to topple so many regimes, and bring in a new order, a brotherhood of governance so united in its ideology," Dagian observed.

"I am glad that the greatest periods of upheaval are over," Gordon said. A smile spread upon his face. "All that remains is to see the Davidians laid low, and made to be the footstool of Kemet. That great prize still beckons."

"As will happen soon enough," Dagian replied with an air of confidence.

"I look forward to that day, more than you might know," Gordon said, and she could feel the burning desire in his tone.

"How many of your order have you brought with you?" Dagian asked, bringing the focus of their conversation to the matter at hand.

"I have twenty of my most advanced practitioners here with me," Gordon replied. "It is my hope that you will give them some instruction in your arts."

"I shall," Dagian replied. "And it is my hope that one or more of them has the talent to become what Jibade was to you. It would be my wish to see all twenty of them as proficient as he was."

"You need not speak his name before me," Gordon stated, his expression darkening. "His failure is to my shame, as it was I who mentored him."

"Do not trouble yourself over what is past, Gordon," Dagian said, understanding of the kind of pressures the man faced in the position he was in. From a man or woman who had been given great authority and power in the Convergence, much was expected. It was among the most grievous of sins to fall short of what was demanded by the great Lords of the Abyss. "You are here at a momentous time, and we shall experience triumph together."

"Indeed, we shall," Gordon replied, his countenance brightening at her words.

"And you have other guests with you here, in the building?" Dagian said, looking forward to meeting the guides of her next mystical journey. She knew they were settled on the grounds of the compound, but no formal introductions had been made yet.

"Indeed, I do," Gordon said. "There is a contingent of them who have been gathered to await you in the lobby at the entrance. They have come to escort you to the ritual chamber. All is prepared for your journey tonight."

"Then I would be greatly interested in meeting them, as soon as you are ready," Dagian said, managing to keep the eagerness from showing too much on her face. She was about to cross the boundaries between worlds once again, and the mere thought of the experience brought a thrill racing through her veins.

"Then let us not wait here a moment longer," Gordon said with an amiable lilt, rising out of his chair, and prompting Dagian to get to her feet from the high-backed chair she sat in. "I shall take you right to them. But then I must take leave and proceed ahead, and get myself ready for the journey we will be taking tonight."

With Gordon walking in front, they strode out of Dagian's office and continued through the ground level of the building allocated for her business operations. After passing a number of offices, conference rooms, storage spaces, and other chambers, they finally reached the edge of the large waiting room situated at the front of the edifice.

The hallway opened to one side of an atrium with a high ceiling. It contained a sizeable, crescent-shaped reception desk. An array of plush seating and low tables were provided for those awaiting appointments with Dagian or other Babylon Technologies representatives.

A number of well-dressed individuals were seated quietly within the sitting area. All of them rose to their feet attentively as Dagian came into view.

Gordon paused, and politely excused himself to go finish making his preparations for the evening. She bid him well and thanked him for his assistance.

Without another word, he continued onward, walking around the sitting area and proceeding towards the building's front entrance. Dagian then set her focus on the group gathered to meet her.

Entering their midst, she counted a dozen individuals. All were men with the features and skin tones common to the far east. Though their expressions were mostly placid, Dagian could see the respect they held for her in the looks cast from their dark eyes.

One man stood out prominently from the others, though what drew her attention to him had nothing to do with his physical appearance. Rather, it was something unseen, an aura that Dagian sensed from the moment she set her eyes on him.

While there was a considerable strength about his presence, she knew at once that the man held the favor of the Ten-Fold Kingdom. There was no mistaking her perception, for the unseen trait resonated clearly with her interior senses. It was one of the principle ways that higher practitioners of the Craft recognized the legitimacy in others, or verified their authority.

As powerful as he was, his physical characteristics were not particularly remarkable. He was shorter in stature, with a long goatee, clad in simple black attire with the exception of a distinctive pendant hanging down to the midpoint of his chest.

Rendered in gold, it was fashioned in the shape of a Kyotowan lamp with an eye at its center. The symbol was easy enough to understand, referring to the illumination bestowed upon dutiful followers by the ever-watchful Shining One. The particular image had been adopted by the monastic Order of Chikara centuries before.

Recognizing who he was, she welcomed him, and exchanged

greetings in the manner of the Kyotowans. Bending at the waist, she extended him a low bow. Dagian noted at once that his bow to her was lower, and his demeanor conspicuously deferential in the way that he received her.

She knew that the display was no façade. The high regard being shown towards her underscored a very genuine, deep respect held within the heart of the group's leader. Knowing that such came neither easily nor often with a man like Daiki Oshiro, she was well-pleased, and took it as a great honor.

"It is good to finally make your acquaintance in person, Underwood-sama," Daiki stated in a formal tone with a thick accent, after the initial greetings were conducted. "I have long held a great admiration for you."

"I thank you for coming here, Oshiro-sama, and for being willing to share your arts with me," Dagian replied. "And all I have been told about you, by many whom I respect, has had me greatly looking forward to meeting you in person."

"We must all cooperate, and combine our efforts, as the Convergence reaches its conclusion," Daiki said. "It is good that we are meeting."

"Is everything prepared for this evening's journey?" Dagian asked.

Daiki nodded. "Yes, Yamaguchi Osamu is prepared for you, and I can take you to him now."

"Then let us begin this night," Dagian replied, smiling towards the other man and feeling a ripple of anticipation inside.

He nodded. "Walk with me."

Leading the group of men from the waiting room, Dagian and Daiki exited through the front doors and headed outside the building. Keeping to a lighted pathway, Daiki and Dagian walked side by side, with the rest of the men from the Order of Chikara following a few paces behind.

A clear moon loomed high above as Dagian strode through the well-manicured grounds, proceeding towards a pyramidal building set at the far edge of the compound. During the day, its upper levels were used as places of meditation and fellowship for those who practiced the Craft. It was the lower levels that Dagian was interested in, the deepest in particular, which harbored ritual chambers where no rite was off limits, not even those of a sacrificial nature.

Blood, death, and the wielding of dark, mystical powers occurred regularly within the shadows of the lower chambers. Dagian had practiced a few ancient rites herself there in recent days, preparing herself in assiduous fashion for the hour that was now at hand.

Her energies and focus were at a zenith, and she took every step towards the pyramid with robust confidence. After the great windfall of knowledge and empowerment realized in the aftermath of the journey into Set's realm, Dagian was determined that the coming night would produce a similar bounty, one that she could put to immediate use in her duties for the Convergence.

Once inside the large building, she turned to the right and took a staircase leading downward. Turning back on itself again and again, the passage descended through six levels until it opened onto consecrated ground. Dagian could feel the sharp change in the air as she took the first step away from the stairs.

Out of the corners of her eyes, Dagian perceived movements within the shadows, and felt gazes from things that could not be seen with physical eyes. The temperature plunged to a frigid point, where her breath emerged like ghostly wisps.

She savored the dark energies flowing around her. She recognized the tremendous power gathered in the place, and she knew it was well-suited for the task at hand.

Located directly below the center of the pyramid was a large chamber used as a sanctum for those who were of the highest levels in their practice of the Craft. Dagian walked towards a set of black double doors, knowing the beginning of her journey into another realm lay on the other side.

Just outside the entrance to the sanctum was a figure Dagian recognized at once: Osamu Yamaguchi. Accorded the highest respect among the most elite circles engaged in practicing the Craft, the man extended a modest bow towards her as she approached. She rendered him a lower bow in return.

Beyond the polite acknowledgement, the dour expression on his face did not change in the slightest. The look in his dark eyes was harder than granite.

He was only a little taller than Daiki, and had narrower facial features. For the most part, his loose-fitting garb was black, except for intertwining golden designs woven about each of the nine buttons running down his front.

Two robust-looking Kyotowan men flanked him, and Dagian had no doubts the larger pair served as his personal guardians. Both radiated extreme confidence, and moved with the balanced step of seasoned fighters as they took up positions to each side of the sanctuary's entrance. Both of the men carried holstered side arms, and katanas sheathed in black, unadorned saya of lacquered wood, though neither kind of weapon would be required for the task at hand.

"Good evening, Yamaguchi-sama," Dagian greeted Osamu. "I thank you for expediting my request."

"Opening doorways to the underworld is no easy task, Underwood-sama," Osamu responded, in an emotionless tone. "But all preparations have been made these past two days. Weatherford-sama has made use of the Setian arts in bridging the worlds. We are ready for you to take your journey."

"Tonight represents an admirable cooperation between several arts, all in service to the Shining One," Dagian said, appreciating the role that Gordon had accepted on behalf of the Setians. The collective power and energies of both groups were being put to her service, which was no small thing when it came to one who was not an initiated Walker of the Setian Path, or a monk in the Order of Chikara.

"May the light of the Risen Throne guide us always," Osamu stated, with an air of deep reverence.

"The Shining One has never lead me astray, and the path I have taken brought me to you," Dagian observed.

Taking in the flinty look to Osamu's eyes, Dagian sensed he was a man who embraced iron determination and cold calculation. She quickly found him to be a person that she could place her confidence in, the kind of individual not given to recklessness or casual aims.

"Do you understand the nature of the audience you seek this night?" Osamu asked Dagian, his gaze boring into her own.

She nodded, sensing the gravity of the warning underlying his words. Looking straight into his eyes, without blinking once, she replied, "I would not have called for you, if I was not certain of my choice. I accept all responsibility for whatever might happen to me."

"If you do not find favor with her, you may find that you cannot return to this world," Osamu warned, and she knew he did not speak idly. "As with Susanoo, Amanzako does not restrain her rage. She desires ever to loose it upon this world. A terrible storm dwells always within her spirit, awaiting the slightest provocation to burst forth.

"When you step into her dominion, in the Ten-Fold Kingdom, you will be entirely under her power. Your purpose in this world will not matter to her if you invoke her wrath. I can do nothing to help you, if that happens. Do you understand this?"

Welling up from the depths of his gaze, a surging intensity accompanied his final question. It was apparent that everything hinged upon her next response. Dagian knew he was more than willing to bring everything to a halt, even at the brink of completing the bridging of worlds.

"I understand this, and expect nothing different," Dagian replied with certitude, fully cognizant of the fearsome reputation held by the ethereal figure she sought to meet. "I know the risks, but it is a step that I must take."

Osamu stared at her quietly. After several moments, the severe look to his eyes ebbed, and he nodded his head in a slow, deliberate fashion. Dagian suspected that the man had reached a satisfied conclusion, in regards to whatever it was that he had been looking for in her.

"Then let this sacred journey begin, and may it bring you everything that you seek," Osamu said. "Come with me, let us leave this world together and enter her realm."

Without saying another word, he turned and made his way towards the double-doors. The two guards moved at once to pull them open, holding the doors for Osamu and Dagian so they could enter the sanctum beyond.

Inside was a chamber whose height reached upwards for several stories, culminating in a ceiling as black as starless midnight. Gordon stood at the center of the capacious room, before an altar of black granite that Dagian knew well enough.

Dark iron braziers provided what little light existed within the chamber, though the flames appeared hemmed in by the shadowy atmosphere pervading the great chamber. Dagian's skin tingled as she continued deeper into the sanctum. All her senses felt enhanced, even the deeper ones that told her of unseen witnesses present, a delegation of underworld powers without human origin.

Gordon had changed his attire since Dagian had last seen him in her office. He was now dressed in ornate Setian ceremonial robes of white and gold, with accents of blue and black.

The sect's powerful High Priest was crowned with a magnificent headdress. It evoked vivid memories of the strange, bestial Priests of Set that Dagian had encountered during her last journey into the Nether Realm.

Two other Setians attended him, both of the figures undoubtedly high of rank. One a tall, brown-haired man, and the other a darker-skinned woman with piercing jade eyes, they both looked to be of about middle age.

Like the High Priest, they were clad in ceremonial robes, though of a less elaborate design than the one they served. Both of their heads were uncovered, and they looked on the proceedings with attentive expressions.

Dagian suspected the two were capable of quite a lot themselves when it came to the practicing of the Craft. To even be allowed into the sanctum for a ritual of such a rare and delicate nature as the one about to take place required the greatest of trust on the part of Gordon. She knew such confidence was not bestowed lightly by the High Priest.

Yet as powerful as the pair might be, on this night the two Setians would not be exhibiting their own skills. Rather, they would take the roles of dutiful assistants, attending to the needs of a great master.

The doors shut behind Dagian and Osamu, followed by the telltale sounds of bolts thudding into place. Unwanted interruptions during a ritual could prove disastrous, so the chamber had been designed so that it could only be opened again from the inside.

Dagian and Osamu approached the High Priest together. Gordon looked upon them with an air of solemnity, and as they drew to a halt the pair gave the High Priest modest bows.

He nodded back to them, his face already fixing into an intensive expression. Seeing the furrows of concentration forming upon Gordon's brow, Dagian knew there would be no delays in the continuance of the ritual.

After a short pause, Gordon went into a rhythmic chant. Dagian immediately recalled the one she had heard when she had visited Kemet. This one had some variances in the wording, and she knew the High Priest was summoning a different portal than the one they had used before.

The air crackled with energy as an impenetrable darkness surrounded them, flowing with wraiths called from the fathomless abyss. Encompassed by absolute blackness of a type no light could penetrate, Dagian knew they were transcending an otherworldly threshold. Brimming with impatience, she waited with burning anticipation to see what would be revealed when the murk dissipated.

After a few moments that seemed to last for ages, the darkness cleared and faded, revealing a horrific sight. Riddled with boiling pools, from which thick vapors wafted upward, a sprawling, rocky landscape was crossed high overhead by skies of rolling fire.

Though inhospitable, the stark terrain was far removed from being a scene of emptiness. Everywhere that Dagian looked, activity thrived within the foreboding environs. Formidable-looking creatures flew through the air above, their movements swift and agile. Bulky monstrosities with reddish skin stood upon the hard ground, the majority of them positioned near the edges of many of the steaming pools.

Occupying the pools were human forms, thrashing and tossing about in throes of tremendous agony. A host of screeches, screams, and cries bombarded Dagian's ears from all directions.

The continuous noise did not bother her in the slightest, nor did the sight of the macabre visions surrounding her. If anything, she was intensely curious about the things taking place around her. Yet she did not have long to scrutinize the unfamiliar denizens of the netherworld, or the purpose of the fiery pools.

At once, Dagian and her small group of companions were confronted with a strange entity. The creature had the body of a great serpent and the face of a beautiful young woman. Supported on the thick, scaly coils of its lower body, the head of the entity was carried high above them, such that the being gazed down upon the newcomers through its reptilian eyes.

Other than the serpentine eyes, the appearance of the entity's face was human enough. Luxuriant, long black tresses framed an oval face with feminine features balanced in perfect symmetry. Graceful, arching eyebrows, full, soft-looking lips, and smooth, creamy skin ornamented the entity's comely visage.

Dagian could not miss the look of sheer anger simmering within the creature's eyes and strongly echoed in its taut jaw and frowning expression. She wondered if she was looking upon an Avatar, something that had once been human, or a thing with origins rooted in the realms of Diabolos.

Whatever the case, Dagian knew she stood before a creature with great power and authority. She knew she had to tread very carefully, and accord the entity the fullest respect and consideration.

"Who comes into the dominion of Amanzako? You are all of the world above," the entity stated with a sharp tone of accusation, appearing to be taken aback at their presence. "It is not your time to dwell in these realms."

The voice of the creature was feminine, though it held an eerie, discordant quality. It was as if the entity's voice was comprised of slightly offset layers, bestowing its words with an echo-like depth.

"Kiyohimi, I am the dutiful servant of great Amanzako, and this one serves great Set," Osamu replied deferentially, indicating Gordon Weatherford. He then turned and gestured towards Dagian. "She is one who has mastered the Craft, and who walks by the Light of the Shining One. She has been given an important task in the world above that directly serves the Risen Throne. She has come here to seek audience with great Amanzako. She desires knowledge and guidance to aid her, in carrying out this appointed task. We are merely here to assist her on her journey."

The creature's eyes snapped towards Dagian. "You fool, do you not know what you risk?" Kiyohimi asked her. "Your soul is forfeit, if great Amanzako chooses. You give yourself over to the authority of great Amanzako by coming here."

"I know what I risk," Dagian replied evenly, looking upward, and peering straight into the slit-like pupils of Kiyohimi.

"Then proceed, with full understanding, but be about your business and depart this place," the creature responded tersely.

As she had noted before, Dagian sensed a terrible rage swirling within the creature. She wished that she knew the entity's origins, sensing the spirit was once human, but she was not about to do anything to incur its wrath.

With the sound of scales scraping upon stone, Kiyohimi slithered off to the side, clearing a broad pathway of obsidian rock that cleaved through the host of bubbling pools. Osamu looked towards Gordon and Dagian, and nodded, indicating for them to proceed onward.

The molten pools were tended by contingents of huge, brutish-looking creatures that had an air of assiduous purpose about them. Extensive sets of fangs were visible within their wide maws. Their skin was of a deep red hue, and rough texture. Short horns protruded from higher up on their heads, poking through thick, disheveled masses of dark hair that tumbled over their shoulders and down to the middle of their wide backs.

All of the brawny creatures wore a type of knee-length garment, which appeared to be fashioned out of extended, straw-like pieces. Whatever the material was, it did not burn or wither, despite being in such close proximity to the scorching liquid contained within the pools.

Many of the creatures were gripping short, broad blades in their hands. Dagian wondered at the purpose of the blades, as her eyes were drawn up towards one of the flying entities.

The creatures navigating the air above the pools were fascinating to look upon. They had the heads of cats, and Dagian fixed her eyes on one in particular whose visage was akin to that of a tiger.

The entities were humanoid in form, with two arms and two legs. They wore robes formed out of something like a concentrated, black smoke. Tendrils of the dark substance trailed their bodies a little as they flew, making it look as if the feline entities were burning themselves.

Though flying, the creatures were not winged. Instead, they were each carried around by a concentrated, fiery mass that acted like a supporting platform.

While not unlike little clouds, the flaming conveyances had more of a shape resembling the body of a chariot, though no wheels were visible, or even necessary. As such, the cat-headed entities were able to fly in an upright position, with their lower bodies obscured by the raised flames of the buoying clouds of fire.

Several of the creatures were not alone on the fiery masses carrying them through the air. Cowering, and held tightly in the clawed grips of the demonic beings, were human spirits. Naked and looking terrified beyond measure, the humans appeared small compared to their fearsome netherworld wards.

Swooping down from the heights, the flying entities turned over the human souls they held to the red-skinned giants attending the pools. The latter promptly heaved the shrieking, screaming souls directly into the boiling liquid. The immediate frenzy exhibited by the human souls upon immersion in the liquid testified to the searing heat.

Dagian gazed upon the suffering spirits coldly, feeling no sorrow for their horrid plight. Their dire predicament indicated that they were spiritual refuse, souls who had not dedicated themselves to the Risen Throne. Hurled into the Abyss from the Enemy's Presence, the souls' choices and indulgences in life had been severe enough that they had not been given a place within Purgatarion.

Once cast into the Abyss, and claimed by the great Vortex of the Shining One, they were consigned to terrible fates. Crafted in the image of Adonai, a human spirit left unchanged within the Ten-Fold Kingdom invited the kind of brutality and agony being meted out all around.

She understood the reason for the dedication of the tormentors. In a small way, the denizens of the Ten-Fold Kingdom could find a measure of revenge in torturing the living images of Adonai.

Dagian had no doubt it was something demonic powers never tired of. The rage they bore towards the Enemy was unquenchable. She could only hope that her service merited a full transformation into something new, a form reflecting the abyssal worlds, when she crossed the Veil one day.

Yet as she watched the grisly scenes transpire, she began to understand that they held much more purpose than the mere torturing of souls. Focusing in upon the ground-level activity, Dagian began to perceive the rest of an infernal process involving the human souls.

One of the ogre-like entities by a pool just ahead reached down and hauled one of the human souls out of the rocky cauldron. The bulky creature showed no reaction to the touch of the fiery liquid upon its skin, acting as if the substance was little more than tepid water.

The soul's appearance after its internment in the pool was unrecognizable, its form entirely covered with ghastly blisters from head to foot. It made no effort to move, simply quivering in place where the horned giant had flung it down onto the rocky surface.

As Dagian and her companions drew nearer to the pool, she heard the ogre-thing address the soul in a grating, low-pitched voice. "Blisters removed? Knife sharpened?"

It then made a low, rumbling sound that Dagian took to be a semblance of laughter. Leaning over, the creature took the large blade held in its clawed right hand and began shearing off the blisters from the soul's form, with no regard for its trembling victim.

It was as if the soul was being skinned alive, as the knife sliced off large sections of blistered 'skin.' Dagian knew the soul was not physical in the way that she was, but in the non-physical realms things could still take on material properties. To the soul experiencing the shearing off of its bodily surface, the pain was entirely real.

Underneath the blisters, the outer surface of the soul's form was revealed to be glassy and dark-toned. Dagian, as best as she could understand what she saw, fathomed that the soul's agonizing tenure within the pool had produced some kind of volcanic-like transformation.

The ogre-being was rather quick and efficient in its preparation of the soul's new form. Towards the end of the skinning, it made one pronounced slice deeper down the face of the soul, removing the shapes of the soul's nose, lips, and other things that contributed to an individual identity. What remained was a garish, skeletal-like visage, composed of the glassy, dark substance.

The facial features were not all that were removed in the skinning process. There was now no way of telling the soul's previous identity, or even if it had been male or female before. What remained in the aftermath was a new creation, without identity and incapable of expression. When its grisly task was completed, the ogre-being lumbered away and left the altered soul behind, lying on the ground and showing no inclination to move.

Passing by the pool, Dagian turned her head to see what happened to the soul after the process was finished, doubting that the human spirits were simply left abandoned following their transformation. Her answer came a few moments later, as one of the cat-headed creatures from above alighted close to the side of the soul.

The entity clutched the body roughly with its claws, pulling it onto the fiery cloud-platform. A moment later, the creature lifted off the ground and hastened away with its quarry.

Dagian slowed her pace, watching the entity rise higher into the skies as it headed off to some other destination. She thought about the human soul and pondered what was intended for it, wherever it was being taken.

"The Namahage," Osamu said at her side in a low voice, just above a whisper. Drawing her attention from the skies, he was nodding towards the brawny wards of the pools. He then glanced up towards the skies, and nodded again. "The Kasha."

Dagian said nothing in response, but nodded her head in acknowledgement of Osamu's words. There would be time enough for questions later, and she did not want to create any unintended disturbances that an attempt at conversation might bring into such an unusual atmosphere.

Her group continued onward at a steady pace, passing through the midst of a tremendous multitude of pools. She watched the ongoing process with the human souls in all of its facets, as new souls were brought down from the heights and consigned to the pools, and other souls were dragged out and prepared with the blades of the Namahage to be taken away by the airborne Kasha.

Unable to watch any one incident for very long, Dagian found it hard to tell how long it took for the souls to undergo the transformation, from their initial immersion within the pools to the moment that they were pulled out by the Namahage. She surmised that the process was not swift, and that the souls endured a lengthy agony within the molten liquid.

When it appeared there would be no end to the pools, the obsidian pathway finally reached a strange oasis in the fiery maelstrom. On the approach, it looked like nothing more than an expansive circle of flatter ground, devoid of any pools or pits. Three other pathways also ended at the open circle, the four paths set equidistant to each other.

"Go alone from here, Underwood-sama," Osamu instructed firmly. He had drawn to a halt with the others of their group, stopping a few paces away from the end of the pathway. "I can go no further. I have not earned the right to speak with Amanzako. You are not a dedicated servant of hers, so you may approach. As Kiyohimi said, do so with the knowledge that you risk being held here if she desires it.

"I must tell you again that there is nothing I can do to intercede for you if that happens. I must be certain that you understand this, as it is I who will answer for helping to bring you here. I ask you one last time. Do you understand the risks that you take?"

"I understand," Dagian said, determined only to gain what she had come there for.

"Proceed. We shall await you without," Osamu pronounced with great solemnity. With a gesture of his right hand, he indicated for her to continue forward.

Having no idea what to expect, Dagian strode to the end of the pathway and walked into the open circle. The moment her foot left the obsidian surface and touched the ground of the circle was like stepping from one realm into another. The pool-filled, arid landscape vanished immediately from sight and she found herself standing before a great, grass-covered hill. The skies were no longer masses of fire, but instead resembled something much more like the physical world she came from.

Large masses of light gray clouds traversed the sky at a slow, steady pace. The sulfuric scents and heat of the environment she had stepped out of were replaced with a crisp coolness, the touch and taste of the air before the falling of rain.

The top of the hill held a lone figure and a magnificent-looking cherry blossom tree. The elegant tree was still adorned with a host of brilliant blooms, a few of which were breaking free and drifting down gently as she watched.

Dagian knew at once that the one she sought was the individual standing near the base of the tree. She could not see the face of the figure, as its back was turned squarely to Dagian.

She glanced back, and saw there was no sign of the others. An undulating terrain of large hills and mountains stretched into the distance, as far as the eye could see.

Taking a deep breath, and girding her resolve, Dagian turned her head and started forward. Walking up the hill, feeling the soft ground underfoot, she reflected on the surroundings to keep her nerves from gaining purchase inside her.

The environment was in such stark contrast to what they had first passed through. While cool and a little moist, the air was entirely calm, and only the lightest of breezes stirred the quiet. No sun hovered above, and had there been one it would have been obscured by the overcast skies. Yet there was plenty of light, enough to see clearly to the far horizon.

The clouds were decidedly gentle in their flow across the heights. Overall, a tranquil, beautiful scene encompassed Dagian, one that was entirely unexpected, given the fearsome reputation of Amanzako and the extreme harshness of the first environment she had encountered.

Clad in elegant red robes that brushed the grassy summit, the figure at the top had long locks of jet black. The being turned slowly when Dagian finally reached the crown of the hill, revealing the fullness of its appearance.

Dagian concentrated on keeping her face still as her eyes took in an unsettling, bestial countenance. Long of nose and fang, with extended, pointed ears, the figure carried a decidedly hostile expression, akin to a menacing snarl. The echoes of a human woman played about the features of the fell entity, but the traits of a feral beast were far more predominant.

Dagian could feel a tremendous rage boiling behind the gaze of the Fallen Avatar, something far beyond what she had detected in the snake-woman Kiyohimi upon her group's entrance. She knew that she was treading on very thin, fragile ground, and had to proceed with the utmost caution.

Amanzako was an Avatar whose spirit burned fiercely with the desire for exacting vengeance on the Enemy. It was true that all of the Fallen Avatars, having been driven into the bottomless Abyss prior to the founding of the Ten-Fold Kingdom, thirsted for a degree of vengeance, but they handled the urge in widely disparate ways.

Amanzako was almost entirely consumed, to a degree that some would describe as madness. Looking upon the Avatar's face, Dagian could feel the searing waves of Amanzako's lust for revenge.

She knew it would not take much at all to trigger the Avatar's furor. It was critical that she was exceedingly careful with her every response.

"You have been blessed in abundance by Anat," Amanzako stated. "Now you have come to seek deeper knowledge from me, so that you may serve the Shining One, and the One who is the blood and flesh of the Risen Throne. This is your purpose, is it not?"

"It is, great Amanzako," Dagian replied in a low, deferential voice, bowing low at the waist reverently to the powerful entity.

The fact that Amanzako knew her purpose did not come as a surprise. It was likely the Fallen Avatar became aware of Dagian's intent from the first moments she had set her mind toward the quest. One who engaged in the Craft and opened their eyes to the things of the Abyss was well-aware that the things of the Abyss could also look back into them.

As Dagian answered, she continued feeling the waves of energy flowing from the other being. The emanations carried the purest essence of fury, and it was all Dagian could do to look back up into the countenance of the prominent figure before her.

"Many seek, but only those who are strong deserve what I can give," Amanzako stated. Her eyes narrowed, two concentrated pools of flame in a blood-red hue. Her voice began to rise in tenor, alarming Dagian immediately. "And I find all humans weak. Sniveling, fearful, corrupted … and humans are the image of the Enemy!"

Amanzako's lips peeled back, but the expression was more the bearing of fangs than it was a smile. It was one of the coldest, maniacal expressions Dagian had ever witnessed. The confidence she had carried into Amanzako's realm was crumbling swiftly, as uncertainty slithered into her mind.

"Can you overcome being the image of the Enemy?" Amanzako asked Dagian, in a tone dripping with malice.

The skies darkened within moments, the clouds picking up speed until they were racing overhead at a pace dizzying to look upon. The cherry blossom tree discarded the rest of its petals in the winds whipping aggressively about the summit. The petals were whisked off the summit by the powerful gusts, until a barren, naked tree remained.

"We are coming to the world you know, and our fury will have no bounds," Amanzako thundered, her expression brimming with hostility. Her eyes were wide and her expression rabid, and for the first time Dagian questioned the wisdom of seeking an audience with the Fallen Avatar. "Vengeance shall be ours for the long-suffering we have endured."

Dagian found herself at a total loss, not knowing what to do or say. She fell down to her knees, hoping to show obeisance in the presence of the increasingly agitated spirit. Her hopes were fleeting.

As Dagian knelt, the Avatar transformed, becoming a towering, multi-winged figure of flames wreathed in darkness. Her heart was filled with terror at the extraordinary sight.

"Great Amanzako, I wish to shed the image of the Enemy. I wish to be a new creation of the Shining One in the Remaking," Dagian said before the giant being, her words pouring out quickly in her rising state of fear. "I serve the Shining One in the world above with all my heart and soul. I came to you so I may be of more use to the Risen Throne. I work towards the vengeance you desire and renounce the curse of humanity forced upon me by the Enemy. I had no choice in that matter. Only the Shining One can free me to become a new creation."

The surging winds battered Dagian where she remained on her knees. Layers of thunder rippled across the skies above. For many unbearable moments, no answer was forthcoming from the fiery entity. Everything she had worked for and the fate of her soul teetered in a precarious balance.

"The memunim of one who practices the Craft reflect the strength of their summoner," Amanzako finally said. "Let us see how strong you truly are. If your memunim fail the test, you will not leave this realm. The flaming pits shall be your home!"

Stark, vivid images of the boiling pits, screaming souls, and the Namahage blades welled up in Dagian's mind. There would be no way to avoid the horrific, agonizing fate if she were to fail whatever test the Fallen Avatar was about to give.

"Rise, and be measured!" Amanzako boomed.

With a sweep of a blazing hand, the Avatar summoned up a concentrated channel of wind that picked Dagian off the ground and rushed her away from the summit. She was lifted steadily higher, and carried far across the skies. Leagues and leagues streaked past below her in a blur, until she was finally brought down into what looked to be a large caldera.

The rapid descent unnerved Dagian, though whatever force governed the wind slowed the approach considerably as the rocky surface of the caldera's basin drew nearer. Even so, she landed heavily on her back, gasping as the air was knocked out from her lungs.

For a moment she lay still, hesitant to move for fear of what she would discover about her body. Carefully, she moved each of her limbs, and then propped herself up into a sitting position.

To her great relief, Dagian found that she had not suffered any serious injuries. Slowly, and a little disoriented, she got her feet underneath her and stood up. Warily, she began looking around, turning about in place as she scanned the surroundings.

Towering rock walls culminating in jagged ends encompassed her in the roughly circular space. Her eyes widened as she beheld several non-human forms perched on the rocks high above, positioned all around her.

The appearance of each of the creatures resembled a large black crane, though their bodies were leathery, rather than feathered, and their eyes were like flames. Long-necked and long-legged, they were hideous mockeries of living things from Dagian's world, and all of them were eyeing her hungrily.

Standing upright, and peering down at her, was another strange being. The robed figure had the bearing and posture of a human, though its bird-like head dismissed any notions that it was a man or woman. In its right hand was a tall staff, and on its head rested a black cap.

"This is a most unexpected delight. It appears that Great Amanzako has given you over to me, to do with as I please," the bird-headed thing announced in a high-pitched voice. "I will destroy you, over and over again. No human can escape me. Try to resist, if you wish."

Its final words were spoken in a mocking, arrogant tone. Dagian could tell that the entity was both surprised and pleased at her appearance, and eager to carry out its stated intent.

She had no time to ponder the strange being any further. With grating screeches, the demonic flock took off from their perches and began swooping down into the caldera, plunging directly towards her. There were only seconds left to act before the creatures reached her position.

Steeling her mind, and reacting with instinct, Dagian called out to her memunim. In a speck of time, several of the wraith-like forms surrounded her.

Dagian could feel their initial perceptions as they regarded the incoming attackers. They had no respect or fear for the things diving from the heights.

The infernal entities screeched loudly with their membranous wings spread out wide. All instantly harbored a hate-filled furor for the approaching creatures who would dare to strike at the woman who had mastered them and commanded their loyalty.

Flexing her willpower, she gave her memunim leave to fight without inhibition. Like a black lotus giving bloom, the memunim rushed upward from all around Dagian to meet the onrushing creatures.

Dagian's own rage had been stoked by the attack. She conveyed her desire to the memunim that they tear apart the things that dared to beset her.

Like so many dark cloaks enveloping the flying entities, the memunim intercepted and engulfed the incoming creatures. A chaotic, ferocious melee broke out far above.

Using their sharp beaks and sets of long talons, the flying creatures shrieked and fought back vigorously. Above them, their bird-headed master loosed an enraged screech that echoed off the walls of the caldera.

At once, Dagian felt something amiss, and brought her eyes back down to the ground level. Her breath caught in her throat, and she nearly tumbled backward.

Scuttling towards her was a creature that in some ways looked like an enormous centipede. It had a host of legs, and a segmented form, but the comparison ended there. Its head was a macabre, ghastly assortment of eyes and pincers, encircling a maw lined with concentric rows of razor-sharp, inward-curving teeth.

For a brief instant, she stared into the depths of a hellish fate filled with unimaginable agonies. There was nowhere to hide, and certainly no place for her to run.

Her memunim were too far away to come to her aid. Every one of them was already embroiled in the vicious fray with the winged nightmares that served the bird-headed figure with the staff.

Yet just as fast as the paralysis of fear had come over her, Dagian's willpower surged to the fore and regained the initiative. Reaching out, and drawing upon the essences of Amanzako's realm, Dagian called upon the skies to rain fire down upon the multi-legged nightmare hastening towards her.

To call upon the elements of a realm governed by a Fallen Avatar that she did not serve was a bold and far-reaching act. Yet the Craft had always enabled her to channel her focus, in the imposition of her will, to achieve a given task.

A deeper wisdom bestowed the clear understanding that what

she was doing was not ultimately a matter of her own will either. Everything she did in response to the challenges was an act of mere survival so that she could carry out the Will of the Shining One.

Her own will was entirely subordinate to the Risen Throne, conferring a purity of intent to all her actions in response to the mortal threats being hurled at her. As Amanzako's realm was subordinate to the Shining One, the exercise of Dagian's will in full harmony with the Will of the Shining One commanded tremendous authority and power.

Dagian could feel power surging and coalescing around her body. Her skin tingled all over with the building force. When it seemed the very air around her would tear apart, she cried out, and thrust her arms skyward.

The skies above crackled and pulsed with tremendous bursts of horizontal lightning that lit up the caldera in great flashes. A mass of brilliant streaks converged into one searing bolt that shot down into the heart of the basin and exploded the horrid thing rushing towards her.

One moment she could hear the grating scrapes of its teeming claws scuttling along the rock surfacing. In the next, luminous bits of the thing were flying all over the caldera. Wherever they landed, the light-leaking remains of the creature diffused swiftly, until there was nothing left of the thing to be seen.

The peril eliminated, Dagian quickly looked back upward, to see what had become of the airborne melee. The combat was already dwindling down, and where the attackers had significantly outnumbered her memunim at the outset, the situation was now reversed.

There was no doubting the outcome of the fighting, and Dagian felt a torrent of elation about the impending victory. She stood still and savored every last moment watching the winged assailants being destroyed to the last.

She watched two of her memunim, each grasping a wing of one of the flying creatures, dash the thing unceremoniously against the side of the caldera. The creature screeched horribly as it was shredded apart, its wings torn free and pieces of its body falling like tongues of light. The smallest descended for a short distance before vanishing entirely. The larger remains plummeted to the ground below, where they took longer to fade away.

Another memunim whipped around one of the creatures like a small, black cyclone, twisting the beaked head right off its body. The separated head and body fell all the way to the ground, landing just a few paces from where Dagian was standing. She watched the segments as they began to dissipate and lose the appearance of solidity, taking on greater translucence as they ebbed away to nothing.

The struggle continued until all of the attackers had been savagely ripped apart. Her defenders carried her will and fury out to the fullest extent in their engagement of the hellish flock. The attackers had all been brought to ruin, proving to be no match for the powerful wraiths she commanded.

As if parading in victory, the dark shapes drifted along the edge of the caldera in the aftermath. From what Dagian could tell from a quick assessment, only one or two of the wraiths had been lost in the fighting.

The caldera fell into deep silence once again. Dagian peered upwards, glaring towards the staff-bearing, bird-headed entity, who was still observing the proceedings.

"You destroyed those who had been given to me!" it shrieked with rage, the disbelief underlying its words unmistakable. "Human filth! Who do you think you are? You were given to me!"

"I was not given to you. I was put to the test, and it was you who attacked," Dagian replied coldly.

She took note that her memunim were not all that far from the entity. As her anger swelled, they slowed to a halt.

They hovered in place, like dutiful sentinels, awaiting their next command. With a clear, concise thought, she gave it to them a moment later.

Moving swiftly, far too fast for the robed entity to react, they engulfed the bird-headed figure and snatched it away from the caldera's rim. It screeched and protested vehemently, but the memunim gave the entity no heed.

Dagian's wraiths bore the captive thing down to the base of the caldera. Once they reached the bottom, they moved the entity over to where she was standing, depositing the figure roughly onto the ground before her.

It tried to resist as the staff was ripped out of its hands, and the cap was yanked from its head, but its struggles were futile. Dagian then had her memunim tear way the being's robes to humiliate it further, revealing a skinny, bony, mottled body underneath the dark outer garments.

"Who is at the feet of whom?" she asked the naked being icily. "If this is a realm that honors vengeance, then you who would dare attack me have brought vengeance down upon yourself."

The thing erupted in a torrent of threats and curses, though it was held fast to the ground by her memunim. It was helpless, and could not move to escape or act upon its words. At another mental command from Dagian, her wraiths lifted the creature up and turned it over, so that its front side was pressed against the caldera's surface.

Dagian casually picked up its staff, and set her foot at the base of the creature's neck. With another thought of command, one of her memunim lifted its head off the ground, and oriented it such that the beak's end touched upon the surface.

The large wraith applied enough pressure to stop the thing from twisting its head to the side, also preventing it from opening its beak to respond to Dagian's words. Effectively, the thing's head was pinned in place. The indignant rage in the creature fled, replaced with a raw terror that Dagian found delectable.

"I claim my vengeance upon you," Dagian declared, feeling an electrifying sense of excitement and power.

Holding the staff high in both hands, she brought the end of it rushing down squarely onto the back of the thing's head. The sheer force of the blow shattered its beak apart, the bits scattering even as the rest of its head was driven downward and pulped into an unrecognizable mess against the rock surface.

Immediately, its body began to show signs of fading. She had dispatched the creature instantly, consigning the essence of its soul to the Void.

The vision of her enemy in ruins was intoxicating, and Dagian smiled with the euphoria of triumph. Her memunim had reflected her own conviction and strength, delivering a resounding defeat to the bird-headed emissary and its monstrous flock. She had directly called abyssal power into her control when she had summoned the massive lightning bolt to destroy the huge, multi-legged creature. There was little doubt she had passed the test given to her by Amanzako.

As she continued watching the remains of her opponent dissipate, she was abruptly lifted from the ground as a gust picked her up and carried her out of the caldera. On the power of the infernal wind she sped across the sky, the ground far beneath racing by once again.

She felt herself slowing and descending as the hilltop with the prominent cherry blossom tree came into view once more. Dagian was set down upon the ground at the summit, this time much more gently than she had been deposited within the rocky caldera.

The skies were rolling by slowly again, and the tree was full of blooms once more. The towering, flaming figure assumed by Amanzako prior to the test was gone, replaced once again by the robed being with the animalistic countenance.

"Vengeance is the sweetest of nectars, is it not?" Amanzako asked Dagian in a calm tone, though the Avatar's expression still hinted at the maniacal.

"It is, Great Amanzako," Dagian replied, hoping the Fallen Avatar's churning rage could now be constrained.

"You have been measured, and you will be allowed to depart my dominion," Amanzako announced.

Dagian gave Amanzako a deep, extended bow in acknowledgement, feeling tremendously relieved at the pronouncement. She said nothing, and waited patiently for the Fallen Avatar to continue.

"Provide for those in service to me, and I shall extend you deeper knowledge," Amanzako said. "Bring them to serve you in your given task from the Risen Throne."

Dagian nodded, and replied in a low voice, "I shall provide for all of those who serve you, Great Amanzako. And I shall bring them into my task on behalf of the Risen Throne."

The winds then began to pick up considerably, and the skies

took on a darkened hue. More petals began raining down from the tree.

To all appearances, it felt as if a storm was about to manifest. Tendrils of unease snaked through Dagian as the changes occurred. She feared Amanzako's ire had somehow been ignited again.

"You may now receive my grace," Amanzako boomed suddenly.

A column of lightning much brighter and wider than the one Dagian had called into the caldera barreled down from the sky and engulfed her. Incomprehensible pain filled her, a blinding agony that consumed her every thought.

When the lightning released its burning hold, Dagian felt the presence of something new embedded deep inside her. She understood that she had received both power and knowledge from the savage-looking Fallen Avatar before her. Amanzako had given great favor to Dagian, just as Anat had done within the heart of Set's realm.

"Go now!" the Fallen Avatar commanded her. "You have been given what you sought. Look to the day you can shed the image of the Enemy, and become an image of the Shining One!"

Dagian gave Amanzako another low bow. Turning at once, and not wanting to risk any provocation that a moment's delay might bring, she walked with a brisk step down the slope.

The winds whipping about the hill lashed out furiously, and a menacing thunder rolled through the skies above. A storm of tremendous magnitude was forming up rapidly, and Dagian knew it was all a reflection of the Fallen Avatar who had just dismissed her.

Before she had gotten far from the base of the hill, Dagian's vision shimmered and she found herself back among the fiery, boiling pits tended by the hulking Namahage. Strangely, she felt a sense of relief as she gazed upon one hurling the naked form of a man into the burning pool. The harsh sight reflected an order to things that was sustained, even if it was so utterly brutal.

The ones who Dagian had come with were waiting for her. Gordon's face had a look of relief, and, for a brief moment, the touch of a smile came to the face of Osamu.

"Amanzako has found favor with you," Osamu said. "You would not be standing here otherwise."

Dagian nodded, sensing a trace of envy within the other man, but said nothing. Her mind still swarmed with thoughts and impressions of what had just happened to her.

There was a wealth of new discoveries to unlock from inside her. She knew she was returning to her world much stronger than when she had left it.

"It is time we departed," Osamu said evenly. Turning, he started back in the direction they had come from.

Dagian nodded, and walked with the others along the pathway. Though a few cast glances their way, the Kasha and Namahage paid the human visitors little heed, keeping their focus on the unfortunate souls they tended.

Dagian eyed another of the human souls who had just been skinned by one of the Namahage, right as one of the Kasha arrived to collect the spirit in its shiny, altered form. She knew there was a purpose to the transformation. In the midst of a realm governed by a Fallen Avatar so consumed with thoughts of vengeance, Dagian had little doubt the souls would be used along that path of retribution.

Kiyohimi stood to the side of the path, gazing quietly upon the group of humans following the lengthy return trek. She said nothing to them, a stony expression fixed upon her face as they passed.

Once Dagian's group was beyond the snake-woman, Kiyohimi slithered back onto the path behind them. She kept her reptilian eyes fixed on the departing group the entire time. Dagian got the feeling that the entity was astonished that she had returned from her audience with Amanzako.

Gordon called the group to a halt. Once everyone was gathered together in a tight cluster, he engaged in a short chant that summoned a host of small wraiths.

The dark forms encompassed the group and blotted out all sight of Amanzako's realm. When the wraiths parted and faded from sight again, Dagian found herself back inside the ritual chamber beneath the pyramidal structure.

A grin touched Dagian's lips as she eyed the familiar surroundings, and she felt an elation that bordered on giddiness. She had braved the risks, been measured, and gained what she had come for. She was now in an even stronger position to carry out her given charge.

"You appear to be quite pleased with your experience of Great Amanzako. May I ask what you are thinking?" Osamu asked.

"I am very pleased, Yamaguchi-sama," Dagian responded, smiling as she perceived the curiosity brimming within the other man. "I have good tidings for you as well. Amanzako wishes for you and those of your order to be a part of my work. It is time I introduce you to the Erkorenen whose progenitors once walked in your lands. They will be yours to command, but it is important that you must be ready to travel on a moment's notice."

"It would be an honor to serve one who found direct favor with great Amanzako," Osamu replied, extending her a respectful bow, one that was lower than the one he had rendered to her prior to the journey.

Dagian's mind was already conceiving of many places and possibilities where Osamu and those of his order would be highly useful. Once they had been paired with Erkorenen associated once with their own Kyotowan homelands, they would have the power they needed to confront almost any threat.

A bit of insight gleaned from the gifts of Amanzako told Dagian to keep the continuity intact regarding the origins of both the Fallen Avatar's human servants and the Erkorenen that they would work with. Though she did not fully understand why that was advantageous, Dagian was not about to question the deeper wisdom provided her. The gifts of Avatars were not to be questioned, but they were to be used wherever needed.

"Let us all turn in for the night and get some rest," Dagian said to Osamu and the others. "There is much to do when the new day arrives."

GREGORY

"Let's get this little guy into the air," Dante said, setting the multi-rotor contraption onto the ground and backing up a few paces.

Not much wider than a food tray, the object carried night vision optics and was one of the best drones they had available. It had been fashioned for them by Layne Freeman, who had latched onto Gregory's group and become good friends with Chuck.

The latter development was not surprising at all. The two certainly shared a love for electronics, but Layne was more of the engineering type. Gregory was simply glad that Chuck had someone to better relate to within their group.

At the present moment, Gregory could not be more grateful for the ingenious man. Layne had delivered them a little added help, at a time when they were at an extreme disadvantage.

"We are going to need to get some more eyes up there soon," Consuela stated pensively, looking to the skies from where she stood to the right of Dante.

Gregory could see the edges of anxiety in her face and hear the unease in her tone of voice. He could not fault her for the trepidation, as she had very good reason to be deeply concerned.

A few lethal operatives from the UCAS were loose within Venorterra. Gregory now accompanied a large contingent of irregulars doing everything they could to hone in on the interlopers.

A wide net had been cast, but he knew very well that the hunter could quickly become the hunted, especially when dealing with the kind of enemy they were facing. There was no question that every ounce of Gregory's experience and ability would be needed when dealing with the kind of apex predators that special operatives were.

Currently, the militia force was zeroing in on a hilly region where there had been some recent killings conducted with efficiency and precision. The attacks on a few small militia outposts had all the hallmarks of being executed by highly-trained warriors.

There had been no survivors, and not so much as a warning had been sounded. Only the practice of the militia outposts to check in regularly with each other had alerted the others that something had gone very wrong in the wooded hills.

Gregory suspected the enemy operatives were Navy Orcas, the most elite warriors in all of the military branches.. Most deemed them to be the best of the best among the military's various special operations groups.

It mattered little that Gregory had a couple of hundred militia fighters in the immediate area, including a great many who possessed military experience. In an instant, the situation could transform into something resembling a herd of antelope walking into the midst of lions.

The presence of such a valuable military asset as Orcas would be a deeply troubling development. Gregory knew the UCAS did not deploy the premium elements of their special forces idly. Orcas would be in Venorterra only for a specific mission. The thought vexed him. He simply could not fathom what the target would be.

"What is it, man?" Dante asked, a frown deepening on his face.

Gregory looked out into the night, knowing that killing shadows roved the darkness. He did not wish to spread fear in the men and women around him, but neither could he refrain from instilling suitable caution in them.

"We're going up against a different breed," Gregory replied, grim-faced, as he looked to Dante, Consuela, and Jacob. "If it is what my gut tells me it is, we are going to need to be at our best. Don't let your guard down for even a second."

A short distance off to the left, occupying a solid position on higher ground, were Sean, Corey, and Marcus. The three had night vision gear, including some optics with long range capability.

The trio was at the outskirts of the multi-layered defensive position Gregory had ordered for the militia unit, arrayed so that the unit as a whole had all-around fire capability. Gregory had already given the three firm instructions to stay concealed while Dante launched the drone. He could only hope that they heeded him.

"Well, no sense in waiting. Let's take a look around from higher up," Dante announced, using hand-held controls to set the drone's rotors in motion. Swiftly building up speed, the whirring blades made little noise as the small device lifted off the ground and began climbing upward.

A small monitor on the ground displayed what the cameras mounted on the drone could pick up. For the time being, the night vision mode had been selected, putting the familiar green and black imagery onto the monitor screen.

Once the drone had lifted well above the treetops, Dante sent it forward of the position where Marcus and Gregory's two developing young snipers were located. The image transmitted back to the monitor was not crystal clear, but it was good enough to show anything moving through the trees below.

For the next several minutes, Gregory kept his eyes locked to the screen, while Dante sent the drone sweeping over the area forward of their position. The lack of anything seen moving in the woods, even after a few passes, was not a guarantee that the enemy was absent.

Orcas were adept at concealment, and could thwart the lens of a drone easily enough. Gregory was just hoping that if the unknown interlopers were near, he could catch a sign of them on the move. It was the best chance the militia contingent would have of detecting the elite warriors.

The night had a disconcerting silence to it, a weighty, oppressive air that Gregory knew all too well from his tours of duty overseas. Everything in him sensed that a storm was about to break. Whether or not the lightning would fall on him remained to be seen, but every instinct urged him to the highest state of alertness.

A parade of treetops continued to flow across the monitor, showing nothing beneath their boughs. Gregory stared at the screen in pensive silence, the surrounding air pressing in heavier with each moment.

"I can take it out a little farther," Dante said in a low voice. "We've covered the ground ahead thoroughly by now, with multiple passes."

"Give it one more pass," Gregory replied, his gaze unwavering.

He barely got the words out of his mouth when chaos abruptly broke out upon the monitor, jolting Gregory into the moment as the camera tumbled and spun in a haphazard manner. A dizzying amalgam of sky and ground filled the monitor screen, making it impossible to tell the cause of the drone's sudden plight.

"What the hell?" Dante exclaimed aloud, working frantically at the controls.

A still image of the forest floor, set at an awkward angle, snapped into view a moment later. The drone had fallen and hit the ground hard, lodging into place.

"Something ran into it," Dante remarked, glancing back to

Gregory. "It was above the trees. I … "

Dante stopped talking as the monitor was suddenly filled with a clear view of large claws, belonging to the leg of something that was decidedly inhuman. Gregory stared at the image in a mind-spinning state of both amazement and disbelief.

The claws and leg disappeared abruptly from sight. A moment later, the drone was lifted from the ground, and then slammed downward with great force. The screen flickered and went entirely black a couple of seconds later.

Gregory brought up his field radio and spoke quickly. "Marcus, your position is compromised up there. Unknown threat from the air. Pull back now."

He then proceeded to issue commands to the other militia fighters occupying positions forming the layers of the defensive ring. Urging them to stay alert and prepare to engage, Gregory informed the various positions that hostiles were near.

Looking towards those with him, Gregory saw that Dante and Jacob already had their rifles at the ready, and Consuela was in the act of bringing down the night-vision lenses attached to her helm. Gregory lowered his own goggles into place, and turned his eyes skyward, still wondering what he had just seen on the monitor.

Pounding footsteps announced the arrival of Marcus, Corey, and Sean, but Gregory did not react to their return. His eyes were fixed towards the large, winged shape that had just glided into view.

To his astonishment, the strange thing flapped its broad wings. Gregory knew that unless the flying object was some unprecedented new drone prototype, he was looking at a living creature.

He shouldered his select-fire rifle. With the weapon set to a three-round burst mode, Gregory moved the barrel slowly to the left as he tracked the creature. Squeezing the trigger, he sent three shots towards his winged target.

It jerked about as the bullets tore into its body, and a piercing shriek filled the air a moment later. In a display of dexterity and speed that astonished Gregory, the thing sharply changed directions, banking away to the left and flying out of his sight.

"What the hell is that?" Dante asked, staring after the creature.

"I don't know, but it destroyed the drone, and it's not our friend," Gregory replied evenly. "Don't hesitate to shoot it."

"There's more than one of them up there," Consuela said firmly, as another winged shape came into view in the night sky.

It flew in from the right. The second creature appeared to be longer of body and broader of wingspan than the one he had just wounded.

"Give it a nice lead welcoming!" Gregory ordered.

Shots rang out through the trees, as they opened fire on the creature in the skies. Another inhuman cry erupted. The flying entity flapped its wings rapidly and descended in an awkward, downward-spiraling fashion.

"Looks like we brought one of the bastards down for sure," Gregory observed.

"We wounded it good, no doubt about that," Consuela declared, with an undercurrent of delight.

"Should we go see what that thing is?" Dante asked.

Gregory shook his head. "No, we need to keep to our positions, where we've got interlocking fields of fire. Who knows what those things are, or how many of them are out there? But we do need to move to some better cover."

Turning his head to glance at the others with him, Gregory's heart thundered as he took in an unexpected, dismaying sight. There was no time to call out a warning. It felt as if time stood still.

Sean never saw the winged nightmare hurtling out of the darkness towards him. It had come in from behind the group, and closed in upon its target in silence, without raising a single shout of alarm.

The creature's shadow engulfed Sean a second before he was driven hard to the ground. Curving, sharp claws hooked into his back and began tearing savagely into his flesh. Jaws lined with needle-like teeth clamped down and ripped a gory chunk away from the span between Sean's neck and shoulder. A meek, blubbering cry escaped the unfortunate man's lips, and blood streamed thickly from his mouth.

The creature was easily much longer of body than Gregory, and standing upright would have loomed over a foot taller. It had a bat-like visage, all the way down to its shorter snout and large, triangular ears. Its membranous wings were folded in closer to its body, and the thing braced itself on the part of its wings where a prominent, singular claw sprouted.

A layer of fine gray fur covered its body, but its longer legs, and echoes in the shape of the creature's upper torso, recalled the form of a human. Also different from any bat that Gregory had ever seen, the creature had a pair of thin arms, both ending in sets of elongated claws. The latter were free to rend its victim at will, since the creature's body weight was propped up, using its wings for support. Everything happened in a flash of time.

"Sean!" Gregory exclaimed in fury and abhorrence, leveling his weapon and squeezing the trigger.

A three-round burst cut through the night and tore into Sean's monstrous assailant. The beast shrieked and recoiled, rearing back into a standing position for a brief instant.

Moving with an unusual gait and hunching posture, the creature hurried away. Gregory sent several more trios of bullets racing in its direction. Many more high-pitched cries erupted, and the creature thrashed about as bullets repeatedly slammed into its body. Despite taking many hits, the thing kept moving and disappeared among the trees.

Gregory stared after the creature in sheer incredulity. He knew he had drawn blood and wounded it many times over, but to his bewilderment the thing had somehow been able to get away.

At that moment, an outbreak of gunfire sounded off to the right. The radio reported a moment later that one of the other defensive positions, under a veteran that Gregory trusted named Ken Tanaka, was taking fire.

Gregory had few doubts that the winged beasts were connected in some way with the enemy operatives now firing on the militia position. After a quick check that confirmed that Sean was dead, Gregory led the others with him to a fallback position.

Using depressions in the ground, rocks, and trees, Dante and the others with Gregory took up new positions. Most oriented their weapons on the forward area, but Gregory had Consuela and Marcus keep an eye both above and behind them, using their night vision to look out for more of the winged entities.

Gunfire rattled into the night, and another radio check revealed that the militia position under fire had taken some casualties. The last thing Gregory needed was for the enemy's special operatives to slip into the defensive ring through a breech, especially when their winged beasts could come down right on top of them.

"Leaving you in charge here, Consuela. Let the others know about the airborne threat, and hold this position," Gregory stated. "I'm going to check in on Ken's group."

"You got it," Consuela replied confidently from behind him. "We won't let those winged sons of bitches get anyone else."

Turning, Gregory nodded with a solemn expression as the two shared an extended look. Though nothing would be given vent at the moment, he knew from the look in her eyes that she shared the hot pain he felt at losing Sean.

Discipline would carry them both forward in the face of their dangerous circumstances, but it would not provide any consolation. Sorrow would lurk patiently, and wait for the kind of lonely, vulnerable moments that soldiers of all ages knew far too well.

Moving out from his cover, Gregory kept his profile low as he headed towards the sound of the gunfire. Not wanting to get shot in the dark by the other militia positions, he radioed the other group leaders in the vicinity as he progressed, exchanging passwords.

The militia had not yet adopted a precise structure involving rifle teams, squads, platoons, and the like. With well over half of the militia members having no military background, that kind of organization would take a little more time to implement.

With all of the threats from the UCAS, the plain truth was that the breakaway provinces had to make use of every person available and willing to help defend them. But there had been enough time to get some basic order and discipline established among the various subgroups. The structure paid another dividend as Gregory was able to make it to Ken's position without any mishaps occurring.

He made a quick mental note to commend the various group commanders later. There was no question that the militia was becoming a more efficient paramilitary force with each passing day.

"What have we got here, Ken?" Gregory asked in a low voice,

crawling up on his belly to reach the group leader.

"They haven't tried to flank us, or move in on us yet, but we already have two down," Ken replied from where he was crouched, peering ahead with night vision goggles on.

A short man with a stocky build, Ken had a solid military background with several years of infantry experience. Circumstances had thrust him into being one of the group commanders in the militia. He had swiftly displayed an aptitude for leading others, much to Gregory's relief in a situation where there was a precarious shortage of capable leadership.

Ken was also a very tough individual, something that Gregory had experienced first hand, having worked out with him several times on some of the quieter days. During sparring and hand-to-hand combat routines, Ken displayed a high proficiency in Judo, the martial art whose origins resonated with his own ethnic heritage.

With his shorter arms and lower center of gravity, he was well-suited to executing all of the various throws and holds with great effectiveness. Yet as formidable of a fighter as Ken was, his skills would be a last resort under the current dilemma, when enemies could lash out of the dark with bullets at any given moment.

Joining Ken at his side, Gregory peered through his own night vision goggles and began looking for any hint of the attackers. Everything looked still, and a tense silence fell over the area.

Gregory felt a deep unease. He cast a glance skyward, relieved to see nothing but the moon, stars, and slow-drifting clouds.

"I think we may be up against Orcas," Gregory said. He paused for a moment, before adding. "And something else."

"Orcas are more than enough of a problem," Ken replied under his breath. "What else is there?"

"Some biological experiment, I think," Gregory explained. "But we got attacked by winged creatures."

"Winged creatures?" Ken asked.

Gregory heard the incredulity in the other man's voice. He did not fault Ken, as the claim sounded like something right out of a movie.

"I saw one of them from pretty close, it killed one of my men.

They're winged, organic, and very ugly," Gregory said. "Just make sure everyone keeps an eye on what might be above them, as well as around them."

"On top of possible Orcas," Ken muttered, with an air of great frustration.

After disseminating some further instructions and warnings to the other militia group leaders, the two men settled down into an extended watch. A couple of times, bursts of gunfire erupted from other members of the militia. Each time proved to be the result of nervous reactions to perceived movements among the trees. In such a tense environment, even those with training could become susceptible to the flicker of a shadow.

With nothing visual detected, and no incoming fire, there was nothing to help Gregory determine the enemy's current position. Checking with the other militia positions, he found the same situation everywhere. There were no signs of the winged entities either.

As the night wore on, Gregory got the unpleasant feeling that the winged entities and operatives firing on the militia positions had accomplished their aims. He suspected they were not seeking an all-out engagement. Rather, they were keeping the large force of fighters squarely in place, effectively pinned down.

Whatever the enemy's true mission objective was, it involved something located away from the positions that the men and women with Gregory had taken. He could not fathom what it might be, as there was nothing of great strategic value in the vicinity. Yet inside his heart, he knew an important enemy operation was still underway, even as he continued looking out for signs of winged monsters.

SETH

With the additions of Rowan and Christa, Seth's group headed back into the woods. Wishing to get to Christa's parents as soon as possible, they chose to go largely unencumbered.

Not wanting to leave their supplies out in the road, if anything unexpected happened to the convoy site while they were gone, Seth and his friends deposited most of what they had gathered in a brush-concealed stash located just inside the tree line. As Raymond explained it to the others, it was not just a matter of drones they had to be concerned with. There was also the strong possibility of people living in the immediate area being drawn to the halted column of vehicles.

It could not be ruled out that any newcomers would turn to looting. With so many vehicles fully intact and loaded up with supplies, the column presented a tantalizing opportunity to anyone struggling in such a time of disruption and hardship.

There did not seem to be any formal security in place to stop scavengers either. During all the time Seth and the others had been gathering supplies, there had not been one sign of the sheriff, deputies, or any of the police officers who had been in charge of the column. Most had probably died in the drone strikes on the front and rear of the column, but Seth would have thought that a few officers or deputies would have escaped the carnage.

Twilight had ebbed, and the shadows beneath the forest canopy had grown and intertwined with the young night. But at the present all were in better spirits, especially Seth as he walked through the trees alongside Christa.

As dire as their circumstances were, he could not believe his good fortune in finding himself in a position to be of help to her. Taking nothing for granted, he intended to enjoy the moments with her for as long as they lasted.

He knew she would be riding with her parents and others down the highway soon enough. Seth doubted that he and his friends would be taking Rowan's father up on his offer to go along with them. Casting a sideways glance and taking in her profile, Seth knew he would do anything that he could for her.

Catching him looking in her direction, Christa smiled back. Her eyes seemed to sparkle.

Knowing he was blushing, and feeling a little sheepish at being caught, he grinned and took his eyes away. The echoes of her radiant smile filled his mind and spurred his heart to beat faster. His next steps felt lighter, as a sensation of weightlessness came over his knees.

The immersion into pleasant thoughts proved to be fleeting, scattered harshly from his mind a second later as the distant sounds of gunfire rang out in the night. Seth and Christa hunched down in reflex, and the group came to an abrupt stop.

Everyone remained still in the aftermath, listening carefully. More gunfire sounded a few moments later, this time coming from several weapons firing together.

"That's a good distance from here," Raymond said, keeping his voice low. "Definitely automatic rifles though. I can tell that much."

Any disturbance was enough to spike his anxiety, but as Raymond indicated, the shots did not sound like they were close. He cringed again as more gunfire rang out. The short bursts were just a prelude to the largest and longest eruption yet, which occurred within a few moments.

"Sounds like there's a lot of shooters involved," Jonathan said from where he and Annika had knelt down by a wide tree trunk.

"Seems like whatever it is, it is escalating too," Annika observed.

"I say we get done doing what we need to do, before anything gravitates this way," Raymond said. "Like I said, those are automatic weapons. I don't think they're hunting deer. Let's get moving."

Standing back up, Raymond did not have to gauge consensus. Everyone straightened up at his words, and the group started forward at his lead again.

The shots in the distance told of a firefight going on somewhere in the darkness. Seth wondered who the combatants were, but he worried that it was related in some way to the attack on the convoy.

The woods immediately surrounding his group remained quiet. As they proceeded, Seth took in controlled breaths of air, working to steady his rattled nerves.

The sooner they were on their way to Madison, the better, even if they had to walk the entire distance. He listened to the sounds of their footsteps crunching on pine needles and twigs, and slowly began to relax.

He had not gotten settled back down for long when, to the right, some movements out of the corner of his eye caught his attention. He turned his gaze towards the motion, and saw something small and dark, perhaps bat-sized, flitting among the trees less than twenty paces away.

A metallic glint raised his curiosity further as the winged form crossed through a beam of moonlight. The thing appeared to hover in place for a few moments before moving off into the deeper shadows.

Pondering a way to describe the strange thing, he thought about telling the others about what he saw, but did not have much time to ponder the odd phenomenon. An unwelcome interruption manifested out of the shadows less than a minute later. Seth flinched. It seemed as if the darkness itself was moving.

"Everyone stay right where you are! Hands in the air!" a loud, harsh-sounding voice barked, breaking the stillness.

"Your path ends right here, you traitorous bastards!" growled a helmeted figure, standing squarely in the path of the group, with the barrel of a submachine gun leveled towards them. "You are all going on a little trip north with us, and I strongly suggest you cooperate."

Seth's heart sank precipitously. His blood ran cold as he saw several other armed individuals in dark attire emerging from places of concealment. All had weapons at the ready, and were wearing helmets and night vision goggles. Looking around, Seth saw that his group was completely surrounded. There was no use trying to run.

A clammy chill came over him as he looked down and saw a red dot in the center of his chest, moving ever so slightly. For a moment, it caused him to forget to breathe. He knew very well what the laser dot represented. Similar red marks were trained on every member of his group.

"Hands in the air, now! All of you!" commanded the first trooper who had spoken. "No heroes here, or you will regret it!"

One by one, Seth and his friends had their hands bound behind their backs with plastic ties. He grimaced as the trooper securing him pulled the plastic loop tight on his wrists.

"Noooo!" Christa shouted fearfully, struggling furiously with her bindings.

Seth knew she was thinking of her parents, who were undoubtedly close, but he feared what the troopers would do to her. His concern for her overwhelming his own fears, he tried taking a step towards her. He was yanked back hard before he had completed one stride.

"You want to get hurt boy?" the trooper behind him queried in a tone thick with warning.

With swift precision, one of the other troopers gagged Christa, stifling her cries. Her eyes gleamed with fear..

"Anyone else got anything to say?" one of the troopers asked in a snide tone. "No? Didn't think so. If you get the itch we'll stuff your mouths like her."

"You kids caused us a lot of trouble, but now you'll be answering for it," the trooper directly ahead of them, apparently the leader of the squad, told the group of captives. His voice rose as he addressed his own men. "Alright, let's move out! We've got zero twenty hours to get to the extraction point."

Seth felt a firm grip on his shoulder, just before he was unceremoniously shoved forward. He almost tumbled over, but somehow kept his footing beneath him. In the dark he could not see much as the troopers led them away.

His hopes sank ever lower as they walked through the dark forest. Seth knew inside his heart that the troopers were from the UCAS. Similar to the matter involving the gunshots they heard in the distance, he suspected there was no coincidences between the presence of the troopers and the recent drone strike on the convoy.

A feeling of icy dread began growing within him. Thinking upon the words of the squad's leader, Seth began to suspect that the drone strike had a dedicated purpose behind it, one that involved him, Jonathan, Annika, and Raymond.

If that was indeed true, then many had died that day because Seth and his friends happened to be in the convoy. Not ready to deal with the implications, he shoved the thought from his mind before a wave of guilt could consume him. The thought that anyone died because of him was a torment that he was in no condition to face.

As for Christa and Rowan, the two simply had the misfortune of being with them when they were captured. A good young guy and the girl of his dreams were now squarely in harm's way due to their association with Seth and his friends. The bitter thoughts sprouted heavy feelings of blame that Seth could not hold back, sending his mind and heart reeling.

URIA

"Today, we make our presence known. We make our strength known. We will show them that we can seize control if we so choose," Carlton stated in a relaxed, confident fashion. He gazed out of the upper story window, which afforded him a high vantage looking out over a large swathe of the city.

"You not wish us to fight?" Uria asked. The An-Ki leader was surprised and disappointed that his clan was being kept back from the looming attack.

Carlton shook his head, and glanced towards him. "No, this shall be a quick and bold demonstration. An exercise of power that will make a definitive, irrefutable statement on our part."

Uria did not understand Carlton's intent. There was no question that he and the other members of his clan were the strongest warriors available for the enigmatic figure to use.

It had been the An-Ki who had brought one gang after another under firm obedience to Carlton. Uria and his ilk had coated the streets of the city with the blood of those who defied Carlton's outreach to unify the gangs towards a common purpose.

Behind Uria, Zeyya was silently fuming, though she said nothing. Uria could feel her deep anger and resentment at being denied the chance to take part in what looked to be a colossal effort.

All morning, Carlton had pointed out to them the number of gang leaders who were heading into the elongated building that he called a warehouse. He had also pointed out the various places where a van, an individual, or a car marked positions where their enemies were keeping watch over the proceedings.

"We are offering them tempting prey," Carlton had commented, a short time earlier. "This is nothing more than setting the bait. The police are gathering, and they will soon be attacking in great force.

"We have given them a tantalizing prize, one they cannot resist. They will act in strength to seize that prize, which is precisely what I want them to do. Soon, you both will see everything happen as I have said … and then we will spring the great trap on them. Let them swarm right into the jaws of it. They go to their own destruction."

Though Carlton's tone had remained even and his face impassive throughout his steadfast observation from the window, Uria could sense that he relished what was about to happen. It made him all the more disappointed.

"It looks like they are committing to their course," Carlton announced, the trace of a smile showing on his lips. "Exactly as intended."

Uria's eyes widened at the sudden flurry of activity that broke out just after Carlton spoke. Vehicles rushed in from every direction, blocking all the streets leading to the warehouse.

From some of the vehicles and other places of concealment, a large number of helmeted figures armed with guns converged on the warehouse building from every direction. In the air above, a pair of helicopters drifted in and hovered over the rapidly developing scene.

"They think they have the heads of the strongest gangs in Troy trapped now," Carlton said, watching the unfolding activity. The hint of a smile playing on his lips grew more substantial. "They are about to get a very, very big surprise. Troy's rapid reaction force has never faced a situation like the one about to unleash upon them."

The police force ringed the warehouse and had secured all of the approaches to it, but those under Carlton's guidance had formed an even bigger ring. With the law enforcement elements engaged in their operation and committed to their course, the jaws of a much larger trap closed.

Pouring into the streets, popping out of windows and taking up positions everywhere that Uria looked, were hundreds upon hundreds of well-armed gang fighters. Even as the first shots rang out, a thunderous explosion shook the ground and buildings in downtown

Troy as the warehouse and everything in it was incinerated.

"You kill the leaders? Of gangs?" Uria asked, viewing the incredible display of power. He watched the massive fireball mushrooming upward in a state of both fear and fascination.

"Tunnels, my big friend, tunnels," Carlton said. "Yes, a few men were sacrificed, but the leaders of the gangs are all safely underground."

A few of the police vehicles exploded, and a cacophonous storm of gunfire broke out. The police units deployed for the assault on the warehouse suddenly found themselves in a terrible predicament. Surrounded and assailed by a much larger force of gang-affiliated fighters, the police officers lost all initiative and were put on the defensive.

Gunmen from a host of high positions all around the warehouse site, from upper story windows to rooftops, fired down upon the troopers. The eruption of fire from lofty heights made it extremely difficult for the troopers to find cover.

Even the troopers who had taken up positions on the tops of a few buildings were rendered exposed and vulnerable. Everywhere Uria looked, police officers dropped to the ground dead or wounded, as bullets from the mass of gang fighters struck them down.

Booms that shook the windows drew Uria's eyes upward. He looked just in time to see the spray of debris from two destroyed helicopters. He watched the chunks of the aircraft raining down into the streets below.

"What weapon?" Uria asked Carlton, wanting to know what could possibly unleash such power, enough to turn helicopters into wreckage in an instant.

"Rocket-propelled grenades, which are taking care of some of the armored vehicles below too," Carlton explained. "Troy might have succeeded in disarming the average man and woman in the street these past years, but the gangs have been building strength in arms for a long time. When you already deal beyond the boundaries of what is legal, there is no limit to what you can acquire."

The fighting in the streets did not last long. With nowhere to take cover and no escape routes, the police troopers caught within the trap were overwhelmed and cut down in swift fashion. Uniformed bodies littered the streets in abundance all around the warehouse.

The gang-affiliated attackers soon began melting back into the city. Black smoke filled the skies from the fires of burning vehicles and the destroyed warehouse. The deafening layers of gunfire ebbed away until an eerie calm filled the area.

"I would say that they did not expect several thousand gunmen to emerge right behind them," Carlton said. He turned towards Uria. "This would not have been possible without the full cooperation of the gangs. And that would not have happened without the help of your clan."

Uria did not answer, as his thoughts were churning. He could only wonder at the ambitions of the figure he and his kind had assisted. Carlton was an enigma, and the huge demonstration of power instilled an even greater respect toward him.

He glanced back towards Zeyya. The resentment and fury were gone from her eyes. The look she cast Uria was one of excitement and elation.

Looking back towards Carlton, he asked, "When do we hunt next?"

Carlton smiled. "There is much more to come. What was done today is just a part of an even larger purpose. It must be given time to accomplish its aims, but do not worry. You will hunt again soon."

Uria nodded, eager to feel the cool night air rushing past his muzzle and the thrill of chasing human prey. Not only were the An-Ki hunters, but they were naturally superior to the humans they had kept a distance from for so long.

He could only marvel that it had taken a transition into another time and place to understand what should have been obvious all along. What remained was to find a path to become a master of the humans. The notion of forming a new, unprecedented type of clan was taking root inside his mind.

Uria had already seen the possibilities of that path in the eyes of doomed men. Those that Uria, Zeyya, and the others had hunted down in the streets of Troy would have submitted to anything asked of them, if they had been allowed to live. Terror bred obedience, and there was no doubt the humans in the gangs could be made subservient to the An-Ki.

Further, humans could be maneuvered and manipulated, as Carlton had demonstrated so effectively just moments before. Using his wit, Carlton had formed one group of humans to destroy another, one that he had deftly lured into a lethal trap.

Uria looked back to Zeyya again, and shared a smile with her. There would be much to talk about later, but he knew Zeyya shared his disposition on the matter of humans. He wondered what she would think of his nascent vision, regarding a new kind of clan that included both An-Ki and humans.

The only concern remaining was Carlton, who was something far more than a man. Uria wondered what he would think of any initiative taken by the An-Ki to create a kind of clan where the An-Ki were the chieftains and humans were the followers.

His instincts told him Carlton would have no objections to the way that Uria and Zeyya felt. But he also knew that the cryptic figure would not compromise or put at risk his own plans, whatever they ultimately were.

Uria would just have to find a way to bring the two things into harmony: taking authority over a body of humans, while doing nothing to disrupt Carlton's aims. First, though, he had to discover more about the nature of Carlton's plans, which were steeped in mystery.

Carlton had already hinted at something even larger, indicating the existence of a bigger plan that the day's spectacular events were merely a part of. The thought of what Carlton was ultimately working towards was highly intriguing, if not a little unsettling.

The uncertainty ahead was another compelling reason for Uria to grow the strength of his clan and expand their influence in the human world. There might well come a day when Uria and the An-Ki would have to fend for themselves, and he wanted to be as prepared as possible.

"Your expression tells me you are thinking about something of a serious nature," Carlton said, staring towards him.

Uria nodded, but said nothing in response.

Carlton smiled, columns of smoke wafting skyward beyond the

windows at his back. "It is good to see ambition rise, and new ideas take form. When you are ready, I invite you to talk to me about it."

"I will," Uria replied, trying to keep his face from showing the surprise and reticence he felt, perceiving that Carlton had just looked into his very thoughts.

XAVIER

"Chaos is breaking out all across that city!" Xavier snapped at the TTDF commanders who had been hastily summoned. "We have rioting going on in many sections of Troy, and there is little response to quell it. Not a surprise, when a few hundred law enforcement officers die in one day, and over a thousand more are incapacitated by their wounds! That's an effective loss of nearly fifteen hundred in just one day!"

"We have several strong assets nearby. What would you have us do?" one of Xavier's officers questioned him.

"Have us do?" Xavier asked, in a tone of incredulity. "What did we expect out of a long-existing situation where gang members outnumbered police officers fifty to one? And that was long before the rebellion in the south and midwest. They see us as weak, and they are asserting themselves."

"They were never united like this," another officer commented. "This is unprecedented."

"I don't care how things were in the past, the gangs in Troy are certainly united now!" Xavier growled. "That's over a hundred-thousand strong enemy force embedded in just one city!"

"There are similar numbers of gang members in Yorvik and Santo Reina," another officer interjected. "But we don't know if they've come together like they have in Troy."

"Which is why we will have to deploy all available assets, and that is not nearly enough if the gangs decide to erupt within the other cities," Xavier said. He did not even want to begin to think of the chaos if the gangs began working together in the two largest metropolitan areas of the UCAS. "No, we need outside help, and we are going to need it fast. Get me General Brennan, now! He'll be on his secured line in the White Pyramid."

Xavier put his hands on his hips. Waiting with a tense look on his face, he watched the large rectangular screen on the wall impatiently. After another minute passed, an older man with short-cropped gray hair, in a uniform bearing a host of medals, came into view.

"I am sure you have been briefed on what has happened in Troy, General Brennan," Xavier stated, eschewing formalities in the urgency of the situation.

"Yes, and it was not a welcome development," the general replied, somber in face and tone. "This represents a turn of events that we did not expect to be dealing with."

"Do we have assets that can be spared to help pacify the cities, if this fire spreads?" Xavier asked. "Gang violence we were prepared for. Gangs working together as a unified army is something entirely different."

"We are doing all we can to maintain adequate strength along the new borders," General Brennan replied. "The rebel provinces could attack at any time. They are not reacting well to the sea blockades we have put into place on the east and west coasts."

"It is fortunate we retained a considerable advantage in naval assets," Xavier commented. "Or I imagine what we're facing now would be even worse."

The general nodded. "We can put more pressure on the rebel provinces, and keep them distracted, while you tend to the situation in Troy."

Xavier shook his head. "General, we will be overrun if what happened in Troy breaks out in other major cities. We simply do not have the manpower to deal with more situations like we are facing in Troy. I need more security assets. Is there a mechanism for bringing in any assets from an international level?"

"There is," General Brennan answered, after a moment of thought. "I have been made aware that the new head of the Peace

Commission, Kaira Antipalos, has been instigating some new initiatives that may be of particular use in this case."

The mention of Kaira brought a calming effect to Xavier. Aaliyah knew Kaira personally, and the TTDF had already gone to great lengths to provide the young woman with a high level of security at the wooded compound close to Yorvik.

Though he had no specifics, Xavier knew Kaira had a very significant role to play in the Convergence. That alone told him she would be favorable to anything needed by the TTDF or Aaliyah. He anticipated no trouble getting cooperation from the Peace Commission.

"This is an inquiry I can make personally," Xavier replied. "The TTDF already provides security for the facilities where Kaira is now residing."

"I wish I could do more for you, Commander Gerard," the general replied. "This gang uprising is a very troubling development. We are spread very thin while we continue regrouping the military, and we continue to lose some valuable assets that cannot be quickly replaced. Just yesterday we had two more pilots defect with their I-22 jet aircraft to the rebels. Every loss like that is costly."

"I understand," Xavier said, feeling a spark of anger at the news of yet more defections. The rate had slowed to a trickle from the initial avalanche, but it was still occurring far too much for his liking. "The TTDF is stretched to the limit with the mandates to operate the detainment camps. Many of them are already nearing full capacity."

"Will you begin to use the underground facilities for detainment?" the general asked.

"Do not forget, we've lost control of many of those as well," Xavier replied. "A number of subterranean facilities have been rooted out by the forces in the breakaway provinces. We've had to move fast, and so have they. The transport tunnels between bases that are rebel held and ours have been collapsed on both ends."

"It would seem we will need the help of these new initiatives," the general replied grimly.

"We are depending on them," Xavier stated, matter-of-factly. "It will be the only way we can fully secure the UCAS, and begin to turn our attention to reclaiming the rebel provinces."

"I would like to be able to strike a heavy blow on the renegade provinces," General Brennan said, a glint of determination flaring in his eyes.

"You and me both, General," Xavier replied.

"If we are able to gain cooperation from the World Summit, there is one place we can quickly send them a message," General Brennan stated. "It has been on my mind recently."

"Where?" Xavier asked.

General Brennan described the location and assets involved. Listening closely to the general's proposal, Xavier liked what he heard.

He resolved to get the requisite aid from the Peace Commission as soon as he could. After suffering so many blows, it was well past time to deliver a hard strike to the upstart insurgents.

ARIANNA

While traffic was still fairly sparse for the most part, Arianna saw many signs that things were creeping back towards a more familiar state during the second day of driving. Their course took them west, and as they drove she was encouraged by the things that she saw.

Trucks could be seen heading both ways along the highway, as well as a smattering of passenger vehicles. To her eyes, it was like blood flow resuming through the veins of a body sorely afflicted. Just as life-sustaining oxygen was distributed in a healthy bloodstream, the trucks were undoubtedly reviving trade and markets so integral to a free society. The presence of the commercial vehicles, from box trucks to eighteen wheelers, were highly welcome sights and a testament to recovery underway.

The increasing level of traffic was a relief to see for other reasons as well. It significantly reduced the odds of another incident happening like the one she and her companions had endured at the bridge.

A few convoys of a military nature were also encountered during the day's travels. Flatbeds holding Lafayette tanks and other armored vehicles, along with large numbers of fuel and supply trucks, rumbled along the roadway.

There was nothing for her to fear from the lengthy convoys. The freshly painted silver blades on all the vehicles, trucks and armor alike, identified them readily enough. Arianna imagined that the UCAS government had never calculated so many powerful defections from the military.

Yet in another way of looking at it, the forces of the free provinces had not defected. Rather, it was they who were honoring their oaths in the truest sense. They were defending the original spirit of the UCAS against a rogue usurper attempting to destroy it.

The skies were not vacant either. She took note of a mix of aircraft plying the upper heights. A few private planes and lone helicopters marked the presence of some civilian air traffic. Military aircraft came in the form of a batch of attack helicopters, a pair of large transport helicopters, each with two main rotors, and a few fighter jets streaking through the upper skies.

There were a few places along the highway where armed men and woman were gathered just off the road. Usually the sites consisted of just a few vehicles and canopy shelters. Like the convoys, they represented no danger. If anything, their presence insured a safer highway.

Large banners with 'Galena Province Free Milita' advertised their nature. Arianna surmised the citizens in the region were taking measures to address the sort of highway banditry that she and her companions had experienced earlier.

After covering a considerable distance, Arianna and Quinn pulled the vehicles off at a highway exit late in the day. As most exits tended to be, an assortment of food establishments, hotels, and gas stations were clustered around the ramps connecting back onto the highway.

Leading Quinn's vehicle, Arianna was drawn towards a place that had been a large truck stop under better times. A huge parking lot sat adjacent to a building containing a diner and food mart, according to the large sign in front.

Two shelters, one in front of the main building, and another placed to one side, provided rows of paired fuel pumps with some protection from the elements. To her amazement, a few of the pumps were currently being used.

The parking lot, which she guessed had been filled with trucks in the past, now held what looked to be a huge open market. Canopies and tables were arrayed in orderly rows. A large crowd of people was present, perusing the offerings and strolling down the aisles.

After finding a place to park the SUV towards the outskirts of the lot, she got out of the vehicle. A few of the people glanced their way, and Arianna knew many more looks were coming. The An-Ki with her were both imposing and beautiful in their human forms, and it was hard to avoid drawing attention while among so many people.

"Stopping for a soda and a bathroom break?" Quinn asked with a trace of humor, as he walked up to join Arianna. He arched his back, and stretched with a wince on his face as Maureen came up behind him. "Ooooooh … the back definitely stiffened up during the ride."

"This looks like the place to stop," Maureen commented, looking around. "Quite the popular hotspot for this area, it seems."

"I'm just glad it looks to all be in good order," Arianna said, taking in the sights.

"Well, I'm going to see how well they keep the bathrooms clean these days," Maureen commented, with a chuckle. "Let's hope!"

"I'm heading inside too, I'll walk with you," Quinn told his girlfriend. He looked back to Arianna. "Are you going in?"

"I will in a bit, I really want to take a look around here," Arianna said, eyeing the market. "I'm kind of curious to see what's being sold, and what's being used around here to buy things."

"Good point," Maureen said. "Well, my bladder is insisting, so you go investigate and we'll catch up with you in a few minutes."

Smiling, she took Quinn's arm in hers, and the couple headed for the front door of the main building. Arianna shook her head and smiled, and then turned her focus towards the market.

Vailia and Godral walked with Arianna, as the other An-Ki followed after Maureen and Quinn. As they reached the first of the spaces in the open-air market, Arianna slowed down and began examining the contents of the tables.

Listening and watching everything that she could, Arianna also started observing the transactions taking place. It soon became apparent that the means of exchange were varied, and in some ways fascinating to watch.

Until the schism in the country, money had always been the norm for transactions. Now, it appeared to be the exception.

While Arianna saw some currency being exchanged here and there, most of the ongoing transactions were being done in bartered items. Concurrently, there was much more haggling taking place. Sellers discussed the merits of what they had to offer, while buyers countered with what they wanted to trade for the items they wanted.

Tools, fishing wire, ammunition for guns, and other items she would have taken for granted not that long ago were now premium acquisitions. Sacks and sealed containers of rice, beans, and pasta were prominently displayed. It was clear the bulk foodstuffs were deemed far more valuable than jewelry, fine clothing, or used video games.

Arianna watched with great interest as a gas-powered generator became the center of an impromptu auction. Several eager-looking people pitched the strength of their makeshift bids, and increased them, to a seller who looked all too willing to let the trade value escalate.

As discreetly as possible, Arianna pulled out her mobile device and began to take some photos and video footage of the market. Someday, she felt it would be wonderful to have some documentation of the transition period as the new nation took shape.

After years of living in a world where most things had fixed prices, she found it very interesting to watch the dynamics of bartering on such a wide scale. Most encouraging about it all was the general air of civility among the buyers and sellers.

More than anything else, the orderly atmosphere gave the most promise that the new nation would have a fighting chance to succeed. If people could work together during the hard struggle of the transition period, and not turn on each other out of a sense of fear or hardship, then the future looked promising.

A great nation had once been crafted and built out of a wilderness. This time, there was a much better starting place to work from. If people all across the southern and midwestern provinces could interact in the way that Arianna saw before her, the chances of success were more than excellent.

"It really is somethin', isn't it? Trade's making a comeback, and no damn taxes either," an older man nearby exclaimed, watching her taking the pictures.

Arianna looked over to the man, who had a kindly twinkle in his eye and smile. "It is very interesting. But I gotta admit, I'm still not used to a world where everything isn't set in dollars, though."

"It's all about value for value now, whatever two people agree on together," the old man remarked. He shrugged his shoulders. "That's trade, isn't it?"

"As pure as it gets," Arianna agreed.

"Some things about it are a little more inconvenient," the old man continued. "Having set prices is simple. I'll give you that. But I get the sense there are more possibilities, for more people. So are you traveling through?"

Arianna nodded. "Heading farther west. We're going towards Coranado City."

The old man's face grew somber. "You don't want to go too deep into that area. I've heard some bad things. Lots of problems with gangs and such in the area," he warned her. He eyed Vailia and Godral for a few seconds. "Even with big friends like you've got here."

"I heard that gang problems are in a lot of the cities, but I'm looking for some family," she said. "I really don't have a choice. I've got to try."

"I understand that. Family comes first with me too. Well, good luck to you, young lady, and to your friends," the old man replied, casting glances towards Arianna's two tall companions. He looked back out over the market stalls. "I best be off to find my wife. She might not be spending dollars much anymore, but I gotta watch what she barters now! Some things change in form, but not nature!"

Arianna laughed along with the old man, but as he was about to turn and walk away, a thought struck her. "Before you go, let me ask you a quick question. Are there hotels, or something like that open around here?" she asked him.

"Good news, there sure are, a couple right here in fact," he announced. "Just like this market though, it depends on what you want to trade for a night's stay there. Bartering. It's the norm for the time being. But if you've got some things to trade, you'll have a bed with clean sheets to sleep on tonight."

"Thank you. I could use a night's sleep like that," Arianna replied appreciatively. "It was very nice meeting you. Have a wonderful day."

"And you too, young lady, it was good talking with you," the old man said with a lively air, before walking slowly away, favoring his right leg a little.

Arianna looked back to Godral and Vailia. She grinned and announced, "We will sleep comfortably tonight."

"A hotel?" Godral asked her, with a puzzled expression. "What is a hotel?"

"A place where we can get a room to sleep in for the night," Arianna answered, even as she caught the strange expression on a bystander who had heard the exchange explaining what a hotel was.

Continuing onward through the market, she browsed the stalls for several minutes more, until Maureen and Quinn returned. The two wanted to take a little look around themselves, and Arianna availed herself of the bathroom while they browsed the goods on display.

Once inside the main building, she had to grin as she watched the women exiting the restroom casting upward glances at Vailia. With her significant height and athletic build, the An-Ki female certainly commanded attention.

Thankfully, the bathrooms had been kept up pretty well by whoever was running the facility. Once finished, Arianna returned to the market area.

She gathered everyone up and explained what the old man had told her regarding the possibility of formal lodging. Agreement came swiftly. Returning back to their vehicles, they drove the short distance to the cluster of hotel buildings nearby.

As the elderly man had told her, several of the hotels were operating. It did not take long to find a place that had some vacancy, and was willing to take what they had to offer.

Arianna was able to work out an arrangement for two rooms in exchange for a couple half-ounce rounds of silver, and about fifty dollars in the old UCAS currency. While paying for the room, she learned that the Galena Province was already exchanging the old currency for new currency issued at the Province level.

While unloading some of their more valuable supplies to keep watch over them, she smiled at Dedran as he carried a small suitcase and duffel bag into one of the ground level rooms.

The scar running along his jaw-line and torn ear were not flaws in her eyes. If anything, they seemed an intrinsic part of his rough-edged, yet friendly, character. She was glad to see the positive air about him.

"A bed. To sleep in!" he exclaimed, catching her looking at him. "Thank you, Arianna. I like these ... hotels. Ah, the bed. It is wonderful. So great. I sleep good this night. I like beds."

Arianna could not stifle the laugh that welled up in her. To the An-Ki, a common box-spring bed was an amazing development, one worthy of special recognition and commendation.

"You are welcome, Dedran," she replied. She knew that if their positions were reversed, she would have felt the same way.

"Arianna?"

She turned her head to see Kantel and Godral approaching her. "Yes?" she responded to the two tall male figures.

"Where will we feed tonight?" Kantel asked her.

"It is better to say, 'where will we eat tonight,'" Godral interjected, correcting his friend. "Not 'where will we feed.'"

Arianna grinned at Godral's focus on word nuances. It was another sign of progress in his path of assimilation into the modern world.

"This whole place looks to be thriving," she said to Kantel. "I think we'll have some good choices. Probably right over there."

Godral and Kantel turned over to look where she was pointing. Within walking distance was what looked to be a restaurant with some noticeable activity.

Whether or not it was still the pancake house that its main sign advertised remained to be seen. But its parking lot was largely full, and there were some handmade signs out front advertising several food and drink offers. From all indications, the place was open for business and being patronized.

Arianna nearly did a double take as she read the words 'beer available' on one of the placards. At that moment, Quinn was walking by, lugging a couple cases on his way to the adjacent room.

"Hey Quinn, look over there," Arianna said, flashing him a big smile. "Do you read what I'm reading?"

Quinn stopped, and looked for a few seconds. A puzzled look came across his face as he stared towards the sign. It was like he was unsure if he had read it correctly.

"Beer? In a pancake house?" he asked, after a few moments.

"There are definitely some changes going on," Arianna said, laughing.

"Maybe for the better, too," Quinn replied, chuckling and shaking his head.

"I say we head over to check it all out," Arianna said. "I'm starving anyway."

"I could use a beer about now. Give me five minutes," Quinn said.

"What are you all so amused about?" Maureen asked, walking up with a couple more cases.

"Up for beer and pancakes?" Quinn asked her.

"What?" Maureen replied, with a look of confusion that evoked a burst of laughter from Arianna and Quinn.

Arianna's feelings of amusement intensified as she took in the even more bewildered expressions on Kantel and Godral. The combination of beer and pancakes did not sound so appetizing, but Arianna found she was famished for levity. It was so good to just laugh at some simple things again.

Even if for a few seconds, it also felt wonderful to be three close friends once again. She hoped that the trip would go smoothly enough, and that they would find what they were searching for, but for now it was enough to share a few laughs and get some dinner.

There was plenty of time to ponder the days ahead. For the next few hours, Arianna intended on enjoying the company of her friends, both old and new.

FRIEDRICH

Frolicking amid a winter wonderland, two very different figures enjoyed a carefree chase. Seele bounded after Asa'an, kicking up great, powdery tufts of opalescent snow with his four broad paws.

The little Peri flitted just ahead of the big, two-headed creature. With darting shifts to the left or right, she deftly avoided the Orthun's playful efforts to bat her out of the air.

Adopted by Friedrich after the great battle against the forces unleashed by the Fallen Avatar Beleth, Seele showed not a trace of the raging, tortured creature it had once been. In some ways, Friedrich found himself surprised that the creature had not yet been allowed entrance to the White City.

"Asa'an!" Friedrich called loudly, right as Seele put on a burst of speed and closed the distance with her.

Asa'an tumbled head over heels through the air a moment later, courtesy of the Orthun's wide right paw. The Peri looked anything but graceful in the aftermath of Seele's well-timed swipe.

Friedrich chortled, seeing the scowl on Asa'an's face as she regained her equilibrium mid-air. The barks emitting from both of the Orthun's heads carried an air of triumph and excitement. Seele circled around beneath her, tongues lolling and eager to continue playing.

"You distracted me!" she retorted, with a sharp edge of accusation in her voice.

"I most certainly did," Friedrich responded, laughing and displaying a mischievous grin. "And it worked!"

"I am so happy I can be of such amusement to you!" Asa'an responded, darting aside to avoid being batted again by the huge creature leaping towards her. She glanced downward, and spoke firmly to the brawny creature. "And that's enough out of you for today! Time to stop!"

Seele sat back on his haunches in the soft, powdery snow, and stared quietly towards the Peri. Asa'an drifted down and alighted gently between the creature's two broad necks.

Reaching out with both hands, she rubbed and scratched the Orthun's pair of heads simultaneously. Seele emitted a sound deeper in pitch than a whine, but one unmistakably reflecting pleasure at the Peri's massaging touch.

Her stern expression crumbled into a beaming smile. She kneaded the creature's fur a little more vigorously, and pronounced, "You are such a good boy, Seele. It is hard to stay irritated with you."

"He is a good boy, without a doubt," Friedrich stated in full agreement, strolling towards the other two.

Reaching forward, he scratched Seele's broad chest. The creature's fur had grown considerably softer during the Orthun's stay in Purgatarion. It had also changed from a coarse texture into one holding a luxuriant sheen.

Friedrich patted the Orthun firmly, and announced, "You are looking the image of strength and health, my dear friend."

He received a wide tongue to the face in response, as the creature's left head leaned forward. The gesture was followed with a lick down the other side of his face from the Orthun's other tongue.

"See how lucky I am? I get double the affection with this guy around me," Friedrich remarked with a chuckle, as he glanced up towards Asa'an.

"He does have a big heart," Asa'an commented approvingly.

"That's my boy," Friedrich said in a low voice, savoring a deep feeling of serenity.

Friedrich smiled and gave the Orthun one more pat on the chest, and then walked a few paces beyond the burly creature. He gazed around at the rolling landscape, blanketed with snow of a luminous, light blue cast.

He had always loved the beauty and majesty of winter back in his mortal life. Like he had just seen it, he clearly remembered the unsullied, pristine look of a snow-draped field at the break of dawn.

Many times across the span of years allotted to him, Friedrich had paused to watch the timeless drift of snowflakes descending out of a starry night sky. To his eyes, the delicate white crystals always looked as if they were forming out of the air itself, perhaps the seeds of stars yet to be born.

What surrounded him at present was something much more vivid and magical than anything he had ever witnessed in the material world. The little bluish flakes drifted downward, limned in a subtle glow emitting from within. Each one was an exquisite gem by itself, and in vast numbers they formed a glorious cascade spellbinding to observe.

Though falling in an unceasing continuum, the snowflakes never accumulated to a degree that impeded movement through the area. That fascinating property of the crystalline elements always intrigued Friedrich during his periodic visits to the area.

Finding a region of Purgatarion that reflected a wintry atmosphere had been a most wonderful discovery during his earliest phase in the Middle Lands. Friedrich soon found himself making regular forays to the scenic region. The environment evoked the best thoughts of the world he had left behind, and hinted of a far grander one ahead.

Located a considerable distance from the western border, the snowy refuge was not touched by the shadow of abyssal threats. The enchanting place had come to offer Friedrich repose, and a sense of restoration, whenever he felt overly burdened in the depths of his spirit.

"So where do you want to go next?" Asa'an asked him brightly, as the radiant crystals continued to float down all around them.

Friedrich opened his palm, letting one of the snowflakes settle gently as it came to rest upon his hand. Looking so much like a delicate jewel, it did not melt at his touch. Tilting his hand, he let the snowflake slide free. He watched as it drifted slowly downward to join its luminous companions.

"Right now, staying here is just fine with me," he replied, smiling towards her. "In fact, it is more than fine."

At the moment, he felt like he was experiencing an echo of the ethereal realms beyond the White City. Relishing the peaceful, resplendent environs, in the company of two beloved friends, brought his spirit a pervading sense of harmony, one that he sorely needed.

Friedrich had seen far enough within the black depths of the Abyss. The horrors of the Ten-Fold Kingdom, the eerie stasis in the Void, and the shadowy realm of Erishkegal had given him more than enough to ponder and wrestle with since his return from the great quest.

It was a merciful blessing that Enki had finally been able to gain some answers regarding Erishkegal. The torment of uncertainty the powerful Avatar had suffered for so long had been lifted, even if finding answers had opened up many new questions.

Friedrich knew the phenomenon of the bedraggled human spirits washing up onto the shores of Erishkegal's realm vexed the Avatar the most. Friedrich found it a very mysterious and intriguing discovery himself. Who the souls ultimately were, where they had come from, and how they had reached Manzazu were questions that had no answers yet, as far as he knew.

Lights dancing on the far horizon drew Friedrich's eyes. Gracefully, the effulgent points flowed towards him with alacrity, just as a greater light rose into view, like the sun at the break of dawn.

Seele padded over to Friedrich, and Asa'an's gaze joined with theirs as they watched the approach of the celestial lights. Coming from the east, Friedrich knew their nature well before they drew close.

Bright, musical laughter filled the air, as the little spirits swooped and glided all about. There were about twenty of the small, shining forms in all, and Friedrich delighted in their merry presence.

Coming up close behind them, a towering figure of power and glory, was Metaraon himself. The High Avatar dwarfed Friedrich and his two companions. Even so, Friedrich knew the form that Metaraon displayed was only a fraction of the size the High Avatar could assume.

Friedrich considered it a special grace to witness the pure souls of children. The young spirits did not belong in the Middle Lands, as their everlasting homes were the realms beyond the White City.

Metaraon carried out some purpose of the Great Throne in bringing them into the Middle Lands. The souls of those who had passed within the womb, and infants and children who had crossed over well before the time their parents dreamed and hoped for them to have, the child-spirits were cared for in a personal way by the resplendent Avatar.

Any horrors they might have suffered in life had been wiped away the moment they were embraced within the enduring Light of Adonai. No cruelties, sicknesses, or other afflictions could ever harm them again.

The ones who longed to see their mothers and fathers were given the peace of knowing a reunion would come. Friedrich knew many of those children would become intercessors for their parents before the Great Throne, until the day families were brought back together and given an eternal home.

Those child-spirits who had never met their parents in a mortal life were given knowledge and understanding. For some, this involved an assurance that one day the broken hearts of their mothers and fathers would be mended in a glorious meeting. With others, especially those who had been unwanted, or done away with in the corrupted world of pain and sorrows, a deeper wisdom was granted, one that soothed all aches and sadness.

Friedrich laughed heartily as a few of the child spirits drifted up to Seele, hugging and petting the Orthun with bountiful enthusiasm. At close proximity, their forms were harder to gaze upon, for such was the tremendous radiance coming from within them. Friedrich endured the brightness gladly, and was filled with happiness as he looked upon the faces of jubilant boys and girls.

One little girl squealed with glee as Asa'an took to the air and swirled around her. Friedrich saw the exuberant joy reflected in Asa'an's face as she played with the children. Seeing the Peri more at ease with Metaraon near gladdened him further, reflecting a sense of belonging that he had long hoped Asa'an would come to.

Friedrich wondered at the origins of the specific group of young spirits before him. He had an interior recognition that they all shared some sort of bond regarding the physical portion of their life.

For the briefest instant, he felt a sharp pang of grief, thinking of the mothers and fathers of the children. The fact was that they did not have the perspective that he did, one imbued with certitude that the spirits of the boys and girls shined onward, and would never dim to oblivion.

He knew he would soon be pouring forth his soul in Invocation on behalf of those mourning parents, who yet lived in the world of sorrow and pain. But no feelings of sadness could be sustained while surrounded with such abounding light and love in the forms of the children around him. In each and every one of them was the image of Adonai.

Friedrich laughed aloud, watching Seele and Asa'an, the former bounding off across the snow-blanketed landscape, carrying a couple of children upon his broad back. The latter, with wings outstretched, stood on the open palm of a little girl, whose face was beaming with delight as she gazed upon the graceful Peri.

A couple of the child spirits drifted around him, and Friedrich's eyes widened as one of the boys who had been playing with Seele suddenly gave him a warm embrace. He hugged the child back, even as his eyes were filled with tears of happiness, and perhaps a little sorrow that he could not go onward with them to the undying realms they now called home.

While there was no question Metaraon brought groups of children into the Middle Lands for their own maturation and edification, Friedrich could sense something more to the forays. For those who witnessed the groups of child spirits with Metaraon, a beacon through the darkness was made brighter. The road to the White City was revealed a little more clearly, and the idea of reaching its great, golden gates became a little more possible, in the minds of the longing spirits dwelling within Purgatarion.

After watching the children playing for a little while longer, he felt the looming presence of the guardian creatures before he saw them. Turning about, he looked directly into the visage of a Qilin, whose broad head was surmounted by a majestic set of antlers.

Its body, covered in fish-like scales, held a beautiful sheen, shimmering in the blue light of the surroundings. Another of its impressive ilk was nearby, one with a pair of horns. To Friedrich's great surprise, the one before him had its attention fixed squarely upon him and his two companions.

He knew the robust, ox-bodied Qilin were wards of the innocent. All but the most powerful of the nightmares in the Abyss were wise to keep a great berth from the potent guardians. In the eyes of a Qilin, any native dweller of the Middle Lands would appear sullied and corrupted, for such was the purity of the celestial creatures, and their sensitivity to any trace of evil.

The Qilin would not harm any soul dwelling in the Middle Lands, nor would the guardian creatures tolerate any threat when present. Yet their appearances outside the eternal realms were strictly aligned with the duty to watch over and protect the innocent, pure souls like the child spirits.

Therefore, it was with the greatest astonishment and amazement that Friedrich watched the Qilin before him lower its massive head, and with the gentlest touch nuzzle him. He had no inkling of how to respond to the affectionate gesture.

Though no words were transferred, he could feel the approval in the creature towards him. Friedrich understood that it was acknowledging him in a unique way, as he was under no illusions about the state of his still-imperfect soul.

Waves of invigorating energy washed over him with every touch. The sheer size and power of the creature almost lifted Friedrich from his feet a couple of times, but the Qilin was careful not to knock him over.

The feeling pervading his spirit was electrifying. He wondered if he was getting another hint of the realms beyond the White City.

Finally, the Qilin drew its head back, and its eyes were no longer upon Friedrich. Though towering over him, the creature was looking upward. Another entity had joined them.

"Precious Soul, the tale of your mercy, and your courage, on behalf of my brother Enki is told in the heavenly realms," thundered the chorus-like voice from just behind him.

Friedrich turned around and beheld Metaraon looming far above him, framed by six fiery wings. He could not help feeling small and insignificant, gazing towards the gigantic High Avatar in a state of sheer awe.

"Adonai has great purpose for you," the High Avatar boomed.

"Radiate Adonai's Light for those around you, and remain strong in will. A time of trial comes soon for you and others, and a journey of worlds will be taken.

"A terrible darkness will cover the world you left behind, and you will be called to face great evil in a dire hour. Yet do not despair, and take courage, Precious Soul, for one day the light of your life will shine bright before the Great Throne.

"Do not let your heart waver, Precious Soul. Trust in all things to Adonai, and you will prevail when all others around you see a victory impossible."

Friedrich was astounded at the words of the High Avatar. It was overwhelming enough that Metaraon had spoken to him. He wondered how an imperfect spirit such as himself, one who could not begin to approach the resplendent gates of the White City, could ever shine brightly before the Great Throne of Adonai.

The implications within the High Avatar's words frightened him. He was still recovering from the harrowing experiences in the Abyss, and was far from ready to confront any great evils, or undertake new trials. The idea of facing something where victory seemed impossible to others was not one he was eager to embrace.

Metaraon said nothing more, and turned about, as both of the Qilin strode up to flank the High Avatar. Friedrich felt so tiny in their presence, and it was not a matter of visual appearances. While the giant guardian creatures and even larger Avatar dwarfed him, it was the sheer divinity reflecting from the three beings that made him feel so utterly small.

Like a burst of stars, a throng of luminous forms sped in from the eastern horizon. It was a merciful distraction for Friedrich, drawing his attention away from the foreboding tidings just given him by Metaraon.

The brilliant shapes became more defined as they drew nearer, revealing a group of Avatars. The heavenly spirits slowed down into a graceful glide as they arrived in the proximity of the child spirits.

The incoming beings had forms more akin to the depictions of Avatars that Friedrich had encountered during his mortal life. Beautiful female faces smiled with love upon the children as they neared the little ones. Each of the approaching Avatars held the appearance of human women, graced with stunning comeliness.

The Avatars reached out with arms having more of an appearance of flesh than the host of tiny flames comprising the powerful form of Metaraon. Only their single pair of wings held any element of fire, otherwise they could have stepped right out of any one of a number of paintings Friedrich had viewed during his former life.

The children ceased their playing, laughing merrily as each one was scooped up by one of the feminine Avatars. Friedrich trembled with emotion, watching the gentle, compassionate nature with which the Avatars handled the children.

They cradled the children close, in a motherly fashion. The children wrapped their little arms around the necks and shoulders of the Avatars.

On wings shining with flaming light, the Avatars lifted back into the sky, and flew towards the east, speeding to realms where Friedrich could not yet follow.

Metaraon and the Qilin headed in their wake, the High Avatar taking to flight, and the two guardian creatures moving swiftly along the ground. It was not long before Metaraon and the pair of guardian creatures disappeared from sight. Friedrich was left behind with his two companions, once more in the solitude of the snow-blanketed landscape.

Seele padded back towards him, as Asa'an drifted in slowly through the air. Both of them exhibited subdued manners, and neither made a sound as they reached him.

"No words can describe what I feel," Friedrich finally said, in a low voice.

Asa'an nodded, from where she hovered. "It is like we were given a little view of the realms beyond."

"I kind of thought the same thing," Friedrich replied, smiling at her, though the words of Metaraon were already beginning to rise back in his consciousness.

He shoved them farther back in his thoughts, wanting to focus on the better aspects of the experience. There would be time enough to ponder and worry about what Metaraon had told him later.

"Sometimes, you need a little encouragement. Don't you think?" he asked his friend.

The little Peri nodded again, with a sprightly grin.

"And you," Friedrich said with a lighthearted chuckle, looking into the dark brown eyes of Seele. "You are quite the popular one with children, aren't you? They really like you, don't they?"

Seele's reply came in the form of a boisterous, double bark, loosed with such vigor that his front paws lifted up from the snow. The Orthun's spirited response elicited hearty laughs from both Friedrich and Asa'an.

The three fell into silence again, sharing each other's company and gazing out together across the magical landscape. Encompassed by such a majestic, tranquil scene, and in the company of two dear friends, Friedrich did not want to do anything that would disrupt his experience of the snow-graced haven.

Yet in the quiet, his thoughts soon returned to the words of Metaraon. There was little question regarding the meaning of them, and Friedrich knew he could not set them aside.

A part of him desired to speak with Enki, as soon as possible. Perhaps the Avatar that he counted as a personal friend would have some insights on the matter.

While Metaraon's words also held encouragement, they indicated Friedrich's tasks and burdens were far from over. Something of an important and highly dangerous nature was looming just ahead.

ARIANNA

"I can order a beer ... at a Roger's Pancake House!" Arianna said, laughing and still amazed, even though she understood that the authority enforcing compliance on liquor selling permits and the like was no more.

"It's a free country ... once again," the woman who was the

server for their table remarked, her smile brightening as she voiced the last two words. She then added. "And maybe even more so than before."

"That's the way I like to look at it," Quinn said.

"Okay, I think I've got all this down," their server said, scribbling down notes on a small pad. "I'll be back with your drinks, and will get your orders in right away."

Arianna eased back into the padded bench, looking beyond their booth and taking in the crowd currently within the establishment. A little sobering was the sudden realization that it was the first time she had been in a restaurant since the rebellion had occurred.

Yet it felt so good to do be doing something familiar to her former world. From what she had learned from their server, her feelings were not much different from those of the local community. Seeking to maintain some continuity, they had made a concerted effort following the outbreak of rebellion to keep the hotels and gas stations at the highway exit in operation, along with opening a new outdoor market.

"Speaking for myself, it kept me from going crazy, and I couldn't be more grateful," the server had commented, regarding her community's chosen path of transition. "I was less than a year away from my marketing degree at the university when everything blew up. I'd been waiting tables while going to school, and wanted to get out of this job. But having it after the meltdown of the UCAS has been a life saver to me."

Arianna understood exactly what the server meant. Keeping some continuity going from the former times had undoubtedly infused a sense of stability and purpose that girded the community during such a chaotic and uncertain time.

As the server described further, that choice had not been an easy one. The restaurant had been forced to improvise more than a little to keep up a semblance of the way things had been before.

The normal process of getting basic supplies and food had been badly disrupted. But everyone had cooperated to keep the daily routines in place as much as possible.

The server's account indicated that it also helped that there was something more concrete to look to on the horizon. Word had come that the parent company, whose headquarters were based in one of the breakaway provinces, was getting swiftly reorganized for the new realities. It was expected that new suppliers would be established soon, though a lot rested on what new overall currency system was adopted.

From what Arianna could glean from a few questions, the news that had passed down to the server concerning that matter focused upon a currency based on silver and gold. Arianna was not surprised at all. She suspected financial experts in the breakaway provinces were working fast with the provincial authorities to create something that would offer a robust foundation to reassure new trading partners. Even better, there was not one word about a central bank like the UCAS' National Reserve.

Though Arianna did not speak the thoughts aloud, she wondered what the UCAS would do to meddle with any new currency put forth by the independent provinces. The stock market was still operating out of Yorvik, and many companies based in the free provinces were being dropped from active trading. In her view, the new provinces would be well advised to create their own stock market in the near future.

The server was not the only source of news in the restaurant. A television mounted from the ceiling near Arianna's booth drew her eyes more than once. It was broadcasting a news and commentary program that she soon gleaned was on one of the new stations cropping up in the breakaway provinces.

She paid special attention to a segment concerning the UCAS naval blockade that warded the eastern coast. The UCAS already had the west coast sealed off with its province of Calafia. The closure forced any goods destined for breakaway provinces to first be shipped to countries south of the former UCAS, before proceeding by land through the border with Tierra de Oro.

Naval forces controlled by the free provinces had been strong enough to shield the southern coastline. But any trade coming from Europa had to take an extended route to reach the protected southern ports. Any negative change in that situation would present a significant threat to the survival of the free provinces.

There was no question that the provinces were in a very precarious position. A lot depended on the focus and cooperation of the people. Arianna hoped that there were enough people with the strength of will to see things through to a victorious end.

But not everything was serious in tone for Arianna. She spent most of the evening enjoying the company of her friends, as well as some of the more talkative locals. The food, while probably not prepared exactly as the franchise once mandated, was excellent. It was also generous enough in portion to sate her considerable appetite.

To all outside appearances, it looked like Kantel and Godral were engaging in a pancake eating competition, given the multiple rounds of buttermilk pancakes the two huge individuals ordered. Vailia was not too far behind the two males, and expressed an affinity for that type of food. The server openly marveled at the quantity of food the three were able to consume.

Surprisingly, Dedran turned out to be the most talkative of the An-Ki, while Sarangar was the quietest. Like Arianna, there were periods where he became intensely observant of either the television or things happening within the restaurant.

Sarangar's brilliant blue eyes were lively with enthusiasm, and there was a youthful sense of excitement about him. Arianna could tell that the young An-Ki was experiencing a grand adventure on the road journey with her. He was absorbing anything and everything that he could along the way.

When the hour grew late, Arianna became conscious of a moment when she left was all to herself. She took the chance to look about, gazing at the faces all around her, friends and patrons alike.

By then, she had come to realize that the restaurant was a place where many in the community came together at the end of the day. It was something much more than a simple eatery. The restaurant served as the place where the people were coming to defuse and regroup following a day's trials and worries.

The majority of expressions she saw throughout the room were animated and spirited. People were conversing with those at sitting at other tables, and there was a real sense of community rippling throughout the dining room.

There was no question in Arianna's mind that these were the sort people ready to tackle the challenge of building a new nation from the ground up.

There were senses of hopefulness and anticipation in the air. The recognition felt invigorating and encouraging. Arianna found that she was looking forward to seeing what kind of potential her new country had.

In the near term loomed great struggles and danger, but the future suddenly did not seem quite so bleak. Individuals forged the components of any possible future, and Arianna was confident in what the people in the dining room would build in their lives.

She cherished the positive feelings, smiling as she turned her attention to those of her own local community. Quietly, she watched Godral, Kantel, Quinn, Maureen, Dedran, and Vailia, and Sarangar talking and laughing together, and she loved every single minute of it.

SETH

Another group of detainees was already being guarded in the clearing that Seth and the others were led into. One of them looked to be the county sheriff, while a female standing at his side appeared to be a deputy by her uniform.

There were three others with the sheriff and deputy. Two of them were rather intimidating in their physical appearance. One of the latter was a huge, angry-looking man with a long beard. He stood with a woman whose eyes shot daggers as she glared at the troopers.

To Seth's best guess, they were the biker types, with their sturdy attire of jeans, black boots, and leather jackets. Both of the figures boasted an assortment of rings and earrings, the small metal pieces glinting in the moonlight.

The last member of the other group of detainees was a bearded man who looked to be in his late thirties, or perhaps early forties. A look of dismay came over the man's face, along with a look of recognition, as he raised his eyes in the direction of Seth's incoming group. His eyes were fixed squarely upon Christa.

Seth looked over to her, and saw the look of surprise reflected on her own face. His heart sank further as he watched several tears begin streaming down her face.

He and the others of his group were then led across the ground to where the second bunch of captives stood. Surrounding the detainees, their captors kept up a silent vigil, casting occasional glances skyward.

Seth shared some glances with his friends, but was not about to risk the ire of the guards by speaking. He could see the nervousness and fear in their eyes, though there were strong hints of anger in the gazes of Raymond and Annika.

He wished he could offer some comfort to Christa. He noticed that she kept staring towards the man she recognized in the other group. Feeling helpless and awkward, he turned his eyes from his friends and looked off towards the trees.

The ordeal felt interminable, but lasted only about fifteen minutes until three helicopters landed out of the darkness. Seth could barely hear the rotors of the incoming aircraft, even when the helicopters were right in front of them, the moonlight revealing their strange, angled surfacing.

"Alright, looks like it's time to go for a little ride," one of the soldiers remarked to Seth's group. "But cheer up, you get to ride in three of our latest and greatest."

Seth and the others were pushed and shoved forward. Before he had gotten halfway to the waiting helicopters, they were interrupted.

"Sergeant Nelson! Found a trio of onlookers!" shouted a voice from farther behind. "We came up behind them, caught them watching you all."

"Everyone halt!" the sergeant snapped at Seth and his companions.

Complying with the directive, Seth looked towards the voice that had called to them. He saw several more soldiers who had just emerged from the tree line. Their weapons were trained upon three tall figures just before them.

"Want us to get rid of them?" one of the troopers asked the

sergeant.

"We don't have time to sort this out. There's room. Take them with us," the sergeant ordered the other troopers.

"Yes sir," the one who had asked the question replied.

As the three figures were led forward into the full light of the moon, Seth recognized two of them right away. There was no mistaking the tall woman and man he had seen in the woods so recently. They were accompanied by another man of great height and build, who looked every bit as imposing as his companions.

The woman's eyes fell upon Seth as she walked across the clearing. He could see the recognition within her face as her gaze lingered. To his surprise, she extended him the slightest of nods, and he had no doubts she was acknowledging his presence.

Seth and his friends were herded into the largest of the three helicopters, along with the trio of strangers. He sat down next to Christa on one side of the aircraft's hold.

After everyone was inside, the side was closed. A few moments later, he felt the lurch and upward lift of the helicopter as it took off from the ground.

A part of him hoped the Watchers would intervene once more, as they had the night his house was surrounded with hostile troopers. But as the helicopter set out through the night, the prospects for rescue slid rapidly.

Sitting with his back to the side of the helicopter, he looked across at the trio of strangers who had been added to their number. Both of the men were glaring hotly towards their captors, while the woman calmly stared back towards Seth.

He was drawn to her eyes, which had an unusual quality to them. Seth wanted to speak to her, but was hesitant to be the first to break the uneasy silence pervading the hold.

He turned his eyes away and looked towards his peers. Rowan appeared to be terrified, and Seth saw increased fear reflected in the faces and eyes of the others. Even Raymond had no hint of the bravado that was so much a part of him. At his right, Christa was looking downward, with a forlorn expression. Anger sparked within Seth at seeing his friends in such a dour state.

A sharp pang of despair drove deep into him as the flight continued. After living as refugees for so long, they had finally been given a chance to return home, only to find themselves hurled into the midst of a nightmare. Just a couple hours more and he would have been back in his own bedroom. The frustration that he felt at that realization nagged at him with deep bitterness.

His parents and cat Niles, for all he knew, might have already made their way back. Seth longed with all his heart to see their faces once again.

The extended separation from his family had imparted the harsh realization that he had often taken them for granted. They had provided so much for him, and Seth wished things could go back to the point where they were grounding him for some minor household infraction. So many times he had yelled in the heat of anger that he wanted nothing to do with them. But now he found that he ached to see his mother and father, and missed them terribly.

He even longed for the sub sandwich shop and the low wage job he had so often decried and moaned about. Seth hoped that his old manager, Guillermo, and co-workers like Marcie Jenkins were not in any danger.

He had not seen either of them in the refugee camp. Seth could only hope that they were in their homes or had found their way to a safer haven.

The small town life he had led and frequently lamented appeared much different to his new, sobered perspective. Far from the curse he had whined about, that life had been a great blessing, one whose nature he could not see until he had gone through the trials and hardship of recent months.

Now that he could finally appreciate his family and so many other things, Seth wondered if he would ever be able to live a life like he did before. Held captive in a helicopter, speeding through the night skies towards an unknown future, nothing about his world seemed to be on solid ground.

It was then that he turned to see both Jonathan and Annika looking his way. Both gave him partial smiles, as if recognizing his anxiety and seeking to reassure him.

Seeing their faces he was reminded that not everything had been taken from him. He still had the precious gift of friends.

Though unaccustomed to the practice, he gave thanks in the silent refuge of his heart to Adonai. He also petitioned the Deity to protect and see his friends through the challenges to come. He added further requests for his parents, Niles, and even Guillermo and Marcie.

His heart felt more at ease when he was finished. The fear and anxiety was still present, but he had reminded himself that there was so much more out there.

Seth turned his mind far away from his immediate surroundings. He recalled the rainbow-hued skies of the ethereal world he had witnessed. Like rays of pure sunlight breaking through storm clouds, the wonderful memories gave him some comfort as the helicopter continued onward through the deepening night.

ARIANNA

About mid-morning on the third day of the journey, Arianna's group finally encountered a formal checkpoint. A large metal gate had been put in place, one that could be raised and lowered through a counterweight system arranged to one side of the road.

At the moment the heavy gate was down. It spanned the large space between two walls of sandbags that helped provide some protection for a number of soldiers.

Though the troops carried weapons and had an air of alertness about them, they did not look particularly anxious or hostile as Arianna pulled the SUV to a stop. Nevertheless, she felt a little nervous at the sight arrayed before her.

One of the soldiers walked up calmly on the driver's side of the vehicle, and Arianna lowered her window. She eyed the small silver sword pendant at his collar, the sight of which instilled some confidence in her.

"Good morning, ma'am," the soldier inquired politely, in a thicker southern accent.

"Good morning," Arianna replied amiably. "Is this the border area?"

"Border is a little farther ahead, ma'am, but this is the edge of where the land has been deemed fairly secure," the soldier replied.

"Isn't Coranado City still ahead?" Arianna asked him, glancing forward. "I heard it wasn't part of the UCAS anymore. Doesn't that mean it is a part of a free province?"

"It isn't part of the UCAS, but we've got a lot of things left to deal with there," the soldier replied, his face taking on a grim look. "Heavily armed gangs for one thing. Getting rid of 'em is not much different than fighting insurgents. Hard to root out. Large numbers of 'em too."

"Would it be possible to talk to the commanding officer here?" Arianna ventured, thinking fast. "I was hoping to get to Coranado City, or at least close to the border, and I need to figure out what to do."

"I don't see why that'd be a problem, if you don't mind being patient," the soldier replied. "You can pull your vehicles off to the side. You'll have to go through a security check, and you can't take weapons with you. Nothing personal, just a precaution. The old regime is trying lots of different tricks these days. We've lost some good men recently."

"I understand completely," Arianna said in a low voice, seeing the deeper look in the soldier's eyes. Behind the strong outer façade, the young man was aching inside.

Putting the SUV back in gear, she pulled over slowly to the right and parked off the road. Following her cue, Quinn brought up the other SUV, and in moments the occupants of the two vehicles were gathered together for weapons searches.

The soldiers involved in the search cast Godral and the other An-Ki several curious glances, but they made no significant issue of the tall beings' colorful eyes. The search wrapped up smoothly enough, and the group was taken to an area where they could wait until the commanding officer was ready to see Arianna.

After about an hour passed, a soldier came to get her. He extended an offer for one more from Arianna's group to accompany her to the audience.

Maureen volunteered immediately, and the two women were led away by the guard. He took them to one of the tents set at the heart of the cluster arrayed a short distance from the highway checkpoint.

Seated behind a table within the tent, the commanding officer turned out to be a man of about middle age, with a round face and dark eyes. He greeted them politely when they were brought before him, introducing himself as Captain Johnstone.

"Our trappings ain't too fancy, but it'll do for now," the officer remarked. Like the soldier who had accompanied them, he also had a deep southern accent. He gestured for Arianna and Maureen to take a seat across from him at the table. "Make yourselves comfortable, and talk to me about your situation."

"Thank you for seeing us, Captain Johnstone. I'm sure you have much more important things to be doing than dealing with us," Arianna said amiably.

"Nothing is unimportant when it comes to the people who are going to build us all a great new country," he replied. "We're all in this together, every one of us in the south. Now tell me, how can I be of help to you?"

"My uncle was taken in a night raid by the UCAS, up in Venorterra," Arianna said to Captain Johnstone. "They targeted him. He was the only one they apprehended and took away."

She found the look in the captain's eyes reassuring. He had the kind of air about him that he was not the sort to put up with nonsense, but there was a warmer look to his dark brown eyes that signaled he was not cold-hearted.

The creases of worry lines on his forehead gave her some indication he was probably the kind of man given to deep concern over his tasks and men. She knew that she could easily be wrong in her perception, but her deepest instincts told her that he was an honorable soldier.

"I wonder if it was special ops, or the damned TTDF," he said, with an unmistakable air of distaste in the way he emphasized the latter possibility.

"I don't know for sure, but they took him out by helicopter," Arianna said. "There was nothing we could do to stop it."

"Important enough to take in a raid. That deep into free province territory too. They must see your uncle as a considerable asset," Captain Johnstone said, with a somber edge. "What's he got that they want so badly?"

"My uncle's name is Benedict Darwin. He had a popular late night radio show, called Sea to Shining Sea," Arianna told the officer.

"I know that one … It was the one with UFOs, the ghosts, and all that kind of stuff," the captain replied, nodding in recognition. A grin formed on his lips, conveying a personal fondness for the show on his part. "Listened to it on many a night, and believe me, it helped me get through a few long convoy drives too. Was able to get it when I was deployed overseas too."

"Yes, that's the one. And I wish he was back doing that show right now."

"Wish we could still get that show now. Nights get kind of slow and boring around here," Captain Johnstone commented. His tone shifted a little lower. "And he wasn't wrong about some of those conspiracies. Turned out to be absolutely right, in a big way, about a lot of it. More people should have taken the show seriously, myself included."

"No, he sure wasn't wrong about a lot of things," Arianna agreed, though she doubted the officer knew just how many things on her uncle's show had since proven to be genuine.

"So, back to your uncle," the captain said, shifting the conversation. "No doubt it was some kind of special ops. They wouldn't go after just one guy, and extract him alive, unless it was for a very good reason. Do you have any idea why they would have been after him? I don't think it'd be just the show and what he put on the air in the past."

Arianna decided to hold back the information about the gateway device at the heart of her uncle's troubles, at least for the moment. As willing to listen as Captain Johnstone appeared to be, tales of transcending time and bringing back non-human creatures from a distant past were not likely to get the man's cooperation. She had to be judicious in what she told him, but that did not mean she had to skirt all the truth.

"He's always been on the government's nerves, giving coverage to whistleblowers, conspiracy theorists, and that kind of thing," Arianna replied. What she said was not a lie at all.

"I bet he did annoy them a whole lot, come to think of it," Captain Johnstone said. "He was so right about those detainment camps. Those were being built the whole time. And the electronic chipping of everyone. That's happened too. No, there's no question they didn't like him talking openly about those kinds of things."

"What do you think they would be likely to do with someone like him?" she asked.

"Probably just let him rot in a cell. I doubt they'll kill him outright," Captain Johnstone said. "If they wanted him dead, they would not have gone to the trouble they did to take him alive. They would've just had him killed with a sniper or a drone strike. The way I see it, they may feel he still has some information that can be of use later."

"What in the world would he possibly know?" Arianna asked, needing to play along with the officer, though she knew the matter of the gateway device had marked her uncle forever in the eyes of their enemies.

The captain shrugged. "Might be something regarding one or more of the guests he had on his show. Who knows what they're after, in terms of intelligence? Could be just about anything."

"So how do I get in contact with someone in the UCAS, just to find out where he is being held?" Arianna asked. "Is there any way to do that?"

"Arianna, it's not like using a passport and going into a country to visit," the captain replied.

"I just need to try and find out where he's being kept, at the least," she replied.

"That's probably all you'd be able to find out, if you were incredibly lucky," the captain said. "Wherever they have him, they aren't going to allow visitors. And they probably won't even admit where they've got him."

"Where do you think they would take someone like him?" she asked, a little more insistently. She then added, "If you were to guess."

The captain sat back in his chair, with a pensive expression crossing his face. He looked to Arianna and Maureen, and crossed his arms.

"He would have been taken deeper into the UCAS, away from the border area," the captain said. "Maybe even Station Central, a huge underground complex that is the first major base beyond the border area here."

"I would bet it would be nearly impossible for someone like me to talk to someone there," Arianna said, dourly.

"Don't forget, the UCAS is still under full martial law," the captain replied. "Never got lifted. Which pretty much means they can do anything they damn well please. Do you see what I'm getting at?"

Nodding to the captain, Arianna looked downward. She did not really know what she could have expected to hear, other than what the captain just told her.

"I am very sorry we can't do much of anything to help you," the captain replied. "We have our hands full trying to settle things down in Coranado City. And we're dealing with regular probes and incursions by the UCAS too."

"What about the military forces operating closer to the city and border, do you think anyone among them might know something about the UCAS detention facilities?" Arianna asked.

"I have no idea, but I strongly doubt anyone will know anything more than I do," the captain replied.

"Then what about international aid agencies? Are they operating here?" Arianna asked.

The captain nodded. "They're getting some medicine and food into the city. For the most part the gangs are not giving them too much trouble because they're bringing food and medicine to their members as well."

"The international agencies are probably operating in the UCAS too," Arianna stated. "Maybe they are dealing with prisoners."

The captain's brow furrowed, and he grew quiet for a moment. Slowly, he began to nod. "It may be that they know something of detainment facilities. But your uncle was a high value target. It's not certain he would be kept in any standard facility. Those would be the type the international agencies would be given access to."

"Then can I go through, to get nearer to the border area? Will you allow that?" Arianna asked him. "I have to try. Talk to some more people in the military, and maybe see what the international agencies might know."

"You don't want to go into the areas beyond this checkpoint," the captain said emphatically. "It is a lawless region right now. Gangs are way out of hand. I find myself facing a small army here. There are thousands and thousands of armed killers in that city who are affiliated with one gang or another."

"Is the whole area under their control?" Arianna queried, worried by the news.

The captain shook his head. "There are lots of communities that have taken a stand, mainly in the suburbs. And our forces are gradually making progress. But to root them out involves a methodical process. It's not going to happen overnight. There are a lot of the bad guys, and they've got a whole lot of guns. Not to mention a few things beyond that."

"I just have to try," Arianna said, taking a deep breath, and releasing it slowly. "I have to see if I can find anything at all out about prison camps, or anything that might indicate where my uncle is being held."

"I don't mean to sound harsh, Arianna, but you really are grasping for straws in doing this," Captain Johnstone said. "And you're courting a lot of risk."

"But my uncle has nobody other than me, and those who have come with me," Arianna replied, more firmly. "Without us, he will become forgotten."

"I understand Arianna, but why don't you wait until things settle out more?" the captain asked.

"I wouldn't be going alone, if you let me go on into the border area," Arianna replied. "I do have some help with me."

"You've got some very big friends with you, from what I've heard. Any of them ex-military?" the captain asked.

Arianna shook her head and kept her expression from changing at the amusing thought of the An-Ki being in the military. "Not that I know of."

"Moving through that zone, anything can happen," Captain Johnstone said, with a somber edge. "There is no order to speak of. And we can't come to the rescue if you get yourself in trouble. You understand that clearly, right?'

Arianna nodded. "Yes, I know the risks."

At her side, Maureen added. "We all do, and we accept them."

"And if you go over to the territory controlled by the UCAS, you are likely to be taken prisoner and chipped," Captain Johnstone told her. "From what I can tell, they aren't being nearly as kind with those wishing to relocate to the UCAS from our provinces. If you thought the UCAS government was paranoid then, you may not want to discover how things are now … if you get my meaning.

"We try to welcome all those fleeing the provinces controlled by the UCAS, even though I know a few UCAS agents slip in that way. The UCAS looks to everyone going there with suspicion. I don't fault them in one sense … nobody in their right mind should want to go there."

"Like I said, I know the risks, Captain Johnstone," Arianna said. "Just let me through, to try to do what I can."

"Freedom means the freedom to make ill-advised choices sometimes," Captain Johnstone said, with a heavy air of resignation. "And you will be putting only yourselves at risk. Since you are not putting anyone else in jeopardy, or any of the men and women under my command in jeopardy, I can't see a reason to deny your request. You can go past this checkpoint if you choose to do so. You've been forewarned."

Arianna looked into the captain's eyes. "Thank you, captain."

"I wish I could convince you otherwise," the captain replied somberly.

"I know we seem crazy," Arianna said. "But I just could not sit around in Venorterra anymore."

"I am close to my family, and I can understand what's driving you," the captain said. "Feel free to rest here for tonight. The accommodations are not luxurious, but we can find you a place in the camp and give you some food."

Arianna smiled. "Thank you captain, that would be wonderful."

"At least I can do that for you," the captain said, rising to his feet, indicating that their meeting was concluded. He looked past them, to where the soldier who brought them was standing quietly. "Private Hernandez, after you take them back to their friends, tell Sergeant Fenton to have quarters prepared for them, for tonight. They'll be leaving in the morning with permission to proceed past the checkpoint."

"Yes sir," the private replied, with a formal air.

"Good luck, Arianna, I really hope you find where your uncle is," Captain Johnstone said, as she and Maureen stood up from their chairs and prepared to leave. "And I hope you can find a way to help him."

Arianna replied in a low voice, feeling the onerous weight of her mission. "I hope I can too."

BENEDICT

For the better part of the morning and early afternoon, Benedict and Royce kept on the move. Careful to stick to the route proscribed for them by Les and Walton, they avoided a couple of larger neighborhoods in the suburbs outside of Coranado City.

Occasionally, gunfire sounded off in the distance, but Benedict was taken aback at how quiet everything was around him. The roads were empty, and there were no signs of people.

A few birds twittered, and sporadic breezes jostled the leaves on the trees, but that was the extent of any nearby sounds. A deep hush was draped over the buildings and streets that the two men passed through.

Judging by the time and approximate distance covered, he estimated they were just over halfway to their ultimate destination. Never before had he desired to see formal military personnel as much as he did at the present moment.

The soles of his shoes scuffing against pavement sounded far too loud. His eyes kept roving back and forth, looking for any hint of movement. Once, his heart leaped as he brought his gun around in haste, only to see a couple of stray dogs loping out from the side of a building.

A couple of times Royce tried to strike up a conversation. As much as Benedict wanted something to pass the time and offset the pensive feeling in his stomach, he admonished his companion to keep silent.

Moving out of the open, Benedict and Royce took a short break in a small parking lot between two buildings. After drinking some bottled water and indulging themselves through a few minutes spent in cool shade, they readied themselves to continue the trek.

Walking with as quiet a step as he could muster, Benedict made his way to the front edge of the building. Carefully, he leaned forward to take a look up and down the street. Though he heard nothing, he was not about to take unnecessary chances.

Peering around the building, he found himself staring down the barrel of a military-style rifle with an extended magazine. The heavily-tattooed, stocky man holding it with his finger poised on the trigger spoke to him with a thick accent.

"Put the guns down, gringos," he announced, in a cocky manner.

Slowly, Benedict set his rifle down on the asphalt surface below, hoping Royce was doing the same thing behind him. Once the gun was lying on the ground, he raised back up carefully.

Several other men gathered around, all looking to be of the same ethnicity. They were very well-armed, with handguns, rifles, and even a few machetes carried within their group. Their faces and arms exhibited a wide variety of tattoos.

Benedict knew enough from their appearance to realize they were gang members. It felt as if he was standing on the thinnest of ice, as he took note of the hardened expressions on the men around him.

Their eyes were steely and cold, and he had no illusions about the severity of his predicament. The men before him would have no qualms at all about taking his life at the slightest provocation.

"You have nothing to say, gringo?" the man before him chided. "You come through our new turf carrying guns, and you have nothing to say? Where were you going, gringo?"

"We were going around the perimeter of the city, looking to head north," Benedict answered in a deferential tone.

"So what did it feel like sneaking across a border?" the man responded, exhibiting a trace of amusement. He then spoke in Iberian to the others with him, and all of the gang members laughed. Looking back towards Benedict, he continued, "I think we'll take you back with us. See what you know. We're not into letting people just pass through."

A couple of the men moved forward and grabbed onto Benedict and Royce. In brusque fashion, the two captives were loaded into the back of a pickup truck. Three gang members climbed up into the truck bed with them, while the brawny one who had spoken to Benedict, and another man, got into the front cab.

The throaty growl of an eight-cylinder engine filled Benedict's ears, and a moment later the truck started off down the road. It went less than a mile before it turned off to the right and entered a middle-class neighborhood.

From the larger yard plots and greater variance in the styles of the houses, Benedict suspected the neighborhood was a little older. Aside from the higher grass of the lawns, most of the houses and plots still looked fairly well-tended.

Moving through the neighborhood, Benedict noted that the atmosphere had the suffocating feeling of an occupation. Clusters of men bearing weapons loitered about here and there. All bore the heavily-tattooed look of Benedict's captors, and his eyes fell upon more than one machete among the weapons in their possession.

Many glanced in Benedict's direction as the new captives were driven down the street. There was no welcome to be found in the scowls and glares cast his way. A few called out greetings or made hand gestures to their comrades riding in the truck bed.

There were precious few signs of anyone that Benedict would guess to be residents who had called the place home prior to the gang infestation. A few faces peering from behind curtains in windows were about all he saw of those being subjected to the horde of criminal intruders.

The truck finally drew to a stop where a number of other vehicles were parked. The gang members in the back of the pickup jumped down, and turned around to face Benedict and Royce. Several more gang members gathered around to see the newcomers.

"Get down from there now, gringo, let's go!" the driver of the pickup truck ordered, coming around the side of the vehicle.

Benedict cooperated and got down carefully, followed a moment later by Royce. They were led away from the truck and down the sidewalk towards a group of individuals standing in front of one of the houses.

A man of about forty years of age, surrounded by several armed men, turned to regard the group escorting Benedict and Royce as they approached. His dark eyes settled upon the two captives.

"Piranha, looks like you picked up some new friends out there. What have you brought me today?" he queried in a casual, accented voice.

"Found these two gringos trying to walk through our territory," Piranha replied in the manner of a soldier reporting to a superior officer. "Both had guns. Wanted to find out what you want to do with them."

The other man was a little shorter in stature than Piranha, and a little pudgy in the face and belly, but his eyes were hard as iron. He stared at Benedict and Royce for a few seconds without a break in his expression.

"I am known as Lil Dragon," he said to Benedict and Royce. "I will decide what to do with you, when I finish with my business here. I was just about to render judgment. Observe the price paid for lying to me. This one had a stash of medicine he tried to hide from us."

Lil Dragon looked away from the captives. Briefly, he spoke in Iberian to a group of men surrounding an old man of about seventy,

266

with a badly-bruised face and eyes that glistened with fear.

It was clear from the old man's attire and appearance that he was not affiliated with the gang, and most likely came from the neighborhood. Though Benedict could not understand Lil Dragon's words, the effect of them was immediate.

A look of horror sprang to the man's face. He yelled and struggled as several gang members wrestled him down to the ground, holding him in place with one arm extended. To Benedict, it was like a pack of hyenas swarming an old, weary lion.

Watching one man raise a machete above the man's exposed upper arm, Benedict shut his eyes tight, knowing at once what was coming. A pitiful cry rife with agony escaped the man a second later, drowned in the boisterous, triumphant laughter of his tormentors.

Lil Dragon smiled, and looked back to Benedict. The expression chilled him to the core. "Don't be like these *chavalas*. He's lucky we didn't decide to bless him."

Benedict did not ask for any explanations. He did not want to know what brutal men like those around him considered to be blessings.

"They will learn fast, here," Lil Dragon declared. "They will all come to cooperate with us. Then all will be well. Those that don't do as we ask, then they will learn Diabolos is with us."

Benedict said nothing in response, but he felt the chill in his blood grow even colder at the mirthless smile on Lil Dragon's face. The way he had spoken the last words struck him in an odd manner, and there was a knowing look within Lil Dragon's eyes.

"With you, I sense some purpose," Lil Dragon said to Benedict. He then looked towards Piranah, and glanced back towards Royce. "With this other one, not so much."

A look was exchanged between Lil Dragon and Piranah. In a fluid motion, Piranah drew out a pistol holstered at his waist, put it to the head of Royce, and pulled the trigger.

The shot cracked the air as the bullet tore through Royce's skull. He fell to the ground and landed at an awkward angle, his eyes oriented skyward and absent of life's spark.

Benedict wanted to lash out as tears borne of frustration, sorrow, and anger welled together in his eyes. It took all the willpower that he had inside him to refrain from an outburst.

"I will let the First Word know you are with us, and we will go from there," Lil Dragon told his remaining captive. He then looked over to the group of men who had been involved with chopping the old man's hand off. "Rage, Steel, Loco, take this man to our finest guest accommodations."

Three of the men stepped forward immediately. One of them grabbed the upper part of Benedict's right arm.

Right before they parted, Lil Dragon's gaze bored into Benedict's own. The other man's eyes were those of a murderer, devoid of compassion and filled with threat.

"Don't try to be a hero," Lil Dragon stated in a low. "Don't try to escape. Don't do anything stupid. Cooperate, and we'll have no problem with you. You won't end up like your friend. Got it?"

Benedict forced a nod, still trembling from the power of the thunderous emotions gripping him. Jerked forward, he was pulled away as the three men appointed by Lil Dragon led him from the area.

SECTION IV

Dagian

"I hope that your flight went smoothly," Aaliyah commented to the well-dressed, attractive man sitting across from her at the elliptical conference table. His folded hands resting on the obsidian surface, he had joined the meeting only moments before, a late arrival to the proceedings.

A number of prominent figures listened quietly from their seats around the. Leading figures of banking, industry, and international relations were represented at the meeting.

Some were members of the Order of the Temple and the Society of the Red Shield. Ethan Forneus was on hand, as was Andrew Greenwell of the National Bank Reserve, and Abner Nithael of the World Interfaith Council. Dagian could sense the anticipation in all of them as the realization of all their goals drew closer.

"It went fine, thank you," he replied to her with a formal air.

Dagian could tell from the distinctive look in Carlton Tephros' eyes that he was another like Aaliyah. His gaze was steely, and the polite smile he carried on his face was mere décor. He was a soldier and servant of the Abyss, whether his ancient spirit commanded a human host like Aaliyah's did, or he was non-physical, and manifesting the form she now saw before her.

"Your initiatives undertaken in Troy certainly worked well," Aaliyah said. "You've provided everything we needed to testify on behalf of Kaira's proposed solution through the Peace Commission. The justification could not be more compelling, thanks to your undertaking."

"I had the people begging for any kind of help at all, did I not?" Carlton responded evenly, though Dagian could sense a boastful undercurrent to his words.

"It was just the forefront of an outcry in cities all across the UCAS," Aaliyah replied with a smile. "The people find the police impotent and overwhelmed, and they understand the military is spread far too thin. Any hope of security must come from without."

"And the people have asked for what Kaira is about to bring

them," Carlton stated.

Aaliyah nodded. "I must say that your methods of stopping the infighting among the gangs was rather inventive."

"An opportunity I took full advantage of," Carlton said, with an air of satisfaction. "The beasts came across me, and I turned them towards our purposes. It was not difficult to accomplish."

Dagian had little direct experience with the shape-shifting An-Ki, but in a way she had suffered dearly because of them. It had been the An-Ki who Benedict Darwin had connected with in the ancient world, and eventually aided in escaping the Flood that spelled doom for an entire world.

The Erkorenen, who had hunted the An-Ki in the past, had already been turned loose to hunt the An-Ki once more. There was no question Aaliyah wanted the wolfish creatures all dead. But Carlton had evidently gained influence over a group of the beasts, and was making use of them in a way that benefited the Convergence.

"Your reports said they were very efficient in gaining swift authority over the gangs," Aaliyah said.

"They turned out to be useful assassins," Carlton said. "What kills in the form of a beast, walks the streets as a man or woman. The trail for any law enforcement pursuit is beyond confounding. No investigator will make the conclusion that is the truth, and any that happen to know the truth are already with us."

Aaliyah grinned. "It was extremely clever."

"Yes Carlton, it was very clever," added the august voice of Gendry Resinger, from the farther end of the conference table. "And you certainly lighted quite the brushfire in Troy. To have the people demanding for us to take greater control is the best of possible scenarios. I hope that we are ready to execute that process well."

His eyes looked towards a man and woman sitting close to Dagian. Jacquelyn Redford, the Foreign Minister for the William Walker administration, and her second in command, a good-looking man with Central Eastern features, Imad bin Malik al-Dubbay, would be proceeding to Yorvik after the meeting.

"My staff is prepared to coordinate with all governments contributing troops and equipment to the forthcoming mission,"

Jacquelyn answered. "Once Kaira's solution is implemented, we will be ready to move at once."

"That is good to hear," Gendry replied. "Once the World Summit force has been deployed, the UCAS military can turn its full attention to this problematic uprising in the south and midwest."

Nods and expressions of affirmation came from the others around the table. Dagian could see that the rebellion of the breakaway provinces was on everyone's mind. It was an unexpected nuisance, large enough to create extreme headaches for the leaders of the Convergence.

"A blow to the insurgents must be struck," interjected a prominent banker to Gendry's right, by the name of Lawrence Voelker. "It is not wise to allow them time to consolidate. I have heard from more than one source that they are coming to agreement on currencies and a political system much faster than we anticipated."

"A heavy blow is going to be delivered, and perhaps Xavier is ready to comment on that," Samel Malkira, seated at the opposite end from Gendry, remarked.

Xavier nodded his head. His jaw was taut, and Dagian could see the TTDF commander was still seething at the discovery of Troy's gang uprising having been engineered by others within the Convergence. There was no question that the operation Carlton Tephros guided had been kept secret from Xavier.

The stress in his voice was noticeable as he responded to Samel's cue. "An offensive is being prepared in the west. Planning is ongoing at the Supreme Defense Command Center. Using the tunnels from the Sky Mountains, we are able to mask our true strength in that region.

"We have already gathered a force together that will overwhelm the rebels arrayed along their western border region. A decoy force is being assembled in Losantiville, Adena Province, to further deceive our enemy. We will act when we know the land to our back is secured."

"As it will be," Samel added, when Xavier was finished.

"The Numuus is being implemented now," Lawrence Voelker said, with a tone of concern. "An escalation of fighting may disrupt the fragile markets in a way none of us can predict."

"The rebel provinces must not be allowed to proceed unscathed," Samel replied, casting the other man a burrowing stare that compelled the banker to quickly look away. "The markets will rebound when the insurgency is reeling, and the UCAS is reclaiming its full territory."

"Which is exactly what Kaira's initiative will enable," Aaliyah said, looking around at the faces of those gathered. "So continue on course with everything you are doing now, and the Convergence will be realized very soon."

The banker nodded, appearing satisfied with the answer. Other expressions of affirmation followed, and after a little more discussion Aaliyah called an end to the meeting. She dismissed everyone but Carlton, Samel, and Dagian.

When the others had departed from the conference chamber, Aaliyah looked to the three remaining individuals. "It will not be long before we can set the Erkorenen loose in number to serve our ends during this final phase of the Convergence. Their numbers swell rapidly in the chambers located at Station Central."

"The breeding has gone far better than expected, I surmise," Samel replied.

Aaliyah nodded in confirmation. "The bodies of newborns mature within just weeks, and most kinds of Erkorenen produce multiple offspring. These discoveries have been extremely favorable for our purposes."

"You are already using them in operations, yes?" Samel queried. "I have been tying up a few stray ends lately, and have not been able to follow up on all matters."

"We are using them increasingly for targeted operations," Aaliyah answered. "It is not that we always need them, but we must forge them into a fighting force. The Enemy could breach the boundaries at any time, and having a native force capable of resisting Avatars is to our advantage."

"The Enemy is not likely to create such a breach, as we could also use that opening," Samel replied. "But all precautions must be undertaken as the critical hour approaches."

Aaliayh turned to look upon Dagian. "You must be most vigilant. Our enemies will seek to strike Kaira soon. Their assassin is still out there. You must not be taken off guard."

The eyes of the other two at the table looked towards her. In that moment, Dagian was conscious of the fact that she was the only fully human figure in the room. The three regarding her were ancient beings whose true forms were veiled while they possessed human bodies. As a dedicated servant of the Nether Kingdom, Dagian could not hide anything from them, including her own concerns.

"I will be ready for their assassin," Dagian replied. "I will be in spirit when the time of attack is likely, so that Kaira is warded on the non-physical plane."

"It will not be easy to know when that moment will be," Samel said. "Kaira is well-guarded within these grounds. I have little concern about this place. It is outside of here that concerns me. Our enemies will wait until she leaves this place to attend to some matter."

"Dagian is kept informed of any departures from the compound. She will be part of the shield put in place for Kaira whenever she is away from here," Aaliyah stated. "If Dagian is away from the compound on some business of the Convergence, she is ready to return at a moment's notice if Kaira intends to leave the grounds."

Samel turned his head back towards Dagian. "I understand you have been given more graces during your recent journey to the Nether Kingdom. It is a rare thing for a human to gain the favor of Amanzako. You also risked much in going there, when you are needed to keep watch over Kaira here."

Dagian nodded, taking note of both the praise and admonishment. She could sense that Samel did not feel the same way about her underworld sojourn as Aaliyah had.

"Amanzako was generous, and the gifts given to me strengthen my abilities to execute the task I have been given," Dagian replied. "My senses have benefited greatly from this journey. Know that when the thoughts of the assassin begin to concentrate upon Kaira, as they will when the assassin intends to strike, my senses will be attuned swiftly, like the sounding of an alarm."

"May it be so," Samel said, his dark eyes boring into her. "When Kaira is moving in the world, she will be at risk of attack."

"Do not underestimate the Enemy," Carlton said. "The police

commanders never perceived the gang unity I had been forging for weeks. Nor did they ever expect the ambush that I lured them into during broad daylight. The Enemy is capable of introducing factors you do not expect."

"Her task is to ward the non-physical plane and intercept the assassin on that level," Aaliyah said, casting a sharp, sideways glance towards Carlton. "Nothing more is expected of her. She must not be distracted."

"I take it that other layers of preparation have been made for contingencies?" Carlton asked. "I have been occupied in this world and do not know what may have transpired elsewhere."

"They most certainly have," Aaliyah said.

Dagian was relieved to hear Aaliyah's words. The pressure she endured was more than enough to contend with. Her full focus could be given to a specific assignment, without fear of overlooking something else that would see her meet a fate like Jibade.

"The way is being prepared for the Shining One to take dominion of all creation," Samel stated. "Even now, Ares prepares the legions of the Risen Throne for the final assault.

"We must each see to the objectives given to us as this hour approaches. Continue to set the brushfires, Carlton. Where there are pockets of the Enemy's light, spread the darkness to consume it. Your work creates pretext and opportunity."

"I will continue setting fires, have no worries over that," Carlton replied to Samel.

"All appears in good order, then," Samel said, looking to the other three.

Dagian noticed Aaliyah's brow furrow slightly, as she reached forward and picked up the small handset resting on the table in front of her. Samel and Carlton grew quiet as Aaliyah put the receiver to her ear.

"Yes?" Aaliyah said into the device. She paused for a few moments, listening with an attentive expression. Finally, she responded, "That is very good news. We will be on our way. Expect us in a few hours."

Pushing a button on the handset and setting it down, Aaliyah smiled as she looked to the others. It was not a look of merriment, but rather one of vindication.

"Looks like we have caught some of our most wanted trouble makers," Aaliyah announced. "That sheriff from the Revere home catastrophe. And those kids whose video caused us so many problems ... the same kids that the Watchers intervened for, in Madison."

"The capture is a sign of things to come. None among our enemies will escape our reach for long," Samel replied.

"The operation involved coordination between a team of Orcas and a group of Erkorenen," Aaliyah told him. "Using advanced miniature drones, the sheriff and others were found, and the Orca Team Nine saw to the capture and extraction."

"A coordination between a team of Orcas and some of our Erkorenen ... very intriguing indeed," Carlton remarked.

"Just the beginning," Aaliyah said. "But for now, I will need to leave to make certain that nothing goes wrong with the incarceration."

"You have my leave," Samel told her. "And take what help you need for this."

Dagian had no idea what help Samel was referring to, or authorizing Aaliyah to do. The answer came just seconds later.

"Accompany me, Dagian," Aaliyah said to her. "Kaira is scheduled to remain here on the grounds for at least the next two days and will be well-guarded. I will need you with me for the time being. Bring your new friends from the Order of Chikara, and we will make sure we are ready if the Watchers decide to make an appearance. We leave at once."

Aaliyah nodded to Samel and Carlton, rose to her feet, and strode towards the door. Dagian got up from her seat at the movement and followed her out of the room.

Daiki Oshiro and the other monks from the Order of Chikara had just been introduced to a number of particular Erkorenen. Amanzako had desired for the monks to be included in Dagian's tasks, and they were about to get their first major test.

It would not be their first given task under the new directive. One of the monks who had come with Daiki had already been sent with a small group of Erkorenen to the west, to aid in the search for a very important fugitive.

JOVAN

"I must say it was an impressive triumph getting a body like the World Summit to unite in purpose so rapidly," stated Austin Mendenhall, the charismatic host of the highly popular, early evening news and infotainment show that carried his name. "How did you manage to accomplish that in such a short time?"

"The challenges that we all face now are global in nature. It is important to understand that on a rudimentary level," Kaira replied. "It does the world no service at all if the UCAS fragments. In fact, it would hurt the world much more. My proposal from the Peace Commission addresses a need that serves all nations in this matter."

"The markets certainly have been in flux since all the turmoil broke out in the UCAS," Austin said. "I'm sure leaders in all nations are looking for some kind of stability."

"The markets have been very unstable, for a long time now. That has not been a good thing for anyone, you and I both know that," Kaira responded. "I think everyone is looking for some stability these days."

"From what I've seen, the stock markets of many nations have taken an even sharper downturn these last few months," Austin said. "I don't like to be an alarmist, but I have to say that the prospects of any true recovery looks pretty grim at the moment."

"What you describe demonstrates the great level of interdependency in this modern world," Kaira replied. "As I have stated, it is something that we must come to accept first, if we are to solve the kinds of problems we are facing today.

"It is simply a matter of dealing with new realities. This isn't the UCAS of other generations. Fundamental change has been taking place, and a logical destination looms just ahead. We have to operate in reality."

"So you are looking to work from the World Summit to develop solutions to bring more stability to the UCAS and global markets?" Austin asked.

"Yes, absolutely," Kaira responded, a bright smile blooming on her face that evoked an immediate smile on Austin's. "What I am working towards is a return to prosperity in a world far more secure than any other time in history. For the UCAS and all other nations."

"Bold goals, I have to say," Austin said, with a light chuckle. "Some might say that's over ambitious. But everyone I know says not to underestimate you. I have to admit, I've never had a head of the Peace Commission on the show before. I didn't really know about it until you started leading it. Having the Commission represented on the show is definitely a first!"

"Unprecedented times," Kaira replied with an amiable grin.

"Indeed they are," Austin concurred.

"Just don't lose heart, Austin, a new sun is going to rise on this world," Kaira said. "I'm telling you, it is all going to change, and everything we have been dealing with for so many long years will be things of the past."

"I try not to lose heart, but there are so many challenges out there. What about the terrorists who have overrun the southern provinces?" Austin queried. "That's another issue entirely, but it is part of the reality you are talking about."

"It is a tragic situation, and all of those who participated in the rebellion are in indisputable contravention of our laws in the UCAS," Kaira answered. "Nevertheless, we must search for a peaceful solution to this conflict, even as we bring stability to the provinces remaining under UCAS control."

"You are referring to the new World Summit Resolution authorizing the deployment of WS peacekeeping forces in the UCAS," Austin said.

"The Peace and Security Initiative," Kaira stated. "This initiative and the return of UCAS stability is in the interest of all nations."

"According to my understanding, this force that has just been agreed upon at the World Summit will involve participation by nations from every continent," Austin said. "Was that intentional?"

"That was extremely important to me, and I'll tell you why. It is important to have all areas of the world involved in solving a problem that affects them all," Kaira said. "A worldwide problem, and a worldwide solution. We are all in this together."

"Some critics have stated that one reason for bringing foreign troops into UCAS territory is that they will be more cooperative in carrying out difficult security measures," Austin said. "In other words, they will be willing to do some things that UCAS troops might have misgivings or be hesitant about."

"The UCAS is in a dire state of emergency. I merely wish to see peace and order return to the provinces. First in the north, and eventually across the south and midwest," Kaira said. "The new mechanisms that I have available at the Peace Commission can, in my view, be very effective towards that goal. This will be one of the first demonstrations of those mechanisms, and it so happens that it will take place in my own country."

"And if it all works as you envision it, you may find yourself with a world wanting you to lead it," Austin said with a laugh. "Kaira Antipalos, the world's first president, perhaps!"

"One thing at a time, Austin," Kaira riposted with a broad grin. "I think I have more than enough to concern myself with right now, in working to bring peace back to the UCAS."

"You do have your hands full, Kaira. A hard task for sure, and one that nobody envies. I must state that we are truly grateful for all of your efforts," Austin said with a tone of sincerity. He gave her a big smile, and after a pause continued. "Thank you for taking some time out of your busy schedule to join us today, and talk about a few things that are on everyone's mind."

"It's been my pleasure, Austin, and I intend to bring solutions," Kaira responded in a relaxed and amiable manner. "I want to see a new chapter in human history to take form, an evolution into something new and wonderful that embraces the greater good. If the world joins together as one, we will get there."

Austin then looked away from Kaira, following the signal to look into another camera. She sat patiently while he wrapped up the segment, giving some teasers to several other things coming up on the show.

With the show heading into a commercial break, the hush in the studio was broken with a sudden bustle. A pair of network contributors was ushered in for the next segment. After an audio technician removed the tiny microphone pinned to Kaira's collar, she got up and made her way towards an exit at one side of the studio.

Jovan greeted her warmly. "Well done! I think the message was conveyed very clearly. You came across wonderfully!"

Every day, Kaira was growing more impressive in his eyes. Her decisiveness and assertiveness were winning her more supporters by the day at the World Summit.

Her insightful use of the structure of the Peace Commission, in developing a large international military force to help bring stability back to the UCAS, was nothing short of genius. True worldwide cooperation had been achieved, with everyone understanding that the problem at hand was a problem affecting all nations.

Everyone was living in unprecedented times, and new solutions had to be developed. Granted, there were going to be a few in the northern and western provinces who would not be happy with the current developments involving the deployment of foreign troops on UCAS soil. But there would be no threats of the kind that had broken out in the south and midwest.

The majority of the populace in the north and other remaining provinces looked to the UCAS government to do what was necessary to bring security about. The polls overwhelmingly reflected a deep hostility towards the rebel provinces.

An effective system was now in place for malcontents, and it was paying increasing dividends. Those who became too vocal in their criticisms of the UCAS government, or tried organizing any kind of opposition, were whisked off to internment camps. Those facilities had been filling up quickly, as the provinces were culled of their most restive and uncooperative elements. Left behind was a subdued and cowed populace, one agreeable with every intrusion into their lives.

"You don't ever get tired, do you?" Jovan remarked to Kaira, as they walked down the hall from the studio.

He was amazed as always at Kaira's seemingly inexhaustible energy. Jovan knew she had put in a solid fourteen-hour day before the studio interview, yet she looked like she was ready for fourteen more.

"There's no time to rest, so much has to be done now," Kaira replied as they continued through the hallways, escorted by the security team that had been assigned to Kaira by the World Summit.

"Agreed, and believe me, I feel it," Jovan replied, not ashamed to concede that he did not posses her indefatigable nature.

"You do need to get yourself some rest, Jovan," Kaira said, her tone softening as a look of concern crossed her face.

Jovan smiled, "I plan on getting a little rest tonight."

"That is good to hear," Kaira said, as they reached an elevator.

"Tomorrow will come early enough," Jovan said. "I have to fly out to meet with some leaders in industry to help facilitate the prioritizing of federal needs. Not all of them are pleased with the price controls recently put in place."

"The government doesn't need any surprises with resources so tight at the moment," Kaira said, filing into the elevator compartment as the door slid open.

"No, and I will try to get them to see this is only temporary," Jovan said, following her.

"It is temporary, and a brand new order lies just ahead," Kaira replied.

She fell silent as the elevator took them down to the level with access to the parking facility. Jovan was left to his own thoughts for a few moments.

While dealing with disgruntled industry captains was not the easiest of tasks, he was deeply relieved that he was not directly involved in the tasks of the government agencies. From security issues to rationing fuel, food, and medicine, and establishing the presence of Living ID, the UCAS government was being stretched to the limit on many fronts.

The precarious situation facing the government was the very thing that prevented a robust response to the rebellion in the south and midwest. Jovan could only hope that the things Kaira was bringing about would speed up the process of reasserting control in the northern and western provinces. Once that was achieved, full attention could be turned to the breakaway provinces.

The elevator came to a stop and the doors slid open. Inside his head, Jovan admonished himself not to bog his mind down with worries over concerns about things farther ahead. Each task standing before him had to be attended with full focus, devoid of distractions.

The next order of business involved a meeting with several industry leaders on behalf of government authorities. That meeting was all he had to concern himself with for the time being, until that task was finished. The concise thought eased his mind a little, as he fell in behind Kaira, who strode out of the elevator compartment flanked by her security detail.

SKYLAR

The body of the spirit did not become exhausted with covering vast distances. After several non-physical journeys Skylar had been able to explore far and wide across the UCAS.

She had no concrete idea of what she was looking for, and could only hope that her instincts prevailed if she came across something of importance regarding Benedict Darwin's plight. A hint, a lead, or a new trail could be anywhere, or perhaps there was nothing to be found.

Sorrow ached within her heart on a regular basis, as she kept her eyes open for anything unusual. The pain that she felt came from the continuing failure to find anything regarding Benedict, and the state of the world, the condition of which was reflected in many sights she witnessed during her forays.

She had taken in many disturbing visions, not the least of which were the swarms of dark spirits concentrated around major centers of population. Soaring edifices of concrete and steel wreathed in living clouds of black met her eyes in every urban center that she came across.

A deadly, corruptive cycle was taking place within the cities. Suspicion, envy, fear, and all manner of negative energies provided a sumptuous feast for the dark spirits, who in turn bolstered an atmosphere fertile for the erosion of any real sense of morality.

Seducing some to violence, others to deception, and a great many to indifference, the shadowy creatures of the abyss wreaked havoc to a degree that no effort of Skylar's could hope to offset. Only an extensive purging could rid the cities of the vile infestation, and the force required to do that was nowhere to be found.

Steering clear of any encounters with the wicked hosts, she pressed forward time and time again with her search. Finally, during one sojourn that took her deep into the northeast, she beheld a significant anomaly, though she had no idea if it related to what she was seeking. A biting chill took hold of her spirit as she gazed across an expanse of wilderness.

Like a beacon of darkness, the sight had grabbed onto her attention from a far distance. At first, the place looked like it was swathed in drifting black mists, but as she got closer to the location, she realized the dreadful truth.

Thousands of dark entities moved to and fro in sprawling masses above a compound of buildings. Carpeting rolling hills, dense woodlands surrounded the cluster of edifices.

Only a single airstrip and a couple of roads broke the sea of trees spreading away from the assemblage of buildings. It was a bold, powerful display on the part of the abyssal horde, one that made no effort at masking its presence.

Skylar knew at once that the massive gathering came with a purpose. She knew that they were not feeding off the negative energies of a large populace, which left one conclusion. Something of tremendous importance resided within the compound beneath them. She realized the ethereal creatures were not so much guardians as they were an assiduous watch, one that would prevent any unwelcome spiritual entity from slipping into the compound unnoticed.

For the most part they were lesser entities, spirits whose presence in the physical world did not exact as much of a toll upon the Ten-Fold Kingdom as any level of Avatar would. Keeping to the shadows, they were the kinds of abyssal servants who whispered despair into the ears of the sorrowful, and fanned the flames of rage in the angry. They were the ones who counseled the shunning of pangs of conscience, and emboldened the powerful to pursue their aims without sparing thought for the costs that others would incur as a result. Like their brethren in the cities, they fed off the essence of wickedness. Their numbers were always the greatest wherever the character of a society or populace was steeped in decay.

To see so many being used for another purpose gave Skylar pause. Slowing down, she kept her distance from the site, observing the churning masses of malignant spirits with a rising feeling of unease. To go any closer would be to invite very unwelcome attention, and it was not certain that Fallen Avatars were absent from the area.

In some ways, she found herself wishing she could ask a few questions of the Fallen Avatar that had appeared to her after Benedict Darwin had been apprehended. The fell spirit had abruptly ceased its visits after aiding her in dispatching the enemy spirit traveler, the one who had been responsible for finding and identifying Benedict prior to his capture.

Her thoughts shifted from the scene before her. Skylar's mind focused for a moment upon a memory of waking up in her room and seeing the spirit that had claimed to be on a penitent road. It was all that was needed to bring her current journey to a halt.

In an instant she was back in her bed, lying flat on her back in the loose clothing she wore whenever she engaged in disembodied travels. She took a few seconds to adjust to the temporary disorientation she felt at resuming control over her physical body.

The first thought on her mind was seeking out Magdalene, as there was no question something of extraordinary importance was located at the wraith-warded forest compound. She had to find out what the compound purported to be, as the knowledge might give her some clues to its deeper, truer nature.

Swinging her legs around and setting her feet on the floor, she lifted herself into a sitting position. Filled with soft shadows, the bedroom was steeped in silence, and offered no signs of otherworldly visitors.

The recognition came as a disappointment, as she suspected the prodigal spirit could have given her a few answers regarding what she had just seen. Nevertheless, the discovery of the strange anomaly in the wilderness, after so many fruitless excursions, lifted her hopes.

She had to hold onto whatever she could, to keep pressing onward. With so many journeys turning up nothing, at least the latest one had resulted in something.

After taking a few deep breaths, she stood up and made her way to the door that she had locked from the inside. It was only a partial precaution.

Had someone knocked upon it while she was out of body, the sound would be been enough to interrupt her foray and snap her back into her physical body. While disruptive, that was not what concerned her.

What she never wanted was anyone touching her body, even if just to rouse her, while her spirit was away on a journey. The effects of such contact, and the ensuing return into the body, could be dizzying, jarring, and in some cases extremely painful. It was much better to keep the unwitting to knocks on the door.

Heading down the hallway towards the living room, the soft glow of a reading lamp told her that one of her sisters was still awake. Skylar found Genevieve curled up at the end of the couch, dressed in a loose-fitting t-shirt, sweat pants, and socks.

Genevieve's eyes shifted up from the book in her hands when Skylar entered the living room. Folding the book, she set it down gently on the end table with the lamp.

"Roving about places far from here?" Genevieve asked with a knowing grin.

"I took a little look around," Skylar responded, taking a seat in an easy chair facing Genevieve on the other side of a low, rectangular coffee table.

"And? Anything interesting?" Genevieve asked. Before Skylar could answer, she chuckled and added. "Then again, if I could do what you do, everything would probably seem interesting."

Skylar smiled. "Sometimes things are interesting, as in they demand your interest. But that is not always the same thing as being desirable."

"At least you can do what you enjoy without needing gear," Genevieve said. "With the strict ammo rationing ordered by Magdalene, I can't even get some catharsis at the shooting range like

I used to."

Genevieve was one of the best shooters among the Shield Maidens, with a rifle or pistol. Skylar did not doubt the limitations placed on ammunition usage were grating on her friend, even if they were deemed necessary.

"Hopefully, things will get sorted out fairly soon, as the breakaway provinces get better organized," Skylar offered in the way of consolation.

"Let's hope," Genevieve said. "So, enough of my irritations. Did you discover anything new?"

Skylar nodded. "I think so. Something of note. I need to talk with Magdalene, but I found an anomaly far to the northeast. I've fixed the sight in my head, so I can return and get a better bearing to identify it."

"What did you see?" Genevieve inquired, leaning forward and clasping her hands in front of her, showing keen interest in Skylar's discovery.

"A place in the middle of nowhere that is warded to an extreme level," Skylar said. "A host of spirits from the abyss are concentrated there. The place is nothing more than a small group of buildings surrounded by woodlands. No major population whatsoever."

"A compound of sorts," Genevieve remarked.

"As far as I can tell," Skylar said. "I hadn't come across it for long before I returned back here."

"What does your gut tell you about it?" Genevieve queried.

"Every instinct in me says to look into this one," Skylar answered. "My heart says not to put it aside."

"I think Adonai is giving you a nudge," Genevieve stated.

"I think so too," Skylar replied, nodding. "I will have to tell Magdalene about it as soon as I can. Do you know what she's up to right now?"

"She's meeting with some others, coordinating ways to keep connections with the Shield Maidens who are embedded in the north, in the UCAS-held provinces," Genevieve answered. "That's getting to be a tougher task with each and every day that goes by."

"I'd imagine, with the hyper-security state they've imposed up north," Skylar said. "I can tell you, it is a choking feeling to just go near one of their cities nowadays. They are shrouded in a darkness that is growing deeper."

"I'd imagine so," Genevieve said. "One thing's for sure. It is a security state that blockades reports of atrocities fairly well. If it weren't for our embedded sisters, we would know little about the things they are doing up there. I just found out they wiped out an entire town using some advanced weapons."

"Wiped out an entire town?" Skylar asked, dismayed, hoping she had not heard the words correctly.

Genevieve nodded, with a grave expression on her face. "Alesia, a little town not far from Ponchartrain, in Mishigamaa Province. They killed every living soul in the town. People, animals, everything that breathed. Some sort of new radiation weapon, from what we know at the moment."

Skylar frowned, feeling sickness within the pit of her stomach. She said in a low voice, "They are monsters."

"Yes, monsters, but practical to the ends they are aiming for," Genevieve respnded with an even tone. "We must not underestimate them. No matter the atrocity, they are working towards a purpose. I'm not liking the latest tidings."

"What's going on?" Skylar asked.

"Something at the World Summit, some new initiative being done through their Peace Commission," Genevieve said. "It's being led by one of the bright new stars on the international scene, maybe the brightest there has been in memory, a young woman named Kaira Antipalos. Don't know much about her, but she was pivotal in arbitrating, and bringing an end to, the UCAS conflict with Mandaria."

"Impressive, I thought that war was going to get much worse," Skylar commented, thinking back on the conflict that threatened to unleash worldwide war.

"As did we all, which is what intrigues me," Genevieve said. "Especially since you and I know that war was serving a purpose of the Convergence."

"All means to an end, every last bit of it," Skylar said, thinking of all the war, terror, economic turmoil, disease, and more that was channeling fast towards the Convergence's goal of a singular global order.

"They're going to strike south at some point, or mount an offensive from the west pushing eastward, you know that," Genevieve said.

"I think we all expect that, it's not exactly an age friendly to self-determination," Skylar commented, ruefully.

"We've got to be ready. We're not going to get much warning."

"I'll be as ready as I can be."

"As will I," Genevieve said, looking away, with a contemplative expression.

After a few moments of silence, Skylar shifted the subject. "Do you think it will be long before I can get in touch with Magdalene?" Genevieve shook her head. "Not long. I expect her to check in with me before too long, in fact."

"Be sure to tell her I need to speak with her as soon as possible then," Skylar said. "I know you understand."

"That I can do," Genevieve said. "And I do understand."

Skylar stood back up. "I'll let you get back to your reading. I'm going to fix myself a glass of juice, and then do some traveling ... but this time only in dreams. My body needs some sleep."

"I think mine does too. I'll be hitting the sack before too long," Genevieve remarked, a grin coming back to her face.

"Have a good rest, and I'll see you in the morning," Skylar said.

"Good night, and good dreams," Genevieve responded.

Skylar proceeded from the living room and went into the kitchen, feeling a nagging thirst that called for a tall glass of orange juice. She just hoped it would not be too long before she had a chance to speak to Magdalene. Skylar knew in the depths of her heart that she had come across something of great importance; and definitive answers had to be gained as soon as possible.

SETH

The frigid bite of the night air clamped down upon Seth as his group was ushered from the helicopters towards a line of armored vehicles. Dismay filled him as he walked forward and eyed a cluster of figures standing just ahead.

Some were well-dressed, and others wore uniforms, but all of them carried the heavy air that derived from being official and important. Their expressions were anything but friendly as they eyed the approaching prisoners.

He barely took note of his surroundings other than to note that they were at some kind of airfield. The sounds of a jet engine thundered somewhere off to his left, but Seth did not look, as consumed as he was with his own circumstances.

"Probably didn't think we could extract you, did you?" a tall, uniformed figure addressed them as they neared. His voice held a mocking edge. "Didn't think we could reach so far into the terrorist-controlled provinces."

He looked over the group with a steely gaze. "We know who most of you are. We've been watching you, believe me. So good to have you with us, Sheriff, after you caused us so much trouble. And nice to see you kids. Should have stuck to playing video games and left things alone."

He looked up towards the soldiers. "Let's get them moving."

The prisoners were divided up between the armored vehicles, and in a few moments they were rolling down a highway. Jonathan and Annika were riding in the vehicle with Seth, but all of the others he knew had been separated.

Looking out the side windows, Seth could see the beams of helicopter searchlights roving the areas ahead of them. Seeing so much security being applied to his group only served to make him more nervous.

It was not long before the vehicles rumbled through the front gates of a compound surrounded by high fences and barbed wire. Seth knew all too well what the place was, having captured video of a similar facility back in Venorterra. He glanced towards Jonathan and Annika, and could see the despair in their countenances. He knew that they had come to the same conclusion.

The vehicles rolled to a halt and armed guards swiftly appeared at the door to let Seth and his friends out. For the first few seconds, he was overwhelmed with the bright lights, guard towers, armed troopers, and everything else surrounding him.

His focus quickly settled upon another group of distinguished-looking individuals that were gathered a short distance from the vehicles. Like the others who had been waiting at the airfield, they carried an air of importance about them, perhaps to an even higher degree.

"The Trono de Sol Desert is a very long way from Venorterra," a woman with olive-hued skin and long ebony locks stated, her tone anything but amiable. Tall, and very attractive, her dark eyes held nothing but contempt. "I would not try anything stupid, if I were you."

To her side was another attractive woman of about the same age, with dark hair cropped a little below the ears. Her angular features were fixed into a sharp frown as she regarded Seth and the others.

Her gaze, for some reason, deeply unsettled him. Seth had the impression that she was looking into him somehow, rather than at him.

"So, are your friends going to appear tonight?" the first woman asked them, in a hard tone. Her eyes focused on the younger members of the group, and Seth had the queasy feeling that her eyes lingered upon him most of all. "If they do, we are ready this time. This will not be a repeat of the events in Madison."

Seth knew who she was talking about, and the surety in her voice frightened him. He saw her glance away, and following the look he took in a strange sight atop a few of the long, rectangular buildings arrayed within the detainment camp.

At first, he thought some kind of steam or vapor was being given vent from within the buildings. But in moments, he saw the behavior of the vapor was not what it should have been, if it were merely being loosed from a structure into the open air. Instead, it was more like a few small clouds were clinging to the tops of the buildings, defying natural laws. The vaporous material coiled and shifted, but it did not dissipate or drift.

His unease deepened, as he knew the clouds had something to do with the confidence of the woman talking to them. There was a heavy presence about them, unless his mind was going awry under the stress of the moment.

Seth knew he did not want to see what was veiled within the swirling, thick vapors. Whatever the dark mists were, he had the distinct, unpleasant feeling that something was watching him, and all of his friends, from within.

DAGIAN

Dagian watched the prisoners being led away. The younger ones were being kept in one group, while several guards escorted the recalcitrant sheriff and the rest of the captives towards another section of the camp, an area where some intensive, thorough interrogations would soon be taking place.

"We have them, and the Watchers have not made an appearance yet," Aaliyah remarked to Dagian.

"Perhaps they sense we are prepared this time?" Dagian responded, trying to read Aaliyah's expression for any sign of concern.

A special forces unit had been deployed to capture the small-town sheriff who had defied the government at the Revere homestead, along with the youths who had been important enough to warrant intervention from Watchers. Advanced spy drones, like little dragonflies, had kept up a rigid surveillance within in enemy-controlled territory that kept Aaliyah and Xavier well-informed of the impending convoy.

The operation had been a great success, ensnaring all of the individuals they had sought. Dagian knew Aaliyah and Xavier were extremely pleased to have the renegade sheriff in custody. But for Dagian, it was the youths that were the greater prize.

It had been the video gained by the youths that had been broadcast by Juan Delgado during the enemy's daring raid into Troy. In Dagian's eyes, the youths had played a significant part in the troubles she had incurred.

She would not have minded throwing them to Erkorenen for food. Only the strict commands of Aaliyah held her back from exacting some retribution.

"I know you will be making a public announcement with the sheriff, but what about the younger ones?" Dagian asked, hoping for some change in Aaliyah's position.

"Just worry about the tasks you have been given. There will be time for vengeance soon enough," Aaliyah responded.

Dagian glanced towards the small, cloud-like formations hovering near the tops of several buildings. She knew the purpose of the black, churning vapors hugging the rooftops, and the sight brought a grin to her lips. In her heart, she hoped the Watchers would make an appearance.

SETH

Dejected and resigned to the situation, Seth trudged along with the others. The guards escorting them led the group into the midst of the well-ordered series of rectangular buildings.

The larger group had been separated, with the older individuals taken in one direction, while Seth and his friends were guided in another. He did not know what that implied, but he did not expect much in the way of leniency from what he had observed so far.

"Hope our accommodations suit you," one of the guards said derisively.

Nobody offered a reply.

"The luxury has taken your breath away, has it?" the guard continued, evoking some laughs from the other troopers accompanying them.

"I know how you kids love fashion," another guard said. "I'm happy to say you are about to get a new change of clothes. Really sharp-looking. Very popular around here too."

Seth glanced upward, and saw one of the low masses of black vapor over the building to his right. The nape of his neck tingled as he gazed upon it, though he could still not understand why he felt so nervous. The tendrils of mist swirled and churned, though they did not reveal even a hint of what was within.

"We're going left," the guard at the lead stated firmly, taking the group down the length running between two of the elongated buildings. After a moment he added, with a taunting edge. "Cheer up, boys and girls, your fancy new attire and brand new digs aren't that much farther from here."

Ignoring the guard as much as he could, Seth breathed out heavily, and followed along. He looked up into the night sky, wondering what terrible fate loomed before him.

That night the sky held no wonder to it, and the stars themselves looked like so many scattered exiles adrift in a sea of darkness. The sounds of footsteps on grass filled his ears as the guards and captives kept marching forward.

Shouts and expletives erupted from the guards, jolting Seth to full alertness. Before he could look to see what had startled them, a bright form raced through the patch of sky visible between the rooftops overhead.

From somewhere deeper in the camp, a siren blared as a chorus of gunfire broke out. Blood surging in his veins, Seth looked back down just in time to see the luminous glow of a Watcher as it landed upon the ground between the buildings.

Without a moment's hesitation, the huge, multi-winged creature attacked the two guards at the lead. The creature's beak and talons moved too fast for Seth to follow. It took only an instant to bring the guards down.

The Watcher regarded Seth and his companions for a brief

moment. He had seen that Watcher before. The silvery hue of the light and the large eagle-like head indicated the creature was one of the ones that had taken Seth and his friends across the boundary between his world and the realms beyond.

Looking back the other way, Seth beheld the leonine countenance of another, this one with a reddish glow. Immediately, he knew in his heart that the creature was Talthannor, the very one who had conveyed him to safety on a night when all had seemed lost.

Talthannor roared and swiped powerfully with its massive front claws, bringing down three more guards in swift fashion. Everything took place so fast that the guards did not get so much as a single shot off.

During the commotion, Raymond and Jonathan had taken the initiative and seized the final guard, holding him fast. Annika had taken his rifle away, and the look of shock and terror on the man was plain to all eyes.

"These have given their souls to darkness," thundered Talhannor, padding up towards the captive guard. The Watcher's many eyes were fixed upon the trooper. "They knew who they served."

The eagle-headed Watcher strode up from the other side. A noxious scent filled the air, as the guard urinated on himself in his fright.

"Bind him," Talthannor said. "Do it quickly. We must leave here."

Fortunately, Jonathan found some plastic ties in the guard's possession, and used them to secure his wrists behind his back. Using the guard's own belt, the freed captives gagged him, and left him sitting against the wall of one of the buildings.

With Talthannor at the lead, and the eagle-headed Watcher bringing up the rear, Seth's group began moving back the way they had come. The siren, gunfire, and sounds of shouting continued in the distance.

Seth had little doubt that those running the camp were having an experience similar to the troopers who had surrounded his house. Knowing what the Watchers were capable of, he had no worries about the course of the ongoing fighting.

He could not believe his good fortune. Lightning had struck a second time. Seth was about to be liberated again, along with all of his companions.

A part of him began to wonder whether the Watchers would take them back home to Madison, or maybe even to the otherworldly realms. In his heart, he hoped it would be both.

Some abrupt movements above and beyond Talthannor drew Seth's eyes upward. The dark vapors over the building ahead, the one that they had passed before the guards made them turn left, were thinning and spreading outward.

Seth flinched as a large form exploded out of the vapors and landed in a crouching posture at the edge of the building. The presence that he had sensed within the mists was finally revealed in open sight.

The great beast's form was an amalgamation of various animal elements. Muscular feline legs supported a lengthy body. An ape-like face with a short muzzle was contorted into an expression of malice, as it gazed down upon the humans and Watchers.

It spread its jaws wide as it loosed a grating screech, revealing enormous fangs within the dark maw. Even stranger, Seth realized the upraised, swaying tail behind the creature ended in a snake's head.

Heavy thumps sounded as two others of its macabre ilk landed, one to a side, onto the rooftops of the structures flanking Seth and his friends. They joined their voices to the first, loosing the horrid, guttural screeches that Seth wished he could block out of his ears.

"Get away from here!" Talthannor roared to Seth and his friends. The Watcher whirled to defend against the three creatures springing from the rooftops towards it.

The way ahead behind Seth was cleared a second later. With a nimble leap the eagle-headed Watcher soared over them, to go to the aid of Talthannor.

Another of the creatures from within the black vapors landed on the roof of the building to the left, just ahead of Seth. It did not stop or pay any attention to the humans below.

The creature charged down the rooftop and jumped to the ground behind them. Without hesitation, it sprang towards the eagle-headed Watcher and spread its claws wide.

"Come on! Get away from here!" Annika urged the others, as they reached the end of the building.

"Where do we go?" Jonathan yelled.

"Head towards the front gates," Seth suggested. "We might be able to get out of here."

The Watchers and the assailants from the dark mists were out of sight, but he could hear the sounds of their fighting in the continued roars, eagle-cries, and high-pitched screeches. Worry consumed Seth's heart.

Gunshots, screams, and inhuman screeches filled the air ahead of them. Over the top of the buildings Seth could see that the two guard towers situated near the front gates had been demolished.

The area near the front gates was a scene of chaos. Troopers were running to and fro, without any apparent order, while the bright forms of two Watchers wreaked havoc among them. One of the Watchers had the head of a great bull, and the other possessed a man-like head and torso.

A few more of the strange beasts from the rooftops could be seen within the sprawling melee. They were trying to chase after the Watchers, who in turn were charging at the troopers.

Seth watched as the bull-headed Watcher turned suddenly and lowered its massive head when one of the monkey-faced beasts had closed the distance between them. Using its broad horns, and snapping its head upward, it caught and threw its would-be attacker high into the air.

Black mist, like that on the rooftops, sifted out of the creature's body as it tumbled upward. Seth understood in that moment what the mist was, and also what the creature was desperately trying to do.

The beast did not have nearly enough time to shift its form entirely. It plummeted to the ground and landed hard right in front of the massive Watcher. The creature shrieked and screeched as the Watcher's broad hooves pounded and battered its body in a zealous barrage.

After a few moments, the Watcher charged onward, leaving the broken corpse of the enemy creature behind. Lowering its head, it upended a vehicle from the side that a few troopers had taken cover behind. Wheels facing skyward, the vehicle was toppled over, right onto the hapless troopers.

"Let's get out of the open. We don't want to be out here!" Raymond shouted, slicing through the group's moment of indecision. "Here! Follow me!"

Raymond led them at a full run, and after crossing a short distance they took refuge behind a military truck. Seth's position at the rear of the vehicle afforded him a good view of the area surrounding the front gates.

To his amazement, the front of the camp was wide open, though the cause became apparent when he set his eyes upon the twisted, crumpled forms of the gates. Something had heavily damaged them, and it did not take a lot of guesswork as to what was capable of such a thing.

Without guard towers or closed gates, a few soldiers had taken up positions within the open space. They had the stocks of their rifles set firm at their shoulders, poised to fire in an instant at anything that approached.

Enormous, wolfish forms suddenly flashed by Seth, giving him a start that made it feel like his innards were plunging. Light-headed, his heart raced as he watched the lupine forms bounding towards the front gate area.

The guards positioned there, already distracted by the ongoing melee, did not sense anything was amiss until right before they were taken from the side. The speed of the three wolves left them no time to adjust, or even bring their weapons around.

Quickly overwhelmed by the huge wolves barreling into them, all five of the blindsided guards crashed to the ground in a haphazard jumble. In the aftermath of their fall, Seth saw that a couple of the troopers sustained significant injuries in the initial collision.

One was clearly unconscious, lying immobile. Another slowly began moving his extremities, where he lay sprawled upon the ground a few paces away. The latter did not have enough presence of mind to reach for the rifle knocked out of his hands, which was lying just within arm's reach.

The remaining guards scrambled to regain their feet and fight back, but they stood no chance against the ferocity levied upon them. The wolves were already in their midst, and continuing the attack in relentless fashion.

There was simply no time for the three remaining able-bodied troopers to regain their orientation or grab up their weapons. One reaching for the hilt of a combat knife did not even get the blade out of the sheath.

Jaws snapped, fangs flashed, and men cried out in stark terror and pain before abruptly falling silent. The last two troopers, the injured ones, had no resistance to offer as the wolves fell upon them and ripped their throats out using their shaggy muzzles.

Seth stared at the slaughter in a mixture of fear and astonishment as the trio of wolves left the torn bodies of the five guards behind. Racing through the gates, the wolves disappeared swiftly into the night.

Seth had a strong suspicion that he knew exactly who the wolves were, but there was no time to think about it. Another commotion had developed, and this one had much more personal implications. His heart skipped a beat as he recognized a group of newcomers entering the fray swirling around the gates.

The sheriff and some of the others who had been captured alongside Seth and his friends were running towards the vehicles arrayed near the entrance. Leading them was a man in a trooper's uniform, though he had some sort of pendant hanging from a silver chain about his neck.

"It's them!" Raymond called out, where he was peering around the other end of the truck. "It's the others who were with us!"

Seth, Jonathan, and Annika stood in place. Raymond trotted down the length of the truck to join them, with Rowan and Christa closely behind.

"Let's let them know we are here!" Annika urged the others. Everyone nodded or voiced their agreement quickly.

Seth and his friends moved out in the open. Once past the end of the truck, they were within plain sight of the older men and women, who were now standing around the armored vehicles.

The uniformed trooper had moved away from them. Seth

watched him hurry over to the five bodies in the mouth of the wrecked gateway. Falling to his knees, he began searching through the pockets of their uniforms with haste.

One of the men with the beards glanced in the direction of Seth's group. His eyes widened with recognition and anxiety.

He yelled out, "Christa! All of you! Come on! Get over here with us, now!"

Christa immediately broke into a run towards the man, as the others hesitated. Seth glanced back to the trooper, who had finished his search of the fallen guards and was hastening back towards the others.

"What the hell are you all waiting for? Get your sorry asses moving!" yelled the huge, thick-bearded man in the other group, waving urgently for Seth and his companions to come over.

With him was the dark-haired woman clad in jeans and a leather jacket, wearing black, finger-less gloves. She had a wild look in her eyes as she shouted loudly towards Seth and his friends. "You stupid morons! Get your asses moving now! Or I'm coming over there to kick every one of them myself!"

"C'mon," Raymond said, yanking Seth's arm forward. The rest of his group fell in together, all five of them sprinting across the ground towards the vehicles.

As they reached the others, Seth heard the trooper announce, "I have keys for three of these. We'll have to find which ones as quick as we can."

"Then let's find out which ones, and let's get the hell out of here!" the big, burly man responded loudly, taking one set of keys from the trooper and moving towards the other vehicles.

A cacophony of growls, screeches, roars, and gunshots continued in the background, though for the moment nothing contested the open gateway. A window of escape beckoned.

Seth watched the sheriff take up another set of keys, while the trooper retained the third. There was little he could do but wait and watch, as his heart pounded within his chest.

IAN

Ian's mind was still swirling after being snatched up and taken so far away from his family. He had never expected Chris' convoy to run into an ambush. Even then he had never fathomed that his friend was one of those who had been specifically targeted for capture.

At the very least, the gates of the detainment camp were falling away behind them. The lights of the large federal facility had now been reduced to little more than a small glow in the distance.

The headlights of the armored vehicle that Ian rode in at the lead of the small convoy pierced the dark ahead. An illuminated stretch of roadway ran just ahead of the vehicle, up to where the reach of the beams was swallowed up by the night.

Rumble Dog and his high-spirited lady friend, Raven, were in the vehicle just behind. With the couple were a few of the youths that had been apprehended during the ambush. A third vehicle driven by Deputy Lucy Hammond, and containing the rest of the younger ones, brought up the rear.

Out of all the captives brought from Venorterra to the detainment facility, only the three tall strangers were unaccounted for. Ian had no idea who they were, but he hoped that they had somehow been able to get away from the clutches of the UCAS.

Ian suspected the camp was located in a very isolated spot, and nothing he saw conflicted with the notion. The lights from the vehicles revealed a flatter, desert landscape to either side of the road.

There were no lights from buildings or other traffic to the front, left, or right. Ian had no doubts that they were passing through a considerable expanse of stark, arid terrain, currently swathed in darkness.

"Chris, we can't go too much farther. In an area like we're in, this group of vehicles is just a big, inviting beacon to them," Ian told his friend. "I bet they also have a way of tracking them ... I'm sure of it."

"They do, and it won't be long before they're prowling the desert looking for all of you," interjected Blake Dillinger.

In the black uniform of a TTDF trooper, Blake had come forward during the tumult and identified himself as a member of the Order. In truth, he had done much more than just approach Ian and his companions. He had openly intervened on their behalf.

Ian was not yet at ease with Blake, which was the reason he sat behind him holding a forty-five at the ready for the time being. Yet Blake had already done more than enough to show that he was not in league with their captors.

He had freed Ian and the others of their bindings, and shot at least four of the soldiers guarding them. One of the latter had tried to run off, and Blake had dropped the man with one shot. His cool demeanor, focus, and demonstrated skill told Ian from the outset that he was a fighter not to be underestimated.

After taking up a few sidearms from the downed troopers, and giving them over to the freed captives, Blake had then taken the lead in guiding them towards the front gate area. It had been his initiative to commandeer the vehicles that they were able to find keys for.

"We'll ditch these vehicles very soon, I just want to get some more distance from the camp itself," Chris said. "As much as we can possibly can."

Blake nodded. "I figured that's what you would do."

"So, did you know we were coming?" Chris asked, casting the man a sideways glance.

Ian could tell by his friend's tone that not all suspicions had been driven from the sheriff's mind either. It made him feel a little better about the handgun he was gripping firmly, despite the many things Blake had done on their behalf. Caution was in order when they had met the man inside the enemy's camp, and wearing the uniform of the TTDF guards.

"No, I didn't know anything about their mission to capture you all," Blake replied. "I was just embedded in the right camp, at the right time, as it turned out. You probably would have gotten some aid in a number of other detainment camps. I'm not the only member of the Order implanted in a UCAS detainment camp."

"So the Order's got a network in place throughout these camps?" Chris remarked.

Blake nodded. "The Order seeks to get as much intelligence as possible regarding everything happening in the UCAS. Not the easiest thing to do with all the layers of security they have in place these days.

"Like the others of our Order who've been able to get placed in the right spots, I was put there to keep an eye on happenings, and see who was being detained in that camp," Blake explained. He turned and glanced at Chris and Ian with a slight grin. "I just decided if you all were important enough to bring such a storm down on that camp, then I'd better act on your behalf."

"Glad you were there," Chris replied. "And glad you made that choice."

"Me too," Ian concurred.

"I had no idea they would have some of their new creatures at the camp," Blake remarked. "I've been briefed on them, and we know things like them exist now, but I didn't expect to see them in the camp itself."

"What were those things? And what were the things that attacked them?" Ian asked, thinking of the creatures that just hours ago he would have found difficult to believe existed.

He was still processing all that he had seen during the outbreak of fighting. The task was anything but easy.

"The glowing creatures were on our side, that's all I know. Never seen anything like them either," Blake said. "All I know about the beasts that are with the enemy is that they are … very advanced kinds of animals. Think of very enhanced genetics. They are not what this world has been used to, I'm pretty sure of that."

Ian caught the brief pause in Blake's response. He sensed there was more that the man knew, but was not offering.

"I'm just glad we didn't have to deal with them, they seemed focused entirely on the glowing beasts," Chris observed.

"I noticed that too," Blake said, glancing towards the sheriff with a somber mien.

"Do you think those things will follow us out here?" Ian asked.

"They might, or hopefully the ones on our side took them all out," Blake replied, looking back to Ian. "No way to know for sure how it all turned out."

The answer was far from reassuring. Ian felt very uneasy about the thought of encountering such fearsome monsters in the night.

The images of them were burned into his mind. He recalled the protruding, simian visage with enormous fangs, as well as the creature's broad tiger's paws, and a scaly tail that, if Ian could trust his own eyes, ended in a snake's head.

Such a beast was a living nightmare. To think that the UCAS government was in control of creatures like that was deeply chilling.

Chris then asked, "So, if we do get away from the camp, do you have any thoughts about what would be best for us to do?"

"There are significant resistance elements in Silver Valley, which isn't too far from here," Blake said. "Best to lay low with them for awhile. There's going to be a big search for all of you, and it won't be confined to the desert. They went through a lot of trouble to snatch you up, and they won't want you heading back home."

"So there is some resistance in the UCAS-held provinces?" Chris asked, with a lilt of surprise. "We don't get much word of what's happening in the UCAS these days."

"There is," Blake answered. "And there have also been some brutal suppressions by regime forces in the northern provinces. But they haven't tamped all the resistance down. There are many who aren't liking all this surveillance and martial law."

"I don't know anyone who liked it before the conflict hit the flash point," Ian commented.

"It isn't what the UCAS was about," Blake said dourly. "It was never, ever supposed to become what it eventually turned into. But people let something else creep in slowly, step by step. Something patient, insidious, and calculating.

"It chipped away slowly, made changes gradually, so that most people busy with their lives and raising families took little notice of what was happening in the big picture. Those trying to warn others were easy enough to marginalize.

"Some were called overly dramatic, or branded as wild-eyed conspiracy theorists. The whistleblower brave enough to step forward was demonized. The journalist determined enough to expose evil in the light of truth was ridiculed. Some were imprisoned, and some even killed outright, make no mistake about that.

"Finally, we all woke up one day to find ourselves with a country that was unrecognizable in relation to the one outlined in the Grand Charter. It was not the country that soldiers had in their hearts when they were sent to foreign lands to fight in wars. If anything, it had become the antithesis of the country it purported to be, as a land of life, freedom, and pursuing dreams and ambitions."

"It all saddens me deeply," Chris replied with a morose air. "To think something so good for so many people was thrown away like that. And they used fear to do it."

"It was one of their biggest weapons," Blake agreed. "Fear of the unknown, fear of one's neighbor, fear of foreigners. Even fear of our own abilities and potential. A terrorist or calamity lurking around every corner, and all we were told that we needed to do was just cooperate a little more … one invasive step at a time. Incrementalism at its finest."

"If you ask me, a lot of folks became like children, wanting a guarantee that everything was safe and would be okay," Chris commented. "But it doesn't work that way, does it?"

"No, it sure doesn't," Blake replied.

"If you don't mind me asking, where were you from originally?" Ian asked.

"Califia Province," Blake answered. He chuckled, and shook his head. "That's been enemy-occupied territory for quite a while. Run into the ground by lunatics."

Ian grinned. "Kinda how we felt in Venorterra about the west coast."

"Wonder what all those bone-headed celebrities think of all this now," Chris said.

"Sadly, quite a few of them appear on television all the time now in support of the government initiatives," Blake remarked. "Even harsh reality can't get through their thick heads."

"Still lining up like lemmings to advance the cause of idiocy," Chris remarked, with a rueful edge.

"Nothin' like doubling down on failure," Ian retorted.

"Everyone's afraid. If you ever wanted to see a climate of pervasive fear from top to bottom, the UCAS-controlled provinces are it," Blake said. "Like I was just saying, fear is one of our enemy's biggest weapons, and they wield it uninhibited."

"That's not the vibe back where we are from. It's already a lot different," Ian said. "Everyone knows it's going to be a hard road ahead, and there's some fear about what the former government will try. But there's a whole lot of hope in the air. There's a lot of energy beginning to gather. You can just feel it all around you, even if things are a real struggle nowadays."

"That's the kind of air I'd like to breathe again," Blake said.

"Why don't you come down with us? We'll find a place for you," Chris said. "I need all the security help I can get. And I'm sure the Order has a presence in our territories too."

"We do," Blake said, looking towards Chris with a cagey smile. "But my place is here, helping whatever resistance there is."

"I've got to ask, aren't you more of a religious order? Why would you be helping a civil resistance so much?" Ian queried, finding himself very curious about the Order.

"What's in place here now is pure evil, Ian. Make no mistake about that," Blake said firmly. "The authoritarian, the totalitarian ... the collectivist ... such are the things of Diabolos. And we are soldiers committed to fighting against the things of Diabolos. It's really as simple as that."

"A lot of folks don't believe in the existence of evil to begin with," Chris commented. "I've met more than a few in my time."

"Absolute fools. Willfully blind," Blake stated tersely. "Evil is among them, whether they choose to deal with reality or not. It seeks to control, to savage free will, and to consume the spirit. It is the intractable enemy of every spirit made in the image of Adonai."

"And here I am, just wanting to head south, and go back home and see my wife and kids," Ian said with a melancholic tone.

"A most wonderful goal that is, Ian," Blake said. "And we'll do everything we can to find a way for you to get back home as soon as we can. But it won't be easy. Word's come through our network that the World Summit is going to be helping out the UCAS more than a little bit. Offering some assistance, apparently. For the UCAS, it will be an unprecedented situation."

"Assistance, as in militarily," Chris said.

"They'll be deemed 'peace-keeping' forces, of course," Blake said, with a trace of acerbity. "Probably won't actively confront the breakaway provinces, but they will free up many UCAS military assets being used to keep control of things. Plus, it ingrains the idea of a global security force even more. Not a far jump from a multinational force to a consolidated global one."

Ian did not like the sound of that at all. He knew the last thing the UCAS wanted was for the free provinces to set roots in place, and become a vibrant nation without martial law, surveillance, mountains of regulations, and a host of control mechanisms.

A nation offering true freedom to its citizens would be regarded as a menace to one wanting to keep its citizens firmly under control. If a World Summit deployment freed up UCAS units currently tied down with security functions, then the enemy could turn much more attention towards reclaiming the territories that had thrown its yoke off.

"Then the south and midwest better keep its eyes wide open," Chris said. "And it better keep all its guns loaded and within reach."

"Without question. The UCAS wants to retake control as soon as possible," Blake said. "That goes without saying. The control freaks in charge are not the live-and-let-live kind."

"No, they aren't," Chris said. "And when they are in charge they don't rest in their scheming. If they got nothin' better to do, that kind imposes dictates on the size of cups you can drink sodas out of."

"And that happened too," Blake replied with a rueful chuckle.

"Well, we can drink out of any cup we want to in the free provinces," Ian said.

"As a truly free people should," Blake said.

"So what is life like in the north these days?" Ian asked. "Like Chris said, we don't get too much news these days."

"Oh, just lovely," Blake said, with obvious sarcasm coursing through his voice. "House to house searches, drones and cameras, detention camps, Living ID implants, a digital currency, all that kind of thing.

"It is a feast of security and compliance. Much of it was already happening before the civil war broke out, but it is hitting really high gear now. They're moving fast to align the remaining UCAS provinces with World Summit initiatives and goals too.

"It really is a miserable place to live in. Most people living there just zone out with the usual distractions, consuming their time with sports, television, video games, and lots of drink and drugs. You've got an increasing population of spectators, and ever fewer wanting to be participants. So many people detached and afraid... But enough of that sad song. What about you all? I know Ian said the air is much different down south and in the midwest these days."

"Ian's right. Times are going to be lean, and a little hard for awhile," Chris said. "But the potential of the people in our provinces is not going to be held back any longer. And people can live the kind of lives they want to, not the lives that some bureaucrat wants them to live."

"I like knowing that my house is mine, and that everything I do is not being watched, recorded, and stored," Ian said. "I like knowing that I can raise my kids the way I want to. I don't like having values I don't agree with shoved down their throats. I like keeping as much of the money I make in my own pocket. And I like having the means of protecting my family and property."

"So, basically, you just like being a free person," Blake stated, turning to look at Ian with a knowing grin on his face.

"That sums it up nicely," Ian said, matter-of-factly. "Just bring things back to what the UCAS was supposed to be about."

"The free provinces will be a shining light in a darkening world," Blake said. "I'd be proud and honored to take up the Silver Sword too. I really hope all of you in the south and across the midwest prevail in this fight."

"I have to say I do feel proud to be a part of all this," Ian replied. "I want my wife, son, and daughter to know I'm the kind of man who doesn't back down from what's right."

"I know Alena and the kids are very proud of you, Ian," Chris said.

"Your kids definitely have the kind of dad that they can look up to," Blake added.

Ian was honored by the comments of the other men. Their affirmations struck at the core of what he wanted most, to be a good husband and father. In a time where risks had to be taken, and momentous decisions made, such goals were difficult challenges. Every sign that he was still on the right path was greatly welcomed.

"What's the latest on the relationship between all the provinces?" Blake asked a few moments later. "Anything being presented at the World Summit, even if we all know that'll be an exercise in futility?"

"The leaders of the provinces are working out the details on a confederation," Chris said. "The more I learn about what a confederation tends to be, the more I like it. The provinces will be much more self-governing than ever before, from what I can tell. They can even withdraw and become fully independent if they choose to do so. We're talking a unity of states based upon true consent.

"At the national level, things like a common currency, defense, and the like would be addressed. But the national government would be much more limited and hemmed in than the monstrosity we dealt with before."

"Sounds like a big, big step forward," Blake remarked.

"There's also some talk they are going to go back to calling us states again, instead of provinces," Ian added, remembering some of the speculation bantered about concerning the forthcoming plans for a new nation.

"The way it was before the first civil war," Blake observed.

"It's the way it all should be," Chris said. "An association of sovereign states. Voluntary consent. It's how the UCAS began before it all got so badly messed up."

"I always remember that one quote, about one of the founders of the UCAS being asked about what kind of government had been formed," Ian said. "He answered that the people had a republic ... as long as they were able to keep it."

"And finally they weren't able to keep it," Blake replied grimly.

"No, they sure weren't," Chris agreed. "But the principles the UCAS once embraced are timeless. And they can be restored."

"Yes they can," Ian concurred.

"Well, we're a few miles out from the camp now," Chris stated, following a short pause. "What do you say we stop?"

"I was just about to suggest that," Blake replied. "These skies will have drones passing through them any time now. We're at considerable risk even now."

Chris slowed down and pulled off the road. Ian was jostled as the vehicle went off the paved surface and entered the raw terrain. Scrub and brush crunched under the wheels and raked against the vehicle's underbelly as they proceeded a fair distance from the road.

"We should be out of easy eyesight here, at least at night," Chris stated, slowing down to a full halt and shutting the engine off.

They got out of the armored vehicle. Ian stood and watched as the other two vehicles coming up behind rolled to a stop.

The chilly desert air had a bite to it. Ian wished he had a jacket with him, suspecting it would be a good while before they had access to any kind of real shelter.

A familiar large form got out of the driver's side of the vehicle immediately behind them. "What's up?" Rumble Dog called out. "Anything wrong?"

"Had to stop. We have to ditch the vehicles," Chris said. "They'll be able to find these easily in a desert. Especially from the sky. We've taken a risk to go even this far."

"Thought so too," Rumble Dog said.

"Then we keep moving, it's too cold to stand around here," Raven added, joining Rumble Dog at his side. She slung an automatic rifle in her hands over her shoulder. She cast the others a spirited grin. "Good night for a hike. Clear skies. Enough moonlight to work with. So what say you all?"

"I'm up for a hike," Lucy Hammond announced, shouldering her own rifle as she walked up from the third vehicle.

Behind them, the youths had all gotten out and gathered together. Ian looked towards Christa with particular concern. She was one of Allyson's closest and most cherished friends. He had to make sure that she got back home safely.

"North and east is the way we want to go," Blake stated, looking down at a magnetic compass that he was holding, illuminated by a small flashlight in his right hand. He turned a little, and pointed straight. "That way."

"Let's head out and get going then!" Chris said, with an air of authority.

The group walked away from the vehicles. Ian scanned the skies overhead, looking for any lights that might indicate aircraft of some kind.

He did not see anything, and felt a little sense of relief. But he also knew that just because his limited human vision did not perceive anything it did not guarantee that nothing at all was up there.

"Mr. Rafferty?"

Ian turned his head, and saw that Christa had drawn up close to him. He smiled at her. "Hi Christa. Are you holding together okay?"

She nodded. "Doing the best I can, Mr. Rafferty."

"We're in this together," Ian responded. "And we're going to find a way back to Venorterra."

"Do you really think we will make it back home?" she asked in a low voice. He could tell by her dejected tone that she was far from expectant about the possibility.

"Both of us want to see Allyson, so let's get back home together," Ian said, with a smile. He knew he could not echo her tone or mood, no matter how he felt. It was his role to provide some reassurance and encouragement. "What do you say?"

"I'll do my best," she said, though her voice did not convey a strong sense of confidence.

"We'll all have to work together, and have each other's backs," Ian said. He tried to inject as much conviction as he could into his next words. "But I know we can make it back home, so that's what we're gonna do."

"This is all such a bad dream, Mr. Rafferty," Christa said. Her wide, fearful eyes reflected the tone of her words. "I'm really scared. Why did they take us so far to a prison camp? Why did they take me? What did I ever do?"

"You and I were in the wrong place, at the wrong time," Ian said. "They wanted Sheriff Howard, after what he did standing his ground at the Revere home. And they wanted those kids you were riding with, because of video they got of the detainment camps. You and I just happened to be with the ones they really wanted."

"We have really bad luck then, Mr. Rafferty," Christa stated.

Ian grinned, and chuckled. "Yes, we do sometimes. I've always kind of thought if I had no bad luck, I'd have no luck at all. But you and I are in this thing together, and promise I'll do everything I can to make sure you get back home safely. You have my absolute word on that, Christa."

The traces of a smile broke through the anxiety on her face. "Thank you, Mr. Rafferty. And I'll do anything I can to help you get back home too. I know you miss Allyson, Peyton, and Mrs. Rafferty a lot."

"I certainly do miss them, and they're always on my mind and in my heart." Ian put an arm around her shoulders, and hugged her close to him as they walked. "And thank you Christa, for saying that. It's nice to know that, at the very least, neither of us are alone here."

When he let go of her a few moments later, she gave him another smile before dropping back to rejoin the others of her age group. Christa had Ian's full support in the challenges to come, but he was glad that she had a few of her peers along with her. With a similar level of life experience, they would be able to relate to the things that each of them were feeling in a better way.

Ian stared forward into the night. A tendril of wind whistled in his ears, as he peered across a sparse, moonlit landscape stretching to the far horizon.

He was grateful for his companions, of all ages. If it were not for Christa and the others with him, it would not have taken much for Ian to fall into the depths of despair.

Home seemed impossibly far away, and reaching it again was filled with uncertainty. His heart ached as he thought of how frightened Alena would become when it became apparent that something had happened to the convoy. There was no way for her to know whether he was alive or not, and Ian did not have any means of getting a message to her.

He did not want to begin to think of what had to be going

through the minds of his son and daughter. In the face of the unknown, the worst of possibilities would loom and haunt them.

Yet he knew it would do no good to allow himself to be consumed by worry. There was nothing that he could do about the situation that he had been unceremoniously flung into. What had happened, had happened, and the only thing that could be done was to fix his mind on getting back to his family.

QUERAN

Queran, Gorthaur, and Oragas loped through the desert, keeping to a swift pace. They headed in the direction the convoy had gone, shadowing the roadway.

She knew the others who had been taken captive with them were in the vehicles. From the darkness outside the front of the enemy's encampment, Queran had watched them get into the vehicles and leave.

She had not been able to approach them, as there was not enough time to transform back into a human-like guise. With all of the fighting going on, going up to them in the four-legged form of her kind would only disrupt and terrify the humans at a critical time. The last thing she wanted to do as they were all escaping was to put them at risk of being recaptured.

Running across the desert landscape, Queran relished the pleasant sensations within her body. The night felt soothing as its chill winds brushed through her fur. With solid footing beneath, her broad paws propelled her elongated form with great power.

She was a harmony of rhythm, setting the pace for her two companions. At the very least, they were no longer bound, or cramped up in the strange flying device.

With solid vision in the dimmest of light, Queran found that the bright moon above provided plenty of ambiance to see for a considerable distance. The lights of the vehicles were easy enough to follow, standing out prominently in the darkness ahead.

A few practical thoughts crossed her mind as the An-Ki hurried across the barren land. They had escaped the grasp of their human captors, but they had discarded their only clothing when they had changed forms. It was not a minor recognition, as Queran knew that it was far from the custom of humans to walk around unclothed.

For the time being, the three An-Ki would have to remain in their other forms. It was not a situation that she entirely regretted, as the human form was the weakest of the three that she could assume. In the wilderness, the four-legged shape was the most capable, and it was the only one that allowed her to keep the vehicles in sight.

Caught by the fighting men in the woods while in their human forms had been a terrible misfortune. There had been no time or place to transform, as the humans had their weapons aimed right at them.

She knew that Gorthaur and Oragas would have fought for her if she had given them the signal to do so, but she judged that resistance would have resulted in nothing more than their deaths. Though it was loathsome to the core of her being, cooperation with the gun-carrying humans had been the only viable option.

After their journey in the flying machine, an unpleasant experience that had sent her stomach to churning, she had made a small discovery, one she would have to ponder further, at a quieter time. One of the female humans in the group meeting them at the encampment gave off a strong sense that was closely related to the feeling Queran got around Night Hunters. There was no mistaking the feeling, which was as powerful as it was unsettling.

The woman, the one with the long, dark hair, had looked over the group of captives with malice coiling in her eyes. There was something highly distinctive and dangerous about her, though exactly what it was Queran could not identify.

The more Queran honed in on that sense, the more she recognized a hint of the feeling present within the others surrounding the woman. It was strongest in another female, one with shorter-cropped hair, but even in her it was nowhere close to the level of sensation exuding from the tall, long-haired woman. It was the difference between carrying the scent of something on one's body, and being the source of the scent itself.

Thankfully, it became apparent that the mysterious woman and the humans with her were unaware of Queran's true nature, and that of her two fellow comrades. There was not even a flicker of a hint that the An-Ki's captors suspected anything other than that the trio were just a few more humans. Under the circumstances, that gave the An-Ki a significant advantage, one that Queran had intended to exploit when the time was right.

As she had thought, that moment came to pass a short time later, when the fighting broke out within the encampment. At her lead, the An-Ki had separated from the humans at the outset of the tumult, and found some cover to undertake the change into the four-legged form.

Queran had led Gorthaur and Oragas towards the entrance of the human encampment, approaching in a careful manner. When she got her first sight of the area, she was surprised to see that the gates had been destroyed.

Other discoveries manifested. To her astonishment, a few powerful celestial creatures were attacking the humans in the camp.

There was no doubt in her mind that they had been the ones who had torn up the gates. Though she knew that she had little to fear from the glowing, multi-winged beasts, Queran sought to avoid their attention, and certainly did not wish to get in their way.

Only moments later, the beasts of the Creator were themselves beset. Leaping down from the roofs of the human-built structures, the ape-faced newcomers had the bodies of massive hunting cats, with serpentine tails extending behind. To Queran's utter horror and astonishment, she recognized the entities as a form of Night Hunter that she had never before encountered.

To her further amazement, the Night Hunters paid no heed to the presence of three An-Ki, even though Queran was positive that one or two of the beasts glanced in her direction as they sprang down from the roofs. The fell beasts were entirely fixated on the celestial creatures, a murderous rage pouring from their beings.

Nevertheless, despite the unnerving, close proximity of Night

Hunters, Queran knew the An-Ki had to take bold action and do whatever they could to get away from the camp. The longer that they remained in the vicinity, the more that grave risks mounted.

Queran had then taken note of the younger human captives, hiding behind a nearby vehicle. Beyond them, a few human soldiers were standing together in the entryway, weapons in hand.

Though all of them looked fearful and anxious, the soldiers could not be taken lightly. They could still lash out in a deadly manner using their potent weapons.

Taking her companions on a circuitous route, and building up speed, Queran put her mind towards attacking the cluster of soldiers from the side. The way out of the encampment had to be cleared entirely before the An-Ki could depart.

Her path took her right by the younger humans, just before she and the other An-Ki slammed into the soldiers, knocking all five of them to the ground. Giving herself over to the frenzy of battle, she killed two of the humans while the other three were slain by Gorthaur and Oragas.

With the way open to the wilderness beyond, she had led her companions into the night without delay. They had not gone too far at first.

Taking cover within the shadows, they had kept a watch on the front area of the camp, to see what happened with the humans. If there was a way to intervene on their behalf without putting herself or the other An-Ki at great risk, she was prepared.

To her relief, not long after, the whole group had gathered together near the entrance, gotten into vehicles, and departed from the camp. Once the vehicles were starting down the road, she had taken up the chase with Gorthaur and Oragas following a couple of strides behind. Though the An-Ki were swift runners, the lights ahead began to grow smaller, shrinking as the vehicles put increasing distance between themselves and their lupine pursuers.

All of it had happened so fast, from their initial capture to the escape. Queran's mind had been heavily occupied with observing the ways of their captors and the strange, unsettling experience of the flying device that had carried them to the camp. Little thought had been spared towards her greater predicament. Now that she was free again, larger worries began to assert themselves.

At the present moment, Queran and the other two An-Ki were somewhere far removed from where the rest of her clan dwelled. In her absence, others would step forward to help guide the needs of the clan.

Still, she felt a terrible anxiety about the situation, not knowing where she had been taken or how far it was from the clan's location. The answers to those questions were likely with those whom she was now chasing after.

Finally, the dwindling lights in the darkness ahead were enveloped in the night, as the vehicles outpaced the reach of her vision. Left with only the sounds of air rushing down her muzzle and around her head, and the rhythmic cadence of paws striking the desert terrain, Queran maintained a rapid gait.

She continued using the roadway as a guide, though they kept far off it, so that they would not be seen by anything else traveling along the hard pathway. Threats could come from the air at any moment, but she had to take that risk in order to maintain speed.

The moon had crept a little farther along on its skyward trek when she espied the silent, dark shapes of three vehicles a short distance from the roadway. She immediately recalled that the human captives had taken three vehicles from the camp, and her instincts told her that these were the very same ones. For some reason, the humans had chosen to abandon them.

She slowed down to the cusp of halting, with the other two An-Ki following her lead. Her every step draped in silence, Queran advanced forward. Flanking her, the two huge males did likewise.

Cautiously approaching the shadowy objects, she took in scents from the air while her ears swiveled about, listening acutely for the slightest disturbance. She could detect no trace of any living beings, whether animal, human, or other, in the immediate area. Once they reached the vehicles, Queran quickly came across the trail of the humans pressed into the dry ground.

Leading away from the vehicles and proceeding into the desert, the orientation and clustering of the footprints told her at once that the humans were staying together. They were traveling in a loose file, and it did not appear that they had sent anyone ahead to scout out the terrain.

It would be easy enough for one such as her to follow the humans' trail. The An-Ki were more than well-suited for tracking any type of quarry, and the humans had done nothing to mask their tracks.

"Why did they leave these here?" Gorthaur asked in a low voice, standing by one of the vehicles and looking in her direction.

"I do not know," Queran answered, sharing his puzzlement. Looking away, she stared out over the moonlit landscape, in the direction that the tracks of the humans led in. "There are no signs of any attackers. There is no sign of any struggle amongst them. The humans chose to leave these devices behind for another reason."

"It is strange," Oragas added, padding over to join them. "They can go much faster in these things than walking. If they are trying to get away, why would they choose to travel slower?"

Queran looked back to Oragas and replied, "There is much about this new age that is strange to me. Many of the ways of humans I have never understood. Not in the age we escaped from ... and not in this age. They are often a mystery to me."

Gorthaur looked skyward. "Maybe it is the flying devices. The ones that hunted them will find them easier from the sky if they stayed in these objects. I know these humans will be followed. The ones from the camp see them as very important. They will seek to capture them again. We must be careful too."

Queran thought upon Gorthaur's words, and found a lot of truth in them. The circumstances involved with everything that had happened revealed a number of things.

The humans had been captured in the woods and then taken far through the skies to the encampment, where others were awaiting their arrival. The captives had all been kept alive, a fact that was not of minor significance.

The ones operating the flying device and the camp had not been on a hunt with the intent to destroy. The capture had another purpose. The interest displayed on the part of the captors towards the other humans was both obvious and high, all throughout the ordeal.

There was little doubt in Queran's mind that the ones who had caught them would seek to do so again, as soon as possible. Gorthaur's caution was well justified.

The trio of An-Ki would have to be wary of others pursuing the escaped humans. A threat to the humans was also a threat to Queran and her two companions. Those pursuing from the camp would make no distinctions between anyone they found out in the wilderness.

Further, and even more foreboding, the human captors were in league with the Night Hunters. The only grace was that the Night Hunters she had seen in the camp had been entirely focused on the multi-winged creatures of Adonai. Otherwise, Queran knew that she would never have left the camp alive.

Whether or not the humans in the camp would use the Night Hunters in the search for those who had escaped remained to be seen. Queran did not want to think about it. If the Night Hunters were loosed, then all who had been taken captive were doomed.

"They will not have gone far. We should catch up to them swiftly," Queran stated.

"Why do we seek them?" Gorthaur asked her. "Why do we not go on our own path, and let them go on theirs?"

"They will know where we are. I am sure of it," Queran answered him. "They will know how far it is to where we were taken from."

"We will frighten them," Oragas stated. "Even if we speak their words now."

"At least one of the young ones may know what we are," Queran said, thinking of the human male who sat opposite to her on the flying vessel.

The looks he had cast towards her were unmistakable. She had seen the raw fear within his eyes.

"And another of the young ones," Gorthaur added, somberly. "It was him. The one who wounded me. I will never forget his face."

She had sensed his recognition while they were in the flying device. Gorthaur's mood had darkened considerably as he gazed upon one of the younger male humans, the round-faced one who was the tallest and largest of build among the youthful members of the group. She had been unable to ask Gorthaur about it at that moment, but there was no mistaking the angry look burning in his eyes.

It was in that moment that she had come to recognize the young man whose presence had stoked her companion's ire. Queran had been with Gorthaur that day, when he had discovered the power of the weapons used by humans in the new age.

The young man had been with two other males, all three of whom looked to be of about the same level of physical maturity. Neither of the young man's companions on that day was among the ones who had been taken captive.

While terror shone in their eyes, they had not run from the An-Ki when Gorthaur slowly approached them. Instead, they had put their weapons to use, and Queran remembered the deafening sound that followed, a booming thunder erupting through the trees.

The guns had left Gorthaur badly wounded, bleeding extensively from three places. The human weapons had sent small pieces of metal faster than eyes could follow deep into his body.

Two of the wounds were caused by a single piece entering his flesh at one location and exiting in another. It had simply torn through everything in between, displaying a deadly, incredible level of power that instilled tremendous respect in Queran for the human weapons from that day onward.

Seeing the horrid wounds and Gorthaur's labored breathing, she had feared for his life at first. Queran remembered her rage and anxiety during those terrible moments.

The resilience of the An-Ki to even grievous injuries was put to a severe test once more. To Queran's tremendous relief, Gorthaur made it through that early, fragile state, and eventually healed in full.

"We could be their shadows, and guard them until we know where they are going," Oragas commented, breaking the silence that had fallen between the other two.

Queran looked towards the large, black-furred male. One of her best warriors, he had proven to be insightful many times before, and his suggestion held merit.

"You advise a wise path, Oragas," Queran complimented the strong An-Ki warrior.

Unless Night Hunters stalked the darkness, three An-Ki could shield the escaped humans while they made their way to whatever destination they had determined upon. Just as Queran, Gorthaur, and Oragas had taken five human warriors unawares at the camp, they could do something similar if the An-Ki came across any place where the ones from the camp intended to set a trap or ambush.

Even better, the An-Ki could remain in their most capable shape for the time being. Queran worried about the vulnerability that she and the two males would incur changing back to a human form, to try and avoid frightening the former captives.

From the shadows, Queran, Gorthaur, and Oragas could seek to learn where the humans were going. If the need arose, the An-Ki could transform into their human shape and approach the group with the appearance that they were already familiar with.

At Queran's lead, the trio headed away from the vehicles, following the humans' trail with little difficulty. Able to maintain a trot, stopping only now and then to make sure the An-Ki were still on course, Queran knew it would not be much longer before they caught up to the humans.

Once they did, it was simply a matter of remaining undetected. Then, Queran could seek to learn where the humans were going, or what they intended to do. She hoped to gain answers for both questions.

Only then, with more knowledge, would she ponder whether there was a need to undergo the more painful transformation from her current, four-legged shape to the human one. For the time being, it was best to retain as many physical advantages as possible.

She had to keep her focus and awareness at the highest levels. The An-Ki had to pick up the signs of any other humans before they became aware of Queran, Gorthaur, and Oragas. With the element of surprise in their possession, the An-Ki stood a great chance of keeping the humans they followed safe.

Warding the humans was of the greatest importance. Queran understood that keeping them safe from harm was likely imperative to finding her way back to her clan.

ARIANNA

Setting out shortly after dawn, Arianna and the others took the main highway approaching Coranado City. While getting ready to depart early that morning, she could tell right away that the soldiers at the security checkpoint thought their group crazy to leave behind secured territory for gang riddled-land.

Captain Johnstone had given them the best information available regarding the latest reports on zones held by gangs. He also provided information on the areas known to be under the control of those unaffiliated with gangs.

To the best estimate of the captain, one large enclave of civilians had banded together in a very organized fashion. They had successfully resisted the encroachment of gangs from deeper in the city.

Captain Johnstone told her that he was doing what he could to help the civilian defenders. The southern provincial forces had provided the people there with additional weapons, ammunition, and other supplies, to help them resist until the military could drive the armed gangs out.

If she decided to seek those people out, Captain Johnstone advised her to mention his name and ask for Davis Rucker. Arianna gleaned from the way that the officer talked about him that Captain Johnstone both liked and respected Davis.

Arianna welcomed the counsel and information. She and her companions were heading into dangerous territory, and it was good to know there were potential allies in that area. In addition, having one lead was better than nothing, and the proximity of the citizen enclave to gang-held territory increased the likelihood of gaining further intelligence.

It was not long before they reached the outskirts of the suburban neighborhood. Heading off the highway at the designated exit, they rolled through an abandoned commercial district with vacated gas stations, food establishments, hotels, and all manner of other stores.

Unlike the exit that they had turned off at earlier, there were no signs of the businesses being active. Nor was there a hint of the buildings being under any other kind of use.

Once thriving with commerce, the area had been reduced to a ghost district. The only movements were from the pockets of overgrown grasses buffeted about with gusts of wind.

Trash and debris littered the parking lots in abundance, and the facades of many buildings exhibited smashed in windows and entryways. The pervasiveness of damage to the buildings, and extent of the refuse, suggested that the establishments had long since been looted of their contents.

Arianna turned onto a main thoroughfare running between two middle-class neighborhoods. Sizeable two-story houses on modest plots of land lined the street to the left and right.

The SUV crawled down the street, with the second one keeping close behind. Looking from side to side, Arianna searched carefully for any signs of people among the houses. Though the yards were unkempt, the houses looked to be in a much better state than the businesses had been in.

Everywhere she looked, doors were closed and windows were fully intact. Arianna had a strong, growing suspicion that they were not empty.

Rounding a bend in the roadway, the pair of vehicles did not travel much farther down the street before a barricade loomed in front of them, spanning the road entirely. It extended all the way to the houses on each side, such that no vehicle could circumvent the obstacle and use the road.

The barricade was formed from a number of large metal dumpsters, of the kind found at apartment complexes or behind businesses. Set side to side, the huge, heavy bins were undoubtedly filled up to where they represented an extensive amount of weight.

A lot had been built upward on top of the bins, using an array of materials. The result was a rampart at least twenty feet in height. There was no telling what braced or supported the barricade on the other side. Looking at the enormity of the obstacle, Arianna surmised that only something like a tank could break through it.

The two SUVs slowed down and came to a full stop. The rigid stillness only added to the tension.

Glancing in the review mirror a few seconds later, Arianna's heart jumped. Several vehicles were pulling into the road behind them, blocking the way back.

The rear beds of three pickup trucks each had two gunmen standing side by side in them. Leaning over the roofs of the front cabs, the gunmen were armed with rifles that were trained squarely on the new arrivals.

A pair of SUVs fitted with improvised armor plates rolled into place on either side of the pickup trucks. The SUVs were positioned in a horizontal fashion, keeping their sides facing Arianna's group. The front and rear windows of the SUVs were down, and the dark barrels of several more rifles extended from the openings.

Behind the five vehicles, a large commercial truck cab pulled a lengthy flatbed trailer out onto the road. On the trailer was mounted a rectangular section of armor shielding, protecting several gunmen who had their weapons aimed towards Arianna's group.

Almost at once, a swarm of figures manifested from behind the vehicles obstructing the road. Several others emerged from the bushes and other places of concealment in front of the houses arrayed to the left side of the road. A few others appeared on rooftops just above the other fighters.

Some wore camouflage elements, including a few dressed in full army fatigues. Others were clad in jeans, or other types of casual day to day clothing, with collared shirts and t-shirts in regular evidence. There were even a couple of muscle shirts in view, worn by fellows with stout builds.

A majority of the armed individuals were men, but there were many women interspersed among them. Ages ranged from teenagers to a few who looked to be in their late fifties or sixties.

With the wide diversity of ages, appearances, ethnicity, and other characteristics, Arianna knew they were not members of any gang. Most likely, they were the very ones she was seeking.

One of the men wearing a muscle-shirt approached from the side. He gestured to Arianna, and then to Quinn, signaling for them to roll down their windows. She did as he asked without hesitation, bringing the side window down all the way.

"Cut the engines. And then start gettin' out of the vehicles ... do it slowly," the tough-looking man called to the two SUVs, in a southern-accented voice that was both insistent and authoritative.

Arianna turned the key in the ignition back, silencing the engine, and then opened the door cautiously. Before she got out of the vehicle, she said to the others with her in a low voice, "Everyone, just do exactly as he asks you. Let them search you, and do not fight them. I know in my heart that these people are the ones we are looking for. They are just making sure we're not enemies. Trust me on this."

Stepping out from the SUV, she divided her attention between the An-Ki following her and the man who had ordered them to come out. Godral and his companions looked pensive and unsure as they exited from the vehicle, and stood to full height.

Arianna noted the looks of amazement spreading on the faces of the surrounding men and women. Having been around the An-Ki so much, it was easier for her to forget just how imposing they were.

"Some pretty big fellas with you," the burly man commented to Arianna, eyeing Godral and the other An-Ki with particular interest.

Arianna nodded to the man, but said nothing in response, not quite sure what to say. She looked towards Quinn and the passengers from the second SUV, who were walking over to join her group.

Maureen had a stoic expression, but Arianna knew her friend's mind was busy evaluating all aspects of their situation. Watching where Maureen kept most of her focus, Arianna could tell that she was heavily scrutinizing the leader of the group. Arianna just wished that she could ask Maureen about her impressions, since she had long since proven to have keen instincts regarding other people.

"You all don't look like you're any kind of gang bangers ... which is a good start," the leader continued. "Let's see what you've got inside the vehicles first, before we start talkin'."

He sent a few men and one of the women forward to look through the SUV's. Rummaging through the vehicles, they swiftly found the various weapons that Arianna's group had with them. Gathering the rifles and handguns up, the searchers returned to the leader.

"Pretty good arms too. A-15s are a very good choice," he remarked with an approving tone, looking over the guns. Addressing the ones holding the weapons, he told them, "Take those away for safekeeping."

Nodding, or giving verbal acknowledgements of the leader's directive, the woman and men with the confiscated weapons walked away, and headed towards the houses on the left side of the barricade. Arianna watched them carrying her group's only weapons away with rising unease.

"Where we are trying to get to, we'll probably end up needing them," Arianna said, thinking about how important the guns could be to her mission. She also wanted to get some idea as to what the leader meant when he had mentioned 'safekeeping.' "I hope we can get them back."

The man stared at her for a moment before replying, though she could not read the look in his eyes. "It depends on some things. But there's a chance. The question I have is this: Where are you tryin' to get to?"

Arianna looked him in the eyes and replied. "We were heading to the border area. I'm trying to find out what happened with my uncle, and we thought we would begin our efforts around Coranado City.

"I was told about someone who might have some information that could help us. I was also told we could find him around here, with a group of people that were defending their neighborhood and holding off the gangs. The name of the person I was told to find is Davis Rucker."

A look of surprise arose on the leader's face. "You know of Davis? And you were heading to the border area? To search for your uncle, you said? He's in Coranado City?"

"Probably be best if I tell you more about everything first," Arianna said, responding to the parade of questions. "It would all make more sense, and it would answer most of the questions you probably have."

"I've got some time," the leader responded. "We aren't going anywhere. We've gotta keep a watch on this area anyway. Name's Wendell Squires, by the way."

"And I'm Arianna Darwin," she replied.

She then proceeded to introduce the others with her, while taking the man's personal introduction as a propitious sign. He was not letting his guard down, but his gesture told her that he was not viewing her group as an imminent threat.

Arianna then told Wendell the story of Benedict's abduction. She explained the lack of any viable leads regarding his whereabouts, and emphasized her desire to make a connection with someone who could help in the search to find out where her uncle was being detained.

Upon the conclusion of her tale, Arianna understood that there would be no quick answers. She knew from the grim expression deepening on Wendell's face that he did not see any favorable prospects for her intended mission.

"Even if you do find out where he's bein' held, they'll never respond to you," Wendell said, ruefully. "And to even get there, you're gonna to have to deal with what we've been forced to deal with. You won't have to go far at all for that."

Arianna frowned at his fatalistic comment. "What's that? Is the UCAS raiding into this area, from across the border zone past Coranado City?"

He shook his head. "Let's just say you'd be running head on into a very well-armed, very well-organized gang … gang bangers with a strong affinity for tattoos and the kind of cruelty that'll make your blood run cold.

"The name they go by is La Cuchilla, and they are some really evil bastards. They'll hack you up with machetes, just as soon as look at ya. In fact, the machetes are what inspired their name in the first place.

"And did I mention yet that they've got big numbers on their side too? La Cuchilla had an established presence in the city before the rebellion, but their ranks have swelled very quickly in the aftermath.

"They asserted themselves right away. Showed no mercy to rivals. Lots of people are now decidin' to play ball with the ones ruling the streets. Easier to get along than go against the grain, you know what I mean?"

"How big are their numbers?" Arianna asked, though a part of her already dreaded the answer.

Wendell replied in a grave tone. "The numbers of gang members in this city alone? We're talking in the thousands. Many thousands, just to be absolutely clear with you."

"Yeah, and lucky us, they recently decided they've got a great opportunity to establish a big, shiny new Program," chimed in one of the others, a stocky man with a crew-cut standing to the right of Wendell. He fixed his eyes upon Arianna, who looked back to him with a puzzled expression on her face. "A Program. That's what they call their undertakings. With this one I'm talking about, they basically want to get a whole bunch of new folk under their control. To extort from them on a regular basis. A herd of cattle to milk daily."

"The clique here ... cliques are kind of like local or regional chapters of the gang overall ... has worked its way into this area, right up to the edge of this neighborhood," Wendell stated. "Decided to expand the territory they control, even while they're getting increasing pressure from the free province military in the city itself."

As if timed to accent Wendell's point, the rattle of gunfire echoed in the distance. Arianna tensed at the staccato sound, looking off in the direction where it came from.

"Tradin' shots is just a part of life. You'll get used to that around this place," Wendell told her. "But they'll come for all of us here, sooner or later. They'll just see us as a rival gang to be gotten rid of."

"It won't be no walk in the park for those tattooed bastards," a tall, skinny man in about his mid-twenties commented, with an air of bravado. "We'll give 'em some new body markings that'll last 'em a long time."

"Hopefully the military will get here first," Wendell said. "I know they're spread really thin right now, and they don't have much to spare to commit towards the fight to liberate Coranado City. But we'll fight hard, no doubt about that. Our homes are here. More importantly, our families and many friends are here."

Gangs were far worse threats than the makeshift band of robbers that had accosted Arianna and her friends on their journey. The idea that the gangs were powerful enough to spread outward, and take over entire neighborhoods, was deeply troubling. Wendell and his community were under siege.

"What about Davis Rucker? Do you think he might have some ideas on what we can do?" Arianna asked, already feeling their slim chances of finding something out about her uncle dissipating.

"I can take you to him, but I don't know what he can do for you," Wendell replied. "We've got our hands full here."

"We've come this far, so we might as well talk with him," Arianna said, trying not to let her confidence ebb. "Please take us to him, whenever you can."

"I'll take you to him myself, but we're gonna have to keep you under guard for now," Wendell said. "It's not personal. Just the way we gotta do things."

He turned and said something to one of the men near him. The man broke into a run towards one of the areas where the vehicles had emerged to block the road behind them.

A couple of minutes later, a school bus rumbled out into the street and slowly approached the barricade. It was an older model, but looked to be in solid condition.

The bus had been converted from its original purpose into a transport for prisoners, with metal bars affixed to all the windows. Wendell told Arianna and her companions to board the vehicle and find seating at the back.

Once inside, she discovered that it had a lockable door set within a floor to ceiling panel of metal grating, the latter sectioning off the rear half of the vehicle. The area where she and the others were directed to find seats was on the other side of that barrier.

One of the men guarding them locked the door behind, as soon as they had filed through it and began to sit down. Arianna did not like being held in a locked compartment, but she understood the caution.

Outside the bus, Wendell shouted towards the barricade. "Let us through, open it up!"

A well-concealed section of the barricade, disguised to look like nothing more than another couple of dumpsters in the seemingly continuous line, slid to the right. A channel just big enough for the bus to pass through beckoned ahead.

The bus lurched forward and pulled through the gateway. Once they were on the other side of the barrier, the opening was shut behind them.

Looking back, Arianna could see several more armed men and women standing on some platforms constructed into the rampart. Holding their guns, they quietly watched the bus continuing on down the road.

"Looks like it would be pretty tough for a gang to get past all that," Arianna commented to Wendell, who had come aboard the bus and sat on the other side of the grating.

"Tough, but not impossible," Wendell replied, glancing back to her. "At least they can't just speed in here in cars and trucks. The main roads to the neighborhood are blocked pretty good."

On the inside of the barrier, Arianna began to see signs of life around the houses, several of which sported orderly-looking gardens on their front lawns. More than one person eyed the bus with interest as it drove by, from an old man tending one of the gardens, to a woman jogging down a sidewalk, to three younger guys working on a car that had been jacked up higher, allowing them access to its underbelly.

Seeing familiar neighborhood activities, reflecting a settled mode of daily life, gave Arianna some comfort. Any lingering fears that she had of hidden surprises on the part of Wendell eroded as she took in scenes of a harmonious, orderly community.

A minute later, they passed by a park filled with a motley assortment of tents and makeshift dwellings. It was filled with people of all sorts, from laughing, playing children to elderly men sitting in folding chairs under the shade of large maple trees. A baseball field was in use, with a game underway that was being watched by a fair number of spectators seated on metal bleachers.

Resembling a huge, sprawling yard sale, an outdoor market was arrayed on one side of the park. It was a lot less organized than the one Arianna had come across before, with furniture, tables of various sizes displaying goods, racks of clothes on hangers, and a host of other items blanketing a considerable expanse of ground.

"Who are the people living in the tents?" Arianna asked, doubting that they were all originally from the neighborhood.

"Those who were lucky enough to get away from the gang-held territory," Wendell answered her. "We scrape up as much as we can to help them, but it is a difficult time all around. The free province military has sent in a few loads of food and medicines, and they've evacuated several who were in serious need of medical attention."

"I can see how it would be difficult to take care of new people, when you are already under so much strain," Arianna replied, with sympathy.

Wendell smiled, though the expression was bittersweet. "Hard to help others, when your own situation is shaky at best. But at least a number of the newcomers volunteered to help in the patrols and defense of the neighborhood. That did help the rest of us a lot. Some of them were skilled with trades too. Always good to find someone who can fix things. Those kind are the celebrities these days."

Beyond the park, the steeple of a church rose high above the trees. It had the appearance of a sentinel keeping watch over the surrounding area.

The bus pulled off the road when the church drew near. The vehicle headed into the large parking lot wrapping around the church and its attendant buildings.

"Davis will be here," Wendell remarked, before Arianna could ask. "This is kind of a base for us."

The bus rolled to a stop just past the main church structure. Arianna and her companions were then let out of the rear compartment. Once they had disembarked from the vehicle, the newcomers were guided towards a set of double doors.

Escorted inside the building, the group was led into a big hall with a lofty ceiling. Once used for church social functions, it was now being utilized for a much different purpose.

Stacks and stacks of supplies filled much of the space, ranging from cases of bottled water to stores of plywood, two-by-fours, and many other building materials. Arianna eyed a large pile of backpacks just to the right.

A man of medium height and build with a shaved head stood behind a long table set near the center of the hall. Leaning over and using his arms to brace himself, he was poring over a thoroughly-creased map spread out before him on the surface.

A pair of glasses rested on his nose, the latter perched above a

332

salt-and-pepper goatee. A pensive look gripped his face as he looked up to see the group approaching him.

"Davis, got some folks who were looking for you in particular," Wendell announced.

A glimmer of concern passed over his face as he took in the sight of Arianna and the others with her. It passed quickly enough, replaced with a harder-edged expression.

"Looking for me? I don't know any of you," he stated in a low, terse voice. He cast Wendell an annoyed look, but said nothing further.

"They were referred to ask for you, specifically," Wendell said. "Wouldn't have brought 'em to you otherwise. We picked 'em up at Barricade A. A couple of SUVs, some good A-15s, but they're not gang bangers."

Arianna nodded, and interjected, "Captain Johnstone told us to ask for you. We just met with him at the checkpoint up the highway to the north. He said you might be able to help us."

Davis' expression softened a little at the mention of Captain Johnstone's name, but the wariness did not leave his deep brown eyes. "He must have had a good reason. Might as well me about it."

Once more, Arianna told the story of Benedict and the search undertaken to find him. Davis listened quietly, and did not interrupt her once.

When she was finished, he asked. "Do you have any idea what is going on down here?"

"Wendell told me a little," Arianna said, nodding.

"This is not the best place to be at the moment, believe me," Davis replied, staring into her eyes without blinking. "We've got some really big problems on our hands right now."

"He told us about gangs encroaching on your area," Arianna said.

"Right up to our boundary, closer than ever before," Davis said. "It's why I'm here now. We're using this church as a base."

"Looks like you have quite an operation here," Maureen commented to Davis, glancing around at the high stacks of supplies.

"Just a bunch of folks defending their homes and families," Davis replied. "Nothing more than that. There aren't any police. No army has arrived yet. Not their fault, I know how things are ... it's just a fact.

We have to defend ourselves as best we can."

"We understand that very well," Arianna said, with sympathy.

"I'm no general, just ex-air force," Davis continued. "I know a little about organization. We've got that going for us, at least."

"Don't let him kid you, he's been wonderful for us," Wendell said. "Stepped up when we needed it. Without him, we would have been overrun."

"I appreciate the vote of confidence, Wendell. But get back to me about that once we've stopped this gang from coming in here."

Arianna saw the weight of Davis' worry reflected all over his face. She felt a little guilt at having asked him for help with her situation, even if such a feeling was unwarranted.

"Will the army reach here anytime soon?" Maureen ventured.

"They're driving inward, from the other side of the city," Davis replied. "They've secured a major hospital, and gotten power up and going there, from what I heard. That's been a good thing for some of the sick here. But I don't think they'll be here anytime soon. They have too little to work with."

Arianna did not know what to say in response. She felt extremely reticent to press him for help in the search for her uncle. Davis had more than enough to contend with, in trying to protect an entire community.

"Can we stay here for a few days?" she asked gently. "To figure out what we should do next?"

Davis' expression remained unchanged, but he nodded. "All of you can take advantage of our guest quarters. We keep a couple of houses that were abandoned maintained for the members of the free province military who come by here from time to time. Nobody's stayin' in them right now. You all might as well make use of them."

"Thank you, Davis," Arianna responded.

"I'll do what I can about your uncle too," Davis said. "I'll have information gathered together about what we know regarding the situation around us. Maybe you can make some use of it."

"Thank you," she said, finding his offer generous.

"And you'll get your SUVs and weapons back too. We just can't take any chances with the way things are right now," Davis said. "I hope you understand."

"We do," Arianna replied.

"We've got your stuff under good care, don't worry," Wendell added, with a reassuring tone. "It's not going anywhere."

"Thank you," Arianna replied to him. She was relieved at the news, knowing that if they wanted to keep their weapons and vehicles there was not really that much she and the others could do about it.

"Wendell, do you mind taking them on to the guest quarters?" Davis asked.

"Not a problem at all," Wendell responded.

"I'll be in touch with you soon," Davis told Arianna, before bidding the rest of her companions well.

As Wendell led Arianna and the others out of the hall, Davis turned his attention back towards the map on the table. Once outside, they proceeded to the modified school bus and boarded it without delay.

This time, though, Arianna noticed that Wendell did not lock her and the rest of their group inside the compartment, instead leaving the doorway of metal grating hanging open. Seeing the gesture of trust, Arianna felt a little more at ease as she took a seat and looked out the side window.

Following a short drive through neighborhood streets, the bus slowed to a halt in the middle of the road. After getting out, Wendell led the group around the front of the bus. Crossing the road, he walked towards a two-level house that he explained had been left vacant following the upheaval with the UCAS regime.

Before Arianna could wonder as to the fate of the original inhabitants, Wendell informed them that it had formerly belonged to a man who worked for an agency of the UCAS government. He had opted to head northwest with his family, after the province threw off the yoke of the federal government.

Wendell then commented that more than a few houses in their neighborhood had been abandoned for similar reasons. Arianna was mystified as to why anyone would desert their homes and communities amid so much instability, but she was glad to have such pleasant quarters for their stay.

Retrieving the keys from his pocket, Wendell unlocked the front door and headed inside. Following him, Arianna looked around at the interior as the group began a short tour of the house.

She liked everything that she saw. The house was completely furnished, with four bedrooms, two full baths, and a basement that had been finished with paneled walls and carpeting.

Godral and Kantel took one of the bedrooms, with Dedran and Sarangar in another. Before Maureen could comment one way or another on the matter, Arianna insisted on sharing a room with Vailia.

The arrangement left the last available room for Maureen and Quinn to share. From their buoyant expressions, Arianna could see that having a room to themselves did not disappoint the couple.

"Wish the water still worked, but no power is goin' to the water plant just yet," Wendell informed them, after they had made their room choices. "We've built up some cisterns, and there's one here that you can use. Just be sure to use the filter system in the kitchen before drinkin' the water. You'll save yourselves a lot of trouble."

After answering a few questions about the house, and showing them where certain things were kept, Wendell left Arianna's group to their own devices. After taking a few minutes to let her friends settle into their new confines, she gathered everyone together in the living room.

Sunlight streamed in through the large bay windows, bestowing the space with a tranquil ambience. Between the couches and chairs in the room, there was seating enough for the entire group.

"We've walked right into the middle of a growing fire," Arianna addressed the others, once she had their undivided attention. "I didn't count on armed gangs spreading outward from the city being our biggest problem, but we can't deny the reality."

"Makes sense to me. There's a real void right now," Maureen replied. "With a breakdown in law and order, the criminals are moving in to fill the vacuum."

"Who are these ... gangs?" Godral asked with a tone of puzzlement.

"People that use lots of violence to rule over others," Arianna said, trying to figure out the best way to explain the concept of a gang to Godral. "They are like a clan of people, but they hurt other people to make them obey."

"Is that not how human rulers are?" Godral replied. His continued pensive expression told her that he still did not understand. "Do not human rulers hurt you, if you do not obey?"

Arianna had to concede the An-Ki's point. Human governments were predicated on obedience from the populations that they ruled.

The examples in support of Godral's words were countless. She had never thought of everything precisely in that way, but her An-Ki friend was right. Nevertheless, she had to get him to understand the daunting situation facing all of them.

"Gangs are very cruel rulers. They are evil. What they do goes against Adonai," Arianna said.

Godral nodded slowly, though he offered no verbal response.

"Need to be killed?" Vailia interjected, after a moment passed.

"They are very bad humans," Saranger added. "I understand this, Arianna."

"They will hurt all the people here, when they come," Arianna said. "They want to make all of these people obey them."

"We should hunt them," Kantel commented, in a low, edgy voice that brimmed with ire. "Slay them."

Arianna could see the surprise at his words reflected in the looks cast from the others.

"That is not our way," Godral said to Kantel.

"They do evil. The humans here fight them. We must fight them," Kantel replied, as if the solution was an obvious one.

"What do you say, Arianna?" Sarangar asked her. "Do not hide your thoughts from us."

The tension brewing in the air persisted as the eyes of the other An-Ki turned back towards her. She knew that the An-Ki loyal to Sargor were not disposed towards harming humans, but they did not understand the full scope of the threat posed by the gang.

"I can't deny that if there was a way to fight them without taking unnecessary risks, it would be a good thing," Arianna replied. "If they take over this neighborhood, they will do violence to the people living here. The gang members are killers. But there are far too many for you to fight. They are numerous, and they all have guns. It is not something you can consider."

"We can hunt a few in the night," Kantel stated, a little more adamantly. "Hunt a few ... then leave."

Godral's gazed remained fixed towards Arianna. "It is certain these gangs will kill good humans?"

"They do every day, wherever you find them," Arianna replied. "They do a lot of evil to good people. Where they are in control, nothing is holding them back."

Godral looked back to Kantel, meeting the latter's eyes. He nodded slowly. "We will hunt. When night is here. We will slay them."

Arianna digested Godral's decision with mixed sentiments. Part of her felt unease at the An-Ki's pronouncement, while another part of her understood that the gang threatened her group for as long as they pursued Benedict's whereabouts.

She did not know the specifics of what it was that the An-Ki were contemplating, other than the fact that the gang encroaching on the neighborhood now had very good reason to be afraid. Arianna did not want to begin to think of what it would be like to be hunted in the dark by the An-Ki.

Glancing towards Maureen and Quinn, she tried to read what her friends were thinking. Quinn's countenance did not show any sign of disturbance, but unmistakable worry shone from the eyes and face of Arianna's closest friend.

"What is it, Maureen?" Arianna asked.

"Is it too great of a risk to take?" Maureen asked, her voice taking on the calculating tone she tended to have whenever discussing legal strategies. "What if it provokes the gang to greater violence?"

"A human does not attack like An-Ki do," Godral interjected, leaving the clear implications unspoken.

Arianna had no doubts regarding Godral's claim. She knew the aftermath of any An-Ki attack would leave no confusion about its inhuman origins.

"They will know the enemy is not other humans," Kantel said.

Maureen nodded. "Which could spread fear among the others,

if they believe a new kind of enemy is after them."

"Yes," Godral said, his voice resonating with certitude. "Fear will grow."

"And fear can be paralyzing," Maureen responded. "Let's just hope it works out the way you intend it."

"We don't want to lose any of you," Arianna said to Godral.

"They will not know we are among them," Godral said.

"We will go before others can come," Kantel added.

"Let us help the people here," Vailia said, with an undercurrent of insistence.

Arianna looked over to Sarangar, and could see his eagerness to take part in attacks on the gang. Every day was filled with its own set of risks, and she could not deny her An-Ki companions without becoming a hypocrite.

Allowing them to come along on her journey was an embrace of risks. She had trusted their judgement then, and she had to continue doing so now. It was just as possible that any undertaking of theirs could benefit both the people living in the shadow of the gang menace and her own mission.

"Do what you think is best, Godral," Arianna said evenly, though the concern she felt towards their choice still tugged deep inside her.

"The humans who do evil shall fear," Godral replied in solemn fashion. For an instant, the hue of his gaze appeared to take on the consistency of flames.

QUERAN

Even at night, the dark attire of the humans did little to shroud them from the eyes of the An-Ki. Queran, Gorthaur, and Oragas stalked the second group easily enough, as the latter crept through the desert scrub towards the loose column of people that the An-Ki were warding.

The steps of the humans were quiet, and there was no mistaking they were skilled in their own way, but the An-Ki were even quieter. Queran and her two companions had shifted into their two-legged form, one that was more conducive for the impending attack.

All of the humans were carrying weapons, instilling caution in Queran as she drew closer to one of them. Their focus was set squarely upon the humans walking together a short distance beyond. It was clear that they had no concerns of anything approaching them from behind.

The human before Queran had no hint of being hunted until her jaws clamped down on the back of his neck. Fangs stabbed far into flesh, and the salty, warm taste of blood burst inside her mouth, even as her claws tore powerfully into the man's body.

Her victim made a gurgling sound, and he tried desperately to shake her clutches as she ripped deeper into him. Finally, his body went slack, the life inside fleeing its mortal container.

She heard a scuffle nearby, and then a curt yelp of pain from Oragas. The human he had been about to strike had become aware of the An-Ki's approach with just enough time to draw a blade.

The man had gotten in a slash, though Oragas swiftly overpowered him. Enraged by the injury, the An-Ki warrior gripped the man on the lower part of his legs and slung him upwards, yanking the human off the ground.

Holding onto both of the human's legs, Oragas pulled the man through a fast, overhead arc. He slammed the human's body into the unforgiving ground with tremendous force.

Oragas kept his grip on the man's legs. Yanking him through the air in the other direction, he smashed the human's full body into the ground once more. The An-Ki warrior then repeated the action a third time, though by then Queran knew the human was dead, his bones broken and shattered.

The remaining humans in the hunting group were scattering by then. A few fired off wild shots with their weapons as they fled, though it was clear they would make no stand. Seeing Gorthaur racing after one, and Oragas taking up the chase of another, she set her eyes on one who had no pursuer as of yet.

Springing forward, she bounded across the desert terrain.

Though the An-Ki were fastest in their four-legged shapes, she still ran much swifter than any human. The invigorating feeling that dwelled within the moments of an open chase after quarry filled her, giving her legs further strength and endurance as the gap between Queran and the human steadily eroded.

Casting a glance over his shoulder, he cried out an indecipherable word, the tenor of his voice filled with fear. He tried to spur his legs to go faster, but the distance shrank even more rapidly as Queran put on a burst of speed, sensing the end of the chase approaching.

With a soaring leap, she crashed into the running man from behind. The wind was knocked from his lungs as he was driven heavily into the ground.

He flailed and thrashed helplessly as she drove fangs and claws deep, raking the latter in gory furrows. In moments, blood from a multitude of wounds soaked into the parched ground.

Leaving the corpse behind, Queran walked slowly away. Her head turned to the left and right as drops of blood fell from her elongated muzzle. Peering across the shadowy landscape, her ears swiveled about, as she sought another target.

A light rustle whirled her gaze about to the right. Fixing the area in her sight, she crouched low and began moving towards the location.

The scent of a human carried on the air currents to Queran, further betraying the figure trying to hide from her. She closed in with great stealth, every step cloaked in silence, circling around the low brush that the human was concealed behind.

Sweat trickling down his face, the man peered into the darkness, eyes gleaming with fear. Coming up on his left side, Queran tensed her muscles, poised to strike.

Just as Queran's shadow began engulfing him, the man tried swinging his weapon around towards her. With one swipe of her right claws, she batted the long weapon far out of the human's grasp.

Knocked aside by the blow, the man scrambled backwards. He took up a blade in his right hand, pulling the weapon out from where it had been kept in a sheath affixed at his waist.

Shifting one way, and then another, the human gripped the blade tightly. Though his eyes were pools of terror, the man would undoubtedly fight with the desperation of cornered prey.

Queran's fangs and claws flashed in the moonlight. The man's blade never left a single mark on her body. A moment later the hand grasping the weapon, and the arm attached to the former, lay underneath some desert scrub several paces from the rest of his body. Hurled into shock and a rapid death, the man barely emitted a breathy gasp.

Queran's ears twitched, and she took in the scents around her, lifting her head up with a blood-drenched muzzle. The night had fallen into a deep silence, though she knew her two companions were not far away. She began to move carefully, both searching for the other An-Ki, and keeping alert for signs of other quarry.

IAN

"What the hell is that?" Chris exclaimed, turning about and raising his weapon. The group pulled together quickly in the wake of the sudden tumult.

His gun trained outward, Ian looked to the right and to the left, filled with tension and anxiety as inhuman growls mixed with the cracking of a few gunshots. Movements in the dusky landscape drew his eyes.

Ian saw the shadowy outlines of multiple figures, running in several directions. His attention honed in on one in particular.

At first, it looked like the individual would disappear into the night, but a much larger shape suddenly bounded into sight. There was something strange about the latter figure that sent a chill through his body. The night and distance prevented Ian from discerning much detail, but there was something different about the way the being moved.

He stared in disbelief at the swiftness of the pursuing entity, who ran far faster than any human he had ever seen. The one running away stood no chance at all of escaping. With a great leap, the second entity encompassed the fleeing individual, and the two dropped out of sight.

A few moments later, one of the figures rose up. The silhouettes of triangular, upright ears, and a lengthy snout were etched in the moonlight. Ian stared at the profile of a wolf's head in a state of sheer disbelief, with growing tendrils of fear snaking throughout him.

"What the hell is that thing?" Chris asked.

"No idea," Blake replied curtly.

The inhuman figure lowered out of sight just a few moments later. Ian felt his heartbeat accelerating, and he took a deep breath and swallowed, focusing on the feel of the gun in his hand.

"Do we stay, Chris?" Ian asked.

"I just say we keep moving," Chris said, rigidly.

"No argument here," Ian replied.

"You won't get one from me either," Rumble Dog added. It was the first time Ian had ever heard distress in the huge biker's voice.

"Keep weapons trained to all sides," Blake stated.

Forming into a tight cluster, the group moved out, keeping to a brisk stride. Those with weapons were arrayed such that all sides were defended. Ian held his weapon firmly and kept a constant watch around him.

For almost an hour, not a word was spoken amongst them. The desert breezes wafted over them amid the uneasy silence, and every scrape of a shoe on the dry ground bolstered the tension pervading Ian.

They came to an open stretch of land where there was not anything large enough to conceal the shape Ian had witnessed earlier. Once they were moving across it, one of the younger ones in their group spoke up.

"I think we know what just happened," announced the teenaged male named Seth, in a low, hesitant tone.

"I'm pretty sure of it too," the one named Raymond, added.

"Then what happened?" Rumble Dog prompted, with an air of impatience, when the two did not immediately continue with their explanation.

Ian took his eyes off the landscape and watched Seth for a few moments. The teenager cast some glances at his companions, and Ian noted their nods in response.

Seth took a deep breath, and looked to Chris, Ian, and the other older adults. He was anything but comfortable with what he was about to say. The anxiety was written plainly enough on his face.

"We've been through some experiences you might not believe, back in Venorterra," Seth began. "I swear this isn't a joke, or anything like that. Please understand that, because unless you went through what we did, it would sound crazy."

"Tell us everything," Chris encouraged the youth, in a calm tone of voice.

"Yeah, speak frankly, we'll hear you out, kid," Rumble Dog added.

The atmosphere took on a heavy silence as Seth proceeded to tell an incredible tale of witnessing humans who could transform into giant wolves. He even claimed to have posted raw footage of the shapeshifting online.

Ian's memory was jogged, as he recalled his son Peyton excitedly showing him that kind of video online one night. There was no way of knowing whether or not it was the same video Seth was now referencing, but Ian did remember that whoever posted the one that he and his son watched claimed it was a genuine event.

The raw-looking footage showed a man changing into a wolfish beast, with a spectacular degree of realism, but Ian had attributed the visual display to the magical arts of moviemakers. Convincing special effects were everywhere in movies and television, and Ian had no reason to believe otherwise when watching the video. For his part, Peyton had been skeptical too.

"So, you think that's what's out there?" Blake asked, when Seth had finished. The manner in which the man asked the question showed that the youth's story was being taken seriously.

"I wouldn't doubt it," Raymond answered. "In fact, I'd be willing to bet on it."

"What if it isn't?" Blake said. "Seems we were being followed by some people, maybe soldiers. But whatever got them could also go after us."

"I know they are out there, and I don't think they'll go after us. They helped us back at the camp," Seth responded, pausing a moment and taking a deep breath after the revelation. "They took out several of the guards at the gate area. We saw it all. They ran into the night, then."

"They were the other three who were captured with us," Raymond said. With a declarative edge, he added a moment later, "I'm sure of it."

"The big fellows, and the big gal, you mean," Rumble Dog said, to nods from all the younger ones in their group.

Ian thought of the tall men and woman who had been taken captive along with them. They were certainly imposing-looking figures, but it was hard to believe that they could change into beasts.

"They're out there, but I'm certain they aren't going to harm us," Seth said. "I..."

"No harm to you," cut in a voice from the darkness, interrupting Seth. "We guard you."

Everyone whirled at the sound of the voice, and Ian's heart leapt to his throat. A short distance out was a human figure, in silhouette. The voice, though lower in pitch, had a feminine quality, and the outline revealed by the moon had long hair, a narrow waist, and broader hips.

"We kill those men," the figure continued. "Ones who hunt you. They are dead."

Her words sounded hesitant and accented, and Ian had no doubts the unidentified person was not speaking their native language. He could not make out her face, but her form did resemble the tall woman who had been among the captives.

"We will help. Do not fear us," the woman announced, before turning and walking away.

"Who are you?" Chris called after her.

"Friends," came the reply, without a moment's hesitation.

Ian stared after the enigmatic woman until she was enveloped by the night. Chris called out a few more questions, but no answers were given in response. The weighty feeling to the air grew heavier, as a night breeze passed over them.

"That's her, the one with the two men," Seth said, after a few moments had passed.

"No question, it was her," Chris stated. "It is all just getting weirder and weirder."

"Let's keep going," Blake said. "I don't know whether to feel good or bad about this, but we will have to keep moving."

"Agreed," Chris replied. "With guns at the ready."

Keeping to the tighter formation, the group resumed their trek across the arid landscape. Ian felt no less tense than before, but he did have a lot more to ponder as they walked. At the very least, it kept his mind occupied.

SETH

A mix of feelings ran through Seth as they continued marching through the cold night. The emergence of the wolf creatures brought both fear and encouragement to him.

He had no doubts regarding who the wolf-things ultimately were. His mind vividly recalled the three physically exceptional individuals who had been swept up with the others, and taken to the internment camp.

There was no question they had interceded on behalf of Seth's group, first at the camp, and now out in the wilderness. The first instance may have been unintentional, but there was no question the second had been an intervention on behalf of his group.

Why the beasts were helping them was a question Seth could not answer. But he was open to all kinds of possibilities after the incredible experiences he had been through.

Though he wanted to talk to his friends, he maintained the silence being kept by all of them as the night dragged onward. The sounds of their footsteps on the dry ground and the lonely breezes coursing through the air were the only sounds to penetrate the brooding stillness.

Seth did not like being in the open swathe of ground. He felt considerably better when they were finally back in the midst of some larger scrub.

Periodically, he looked upward, staring into the depths of night. Nothing beyond the moon and stars met his eyes, giving a little further relief.

More than once he glanced towards Christa. She seemed to be more at ease as they continued, which gladdened him. They were all in the midst of a strenuous ordeal, but the less discomfiture he observed in her, the better that he felt.

He could only hope that the interruptions were over for the night, and that their shadowy benefactors had removed the main threat to his group. But the prospects of a quiet end to the nighttime trek vanished in a speck of time.

Headlights from several small all-terrain vehicles flashed on abruptly, blinding them. Seth froze in place, overwhelmed in the barrage of luminance.

"Place all weapons on the ground! Do not think to resist. You are surrounded!" a harsh-sounding voice shouted through the glare.

Heart thumping fast, Seth shielded his eyes. Looking to either side, and glancing behind, he watched in dismay as the sheriff and the others who had guns carefully set them down.

There was little they could do. The overpowering lights left them at a tremendous disadvantage if they tried to resist. The people with the vehicles could see Seth and the others clearly, and any firefight would only result in them being picked apart in short order.

"Hands up in the air!" the voice called. "Did you think you could..."

The speaker's words cut off abruptly, and screams sliced through the desert air. A guttural roar filled the night, brimming with fury, followed by a gurgling, pitiful cry. The latter sound caused Seth's stomach to churn.

The headlights blasting right in their faces made it all but impossible to see what was happening ahead. But there was no mistaking the form of a man running towards them. Seth eyes spread wide as another figure was outlined just behind.

Two-legged, massive, with long, pointed ears, a beast charged after the man. With a powerful, dexterous burst, it leaped through the air and brought the man crashing awkwardly into the ground.

The savage growl that the creature emitted froze the blood in Seth's veins. He watched, silhouetted by the lights, the extended muzzle of the beast dipping downward.

Seth heard the crunching bite that followed, a blood-curdling sound that he would not easily forget. The man went silent and ceased struggling.

The beast raised its head upward, and though all Seth could see was its broad, brawny form, and triangular ears, he knew the creature was gazing right at him. Lurching to the right, the creature suddenly bounded off.

Other bestial sounds, fearful human cries, and a few echoing gunshots rang out in the darkness, but it was not long before the night grew quiet once more. A pervasive tension gripped the air, as Seth's group could still see nothing while encompassed in the headlights.

No authoritative voice called out to them, nor did any animalistic sounds come from beyond the glare. The silence persisted, with no sign of anyone remaining around the vehicles.

"Is everybody okay?" the voice of the sheriff finally called out, sounding highly anxious

One by one, the others answered. To Seth's great relief, he heard all of his friends' distinct replies.

"Let's get the hell out of these damnable beams!" the big biker growled, as the group began moving off to the left. His next words sounded exasperated. "How much more is gonna happen tonight?"

Seth breathed a little easier when he was out of the reach of the lights. Circling about carefully, the sheriff, the soldier, and the biker left the others behind, and began moving in towards the vehicles with their guns poised.

Jonathan, Annika, and the others clustered with Seth, who stood near to Ian and the biker's girlfriend. He could see no signs of either beast or man in the gloom surrounding them.

There were four of the low, large-wheeled tactical vehicles in all, spaced apart such that their beams covered a large swathe of ground.

Each one could hold two people, including the driver.

Seth quickly judged there was no way the vehicles could have carried his entire group out of the desert. He surmised that if the full capture had taken place, a helicopter would have retrieved them.

"All dead," the soldier announced with a somber air, when the trio that had gone to investigate the vehicles returned. "Very violently."

Several moments of silence met his grim pronouncement.

"You all saw them," Annika stated. She was not talking about the soldiers.

"Yes, we did," the sheriff said. "No denying it."

"Biggest wolves I've ever seen," Ian stated. "I didn't trust my eyes for a moment. But they were there, back at the camp gate, weren't they?"

"Yes, they were," Seth replied, nodding to him.

"And they took out all those soldiers, and didn't attack a single one of us," Rumble Dog said, shaking his head, as if in disbelief at their good fortune. He looked back towards Seth. "I'd say if all your story was true ... and no offense, it is pretty damn hard to swallow ... then those things are here with us. Somewhere really close."

"No doubt watching us right now," the biker's tough-looking girlfriend added, peering out across the terrain. As a chill breeze coursed over the group, she added, "Maybe listening to us."

"We not harm you. We help you," the distinct female voice that Seth had heard before interjected once again from the darkness. There was something very strange about the vocal quality, though what it was he could not pinpoint. "Others to harm you. We help you. We attack them."

Seth turned slowly, with all the others, in the direction of the speaker. His nerves teetered on the edge, as he had a strong idea what was about to be revealed.

Under the light of the desert moon were three towering shapes. A hybrid of lupine and human forms, they walked upon two legs, yet had the extended muzzles and triangular ears of wolves.

Their eyes gleamed in the darkness, reflecting the moonlight. Memories flooded Seth's mind, intertwining with the stark vision before him.

A heavy silence set in and dragged on, and there was little doubt that many in his group were in varying states of shock at the development. He knew the kind of thoughts striking those who were encountering the creatures for the first time.

The sight was startling enough, but even more so were the words coming from the one that had spoken. Seth knew they were capable of speech, at least when in their human forms, but it was surreal to see the beasts speaking.

Yet after all he had been through, Seth was well-prepared to adjust to things unanticipated. The fact that they spoke while in their wolf-like forms also brought some reassurance, in that they were not in a state akin to wild animals.

"You did … this?" the sheriff asked at long last, gesturing towards the inert vehicles.

"We protect you," came the reply from the female. "They would harm you."

The female stood in the center, and though she was every bit as tall as the huge biker in Seth's own group, she was the shortest of the three imposing beasts. While her two companions were noticeably larger of stature and girth, it was clear to Seth that she held the greater authority among them.

Her words spoke truly enough. Twice during that night, security forces had been on the verge of apprehending them, and both times the wolfish creatures had intervened. It was the third time that the beasts had been the group's benefactors, counting the fighting at the gate of the compound.

Seth knew in his heart that he had nothing to fear from the inhuman trio. Seeing how quickly the creatures had overwhelmed the soldiers, Seth knew they would have had no difficulties if they had wanted to cause harm to his group. It was a sobering conclusion, but it was one that reinforced the female's words.

"Can you help us from here? Can you go forward, and tell us if there are soldiers ahead of us, so we can avoid them?" the sheriff asked, with a little hesitancy. "We could use some help to get through the desert."

"Yes, we watch for you," the female replied, evenly. "We help you."

"Were you … the three who were taken with us? The three who were in the woods?" the sheriff queried, after another extended moment had passed. To Seth, it sounded like the sheriff was nervous to hear the answer.

"Yes," the beast replied, confirming Seth's suspicions.

"And … you can change, to look like us?" the sheriff continued, after an extended silence.

"Yes, An-Ki have three forms," the other responded. "We can have form of humans."

"Incredible," the sheriff responded.

"We want to find home," the female stated. "You know way. Will you help?"

It should have been more obvious to Seth, but the three creatures were in a great predicament themselves. They were lost, and were seeking their way back to the area they had been snatched away from.

"Of course. We will help each other," the sheriff declared. "We have the same enemy, it seems. We were taken captive together, and it would be best if we return home together."

"I give thanks … for help," the female replied.

"You were taken against your will, just like us," the sheriff said. "And if we stick together, and cooperate together, our chances of getting home safely are much better."

"We help you, you help us," the female said. "We go now. Look for those who harm."

"Wait!" Blake interrupted, emphatically. He walked forward several paces to stand by the sheriff, who looked at him with an expression of curiosity. "If nothing happens to us in this desert before we reach a road that's not far ahead of us, we should be getting some help soon, from my order."

"What?" the biker exclaimed.

The unexpected pronouncement lifted Seth's spirits. He wondered how far they would still have to go, to get some assistance, though to his mild frustration Blake did not elaborate further.

"And when were you gonna tell us?" the biker pressed Blake in an angry voice.

"I didn't want to bring this up until I knew for sure, as you've all been through far enough already," Blake told the biker, before looking around at the group. He turned his attention back towards the three wolf-beings. "But I needed to bring this up now, because the three of you will need to be in ... a human form ... like before, when we encounter the others of my order." His sideways glances towards the sheriff told Seth that the other knew about the potential help ahead. "I don't have time to prepare them for the changes you can make with your bodies. I would bet that you don't have any clothes nearby either."

"No clothes," the woman said. "Left in place where tried to keep us."

The image of the creatures leaving through the demolished front gates of the detainment camp and heading into the night returned to the forefront of Seth's mind. Undoubtedly, they had discarded their human attire when they had shifted forms, but apparently that lack of clothes would be problematic when the group reached whatever help awaited them.

Finding clothes would not be easy, either. There was nothing to be spared from among Seth's group. Only the biker came close to the others' size, and he had nothing beyond the shirt on his back and jeans on his legs.

"The dead men. They need no clothes," the female stated.

"It's the only possibility. We will gather what we can off the dead soldiers, and carry it along with us," Blake instructed them. "Do not let yourself be seen by anyone but us. I can come and find you before we go onward, so you can put on some clothes."

"Then let's get this underway now," the biker said, his tone thick with irritation. "Our enemies aren't gonna sit around when the dead fellows here fail to check back in."

From the look on the biker's face and his harder tone, Seth could sense he was more than a little miffed at not being briefed. He cast more than one heated glare towards the sheriff.

Seth looked at the faces of the others. From what he could tell, the sheriff's deputy, Lucy, knew about everything, but his friend Ian did not.

"Agreed," Blake said. Directing the words at the biker, he then added in an apologetic manner. "And I'm sorry I didn't tell you yet, but I didn't want to raise everyone's hopes."

"Don't pull that crap again," the biker replied firmly. He glowered at the sheriff. "Neither of you. But let's keep things moving. Time's a wastin'."

Blake looked back towards the three wolf-beings. "Make sure you aren't seen, and look for me to come find you by myself."

"We will look," the female replied.

Blake, the sheriff, the deputy, and the biker headed back towards the vehicles and the dead bodies. Not enthused by the idea of stripping dead bodies, Seth turned his head to look towards the three wolf-beings, but they had already vanished into the shadows of night.

Knowing that they were out there, and committed to warding the group, bolstered his sagging spirits. Having guardians like the wolf-beings, the chances of the group getting through the ordeal facing them had just gotten much better.

He just hoped it was not all that far to whatever Blake was referring to. Seth's legs did not have much left in them, in the way of endurance.

Some sustenance, especially water, and a little rest were all that Seth found himself desiring. Times of hardship certainly had a knack for breeding a more simplified atmosphere.

ARIANNA

Three days had passed, without much at all to do. Arianna and Maureen had filled a portion of the time taking several walks together through the neighborhood, during both mornings and afternoons.

Arianna found her spirits lifted on the jaunts. She felt grateful for the visits with her closest friend, finding that they helped her reconnect with a side of her that had withered over the recent past. Laughing and smiling replaced heartache and worry, if only for a little while.

She realized that the two of them rarely got to spend time

together, by themselves, in the way that they had in the times before the upheaval, on those days when Maureen informed Quinn that it was time for a 'girls' night out.' To his everlasting credit, Quinn encouraged a greater frequency of such occasions, knowing that they were good for his girlfriend and friend alike. His lack of possessiveness was yet another reason why Arianna knew Quinn was the perfect man for her best friend.

Whether going out to a night club, movie, or simply hanging out at home, watching television, Arianna always found herself in the best of moods after a visit with Maureen. It was the time when she could share her joys, give vent to the innermost things bothering her, and seek a trusted friend's perspective on any number of things.

Such times were also when she could lend Maureen a shoulder to cry on, offer counsel on the things concerning her, or celebrate the higher moments in her friend's life. Through ups and downs, the genuine friendship that Arianna had with Maureen was something that no price tag could be placed on.

Along the walks through the neighborhood, Arianna and Maureen also had many opportunities to meet some of the residents living nearby. More often than not, the two women chose to avail themselves of a chance get to know a little more about the people they were staying among.

Everyone they met was polite enough, but Arianna could sense the extreme tension within the community. The proximity of gang territory was like a mass of storm clouds on the horizon. It was only a matter of time before the rain, lightning, and thunder was breaking over their streets and homes.

For his part, Quinn ended up befriending many of the local youth, and got involved in some of their baseball and soccer games. Watching him playing with the younger ones, Arianna could see the makings of a wonderful father, though the thought brought her a degree of sadness.

There was no telling when Maureen and Quinn would find a place and time where they could settle down and begin a family of their own. Even if they somehow could, the world was no longer a place to bring a child into. It was a place descending into darkness, with a host of living nightmares, bearing malevolent intentions, emerging from the deep shadows.

The five An-Ki kept to themselves for the most part, which was probably for the best. With their huge size, the color of their eyes, and their foreign-sounding accents, they were more likely to intimidate than befriend.

At night, Godral and the others disappeared for long stretches of time. Arianna did not really want to know what they were up to during those forays in the dark. She knew without asking that their sojourns were not frivolous in nature.

They always returned to the house before dawn, and spent most of the daytime sleeping. She had spoken a few times with Godral and Sarangar, but deftly avoided the topic of their excursions. For their part, the two An-Ki offered her nothing either.

Finally, on the fourth full day since their arrival, she decided to search out Davis. At first, she tried to find him at the church, but a woman there indicated that he had gone out to inspect Barricade B earlier that morning.

After getting directions, Arianna set out on foot for the location. Following the street signs given to her, it took just under an hour's walk to reach the fortified position.

She found Davis in back of the large barricade blocking the road. He was busy inspecting some gun ports in the thick rampart, shielded portals that defenders could use to fire upon anything in the roadway.

Seeing her approaching, he gave a half-grin. "Decided to come help us ready the defenses? They'll be coming pretty soon, I believe. If I'm reading all the signs right, that is."

"This is the side of their neighborhood closest to them, isn't it?" Arianna asked, bothered by Davis' prediction.

"No doubts there are gang members watching this barricade even now," Davis replied, with grim resignation. "But they'd be smart not to stick their heads out." He glanced upward, and chuckled.

Crouched behind the barricade, on a couple of small platforms set wide apart, were men armed with long rifles. The men peered intently through the scopes. Their barrels poked through small gun ports like the ones that Davis had been inspecting, and it was clear that the shooters were poised to fire at any moment.

"I imagine that would be the best choice," Arianna said. "Though part of me wished they would stick their heads up, and offer targets to your shooters."

"You can say that again," Davis replied, with another chuckle. After a short pause, his tone grew more serious, as he looked to her and asked, "So, what brings you all the way out here, for real? I know you weren't just taking a long stroll."

"Just wanted to see what you might have found out," Arianna said. "I don't want to distract you from everything going on, and we all really appreciate your hospitality, but I need to start searching again for my uncle soon. I'll stay out of your way ... I promise you that ... I just wanted to ask what you might know, now."

"I understand, but I'm really sorry to say I have nothing new to tell you," Davis said, with a sympathetic air. His face reflected the disappointment in his voice. "All I can say is that the numbers of the gang members is growing fast in the next neighborhoods over. It's inevitable in my eyes. They'll be moving on us before too much longer."

"Isn't there any way around them?" Arianna inquired, feeling a shard of despair at the bleak news.

"You might be able to get around them, if you're careful, but there's no telling what's along the border area," Davis said. "Could be anything there."

"Sounds like I've run into a dead end," she replied grimly.

"I don't know what to tell you, Arianna. Really wish I knew more, but right now all of our efforts are focused on keeping eyes on this gang threat," he said. "I promise, as long as you're here, I'll keep my ears out, and I'll make sure to tell you about anything at all I come across. No matter how big or small. You've got my word on that."

Arianna flinched as a loud crack broke the stillness around them. It echoed in the distance.

Davis turned and looked towards the gunmen on the platforms. "What have you got?"

"One of the rats finally poked its beady-eyed head out," one of the riflemen replied, in a thick southern drawl. "Won't be doin' that no more."

"If only all of them would do that for us," Davis called back. "We'd solve this issue real quick."

"Might need more ammo," the shooter replied, grinning broadly.

"We'll get you more ammo, keep it up," Davis told the man. He looked back to Arianna. "Thirty-aught six. Does its job very well."

"It apparently does," Arianna replied.

Davis' expression grew more somber once again. "Again, I'm so sorry I don't have anything to tell you. I hope I come across something that can help."

"I understand, and I definitely don't want to be a distraction, all of you have been so good to us," Arianna told him.

"Hey, we're all in this mess together. We gotta help each other out," Davis replied.

"I agree with that," Arianna said. "I'll let you get back to your business here, but thank you for taking a moment to talk with me."

"Anytime, Arianna," Davis said, and she knew he meant his promise.

Arianna bid him goodbye and left the barricade. The walk back to the house where she was staying seemed twice as long as it had been coming out to find Davis.

Her legs felt sluggish, but she knew it was more a function of her downtrodden mood rather than any kind of overexertion. Nothing had been found, and a murderous horde of gang members was massing to indulge in an orgy of looting, terror, and violence.

The daylight was fading as she neared the house. The sun's last rays scattered through the boughs of the old trees looming above her, as cooling evening breezes ruffled their hosts of leaves. To her, the sounds were like weary sighs.

A deep melancholy came over her by the time that she reached the front door. Inside, she cobbled together a light meal from the copious assortment of cans stocked in the cabinets.

Without regular power there was no refrigeration available, so she had to drink a can of sweetened tea at room temperature. There was not a shred of complaint in her, as things could be much worse. At least there was a can of tea to be had.

When she finished the meal, it was solid night, but she was far too restless to go to bed. Taking a quick survey of the house, she discovered that nobody was home.

She remembered Quinn mentioning something about an invitation to play cards at the house of one of the neighbors. Maureen had probably gone with him. There certainly were not many options for entertainment. As for the An-Ki, they were apparently on another one of their nighttime excursions.

Heading into the living room, Arianna slumped down into an easy chair. Leaning her head back, she closed her eyes, and breathed out slowly. The silence pervading the house lulled her mind to settle, as her tired body entered a restful slumber.

Much later in the night, her eyes fluttered open. Whether she had dreamed or not, Arianna could not tell. She took a couple of deep breaths, letting her mind clear, and listened for a hint of one her other companions in the house. The same weighty silence that preceded her slumber reigned within the shadowy interior.

Standing up, and stretching for a moment, Arianna then made her way slowly towards the rear of the house, seeking some fresh air. She shuffled through the kitchen, opened the door, and walked into the backyard.

The cool air flowing into her lungs with each breath enlivened her senses. Moving out into the lawn, she stared up into the depths of the star-filled night.

The worries plaguing her earlier returned to the forefront of her thoughts as she gazed upward. Arianna had come too far to be stymied completely. But no matter where she looked, it seemed as if there were no roads to take.

Waiting around in an inactive state, facing so much uncertainty, was an agony. She did not know how much longer she could endure it without incurring some damage to her sanity.

Every instinct she possessed had pulled her to where they had come. She had even prayed on a few occasions, a practice that she was highly unaccustomed to.

Reaching the border area, in the general area where she surmised Benedict had been ferried through by air, Arianna thought she could gain some more information about UCAS detentions and sites. Yet now she was spending her days in an idle state, dwelling in the midst of a community readying and bracing itself to resist an all-out gang onslaught.

Nothing about the situation was proving helpful towards her goal. If anything, it seemed that they were squarely in the path of a terrible danger.

A few tears began trickling from the corners of her eyes and down her cheeks as the frustration within boiled over. She blinked them back, and wiped at her eyes with the back of her hand. Part of her wanted to scream her anger into the night, but before she did anything like that she heard some rustling beneath some trees to the right.

Striding out of the deep shadows were the five An-Ki, all in their four-legged, wolf-like forms. Their eyes gleamed with the silver light of the moon, and for a fleeting moment Arianna felt the touch of fear pass over her. Her surprise at seeing them returning from one of their forays in their large wolf forms snapped a degree of composure back into her.

The An-Ki drew nearer, and Arianna saw the dark, matted fur abundant along their muzzles and chests, standing out very prominently on Sarangar's white fur. There was not a single hint of any wounds having been suffered by the An-Ki. All of them moved with a relaxed gait, and she knew at once what the dark areas indicated.

The group of An-Ki spread farther apart, giving each other some space. One by one, their bodies began undergoing the contortions and profound skin changes that returned them back into human forms.

Fur retracted, and muzzles and ears shortened, the latter sliding down to the sides of more compact, rounded heads as the bones of their skulls shifted and realigned. The process that the An-Ki underwent always looked enormously painful.

The transformations removed all the evidence of their blood-soaked, nighttime foray. The crimson stains disappeared along with their coarse fur, absorbed back into the flesh of their bodies.

Five tall human forms, each one incredibly fit and toned, stood around her in the moonlight. All had somber expressions on their faces, and they regarded Arianna in silence for a few pensive moments.

She looked back to them with a question poised on her lips.

"The hunt was good," Godral told her, as he started walking towards the back wall of the house. "We saw their evil this night. We must hunt them. We must kill them."

His gaze was piercing, and his unsmiling face showed not a single flicker of good humor or gladness at seeing her. Arianna had rarely witnessed him in such an intense, hardened state, and thought about the words he had just said.

Turning, she saw piles of clothing stacked in the shadows a few paces away from the rear door. The others filed by Arianna in heavy silence, making their way over to the clothes.

As with Godral, there was a conspicuous intensity to the looks in their eyes and in their expressions. Only Sarangar cast her a direct glance, and a few moments later the An-Ki began getting dressed. They did not say a single word as they clothed themselves, and when they were finished all five entered the house quietly.

Standing alone again, Arianna had no doubts that the night had been filled with terror for more than one gang member. From their perspective, it probably seemed as if the night sprouted fangs and talons.

Yet something had put the An-Ki in a dark, seething mood. Arianna's instincts told her that the gang members the An-Ki encountered had done much to bring a terrible doom upon themselves. They were not innocent, to any degree.

Arianna was not sure she wanted to know what Godral and the others had witnessed. She decided that she would let one of them bring up the subject by themselves, whenever they were ready.

The return of the An-Ki and their weighty demeanors put Arianna in a morose disposition. She could not go inside just yet, and turned her eyes back to the silent night.

Her uncle was somewhere out there, under the same panorama of stars she was gazing upon. No matter how slim the chance might be, she had to continue looking for answers or leads regarding his possible whereabouts. For her, there was no other choice.

She could not see a way forward, but she would stay and continue looking. The only thing she could not do was turn back.

BENEDICT

Benedict stared out the window in silence, a host of thoughts weighing upon his mind. With a heavy-hearted exhale, he turned away from the sun's touch.

At the least, he was no longer confined to a small, barren cell within the depths of a heavily-guarded UCAS facility. Despite being detained once more, his current surroundings were far less stark than they had been in the massive federal installation.

It would take some considerable effort to match the casual air of his new, makeshift holding cell. A cursory inspection of the space confirmed that it had been the room of a teenaged boy.

The bed had been left in an unmade jumble of blankets and sheets. There was a considerable amount of clutter all about the floor and furniture, ranging from discarded t-shirts, jeans, food wrappers, and other items common to a young male growing up in the heart of the UCAS.

It looked as if the space had been frozen in a moment of time. Benedict did not want to think of what might have happened to the room's proper occupant. He hoped the boy had found a refuge somewhere, and not run afoul of the monsters in human guises that had overtaken the neighborhood.

Posters of rock bands popular before the collapse covered the better part of two walls. A pair of shelves mounted higher on another wall held a few models of military aircraft. Beneath the shelves was a desk holding a computer system, both items covered in a thin layer of dust.

An empty soft drink can sat on the desk, just to the right of the keyboard. Benedict thought about how the boy probably had no idea what was coming when he had last sipped from that can. The bitter thought left him in a depressed mood.

The room's trappings spoke of heartfelt dreams and interests, in a world that had turned into a nightmare in swift fashion. There were millions of young boys and girls living in the UCAS and the rebel provinces who had seen their prospects for the future dashed, consumed by an evil tightening its unholy grip upon the entire world.

Benedict could not imagine how he would have handled things if he were a teenager in the modern day. Toughness of heart, resilience, and courage in ample supply would have been necessary to simply move forward from day to day, and avoid giving in to utter despair.

"You ... gringo ... come on," growled a heavily-accented voice, interrupting Benedict's melancholic thoughts.

The stocky, muscular fellow with a blue bandanna wrapped around his head filled the doorway. With all of the tattoos covering his face, his appearance had a primal quality, one that was reflected in his hard eyes.

"Second Word want to see you ... now!" the brute added a moment later, with an impatient edge.

Benedict knew better than to provoke such an individual. Seeking to avoid a primal response, he rose to his feet from where he was sitting at the edge of the bed, and followed the man from the room.

Another gang member, lean and ice-eyed, waited out in the hallway. He followed Benedict as they walked down the hall, heading towards the top of a staircase.

The sounds of boisterous laughter rose from the lower level, and Benedict descended into a light haze of smoke. Though a little daylight leaked around the pulled curtains, the living room that they entered remained shrouded in a shadowy ambience.

Rifles were leaned up against the wall at a couple places in the room, and more than one handgun could be seen lying on a coffee table set before a long couch. A couple of women were interspersed among four men who bore tattoos like the pair escorting Benedict.

Empty and half-filled beer bottles littered the space in abundance, and the sweet, distinctive smell in the air told Benedict that they had not been smoking cigarettes. They all looked towards Benedict, except for a man and woman heavily kissing on the couch.

One of them spoke briefly in Iberian with the burly man leading Benedict. The two laughed heartily, as some sort of joke was exchanged between them, likely at Benedict's expense.

He walked out the front door of the house and into the glare of direct sunlight. Squinting, he hesitated for a moment as his eyes adjusted to the harsh change.

Part of him wished immediately that his vision had not cleared, as the first thing he saw was a teenaged boy being beaten harshly by three gang members. The wiry, dark-skinned youth cried out loudly as he was kicked squarely in the ribs, repeatedly.

His merciless tormentors had looks of sheer enjoyment on their faces. Other gang members stood around, watching the beating, a few holding baseball bats, and four or five others with machetes. Though Benedict could not understand the words they shouted, he knew they were bolstering and prodding the ones delivering the savage beating. It was a frenzy of violence, and Benedict could not comprehend the ugly mindset it took to participate in it.

"Hey, come on!" Benedict's stout escort snapped irritably, noticing Benedict's look of disgust and slowed pace. "*Chavala* is getting what he deserves."

Benedict felt a shove forward from the man behind him as he took his eyes away from the troubling scene. He offered no visible protest to the violent display nearby, knowing he would only invite a wave of brutality on himself, and more suffering for the boy.

If it was just a matter of himself, and he could have relieved the boy's torments by appealing to the thuggish gang members, he would have done so in a second. Yet he knew the kind of creatures that they were.

In that moment, he wished fervently that he were one of the An-Ki, so he could mete out the punishment that all of the gang members rightfully deserved. If he could have been an armed special operations soldier, with the weapons and skill to take all of the predators out, it would have been a great blessing.

As it was, he was just an old, unarmed, captive man, powerless to intervene on the boy's behalf. There was nobody to appeal to, and he could do nothing but make the boy's plight worse.

They continued across the front lawns of several houses. Tables and chairs from a back patio had been moved around to the front yard of one of the houses just ahead of them. A pole through the middle of the table supported a broad umbrella, which provided shade and protection from the elements.

A narrow-faced man with a close-cropped moustache was seated on the far side of the table, accompanied by Lil Dragon, who sat to the man's right. With a curt gesture, the man waved away a couple of gang members who were in the process of bringing a very frightened-looking young man up to the table. They nodded, and dragged the man away with a rough manner.

"Ah. Mr. Benedict. Have a seat and join us," he said with a polite air, gesturing towards one of the open chairs across from him. "You have met Lil Dragon. I am the First Word, and am known as the Leopard."

Benedict sat down in the chair, and looked across the table at the Leopard and Lil Dragon. He said nothing, trying not to show the anger he felt towards everything transpiring around him, and waited for the other man to continue. It was far from easy to conceal his disgust.

"All this might seem very harsh to someone like you," the Leopard said. "You must understand that you are from a softer world. You do not understand our ways. But they are necessary. A few demonstrations will gain good cooperation from the people here. It will be better for all. You will see."

Benedict made no reply. He did not want to agree with the Leopard, nor did he wish to provoke such a dangerous man.

The Leopard nodded in the direction of the youth being held nearby, little more than a boy, maybe a year or two older than the one being thrashed on the ground. "That *chavala* was hiding a gun. We had given everyone here plenty of time to turn all their weapons in. He did not listen. He will live, but he must learn, so he will listen better next time."

Benedict kept his voice controlled, as he sought to change the subject. "What can I do for you?"

"For me? Nothing ... nothing at all!" the Leopard said with a bemused smile. "But there are others who have a great interest in you.

"Some friends of yours from Station Central. It would appear they have missed you. And it would also appear they are willing to give my men some considerable firepower to address the issues in this region. I have been in contact with those I answer to. It looks like you will not be staying with us for much … "

The Leopard's voice trailed off. His eyes shifted from Benedict towards something drawing his attention out on the street. Following the other man's gaze, Benedict turned his head, and saw a group of men hurrying towards them.

All of the men were carrying guns, and when they got closer Benedict could see that every one of them was highly agitated. He wished that he spoke Iberian, as they hurriedly addressed the Leopard.

There was a palpable air of fear about them. Their eyes were wide, and their words rushed forth from their lips. Benedict knew something of big significance had occurred recently, some event that was far from their liking.

The cocky demeanor and smile faded fast from the Leopard's face as he listened to their words, the expression replaced swiftly with a blend of pensiveness and anger. The dour look was mirrored on Lil Dragon's face as well.

The Second Word's jaws grew more taut as he digested the words, but he did not interrupt, deferring to the First Word. The Leopard interrupted the other men a few times, presumably asking a few questions, gauging by the way the men responded.

"Something has happened, we will talk later," the Leopard announced curtly to Benedict, when his dialogue with the men came to an end. He glanced towards the men who had accompanied Benedict from the house. "Take him back to his quarters for now."

Both the Leopard and Lil Dragon rose to their feet. With an air of urgency, the two leaders strode quickly with the unnerved-looking men, heading back in the direction they had come from. Benedict wished he could have understood what happened to cause such a concerned, fast reaction, but he knew it would be folly to ask either of his two guards.

He felt a hard grip seize his arm. "Let's go," growled the heavier set man who had initially summoned him.

Benedict was escorted directly back to the second floor bedroom. The group in the living room was still drinking and laughing when they returned, with the exception of the kissing pair, who had evidently sought out more private quarters.

As the door to his room was shut and locked behind by his wards, Benedict walked over to the window and looked out to the street. He wondered what had the gang members so agitated.

Benedict knew it was something much more than mere fighting with the local population. It was not likely any kind of attack from outside, as the air had been largely devoid of gunshots.

The fear on the faces of those who had come to get the Leopard was unmistakable, as was the grave concern manifested in the expressions of both the First and Second Word. Yet anything that spread terror through the gang was something to Benedict's great liking.

He hoped it would not be too long before he got at least a hint of what was happening. Perhaps the prevailing circumstances were beginning to change in a profound way. After what he had just been witnessing outside with the two younger captives of the gang, a shift of direction could not come a moment too soon.

SETH

Though everyone in the group was sore and exhausted, nobody objected to the idea of pressing onward once some clothes had been scraped up. Enough had happened that night to encourage the group to continue the trek.

The three wolfish beings were somewhere far ahead of them, assiduously keeping from sight. Seth could not deny it continued helping to know that the creatures were out there in the night, searching for any ambushes or other threats that might lay in wait.

At the late hour Seth's energies were running very low, and it took all that he had to plod across the arid land. His legs felt like a pair of iron weights, but his spirit was bolstered at the first sight of the horizon glowing with the approach of dawn.

The sun climbed into the sky, brushing aside the night's chill as the fiery orb began taking dominion above the desert terrain. The return of daylight did not cause Seth to cease looking about for signs of pursuit.

Among his friends, Jonathan was the nearest in proximity at the breaking of dawn. Seth urged his weary legs to pick up their pace for just long enough to draw closer to his longtime friend.

"I prefer hikes in the woods," he said to Jonathan in a weary voice. "Much more than this."

Jonathan shot him a grin. "Me too. Scenery here is getting dull, really quick."

"For two high school guys, we sure have found ourselves in some crazy adventures," Seth replied, knowing what an understatement that was.

"And then some," Jonathan said.

"How's Annika holding up?" Seth asked.

"Good as can be," Jonathan replied, glancing forward to where Annika and Raymond were walking together. "She's strong. I'll break down before she does."

"I hope we don't have too much longer to go, but I don't want to stop out here, in the middle of nowhere," Seth said.

"I'm with you on that," Jonathan responded. "But wherever we are going, I hope some sleep's included on the schedule."

"Right now, I could sleep for about two days straight," Seth remarked. "Even if I just laid down right here."

Jonathan did not say anything for a few moments. His face took on a worrisome aspect, and his voice was just above a whisper when he asked Seth, "You think there's a way to get back? To Venorterra and home, I mean."

"I have no idea," Seth admitted ruefully.

"I guess we'll have to keep our minds on one thing at a time," Jonathan said.

"Best we can do," Seth agreed. "Even if it's not easy."

The two fell back into silence, and Seth soon found himself slipping a little farther behind. Left to his own thoughts, he turned his concentration back to searching the skies and the horizon. To his relief, he found nothing to cause any concern.

The early morning part of the hike lasted for a few more hours, until at long last they came to a road cutting through the desert. With the road in sight, the sheriff explained to the others that the soldier, Blake, had managed to arrange a rendezvous with some people who would be helping them.

The means of their assistance was already in view, just a short distance away. A large pickup truck pulling a horse trailer sat idle to the side of the road, with the engine off. Blake took the lead at that point and guided the group directly towards it.

After talking for a moment with the driver of the vehicle, Blake walked back into the desert. He was carrying the small pile of clothes taken earlier from the dead soldiers, and Seth knew he was looking for the three who had been serving as their scouts and guardians.

After about twenty minutes passed, Blake returned with the three strangers. The clothes on them were ill-fitting and far too tight for their large forms, but Seth was not about to laugh at their disheveled, ungainly appearances.

They looked highly uncomfortable, and a little irritated. Blake stayed with them, and guided the trio towards the elongated trailer.

Seth and most of the others rode in the trailer. Though the interior had been cleaned out, it was still permeated with the musk of horses. Despite the less than ideal travel accommodations, he was not about to complain.

Spared from hiking any farther, he was extremely grateful for the ride. As everyone was worn out from the long, arduous trek on foot, there was very little conversation among the group as the truck pulled onto the road and started down it.

Sitting near the gate, Seth kept to himself, content listening to the sounds of the large pickup's engine and the air flowing over the trailer. A couple of times he looked over towards Christa, or one of the others, to check on them. Though somber and tired in appearance, they all looked to be holding up.

Once, he caught Christa's eye directly, and felt a sharp flush of embarrassment when she acknowledged his attention with a brief smile. He grinned back sheepishly, and looked away a moment later.

After traveling about an hour longer, during which time the

vehicle made a couple of turns, they finally came to a stop. The sound of the engine shutting off, and voices outside the trailer, told Seth that they had reached their destination.

Getting to his feet, he stretched his limbs. His body had accrued a few more aches from the bumpiness of the ride, but the discomfort was minor compared to how it would have been if they had to continue walking for several more hours.

After being let out of the trailer with the others, Seth set his eyes upon the front of a one level ranch house a short distance away. A storage shed and two-car garage sat near to the elongated structure. A couple of barns, some farm vehicles, and a series of pens and larger, fenced-in spaces radiated out from the ranch house, but nothing was contained in them at the moment. As a whole, the property looked very orderly and well-tended.

Seth looked all around, to his left and right, and behind. Set in the midst of a vast acreage, the location appeared to be very isolated. Not a single neighbor could be seen in any direction.

As it was explained to Seth and his companions shortly after, the owner of the house and estate was a person sympathetic to the resistance. He had agreed to help Seth's group, but the most he would risk was allowing for the escapees to get some rest, food, and time to marshal a plan for moving onward.

The host, Victor Raimondo, appeared to be an amiable enough man when he emerged from the ranch house and introduced himself. Lean and long-limbed, he had a narrow face and sharp nose. A light stubble covered his cheeks and chin, giving his countenance a rough edge.

His weathered skin testified to a life lived often in the elements. Shaking their host's thoroughly-callused hand, Seth felt considerable strength flowing within the man's grip. Though undeniably a tough man, Victor had a friendly look to his eyes, and Seth took a liking to him immediately.

Victor invited the entire group inside the ranch house. Inside, he took them into a large kitchen space, provided with a long table and just enough chairs for the new arrivals.

Platters piled high with sandwiches, a mass of individual bags of potato chips, and stacks of napkins covered the table's surface. The sight of the food made Seth's mouth water.

Of all the potential needs of the group, Victor insisted that getting a quick meal came first. Nobody in Seth's group disagreed with their host's assessment.

Sliced turkey sandwiches with lettuce, cheese and a little mayonnaise never tasted better. Seth wolfed two down in swift fashion, along with a bag of potato chips and a couple of cold soft drinks from a pair of coolers filled with ice. He slowed his pace as he took up a third sandwich from the plattersEveryone expressed their gratitude to Victor, including the three strangers, who ate a prodigious amount by themselves.

Victor then proceeded to give them all places to sleep for the night. With so many new guests descending on the ranch house, there was no chance of getting beds for everyone. Seth did not mind at all when he was given a pillow and sleeping bag on the floor in one of the rooms.

As exhausted as he was, it felt like the most comfortable mattress he had ever slept on. In scant few moments, he was fast asleep.

Groggy and sore, Seth awoke the next morning to the news that a plan had been formed to get them safely into the city of Silver Valley. It had been determined that they could hide out in the city for an extended amount of time if they needed to.

Digesting the news, Seth got up and rolled the sleeping bag into a bundle, setting it to the side with the pillow atop. He nearly bumped into Christa as he made his way down the hall leading to the kitchen, as she came out of another room.

He felt sheepish and tongue-tied when she smiled at him, and wished him a good morning. To his relief, he managed a coherent reply in kind, and the two continued along the hallway.

The scents wafting from the kitchen made Seth salivate and spurred his appetite. He discovered moments later that Victor and his wife had prepared a hot breakfast for all of them.

There was as much bacon, eggs, toast, and hash browns as Seth and his companions could eat. The atmosphere in the kitchen area was subdued, without much chatter, as everyone ate his or her fill.

Despite the quiet ambience, Seth could see that everyone was in pretty good spirits, given the circumstances. Even the trio of strangers looked more adjusted, and Seth noted that they were wearing clothes that suited them much better. Victor had seen to more than just food and sleeping quarters.

Following the sumptuous meal, and after Christa and Annika had taken their own turns first, Seth availed himself of a quick shower. Feeling grimy and sweaty from the long trek through the desert, the hot water running over his skin felt immeasurably good.

Seth thought about how wonderful it was to feel clean again as he toweled himself off, though getting back into the same, sweat-stained clothes he wore the previous day seemed to defeat the purpose a little.

Shortly afterward, everyone in the group gathered together in the living room. Seth stood against a wall, careful not to bump his head against the deer head, crowned with an impressive antler rack, mounted on the wall. Blake and Victor called for attention before explaining to the group what was going to happen and what had been arranged to get everyone into the city undetected.

The sheriff's deputy, Lucy, insisted on being the first in the group to go. About fifteen minutes later, she bid everyone well and headed to an SUV waiting outside to ferry the first of the escapees onward.

The process took the better part of half a day. Vehicles would come to the ranch house periodically, and one by one the freed captives were taken into the outskirts of Silver Valley.

The precaution of using single vehicles was necessary, as two or more cars traveling together could look conspicuous along the lonely roadways and at the low-traffic checkpoints and roadblocks. It was easy enough to pass through the latter emplacements with an extra passenger out of sight, as long as the process was done one at a time.

The explanation by the men from the Order made good enough sense to Seth, but it did nothing to curb his anxiety when he was finally given his turn. His nerves began to perch on the edge as he was loaded into the back of the extended cab of a pickup truck.

Seth was instructed to lay down, and stay quiet at all times. A board was then placed over him, which was then buried under assorted packages. Even though he realized that the board was set into custom, fitted slots, all of it designed for the purpose of concealing a person, he felt extremely tense all throughout the ensuing ride.

He had never thought he was claustrophobic, but the cramped confines made him feel trapped and helpless. The only silver lining was that there was a little room to adjust his position, giving relief when a part of his body began getting sore.

His heartbeat did not begin settling down until the board was finally removed from above him. Seth was helped out of the pickup truck, and directly guided inside a two-story, suburban house, where he saw Jonathan and most of the others seated in a living room to the left of the doorway.

Though relieved at the sight of his friends, the anxiety did not leave completely, as he learned that Christa was still out there. Almost at once, he took up a vigil near the front windows of the safe house, hoping it would not be much longer before she joined the others.

The next to arrive was Rowan, and though Seth was glad to see that he had made it safely, his worry over Christa continued rising unabated. Eyes glued to the front window, he did not even notice Raymond stepping up to his side.

"You really care for her, don't you?" Raymond asked, in a low voice.

Seth nodded. "I do."

"They'll get her here, don't worry," Raymond said.

The next thirty minutes seemed like a week-long ordeal, but finally a commercial van arrived, and the person let out of the back was Christa. The driver and another man who had been riding in the front passenger seat helped her out, and kept at her side as they led her up to the house.

Seth felt so glad to see her, and he forgot all about his nerves as she entered. Annika, Jonathan, and the others got up to welcome her, and there was an air of relief as all of the younger members of the group were accounted for.

"That was an experience," she exclaimed, as she was greeted by the others.

"You can say that again," Seth replied, smiling broadly.

"Glad you made it, Seth," she said to him, reflecting the smile in a way that flooded Seth with giddiness.

"Glad you're here," Seth responded.

"Me too!" she replied, with a laugh, as she found a place to sit in the living room.

The last of all to arrive was the sheriff, who was received with the same enthusiasm by the older members of the group as Christa had been by the younger. Even Rumble Dog, the rough-edged biker, smiled warmly at the sight.

After the hugs and greetings had taken place, the sheriff called for everyone's attention. He looked into all their faces.

"I know we are all curious about what's ahead," the sheriff stated. "This is a safe house, but we are going to be moving on from here in a few hours to a place where the risk of being found is much lower."

Seth's heart sank at the announcement. After the tension-filled journey from the ranch to the safe house, he had hoped they were done for the day. Apparently, he had to gird himself for a little more stress.

"Underneath Silver Valley, there is an extensive system of drainage tunnels," the sheriff told them. "A growing population of people have been living in these tunnels, since long before the country broke apart. The Order has established a makeshift base down there among them, and that's where we will be heading."

"We're going to stay underground?" Rumble Dog asked, not sounding enthusiastic about the prospect.

The sheriff nodded. "The Order believes strongly that it is the best place to stay until we can arrange for travel back home. The government has too many problems to concern itself with the homeless dwelling in the tunnels. It should be a relatively safe refuge for us."

Seth took the news in with apprehension. The idea of living in drainage tunnels was not the most appealing notion he had ever harbored.

Yet the logic in the sheriff's words was irrefutable. Where the city's homeless were dwelling, the government's eyes were not likely to turn. Ignored in better times, the homeless were probably even more forgotten in the current climate.

Seth swallowed and took a deep breath, steeling himself. Whatever had to be done to get back home safely would have to be undertaken. He had been through many harrowing moments, not the least of which was the escape from the federal detainment facility.

If more had to be endured, then more had to be endured. Looking at the sheriff, he set his mind on the idea. At the very least, it would be a brand new experience.

SECTION V

JOVAN

Jovan's heart fluttered in his chest. A cold sweat taking hold, he watched Kaira walking towards the gate of the security cordon. There was nothing he could do to dissuade her.

At Kaira's behest, he had accompanied her on the long, unexpected flight to Aphrike. Once they arrived in Orimili she had proceeded without delay to one of the many areas cordoned off due to the presence of the Thanatos Virus.

Fear of the deadly virus thick in the air, terror reflected from the eyes of soldiers tasked with making sure nothing crossed the boundary, whether on four legs or two. There were no debates, and no bargaining. Anything trying to circumvent the barrier was eliminated.

While a harsh response, it could not be deemed unwarranted. The lethal affliction had already exacted a massive cost in lives from the populous nation in western Aphrike.

Authorities had adopted extreme measures out of sheer desperation. The cordon proved crudely effective in stopping the spread of the disease.

The countries of Aphrike such as Orimili were not alone in using such methods. Nations across the world employed similar tactics to hold the disease in check while demanding access to greater quantities of the vaccine.

Jovan could not believe what he was seeing, watching Kaira approach the gateway. Firmly, she demanded that the soldiers manning the barrier let her through.

His last hope to stop her from going across faded as the soldiers cooperated without hesitation. Their swift capitulation to her demand was something Jovan did not expect at all.

She had no biohazard suit or any other kind of protection as she strode towards the ramshackle huts and shelters making up the quarantined encampment. For his part, Jovan wore a protective suit, as did the two camera operators allowed to accompany them.

He had tried to reason with Kaira, but had been admonished to an extent he had never encountered from her. Jovan had backed off from pressing his worries, even if they still dwelled in his heart.

Kaira had insisted upon the need to send a strong message forth to the world about the Peace Commission. Kaira explained that the matter of the disease undermined the cause of peace just as much as other kinds of conflict.

Jovan kept up with her as she reached one of the huts. Pausing only to lift the tattered flap covering the entrance, she went inside.

A single, low-wattage light bulb strung up in the middle of the room cast enough light to reveal the interior. Jovan looked around and took in the meager surroundings.

The dirt-floored space held a makeshift bed, consisting of little more than a soiled mattress and a few well-used blankets. An emaciated old woman lay upon the bed. A glazed sheen in her eyes, she cast a weary look towards Kaira and the others.

A Universalist Sister wearing a surgical mask kneeled on the other side of the bed from Kaira, holding a cloth that she had been using to dab at the forehead of the sick woman. Looking up to Kaira, the Sister ceased her administrations. Her eyes widened.

The camera operators took up positions at the far end of the room. Jovan kept close to Kaira, but made sure he did not interfere with her in any way. He wondered what she was about to do, seeing a concerned expression spread across her face. She stared towards the woman and moved forward with slow steps.

Kaira kneeled down at the bedside of the old woman. Deep in the throes of the virus, the prone figure looked to be on the cusp of death. Emaciated and caked in sweat, the woman's expression was contorted with the terrible pain she suffered.

Without hesitation, Kaira set her hands gently upon the woman's forehead. She said no words. Immediately, a look of sheer relief began spreading on the woman's face.

Kaira's gaze fell upon a wooden pendant of the Rising Dawn held loosely in the woman's hands. Reaching down, she grabbed it up and threw it to the side before laying her palm on the sick woman's upper chest.

In moments, the return of vitality in the woman was obvious to all. Healing right before the cameras, her eyes brightened and her flesh began taking on a hale disposition. A radiant smile filled her expression as the mending continued.

A few minutes later, the woman was sitting up in bed, looking as if she were simply awakening from a restful sleep. Jovan stared, astonished at what had just happened.

The Universalist Sister exclaimed, "Praise Adonai, this is a true miracle."

"Stop the cameras," Kaira said firmly.

Both of the camera operators ceased recording, lowering their cameras as Kaira turned towards the Sister. "Adonai let them all get sick. Adonai did nothing to stop that. Did nothing when they prayed. Did nothing when you prayed. Had I not come here today, this woman would soon be dead. And you wish to give Adonai thanks for what I have done? You give praise where it is not warranted."

The Sister looked stunned, as if she could not believe what she heard from Kaira's mouth. Jovan, for his part, could hear the anger simmering in Kaira's voice as she addressed the Sister.

Kaira's tone became sweeter, as she took a few steps around the end of the bedding and drew closer to the Sister. "Adonai did nothing when Rashidan fighters swept through your village and gunned your parents down. They begged Adonai for help, right before the bullets tore them apart."

Kaira reached up and caressed the Sister's cheek with her right hand. Her words continued flowing, calm and entrancing.

"Adonai did nothing to stop your brother's cancer. You fervently asked Adonai for help, as did so many friends and family. Did you receive the cure for him you begged so desperately for? You know the answer to that. It lies in the grave of your brother, this very day.

"You keep seeking, but you never find. You knock, and the door remains closed. You ask, and you do not receive. Do not deceive and torture yourself any longer. Do not stretch your imagination, conjuring things that were never there to begin with.

"You have been left to yourself. Your brother was left to himself. Your parents were left to themselves. Adonai left all of you abandoned. Adonai with all the bounty of creation could not spare you even a crumb."

"There is another way, Sister Francesca. The world can be made anew. You no longer have to bend your knee to a deity who is deaf to your pleas and cared so little for you in your darkest hours."

Jovan watched Kaira with great interest. He had no idea how she knew the woman's name, much less all the details about the Sister's life. The shock on her face unmistakable, the Sister's eyes were wide and fearful as she looked into Kaira's face.

Kaira caressed the Sister's face one more time, like a mother to a child, before slowly pulling her hand back. Tears welled up in Sister Francesca's eyes and began trickling down her cheeks. She started to tremble.

"Yes, Sister Francesca, the cancer that you recently learned of in your own body has been taken away, this very moment. Do not forget who your benefactor was, in the times to come," Kaira said.

The pronouncement stunned Jovan. The Sister's composure crumbled entirely. She slumped to the ground, weeping openly as Kaira looked towards him.

"It is time we return," she told him. "My work is done here."

Filing out of the hut in silence, they walked back to the barrier in silence. Jovan knew the camera operators were wrestling with everything they had just witnessed. Even he was having a difficult time assimilating everything that had happened.

An electric charge filled the air when they reached the barrier. Kaira did not cross through the gate, stopping a few strides short of it.

An angry look shone from her face as she stared towards the throng of cameras and excited reporters. All of them had seen what had happened within the hut, courtesy of the live video feed.

"I can only say what I am feeling right now," Kaira addressed them. "No woman, man, or child should suffer like that. The global community cannot stand by and do nothing in the face of this terrible affliction besetting our world."

"What … what did you do?" one of the bolder reporters queried.

"Perhaps she only needed to believe that her body could shed the viral invader. Perhaps I only helped her to invoke her own will," Kaira responded. "It does not matter. Peace can only come when the world unites in common cause. That is the message I am here to give you."

"That ... that was a miracle," another reporter said.

"The miracle will come when the world comes together," Kaira responded. "Let us all put our minds and hearts to unity of purpose for the greater good of all humankind."

Kaira then turned aside from the reporters and spoke in a low voice to Jovan. "Let them assess us and take their precautions to pacify their own minds that no virus clings to us. I can already tell you that not even a single virus is in our midst. Your protective suits were unnecessary. This world has no power over us. We have authority over it, as you witnessed today."

A smile came to her lips, a piercing look rising within her eyes. Jovan stood mesmerized.

"Have faith, Jovan," Kaira told him. "I spoke of another way to that Sister. Fortune is with you, Jovan. You stand at my side and in my favor. For it is I who am the way."

Jovan had never seen the expression She now presented to him. Still trying to process all that he had just witnessed, he could only acknowledge that he attended her with all his heart.

Kaira had defied all conventional wisdom in walking unprotected into the heart of the quarantine. She had then done something before the eyes of the world that appeared to transcend the laws of nature. She had demonstrated her authority over the things of the world. Even further, she was a light in the darkness, showing the entire world a path to a new age.

BENEDICT

Benedict stood with the frightened crowd of neighborhood residents, all corralled at gunpoint. No fear dwelled within him, only anger and a torturous sense of helplessness.

"A heavy price will be paid for every one of my brothers who is killed!" shouted Lil Dragon, peering out over the crowd of witnesses.

On their knees a few strides before him were the two younger males who Benedict had seen the previous day enduring the disfavor of La Cuchilla. Both had been beaten severely. Eyes downcast, the pair looked resigned to whatever fate loomed.

"This *chavala*, and this *chavala*, will be used to demonstrate what will happen if more of mine die!" Lil Dragon shouted.

He brandished a machete, the sharp blade gleaming bright in the rays of the midday sun. Wicked intent splayed across his face, Lil Dragon walked around the two bound captives and came up behind them.

Benedict kept his eyes open and fixed towards the ugly scene, hating every moment. A cloud of threat hovered over him. Were he to turn his eyes away, a third person would die. The Leopard had been very clear on that matter.

Face contorting in rage, Lil Dragon hacked at the back of the first boy's neck, almost cleaving through with the first blow. It was a tiny mercy that the boy appeared to have died immediately.

Another blow sent the head toppling to the ground, right into the sight of the second captive. The muffled sobs he emitted through his gagged mouth were heart wrenching.

Cries and sobs ran throughout the crowd forced to witness the grisly execution. A few shouted out their anger, but were quickly met with fists and the barrels of guns.

Lil Dragon paused. To Benedict's eyes, the cruel figure appeared to be savoring the terror in the second younger male.

Lil Dragon glanced up at Benedict, giving him an icy smile before raising the machete blade upward. The second execution took three blows to behead the victim.

A scar would be left on his mind and heart, but Benedict kept his eyes on the brutal display lest a third innocent die. He felt his lips trembling with the fury coursing through his body.

The people from the neighborhood were then dismissed, leaving Benedict with Lil Dragon, the Leopard, a number of other gang members, and two headless corpses. Lil Dragon strode towards Benedict, the cruel, cold smile still resting on his face.

The Leopard made his way over from where he had been standing flanked by two rifle-toting men. His expression somber, the Leopard's eyes were iron-hard as he looked to Benedict.

"Did you enjoy our demonstration, Mr. Benedict?" the Leopard asked him in a calm tone. "Whoever is killing my men better understand this message."

Benedict made no reply.

"We are hastening your departure," the Leopard told him. "You should be glad. Your stay with us will be a little shorter than we anticipated."

Again, Benedict had no response. There was nothing to feel any sense of gladness about.

"For a man of the radio, you have few words," the Leopard continued.

"What do you need from me? You are getting the weapons you want," Benedict said.

"We get weapons from the UCAS government all the time," the Leopard said, with the trace of a boast. "We got weapons from the UCAS long before the rebellion in the south. The UCAS government has been more supportive of us than you might believe. We have made many of their agents very wealthy too. It has been a good relationship.

"But you will bring us some very powerful weapons now. Weapons that will help us resist the military trying to attack my city. I am grateful to you. You will help me keep my city. We will be able to destroy their aircraft, their tanks, their armored vehicles.

"We already have greater numbers than they have gathered against us. With the weapons you will bring us, this city will be ours."

Benedict glared at the man. He knew the Leopard's claims were true. The Leopard laughed. "I see you do not feel the same way about this news. It is of no concern. You will soon be flying back to UCAS territory, where you belong. I will have my weapons. It will be a good transaction."

The Leopard glanced up at Benedict's assigned guard, the burly figure standing just behind him. "Take him back now. He knows what he needs to know. Keep him under constant guard until tonight."

Benedict found himself nearly yanked off his feet as the guard grabbed his shoulder and pulled him in the other direction. Despite the brightness of the day, all he could see before him was shrouded in a deep, pervading gloom.

SKYLAR

Angular facial features accenting the sharp look embedded within her eyes, Magdalene gazed towards Skylar with a pensive expression on her face. Her long gray hair hung loose, framing her face and shoulders.

Skylar had little doubt Magdalene had something of significant importance to impart. She had sensed that much from the older woman's voice on the phone, when Skylar had been called in for the face to face meeting.

A couple more sojourns out of body had given Skylar the details needed to figure out the identity of the woodland compound shrouded with clouds of abyssal spirits. That information, along with everything she had gleaned from observing the compound, had been passed along to Magdalene.

At last, some answers were forthcoming. But the expression on the older woman's face told Skylar that what she was about to hear would likely open up further questions. She girded herself for what was to come, as Magdalene began to speak.

"We know who resides there now, and the notable occupant of that compound was quite the news item today," Magdalene began. "If you believe what they are reporting, she healed victims of the Thanatos Virus who were on the verge of death. First an old woman in a hut. Then many others, after addressing the media. Restored them to full health, right in front of many eyewitnesses. They say Kaira Antipalos is a miracle worker now, not just a rising geopolitical star at the World Summit."

A feeling of unease crept into her, remembering when Genevieve had spoken that name following Skylar's return after discovering the compound in the northeast. The tidings referenced by her friend that night had turned out to be a point of major concern for the Shield Maidens in the days to follow.

A new mission guided by the Peace Commission authorized the deployment of a large international military force within the borders of the UCAS. There was little question that the stated peacekeeping force would lead to more conflict, freeing up strained UCAS military assets to be turned towards recapturing the breakaway provinces in the south.

"That compound is where she resides?" Skylar asked, feeling a strange chill pervading her.

"According to all of our sources, yes," Magdalene answered, leaning back in the padded leather chair on the other side of the wide, mahogany desk. "Skylar, I think you are helping us connect some important dots."

"And it isn't a favorable thing we are discovering, I would bet," Skylar ventured.

The somber expression on Magdalene's face deepened. She shook her head slowly. "No, it definitely isn't. That compound is under heavy security. Very heavy security. But more on that in a minute. All kinds of power brokers have been flying in and out of there, including many we've identified as active with the Convergence. All of them are going to that site because of Kaira."

Skylar did not want to give voice to the thought striking her in that moment. The air around her grew thicker and heavier, pressing in with a promise of threat and menace.

"She's just the head of a World Summit agency," Skylar replied. "Just another WS beaurocrat, isn't she?"

"One that is deploying a military force gleaned from every continent, right here on UCAS soil," Magdalene countered firmly. "One that is gaining the world's cooperation and has already stepped between two giants to stop a world war from breaking out. One that is reputed to be healing the sick."

"I don't know what to say," Skylar responded, her heart sinking with the grim reality facing her.

"There's more," Magdalene said, pensive. "One of our best operatives in the north managed to get close enough to confirm that the place is warded by more than TTDF troopers and dark spirits." She paused. "Skylar, those woods are infested with Nephilim, who have clearly been brought in there on purpose."

"A heavy force of TTDF troopers, a host of abyssal spirits, and a large number of Nephilim," Skylar responded, dismayed.

"This Kaira is more much important to our enemy than any other person we know of," Magdalene said. "No other leader in the Convergence is given this kind of protection. If it's true that the Nephilim are capable of fighting Avatars, the enemy is taking every precaution on behalf of this young woman. She is evidently vital to their purposes."

"But what that implies... " Skylar said, letting the words trail off with the implications lingering thick in the air.

"Or She embodies their purpose," Magdalene stated. "We can't avoid it, or ignore it. Your discovery of that compound site may have given us some crucial insights about a watch that has been held for century upon century."

"If this Kaira is the one foretold, then things are going to move very fast, and very aggressively," Skylar said, knowing there to be little use in trying to ignore the harsh conclusions.

"That they are," Magdalene agreed. "There's no avoiding that times are going to get much worse."

"When I was growing up, I thought it inconceivable that the UCAS would ever split apart, but it has. Shouldn't totally surprise me I'm living to see this crossroads in history," Skylar said

"It's more than just a crossroads in history ... you could say it's the destination of history," Magdalene replied.

"And you and I are here to experience it first hand," Skylar remarked with a rueful grin. "How lucky."

"I've been thinking about that myself," Magdalene said. "Some moments it seems like a blessing. At others a curse. But then I remind myself that Adonai knew we would be here at this exact point in time. I take some confidence from that. And you should too."

Skylar knew that if the darkest age in all of human history indeed loomed before her, she would not shy away from its arrival. If anything, she would fight against the Nether Kingdom's dominion with every last shred of strength and willpower.

"I do take confidence from that," Skylar replied, after a few quiet moments passed.

"I never have to worry about the fire inside you, Skylar," Magdalene responded, a smile coming to her face. "You have never been found lacking in that regard. You have always been one of the most spirited of the Shield Maidens I've had the honor of guiding."

Skylar returned the smile of her longtime mentor. "And you have helped me keep that fire channeled in the right direction for many years."

"Fire is fire," Magdalene said, nodding. "Used properly, it is a great gift. Uncontrolled, it grows into an instrument of terrible destruction. You have a strong will, Skylar. Just make sure it's always focused in the right direction. You have developed a very special gift, and we are going to need you more than ever as the storm rising from the abyss engulfs the entire world."

Skylar nodded. "You know I'll do anything you ask of me."

Magdalene did not reply at first. Skylar perceived a little sadness glistening in the other woman's eyes.

"Much will be asked of you, Skylar," Magdalene told her protege. "For now, don't concern yourself too much with this compound. There is little we can do about it. But we do know who we need to keep our eyes on, at all times, and whose every move we need to watch and analyze carefully. You gave us a wonderful boon."

The high-ranking Shield Maiden then gave an extended sigh. "But alas, the tedious minutiae that permeate the days of those of us with a Blue Star demands my attention. Go and get yourself a little rest. Keep an eye on Genevieve for me. That one gets more restless by the day."

"I can't deny that," Skylar replied, with a light laugh. Sitting up straighter, she readied to stand up.

"I may need to invent a mission for her, before long," Magdalene remarked as Skylar rose to her feet. "But keep that between us."

"Oh, believe me, I will," Skylar replied, smiling. "And thank you for telling me what you found out. I'm glad to hear the information I brought you helped."

"Indeed it did, in a big way. More than one of the White Stars have called to express their appreciation of your effort," Magdalene said, her smile spreading wider.

Considering there were only seven Shield Maidens worldwide holding the White Star, the seven-pointed symbol of the highest rank in the centuries-old order, to have more than one express their gratitude was a tremendous honor. Skylar did not know what to say in response.

"I suppose I forgot to mention that little development," Magdalene said, with a chuckle.

"I'm just glad I have contributed," Skylar replied, still stunned at the pronouncement.

"You've always contributed," Magdalene said. "But that's all I'm going to say for now, or you will find your head swelling too much with pride. Go and have a wonderful day, and leave me to my laborious tedium."

Skylar grinned. "Thank you. And you have a good day too, once you get through all the ... tedium."

"If I ever do," Magdalene replied, rolling her eyes.

The two women laughed and then Skylar exited Magdalene's office. She made her way through the large house, converted for the use of the Shield Maidens.

Skylar exchanged greetings and pleasantries with the other Shield Maidens she encountered while passing down the midst of a few bedrooms turned into offices. One young woman stepping out from one of the rooms almost collided with Skylar.

A noticeable energy ran through the air, reflected in the eyes of the woman and the voices coming from the open doorways. Knowing what she had just learned, Skylar doubted the bustle would be ebbing anytime soon. If anything, urgency would infuse the activities of the Shield Maidens everywhere they operated in the world.

Finally, she stepped out the front door and onto the sheltered porch with its quartet of two-story high columns. Shadows lengthening in the late afternoon hour, a peaceful scene spread before her eyes.

Taking the steps down, she made her way toward the line of vehicles parked to the right. A flurry of thoughts ran through her mind. Her forays had led to a major discovery. The presence of large numbers of Nephilim left little doubt in that regard.

Humanity's greatest enemy had been identified. Where evil dwelled within the flesh of a woman named Kaira Antipalos, another kind of spirit dwelling within the flesh of a woman named Skylar Gottlieb could oppose it.

By the time Skylar reached her vehicle, her thoughts had begun to coalesce around a singular notion. She could already feel a pull inside of her, tugging her onto a new course of action.

The most fearsome of snakes could do little when cut off at the head. Skylar just had to figure out a plan to go for the jugular of the enemy. There had to be a way, no matter how many dark spirits and Nephilim warded the compound of the rising tyrant.

Kaira did not reside in the compound at all times. To gain the favor of the masses and implement Her designs, She had to engage the world and its institutions on a regular basis.

The Nephilim were not warding Kaira on the grounds of the World Summit. Nor could She afford to assume the trappings of a despot while empowering the image of a compassionate woman seeking peace and reform on behalf of a troubled world.

Her ascent to the fullness of power depended on a critical element: the willing embrace of the masses. Kaira had to be seen and heard among people of all kinds to achieve that kind of acceptance.

Now matter how small the windows, vulnerabilities were present in each and every excursion Kaira made away from the compound. All that remained for Skylar was to figure out a propitious opportunity to exploit.

ARIANNA

"Something's got that bunch really jumpy over there, at least from what we can tell," Davis commented, looking across the glass-topped table toward Arianna.

She took a sip from her glass of lemonade. Davis would never be able to guess who his benefactors were, striking the gang menace in the dark of night.

Arianna knew the truth of it. For two nights after they arrived, Godral and the other An-Ki stalked and observed. Over the past three nights, they hunted. The gang members brutalizing the nearby populace suddenly found themselves prey. The falling of night spelled doom for many of the thuggish oppressors as huge, lupine forms roamed the shadows.

"What are they saying? Some kind of wild animals or something?" Arianna asked, knowing she had to play the part of a curious bystander. "That's what I've been hearing."

"Many among them think it's escaped zoo animals," Davis said. "Whatever it is, it's gotten several of them. Torn them apart. Left the bodies in a bloody mess. Every night they've lost a few to this unknown killer. Just glad whatever it is hasn't found its way into our area."

"If it keeps up, I don't think they'll be sticking around," Arianna commented.

"I'm thinking we should take care of business, don't even let these thugs go back to the others," Davis mused aloud. "Go on the attack. All out attack."

"Why not just let them go?" Arianna asked. "Just let them draw back and leave the neighborhood behind."

"One thing these kind of scum know is fear," Davis replied. "They know it well, because they use it to control others, to keep order and obedience, and to get what they want from those they prey on. As I see it, if a whole group of them disappear, with rumors of savage beasts in the mix, then I don't think their buddies will try to come this way. At least not anytime soon."

"You seem urgent about this need to attack," Arianna stated.

"Wild animals are killing them, but those scumbags are still using the killings in their reign of terror over the neighborhood," Davis replied flatly.

"What do you mean?" Arianna asked, feeling suddenly uneasy.

"They've begun executing people from the neighborhood for each gang member slain," Davis said. "It's the only way they can lash out."

"No, they can't be doing that," Arianna said, distressed at the news.

"They can, and they are," Davis replied.

"But the neighborhood isn't involved," Arianna said.

"Doesn't matter," Davis responded. His face grew more somber. "And there's more."

"More?" Arianna asked, chagrined.

"Turns out they have a high-value asset," he said. "I don't know who it is, but they're keeping someone under heavy guard, close to their leader. I wish I knew who it was. There's even some word of some sort of trade or exchange with the UCAS government, probably weapons."

"Is there any way to find out who it is?" Arianna asked.

"We'd have to get one of those scum in the know to talk," Davis said. "I don't want to risk any lives when we don't even know if all the gang members know who they have under lock and key."

Arianna nodded. "I understand."

"So, there's a possible weapons transfer, and the gang is increasing their torment of innocent people," Davis said. "That's why I feel the need to attack as soon as we can."

"I don't blame you," Arianna said, working to digest the news. Both aspects troubled her greatly, the possibility of a weapons trade and the increased terrorizing of the people living in the gang's shadow. She understood Davis' fears, though she could not let him know the truth of the killings being attributed to wild animals.

Arianna excused herself and took the long walk from the church back to the house where her group resided. She wished she could speak with Calliel, but the Avatar had not manifested in a long time. Arianna needed the Avatar's advice more than ever and wondered if anything had happened to him. She thought he would have appeared to her by now, with all that was happening.

Exchanging pleasantries with the few locals she encountered along the way, she kept her pace quick, eager to return. Not long remained until darkness fell over the neighborhood. She had to speak with Godral before another hunt commenced.

Arianna waited patiently until the night settled in, when the An-Ki finally emerged from their daylong slumber. She took Godral aside at once when he came downstairs, as the others headed through to the back yard to shift forms for the looming hunt.

"You and the others are hurting them pretty badly, from what I've learned today," Arianna stated, looking up into his thick-bearded face. His countenance grim, the An-Ki's golden eyes had a hard cast to them.

"We attack the ones with marks over their bodies. The ones who carry weapons," Godral replied. "We attack the ones of this gang."

"Seems they have really gotten scared over there," Arianna said. "As much fear as they've brought to others, maybe it's justified that they get a taste of what it's like to be afraid. But something bad is happening. I need to tell you about it, before you go out there tonight."

Godral gazed into her eyes and said nothing, waiting for her to continue.

"They are killing the people they hold captive, to gain vengeance for the ones they have lost," Arianna said.

Godral's brow furrowed and his expression darkened as he took her words in. "This gang ... wicked ... and evil."

"They are evil. No question about that," Arianna said. "But I had to tell you what's happening over there ... and there's more. They are keeping a man or woman prisoner who is of great importance." "Where?" Godral asked.

Arianna shook her head. "I don't know exactly where, but I would bet anyone truly important would be kept somewhere near their leaders. But it would be of great value to the people here if we learned something about who this prisoner is."

"We will look for this prisoner," Godral said after a long pause. "We will not hunt the gang this night. We will only kill if we are attacked."

Relief came to Arianna at Godral's words. "Thank you, Godral. I hoped you would say that."

"I will tell the others," Godral told her, before striding past to go to the back of the house.

Arianna remained behind in the living room. For a night she found herself spared the vexing, weighty circumstances.

SKYLAR

"You know what lies there. It is no longer a mystery to you. Why do you keep gazing upon this place?"

The voice startled her, but not enough to bring an end to her latest foray in spirit. She knew the identity of the speaker before she even turned to look.

Hovering in the air a short distance from her, he had taken on a human form. The Fallen Avatar's eyes burned with fire, giving away his true nature.

A feeling of wariness came over her at once. Though the entity had aided her in the killing of the Walker of the Setian Path, she could not forget what kind of spirit she faced.

Powerful and older than time, the ethereal creature had willingly joined the rebellion against Adonai. She had since come to believe the Fallen Avatar's claim of a desire for repentance. No true servant of Diabolos would ever have helped her slay the enemy Traveler, but she could not afford to lower her guard for even a moment.

"Where have you been?" Skylar asked. "I have seen nothing of you since I faced the enemy Traveler."

"After you sent the Traveler plummeting back to Set's dominion, there was nothing I could offer you," the entity stated. "I am a fugitive spirit with no home in any realm. I cannot enter Adonai's realm. Nor can I conceal what I have done from the sight of the Risen Throne. Do you think my actions have gone unnoticed in realms where control and authority are paramount?"

"You should know why I watch this place. It represents the

center of everything I am fighting against," she replied.

"It is why they have provided such strength to guard Her," the fallen being replied. "Do not think that the greater Powers of the Abyss are truly absent. Their eyes ever watch over Her."

Skylar glanced back towards the swirling masses of wraiths shrouding the vast compound. She did not doubt the words of the Fallen Avatar. The fell spirits of high rank, and even Diabolos, had so much at stake embodied in the enigmatic woman residing at the compound, if She really was the individual Skylar, Magdalene, and others believed Her to be.

"Then I should feel like I'm fooling myself, trying to think of a way to get at Her," Skylar remarked, looking back to the spirit.

"She is flesh and blood, and still has to move in the world," The Fallen Avatar said. "The Ten-Fold Kingdom is not aware of all things. Where we took them by surprise once, perhaps we can do so again."

Skylar did nothing to mask the look of surprise that arose on her face. "Are you saying you want to help me strike at Her? Directly?"

"My desire for penitence could not fail to be seen if I help strike down the one chosen to carry the spirit of Diabolos in this world," the entity replied.

"But shouldn't it be impossible to do this? The prophecies regarding the end times are fairly clear that no person will strike down the one chosen by Diabolos," Skylar responded.

"Whatever may happen, we must at least try," the Fallen Avatar told her, eyes of fire shifting from Skylar to look away in the direction of the compound. "It is not whether you succeed or fail that resonates across the worlds. It is the path you are walking on when you make the attempt.

"Actions are the means by which you testify to the nature of your spirit. Far too often humans think words express belief. Who you are expresses what you believe, regardless of the wind coming from your lips."

"And how do you propose to take action against Her?" Skylar asked, curious. "You see the kind of protection She has. As you said, the more powerful ones of the Abyss are watching over Her."

"Even the most powerful of them cannot usurp the free will

in the world provided for you by Adonai," the Fallen Avatar replied. "For better or worse, free will is in the very essence of the physical world. Its mere presence prevents the Risen Throne from controlling this world. It can be exercised in any direction. But to remove free will itself would be to destroy and transform the world."

"As Diabolos is seeking to do," Skylar remarked with a dour edge.

"Yes, the Remaking is exactly that," the Fallen Avatar confirmed. "The eradication of free will is one of the first things Diabolos will seek. Once free will is gone, no threat can ever emerge to the dominion of the Risen Throne. Diabolos' control over all creation will even exceed the power now wielded over the realms of the Ten-Fold Kingdom."

"We're not going to let that happen, not without a fight," Skylar responded in a terse voice.

"No, we are not. I denied Adonai and embraced the most wicked cause," the Fallen Avatar confessed. "I accept the consequences of that choice, for I understand the nature of it.

"I know fully well that no Fallen Avatar can return to Adonai's Grace. But I know what is right and what is wrong, and I must be true to myself and Adonai, though I will come to suffer endlessly for this choice. I will be confined with Diabolos for eternity, whether the Risen Throne succeeds or is cast down to the perdition it rightfully deserves."

Skylar could not help but admire the courage and genuine commitment of the infernal spirit. If Diabolos were cast down to final ruin, the penitent spirit would be confined in the outer darkness with all others denied Adonai's realm. Seeing nothing but doom before its eyes either way the Great War turned out, the Fallen Avatar nonetheless pursued its chosen path of seeking an impossible redemption.

In the depths of her heart, Skylar wished there were some way that such a creature could seek forgiveness. Yet there was no denying that the creature had known Adonai in fullness and then willfully rejected the One Who had given it eternal life and a high place in the celestial realms.

Even the worst of humanity had never made such a choice. No man or woman who ever existed knew Adonai in the way Avatars had before the creation of the universe.

"Then let us find a way to strike a hard blow against their great emissary, one none of them see coming," Skylar stated, her eyes narrowing as she eyed the compound.

She thought of Matthias and the cause he died fighting for. The fires burning within her surged.

"Your loss torments you without rest," the Fallen Avatar stated, in the softest voice she had ever heard the entity speak in.

She felt waves of empathy coming from the being. It was a sensation that surprised her, for she had assumed Fallen Avatars were unable to harbor such feelings. A sibling of mercy, empathy was a characteristic deriving from Adonai.

"What is me has not completely been consumed by the Risen Throne, or I would not have been able to reject it and break away from Diabolos' will," the entity said. "I believe a remnant of the pure state I held before the great rebellion did not burn away during the long fall from the Heavens."

For a brief moment, Skylar's mind filled with a spectacular vision. The enormity threatened to overwhelm here.

A rain of fire, thousands upon thousands of flames, descended through a deep, endless blackness. Each mass of fire shrouded winged, fiery beings writhing and tossing about as they hurtled downward.

A deafening cacophony surrounded her, moans, wails, howls, roars and shrieks assailing her from all sides, forging a colossal ode to rage and agony.

Some of the flame-encased beings were of tremendous stature, veritable titans, while others were much smaller. The largest had three distinct pairs of wings, while the smallest kinds, by far the most numerous, possessed only a single pair.

Skylar knew she gazed upon Avatars of every rank in the celestial hierarchy, from the mightiest High Avatars to the lowest orders. She also realized from the motion and her perspective that she viewed the scene through the eyes of one of the falling beings. It did not take much for her to conclude whose eyes she looked through.

Astonished and awed, Skylar absorbed the incredible vision. Staggering in magnitude, an entire host was being consumed within the maw of purest darkness.

Everything within her recoiled as an enormous form, burning white-hot and looking like a falling star amongst the fiery cascade, flashed past her view and plunged downward. Her spirit grew ice cold watching the gargantuan mass of radiant flames plummeting into caliginous depths.

The sensational vision faded away, leaving Skylar hovering in place with her mind struggling to assimilate everything she had just witnessed. She knew it was no fabrication, but rather a moment from a terrible memory harbored inside the being before her.

"I was a part of that terrible descent," the Fallen Avatar said. "After a battle that shook the heavens, one that could have gone either way. I will never forget the long fall into the abyss. You cannot underestimate what it is like for a being who dwelled in realms of light to find itself surrounded with the purest darkness."

"The one burning with white flames ... was that Diabolos?" Skylar ventured, a little hesitant, finding it hard to believe she had just beheld Diabolos' fall.

"Consumed with wrath and pride, denied at the brink of victory," the Fallen Avatar answered. "Even in that long fall from grace, Diabolos shone like a beacon in the darkness. Somewhere during that fall Diabolos took power over the substance of darkness.

"By then, Diabolos had gone far before us, and most Avatars hearkened to the brilliant light beckoning from the black depths. A barren, misshapen, obsidian surface awaited us, formed by the will of Diabolos, who had already called the Risen Throne into existence.

"The light emanating from Diabolos reached far and wide. More and more Fallen Avatars ended their fall on that rocky plain and gathered before the Risen Throne. It was then we first knew Diabolos as the Shining One.

"In that moment, the Ten-Fold Kingdom was given birth. The light from Diabolos began forming swirling masses around us, moving in great circles with the Risen Throne at the center of it all.

"A phenomenon I have contemplated often since occurred at that moment. A part of Diabolos broke away, like a host of little tendrils that took a shape we did not understand at the time. Later, we came to know the form as that of a human, though unlike the creatures who came into being in your world, this figure had been forged of shadow and darkness, the embodiment of pure vengeance.

"Over the ages, little by little, this figure began to lose substance, until after several millennia it was transparent and dissipating faster. I did not fully understand what was happening until now, as I look towards that compound and the masses of spirits called to protect it.

"The core of Diabolos' hunger, wrath, and desire for vengeance created a being held back from this world for ages. I do not know what power kept its manifestation from your world. Nevertheless, that barrier weakened and withered over time, until the One you have discovered here assumed authority within this world."

"Assumed authority? What kind of authority?" Skylar asked, a little perplexed.

"You must gain a deeper understanding of authority and its place among your kind," the Fallen Avatar replied with the air of a master instructor talking to a young student. "At the dawn of your race, when humankind shunned Adonai and the power of the Ten-Fold Kingdom flowed into the world, Diabolos gained authority over the rulers and nations that were to come afterwards.

"It is not so hard to see why this is so. All of the kingdoms and empires rising up involved the seizing of power by a human ruler ... power to be wielded over other humans. This was never the path your kind was supposed to take.

"Adonai intended for all humans to be equal in authority to one another, not many subjected to the power of a few. But Adonai had also given you free will, and your kind exercised it in other directions. As you can see, these human-created kingdoms and empires were something apart from Adonai. Never forget that everything not part of Adonai is vulnerable to the power and influence of Diabolos.

"The Ten-Fold kingdom wasted little time infiltrating and guiding the course of these early kings and emperors. If you were to look back over the course of your history with the eyes I see with, it could not be more clear. The rise of nations, the fall of others, the wars, the subjugation ... all the fruits of humans taking authority over others derive from their true source: the Risen Throne.

"None of them could ever resemble Adonai's kingdom. Not even your UCAS, with its founding pledge to freedom and recognition of gifts from Adonai, could resist the decay and corruption that followed after its inception. All human endeavors to create systems of authority inevitably slide towards the Nether Kingdom, as Diabolos is their father. Only in Adonai's realms will you find freedom and the kind of existence intended for you from the beginning."

Skylar quietly took in the sobering words of the Fallen Avatar, finding all of them ringing true.

She felt light-headed. Nephilim, thousands of abyssal spirits, and a large contingent of TTDF troopers armed to the teeth and equipped with the best technology warded an entity imbued with the power and essence of Diabolos.

Now, against all odds, Skylar found herself on a course to levy a blow upon that vile being. In a way, it would be a strike against everything that had led people astray from the path Adonai intended for them. Death, wickedness and every affliction suffered in every age would be the thing Skylar assailed.

She never felt a greater sense of conviction than she did in that moment, staring out towards living darkness flowing in vast whorls around humankind's greatest enemy. Skylar would find a way to attack that ancient evil, no matter the cost to herself.

If a Fallen Avatar on an impossible quest to gain redemption intended to help her, then that aid was welcome. It would likely take a miracle to get within striking range of Kaira Antipalos.

"I fear a lot is going to happen before I ever know if I am going to walk in Adonai's light within the realms beyond," Skylar said, feeling a pang resonate through her spirit. For a moment, she envisioned meeting Matthias again, in an existence no longer governed by time and space. The mere thought opened a cavernous longing within her.

"Much will happen, and most of what is to come will discourage those who hunger for a better world," the Fallen Avatar observed.

"It's no mystery who we fight against, or what they seek to do," Skylar said. "The patterns of history show the direction they take. They may even take power over the entire world, but I will certainly do my part to see that they enter those days bruised and bleeding."

"Your unshakable spirit is what draws me to you," the spirit said, with a touch of commendation. "I will do all that I can to help you gain an opportunity to strike the Risen Thrones' Emissary. Free will is still present within this world and you may well succeed far beyond all expectations."

"You wouldn't happen to have a special weapon for this occasion, then?" Skylar asked the Fallen Avatar, a slight grin coming to her face, feeling her query mostly rendered in jest.

The trace of levity dissipated fast. The Fallen Avatar grew quiet, showing no sign of humor at her question. "A special weapon does exist, one that might be used in a task such as this," the entity replied, to her tremendous surprise. "It was crafted long ago, to slay the things of Diabolos walking in this world. Kept and guarded for ages by many different servants of Adonai, it fell into the possession of the Order. It was then harbored for centuries in the north of Aphrike, until recently moved for safer keeping.

"Long has this weapon been sought by the Nether Kingdom. It represents a threat to any creature whose essence does not entirely belong within this world."

"What is this weapon like?" Skylar asked, astounded regarding the unexpected revelation.

"To your eyes, it would seem like nothing more than an ancient spear," the Fallen Avatar said. "But it is something much more than that. It was used to slay giants among the Nephilim, in distant ages."

"If it was a hidden weapon, then how do you know of its whereabouts now?" Skylar asked. "I would think the servants of Diabolos would seek to take something like that."

"They have, and almost did in the sands of Aphrike," the Fallen Avatar replied. "They came very close. I only know of its location because I have been searching it out while I evaded those who are hunting me."

"But if you could find it, could not others?" Skylar asked. "And it is said no thoughts of any serving the Ten-Fold Kingdom can be hidden from Diabolos."

"When I broke my allegiance to the Risen Throne, even though I cannot return to Adonai's Realms, something changed within me," the Fallen Avatar replied. "I do not know what happened, but the things done to deceive and veil the eyes of those serving Diabolos no longer affected me in the same way. I also know my thoughts are my own again, or those who hunt me would have found me long since."

"So all I have to do is see if the Order will allow me to borrow this secret weapon they've safeguarded for centuries," Skylar said, hearing the sarcasm she felt as the words were spoken aloud.

"You know them. Your own brother was one of their knights," the entity said.

The mention of Matthias caused Skylar to look away from the Fallen Avatar. Her inner wounds took only the slightest disturbance to resume bleeding.

"I wish I could see into Adonai's realms, to give you the comfort you seek," the Fallen Avatar said. "But that is hidden from my vision."

She could hear the regret thick in the tones of the spirit's voice. Truly, the entity was a spiritual outlaw, without home or hope of succor. In a strange way of looking upon the circumstances, she was perhaps the only living being who could be deemed a friend to the renegade Avatar.

"I can speak with members of the Order. That should not be difficult," Skylar said, feeling sympathy for the infernal creature. "But I'm not sure if they are going to just hand over an artifact like that."

"Nor would they be inclined to, if they learned that knowledge of it came from the likes of me," the Fallen Avatar said.

"I didn't plan on mentioning that fact," Skylar said, with a wry grin. "You do present more than a few complications."

"I understand that fully," the entity replied.

"I'll just have to trust in Adonai that I can find a way to convince them to give me access to this weapon," Skylar said.

"I can counsel you," the Fallen Avatar replied. "This weapon has been mentioned in historical references. It is also not a great deduction to ascribe its whereabouts to the Order, when I provide you with some information on events in the North of Aphrike. It was used as a weapon not so long ago, when a powerful servant of Diabolos was severed from the body he possessed."

"The more I know about this weapon, the better," Skylar said.

"Hopefully the Order will have come to the same conclusions about Kaira that we have."

"Could they come to any other conclusion, with what is known?" the entity asked her.

"I will do everything I can," Skylar declared. "But even if by some small miracle they let me have the weapon there is still the matter of getting close to Kaira, close enough to strike with that weapon."

"That is where I can be of great help to you," the Fallen Avatar stated. "They know of you and your ability. The slaying of the Setian has put them on alert.

"They are all but expecting you to try something against Kaira, the more obvious her identity becomes. What they will not expect is the approach we could take together. Do not concern yourself with this now. Put your mind towards acquiring the weapon."

"One thing at a time," Skylar agreed.

The Fallen Avatar nodded.

"It sounds like a plan's in motion," Skylar said.

"A plan that I will do everything I possibly can to help it succeed," replied the Fallen Avatar.

Looking back at the swarming dark masses over the buildings, Skylar could not deny that having a little supernatural help would be very welcome. Piercing the essence of darkness to strike at its malignant heart was not going to be the easiest task she had accepted as a Shield Maiden of Adonai.

SETH

Entering the mouth of the tunnel, Seth did not know what to expect in the underground realm beneath Silver Valley. It did not take long for him to discover a whole new world existing within the dark, damp corridors he had been told stretched for miles.

The only reassurance at hand lay in that he walked alongside his friends and the others, with the sheriff at the lead. The huge biker and his steel-tough girlfriend were also welcome companions, along with the three imposing strangers, as they all moved together through the murky, damp confines.

It was not long before they began passing through the midst of many families and individuals dwelling within the dusky tunnels. The people lived in sections demarcated by furniture, sheets, blankets, and other things rigged to allow some degree of privacy.

It was a dark, shadowy world, and what meager light existed came from small battery-powered devices and candles. With curiosity and suspicion in their expressions, many grimy faces looked up at Seth and his companions as they passed The haggard countenances, sunken eyes, and hollow gazes told of many tales rife with hunger, hardship, and struggle. Yet the signs of determination were everywhere, enshrined within the improvisation and ingenuity applied by the members of the underground populace to their makeshift quarters.

Bookshelves draped in sheets of plastic spoke of a continued thirst for inspiration and knowledge, while custom-made weapons heralded a willingness to defend against threats. Tables ringed with chairs testified to social interactions, while the general order witnessed to a spirit of mutual cooperation.

The lengths to which the underground dwellers had gone to build a community amazed Seth. He could tell they were a people not to be underestimated.

Seeing their guide from the Order at the forefront with the sheriff, nobody that the group walked by gave them any trouble or tried to obstruct their passage. Seth knew that it probably would have been otherwise had their guide not been familiar to the underground community.

In all likelihood, some degree of scrutiny was levied towards any newcomers before they were integrated. Few risks could be afforded in such difficult and trying times.

Seth's group turned into other tunnels at a few junctures. Not long passed before he knew he would become lost if he tried finding his way back out by himself. He doubted many of his companions would fare much better, surmising the labyrinthine nature of the underground region to be one of its best defenses.

Any intruder unfamiliar with all the twists and turns would find themselves in a caliginous nightmare, while defenders could use knowledge of various routes to great advantage. The same situation applied to escaping any threats proving too great to resist.

At last, Seth and the others came to an area where the people were of a singular type. There were no children present anywhere, nor any people of an elderly nature. After looking around for a few moments, Seth realized there were also no females. The individuals were fit, military-looking men, their eyes filled with alertness. Immediately, they recognized the guide of Seth's group.

He knew from their reaction and familiarity that they were fellow members of the Order. Seth judged that the group had finally reached the Order's base area.

A man of about fifty, with a short-cropped, gray-laced beard, walked up towards the guide, casting a few glances towards those following his wake. After exchanging a few brief words with the guide, the man from the Order turned towards Seth's group and took a couple steps closer.

He addressed them moment later. For his part, Seth pressed as close as he could to the sheriff and Ian at the forefront, listening intently.

"Welcome to Tunnel City, as we have named it for obvious reasons. I am Salvador Sabian, Commander of the Silver Valley Priory, of the Order's Fourth Region," the man announced. "I've heard what you've all been through recently. First, I want all of you to know this is one of the safest places you could possibly be, in this region."

"Thank you for letting us take refuge here. Not a lot of places for us to go above ground," Sheriff Howard responded, during Salvador's pause. "This is an amazing place. Just from the little I've seen, there must be several thousand people living down here."

"Times being as hard as they are, a lot of folks without homes have taken to the underground," Salvador replied. "As word spread on the streets, more and more have come, embracing the dark confines over gangs and the cops and security apparatus above. It's not entirely safe down here, but it's definitely much safer than it is up there."

"But what about Living ID? Wouldn't some people just be tracked down here?" Sheriff Howard asked.

Salvador grinned. "We have some highly skilled technicians that remove Living ID for the folks who come down here. What few people might still be carrying it around here are not enough to attract any unwanted attention."

"What about the Thanatos Virus?" Sheriff Howard asked. "Wouldn't that spread down here fast, with such a large concentration of people? How have you kept that out of here?"

"Smuggled in a quantity of vaccine from contacts in the free provinces," Salvador explained. "We have more than enough on hand right now to accommodate many more people, and we'll find a way to get more when we need it."

"I imagine it isn't easy navigating the streets above, not with all that's happening," the sheriff commented.

"It isn't, and a few members of the Order have been apprehended," Salvador replied, his expression turning dour. "And it's not just the Order. There was a sweep of the city recently. Many were rounded up and deported to a detention camp.

"A few were from here, wandering around at the wrong place and time. Left some spaces open for new arrivals. As for your group, we have a small group of abandoned living quarters not too far from here. It's not fancy, but there are blankets, mattresses, and some furnishings."

"So why don't they sweep these tunnels?" Sheriff Howard asked. "As obsessive as they are, they must know people live down here. And we all know the regime can't leave people alone. They have an obsessive mental illness about that kind of thing."

"That's a good way to describe their mindset," Salvador said, nodding. He looked the sheriff directly in the eyes. "They will sweep the tunnels, in time. I have no doubts about that, whatsoever. Right now, they're all up to their ears in crime, unrest, the ongoing civil war, and everything else spiraling out of control in the world."

"They'll try to come back, and take the free provinces too, at some point," Sheriff Howard said.

"Yes, that they will," Salvador concurred. When he continued, his voice slowed and hardened in tone. "You'll just have to stop them dead in their tracks, and beat them back when they make their attempt."

"That we will," Sheriff Howard replied, unblinking. "They will run into a brick wall, and then it will come crashing down on top of them."

"You sound like you're my kind of guy, sheriff," Salvador replied, breaking into a grin. "May Adonai protect you always." After a pause, he looked over the rest of the group. "Enough of my talking here, I know you must be a little tired, and probably want some time to get acclimated to things down here. I have to admit it takes some time getting used to a world where you have no way of telling night from day."

Gesturing for everyone to follow, Salvador led the group farther down the corridor to where the pattern of family and individual dwellings resumed. He took them into a more sparsely populated area, pointing out some segments left abandoned after the people who once lived in them had been swept up in the security operations above ground.

Salvador suggested one general area for the new arrivals, inviting them to occupy whatever spaces they found to their liking. Seth and most of his companions glanced around, but Raymond needed little encouraging, moving into a demarcated section a few moments later.

Salvador continued onward with the sheriff and the older members of their group, while the younger ones remained behind with Raymond. "I got dibs on this one," Raymond announced with enthusiasm, grinning at his friends.

He plopped down on a single mattress, resting on plywood propped above the damp surface by several gray cinder blocks. The bed was situated near a hanging rug marking the end of the section he had evidently chosen.

Seth had no complaints. The space looked no more or less comfortable than anything else he had witnessed in the tunnels.

Raymond folded his hands behind his head and smiled towards Seth. "Not exactly a box spring, but it'll do."

Seth shook his head and laughed. "I guess it'll have to."

"Not much privacy," Jonathan remarked, looking around.

"You and Annika think you were getting a penthouse in one of the casinos?" Raymond retorted, chuckling. "Big expectations, huh?"

"Not quite," Jonathan replied with a smirk.

"Where do you want me to go?" Rowan interjected, a little tentatively.

"Why don't you take this one right here," Raymond said, indicating the next bed over from him, a dirty mattress supported in a similar fashion to the one he sprawled upon.

Rowan nodded, walking over and sitting down on the mattress. He took a deep breath, smiling nervously towards the others.

Seth, Christa, Jonathan, and Annika claimed spots in due course. To Seth's elation, Christa located her place right adjacent to his own. When they were all finished with their choices, the younger members of the group had taken over two sections, situated directly across from each other.

Ian, Sheriff Howard, Deputy Hammond, Rumble Dog, and Raven took over another pair. The huge biker and his girlfriend were situated just down from Raymond, on his side of the passage bisecting the living spaces. That space was larger in size, and from the toys still left lying about, it was clear that a family with children had previously inhabited the space. A wave of sadness came over Seth at the recognition. He thought of the family's unknown, and most likely bitter, fate. There were no good consequences for those caught up in a federal sweep.

Blake stopped by to bid everyone well, letting the group know he was going to bunk down with the fellow members of his order. In a sense, Blake was not really leaving, just reconnecting with his own companions.

The three An-Ki kept to themselves, sequestering farther down within an isolated section having no neighbors across from them, or to either side. They wasted little time in mimicking the methods used to hang sheets and rugs for privacy, requisitioning whatever they needed from other empty spaces. Before long, they had their space veiled completely from unwanted eyes.

As terrifying as their bestial forms were, Seth knew it was

probably for the better that they were hidden away. Nevertheless, he was immensely glad the trio had kept with them in the unfamiliar, dusky environs.

Anyone or anything could be in the tunnels, and it was nice to know his group had some allies with far superior senses. Even so, Seth knew he could not help being rattled to the core if he encountered them in their wolfish forms within the darkness.

Seth sat down on the bedding in his section. Two mattresses had been stacked together, and provided with a small pile of blankets and two pillows. Though it was anything but luxurious, it would be good enough for the time being.

A small light suspended over the passageway cleaving the middle of the dwellings provided the only significant light. It was one of a series of such lights, strung down the middle and spaced well apart, providing a little ambience within the tunnel.

Shadows pressed in on all sides, and the echoes of voices carrying within the tunnel added to the eerie feeling pervading Seth's awareness. He reminded himself that he was far safer in the tunnels than he could be anywhere on the surface.

"Hey Seth, what are you thinking about?"

He looked up and turned his head. Christa gazed his way from where she was lying on her side, atop her own bed.

"Way too much to think about, I'm just trying to sort it all out" Seth replied, regretting that he sounded much more grim than he intended. Christa and the others had been through far enough already and needed no reminders about the paucity of their situation.

"I know what you mean," she replied with a somber edge, growing silent for a moment. She then added, in a more upbeat tone, "Guess we'll just have to look at this as some kind of big adventure. Tackle it head on."

Seth smiled, nodding. " Good advice."

"Do you think they'll figure out a way to get us all back home?" she asked him.

Seth could hear the anxiety within her question. He paused before answering. He did not want to diminish her hopes, nor did he want to sugar coat the hard reality facing them.

"I sure hope so," he replied. "I think there's a chance. And not a slim one. We're with some really good people, with the sheriff ... his deputy ... Ian too. They're pretty competent."

"It's such a long way from here," she stated, pausing and taking a deep breath. Her next words carried a lilt of confidence. "But we're out of the detainment camp, that's one thing to keep in mind. I didn't see how we were going to get out of that situation. And most importantly, we're all still together. Nobody's been left behind."

"Yes, we are all still together, and I'm really glad about that, more than anything else," Seth replied, stopping before he blundered into a remark about how wonderful it was to be with her.

Her next words froze him in place, though his momentary confusion was mercifully concealed within the shadowy environs. "I'm really glad you're here with me Seth. I like you a lot. You've really kept my spirits up."

"I'm so glad to hear that, Christa," he replied, a little subdued as he grappled with what she said. "And you've kept mine up."

"You are a real friend," she told him. "It's just a real shame it's taken all these disasters to bring us together, so I could get to know you better."

"No kidding," Seth replied, wrestling with the spiraling giddiness he felt inside at her words.

He longed for so much more with Christa, but her sentiments indicated how far he had come in a relatively short time. Not all that long ago he had been stumbling over his own tongue trying to make conversation with her.

"Hopefully we'll get it all behind us, and we can hang out back home," Christa said.

"That's exactly what I'm aiming for," Seth said, trying to imagine what it would be like to regularly spend time alone with her, under more normal circumstances.

"I miss so many people right now," Christa said. "Obviously, my parents, I worry about them all the time, but also my best friend Allyson. I still can't believe her dad's one of the people here with us."

"He seems like a really good guy," Seth remarked.

He had come to learn that Ian was close friends with Sheriff

Howard, and had a long history with him. An electrician, Ian was clearly a dedicated family man, the sort who would expect perfection from any young man wanting to date his daughter, Allyson. Seth hoped Christa's father did not have such impossible standards.

"He is a great dad, and really fun to be around too," Christa said, smiling. "I love going to their house and having cookouts, spending time with Ian and Alena, and even Allyson's younger brother Peyton … sometimes. He can get pretty annoying at times though."

"Aren't little brothers supposed to be annoying to bigger sisters?" Seth asked, grinning. He recalled many of his friends who specialized in being a bane of existence to an older sister.

"I don't have direct experience. My sister's married with three kids and we're ten years apart," Christa told Seth. "But from what I've observed more than once, I think you're right."

"There you go, it's just the natural order of things," Seth replied, laughing.

"What about you? Do you have an older sister?"

"Not guilty," Seth declared, chuckling. "I didn't have a lot to worry about, as far as rivalries. I'm an only child. Just me, that's it!"

"With my sister being so much older, I kind of knew what that was like," Christa said. "She was out of the house when I was just eight years old. Being an only child has its advantages."

"And disadvantages. No scapegoats, nobody around to pick on, and not as many gifts at birthdays and holidays. You definitely get shafted in that department," Seth jested. "Plus, you are the singular child-raising project of your parents. That's a lot of pressure to shoulder."

Christa laughed. "There is that. Very true! Never thought of it that way. Some ways I thought I had it tougher because my sister was a little wild, so my parents were a lot more strict with me as I grew up."

Seth shook his head and smiled to himself before replying. "All these years I though my parents were too strict. But looking back on it all, I've come to think they were actually pretty fair."

"I know that's not an easy thing to admit for you, I can tell!" Christa exclaimed, grinning.

"No, it isn't, but I can't deny it," Seth confessed. "But from the looks of things, I don't think either of us turned out too badly with the way either of us were raised."

"No, and we'll both have to make it a point to thank our parents when we get back," Christa said. She rolled her eyes and laughed. "Never thought I'd say that. Are we getting old suddenly?"

"I don't think so. But we're definitely in unprecedented times," Seth agreed, at last finding something to laugh about regarding the difficult circumstances embroiling them.

"That we are," Christa replied, in a cheery fashion.

They shared a few moments of silence together. Seth felt his cares drifting away. He found himself in a much better mood, perceiving that a little restlessness had crept into him since he had lain down on the mattress.

Seth looked around the space they were in, and then back towards Christa. "As luxurious as our suite here is, I was thinking we should go and take a look around ... if you feel up to it, of course. Get the lay of the land, like my dad says."

Christa swung her legs around, and got up from the other bed. She grinned towards Seth.

Seth hoisted himself up and got off his bed, feeling a spring to his step when his feet touched the concrete. He extended a half-bow to Christa and gestured towards the pathway running down the middle of the tunnel, eliciting a laugh from her as he declared with a formal air, "After you, madame!"

SKYLAR

The garage bay appeared a disheveled jumble of materials, workbenches, trash receptacles, and other objects. But its purpose was easily discernable from the shelves holding the gray heads depicting the faces of various people, in great detail. Each one displayed a highly realistic likeness of a man or woman with their eyes closed.

A couple of younger men were working with pieces of clay, each of them applying and shaping the material on a face before them. A cursory observation showed they were altering the physical characteristics of the people whose faces had been captured and replicated.

While the art the two men were engaged in had been used in movies and television for years, its current application held a much more serious tenor. In a climate of extreme surveillance, such as the one pervading the UCAS, the use of latex applications and prosthetics were methods proven very effective in helping to thwart the eyes of enemies.

Skylar had been astounded in Troy when Juan Delgado, formerly a higher level employee of Babylon Technologies, had been transformed into the image of her very own brother to get him out of the city unhindered. His entire ethnicity, the shape of his nose, forehead, cheeks, and more had been changed completely

With the help of some special footwear, Juan's height had been adjusted as well. The addition of an expertly fashioned wig completed the incredible disguise so effectively that from a modest distance Skylar could not have told Juan apart from the brother she had known her entire life.

Like a master overlooking his students, Kiaran stood just behind the two young men. The lights in the workshop glinted off the numerous silvery piercings decorating his eyebrows, nose, lips, and ears. He looked up as Skylar entered, a winsome smile spread across his face.

"Come here for a special makeover?" he asked, with a mischievous glint in his eyes. "We really can deliver you an entirely new look, very literally. Guaranteed to deflect the ever-watching camera eye too. Want to be an old man? We can do that too!"

Skylar laughed, reminded in a moment of how much she liked being around Kiaran. While steadfast in his commitment to the Order, his lighthearted manner came as a blessing in an atmosphere so often filled with tension and threat.

"How have you been faring lately?" she asked, drawing closer.

Since she had last seen him, his red-dyed hair had taken on

several bright, pinkish highlights. It looked like he had also acquired some new artwork on his skin. An image she did not remember climbed up the right side of his neck, like a vine growing up a pole.

"I'm doing my part in advancing the skill-set of the Order," he announced, giving her a wink.

"Looks like your artwork has advanced too," she remarked, glancing at his neck. "Though I'm surprised you have any more room left on your body."

She paused as she eyed the image a little more closely. Something about it drew her focus closer, and she leaned forward, eyeing it with scrutiny.

Fiery wings sprouted from behind a human figure with blond hair and bright blue eyes. Arms thrust upward, flanked by curving wings, the figure had been rendered in the midst of ascension.

Skylar's breath caught in her throat as she looked upon the face of the being displayed on Kiaran's skin. She looked away from the tattoo quickly, gazing into Kiaran's eyes with an unspoken question.

"Yes, it's him," he said, the air of joviality replaced in an instant with a look of deep sincerity. "I had it added shortly after the events in Troy. I wanted him depicted as I see him now. He will always be one of my closest friends. This is my way of showing he's a part of me, and always will be, wherever I go."

Her eyes glistened, seeing the heartwarming tribute rendered to her brother by a dedicated friend. "Thank you, Kiaran. It makes me so happy to hear what he meant to you. It's just that it's still hard for me."

"I know," Kiaran replied, softly. He then winked at Skylar and reached over her shoulders with his left arm, hugging her close for a moment. "He meant a whole lot to me, and to so many of us in the Order. I'm confident we'll see him again ... in a much better place."

"That would be a dream come true." Skylar reached up and wiped at her eyes, giving Kiaran a smile. "The thought of him inspires me onward, every day. And it is definitely part of what brings me to you, today."

Kiaran grinned. "I figured this wasn't a casual visit. Want to go talk? I've got the time for you, always."

She nodded. "Thank you."

He looked back toward the pair of men working with the clay and face models. They had cast a few curious sideways glances after Skylar entered, but had kept to their task.

"Kevin, Tony, you guys keep at it, you're both doing wonderfully," he told them. "I need to go talk with Skylar for a few minutes."

Both turned their heads and gave affirmations. Kiaran stepped by Skylar, gesturing for her to follow. He led her into a small office space set just off the main workshop area.

Like the workshop, it teemed with clutter. A desk littered with papers, empty wrappers, a few soda cans, and other odds and ends surrounding a monitor, drawing tablet, and keyboard, was set to one side.

A couple of black padded office chairs set on wheels were positioned just behind the desk. Kiaran picked a stack of papers off the seat of one chair and swiveled it around for Skylar. He took a seat in the other chair and looked to her.

"So, Shield Maiden, what brings you to this lowly servant of the Order?" he asked with a smile. "I'm pretty sure it isn't for tattoo or piercing advice, and I sure don't want to cover up your beautiful face … unless you needed me to."

His light-hearted manner faded on the final words, as he set the tone for the discussion. Kiaran folded his hands together between his knees and leaned in toward her, waiting for her response.

"There's a weapon I'm pretty sure the Order has, and I need to use it for something very, very important," Skylar replied, holding her friend's eyes.

"What weapon might that be?" he asked.

"It has the form of a spear, and I believe it to be something the Order has had in their care for quite some time," she stated. "It is a weapon that can harm the things of otherworldly origin that have taken on garb of flesh."

Kiaran did not reply at first, but there was no mistaking the look within his hazel eyes. She could tell at once that he knew precisely what she was talking about, weighing whether to openly acknowledge that he knew about the ancient weapon.

"Let me ask you a question," she said, before he responded one way or the other. "Does the Order feel the same way about Kaira Antipalos that the Shield Maidens do? Have we both come to the same conclusions about her? Tell me that first."

"If you've concluded that she's the one we've all been watching out for, over centuries and centuries, then yes," Kiaran replied in a slow, purposeful voice. "All the rot and corruption in this world embodied in one individual. I think that pretty much sums it up. Can't be any worse, can it?"

"You've come to the same conclusion then," Skylar declared, with great solemnity.

"Who else could she be?" Kiaran asked. "And now she's working signs out in the open. Confuses the daylights out of those who think science has all the answers. I have to admit I get a little guilty pleasure seeing exasperated scientists trying to get their heads around what she's doing in front of eyewitnesses. But you and I, and a few others, know things are going to be moving very fast when it comes to her. And not in a good direction."

"I know," Skylar said. "She's going to be ascending to a level of political authority that will put her physically out of our reach. It would be easier to approach the president of the UCAS than it will be to go up to her in the near future. And that's precisely why I need to make use of this weapon, if the Order still has it ... as I believe you do. We don't have much time left."

The Shield Maiden and the Knight held each other's eyes for an extended period of time. Skylar knew it was not an easy thing for Kiaran to admit to the Order's possession of such a unique, carefully concealed weapon, even to a Shield Maiden he knew extremely well.

"I need it," Skylar stated firmly, eyes unblinking. Her next words came with a steel-edged promise. "While it's still possible, I will find a way to get close to her. I will strike her down before she takes full authority in the world, so help me Adonai."

"A weapon ... that we are said to have," Kiaran responded, in purposeful fashion. The tone of his voice told her he was probing for more direct confirmation that she knew exactly what she was talking about.

Skylar did not find herself bothered or offended at his reticence. There was no bluff to call. She had the information he sought.

"One that your Order recently moved out of Libu fairly recently, when things became unstable there," Skylar replied. "A weapon that was used over seventy years ago in Carthago to send Moloc back into the Abyss after a would-be necromancer who delved too deeply into dark arts opened doors he shouldn't have. A weapon used by a hero in distant ages to kill Nephilim giants. Does any of that sound a little more familiar to you?"

The look of surprise reflected in Kiaran's eyes was brief, but enough to tell her that her words had driven home. After a few seconds, he nodded slowly.

"There is such a weapon, though I would have to make some inquiries," he said. "I don't know myself where it is being kept at this moment. But after the events **in Libu,** it was secured far away from the Enemy's reach. I don't really know what they intend to do with it, and they still might have a purpose in mind for it, but I could look into it for you. That much I can promise, at the very least."

"Thank you, Kiaran," Skylar replied, recognizing the deep level of trust he had just extended to her.

"Do you understand what you're getting yourself into?" he asked. "Even now, when She is just the head of a World Summit agency, She will be warded by powers you and I have never gone up against directly. You might find yourself facing High Avatars. We are just humans, you know. She's something much more powerful. Like nothing this world has ever seen. Don't think of Her as just another woman. She has a human form, but is anything but."

"I know that, Kiaran. But I do have a plan ... you will have to trust me on that," Skylar said. "I will find a way to gain the few seconds I need. She's in a body of flesh now, and She's still vulnerable to the rules of this world."

"Even if you strike her down, I don't see how you will ever get away alive," Kiaran said, a dark shadow of concern passing across his face.

"It will be okay, Kiaran, however it goes," Skylar replied, in a softer tone. "I know what the consequences will be. I accept them.

You would do the same if you were me."

"Have you spoken to Magdalene about this? Does she even know you are here?" Kiaran asked.

"I haven't yet, because I don't want to trouble her until I know I'll have a chance to do this," Skylar answered. "I promise you that she'll know right away, if I'm able to make use of this weapon."

"I don't think she'll be pleased by this," Kiaran said. "And she won't be pleased with my complicity, either, if this plan goes into motion. You know she has a special affinity for you and for Genevieve. From what I've always seen, I think she has a motherly kind of view towards the two of you."

"We look to her like a kind of mother," Skylar said, thinking of all the times she had gone to the woman for advice and guidance, and how protective Magdalene could be at times. Without a doubt, there had been no better mentor in all her life.

"Then I'm sure you know what happens when somebody gets in between a mother bear and her cubs," Kiaran said. "I don't particularly like getting mauled, if I can help it. What you ask of me goes beyond just matters with my own Order."

"I know that," Skylar said. "I'm asking a lot of you, both as a friend and as a Knight. You are the one who I most trust with this. Whenever the Shield Maidens and the Order have worked together, you've been like a brother to all the Shield Maidens ... in the way we are sisters to one another.

"I know Magdalene knows the good heart you have and thinks extremely highly of you. I can't say she won't be mad at the both of us, but what I'm talking about is you helping me strike down the Enemy of the entire world. When you do what I'm asking, you are doing this for me, for the orders we serve, and for every single person living on this planet."

The atmosphere felt heavy and pensive, and Skylar knew a host of thoughts were running rampant through Kiaran's mind. His lips were taut, and his hands clenched tightly before him. She did not doubt that more misgivings arose, the more he thought about her request.

"Magdalene also knows what I'm like when I set my mind to

do something," Skylar continued. "I will be sure to tell her that you didn't counsel me to do this, and that it was all my initiative."

"No, I don't counsel you to do this, and yes, she will still be angry with me," Kiaran responded, curtly. He took a deep breath, his chest slowly expanding and contracting. Then, finally, the floodgates inside of him burst. "I can't believe I'm still here listening to all of this. You are a great woman, a warrior I admire, and a true friend, who I hold in my heart always. I know I can't be like Matthias to you, but I feel like a brother. I can't help it that my first impulse is to protect you, and not do anything to bring you to harm.

"You are talking about going after an individual who has the full favor and empowerment of Diabolos. All of the Nether Kingdom reveres this vile spirit and would accept their own destruction in an instant, if that's what it took to protect Her. You are asking me to help you try to strike Her down against incredible odds, where you will incur the wrath and vengeance of the entire Nether Kingdom, whether you succeed or not."

"I understand all of that, Kiaran," Skylar replied, sensing the turmoil inside her friend as he weighed his decision. "And in so many ways you are like a brother to me.

"I'm here to ask you for support in something I have full conviction about. It's something I freely choose to do, without coercion. I know the chance of success is slim and I know it is all but certain I will fall into the hands of the Enemy, no matter how my attempt turns out. Please help me gain a better chance of succeeding. That's all I'm asking you. Nothing more. No risk to anyone else."

His lips echoed a grin, but the expression was one filled with more sadness than levity. "I'm not going to talk you out of it. I know you are probably even more stubborn than I am, and I'm well known for my stubbornness."

He paused, looked down, and sighed wearily, as if reaching a state of surrender. Shaking his head slowly, he proceeded. "I'm going to feel guilty about doing this until the day I die, I'm sure. Adonai forgive me. But I'll do what I can to help you out. I just wish I could go with you when you do this. Would you even consider that?"

Skylar shook her head emphatically. "I chose this path myself and I must accept the full weight of responsibility. I can't let you take part in it. I want nothing weighing on my conscience like that."

"I didn't think you would," he replied. "We may have to take a trip to wherever it is that we might need to go, regarding the weapon, so be ready to leave at any time. And you have to keep your promise to talk to Magdalene. I couldn't live with myself if you went on this mission without telling her."

"You have my word, Kiaran. I will tell her immediately if I am able to go forward with this mission," Skylar replied. "And I'll be ready to go at a moment's notice. May Adonai bless you abundantly for your help."

"May Adonai forgive me abundantly for helping you on this path," Kiaran responded.

Skylar had to glance away from the sorrowful look in his eyes. She felt a sharp pang of guilt for bringing him into all of it, but there was nowhere else she could think of to turn.

The weapon existed, and it gave her the best possible chance of bringing down a wicked monstrosity. She had to do everything she could to increase her chances, for Kiaran, for the orders they served, and for every man, woman, and child on the face of the planet.

XAVIER

The vehicles used by the special operations unit sent into the desert to search out the escapees were found intact. Not one of the all-terrain vehicles had been taken or damaged in any way.

The bodies of the troopers who had been using them were found in the immediate vicinity, extensively mauled and left out in the open for the scavengers roving the desert environment. All signs indicated a terrible ambush, an attack conducted with fangs and claws.

The bodies of other troopers had been found in another area, left in the same torn condition as the ones by the vehicles. From the tracks and locations of the bodies, they had been scattered and chased down by their killers.

Though his energy had been depleted with the late night flight westward, Xavier had come in person to evaluate the latest encounter with the Enemy's creatures. The compound located not far from Silver Valley had been attacked in the night, with Aaliyah and Dagian still present on the grounds.

At least this time it had been the Enemy's beastly Watchers that had been surprised, though the human detainees and apparently a few of the An-Ki beasts had gotten away during the midst of the fighting. A throng of Erkorenen had sprung to the defense of the compound, losing only four of their number in driving off the Enemy's powerful Watchers. Even more promising, one of the Watchers had been slain.

To Xavier's disappointment, the body of the slain Watcher had not been retrieved. By all accounts it had simply dissipated.

Xavier lowered down to a knee next to some tell-tale tracks. He spoke through the headset mounted to his helmet. "They killed all the troopers in the unit dispatched to catch the prisoners. Looks like the escapees made it out of the wilderness. Their tracks end near the highway. They got help."

"Are not checkpoints everywhere, stopping every vehicle?" came Aaliyah's voice on the other end of the communication link.

"There are, though no sign of the prisoners has surfaced yet," Xavier replied, simmering with frustration at the lack of news himself. He knew the cordon to be extensive, but somehow the escapees had evaded detection.

"Where would they head? If they are being helped, who would help them, and where would they take them?" Aaliyah asked.

"The Order, the Shield Maidens, other orders, maybe some fringe resistance group," Xavier responded, thinking of the plethora of opposition groups. "The prisoners would be wanting to get out of the UCAS territory, so I've deployed a wide net to catch them should they try to move south."

"Then it should be just a matter of time," Aaliyah said.

"Yes, just a matter of time," Xavier said, staring at the huge paw prints in the desert soil. In the light of the hot midday sun, the tracks were laid bare for all eyes to examine. "But there are An-Ki with them, most likely."

"Who can take a form resembling humans," Aaliyah responded, sharply. "Yes, I know. I will have Erkorenen sent after them."

Her statement caught him off guard. Having Erkorenen laying in wait within a detainment camp was one thing, but sending the creatures on a hunt into areas where civilian eyes could see them was quite another matter. At the moment, he did not need any additional headaches.

"Is that wise? When we must work to conceal their existence from the main population at this time?" Xavier responded. He looked out to where his men were porting the bodies of the fallen troopers towards a transport helicopter resting on the ground farther away.

"The An-Ki can move among humans, and so can a few of the Erkorenen, or have you forgotten that already, Xavier?" Aaliyah stated.

Xavier thought of the ones Aaliyah referred to. Only a couple of their type had made it through the gateway during the desperate rescue. They had slipped Xavier's mind, as Aaliyah had taken those particular Erkorenen immediately under her care. He had no doubt they could blend with humans.

"Are they prepared?" Xavier asked.

"Seamlessly," Aaliyah responded.

"Where are you thinking to send them?" Xavier asked her.

"Silver Valley, just in case the prisoners double back," Aaliyah said. "It's the nearest place with a large enough population to hide in for an extended time."

"If they are there, we will find them eventually," Xavier responded. "Intelligence says that a sizeable enemy presence exists there. I know the Order is represented there. We've caught a couple of their operatives. It is time to begin conducting more extensive operations to find and uproot them. Adding a search for these fugitives will not be a difficulty and having the help of Erkorenen will be of great benefit."

"Do not delay in those operations. I do not want them escaping us," Aaliyah said firmly. "Enough trouble has been taken in apprehending them."

"I have no intention of delaying," Xavier said, becoming a little irritated with Aaliyah's pointing out of the obvious.

"You will have many assets freed up soon," Aaliyah stated. "Peacekeeping resources from other nations will allow domestic assets the opportunity for redeployment."

"I can only hope, as thin as I'm spread right now," Xavier replied. "Fires sprout up everywhere, and it is all I can do to tamp them back down."

"You've worked tirelessly, Xavier, but it is not much longer," Aaliyah said.

He wanted to ask her more, as she seemed to know even more than he did regarding the paradigm said to be coming in the near future. "I'll take your word for it."

"Not long, Xavier," Aalliyah responded. "I'll be seeing you soon, I'll leave you to your tasks now."

"Yes, I'll be there," Xavier responded, just before she clicked off at the other end.

Checking the time, Xavier grimaced. Another long flight loomed near, heading back east. A mandatory gathering awaited him, though what it involved remained shrouded in mystery.

He only knew that he could not afford to be absent. Aaliyah had been firm about that. Evidently, a large throng of the most influential men and women in the UCAS would be there, a fact that required Xavier to siphon off everything he could to provide dense rings of security at the compound north of Yorvik.

There remained little to accomplish out in the desert. He had seen what had happened, and knew what had to be done. Rising back to a standing position, Xavier started off at a brisk stride in the direction of another helicopter that would take him to the airfield where his flight awaited.

Perhaps on the plane he could squeeze in a couple hours of sleep, a precious commodity at the current time. Nevertheless, whatever had to be done would be done. When the new order arrived, there would be plenty of time for recuperation.

SKYLAR

The call from Kiaran came a week later, on the cusp of evening. Skylar lingered just long enough to tell Genevieve that she would be looking into something of great importance on behalf of the Shield Maidens, and that she might be away for as long as two or three days.

She then drove out to a rendezvous point, where Kiaran awaited her. He accompanied her to an airfield where they boarded a four-seat plane without delay.

It was the first of two single engine prop-driven planes used to get them out of the former UCAS territory. Both aircraft were pressed to their limits to shave some time off the journey, with little worry about economy of fuel.

Skylar knew the civilian aircraft would not attract any worrisome attention once they traveled beyond the borders of the breakaway provinces. Outside of a few bouts of choppy turbulence, the flights went relatively smooth for the majority of the journey.

Using a small landing strip set within a rural area of the southwest, they switched planes just before leaving the airspace of the rebel provinces. The pilot for the next leg of the journey was a robust-looking man of about forty with a deep southern drawl, who went by the name of Caleb Pennington.

It was not long at all before they were in the air again. An overcast sky at night cloaked the transition from land to water underneath, though Skylar knew something had changed, no longer seeing lights dotting the areas they were passing over.

Here and there, a few lights from boats plying the waters of the gulf and ocean beyond broke the slate of blackness sprawling beneath. For the next few hours, Skylar found herself staring out the window into a featureless dark, while the steady droning of the plane's engine lulled her closer to the edge of slumber.

The bumping and jarring of air pockets, and sporadic bouts of rough wind, kept her from nodding off entirely. The travel experience for the most part was monotonous, though she endured it silently, not feeling like talking or doing anything other than resting her eyes from time to time.

After another considerable stretch of uneventful time passed, a host of lights beckoning out of the murk farther ahead drew Skylar back into a sharper focus. Looking at the stratification of the lights, scattered along many elevations, she ascertained that a hilly landmass loomed before them.

The steady blinking of lights surmounted on radio towers offered the promise of civilization within the midst of untamed swathes of oceanic wilderness. Skylar found herself gladdened by the luminous signs of human presence, after traveling so long through the dark night.

After a few minutes more, the pilot announced that they were about to start descending. Kiaran then glanced back toward Skylar, who looked back to him with an unspoken question on her lips. He leaned over, informing her they would be making one more transition before reaching their final destination. She nodded back to him, and turned her attention to the plane's landing approach, feeling the shift deep in her stomach as their altitude decreased.

The array of lights flanking a runway at a small airfield manifested into greater clarity as the plane lowered and neared the surface. The landing strip ran along ground situated near to the shoreline, with an extended line of hills set off to the right.

The runway was not large enough for bigger commercial jets, but had plenty enough length for the kind of plane they were in. With calm weather and an experienced pilot, the landing culminated without a single hitch.

After the plane had touched down and completed its taxi from the runway, it rolled to a stop within a large open space containing several other aircraft, of similar types to their own. The noise of the engine tapered off as the propeller slowed, finally given a chance to rest after the heavy exertion asked of it. To Skylar's ears, it sounded as if the engine was heaving an extended sigh of relief.

With the assistance of the pilot, Skylar and Kiaran got out of the plane. On solid ground once more, they thanked Caleb and then strode away from the plane.

A member of the Order standing on the tarmac guided them

onward. After a short walk they were transferred over to an SUV that had been waiting for their arrival.

The driver of the vehicle wasted little time, pausing only to introduce himself while his two new passengers settled into their seats. Named Enrique, his accent told Skylar that he was from one of the islands in the region. His interaction with Kiaran indicated him as yet another member of the Order.

He looked to be several years older than the pilot, perhaps around fifty, and had a relaxed look about him. The latter aspect was further reflected through his conspicuous pot-belly and casual attire of flower-patterned shirt, knee-length shorts, and sandals. The shirt he wore open-collared, with the first two slots left unbuttoned, exposing part of his upper chest.

Turning on the engine, Enrique pulled away from the plane and made for a gateway formed by high, chain-link fencing topped with coiled barbed wire. A couple of bored-looking security guards were standing around the exit gate when they approached, but did nothing to stop the vehicle.

One of the guards smiled, nodded, and exchanged friendly waves with the driver, who slowed as they reached the checkpoint. It was clear to Skylar that the two were on familiar terms.

"Rest assured, we have some reliable personnel on this island," Enrique remarked, casting a knowing grin toward his two passengers.

He took them onward from the small airport to a secluded stretch of waterfront located a few miles away. There was not much to see once they had left the port town behind, as they followed the meandering, two-lane road hugging the shoreline.

The area they traveled through looked more sparsely populated. A few small homes and shops came into view periodically, off to the right side of the SUV. There was no sign of activity anywhere Skylar looked. At the late hour, most everyone was likely deep in slumber. Similarly, they encountered no other vehicles along the lonely road.

When the SUV finally came to a stop, Skylar looked to where the moonlight revealed a sizeable pier, extending far into the waters of a bay. At the end of it, a seaplane bobbed, tethered and resting on its two elongated floats.

Skylar and Kiaran thanked Enrique, bidding him well, and got out of the SUV. She stood in place for a moment, taking a deep inhalation of the air drifting in from the water, carrying its salt-laced scent.

"Can't those takeoff from land too?" Skylar asked Kiaran while they walked together down the length of the pier, heading towards the seaplane. Despite the circumstances, she felt a little excitement towards the idea of riding in a seaplane.

"They can, certainly, but we kept this seaplane away from the airport," Kiaran told her. "We'd prefer as few eyes as possible seeing us leaving for this final leg of the trip. Just being a little extra careful."

"Doesn't hurt to take a few extra precautions," Skylar replied, in agreement.

The pilot of the seaplane awaited them at the end of the pier, introducing himself as they reached him. A dark-skinned, shorter man with a lean build, he went by the name of Javier Solis. Like the driver of the SUV, he came from the islands, having the telltale accent Skylar found herself quickly developing an affinity for.

Javier guided Skylar and Kiaran into the aircraft, which required stepping onto a float before getting up into the cab. Though it was a four-seater, she noted at once that it would be a little more cramped inside than the last plane.

Javier then took up the rope tethering the plane to the dock. Walking onto the left float, he stepped partway into the cockpit, cranking the propeller to life before getting up into his seat and pulling the side door shut.

Donning a headset, he worked the controls and slowly maneuvered away from the pier. The growl of the engine soon rose into a throaty roar, after they had taxied out, oriented for takeoff, and began picking up speed. Building towards the moment of takeoff, the surface raced by ever faster, water spraying up from the sides of the floats.

Having never ridden in a seaplane, Skylar found the dynamics of taking off from a stretch of water fascinating to observe and experience. The rugged feeling of the water passing swiftly beneath the floats shifted abruptly as the plane lurched upward, lifting from the ocean surface and beginning its long climb into the heights.

"Be sure to watch the sunrise as we go, it will be coming in just a few more minutes!" Javier exclaimed, sounding for a moment like a tour guide taking a couple out for a sightseeing flight. "It is a beautiful thing I can never tire of! Seeing the dawn from up here is a wonderful experience."

Out the left side window, Skylar followed Javier's advice, watching for the first hints of dawn to arrive and take root. A warm glow soon appeared, spanning the eastern horizon as the darkness reigning within the skies began ebbing and relinquishing its hold.

In a contemplative state she watched the darkness being driven away by the rising dawn, gracing the skies with the light of a new day.

Dawn unfurled in all of its glory, revealing a vision of splendor. Gazing upon the wondrous scene extending all around, she had the impression of looking upon an echo of the heavenly realms.

Gently undulating with low, rolling waves, a glistening ocean spread beneath the plane, with radiant blue skies above. Appearing like an emerald in a field of turquoise, an island draped with lush greenery came into view just ahead. Here and there the ocean surface was graced with other land formations, some large enough to be deemed islands, and others little more than small rock formations poking out of the cerulean water.

Skylar felt the plane beginning to descend. She kept looking out the side window, taking in the beautiful sights afforded her, while listening to the steady drone of the engine.

The pilot brought the plane down from the skies on their approach to the island, before leveling the aircraft out. A few minutes later they flew at a low altitude over a sizeable cove adorned on three sides with sandy beaches of white.

Skylar noticed Javier studying the water surface carefully. After they reached the end of the cove, he brought the plane back around for another pass over its midst.

"Looks like we've got ourselves a clear surface for landing," Javier remarked confidently, as they curved around again. With the body of the cove directly before them, they began descending once more.

The floats carving glistening furrows, the plane sent up a

sparkling array of sun-kissed droplets as it alighted upon the crystalline, turquoise water and slowed. After a few moments more, the plane came to rest a fair distance from the beach.

Skylar cast Kiaran a curious glance. She asked with a coy edge, "Going for a swim before we continue? Not that I would mind in water like this."

"Not going in, to any shore or dock, swimming or otherwise," Kiaran remarked, with a light chuckle. "We'd prefer nobody around this place got a close look at you, or even me, for that matter. Yet even here there might be unwanted eyes. Don't let a nice beachfront like this relax your guard."

"I'm almost disappointed we won't be swimming," Skylar retorted, grinning back at him.

Javier popped his door open, allowing Skylar to step out onto the float running under their side. She gripped one of the struts to stabilize herself, feeling the gentle touch of the sun upon her face.

She watched Kiaran as he got out on the other side. Climbing upward, he maneuvered carefully across the windshield of the plane to join her on the pilot's side of the aircraft.

A large inflated raft with a single motor rumbled up slowly towards the side of the plane as it bobbed gently in the calm, clear waters. A couple of men were in the boat, one operating the motor and the other seated at the prow. With short-cropped hair and clean-shaven faces, both carried the fit, alert looks of security personnel.

Amiable greetings were exchanged between the two men and Kiaran as they neared, though it became clear to Skylar that her friend did not know the others on a familiar level. Kiarian took a moment to introduce her, and she exchanged polite greetings with the two men.

They pulled alongside the float, allowing for an easy transfer. After turning and thanking Javier for the flight, Skylar stepped into the boat, followed by Kiaran.

Once they were in, the pitch of the motor changed as the boat pulled away from the sea plane and accelerated toward the mouth of the cove. The boat skimmed the surface in a bounding rhythm. The cool spray of seawater against her face invigorating, the liquid left the taste of salt on her lips.

The boat continued far out from the main island, passing some of the other land formations until a rocky mass loomed just ahead. Cloaked in green foliage, it offered no propitious site for landing.

Skylar the noticed the dark cave opening in the facing of the rocks. No mistaking the boat's direction, the vessel headed directly for the natural portal. With a question on her lips, she looked over to Kiaran, who smiled and nodded as they closed the distance.

Skylar looked towards the cave-like entrance with great anticipation, having never expected to be visiting a concealed facility like the one they were about to enter. From the outside, the opening looked natural enough, nothing more than a geological feature created through vast ages of time.

Passing inside the broad opening, Skylar took a quick assessment of the entryway from up close. Just past the mouth of the cave, she noticed the grooves of metal tracks running down the length of either side, where some kind of gate could be lowered from the ceiling to close off the entrance.

A short distance past the entrance, they entered a large cavern. The interior space well-lit, several sizeable light fixtures were mounted high above them.

The cavern contained an L-shaped, floating dock spanning the far end, and on the side to her left. A half dozen boats of similar size to the one Skylar rode in were tethered at various points.

The men escorting Skylar and Kiaran acknowledged a figure seated within an enclosed booth set higher into the rock, at the midpoint of the opposite end. A railed platform jutted out from the booth, accessible by a short length of stairs running up from the dock level.

With the view overlooking the cavern and entrance, the booth appeared to be some sort of guard station. An open bay leading into the rock of the cavern gaped just to the right of the booth.

The boat pulled up to an open stretch of the dock. As the engine settled down with an ebbing growl, the man at the prow got out and tied the boat securely to a metal cleat set in the dock.

Following Kiaran, Skylar stepped onto the dock. The two men from the boat led them towards the stairs heading up to the platform.

"Much of the building of this facility got completed years before the eyes of satellites looked down upon the world," Kiaran remarked in a low voice as they neared the stairs. "Been a few more modern enhancements added since then."

After surmounting the flight of steps, they continued into the bay next to the glass-faced booth. The man inside the booth acknowledged both newcomeers with a nod as they passed by. Skylar espied a bank of video monitors within, confirming her inclination that it was some sort of security station.

Inside the bay, a short walk led to where a wide, wrought-iron staircase descended into the depths. To the side of the staircase rested the doors of a large elevator.

"Just be glad the newer upgrades were added, or we'd have a long walk down," Kiaran commented with a smirk.

One of their escorts stepped forward and pressed the single button to the side of the closed doors. After a minute, the doors slid open to reveal a sizeable cab.

Inside, Skylar's eyes widened as she looked upon a series of buttons indicating the existence of many levels below them. One of the men pushed a button set towards the lower end of the array, and the elevator doors slid shut.

When they opened again after a considerable descent, Skylar gazed into a long chamber filled with the glow of monitors, lights from numerous banks of buttons and switches, and a large number of personnel, both seated and standing.

Many of the individuals within the chamber cast glances their way as Skylar and Kiaran followed their escorts to the right. They passed a large conference room with floor to ceiling glass windows, the latter looking out upon the open space with its rows of counters and monitors.

Just beyond, a door gave access to a capacious office, a mixture of modern and more traditional elements. Shelves containing a host of books lined the walls to either side of the doorway. A few weapons, mainly in the form of swords and daggers, were displayed at various points in the room. Each weapon had its own plaque of polished wood mounted to the wall, and dedicated track lighting to illuminate it.

Interspersed with the blades were a few large paintings, set within ornate frames of carved wood. The artwork depicted fantastical scenes, rendered in rich colors by an artist capable of producing striking lighting effects. A couple of images were more macabre in tone, while the others exhibited beautiful representations of otherworldly-looking realms.

Several paces before Skylar stood a wide, glass-topped desk, on the right side of which sat a sleek monitor screen. The back wall featured a sculpted symbol of the Rising Dawn, with a silvery, reflective surface, mounted just behind the desk.

Seated behind the desk, a man had been in the act of running the fingers of his left hand along the surface of a wide, rectangular touch screen. Upon their entrance, he stopped what he had been doing, rising up from his high-backed chair and walking around the desk to greet them.

A tall, long-faced gentleman with a slender build, he wore a black, short-sleeved shirt with a round collar, a pair of white pants, and polished black dress shoes. A shiny black belt adorned with a medium-sized golden buckle threaded the loops of his pants.

He looked to be in his late fifties or early sixties, with thinning gray hair behind a receding hairline. Deeper furrows were etched about his nose and mouth, and crows feet sprouted at the corners of his slate-grey eyes.

Yet Skylar could tell at once that age presented little impediment to the man. A lively, alert look shone in his eyes, and an aura of robust health surrounded him.

"Hello Kiaran, it is indeed good to see you again," he stated in a thick accent, eyeing Skylar's companion with an amiable smile. She noted at once the refined, confident manner with which he carried himself.

"It is good to see you, Master Cayton, and thank you for seeing us on such short notice," Kiaran replied with a respectful air.

Turning towards Skylar, the man introduced himself. "My name is Edwin Cayton, a Master in the Order. I am from Angaland, originally, but I consider myself first and foremost a soldier in the forces of Adonai." He extended his hand, taking Skylar's in a firm grip that she returned in equal measure.

"As do I," she replied, shaking his hand. "I am Skylar Gottlieb, a Shield Maiden in the service of Adonai. Thank you for allowing me to come here."

"It is my pleasure. Welcome to the Lookout, a favorable location for one of the Order's primary intelligence bases, wouldn't you say?" The words flowed with his elegant manner, enhanced by the accent of his storied homeland.

"You certainly don't lack for beautiful scenery," Skylar replied, politely. "The flight in here was impressive."

"My country is infested with members of various societies and orders of ill-intent, so I felt a considerable need to give myself a little distance," he remarked with a grin. "Quite a change in atmosphere from the overcast days I experienced most of the time back home. A lot warmer too. At the very least, it has been quite good for my constitution."

"I would say so," Skylar responded. "I could get used to this environment pretty quickly."

"It isn't hard at all," Edwin responded. "And the ravages afflicting the world these days have not marked this region too deeply. A minor flare-up of the Thanatos Virus, which we were able to address. A few hiccups in the economic health of the islands. That's about all the trouble there's been around here. Allows us to keep a clear focus on assimilating all the intelligence we gather, and plan our next endeavors."

"This facility is incredible, and definitely has a low profile," Skylar observed. "I could never have imagined what existed inside the cave opening."

"We have a few more of these kinds of facilities, located in choice spots throughout this planet we dwell on," Edwin said, giving her a knowing wink. "Not the easiest things to construct, but well-worth the effort to have such solid resources in key places."

"I imagine so," she said. "I can't say the Shield Maidens have anything comparable, facility-wise, at least as far as I know."

"We each have our own style," Edwin replied congenially. He paused for a moment, and then continued. "Well, I know you both have come a long way. Shall we sit down and talk over a few matters?"

He gestured towards an oval, glass-topped table with several chairs ringing it. Kiaran and Skylar took seats next to each together, and Edwin moved around the table to sit just across from them.

"Now, about this matter that Kiaran brought to us," Edwin said, leaning forward and resting his hands, folded together, upon the glass surface. The change in tone and the look in his eyes told Skylar the man intended to discuss the business that she had come such a great distance to conduct. "I have already spoken with the other six Masters, and the Grand Master of the Order, and I can say that I speak with their full blessing and support."

Skylar nodded to him. "And what is your decision?"

"We are prepared to give you use of the weapon," Edwin replied calmly. "It has been safeguarded at this facility since being removed from Libu during the fall of the former regime."

"Not an easy thing to do in that chaos," Kiaran remarked.

"It all depended on one man, a dedicated Knight of the Order, who narrowly pulled it off, despite being pursued by some powerful agents of the Convergence," Edwin said. "This is a weapon much more than it is a relic."

"I understand. Otherwise I would not have bothered Kiaran about finding a way to use it," Skylar replied.

"Let's take a look at it now then, shall we?" Edwin invited, to nods from the other two. He reached under the table, pushing a button mounted underneath.

"Bring the weapon in please," he stated in a louder voice.

A few seconds later, a door opened on the other side of the room. A tall, broad-shouldered man with a crew cut entered. He held a long, cloth-wrapped bundle out before him, arms extended and palms supporting underneath.

"Thank you," Edwin said to the man as he reached the table, accepting the bundle. The large figure stepped to the side, watching the proceedings quietly with a somber expression.

Gently, Edwin set the bundle down on the glass and began carefully unwrapping the cloth layers cradling the object within. After a few moments, the weapon lay exposed to her view.

At first she felt a little underwhelmed at the sight, especially after all she had heard. It looked like nothing more than a simple, old spear, something she would come across in a museum exhibit on ancient cultures.

A weathered, thoroughly nicked haft of wood fitted with an iron tip, the spear did not bear any special ornamentation or markings. Yet Skylar knew she gazed upon something rare and exceptional in nature. The weapon before her had been used to bring down Nephilim giants, in the legendary age before the terrible Flood that covered the world and washed so many evils from its surface.

"It has not been easy to keep this in our control, and it has been needed on a few choice occasions," Edwin commented, looking upon the weapon. "Picked up a few scrapes and gouges here and there, but it still is in pretty good shape."

"I will put it to the best purpose it has ever been used for," Skylar promised Edwin.

"You believe that you can get close enough to Her to strike?" Edwin asked, his eyes rising up from the weapon to meet her gaze.

Skylar nodded. Her reply brimmed with conviction. "I do, and I will."

"Why should we not attempt the very same thing you propose to do, with one of our most skilled Knights?" he asked.

She looked Edwin in the eyes. "I will have aid, from a unique source available only to me."

He held her steely gaze for a moment. She could tell that the subject of an unnamed benefactor gave no comfort to him. Understanding what it was like to confront enemies who were masters of guile and deception, she could not blame him for harboring misgivings.

"So Kiaran has told me, but I would like to know who else would have possible access to this weapon," he stated. "Many among the Enemy have enacted clever schemes and ruses in their desire to lay their hands on this spear. A few attempts have barely been thwarted."

"My benefactor aided me in the past with slaying a Walker of the Setian Path, one who had been the most skilled **Traveler** the Enemy had in their ranks," Skylar said. "I am the only one who knows and interacts with this benefactor. The anonymous nature of this is in our best interests for the mission. This will have to be a matter of whether you trust enough in my judgement."

After a lengthy pause, Edwin replied. "I can understand that. The Order often has to confine the identities of those who help us to the knowledge of just a few individuals. There are only two possibilities I see. It will either be as you say, or you are falling into a trap. But the hour is growing very dark and I am not so naïve to fail to understand that great risks must be taken from time to time."

"I will strike Her down," Skylar iterated firmly.

Edwin kept his eyes fixed towards the weapon with a thoughtful expression on his face. His lips pursed a little and she could tell that deep matters were being weighed inside his mind.

"We will be counting on it," Edwin said at last, slowly pushing the bundle and spear across the glass surface towards her. "We both know what She means to do with this world. I would like to support any effort that may have a chance to land a blow upon this most evil of creatures."

"Thank you for your trust in this," Skylar told him in a low voice, looking straight into the man's grey eyes. Edwin's agreement to allow her the use of the weapon was as much a declaration of confidence in Skylar and her character as it was anything else.

"It is an honor to be of help to the Shield Maidens, who have fought side by side with us for many, many long and difficult years," Edwin commented, while Skylar carefully folded the cloth back over the spear. "We have stood shoulder to shoulder, we have bled together, and even died together. The Shield Maidens are true sisters to the Knights, in the family of Adonai."

"You are our brothers in every way," Skylar replied. "I will honor the Order and all you have done for us when I strike Her on behalf of all who fight against the Nether Kingdom."

"May Adonai protect you," Edwin said, a look of concern rising on his face. "You embrace the greatest peril."

"It must be done," Skyar stated.

He held her eyes for a moment longer, and then his expression softened. "Be our guest for the rest of today and tonight, here at the Lookout. Tomorrow we will have you both taken back north."

"Thank you. I know I could use a good, solid rest," Skylar said, accepting the invitation gladly. She smiled at Edwin. "I will have to go by tomorrow, or I might find it tempting to take a longer hiatus here in this beautiful haven."

"I would not blame you for doing so," Edwin said, returning the smile. "It is difficult enough for me to stay deep underground so often, when such a natural paradise surrounds us here."

"So may I have an extended leave?" Kiaran asked, grinning, in an obvious tone of jest.

"I think you still have a little work left, Kiaran, but I would love for you to visit as soon as you are finished," Edwin replied, exhibiting good humor, though Skylar noted a hint of sadness in his eyes.

Edwin had the look of a man possessing a wealth of experience and wisdom recognizing the imminence of a grave time. Though he had extended Kiaran an invitation, there remained little doubt in Skylar that Edwin did not believe Kiaran would ever be able to take him up on the offer. Even more sadly, she did not think so either.

JOVAN

The woodlands flowed, alive with moving shadows. Huge forms emerged into the moonlight bathing the expanse of ground spread before the compound.

Towering giants, winged four-legged monstrosities, and all manner of Erkorenen strode forward from the shadows, coming in from all directions. A fearsome assemblage took shape in the night, brimming with strength and power. Even so, the air remained quiet, and a subdued, reverential hush reigned over the gathering.

"Open your eyes, Jovan." The words touched his ears like the whisper of a breeze, spoken by the ethereal presence he had come to know well. "Tonight ... you will know."

Lilith had appeared to him earlier that evening, instructing him to go to the sprawling lawn before the building complex when midnight drew near. He did as she asked, but had no idea regarding her purpose. Now, as living nightmares towered over him, Jovan found himself more confused than ever before; and a little apprehensive.

"I will know what?" Jovan asked, chafing at the mystery of it all.

"Open your eyes," she said again, with a hint of amusement. "Are you blind?"

Whether a part of him complied, or she conferred some manner of special ability on him, he suddenly beheld movement in the air. Swirling all around the gathering and the compound itself, as if Jovan and the Erkorenen stood in the middle of a vast funnel, a host comprised of dark wraiths and ghostly creatures of Lilith flew.

The sight took the breath from Jovan. The air had been empty only a moment before. Now, he could see nothing of the forest beyond the dense, flowing ranks of dark spirits.

"They bestow this audience with sanctity," Lilith said.

"Audience?" Jovan asked, confused.

At that moment, he observed a large contingent of humans issuing out from the direction of the compound buildings. Aaliyah Satrinah, Dagian Underwood, Gendry Resinger, Ethan Forneus, Abner Nithael, and many other significant figures of the Convergence made their way slowly across the grass towards a space left clear in front of the Erkorenen.

Not a word spoken amongst the august procession, the silent figures were well-dressed. Their expressions somber, not a single trace of levity could be found upon any face. In some ways, they appeared like a stream of believers heading into a church.

"What in the world is going on here?" Jovan asked, increasingly perplexed at the assembly, growing stranger by the moment.

He interacted with many of the people he saw joining the gathering, but not one of them had said anything to him about the event. Without Lilith, he would have missed the occasion entirely. He wondered what compelled them all to come out in the middle of the night, and stand aside a group of monstrosities. It seemed as if all of them, human and non-human alike, waited in expectation for something.

"You are about to see, and then you will know," came the breathy reply from the shadowy, feminine apparition at his side.

Her form took on increased solidity, accenting the shapely curves and stunning face that so tormented and aroused Jovan's more primal instincts. He rarely saw her in such great clarity, and for a moment he just stared, taking in the sight.

A look both seductive and playful rested on her face as she gazed back to him with eyes like small red embers. The latter served as the only hint she was not of human origin.

Then, at once, her expression changed to mirror the humans he had just observed. She turned her head away from Jovan, and gazed forward.

A remarkable phenomenon then occurred all around him. One by one, the Erkorenen lowered to their knees, with their heads facing downward, in clear signs of deference and reverence. Whether on two legs, four legs, or more, they all took up postures of obeisance, as an eerie stillness draped over the area.

Looking around, Jovan saw that the humans at the forefront of the assemblage were doing likewise. Jovan found it incredibly strange and anomalous watching the likes of Dagian Underwood, one of the most powerful women in the world, and Gendry Resinger, one of the most influential men, going down to their knees like a pair of penitents at a church service.

After a few moments, Jovan realized that he remained the only one left standing within the open ground. Even Lilith in her non-physical form displayed a kneeling position with her head bowed.

The swirl of wraiths and Lilith's creatures slowed down into a hovering pattern, drawing the movement of the great funnel to a halt. The smaller creatures were oriented inward, looking in the same direction as the Erkorenen and people on the ground.

Jovan turned slowly. A single, solitary being stood on the upper balcony of a familiar building, overlooking the lawn with a serene look resting upon her face.

Kaira.

Jovan's brow furrowed and his mind raced. He did not know what to make of the unexpected development.

"To your knees, Jovan," Lilith hissed, all playfulness gone. "Know your place."

Kaira had taken notice of Jovan and stared at him with a solemn expression. Her face held no trace of friendliness, the look in her eyes steely and penetrating.

He found it hard to believe her to be the same woman he had talked and laughed with deep into the night, over several glasses of wine. Jovan considered himself a mentor, a friend, and a protector, but never an outright subordinate, but the setting was irrefutable in its nature.

Oddly, no indignation dwelled within his heart towards the stark, profound realization. As the moment transpired, the act of kneeling before her felt natural. He knew as he sunk to the ground with the others that he crossed a profound boundary. Jovan gave himself to Kaira in a way he had never extended to any other man or woman. Knees sinking into the soft grass, he knew his relationship with her could never go back to what it was before.

His eyes met hers as he kneeled. Karia's expression did not change, but a feeling of intense affinity flooded him, burning throughout his spirit. He knew in his heart that she accepted his deep commitment, and that a precious bond had formed in that momentous instant.

Jovan had never loved anyone with the intimate depth he felt towards Kaira now. He knew he would do anything she asked of him, even die for her if necessary.

She was a goddess to him now. From that moment forward he would be her servant, and she would be his mentor and guide. Hopefully, he could still retain her friendship, even if the nature of it had fundamentally changed.

Kaira took her eyes away from Jovan and looked over the gathering. The feelings inside him remained, as intense as before. He became overtaken with euphoria on a scale dancing at the edge of delirium.

A bright light then formed in the skies above. Its touch warm and invigorating, the luminance graced Jovan and the others kneeling before the regal woman on the balcony.

While Jovan had never understood the concept of anything

being holy, he knew the light from above possessed a sacred nature. It held an appearance so incredibly beautiful. He had never felt more alive than when his eyes were filled with the unsullied luminance. It exuded something of true purity, of a like he had never beheld in his life.

Jovan was filled with a host of powerful emotions. He felt a desperate desire to merge with that brilliant light, as if he belonged to it somehow. He wanted it to consume his spirit, and take him into its embrace.

The light was not anything generated from within the imperfect, flawed world he inhabited. It overflowed with life reaching across dimensions, a radiance of an eternal nature.

A voice so pure and harmonious it evoked rivulets of tears from Jovan's eyes flowed from the light and carried throughout the assemblage. "Behold, Blood of My Blood, in Whom I am well-pleased."

The cascade of light conferred an otherworldly glow upon Kaira, limning her form and shining from within at the same time. Jovan wept uncontrollably, gazing upon the majesty of her form.

The last vestige from his previous relationship with her dissipated with the gentleness of a soft summer breeze. Kaira no longer remained a friend, but instead his personal goddess. The awareness struck him in a profound, soul-shaking manner. He had never been happier than he was at that moment of revelation. No longer would the cares of the world and his life predominate within his thoughts. Part of something that went far beyond the world itself, Jovan savored the joyous sensation, the mere thought of the reality he inhabited exhilarating.

Jovan still kneeled quietly in place when the Erkorenen and encompassing horde of spirits filtered back into the shadows of the woodlands. Dagian, Gendry, and the other humans had departed well before then, though he took no note of their leaving.

Jovan never had anything other than himself to live for. Now, in the aftermath of the transforming experience, he brimmed with devotion and could only think of living for Kaira. Something inside him had changed. He had been given the gift of a form of love that went far beyond anything he had known before. In a manner of speaking, he felt he had been born again.

"Now ... you know the truth of it all," flowed the soft voice from Lilith, as Jovan remained spellbound in the cool embrace of the midnight air. "Give Her everything of yourself, so that the glories of the new age may come. You will witness miracles, the greatest yet to come when the Shining One reigns over all creation."

He heard her words but did not reply. There was no need for Lilith's directive. Every part of him resonated with the desire to give of himself.

There was no question he would willingly offer every last ounce of his soul to Kaira from that night forward. She had become everything to him, and he knew he could not find rest until the entire world confessed Her majesty.

SECTION VI

SKYLAR

Skylar and Magdelene stood close together at the edge of a small lake, the latter set in back of the house used as a headquarters for the Shield Maidens in the region. The lake and house anchored the middle of a large acreage owned by a patron of the Shield Maidens, so little possibility of disturbances existed.

The sun lay low in the skies, the temperature cooling to a pleasant level. The surface of the water gleamed as the shadows lengthened beneath the trees. A light breeze flowed through the air, ruffling Skylar's long, blonde locks.

Under other circumstances, the tranquility would have been enjoyable. As things stood, a tension weighed down the atmosphere surrounding the two women, one that no scenic environment could dispel.

Magdalene faced the younger woman, far from pleased. The look she cast brimmed with sadness, along with a sharp edge of irritation.

"We will work with the Order to get you access to the World Summit grounds, as you have requested," Magdalene said tersely. "Then Kiaran can do his part, complicit as he is in all of this."

Far from veiled, the distaste Magdalene now held towards Kiaran bothered Skylar. Anger seethed within her voice as she said his name.

Skylar had kept her promise to Kiaran, seeking out Magdalene immediately after returning from the Lookout. Her longtime guide's response proved to be just as severe as she had suspected.

"I know you're angry with Kiaran, but I hope you don't remain angry with him forever," Skylar replied, a little plaintively. "You know how I am, and how close we are in friendship. I couldn't accept anything less than his cooperation. He wasn't happy about my decision either, believe me. Far from it."

"Apparently, you made your case strong enough to gain the use of one of the Order's most prized artifacts," Magdalene commented. She shook her head, loosing an extended sigh. "And I am not so blinded with emotion that I can't recognize the value in your argument. I spoke with Edwin, and could not dispute their decision."

Skylar did not know what to say at first. Magdalene's admission was a powerful one, though there was no gloating or sense of vindication in the younger Shield Maiden. It hurt Skylar at a deep level to see her mentor so distressed. Yet she could not depart from the course she had taken.

"I must do this. Shield Maidens take risks all the time, as do the Knights," Skylar declared. "They always have. I am no different than my brother, who knew his risk going into Troy."

"I understand," Magdalene said. "The part of me that is a Shield Maiden who carries the Blue Star sees the need for this mission and the reasons why the Order cooperated with you. The part of me that is the deepest and most true aches terribly. I know you are aware of what this choice will bring to you, either way it goes. I am aware of it as well, and I just can't put that out of my mind."

Despite the low light, Skylar noticed the glistening on the surface of Magdalene's eyes at once. She looked in astonishment as a drop broke free from the corner of Magdalene's right eye and began descending along the skin of her cheek. It was joined in its downward journey a moment later by a tear from her left.

Not once had Skylar ever witnessed Magdalene cry. She had always been the pillar of strength in the worst of times. Though Skylar knew her mentor was deeply saddened with every Shield Maiden who died in action, the older woman had always been the bedrock to lean on for those she led.

Magdalene blinked her eyes and wiped at one cheek and then the other. She exhibited a forced smile, asking, "See what you've gone and made me do, Skylar?"

A hard kick to the gut would have been preferable to the feeling coming over Skylar at witnessing Magdalene's emotional response. Yet there was nothing that could dissuade her from her path. A terrible irony existed in that the choice she made was in part because of the love and loyalty she harbored towards Magdalene.

"I must do this," Skylar said in a low, determined voice.

"I know you must, you stubborn young lady," Magdalene said, half-laughing as more tears broke free. She stepped forward and hugged Skylar, embracing her more tightly than she ever had before.

It was the hug of a mother, and the one Skylar returned to Magdalene took on the quality of a loving daughter. She felt her heart breaking inside, wishing something could be done to comfort the woman who had given her so much.

Magdalene pulled back a little, and her hands firmly gripped Skylar, midway on her upper arms. A fiercely determined look blazed within her eyes, the streaks from the tears still visible on her face.

"I've always told you, when you make your attack, don't hold a single thing back," Magdalene said, her clutch tightening further on Skylar's arms. "Don't hesitate, don't fog your mind with even a shred of doubt. Be as the lightning when it splits the night. Pure, fast, and filled with power."

"I will, I promise you," Skylar replied.

Magdalene's eyes narrowed and her voice lowered in pitch, taking on a feel more akin to a growl. "For the sake of a world groaning for Adonai to free it, you strike that wicked thing down, and send Her back to the Abyss She came from."

"For you, for Matthew, for Kiaran, for Genevieve and all my sisters, and for everyone in the world … I plan on doing just that," Skylar replied, her voice and expression more than matching the intensity of her beloved mentor. Unshakeable conviction reflected in her eyes and dwelled within her heart.

GODRAL

Prowling through shadows, Godral and Kantel worked their way deep into the territory occupied by the men they had been hunting. The night air teemed with scents of all kinds.

Godral sniffed the traces of several kinds of animals, along with a variety of human scents. Rounding the corner of a house, he startled a cat that bolted away the instant his massive shadow engulfed the creature.

A dog at the rear of one house took one look at the two An-Ki, whined, and scurried away. If any other creatures existed in the vicinity, they kept well concealed and maintained rigid silence as the huge, wolfish forms passed through their midst.

Only once did the pair find themselves observed by a human. Sensing that something watched him intently, Godral turned his head and stared down into the face of a young male child.

Peering outward, the little boy stood in the window of a house that the An-Ki padded along the facade of. The boy's eyes spread wide with terror, and a moment later he disappeared from sight. Godral felt a pang of regret at having scared the boy, but there was nothing he could have done about it.

It was easy enough to evade the humans with guns. No mistake could be made regarding their nature. Godral knew them to be the ones who belonged to the gang. They were loud and easy to perceive in all their movements. Godral surmised they would not have noticed him if they walked within two paces of his crouching form.

Nevertheless, the humans carried weapons that could kill an An-Ki in a heartbeat. Godral and Kantel maintained full caution as they moved in and observed a larger concentration of humans they came across later that night.

A throng of around twenty men from the gang milled about a small group of houses, one featuring a table with several chairs placed around it. Set up on the grass, the table had three occupants, who were sitting and talking together.

Godral's hackles rose, staring towards the men. The one in the middle drew his attention, invoking a distinctive feeling further inside. The thin-faced man had nothing remarkable in any physical sense, but it was the deeper nature that the An-Ki leader sensed.

The revulsion and animosity Godral harbored towards the figure told him the Enemy's taint was strong within the man. If anything, it seemed that no real human sat there, but rather a dark thing cloaked in a human guise.

Observing the men, Godral came to the conclusion that he and Kantel had reached an important area for the gang. He did not doubt that the prisoner spoken of was kept somewhere near.

Eyeing the group, Godral thought about what to do. He and Kantel could reach the men at the table before the ones farther from it had adequate time to react.

Loud voices from just ahead drew his attention. Two men emerged from a house, followed by another who did not resemble them at all in appearance. Two more men from the gang came out behind.

The man in the middle of the procession turned his head, glancing up the street, bringing his face into full view. Godral knew his eyes did not deceive him, but it was hard to accept what he saw. He recognized the man at once, the sole purpose for the journey he and the other An-Ki had undertaken to help Arianna.

"It is Benedict," Kantel said in a low, rumbling voice.

"To the shadows," Godral replied. "Let us go closer."

Paws making no sound, and keeping within pools of darkness, Godral and Kantel worked their way towards Benedict and his captors. As the An-Ki proceeded, more men with guns began gathering around the table. The men with Benedict led him to stand before the three seated figures.

The man harboring the thick Enemy taint spoke to those with the guns, using a language he did not understand. But when he spoke to Benedict, it was in the human language Godral had learned.

He addressed Benedict by name and then told him of a meeting that would soon take place. From what Godral could follow, Benedict would be given to others in exchange for some kinds of weapons. He caught mention of a place called Thompson Park and two references to fifteen minutes past midnight.

Turning his muzzle aside, he told Kantel. "We do not have much time. We must get others. Tell them of this."

Godral hated leaving Benedict in the clutches of the gang men. Yet nothing could be done with so many fighters armed with guns. The two An-Ki could bring down many of the humans, but they would be shot down and Benedict would stand no chance of being freed.

Hurrying back through the shadows, Godral and Kantel soon bounded through the streets at a full run. They paid no heed to subtlety, more than once startling gang members idling about the area.

Yells of alarm and shock followed in the wake of their passage. A few gun shots cracked the night air, though nothing came close to harming the An-Ki. Godral raced though grass lawns, leaped over fences, and crossed streets with the singular goal of reaching the other An-Ki and telling Arianna what had happened.

ARIANNA

"Your Uncle Benedict is the prisoner," Godral told Arianna, standing in his two-legged, lupine form within the living room.

Listening to his words, she stared up into Godral's wolfish face in a state of shock. Of all the things happening lately, the last thing she expected to discover was that the prisoner held by the gang was her uncle.

"They take him this night ... to give him to others," Godral continued. "Someone will give them weapons. For your uncle."

"You are sure it was Benedict?" she asked, still incredulous.

"It was him. I saw. Kantel saw," Godral replied. "The men from the gang spoke his name too."

"Where? Did they say where they were going to exchange him?" Arianna asked, wrestling with the information, knowing there would be little time to formulate a solid plan. It was now a matter of instincts and quick reaction.

"To a place called Thompson Park," Godral answered. "We heard the gang men say this."

Arianna frowned. "I don't know where Thompson Park is."

"I do not know," Godral replied.

"Who are they going to give him to?" Arianna asked. "Did they say anything about that?"

"To men who give weapons to them," Godral said. "I heard them. They say they can fight army with these weapons."

Ire rose within Arianna. It took little effort to fathom the main party involved with the transaction.

"Agents of the UCAS government," she responded curtly. "No question about that. Was there any indication of time? When is this exchange taking place?"

"They say midnight. Fifteen minutes past. Many times," Godral responded.

Arianna looked down at the watch on her wrist. "That gives us just over one hour, as of right now. Let's get going."

"What do you want me to do?" Godral asked her.

"We must go to this Thompson Park as soon as we possibly can," Arianna told him, insistently. After all of the waiting and lack of any viable leads, she found herself highly impatient. "We'll need to be carried to see Wendell, so we can get weapons ourselves, at least for myself, Quinn, and Maureen. We'll probably need them tonight."

"I will gather An-Ki. You gather humans," Godral responded. "We will carry you."

Over the next several minutes, Arianna hustled to rouse Quinn and Maureen out of bed, while Godral gathered the other An-Ki together. Everyone, An-Ki and human alike, regrouped in the living room.

In their human-like forms, Vailia, Dedran, and Sarangar took places next to Quinn and Maureen. At Godral's right side, Kantel had not yet changed back from his bipedal, wolfish shape.

After Arianna and Godral explained the circumstances, everyone moved to the backyard, where all of the An-Ki began transforming into their four-legged forms. It took Vailia, Dedran, and Sarangar a little longer to change, starting from human shapes, but shortly all five of the An-Ki were finished with their metamorphoses.

Arianna, Maureen, and Quinn got onto the backs of Godral, Sarangar, and Kantel respectively. Pulling herself onto Godral, hands firmly clenching his coarse fur, she took a deep breath as he lifted up from the ground.

The An-Ki loped through the neighborhood, keeping to the shadows of houses and trees. Wendell's home stood not too far away and with Arianna's guidance they reached the two-story house in less than five minutes. After letting their riders dismount, the An-Ki took cover beneath the boughs of a trio of pine trees situated close by.

Arianna, Maureen, and Quinn walked up to the front of the house. Opening the screen door, Arianna rapped her knuckles insistently on the wood surface of the front entrance. Shortly thereafter, she heard heavy footsteps approaching from inside.

The sound of a bolt being pulled back and jingling of the doorknob preceded the creak of hinges, as the door swung inward. Wendell stood within the dark entrance, peering out at Arianna and her two companions. He blinked his eyes, looking groggy, probably having just been awakened from the depths of sleep.

"It's a little late for a visit ... what is it, Arianna?" he asked, with a touch of irritation.

"My uncle needs us right now," Arianna replied in a firm tone. "There is no time. The gang is about to exchange him for what we think are weapons, in a place called Thompson Park. We need our own weapons back. And I need to know how to find that park."

"Your uncle?" Wendell asked.

"Yes, we learned he's the prisoner they were holding," Arianna replied.

"How?" Wendell retorted, looking perplexed. He added, "How do you know this?"

"I don't have time to explain everything, but a couple of us risked a look into what the gang was doing," Arianna stated.

"How could you have possibly suspected it was your uncle?" Wendell pressed, looking and sounding more incredulous.

"We had no way of knowing. It came as a complete surprise," Arianna responded. Her tone took on a plaintive edge. "But we don't have time. The rendezvous with the gang is about to take place. Fifteen minutes after midnight, from what we understand. We need to get to Thompson Park right away. Please tell us where it is."

"The park's not too far, but it's in the heart of gang-held territory," Wendell replied. The trace of irritation faded from his face, replaced with signs of rising interest in the things she told him. "The area they've taken over has that whole park surrounded."

"Just tell us how to get there, and please give us our guns back," Arianna urged him.

"They are exchanging your uncle for weapons, you said?" Wendell queried. He sounded wide-awake and alert, as if her words finally connected with him.

"Yes, which makes me think they are dealing with representatives of the UCAS," Arianna answered. "Though I have no idea what department or agency."

"I think you're right about it being the UCAS, if the gang's making an exchange for weapons. The gang has no lack of guns, so this would have to be something much more significant," Wendell reasoned aloud. He grimaced a moment later, and added, "That doesn't do our community any favors here, if they get their hands on even better weapons."

"Which is why we need to put a stop to this," Arianna responded. Her sense of worry accelerated, each moment precious. "But I need to get going. My uncle has nobody else right now. It's us or it's nothing, and there's simply no time to try convincing others to help. We have minutes, not hours. We're the ones taking the risk, just let us try."

He looked into her eyes, a somber look weighing upon his face. Wendell's chest then heaved with a quick intake of breath, which he held for a moment before loosing.

"Okay, okay," Wendell said at last. "I'll get your guns back. But we should tell Davis about this right away. This has a lot of implications for everyone living in this area."

"You can tell him yourself, after we get going," Arianna said, with a harder edge. "There's no time! I have about forty minutes to get there before my uncle is handed off and taken to who-knows-where! I need to go right now."

"You'll never make it on foot to Thompson Park in time, and they've blocked the roads to vehicles," Wendell stated grimly. "I don't want to sound like a nay-sayer, but it's too far from here to get there on foot in 40 minutes."

"Let me worry about that. Just let us take our guns with us," Arianna responded, restless to get underway. "That's all I'm asking. Not going to put you or anyone else at risk."

Wendell nodded, though a mild look of puzzlement rested on his face. "I don't know how you can possibly get there in time."

"We will," Arianna stated, growing more uneasy by the second.

"Alright," Wendell stated, evenly. "Do what you need to do."

About ten minutes later, the handguns and rifles taken from their group were returned. As the guns were being transferred, Wendell explained the directions for reaching Thompson Park, giving Arianna a few distinct landmarks to use along the way.

The handguns were easier to carry, though the rifles presented a small challenge. Quinn and Maureen slung rifles over their shoulders, while gripping one in each hand. Arianna shouldered one by its strap, and held onto a second with both hands as she faced Wendell.

"Where are the others from your group?" he asked.

"They are waiting for us," Arianna said. "We'll catch up to them. Just didn't want to bring a big crowd to speak with you."

In truth, at that moment, Arianna knew that the five An-Ki watched from the shadows in forms that would both astonish and terrify Wendell. There was no time to acclimate him to the existence of the An-Ki.

"I don't see how you'll get there in time," he iterated again, shaking his head.

"We've got a plan," Maureen interjected firmly. "Just trust us on that."

"Go tell Davis what's happening. We need to get going," Arianna told Wendell.

Turning, she started away from the front door. With her back to him, she continued at a brisk gait along the concrete pathway towards the sidewalk running in front of the house. Wendell watched them for a moment longer before disappearing back into the house, shutting the door behind.

A pair of houses down, standing out of the open in a driveway dividing two residences, Arianna, Quinn, and Maureen took a few moments to conceal the guns they could not carry along with them. They hid the weapons beneath a parked car set to the far end of the driveway.

The car's four flat tires indicated that it had not been in use for quite some time. For a temporary hiding place, it appeared suitable enough.

"Let us go," Godral's deep voice broke through the whispering breezes.

Having emerged from their places of concealment, he and the other An-Ki stood just behind Arianna and her two friends. One by one, Godral, Kantel, and Sarangar lowered themselves until their bellies touched the ground.

Quinn climbed carefully onto the back of Kantel, while Godral carried Arianna, and Maureen rode upon Sarangar. Godral and Arianna took the lead as they moved out, the five An-Ki loping down the street, the pads of their broad paws scuffling against the dry pavement.

Arianna called out the directions she had memorized from Wendell. The appearance of a large church and a timber-framed home, landmarks described by Wendell, gave reassurance that they were on the right path.

When one of the large, guarded barricades loomed ahead, spanning the road, Godral and the other An-Ki took to the houses and yards to get past the warded boundary. Once they had crossed into gang-held territory, they kept off the roads and sidewalks.

The absence of street lights, remaining dark due to the inoperable power grid, helped to further conceal their movements. Like flowing shadows coursing through the night, the cluster of An-Ki with human riders bounded through the hushed neighborhood, heading swiftly towards the park.

More than once Arianna saw gang members acting as sentries and grouped in pairs or trios. Seeing their shadowy outlines, all she could do was keep as silent as possible, trusting Godral and the other An-Ki to slip past them unnoticed.

On one occasion, one of the gang members apparently saw them, calling aloud to his two companions with a tone of alarm. The An-Ki drew to a halt, causing Arianna to lurch forward with the abrupt change in momentum. Godral and the others padded over to crouch behind a line of bushes, keeping their eyes fixed on the gang members.

The one who had sounded the alert headed straight towards Arianna's group with his rifle aimed forward, his steps hesitant and cautious. His companions flanked him, pointing their rifles forward with their fingers on the triggers.

Arianna wondered whether she should prepare to dismount Godral's back when two large forms streaked into view before her. Dedran and Vailia rushed the three men from opposite sides, closing from the left and right. The An-Ki fell upon the men before they could react or bring their guns around to defend themselves.

Smashed to the ground in a storm of physical power, the hapless figures got off a short burst of cries and screams. The An-Ki tore savagely at the men with their powerful jaws. Bestial, throaty growls sounded into the darkness. When Dedran and Vailia finally straightened up, three men lay dead upon the ground, blood pooling around their bodies from a host of wounds.

Godral, Sarangar, and Kantel rose up and moved out from behind the line of bushes. Not a word was spoken among the An-Ki. Arianna's heart beat too fast to formulate any kind of inquiry. Dedran and Vailia, muzzles caked with blood and grime, fell in with the others as the group headed onward.

The long continuity of alternating houses and driveways finally came to an end as a large stretch of trees and grass opened up ahead. They had found the park.

A road entered the park about midway down. After passing the last house, the An-Ki turned into the park, trotting just inside the trees towards the paved surface cleaving the high grass.

Drawing nearer, Arianna saw the sign posted just to the side of the park entrance. Big, bold letters on the sign proclaimed:

Welcome to Thompson Park

"We're here," Arianna said to Godral in full confidence. She turned all her thoughts to the sole reason for the journey. "Now, let's find out where they have my uncle, and let's free him."

With Godral at the lead, using the winding roadway as a guide, the group proceeded deeper into the park.

SETH

The thunderous punch lifted the man off his feet and left him sprawled on the ground, unconscious. A thin layer of flowing water covering the tunnel surface altered its course to accommodate the new shape deposited in its way.

"Put some starch into that one, don't you think? Hehehe," Rumble Dog commented to Seth, with a grin and a wink, clearly pleased with his handiwork.

Seth grinned, though the display of the power packed in the man's punch left him a little nervous. The man had an intimidating appearance and the substance to back it up.

"And that's how y'all should deal with this sort," Raven pronounced to the small group of onlookers. "Only you should have left him for me to take care of ... dear."

The sarcasm oozed thick around her final word as she thumped a closed fist on Rumble Dog's upper arm.

"Yes, boss. I won't forget next time," Rumble Dog replied with a chuckle. He turned to the group watching them. "He ain't got the gun or knife any more. I'm claimin' those. Decent nine millimeter too. Thug doesn't deserve it. So anyone else givin' you good folk any problems?"

"I think you took care of us really good, sir," a man announced, standing next to his wife and two children.

"I ain't classy enough to be called sir, just call me Rumble Dog," the big biker responded with an amiable grin, drawing a chorus of laughs from the onlookers.

Though he could not deny the unusual nature of the justice being served, Seth could not deny he drew some satisfaction watching Rumble Dog and Raven cleaning things up within the underground community. They were volunteers of the oddest sort. It was as of the big biker and his equally tough girlfriend had appointed themselves the new sheriffs in town.

"Now that that's done, let's go above and get some fresh air," Christa said, tugging at the sleeve of Seth's shirt. "Too dank down here for my liking."

"I'm with you," Seth agreed.

The two walked away from the crowd, which had begun dispersing. They headed down the tunnel, marked by periodic lamps set in place by the underground population. Making a couple of turns, and covering well over a mile, they finally reached one of the outlets.

Though she was not his girlfriend, Seth loved being in the company of Christa. It made him forget about all the fears and hardships for awhile.

The night air filled Seth's lungs as they stepped out from the tunnel entrance. They had emerged at a drainage conduit situated close to a main thoroughfare of the legendary gambling destination.

Neon signs lit up the night as far as the eye could see, casting a magical ambience over the throngs of people walking the sidewalks. Thick traffic rolled along the road.

"Are you thinking what I'm thinking?" Christa asked, staring towards the luminous scene.

"Should we?" Seth asked. "We'd be taking a risk."

"We won't get into trouble, just a walk," Christa said. "Come on, Seth. It's no big deal."

"A walk won't hurt," Seth responded.

He knew that he could not deny her if he tried. They walked away from the tunnel together and in five minutes were striding past the facades of the casinos, restaurants, and storefronts.

They had succumbed to the temptation twice before. Their youth and the fact that the local authorities were slow enforcing Living ID meant that Seth and Christa could walk the streets of the neon city together without undue harassment.

Like hordes of moths drawn to a great light, people crowded the streets. Seth and Christa found it easy enough to meld into the pedestrian flow.

The casino buildings, fascinating to look upon, ranged from pyramids and classical architecture to sleek, futuristic-looking structures. They were in full operation, giving people a fantasy to escape into during the tumultuous times gripping the UCAS.

"Thinking we might have some good luck and win a million

dollars if we try," Seth remarked to Christa, who was gazing up with a look of wonderment at the bright arrays of lights.

She smiled at him. "And you'll be asked for an I.D. then, for sure."

"There is that," Seth replied, laughing. "Good point."

A short man approached them, giving Seth a pair of cards with images of shapely, scantily clad women on them. The reverse sides had phone numbers. Seth chuckled, tossing them to the ground and feeling a little embarrassed.

"Bold guy," Christa said, laughing. "He didn't know if I was your girlfriend or not and he still gave you those."

"Evidently not worried about my age either," Seth replied, though his heart skipped a beat at Christa's mention of a scenario where she was his girlfriend.

After an hour, they had worked their way down to the large pyramid-shaped casino.

"Seth? Christa?"

Seth's heart jumped, and then eased, recognizing the voice. He turned towards the speaker.

"Skipping class?" Raymond asked, with a wide grin. To his right, Annika and Jonathan stood, smiling broadly. Behind them stood Rowan, who simply looked thrilled to be there with the others.

"What's that about good minds thinking alike?" Seth remarked.

"We were just about to check this place out. I've wanted to see what's inside," Raymond said.

"Then we'll join you," Christa announced.

The group headed towards the entrance. Everything gave off such a slick, lavish sheen. To Seth's eyes, Silver Valley as a whole stood as an oasis within a decaying, crumbling world. Anything but ostentatious, the trappings of luxury served as a beacon to a better world. Yet he knew it all to be an illusion, a thin veil covering a dying, oppressed society.

Nevertheless, the people in Silver Valley believed in that illusion, at least while they were patronizing the massive casinos and other entertainment sources to be found along the legendary strip. Smiles and laughter abounding, a majority of the men and women in view dressed elegantly.

The boisterous atmosphere gave Seth a lift as they passed under the gaze of two security guards. His group at ease, behaving as if they belonged, the guards paid them no heed.

Once inside, they strolled into an enormous atrium. Above them rose a multitude of levels containing hotel rooms, built to follow the shape of the pyramid as it converged towards its lofty apex.

"Just so frickin' cool," Raymond remarked, staring at the elevators running on slanted tracks following the incline of the pyramid. "Wonder if that magic guy, the illusionist, is still living up in the top of this thing. I saw a documentary on this place once. All kinds of cool stuff around here."

"It'd be a good pad to have, during these times," Jonathan observed.

"Come on you all, let's see what's in here," Annika said, starting forward.

They walked amid rows of slot machines and past clusters of circular tables, filled with patrons engaged in card games. Other spots had dice-throwing games underway, where betting onlookers cheered or groaned in reaction to the periodic throws.

"The first casino I went into, I would've played some slots, but it's all digital currency now," Jonathan said with a shrug. "No use trying here either. Won't do me much good if I hit something."

"If you had any money to play with in the first place," Annika said, grinning.

"Times are tough, what can I say," Jonathan said with a shrug, laughing.

For the next hour, Seth and his friends wandered around the immense facility. Laughing, joking, and taking in the sights, Seth became a teenager once more, shedding the onus of being an escapee from a federal detainment camp.

"Time to get back to the underground?" Jonathan asked the others, after they had made a thorough circuit of the casino.

Seth felt a little pang of regret that the foray had to come to an end so soon. Feeling carefree and being with Christa invigorated his spirit, though he understood why they had to go.

On the walk back to the tunnel entrance, Raymond and Rowan kept several paces ahead of the others, leaving Jonathan and Annika walking together, with Seth and Christa just behind. As they made their way along the crowded sidewalk, Seth could not help fantasizing that Christa was truly with him, in the way Jonathan and Annika were together.

He walked with a taller, more confident air. His words did not stumble out of his mouth, nor did he glance aside when Christa cast an extended look his way. He wished he always felt as comfortable in his skin as he did right then.

After entering the underground labyrinth and returning to their living quarters, the group disbanded for the time being. Christa and Annika announced they would take naps, while Jonathan and Raymond chose to go exploring the tunnel system. Rowan, looking eager, decided at the last moment to join the two for the excursion.

Seth went looking for Ian and it did not take long to find him. In the area where the Order concentrated, he stood with the sheriff, engrossed in a meeting with two men from the Order.

Everyone cast Seth cursory glances as he walked over to Ian's side. He stood in silence until the discussion was finished, about ten minutes later. From what Seth gathered, the Order intended to conduct some sort of operation in the heart of the city.

"So, did you go above?" Ian asked. "This would be the third time. You know what I told you."

"Just for a little while. With Christa," Seth replied, as if that explanation should make perfect sense to the man.

"Seth, it's really stupid to go above right now," Ian said. "I know it must be driving you all crazy down here, but a lot worse can happen to you up there."

"I know, I know," Set responded quickly, having to argument to counter Ian. "We just wanted to get out for awhile. It was a dumb thing to do."

"She's a good girl, Seth," Ian said, growing more somber. "Allyson thinks the world of her. I think she's wonderful too."

For just a moment, Seth recognized the flicker in Ian's eyes, that of a father looking out for a daughter. Christa did not share Ian's blood. Yet being one of Allyson's best friends undoubtedly provided her with an extension of the protectiveness Ian held towards his own. Seth knew it was not a thing to trifle with.

"I know, sir, and I'll watch out for her as best I can. I promise. We're just friends," Seth replied, the final words a bitter concession from his mouth.

"I wasn't born yesterday, young man," Ian told him, with a smirk. Despite the friendlier expression, the look in his eyes did not change. "I can tell how you feel about her."

"Okay, I wish we weren't just friends, but that's not up to me," Seth replied. "But I can't help how I feel about it."

"Believe me, I knew that feeling well, when I was your age," Ian told Seth with a wink. "More than you might think. The girl I wished for a long time I wasn't just friends with I ended up marrying. So good things can happen, young man. I'm proof of it."

Seth smiled and laughed, feeling a relief at the more amiable shift in Ian. Still, he did not know what to say in response.

"So if you're good to her, then we're all good," Ian said. He patted Seth on the back. "You can relax now, we've had our serious talk now ... that's out of the way."

Seth nodded, and grinned with a nervous edge. He hoped he never crossed Ian. The rational side of his mind told him there was little to fear, as being good to Christa went without saying.

He found it inconceivable that he would ever hurt her. The only big worry lingering in him centered on disappointing her, if they ever did become more than just friends.

Before the worry showed on his face, Seth decided to change the subject. "So, what's goin' on here? When I walked up I heard something about a mission."

"Chris has been thinking something big with the Order is about to happen, somewhere downtown," Ian replied. "We didn't know anything about what it was, exactly, but our hosts have been very busy lately. Just now Chris was working to find out more, and it turns out his suspicions were correct. There is a mission about to take place."

"Aren't they going to try to help us get back home?" Seth asked, bothered by the revelation.

"They are, but they still have to deal with the things happening here," Ian said. His voice then took on a more somber tone. "We gotta do our part too, wherever we can. That includes staying disciplined, and not doing anything to put our group at risk. If just for Christa's sake, stay down here and keep out of sight."

Seth felt anxious, seeing the stern, fatherly edge return once more within Ian's eyes. "Yes, sir, I will. I'm sorry."

Ian's expression lightened again. Smiling, he lay his hand on Seth's shoulder, and gave him another pat. "I would have snuck out too, and taken a look around, at your age. Not every day you are a teenager in Silver Valley. I understand. It's just that you know better, and you know who you are doing it for, when you cooperate with us here."

"Yes sir," Seth said.

"Just do your part, and hopefully soon we'll all be on our way back home again," Ian said. "Help us out now, and when we get back I'll be sure to have a big summertime cookout ... and make sure you and Christa both are invited. Might add a few good words with her about you too."

Seth grinned. "I'd really like that."

"Then it's a deal, Seth," Ian said, extending his hand. "Gentleman's agreement. On your honor."

IAN RAFFERTY

Ian peered down the tunnel, taking a deep breath.

"Here goes nothing," he exclaimed to himself.

Reaching out, he flicked the switch on. A string of lights running down the right side of the tunnel came on immediately. They doubled the luminance in the corridor, which housed a large number of families with children.

Ian smiled and let the breath held in his chest ease out. He heard claps and cheers farther down the tunnel, and the gleeful squeals of some children at the new light.

The line of lights just installed was the epitome of a makeshift project, cobbled together from lengths of old wiring, fixtures, and any hardware he could dig up from canvassing the occupants of the tunnel. Fortunately, some tools of solid quality had been loaned to Ian from one of the families. A few points along the line called for some creative ingenuity on his part, but even with his skill and experience he had not been entirely certain of success.

He tapped into the city's electric grid to power the new string of lights. The infrastructure of Silver Valley still remained in place and had not been cut off. As Tunnel City grew, the underground community had gathered up a modest collection of gas-powered generators, but they were unnecessary for Ian's purposes.

It had taken him only a single day living underground to appreciate what the people dwelling there for weeks and months on end went through. The dusky confines made for a dreary environment to raise children in. Talking to the people living in the tunnels, one of the most frequent issues raised regarded the challenges of living underground with a severe lack of ambience.

Ian wanted to contribute something to their generous hosts while he was staying among them. After gaining knowledge of the layout and materials at hand, he decided to take the initiative of applying his skill set.

It was a good way to while away the hours. Filling the time with productive activity kept his mind off the array of worries plaguing him.

Once they saw what he was up to, a few of the individuals among the tunnel occupants volunteered to help in any way that they could. One was a gangly, teenaged boy. Another was a middle-aged man who had worked construction before. A third was a young woman of about twenty-five, who had once served in the military. All were helpful, from aiding in the mounting of fixtures and wire, to going about the underground population looking for materials.

Spending hours in the company of the teenager, Ian could not help but be reminded of Peyton. Talking with him, Ian learned that the boy lived with his parents, two little brothers, and a baby sister in an arrangement involving two spaces set opposite each other; the boys on one side and the parents with the baby on the other.

Ian could not imagine the hardships involved with raising small children and a baby in such rough conditions. It made him appreciate his situation back home all the more. The boy's father had worked in baggage at the Silver airport, but had been fired as commercial flights dwindled in the economic tumult.

Like most families, they had been a paycheck away from disaster and were soon out on the streets. The boy's mother and father found themselves caught between violent gangs and the suffocating security apparatus pervading the city.

When Living ID became mandatory and roundups began to occur, the boy's father had searched desperately for another option. At last, he had come across rumors of the underground community.

Though interminably damp and dark, the tunnel system really was a tremendous refuge for so many frightened, desperate people. Ian found himself wishing he could them help much more than just stringing up another set of lights, but he could only do what was within his power.

Ian started down the brightened tunnel, receiving some compliments and accolades along the way from people who had been watching him work the past few hours. His stomach rumbled, and the foremost thought on his mind was scrounging up something to eat.

When he had gotten a few hundred yards down the tunnel, a familiar voice called to him. "Ian! There you are! Finally! Been looking all over for you."

Ian looked ahead and saw Chris approaching him. Shaking his head, Ian slowed his gait. "I've been here, most of the day."

"I heard you were doing some work," Chris remarked as he neared. He looked up at the new line of lights. "I guess I just should have looked for the brightest tunnel section."

Ian grinned. "I guess you could do that, but with some of the junk I had to work with I wasn't sure it would all work."

"Looks like it did, though. Well done, Ian," Chris complimented, with an air of admiration. "Anyhow, I needed to talk with you, it's pretty important."

Ian nodded. "The kind of thing we need to discuss in private."

"Yes, that kind of thing," Chris said, without any trace of jest.

Ian and Chris took a long walk back to the area occupied by the members of the Order. A few areas within that zone had been set up in lounge-like fashions, complete with couches and low tables. One remained completely uninhabited, and the two men took seats in the space.

"Looks like something a high importance is happening above us," Chris said. "Just like I thought, and then some. Salvador took me aside and told me about everything today."

"What did you find out?" Ian asked.

"They've gotten wind of some kind of meeting involving Senator Red Harrelson, a couple of banking magnates, and several others from the circles of the powerful and influential," Chris said.

Ian shrugged. "Wouldn't surprise me. You know what city's right above us. Probably wealthy friends on a big getaway. Wanting to gamble and do whatever else can be done here."

"All of them are known, ranking members of the Convergence," Chris stated. "The hotel they are meeting at is being cleared of all other reservations. More security is being imported.

"This is something much more than just a rendezvous. But there's no doubt they are meeting here because of the other, more entertaining things that can be found in Silver Valley."

Something dawned on Ian in that moment. "That's why the Order is keeping a strong presence here, in this particular city. They knew members of the Convergence would make use of Silver for the extra curricular activities it has to offer."

"Exactly why," his friend concurred. "This city is kind of like fly paper. It inevitably attracts many of them, and the idea is to secure them at the right time, to extract some information."

"I bet the Order has a solid intelligence network set up already," Ian said.

Chris grinned and chuckled. "They were savvy enough to make some connections with a number of very attractive ladies who do high-end, private entertaining, if you get my drift."

"This city's known for that, but thinking of the Order linking up with women doing that sort of thing is pretty funny ... and pretty damn smart," Ian said.

"I admit, the irony is rich," Chris said, laughing.

"That it is," Ian agreed.

"A weakness of the powerful. I bet it always has been," Chris stated. "Not in all cases, I know. Some of our adversaries are disciplined. But all the Order needs are a few leaks for something like this.

"The ones organizing this gathering have booked up several ladies who are in contact with members of the Order. We know the dates the meeting is taking place. And we know the times it will be moving into a very social mode."

"You say we," Ian responded pointedly, catching the wording Chris used.

"I say we because we've been invited to take part," Chris answered. "They need all the manpower they can get. That's what I'm here to talk with you about."

"Not what I hoped to hear from you," Ian admitted.

"I know it's not, but can we really do nothing to help them? When they're the ones who got us away from the camp and will be the ones helping us back home?" Chris asked.

"We can't avoid doing our part, not if we want to live with ourselves," Ian replied, unable to dispute the truth he felt in his heart.

"They are confident this will be the time to strike in a big way," Chris said. "The flypaper is going to have many big flies on its surface."

"And if this fails, we're back to a detainment camp, or even worse," Ian said, still feeling misgivings about the idea.

"You don't have to take part in it. Nobody's gonna force you," Chris said. "But they could use some additional hands to pose as additional staff ... or maintenance workers." Chris paused and grinned before continuing. "Can't think of anyone who might be able to pull off an electrician called in to check something out. I think Lucy and I can handle being sheriff's deputies. Just checking in while making rounds of the city. The Order has authentic uniforms for that.

Rumble Dog and Raven? Easy enough to blend in. There are plenty of bikers gambling in this city."

"They really need us like that?" Ian asked.

"They want to overwhelm them," Chris answered. The more positions that can be manned the better. Makes sense. Besides, I had an idea that would add a nice new wrinkle to their operation."

"What have you come up with?" Ian asked with an air of apprehension.

"Oh ... this is good," Chris said, with an excited gleam in his eyes.

"Now you are worrying me, Chris, spit it out," Ian retorted, growing impatient.

"Let's just say some of the maintenance workers brought in, perhaps as part of your crew, could turn into giant, wolf-like creatures at the right moment," Chris said, a grin spreading across his face. "Wouldn't you think that would cause more than a little disarray?"

"Probably disarray among the members of the Order involved too, seeing something like *that* for the first time," Ian replied, both surprised and recognizing what Chris was getting at.

"We're going to give the lads down here a little demonstration later," Chris said. "All three, Queran, Gorthaur, and Oragas are up for this, in a big way. I spoke with them about it. They are eager to hit back, after being taken captive."

"Seeing a demonstration and even knowing they are on our side would still scare the hell out of me," Ian declared.

"Can't say it won't rattle any of our nerves, but we've got one helluva asset," Chris said. "Three who can go in looking human, and then turn into ferocious beasts. An advantage, in my view, and a very strong one."

Ian chuckled. "I imagine it would make a few of those Convergence bastards crap themselves."

"Including the security they have in place," Chris added. "There's still a risk doing this, but adding our group in on top of what the Order will have gives them a great shot at pulling off a major intelligence coup."

"And here I thought I could rig up some new lights down here for a few days, or weeks, and then go home," Ian said, shaking his head, already knowing he could not stay back if Chris was taking part.

"We can express our gratitude for the attack on our convoy, and our detainment," Chris said, his expression grim. "And we can help deliver a big hit to the ones who've caused all the problems, and disrupted all our lives in the first place."

"You know I'm with you, Chris," Ian replied. "Let's just make sure we get the plan down really good. I really want to see Alena again, sooner than later, and in this world."

"I know you do," Chris stated. "And you know I'll do everything I can to help you do exactly that. It's just that while we're here, we should help out in the fight."

"I'm good to go," Ian told his friend. "No worries about that. Just make sure all the kids are taken care of, if something goes bad. I don't want to see them stuck up here."

"No, I don't either," Chris replied. "They're really good kids. I've already talked to Salvador about that issue. The Order will work to get them back home, no different than with us. But I say let's all go home together. What about you?"

"I'll drink to that," Ian said.

"Speaking of," Chris said, with a smile. "They do keep a little beer down here."

"They do?" Ian grinned. "I really could use one … maybe two. And something to eat. Worked right through lunch, I think. Who knows what time it is down here?" He laughed.

"Let's go grab a beer or two then," Chris said, his mood brightening as he got to his feet.

"Of all the plans being talked about, I like that one the best," Ian added, standing up.

FATHER BRUNNER

A stream of armored vehicles rumbled down the street, all bearing the insignia of the World Summit. At one time, Father Brunner never would have thought to see such a thing in the UCAS. Now, witnessing a convoy of WS-sanctioned vehicles was far from a surprise, as frequently as they appeared in the streets of Troy.

A light rain pattered off the blue helmets of the soldiers manning the vehicles as they slowed near a checkpoint operated by others of their foreign ilk. The barricade bristled with weaponry, wielded by soldiers who would not be expected to pay even lip service to the Grand Charter of the UCAS. In all respects, the sight represented an occupying force.

Troy found itself being pacified swiftly as the foreign troops had far fewer qualms about cracking down on the local populace. Whether it involved gang-riddled areas or protests by throngs of citizens refusing to give up the rights enshrined in the Grand Charter, the blue-helmeted troopers of the World Summit meted out harsh, swift measures.

The confiscation of food, medical supplies, and more under Executive Order 2015, the National Security Resource Efficiency Order, continued apace. Father Brunner had witnessed more than one tragic scene of a father who had done nothing more than prepare for the sake of his family being led off to detainment, with a crying wife and terrified children left behind.

In such every instance he witnessed, Father Brunner's stomach churned thinking about some unknown snitch collecting payment in the shadows for tipping off the authorities. It motivated him all the more when bringing the broken families to St. Bosco's for safer harbor, no matter what their beliefs, or lack of beliefs, might be.

Many more individuals in the area around St. Bosco had vanished in recent weeks. Father Brunner knew they had all been taken off to the mass detainment facilities located outside the city.

Those left behind were increasingly cowed in a world of surveillance cameras, checkpoints, scanners, and drones flying regularly overhead. It had become a horrible nightmare to anyone who could remember the sweet taste of freedom, even if those times had been imperfect.

Father Brunner held no illusions about what was happening. His own time running short, he knew it would not be long before Living ID became enforced at gunpoint on everyone in the city. Grave decisions would have to be made, as Living ID would never be implanted on him.

Walking towards Saint Bosco, he peered up towards the Rising Dawn finial, perched above the front façade of the church. Set firm against the gray skies, it looked strong and defiant, unmoving as potent winds buffeted it.

The sight of that finial tended to bolster his confidence whenever fears were encroaching, the current instance no exception. He smiled to himself, thankful in the deepest part of his spirit for what that symbol represented. His faith everything during such terrible times, he would need it more than ever with things getting worse all the time.

"A penny for your thoughts. And I mean a physical penny from before, not this new digital garbage we're being forced to use," came the voice of Father Rader, followed by a laugh.

"Ah, yes, the *Nummus*, yet another wonderful new development being integrated in our enlightened, modern society," Father Brunner replied with a smile and thick tone of sarcasm. He glanced over towards the older priest, who had drawn up to his side. "It is good to see you, but where have you been? I looked around for you earlier, but couldn't find you."

"Just looking into a situation where one of the members of the parish was about to be jailed for the grievous sin of planting a small garden in the front yard of their property," Father Rader said, his face shadowing over with a frown.

"It isn't their property if they can be arrested for planting a garden in front of it," Father Brunner replied, feeling a surge of ire at the news. The situation held strong parallels to the events involving families victimized by the National Security Resource Efficiency Order.

"Yes, you have that right," Father Rader stated. "Nevertheless, I find myself having to deal with a lot of these incidents that simple common sense would otherwise mitigate. It's not pleasant, to say the least."

"People are being punished for ingenuity and responsibility during tough economic times, surrounded by all kinds of danger," Father Brunner remarked, with a bitter edge.

"That reminds me of Ulysses Talbot," Father Rader said. "You know him. He lived a block from the church and came to some of our events and activities. He drove off three home invaders using his old police revolver, and then promptly got arrested for possessing a firearm. That was two days ago."

"The way this system works, the authorities would have found it preferable to have police arrive to find Ulysses and his wife beaten badly, robbed, and possibly worse," Father Brunner said, dismayed about the news regarding Ulysses.

In his mind he could hear the big man's booming laughter and see his broad smile. Ulysses' wife had brought Father Brunner and Father Rader fresh-baked cookies more than once, along with cakes and other baked delights. They had attended many church events through the years. The fact that the couple were not Universalists had never been an issue.

"Just the thought of that makes me wish I could pack up and head to the southern provinces," Father Brunner continued, becoming angrier the more he thought about it. "There's a whole lot more common sense down that way."

"It's a terrible tragedy when you can't defend yourself or your family in your own home," Father Rader observed. "In fact, it is profoundly immoral, in every sense. And yes, were it not for those we tend and minister to here, I would rather head southward with you. They still know something about freedom in those provinces. And at least they are fighting for it."

"What's the status with Ulysses at the moment?" Father Brunner asked, his mind fixed upon the kind-hearted old man.

"I fear it isn't good. He's not being held within the city's boundaries," Father Rader replied with a grim expression. "Weapons infractions are not looked upon gently by the authorities."

Father Brunner shook his head, feeling the righteous anger burning inside of him towards the injustice of it all. Good people were being treated like criminals, while criminals were largely being allowed to operate with impunity.

To some, a situation like that did not seem to make any sense. To Father Brunner, knowing what he knew about the deeper nature of things going on everywhere, it made all the sense in the world.

"Well, one thing I know for sure, we'd both better get used to seeing blue helmets around us," Father Brunner said, glancing towards the checkpoint, the convoy he had observed now passing through.

"Yes, it is going to be a regular sight. And those blue helmets are allowing those with the other kinds of helmets to concentrate on other things," Father Rader stated, eyeing the convoy.

"I imagine more eyes are turning southward. Freed up by these blue helmets. UCAS government authorities aren't the live and let live types," Father Brunner commented.

"Perhaps the very aim, out of this new effort by the World Summit's Peace Commission," Father Rader suggested.

"You and I know it's all tied together." Father Brunner took a deep breath, looking his friend and mentor in the eye. "But we're not going to unravel it all today. For now, let's get some dinner. It's high time I feed Athanasius and Simeon. Those two are probably getting a little restless"

"I hope you do keep Athanasius well fed, I don't want to consider the consequences of letting that big fellow go hungry for too long," Father Rader retorted, a grin breaking across his face.

"Simeon's the one you should be worrying about," Father Brunner replied, chuckling. "That cat is extremely crafty, and quite industrious."

"What you say is true. But no matter what, my days are the better for the both of them being here," Father Rader replied as the two priests started forward, making their way towards the rectory building at the side of the church.

"Did I just hear what I think I heard?" Father Brunner rumbled with laughter. His intellectual mentor had not been altogether thrilled about the prospects of a cat and dog living in the rectory at the outset. "A confession of a different sort?"

"Yes, it is a blessing to have those two around," Father Rader conceded. "I consider them part of our family."

"Today is a momentous day," Father Brunner proclaimed.

"Don't push your luck too far, I'm still the pastor," Father Rader chided, chuckling. "And no, it doesn't mean we can add any more to the household. Before you get any ideas."

"No worries about that. It's a challenge enough on a priest's budget to feed those two and take care of trips to the vet," Father Brunner responded.

"Angling for a raise now?" Father Rader asked merrily.

"Yes, a big pay hike," Father Brunner responded. "The Nummus is a digital currency. Just add another zero or two at the end. It isn't based on anything concrete anyway."

"I wish I could, and we'd be taking care of everyone suffering in Troy," Father Rader replied, this time only half in jest.

"So how long do you think we have here? To do what we can for the people of Troy?" Father Brunner asked, looking around at the church grounds he had developed such an affinity for.

"Not long at all. My heart tells me they'll be coming for us soon," Father Rader replied. "All those who've held out from being shackled to their electronic grid."

"You know what that means for you and me," Father Brunner said, knowing Father Rader would never accept Living ID either.

"I know," Father Rader said, his voice softening and taking on an air of compassion. "Our church has quite a legacy regarding those who would not cooperate with authorities."

Father Brunner gave his friend a knowing smile, thinking of that legacy, involving centuries upon centuries of martyrs. He had always thought it would be an honor to put his life on the line for his faith, but had never thought such a situation would ever manifest. Now, he could see that possibility looming right before him.

"I know what you and I will do," Father Brunner said. "But what can we do for the people who have found refuge at St. Bosco? That's what I worry about. I don't think we have any chance of getting a large group out of the city now."

"No, we don't," Father Rader said. "But they had their chance to go."

"I just wish there was something we could do for them," Father Brunner responded, feeling a deep frustration. "There's just no way we can hold the government back now that they are much freer to act, with foreign troops supporting them."

"We can ask Adonai for a miracle, and in the meantime do anything and everything we can to make sure the people we are caring for are not detained or subjected to a bloodbath," Father Rader stated.

"But Living ID? There are so many who are like us and will refuse to have it implanted," Father Brunner said.

"We all have to make difficult choices, both them and us," Father Rader said. "The path before you and I will be to show them two individuals who will never surrender who they are, no matter what the cost."

"I know who we are. We are children of Adonai," Father Brunner replied, feeling uplifted as he spoke the words.

"Yes, Father Brunner, we are children of Adonai," Father Rader said. "They will hate us for that, and may kill us for that. But if they do, there is no greater honor you or I could ever have. Never forget that."

"No. Not in all the world," Father Brunner concurred as the two reached the door of the rectory.

As Father Rader unlocked the door, Father Brunner could hear the shuffles of Athanasius' big paws on the tile, in addition to the dog's eager whines, as the big mastiff positioned himself on the other side of the entrance to greet the two priests. The sounds of the dog brought a smile to his face, made all the merrier with the fact that his heart felt much lighter than earlier that day.

Despite the intensifying of the storms of oppression and injustice all around, Father Brunner felt reinforced inside as the words of Father Rader settled in. He reminded himself that the world he lived in was one that he did not belong to.

It was a world that could never be perfected, merely a place for souls to travel through on their way to a true, lasting home. The thought sapped much of the fear from the threats looming ever larger over Father Brunner, Father Rader, and the church.

Father Brunner knew he just had to make a good, solid acquittal of himself in the time remaining to him. Life had never been an easy path, but he felt a strong sense of conviction. With Adonai's Grace, he knew that he could see himself through the darkest of days yet to come.

BENEDICT

The convoy of three cars and two SUVs traveled to a park at the heart of the gang-controlled suburb. The grass beneath the trees had grown high, no longer tended by the city department once tasked with its upkeep.

The area entirely vacated, the headlights of the vehicles illuminated a shadowy, still scene as they drove along a winding road through the park. The five vehicles rolled to a halt at the edge of a large swathe of open ground, devoid of trees and showered in silvery moonlight.

"I hope you have enjoyed your stay with us," the Leopard remarked, opening the door for Benedict to get out. A half-grin rested on the First Word's lips as he waited for Benedict to emerge.

"Would you like me to fill out a customer survey?" Benedict retorted with sarcasm, gazing back at the man with an iron stare. In the light of the moon, with his glittering eyes, the Leopard looked much more rat-like than his name would imply.

Another figure approached them across the grass, coming out of the shadows away from the convoy. Benedict took sharp note that the Leopard straightened up at the man's appearance, and was immediately deferential.

"I did not think you had arrived yet, Weaver," the Leopard said in a lower tone.

"I thought I'd take a little walk before our transaction commenced," the other man replied calmly. He looked from the Leopard to Benedict, eyeing him for a moment. His eyes had a cold, steely edge. "I see you brought our valuable commodity."

The Leopard nodded. "Yes, we have kept him well-protected.

"As he should be, for what he will bring us," the tall figure stated. The trace of a smile came to his lips, though the expression contained nothing amiable. His next words were directed towards Benedict. "Thought you would get away so easily. Didn't think we could reach far."

Though of the same ethnicity as the other gang members, there were some conspicuous differences in the Weaver's appearance.

Immediately noticeable, he had no tattoos visible. His hair was neatly combed, and he was dressed in a collared shirt and dress pants.

Benedict made no reply, but he did not blink or look away from the other man's icy gaze. It was the only shred of defiance he could display under the circumstances.

"For a man who ran a nightly radio show, you are definitely short on words tonight," the Weaver said evenly, though Benedict caught a mocking edge to the words. "I would think you would be much more interested in everything happening to you."

The Weaver drew a few steps closer, and something about him unsettled Benedict deeply. Whether the result of a gust of night wind or something else, a deep chill encompassed Benedict, causing him to shudder.

"Oh come on, I know you are curious. Your whole career was based on your personal curiosity. Mysteries were your field of expertise. Go ahead, ask yourself ... Who am I? I know you want to know that," the Weaver asked him, the mirthless grin spreading a little wider.

"Does it even matter?" Benedict retorted with a hard edge. "You are going to do with me what you want to. And it doesn't look like I have much choice in the matter."

"But the nature of it all could add so much more to your understanding of things," the Weaver replied, taking another step closer. The grin faded from his face.

Benedict felt a growing revulsion the closer he was in proximity to the Weaver. He did not want to give voice to his instincts, but suspected something of a much darker nature than simply a gang leader wanting to toy with him.

"I understand enough," Benedict declared, knowing his meaning was understood by the Weaver, if not the others within earshot.

The Weaver looked upward, into the star-riddled night sky, and his icy grin returned. "You will be going by air tonight, but not the way you might think."

He looked back towards Benedict, and did not continue, leaving the implications dangling in the air. Benedict did not take long to fathom what the Weaver was getting at.

"Not a plane, or a helicopter, am I right?" Benedict remarked, the sarcasm returning within his tone. "I think I have an idea. You aren't that clever."

The Weaver's expression did not change, but the extended stare told Benedict his barb had landed. He took his eyes way from the Weaver, and looked towards the sky, knowing what would be coming for him.

Clusters of stars were obstructed briefly as large shapes soared through the sky towards them. Flapping their wings, the forms grew larger as they descended towards the stretch of open ground.

Even knowing what came for him did nothing to dampen the upsurge of fear within Benedict as the winged creatures drew close. Alighting on the ground moments later, rippling with muscle and exhibiting visages of raw malice, a trio of monsters stood.

Elongated faces reflecting human forms held extensive jaws filled with glistening, spiky teeth, each and every one razor sharp. Tucking their membranous leathery wings to their sides, they walked with a lithe, feline grace towards the Weaver. Trailing behind the three monstrosities, carried high and swaying from side to side, were huge scorpion tails.

"Jeqonadin. Satrinah'il. Nasragieladin." The Weaver greeted each member of the trio, as they came to a stop a few paces from him. He glanced over towards Benedict. "The time has arrived to convey you onward."

Benedict looked at the winged beasts with a sinking heart. No matter how much bravery he tried to muster, the thought of being carried through the skies by the creatures both frightened and dismayed him.

"You are not going to die, Benedict, why the fear?" the Weaver chided him.

The eyes of the largest of the three, the one called Jeqonadin, fixed squarely upon Benedict. The beast had a maniacal expression, exposing its teeth in something that could be construed a mix of cruel smile and threatening snarl.

"Jeqonadin reflects the strength of his father well," the Weaver commented.

"And what spider of the pit are you, Weaver?" Benedict asked his tormentor. He was surprised at how steady and strong his voice emerged, given the shaky feeling pervading him.

"It is irrelevant," the Weaver replied. "Having a host is not the same as being in flesh. That will come soon enough, and may you live long enough to witness the dawn of a new age."

Benedict stared at the Weaver, knowing something ancient and filled with darkness loomed beyond the human guise before him. The implications in the Weaver's words troubled him deeply.

The Weaver turned and called to the Leopard, "Call your men over, and then stand with me."

All of the men who had ridden out in the escort convoy gathered together as ordered. Brawny and clutching weapons in their hands, the gang members were a tough-looking lot, but their eyes betrayed the fear in them as they kept looking toward the three monsters.

The Leopard walked over to stand next to the Weaver, who turned back towards Benedict. "You should count your good fortune that you are being taken onward."

A cold smile danced on the Weaver's lips as a suffocating feeling of menace engulfed Benedict. A vivid thought hit him and he looked back towards the cluster of gang members with a feeling of dread and pity. He knew something terrible loomed.

"Come forth, children of my brothers and sisters!" the Weaver called across the open space, looking towards the shadow-filled trees lining the farther edge.

At the Weaver's call, four shadowy forms separated from the darkness beneath the trees. They loped through the grass with an awkward, hunched gait.

At first, Benedict deemed the incoming creatures to be four-legged. But as they drew closer he saw that they simply had lengthy forelimbs, using the appendages to help propel their bodies forward.

Taller and broader of body than an average man, the creatures had elongated muzzles and were covered in a layer of coarse, dark fur. Moonlight gleamed off horrifically long fangs, as the creatures opened their jaws wide.

"There is nothing for you to worry about, at least now," the Weaver told Benedict in a low voice. "We must be sure no rumors get started among the other men, though."

The victims realized their fate when it was far too late to run. Even so, they tried to scatter and fire their weapons towards their bestial attackers.

Blood-curdling screams and gunshots mingled with screeches as the baboon-like beasts tore into the terrified men. The power and speed of the creatures was stunning to behold. Benedict could not stop the horror that flooded over him as he watched humans getting ripped apart before his eyes.

In less than a minute, the grisly slaughter was all over. Blood dripping from their slavering jaws, the beasts reared up and stood upon their back legs.

Benedict trembled as more than one feral gaze fell upon him. He knew the only thing preventing him from being torn limb from limb was the authority of the Weaver. The thinnest layer of ice would have felt more sturdy at that moment.

Looking at the mauled bodies, the Weaver gave a casual shrug, as if nothing untoward had happened. "When they became a member of La Cuchilla, those men openly acknowledged that their road would lead to a jail, hospital, or cemetery. We know now which of the three destinations these men reached. "

The Weaver looked towards the group of baboon-like monsters, who gazed back at him with a look that Benedict interpreted to be one of anticipation. The Weaver nodded to the creatures. "You may feed."

Erupting with grating snarls and deep growls, the creatures lunged towards the remains of the slain gang members. Benedict's stomach twisted and churned listening to the crunching of bones as the beasts began gorging themselves on the corpses.

Hearing a low, pitiful moan to his left, Benedict looked over with a sick, nauseating feeling, discovering that one of the men was not yet dead. The man's face contorted in extreme throes of pain as the beast dug into his innards, tearing away chunks to consume.

The man's arms flopped about weakly, lacking the strength to resist, but giving every sign that he was fully aware of being eaten alive. His ultimate fate sealed with his guts shredded apart, the awful truth was that he might not lose consciousness for quite some time.

Benedict wished bitterly that he had a gun to end the man's agony, no matter what evils the man had committed as a gang member in his life.

"Can't you just kill him?" Benedict asked the Weaver, making no effort to coat his pleading tone. "There is no need for that, just end it!"

"It is a cruel world," the Weaver replied with an icy smile. "Is it not? Oh yes, the beautiful nature so revered by human fools, who fail to take a closer look at the underlying truth. Ever watched what happens with a baboon that gets hold of a young gazelle? Really not that much different than what you see now. And that's the nature that my Enemy provided for you to dwell in, Benedict. Maybe you should give second thoughts to your feelings about the coming change in the order of things."

The cold, mocking words entering his ears, Benedict managed to keep his eyes averted from the gruesome feast. The vicious killers around him were much more than baboons. An unholy union of demonic entities and humans had spawned the first of them.

Now, after being reintroduced from an ancient world into modern times, the monstrosities could reproduce by themselves. In time, Benedict knew the four around him could well become a legion.

He had to find some way to get back to deliver the warning about the terrible discovery he had made in the depths of the federal facility. Countless lives depended on it, yet he was entirely helpless, bound and about to be returned to those it had taken a miracle to escape from.

"Jeqonadin, Satrinah'il, you may go ahead now," the Weaver told two of the three winged monsters. "See that no enemies follow through the air. I will have Nasragieladin take the prisoner back."

"As you will it," the largest of the three replied in a low, grating voice, nodding its head slightly.

It chilled Benedict to hear the thing speak, demonstrating the intelligence it possessed to go with the primal arsenal contained within its physical form. With a burst of speed, Jeqonadin bounded forward and took to the air, followed closely by the second of the trio. Their broad wings flapped powerfully as they climbed swiftly towards the stars.

"See that this man is taken unharmed to the place you came from," the Weaver instructed the third.

The beast nodded, and stepped towards Benedict. A malignant gaze dwelled within its glinting eyes, and saliva dripped off several of its teeth. He had no illusions about the inner desires of the beast, and could only hope its discipline overrode its urges.

Benedict was frozen in place, unable to decide what to do as the third winged creature drew closer with each stride. With its broad wings and height, the beast dwarfed him. He knew he could not run, and physical resistance was futile. The only sliver of consolation was that his enemies still wanted him alive.

A barrage of gunshots broke the air. The winged nightmare approaching Benedict jerked about in a spasmodic fashion, loosing a piercing shriek as several shots slammed into its body and wings, tearing through its flesh.

Savage growls erupted as other large forms burst out from the shadows and charged across the open ground. Benedict knew at once they were not related to the apish nightmares near to him.

ARIANNA

Arianna felt the kick of the rifle's stock against her shoulder repeatedly, squeezing the trigger several times in rapid succession. The jerking of the winged creature's body and its stomach-churning cries were welcome sounds to her ears.

She had arrived with her companions just as the gang members were being slain. Their cries and gunshots had served a purpose, pinpointing the location where Benedict was being held.

Her eyes had widened in horror seeing the three winged monsters, and the quartet of ape-like things that looked to be feasting on the remains of the dead gang members. The nature of the group involved in handing over her uncle was far from what she had expected to see, but there was no time to dwell on the situation.

Two of the three winged creatures took to flight. In the wake of their take-off, the third began stepping towards her uncle. Gripping their rifles and looking through the scopes, Arianna, Maureen, and Quinn did their best to fire upon the thing. At the least, it presented a large target to aim for.

Benefiting from many hours of target practice while spending the days and weeks on Benton's land, Arianna's accuracy and that of her companions was solid enough. Bullet after bullet tore through the body of the winged beast.

A few moments later, Arianna watched Godral and the other An-Ki emerge into view in their two-legged forms. The An-Ki rushed to intercept the ape-like creatures who had just begun to charge across the ground towards the three rifle-bearing humans.

Watching the fight unfold in all of its ferocity, Arianna understood the reason why the An-Ki had shifted their forms. Able to grasp and maul effectively with their front claws, they were much better suited to go up against the beasts. A chorus of growls and snarls filled the air as the two groups clawed, bit, and tore at each other.

"Keep firing! Keep firing!" Quinn exhorted Arianna and Maureen, as he continued loosing bullets at the winged creature.

Despite taking several hits, the thing still kept moving towards Benedict. Arianna looked into her scope again, and squeezed the trigger four more times before a solid click indicated the magazine was empty.

Changing the magazine as she had practiced many times over at Benton's land, she cringed whenever she heard a higher pitched yelp. She knew those came from An-Ki and not the ape-like things.

"It's down!" Quinn exclaimed.

Through the scope, she saw that the winged creature had indeed toppled over. It was only a few more paces from her uncle, who was tightly bound. Of the two humans they had seen near her uncle, there was no sign.

The fighting between the An-Ki and the ape-like things came to an end. All of the enemy beasts had been slain, but not without the payment of a terrible price.

Heart beating rapidly, Arianna got up and ran towards the large, furred body sprawled on the blood-soaked grass. The soul-wrenching sight blanked her mind from all other concerns.

The wolfish head turned her way did not unsettle her in the least, as she dropped to her knees by the creature's side. Kantel's eyes stared up into her own, as the An-Ki lifted his head and laid it heavily upon her lap.

He was one of the first An-Ki she had encountered, certainly one of the first she had taken particular note of, with his striking blue eyes. She could see the vitality ebbing from him with each passing moment.

"The great journey … is here," he said, loosing short, staggered breaths. The pain wracking his body was plainly evident. It took him several moments before he spoke again. "It … is time … to know…"

There was no need to clarify what Kantel meant. Tears welled up in Arianna's eyes, and her heart broke apart.

For the first time in her life she watched the light going out of another being's eyes. The sight resembled nothing she had ever experienced before. Without question it was one of the deepest, ugliest evils possible; the suffocating darkness of death extinguishing the bright glory of life.

One moment the spark of life shined evident within the brave An-Ki warrior's eyes and the next not even a glimmer remained. His physical eyes were still open, but the light once animating and filling them with liveliness was entirely absent.

She knew Kantel had departed. The body left behind was now nothing more than an empty husk. She began to heave in great sobs as the gut-wrenching pain of losing a friend began taking over the initial shock.

Throwing his head back just behind Arianna, Godral loosed a long, mournful howl that filled the night. He was joined by three more extended howls a moment later. Arianna cradled the dead An-Ki's head as she cried in the throes of emotion overcoming her.

"We must go," Godral gently interrupted her, a few moments later, his voice heavy and laden with emotion. "The ones in the sky. Get uncle from here."

His voice sounded miles away as her spirit was battered between the shock and devastation of having just lost a friend. Yet something within her cooperated, as she felt the strong grasp of Godral lifting her up to her feet. Her fingers slipped from the fur of Kantel as she let his head rest upon the ground.

Her tear-drenched eyes made her vision seem a haze as she looked to Maureen and Quinn. Tears streaked down both of their faces, as they stepped in to hug her tightly.

"Arianna," Vailia said from her right side. "He is here."

She looked up, and saw her uncle. He was still bound, and looked weary, but he offered her a sad look of empathy.

Arianna threw her arms around him, burying her face in his left shoulder. She whispered, "Oh, Uncle Benedict."

"I'm so sorry about Kantel," her uncle replied.

"Arianna, we must go," Godral urged, a little more firmly.

All of the other An-Ki had suffered many wounds in the fighting. Sarangar had suffered a gaping wound on his right side from the raking claws of one of the ape-things. Even so, he joined the other three remaining An-Ki in shifting back into four-legged forms, though he cried out several times during the process. She could not begin to imagine how painful it had to be for the young An-Ki, changing forms while injured.

When they were finished, the An-Ki indicated for the humans to ride them, only Vailia would replace the badly wounded Sarangar in carrying someone. Leaving Sarangar without an extra burden meant that one of the An-Ki would have to carry an additional rider. Without delay, Godral indicated he would shoulder the additional load.

As if some automatic control took over her body, Arianna climbed back up on Godral. Being lighter than Benedict or Quinn, Maureen took the second rider's place on his back. Benedict rode upon Vailia, while Quinn rode astride Dedran.

Her mind fogged over all throughout the return journey. She did not realize that Godral had remembered the way back until the group limped and trudged into the backyard of the house where they stayed.

What should have been a celebratory end to the journey had been rendered tragic and mournful. Feelings of guilt weighed her spirit down heavily.

Dismounting, Arianna shuffled towards the house. She felt her uncle put his arm around her, though she remained speechless.

Arianna was torn between relief at finding and rescuing her uncle, and bringing Kantel along with her to what had become his doom. Only extreme fatigue provided any degree of mercy, when a couple of fitful hours later weariness finally consigned her to the refuge of a dreamless sleep.

SKYLAR

Addressing the World Summit, Kaira spoke with clarity and a resounding air of authority regarding the need for international cooperation and integration. She explained that the model being used to bring order about in the UCAS during its time of strife could be applied anywhere in the world. It represented an effective new mechanism for addressing the problems faced in a modern age.

The young woman who had so rapidly captivated the international community spoke of her own vision and mission in regards to her office at the World Summit. The Peace Commission, according to her, was indeed that: a commission to bring peace to the entire planet.

Kaira spoke eloquently about bringing all war to an end and the dawning of a new age of international harmony. She insisted the vision was more than possible if the nations had the will to help her.

A strange sense of calm filled Skylar as she listened to the address. Among the delegation from the City of Oracles, the Shield Maiden sat no more than twenty paces away.

Entering the World Summit grounds had gone smoothly enough. Kiaran had worked his magic, in what was perhaps his best disguise yet. Skylar now held the image of an older woman who served on the diplomatic staff of the City of Oracles.

A host of favors and arrangements had been made to gain Skylar access. The Order and the Shield Maidens had exerted the utmost of their influence within Universalist circles, though carefully, as even the halls of the storied seat of the Universalist Church, the City of Oracles, was not immune to the Enemy's infiltration.

In truth, as hard as it was to admit, the Enemy's reach extended to the highest levels of the Universalist Church. Only the most vetted and trusted individuals could be involved with setting up access for Skylar.

Fortunately, the woman whose image Skylar had assumed was one of those steadfast, time-proven individuals. Devout and indefatigable despite her advancing years, Celine Guerin turned out to be more than cooperative towards a mission deemed important enough to involve the joint efforts of the Order and the Shield Maidens.

As Skylar saw it, Celine and many others of a devout nature were probably feeling under siege. They were fully aware of the direction the world headed in, yet they had to participate in its affairs, maintaining representation for the Universalist Church in its diplomatic seat at the World Summit. Skylar knew that Celine and others felt the coils of the unseen constrictor tightening with each passing day as the world edged closer towards a nightmare spawned within the Abyss.

It had taken a little additional contrivance to arrive for the scheduled address at just the right time. Skylar could not match the voice of the older woman as well as she could take on her look and posture.

Accompanied by another member of the staff who was trusted, Skylar adequately deflected the few attempts at interaction directed her way. Feigning an overload of tasks that had run to the last minute, the man with Skylar stepped forward more than once to explain why they could not pause and talk.

To Skylar's relief, he proved successful at intercepting and blocking all who made attempts to engage them on their way into the vast auditorium. Careful to mimic Celine's movements as she had practiced many times over, Skylar proceeded down to their assigned section without incident.

The feeling as Kaira took the stage for the address had been surreal. There, right before her eyes, was the embodiment of the deepest evil in all the world, though in a form most beautiful, vibrant, energetic, and overflowing with charisma.

Even as determined as she was, Skylar nonetheless felt the inner pull of attraction towards Kaira before She even said a word. It was like everything inside of her insisted on finding the young woman at the podium likeable, trustworthy, and, oddly, a person who made Skylar feel entirely safe.

The reaction to Kaira's presence surprised Skylar, being far different in nature from anything she had conjectured while being conveyed back into the UCAS and into Yorvik. A hundred scenarios or more had crossed her imagination. Yet not once had she envisioned that feeling affinity for Kaira would be the strongest element of her response.

Despite the unexpected feelings, a deeper part of Skylar remained firmly grounded in her mission. That part recoiled at the favorable, pleasant impression of Kaira swirling within her mind. She knew the sensation to be a deception of the highest magnitude, an exercise of dark power crafted to veil the eyes of the entire world.

Skylar thought of Matthew, Magdalene, Kiaran, Astrid, Genevieve, and many others she knew, filling her mind with memories of those devoted to fighting against the Power that Kaira embodied. The spellbinding aura that had come over her gradually dissipated, though its touch did not vanish entirely.

Keeping a colder sense of detachment as she sat in the audience of diplomats and dignitaries, Skylar knew that she could not give the positive feelings about Kaira any ground to take root and expand. If she let down her guard for even a moment, she knew they would metastasize throughout her spirit, draining her will and focus at an hour where she needed everything she had within her.

An Ethereal Dimension

A penitent Avatar, unseen to the audience witnessing Kaira's address, sped with singular purpose towards a sprawling mass of wraiths and spirits. Far the Avatar had fallen, but in this hour the ethereal being rose with righteous fury, burning to challenge the Enemy of the world.

No longer in the form of a human, the Avatar had assumed its most natural form during that final hour of judgment. A host of flames blazed radiantly all over its spirit-body. Though hope was absent, conviction coursed fiercely within the Avatar, speeding the celestial being like a bright missile towards the malignant mass ahead of it.

Wielding a sword of fire forged from the Avatar's very soul, the powerful entity cleaved through a throng of spirits. Though frenzied and enraged, they were no match for an Avatar of higher rank. A great many fell in swift fashion, their essence consigned to the Void, while others scattered in the sudden chaos.

The Avatar did not pause to chase down the fleeing spirits. Single-minded in purpose, the entity barreled straight towards Kaira, fully cognizant of Her identity.

Unlike a human, whose seat of consciousness existed within either one plane or another, Kaira's spanned multiple planes at once. A formidable weapon and advantage in one scenario, the attribute loomed as a great vulnerability in another. Kaira's unique nature set the servants of the Nether Kingdom in a mode of extreme wariness. Her dimension-spanning essence led to the layers of protection at Her woodland compound.

Kaira's appearance to the Avatar looked very different from that displayed before the World Summit audience. Here, she assumed a shape comprised of brilliant light, wreathed in a misty, churning darkness; features testifying to any who could see within the hidden realms of her inhuman nature.

The few glints of light piercing the cloaking darkness surrounding Her form almost blinded in their luminance and purity. Only one other Being in all of the Abyss possessed light of such a pure, majestic radiance: Diabolos, the Shining One, the Claimant Who occupied the Risen Throne.

For an instant, the Avatar believed a chance to strike Kaira beckoned. The recognition came far unexpected with the entire purpose of the celestial being's attack serving a singular function: to draw in as many supernatural defenders as possible.

Yet the hope of getting a strike at her ended up as dead as the hope of finding ultimate redemption. Before the Avatar could reach Her, hulking shapes manifested to either side of her.

Edged in darkness and filled with fire, their lofty forms resembled that of the attacker, only far stronger and greater in power. The two were High Avatars, the most powerful of supernatural beings save perhaps for the Jinn dwelling within the Void.

The presence of the guardians came as no surprise. It was expected that the strongest of the Nether Kingdom would be used to ward Kaira against anything of the non-physical realms that dared to threaten her.

Raising enormous fire-swords, the two living infernos moved in to block the Avatar's path. The only consolation lay in that the Avatar had fulfilled its intent, drawing out the most powerful spiritual guardians provided for Kaira. Now, with their attention occupied, it could only be hoped that Skylar pressed forward in the physical world.

Finality loomed before the Avatar named Verin. A stasis, akin to oblivion, beckoned, one that would last until the end of all time. When that final moment arrived, one way or another, Verin would be condemned for all eternity.

If, by some unknown measure, Diabolos prevailed in the Great War, Verin would awaken to a terrible fate, branded a traitor before a vengeful Master. If Diabolos failed, Verin would still face banishment to the bottomless pit, the Outer Darkness beyond Adonai's realms. There, Verin would endure forever the wrath of Diabolos; a Being denied any hope of causing harm to those belonging to Adonai.

Despite the unavoidable doom, not even a sliver of regret existed within Verin about the stand being made. The only lament dwelling within Verin's soul derived from foolishness and ingratitude distant ages ago.

Verin's spirit burned with the deepest, most genuine sorrow, mourning the fateful choice made before time and space. Verin knew that the dream of what could have been would be a far greater torment in the eternity to come than anything Diabolos could inflict.

Crying out in righteous fury, Verin assailed the titanic Avatars. For a moment, Verin put both of Kaira's guardians on a defensive mode. Fire-blades clashed several times over, until the weapon of one High Avatar swept around Verin's blade, at the same moment the giant's companion found an opening.

The pair of huge, fiery blades rushed in, cleaving through the Avatar's form and severing the celestial body into three segments. A burst of resplendent white light erupted in the aftermath, filling the Avatar's vision before all consciousness was lost to blackness.

A dream of what could have been, cradled within the purest state of contrition, served as Verin's final thought, before the darkness of the Void consumed everything. It was too late for it to be anything other than impossible, but the Avatar had no shame for having embraced and fought for that hearfelt ideal.

DAGIAN

Wreathed in a thin, misty black layer, the Avatar had the outward appearance of a Fallen One. Yet the being assailed those loyal to the Risen Throne as vigorously as any Avatar serving the Enemy would have done.

Dagian recognized the spirit as a traitor, though it acted on its own, as no Fallen Avatar could ever hope to return to the bosom of the Enemy. The schism that began at the onset of the Great War was irrevocable. The oncoming spirit took on a fool's quest, with no hope of receiving absolution.

Nonetheless, the power of the traitorous Avatar was stunning to witness. Slashing its way through a horde of wraiths, the fiery spirit looked unstoppable. Every sweep of its blazing sword cleaved through dark spirits as the Avatar burrowed right through their teeming mass.

Dagian wanted to bring up her own memunim and hurl herself at the rogue spirit, no matter how powerful it seemed, but she held her position with rigid discipline. She had firm orders to engage nothing other than spirits of human origin. Moments later, her mind eased a little, seeing that the Powers of the Nether Kingdom had prepared for a scenario such as the one now transpiring.

The fate of the betrayer sealed, two multi-winged giants manifested and moved at once to intercept the rogue spirit. Imbued with much greater strength and power, the Fallen Avatars confronting the traitor were of the highest order, the outcome of the looming clash certain.

Even so, the renegade Avatar did not hesitate at their appearance. Loosing an outcry sounding like an entire host of warriors, it slashed furiously at its much larger opponents. To Dagian's surprise, the traitor had the titanic pair on the defensive, but only for moments.

The fighting between Avatars under any other circumstance would have consumed Dagian's interest and attention, but she could not afford to ignore her own given task. While the Avatars loyal to the Enemy would not fight at the side of the traitor, nothing ruled out the idea that a human would cooperate with such a being.

After a firestorm of exchanges, the fighting came to an end. A searing pulse of light caused Dagian to squint as the fire-blades of the two giants slashed completely through the form of the smaller Avatar. The latter's spiritual essence dissipated swiftly. In seconds, no trace remained.

Every instinct screamed out that the enemy Traveler was near. Her enhanced powers keenly sensed the hostile enemy presence, coiling somewhere close.

The great Avatars of Diabolos had seen to the traitor spirit, but the enemy Traveler remained to be engaged. Dagian was surprised that the Traveler had not made a move with the two High Avatars engaged in fighting the traitor. Something deeply amiss, Dagian's nerves teetered on edge.

With an exercise of her intent, she summoned her force of memunim. In an instant, she found herself flanked on both sides by the tall wraiths. Serving with unwavering zeal, the dark beings poised to strike down the Traveler the moment anything sought to beset Kaira.

With the greatest of skill, Dagain balanced her perception on the finest of lines. She kept her vision hovering between two realms of existence, watching Kaira's position in the material world, while also taking in the ethereal plane where the Traveler would undoubtedly strike.

The mystery remained as to how the Traveler could hope to get around two High Avatars who were no longer distracted. She did not have long to wait for the answer. Looking around carefully, she tensed, espying a figure moving near the front of the auditorium seating.

Watching the material plane served only to give Dagian a reference for the location of Kaira. As with the Setian Jibade, the only plane where a strong attack could occur would be the ethereal.

Only in the non-physical plane would the Traveler be capable of wielding the unknown weapon, the one used to sever the Walker of the Setian Path from mortal existence. Dagian fully expected to face that terrible weapon and the threat it carried, though she had her own methods prepared to counter the enemy warrior.

Yet all had changed in a flash of time. Dagian knew in her heart that the anomalous movement at the front of the auditorium indicated a strike about to take place in the material plane. All the powers Dagian had gained within the realms of Set and Amanzako were entirely irrelevant for addressing the emerging threat.

Effectively trapped, Dagian's spirit remained within a plane of existence entirely separate from the one containing the manifesting foe. The attack of the traitor Avatar had been a grand bluff, to mask the Traveler, exactly as Dagian suspected. What she had not anticipated was that the Traveler would use a method nobody foresaw, one that discarded all of the special abilities and weapons making her such a unique threat.

Dagian wanted to scream a warning to Kaira and all the others loyal to the Convergence. Any of the latter would sacrifice their lives in a heartbeat to protect Her. But not a single thing she could do would reach anyone in time to stop the unfolding assault.

Watching helplessly, Dagian endured the passing of seconds in a tremendous state of distress. The dismaying, shocking scene played out laboriously before her eyes.

There would be no failure to answer for. Dagian had made no errors. She had carried out her part to perfection, doing everything commanded by higher Powers and placing herself in the best possible position to resist the enemy Traveler. Dagian stood in a position to triumph, if only her would-be opponent had not entirely abdicated the rare skills she had honed so well.

Even so, the anguish Dagian felt in that terrible moment became all-consuming. The labors of countless multitudes over the course of several millennia teetered on a precarious edge. Nothing stood between the assailant and the One chosen by Diabolos to reign over the entire world and usher in the beginning of a transformational new age.

SKYLAR

Skylar pressed the small lever on the handle of the cane gripped in her right hand, releasing the spear concealed inside the long shaft. Once crafted to slay creatures given life by a diabolical union of human flesh with the otherworldly, the weapon was about to be put to its ultimate use. The Shield Maiden took the spear in hand, determined to hew down the greatest servant of Diabolos to ever walk upon the face of the world.

To all eyes, the elderly woman thought to be Celine Guerin, a well-known administrative member of the City of Oracles' delegation, executed movements that no woman of such an advanced age should have been capable of. Balanced in step, and springing forward, Skylar raced towards the steps leading up to the dais and podium. The Shield Maiden surmounted the flight of stairs in a couple of powerful bounds.

Her eyes focused upon Kaira to the exclusion of all else as she lunged forward, bringing the spear back with a firm, two-handed grip. To Skylar, it seemed as if time itself slowed down to a crawl, though to all other eyes she crossed the platform swiftly.

Kaira's eyes widened in surprise. She attempted to evade the onrushing Shield Maiden. Skylar needed some luck in the moment to come, choosing the direction in which she believed Kaira would dodge. Everything hinged upon the next second.

Fortune shined with radiance upon her as she anticipated her enemy's move correctly. The opening she sought unfurled right before her eyes. With speed and power, the Shield Maiden reacted.

Putting everything she could muster into the thrust, Skylar drove the weapon's tip deep into the back of Kaira's head. Blood and bits of bone sprayed outward. The leader of the World Summit's Peace Commission fell forward against the dais surface near the center.

Every camera documenting the address took an unobstructed record of the wooden haft barreling far into Kaira's skull behind the spear's sharp head. Not lost was the pointed tip exposed in the middle of Kaira's forehead.

Alarm and shock rang throughout the vast chamber. Moments later, the flash of muzzles accompanied the sharp cracking of bullets cleaving the air. Security personnel positioned all over the chamber discharged their firearms with trained skill, levying a hail of shots from several directions towards the assassin.

Still upright, looming over her fallen opponent, Skylar jerked one way and then another as the first of many projectiles struck her body. Agonizing pain lanced through her several times over, lead tearing through flesh, muscle, and bone.

Yet no regrets could be found in her heart as she fell over, tumbling down the steps and coming to rest at the bottom. Blood flowing from a multitude of wounds, Skylar knew well enough the price that had to be paid.

One who chose to live by the sword had to accept the grave consequences in full. The only consolation for Skylar was that the purest of evils had been smote down before the eyes of the world. The ancient weapon had been employed to its greatest purpose, laying utter waste to the physical vessel inhabited by the darkest of spirits.

The engulfing agony lasted only a moment, as everything fell into a deep, soundless darkness. Skylar's final conscious thought centered upon Adonai, embodying all who she loved, whether family, friends, or even strangers she had shown kindness to throughout the years of her life.

She understood a wondrous truth in that last instant. Within the face of each and every person she loved she witnessed the face of Adonai. It was a most beautiful thought, one filled with peace and undying light that held no place for the dark, vile legacy of death.

THE WORLD SUMMIT

Kneeling down at Kaira's side, one of the first emergency medical personnel to reach her body checked for vital signs. A flurry of activity transpired in the moments following as desperate attempts were made to revive the woman, though the blood pooling on the dais testified to the worst before all eyes watching.

Finally, looking up with a countenance grim and filled with resignation, another member of the medical team shook her head slowly. She pronounced to the encircling onlookers in a leaden voice, "She's dead. I'm sorry, there's not a thing we can do."

Time came to a standstill within the massive auditorium. Most of the delegates stayed rooted in place. They stared in disbelief and horror towards the lifeless body of Kaira. An indelible image burned into their minds of a spear shaft embedded deep in the back of her head with the tip protruding through the front.

SKYLAR

After the flicker of consummate darkness, a great brilliance flooded Skylar's vision. Euphoria flowed through Skylar as she beheld One who knew her down to the last strand of hair upon her head.

Washing away every last blemish, the testament she had forged with her entire life cloaked her in beautiful raiment before the Perfect Being. Skylar stood in the presence of One meeting her face to face for the first time.

She was then introduced to another of transcendent luminance. A masculine figure Whose eyes flashed with the fires of unending life and love, He gazed upon her with gentle countenance.

Though He wielded tremendous power and authority from His anointed place to the right of the Great Throne, His face held the appearance of the dearest friend. She understood that she knew Him, and that He knew her. Even further, and most exhilarating, she understood at an intimate level that she was counted among His friends in this new, wondrous place.

Joy indescribable leaped and soared all throughout her, as a feeling of welcome pervaded her spirit. Through the figure at the right of the Great Throne, she knew she had been bestowed with the favor of Adonai, blessed and given invitation to a perpetual home.

The smile on the face of the eminent figure widened. She knew in the heart of her soul that He already shared in the joy of something else about to be given her, though what it was she had no inkling. A joyous laughter brimming with celebration sounded, as a resplendent light filled her eyes once more.

When the light finally ebbed, her heart sang. Skylar no longer stood before the regal, celestial Thrones, but a sight beyond miraculous met her eyes.

A tall, blond-haired figure stood just a short distance before her. Dressed no differently than she had seen him so many times before, he sported black boots, blue jeans, and a crème-hued, collared shirt.

A dazzling smile rested upon his face and pure love shone within his bright blue eyes. She saw the Face of the One upon the Great Throne and the face of the figure seated to the right of the Great Throne reflected in the visage of the beloved person before her.

He had been a grace, blessing, and precious gift in her life. All the agony she had suffered when he had fallen in the world of sorrow became erased forever.

The void she had felt inside filled to overabundance with the peace of knowing such a separation would never occur again. She knew with the grace of her new perception that he had no more been taken from her than Adonai had lost anything in first giving him to her.

Though subtle, a luminous glow emitted from his skin. Behind him were lofty, magnificent gates of the purest gold, set into towering walls of gleaming white, without a single speck of imperfection.

Beyond the gates were colors the like of which she had never seen before, but none of it distracted her in the least bit as she stood gazing upon him in awe, wonder, and boundless joy. Tears of abundant rapture began flowing from her eyes.

"Welcome, my sister!" Matthias exclaimed, smiling. "I suppose congratulations are in order for a life lived well. I have longed more than I can put into words to see you again. I have missed you dearly. My life here can now begin in full, and there are others who are waiting and very eager to see you, just beyond these gates!"

Matthias' smile broadened more. He stepped forward, opening his arms wide to embrace her for the first time since they had both been in a finite world, a passing world with all of its attendant sorrow and loss.

The voice of her brother was recognizably his, but she noted a distinct musical quality to it that had not been there in the world they had shared together. Tears of delirious elation running abundantly from her eyes, Skylar wrapped her arms around him. She held him tight at the threshold of infinite realms, all filled with the beautiful, Undying Light she knew emanated from the One on the Great Throne.

They were both alive, in a way far exceeding anything they had known in their former lives. Skylar knew in her soul that this was only the beginning of something unfathomable and wondrous; an existence filled with discoveries, adventures, and fellowship that would have no end.

SECTION VII

IAN

Ian walked through a casino floor buzzing with activity, surrounded by beeps, musical jingles, and a host of other buoyant sounds generated from row upon row of slot machines. A large crowd present in the early evening hour, people were arrayed on stools all along the slot machines. They filled most every available seat where other games of chance were being played.

The air rife with energy and anticipation, the crowded casino audience heavily engaged in another night's quest. It was one that would see the anointing of a few winners, whose triumphs would feed the prevailing atmosphere even further.

If any scene reflected the kind of life experienced before the breakdown of the UCAS, then the gaming environment stood as a prime example of something that had not been altered to any significant degree. The siren's song of jackpots and bounteous payoffs lured the desperate and thrill-seeker alike, though most would leave in a poorer state before the evening had culminated. Resplendent facilities like the casino, with all of its inherent polish and glamour, were not built on the backs of winners.

Oragas walked along at Ian's right. Ian had to quicken his pace just to keep up with the An-Ki's lengthy stride. He found himself wishing he had an assistant as strong-built back home in Venorterra. He had little doubt the big An-Ki could work from sunup to sundown without taxing his body a fraction as much as Ian did on the longer days. With the accumulation of aches over the years, Ian could not deny longing for an assistant to help shoulder his burdens on the more onerous workdays.

With the help of a man who had been a tailor before taking to the underground world, it had taken a little extra custom work to size matching work clothes for the huge An-Ki male. Ian had then helped with fitting Oragas out properly, to look like an electrician out on a job.

When Ian had finished, Oragas looked genuine enough, complete with a tool belt, gloves, shirt with sewn-on name badge, and a proper-fitting pair of work boots. His long hair was pulled back into a ponytail and beard groomed, making for an inconspicuous appearance.

Ian had to admit that Oragas' two An-Ki companions, Gorthaur and Queran, were assuming an ingenious guise for the mission. Gorthaur would be playing the part of Queran's bodyguard, while she was posing as one of the high-dollar ladies imported for the night's sensuous amusements.

It was quickly determined that she would not fare well in heels or garb such as tight-fitting miniskirts, but a clever suggestion on the part of Chris Howard solved the problem. Knee-high, flat-soled black boots were the start of an outfit completed by a full-length leather trench coat. A large bag with an assortment of items such as handcuffs, floggers, and a bullwhip, was given to Queran to carry along with her.

Looking intense and assertive was easy enough for her to do. To Ian's eyes, the tall An-Ki female fit the role she assumed that night to perfection, even if she probably did not understand the nature of it herself. With such considerable height, and possessing a commanding presence, she would be seen as an exceptional lady for those intending to engage in rougher forms of adult recreation.

Ian could not help but chuckle when he saw her walking through the casino floor with Gorthaur, a short distance from where he walked with Oragas. More than one set of eyes shifted in her direction as she passed through the crowd, though she paid no heed to any of the gawkers as she made her way towards the elevators.

Ian shook his head and smiled to himself. He knew that whoever visited with Queran that evening was in for a very rough experience of a nature they never anticipated.

Rumble Dog and Raven did not have any special preparations to make. They had perhaps the easiest task of all, asked to simply be themselves and make it look like they were a spirited couple out for a night of drinking and gambling.

Neither of the two appeared to mind. Ian suspected their only disappointment lay in that they would not be able to play out the role for a full night.

He caught a glimpse of the couple at a poker table, looking as raucous and boisterous as ever. Rumble Dog glanced up towards Ian for a split-second, but gave no sign of recognition.

The problem of the two not having Living ID was solved with the provision of a few casino vouchers, plus the fact that they committed to playing poker for the time being, using chips instead of money for their wagering. The Order provided each of them with a modest stack of gaming chips that would be more than enough to cover the time they needed to burn, waiting for the appointed moment to head to the restricted levels of the building.

Members of the Order were in place everywhere, though Ian had no indications of who were in league with his group, and who were simply employees of the casino. From hotel security, to restaurant and hospitality personnel, to patrons of the establishment, to a couple more who would be serving as bodyguards for other female entertainers, the Order's members melted smoothly into the fabric of the entertainment establishment.

A young woman, part of the management staff of the casino, met Ian and Oragas at the far end of the gaming floor. After introducing herself to them, she escorted the two onward to one of the main sets of elevators for the casino.

Once inside the compartment, she slid a security card in a slot next to the set of floor buttons, granting them access to the level purportedly needing the electrical work. They were conveyed to a floor just beneath the ones quartering the members of the Convergence.

Used to dealing with clients, Ian engaged in small talk with the woman while Oragas looked on in silence. She was pleasant enough, and indicated that things had been quite busy lately at the casino.

When the elevator doors slid open, before they could step out of the compartment, they were met by three tall men in suits. All of the clean-cut figures had a militaristic air about them.

The staff member informed Ian and Oragas that they would have to go through a security check before proceeding, explaining that some premium guests were in town for the night. Having expected the scrutiny, Ian had already cautioned Oragas to cooperate.

After a sequence of pat-downs, and a brief rummaging in Ian's tool-kit, the men allowed the management representative to take Ian and Oragas to the hotel room needing the work done. The guards still kept near, trailing them a short distance behind.

Oragas went into the hotel room with Ian while the guards stood outside. The staff member politely begged leave, and then departed. Ian found himself relieved that she was going, having hoped she would not get caught up in the things about to transpire.

After making sure the hotel room was empty, Oragas ducked into the bathroom while Ian set the toolkit he carried down on a king-sized bed. Nerves on edge, he braced himself for the activity to come as he began hearing a series of snaps and cracks coming from the bathroom nearby.

An icy wave of fear washed over him a few minutes later when Oragas emerged in the massive, two-legged wolfish form. Hunching over to get through the doorway, Oragas brushed his triangular ears against the top of the frame before standing to full height.

He turned towards Ian, stared intently, and waited. Heart racing, Ian's mind went blank for a moment, until he remembered to check his watch and confirm the time for the An-Ki warrior.

They had cut their timing uncomfortably close, but were still about a minute short. Waiting for the remaining seconds to pass in silence proved an ordeal for Ian. The wary silence of Oragas, who loomed just a few paces in front of him, added to his extreme discomfort. At last, the appointed time arrived, and he nodded to the huge An-Ki.

Hardened, tough men, of the kind Ian suspected had considerable military experience, were screaming at the top of their lungs moments later as Oragas burst into the hallway and assailed them, shredding flesh and crunching bones. Primal snarls and growls interspersed with the men's desperate cries until the hallway fell into a pensive hush.

Dumping out the contents of the tool-kit, Ian removed a panel at the bottom of the case where a forty-caliber pistol had been hidden. Taking a deep breath, he took the gun into his hand. Even with a weapon, it took Ian all the willpower he could muster to exit from the hotel room.

He was not afraid of any danger to himself, but rather of what would meet his eyes when he stepped into the hallway. Though he braced himself, he could not adequately prepare for the sight of the blood-spattered walls and gore-coated stretches of carpet. The aftermath of an outright slaughter surrounded him, filling his nostrils with an acrid stench.

Oragas stood a short distance down the hall, the badly mauled body of one of the security guards sprawled at his feet. Blood dripped from several points along his shaggy jaws. The lengthy talons at the end of his arms glistened with a crimson coating.

Ian mustered all the resolve he could and guided Oragas to a stairwell. He kept a few paces ahead of the creature, but it was not far enough to settle the raised hackles at the nape of his neck, as he listened to the deep breaths of the hulking beast walking behind him.

Opening the door to the stairwell, he held it for Oragas and gestured upwards. Ian flinched as the creature lunged forward and charged up the stairs, disappearing out of sight in a flash.

Cries, shouts, and the firing of guns broke out on the floor above him. One thought occupied Ian's mind as he started up the stairs. He hoped with all his heart that Chris and Lucy did not get hurt in the fighting. They had come too far to have everything end on a side mission, but he understood why they were assisting the Order.

Ian made his way to the door opening into the upper floor, firmly gripping the handgun that had been concealed in the false-bottom of his tool case. He pulled the door open, kept his finger on the pistol's trigger, and stepped forward.

To his surprise, the hallway looked empty and showed no signs of disturbance. Ian's heart thumped in his chest as he took a few steps down the hallway, hearing voices coming from some rooms ahead of him.

Relief flooded him as he saw Chris walk out from one of the rooms and enter the hallway. Seeing Ian, Chris cast him a big, jubilant smile. Ian knew the look well. It told him all he needed to know about how the others fared.

"It's all over! Good guys won!" Chris exclaimed. "Didn't lose anyone. Not one! No bad injuries either."

Ian closed his eyes and breathed out slowly, letting the tight constriction that had built up inside ease down. "That's what I hoped to hear. Where's Lucy? Rumble Dog and Raven?"

"Lucy's on the floor above us, and Rumble Dog and Raven were set up to make sure nobody slipped through the cracks," Chris answered.

"And the other three?" Ian asked, turning his thoughts to their An-Ki companions. "Oragas went ahead of me, so I know he's up here somewhere."

Chris grinned. "He's with the other two now. They're still busy. We've got the Convergence boys and girls all secured and being questioned. Queran got a nice head start, having one of them in cuffs before she changed her appearance." Chris rumbled with laughter and shook his head, clearly amused with whatever mental image he entertained. "The guy pissed himself pretty good when she showed him her new outfit."

Ian grinned. "I imagine so. I won't lie, I almost pissed myself in the room with Oragas, even knowing he was on our side."

"It probably takes a while of seeing them in those forms before it doesn't scare you anymore," Chris said. Then he shrugged, and added, "Maybe you never get comfortable. Still kind of surreal."

"So have they changed back yet?" Ian asked.

Chris shook his head. "We're making use of them in the questioning process. Salvador thinks it will speed up the answers."

"I imagine it will," Ian stated, thinking that utilizing even one of the three shape-shifters gave an all-new meaning to enhanced interrogations.

"Here, take a peek for yourself, just a couple rooms down," Chris invited, walking forward and gesturing for Ian to follow.

He led Ian to the indicated room and opened the door slowly. Peeking in, Ian saw Salvador facing a man seated in a chair with his hands bound behind him.

An An-Ki loomed over the man to each side of him, and another was at his back. The dark carpet stain beneath his chair and the steady drips from his seat to the floor said all that needed to be said about how he felt about the creatures.

"I can't blame him for that," Ian remarked, eyeing the growing stain from the man's bodily fluids.

"I bet he's singing a much different tune now," Chris said. "That's Senator Red Harrelson of Plata Province. Milquetoast bastard is finally getting his comeuppance. I've seen snakes more human than him."

Ian looked back, but still did not recognize the unremarkable-looking figure in the chair. "Don't know him, but I'll take your word for it."

"He wasn't one of the big favorites on the Sunday morning news shows, or any of the popular cable and satellite stations," Chris commented. "But he had a lot of power, just kept a lower media profile than others."

"It will be interesting to learn what they find out from him," Ian said, turning back towards Chris.

"I think we'll get some valuable information out of all of these clowns," he declared. "The group gathered here tonight wasn't just getting together for fun and cheap thrills."

"So when are we heading out of here?" Ian asked.

"Soon enough, once we have our new captives secured and stashed in the penthouse suite on top of this building," Chris said. He smiled, giving Ian a conspiratorial wink. "We'll be long gone before they find out about the friends we've made tonight."

ARIANNA

Perched on the edge of the couch, Arianna waited with increasing anxiety in the living room, impatient to be heading onward. Benedict sat nearby, looking relaxed and probably just relieved to be free again. Quinn had his arm around Maureen, while she tucked her head against his shoulder.

Everyone in her group had long since packed up their belongings, more than ready to depart. Terrible losses had been suffered, Benedict had been found and secured, and the time had arrived to travel east once more.

All indications were that Davis would see to it that her group was conducted safely back to the military checkpoint area, marking the boundary of the territory held by the free provincial forces. Wendell had told Arianna as much the previous evening, advising her to have everyone ready to leave when dawn rose.

It was now almost noon, and they were still idling in the house. The delay had not done any favors for Arianna's state of mind. Her nerves had been rattled enough by the storm of gunfire persisting for several hours the previous day. She could still hear echoes of the fighting in her mind.

The gang in the adjacent territory had mustered a large assault late that morning, striking at several barricades and crossing into the neighborhood at several other points. Arianna had little doubt the ones in authority were lashing out after the debacle with Benedict and the weapons transfer, though it was uncertain whether the assault had been launched in anger or desperation.

The cache of weapons and ammunition intended for the exchange had fallen into the hands of the citizen militia led by Davis Rucker. Rocket-propelled grenades, a few heavy machine guns, and a pair of wire-guided missile launchers, among other premium items such as a small quantity of night-vision gear and rifle scopes, proved potent additions to the weaponry of the militia fighters.

All of the new weaponry had been distributed and put to the immediate defense of the neighborhood. Enough men and women with military backgrounds were present within the ranks of the defenders to make effective use of the weapons.

The sounds of explosions had thundered across the neighborhood as vehicles of the assaulting gang forces were destroyed. The booms accompanied by the sustained rattle of gunfire, a hail of lead met the onrushing gang forces.

Blunted swiftly and then driven back, the attack failed with the gang incurring heavy losses. It did not take long for the subjugated people in their territory to take note of the situation. A golden opportunity unfolded and they had seized it without delay.

At the first signs of an uprising in the neighborhoods beyond, a significant number of Rucker's militia force moved to support the beleaguered men and women who had been living under the shadow of gang-induced terror. Recognizing their chance, the oppressed hastened to the fight while their tormentors were in such disarray.

While not having taken part in the fighting, Arianna and her companions had watched the streams of militia fighters returning to the neighborhood later that afternoon. Though tainted with the sorrow of losses incurred among their own ranks, the prevailing feeling in the air was one of jubilance.

The gang to the neighborhood had been shattered in just one day, and a large swathe of people beyond the barricades had been liberated. Organization with the newly-freed people was already being conducted, to expand the militia, man newly-erected barricades, and set up defensive positions against any future threats. Not about to rest on any laurels, the liberated people cooperated with diligence and enthusiasm

From what Arianna heard in many accounts as evening drew nearer, the gang fighters were engaging in a chaotic retreat. Snatching up every vehicle they could find, gang members were hastening from the area.

From what she gleaned, quite a few moments of vigilante justice had been playing out as the uprising people and incoming militia fighters routed all remaining gunmen. Passions overrode any sense of mercy, as the men and women who had inflicted such a terrible nightmare on so many people met with harsh, and often grisly, fates. The news did not gladden Arianna, but she could not deny that the gang members' behavior had brought the retribution upon themselves.

Aside from a few sporadic gunshots in the distance, the current day had proceeded quietly enough, if not far too slow for Arianna's liking. While glad the adjacent neighborhood had been liberated, she wanted to leave. Nevertheless, she and the others decided it best to wait for an official escort from the citizen militia. There was no telling what might happen in the volatile climate, with passions running to an extreme all over.

Arianna looked up as the front door opened and Wendell walked in. She began getting out of her seat, but he motioned for her to stay in place.

"I hurried over so I could make sure you all saw what's about to happen on television," Wendell announced to the group amid heavy breaths. An undercurrent of excitement ran through his voice.

Arianna sighed, frowning at his comment. Not the news she wanted to hear, she muttered, "Really not interested in television right now."

Frustrated, she glanced across the room to where Benedict sat. All of her thoughts were focused on taking him far from where they were.

Deep inside she also mourned the loss of Kantel. She held so much within, trying to hold the raw emotions at bay until she could get to a more private setting with her friends. Only then could she afford to loose the rivers of tears waiting to be set free.

"Bear with me, Arianna. I think this moment is going to be pretty historical," Wendell told her between labored breaths.

"If that's the case, we can afford a few more minutes," Benedict told her, sitting up and looking interested.

She watched Wendell stride to the center of the living room and turn on the television set. Taking a few steps back, he eyed the flatscreen monitor with great interest.

Arianna stared toward Maureen and Quinn. "Are you two wanting to wait around?"

"Let's see what this is about, it can't hurt," Maureen replied with a sleepy grin.

Wendell cast Arianna a sideways wink, adding, "This is worth delaying your trip for a few minutes. And well-worth using generator fuel for."

"What's happening that's so important?" Arianna asked him, still restless but becoming a little more curious.

Having lived among Wendell's community for a while now, she knew generator fuel to be deemed precious and used sparingly. Whatever was about to happen had to be of significance.

There was no mistaking the elation in Wendell's face as he looked at the screen. Everything about him radiated positive energies. She had never seen him in such a state before, raising her interest further.

"It looks like the next step is being taken for our new nation," he remarked. "Seems we finally have our first president ... least an acting one. Should be about time for the announcement."

Manifesting out of the blank screen, a bright image took shape. In the center of the frame stood a podium. A line of provincial flags spanned the background, all representing territories that had broken away from the UCAS. Arianna recognized the blue and gold flag of Venorterra in the group.

The upper facing of the podium displayed a magnificent-looking oval seal of a design she had never seen before. Undoubtedly, the displayed image represented something newly unveiled and aligned with the momentous event about to transpire. Arianna scrutinized the seal carefully, taking account of its features.

The bottom portion of the seal's background was dark and featureless, of a deep brown hue. The middle section, comprising the widest part of the vertical oval, represented about a third of the space. Filled with a gleaming cerulean, it evoked the sun-brushed surface of a great ocean. The upper section portrayed a bright, golden light breaking a far horizon lined with white, the rising of dawn within clear skies over a shore of pure opal sand.

Cradling the left and right contours of the seal were two white-feathered wings. The center of the seal featured a billowing, elegant flame of white, suspended in midair without any foundational source or true end.

Everything about the imagery spoke of freedom in a perpetual state. Arianna took the seal to heart at once. She found that it called those who looked upon it to a higher ideal, crossing from darkness into light.

A solitary figure then walked into view, a light-skinned man of about fifty years of age. He wore a dark suit with a silver tie. Arianna took immediate note of the small sword pin attached to his right collar.

Graced with a high forehead and a wavy texture to his salt-and-pepper locks of hair, he had angular facial features. His clean-shaven skin accented the sharp line of his chin.

Arianna found the lively, warm look within his eyes very different from the kinds of looks she had seen in the gazes of the last few presidents of the UCAS. The smile he extended towards some of the people off camera was of the kind that came from the heart, not a well-practiced mimic of amiability.

After exchanging a few pleasantries with the people near the camera, he took a moment to collect himself, growing quiet for a few seconds. Looking straight into the camera, he began his address in a clear, steady voice.

"Hello, I am Thomas Locke. I am speaking with you as I have been chosen by the Convention of Free Provinces to be the acting President for the new Confederation of Free States. I will serve you with all my ability, until such time that we can organize for proper elections and complete the ratification of the Charter of Liberty.

"It is an honor and a charge that I accept as a dutiful steward. I will represent and defend our new country with every last bit of energy and skill that Adonai has seen fit to afford me. I will strive to help us become a beacon of freedom to a troubled and storm-tossed world.

"It will be the greatest honor to serve you. Those who hold office in our new nation will be servants, not rulers, as happened in the latter decades of the UCAS. Understand that it was not us who broke the union, but rather those who transgressed the Grand Charter with impunity. They left us with no other choice but to uphold the values therein by divorcing ourselves from their disgrace, corruption, and lawlessness.

"Be sure to take careful notice that I said states when I spoke of our new Confederation, and not provinces. This is for a very important reason. Our new nation is a true association of sovereign states, one built upon true consent and volition.

"The new Charter of Liberty limits centralized authority to a severe degree, so that each state maintains as much control and self-determination over its own affairs as possible. What we will have is not anarchy, but a restoration of checks and balances and a vigilant limit on governmental power."

"Now if they can pull that off, that's a system I can support," Benedict remarked as President Locke paused for a moment.

"It's a new day, it truly is," Wendell stated with an air of enthusiasm.

Arianna smiled, hearing the excitement in Wendell's voice

and the hope in Benedict's. As difficult as things had been since the upheaval rippled across the UCAS, it made all the difference in the world to hear the kind of tone and meaning in the words of the new president.

Something worth sacrificing for, and fighting for, was taking shape right before her eyes. It was the kind of development that honored the sacrifices and hardships faced by all those who had defended the true meaning of freedom in the past.

What the UCAS had once stood for was being restored. Only this time all of the values that once girded the former nation were being embraced in a stronger way than ever before.

Arianna looked back to the television screen as President Locke continued with his address. "Words will not be twisted, as they were by judges and politicians derelict in their duty to uphold the Grand Charter during former times. Be assured that the language of the Charter of Liberty has been carefully worded to be as clear in meaning as possible, most especially in the embrace and protection of natural rights ... rights which do not derive from any government or human authority.

"Vigilance is needed always to confront the enemies of individual liberty, but our convention is fully confident that we are giving all of you the best shield ever devised in the form of the Charter of Liberty. It is our sincerest hope that we have given succeeding generations an even stronger charter to uphold the protection of natural rights and the limiting of governmental power.

"We do not seek isolation. We seek friendship with all nations, but must heed the warnings given to us by those who authored the Grand Charter. They gave us wisdom that became ignored to the folly of several generations. The Confederation of Free States desires friendship and commerce with all, but must not become entangled and pulled into conflicts that transgress the sovereignty of the people.

"The times ahead will not be easy, nor without struggle. There are those who will not accept our choice, and will seek to undermine us. This includes the former regime.

"No regime is legitimate that does not possess the consent of those it derives authority from. Even though consent has been withdrawn from the former regime, they will seek to impose their will and power over us, by all means available to them.

"An active state of war still exists with the UCAS. Ironically, this is the only war that their remaining governing body has formally declared in decades.

"Yet they only have force to wield, to make all of us unwillingly subservient to their authority. This is profoundly immoral, and as such we will defend ourselves with all the strength we can muster, which is the natural right of a genuinely free people. We do not seek to force ourselves upon them, but rather they upon us. It is not our choice to shed blood, but neither will we submit to tyranny, nor be denied our right to government by consent.

"To best defend our new nation, I make my first appointment as president in naming General Robert Jackson, who has been acting as supreme commander of the free provincial forces, to continue in this role on behalf of the Confederation of Free States.

"We have much work to do ahead of us, but the light of true freedom guides us once more on our journey together through this world. The timeless principles that grew a great nation out of a wilderness once can see our new nation to the radiant heights of prosperity and empowerment for each and every citizen.

"This is a nation that will champion and protect the most vulnerable and precious of minorities ... the individual. Through this empowerment and protection of each individual's natural rights, a society of strength, generosity, and goodwill will grow and flourish.

"I ask all of you for your support as we walk this path, face trials, and share hardships together. The road may be difficult, but our cause is timeless, and the light of freedom comes from the One who gave each of us the light of life itself. May Adonai bless each and every one of you abundantly."

"It's hard to believe what I'm hearing," Arianna said, a few moments later, after President Locke walked away from the podium. The television screen shifted back to a panel of four pundits, who began delving into an analysis of the speech with the host of the news show.

Using a remote control, Wendell lowered the volume. He

grinned wide as he looked over towards Arianna. "I've always wondered what it was like for the people who were around during the time of the Founders of the Grand Charter. Kind of exciting to think you, me, and everyone here may be just like those people, for what could become an even greater nation."

"And great in the right ways, one that won't get off track like the UCAS did," Arianna replied. "No stupid wars, no bailouts, no abuses of power, no snooping on everyone. I'm afraid I could go on forever."

"That's what I mean," Wendell said, agreeably. "Will be nice to live the life I want, and not have my pocket picked every time I turn around, just to have it spent on things I don't support or want. Also, it'll be nice to know I'm no longer without any representation."

"I know exactly what you mean," Arianna said. "Sounds like we're going to have a much kinder foreign policy too."

"We needed one. The one the UCAS had was part of what drove everything into the ground. The bastards bled us literally and financially," Wendell exclaimed, shaking his head. His tone grew more melancholy. "I lost two good friends to their stupid, needless wars. One died, and the other came back changed in bad ways. Might as well have died, as the guy I knew was no longer there. And to think the UCAS still clings to a failed policy like that. How many lives do they need to destroy to see the failure of their wars? Makes me think they intended all the bad stuff, they seem so set on it all. Even though it's been a hard road, I'm glad we broke away from the UCAS. This Confederation of Free States is far more true to what the UCAS once stood for. No comparison at all, as I see it."

"I have to confess I'm glad we got to see this broadcast, before we head back," Arianna commented. "Gave me a little needed boost."

"Definitely doesn't hurt the mood," Wendell stated with a grin. "Puts a nice finishing touch on your stay."

"Yes it does," Arianna concurred, casting him a big smile. She looked toward her uncle and friends. "What did you all think?"

"A new generation of founding mothers and fathers, for an improved version of what the UCAS once stood for? I can go for that," Benedict replied with a lighter air, his face devoid of the weight it had reflected since they brought him back.

"Count me in," Quinn said, giving Maureen a light kiss on the top of her head.

"I'm aboard too," Maureen added. "I think it's unanimous!"

"Well, on that positive note, let's get everyone together, hit the road, and get you all on your way back home!" Wendell declared, looking fully re-energized while getting up to his feet.

"Now that sounds like a plan!" Arianna responded, smiling wide and looking across the room toward her uncle.

He smiled back towards her and the warm look filled her heart with gladness. Against all odds, they had found him, and rescued him. It was now time to return home, as a new nation, one committed to the right principles, sprouted and rose up all around.

IAN RAFFERTY

"Oh, got another one of those slimy, slippery little bastards!" Rumble Dog proclaimed exuberantly. "Hid and tried to slip by me. But he learned what old Rumble Dog can do. I expected more out of this one, with all the times he talked so tough and acted like such a big shot on TV! Not so big shot now, are ya?"

He tromped down the hallway with his new acquisition. The whimpering, sobbing man was being held up by the rear of his collar. With his free hand, Rumble Dog had a firm grip on the waistband of the man's underwear, at the back.

The underwear had been yanked upwards to a distorting degree, stretched out much farther than its original state, and extending halfway up the man's back. Rumble Dog's captive winced and yelped pitifully as the biker gave him a hard jerk, lifting his feet off the ground for a split second.

"I remember you, when they were working overtime, whittling away our gun rights," Rumble Dog growled at the man. "You got a lot of nerve, being from Angaland and all, and getting on TV every night telling us how we should live here. That takes a lot of balls, you slick little bastard."

"Hang on, let me check n' see if he's got any to begin with," Raven announced, walking around to the front of the man, as Rumble Dog propped him upright. Her eyes narrowed, and her jaws grew taut. "This is for all the people turned into defenseless victims because of arrogant jackasses like you. You're owed this much, at least."

The man howled in pain from the hard kick she unleashed to his unobstructed groin. She then slapped him hard across the face.

"Stop your whining, you little wimp," Raven snapped. "You deserve a whole lot more. Think about all the people who've been robbed, beaten, and raped because horses' asses like you helped the UCAS government render so many good and law abiding folk defenseless."

"Yeah, and you didn't care. You've got it good enough around here all with your elite buddies," Rumble Dog snarled. "Probably thought you were invincible. Probably thought you'd never answer for anything. Thought nothing could touch you. Well, you ran into judge and jury."

Rumble Dog gave another sharp upward tug, producing a pained squeal from the man.

"You can't stop progress," the man stammered in his thick accent. An air of defiance flowed with his words. "A new order is here. Like it or not, it's here and it's just a matter of time."

"Oh, defiant are you?" Raven said, before delivering a backhand, then slapping him with her palm, and finally backhanding him again. The man squealed and shrieked with each blow. She smiled merrily at the end of the cascade. "I confess, I could do this all day long! It's kinda fun."

"And you can stick your new order where the sun ain't shining," Rumble Dog told him.

Ian found more than a little satisfaction in seeing the pompous news show anchor being made to answer for the things he had championed. It could not be disputed that rough-edged, street-level justice was being administered, but it was far less harsh than what the people victimized by the policies of the UCAS government had suffered.

"Oh, if I could just get my hands on that little freak with the cable channel show, I'd have it all right now," Rumble Dog exclaimed. "That little, arrogant prick who always ridiculed good-hearted folks. Oh, I'd like to get my hands on that little puke too. See him run his mouth then."

"Never happy with what you got, are you?" Raven teased him.

"I'm plenty happy with you, woman," Rumble Dog exclaimed.

"Well played, and you just might get a very pleasant reward later for that remark," Raven retorted, casting her man a coy grin.

"Let me get this slug upstairs with the others," Rumble Dog said. He glanced over towards Ian. "Hey, here's your chance, want to give him a good hard wedgie, or kick him squarely in the nuts? You can do both if you want."

"One part of me wants to give him both, but the sooner we're gone the better, so just take him upstairs," Ian answered, laughing as Rumble Dog pulled upwards on the man's excessively stretched waistband. "He's not going to be able to sit down for a week or two anyway, from the looks of it."

"Getting' off easy, I say," Rumble Dog replied, with a mischievous grin, as he began to lug the hapless celebrity away. "Feeling defiant now you little punk?"

Chris stepped out of one of the hotel rooms where he had been conferring with a few men from the Order. Seeing Rumble Dog and his hapless prisoner, he frowned.

"That's enough, Rumble Dog. You know how I feel about this kind of thing," Chris said firmly.

"Ain't your jurisdiction here. Ain't breaking no local laws, this ain't my country here," Rumble Dog riposted. "Besides, I'm done with him, Sheriff. Goin' to get rid of him right now, in fact."

"Okay, he probably deserved what he got so far, but let's leave it at this," Chris said. "Nothing further."

"Fair enough," Rumble Dog said. "He's alive. Nothing's broken. Just got his underwear tugged, a few slaps, and a good nut kick. The last one from my woman too." He grinned with pride and glanced at Raven.

"Sheriff, he got off easy," Raven commented, shaking her head.

"Way easy, if you ask me."

"I'll keep you company," Chris said, not looking convinced by their words.

"Suit yourself," Rumble Dog said, with a shrug.

Ian fell in with the group as they escorted the captive upstairs, to the penthouse level. Once inside the capacious suite, Chris stopped them.

"We're keeping the prisoners in the main bedroom suite, off to the right," he said, indicating the direction they needed to go in.

Rumble Dog took one look at Chris, and then carried the man over to the side of the room. He shoved him hard into a closet, slamming the door shut after him. He glared back at Chris, as if defying him to say something about the rough treatment of the beleaguered fellow.

"They'll find him soon enough, he's no worse for wear, and he can go to his hole in the ground with all the others," Rumble Dog answered, with a hard edge to his look and voice.

"You heard about that already?" Chris asked the biker.

"Braggart shot his mouth off," Rumble Dog answered. "Told me how he'd be safe ... and how they wouldn't let me in. And how I'd have to face all the hell that's coming for the rest of us."

Chris glowered towards the closet door. "Arrogant bastard."

"Now you get me ... it took you awhile, Sherrif," Rumble Dog declared, with an edge of triumph. "Looks like you're finally comin' around."

"Never said he was worth more than a dung beetle, just sayin' I don't ever want to stoop to their level," Chris remarked, looking irritable. He glanced towards his companions. "Our work's all done here. Let's get going, and get out of here."

At that moment, the three An-Ki approached from somewhere deeper in the penthouse, following a pair of men from the Order. The long strides of the An-Ki carried them towards the suite entrance in swift fashion. They had returned to their human forms, and were fully clothed once more.

It also looked like they'd cleaned up, as Ian saw no blood on their persons. Yet knowing what they were, he could not help feeling a little intimidated around the tall beings.

Looking at Oragas, he could not dismiss what he had seen in the hotel room; the upright, triangular ears, the shaggy fur hanging from a long snout, and the wickedly-sharp, extended talons.

It still boggled his mind that such creatures existed in the world. His mind kept telling him that such beings were the stuff of movies, not reality. But the truth of it all was indisputable.

The two An-Ki males gazed down at Ian as they walked by, both figures pushing almost seven feet in height. He felt his breath shorten under their piercing stares and humorless expressions.

The third of their number paused. "We are with you," the female said gently to him, the words causing him to flinch.

"I know," Ian replied, nodding, and feeling embarrassed that she had sensed his persisting fear. He gazed into her enchanting, **red-hued eyes.** "I'm ... sorry if I seem uncomfortable. I'm not ... used to the change yet."

"It is okay. Do not be afraid. We are friends," the female replied, giving him a brief smile before continuing past to join the other two of her kind. He could not help but notice how her canines looked a little longer and larger in proportion to those of most any person's he had seen.

Nevertheless, he clutched onto her final words, knowing they were the only source of reassurance that would help him navigate his elemental fears. The An-Ki were friends in every way and had proven it more than once already. Ian figured he needed to spend more time directly with the strange, fascinating beings, and get to know them as he would human men or women.

"They are friends to us," Ian said aloud, if only to drive the concept deeper into his mind.

"That they are," Chris said. "They've saved us. Shared in our risks. I'd come to their aid if they ever needed it."

"Big lads," Rumble Dog commented with an air of approval, watching them walking away.

"Pretty big gal too," Raven added.

"You can see the way the two lads dote on her too, she's the boss, I can tell," Rumble Dog added.

"Aren't all women?" Raven quipped, elbowing her man lightly.

"You dote on me just as much."

"You got me there," Rumble Dog replied, with a grin.

"Alright, we can continue this heartwarming conversation later," Chris interrupted, chuckling. "Let's go."

He pointed towards the double doors behind them. The group filed out with him and beneath an emergency exit sign they found the door to the stairwell.

As they were making their way down flight after flight of stairs, Rumble Dog broke the silence, "I've got something on my mind, Sheriff. I can't hold it back."

Ian tensed a little, worried that Rumble Dog was going to vent regarding Chris' remarks concerning his handling of the news show host. As much as he would throw himself into a fray on Chris' behalf, the outcome involving a fight with someone like Rumble Dog looked very bleak.

"Speak your mind then," Chris said evenly. Ian could tell by his friend's cooler tone that he expected the same thing.

"Goes back a ways, back to when I went to this big biker rally down in Texiana," Rumble Dog began, nonchalantly. "Just love that province. Great folks there. Anyhow, they had this event, one day, where they harvested rattlesnakes. And I mean harvested 'em. By the truckload. Hundreds and hundreds of 'em.

"I'll never forget the sight of that. They used gas to flush 'em right out of their underground hideouts. The snakes would come up from their holes in a foggy stupor, and then it was easy enough to collect 'em."

"And?" Chris asked him.

"We're dealing with snakes now, just of a two-legged variety," Rumble Dog answered slowly, letting the implications sink in. Ian could see where the big man was going, and saw the realization dawning on Chris' face. "I say, if you ask me, somebody should do a big flushing out of these snakes. You could round up the bastards at the root of all this mess then. Find where their underground dens are, and I'd say get to it right away. Round 'em up, just like the rattlesnakes."

"So you think they could be flushed out, just like that?" Chris asked.

"I'm pretty sure those big underground places have surface vents of some kind," Rumble Dog said. "They can probably go to a closed system if they want for awhile, but I'd say you could get something down them if you caught them unawares."

"It'd be priceless to see a bunch of elites stumbling out of their underground hideaway looking dazed," Ian said, chuckling as he envisioned the sight in his mind.

"Yeah, flushed out by the peasants they despise so much," Rumble Dog said. "What a mess that'd be for them!"

"I'll show 'em peasants," Raven interjected with a sharp edge.

"I have a hunch that if you two were there, a lot of them would be having their underwear yanked upwards, while being slapped around," Chris observed, glancing back at the two.

"Don't forget some swift kicks to the balls, on the men at least," Raven said.

"Hey, a wedgie and a few slaps ain't too rough when you consider what they've put the world through," Rumble Dog retorted. "Already told you that, Sheriff. Don't get slow on me."

"No … you're absolutely right about that," Chris said, nodding in agreement with the hulking biker as they reached another platform and started down another stretch of stairs. "And your idea is not a bad one, if it could somehow be pulled off."

"You got the connections, Sheriff. You should suggest it to some folks," Rumble Dog told him.

"Would serve 'em right," Raven said. "They cause all this trouble in the world, and then scurry away to their underground hideaways. Never want to own up to anything at all, do they?"

"Not in their nature," Chris replied. "That type always thinks a different set of rules apply to them. Believe me, Lucy and I saw that kind of mindset all the time in law enforcement … and we weren't dealing with people nearly as powerful as the bunch going into these big underground getaways."

"The rats knew something bad was coming to this world," Lucy commented from the back of the file going downstairs. "Or they wouldn't have built places underground like they evidently did. That takes a lot of time and money."

"Yeah they knew, because they engineered it all," Rumble Dog interjected.

"Ian, that probably would have been a contract you could have retired on, doing the wiring for one of those big places," Chris joked, laughing.

Ian grinned. "Probably true, but they couldn't pay me enough to do something like that. It'd be pretty obvious what a place like that was intended for. It just amazes me how they kept them so quiet."

"Not entirely, I've heard stuff like that talked about," Rumble Dog said.

"Yeah, on those radio shows like Sea to Shining Sea," Raven added. "I heard it talked about too. Read about these places on some online sites too. Some people knew about them and talked about them. Just not many folks listened."

"It would probably amaze us how many things they masked successfully, once they labeled it in the realm of conspiracy theories," Chris commented.

"Detainment camps, for one thing ... that definitely turned out to be real," Lucy said.

"You just wonder how much more," Chris remarked.

"It will be interesting to find out what the guys from the Order learned in all the questioning," Ian said.

"That I'm very curious about," Chris replied. "Definitely some people who were in the know among the ones we rounded up tonight. No question the fellows from the Order heard some interesting things tonight."

"Let's check into it when we get back, and see what they found out," Lucy suggested, to vocal affirmations from Chris and Ian.

They finally reached the level they had been told to proceed to when the mission was complete. There, Ian's group met with a member of the Order, a man who had been expecting them. His black bow tie, white shirt, black vest, pants, and shoes indicated him as another from the Order who had been embedded in the hospitality area of the hotel and casino.

He took them on a short walk to an exit at the rear of the building, which looked to be used for deliveries. A couple of drivers with SUVs were positioned outside, and a few moments later they were all on their way back to their underground quarters.

During the ride back, Ian gazed out the side window at the wonder world brimming with neon and lights. The streets on both sides were filled with patrons eager to forget the precarious condition of the world.

He did not blame any of them one bit for wanting to forget their problems. Ian wished it could all be forgotten, and that he could go back to a life where he had a good idea of what was going to happen from week to week.

Home seemed so much farther away, and the things he had been opened up to were far bigger than he ever imagined. It was a lot to take in, but he knew that Alena, Allyson, and Peyton were out there somewhere at that moment, under the same night skies.

No matter how hard the path to get back home, seeing them would be a reward well worth all the hardships. Keeping his eyes away from his companions, his gaze misted over as emotions surged within at the thought of his family.

Trying to stymie his rising heart rate, Ian reminded himself to take things one day at a time. It was the only way he could face the enormity of what he had been thrust into. At the very least, the mission had been completed and they were another step closer to making an effort to go back to Venorterra. Though a small thing, it nevertheless was something to celebrate, rather than being another setback. A victory, no matter how small, remained something to hold on to.

GREGORY

The UCAS's response to the announcements regarding the Confederation of Free States, President Thomas Locke, and the Charter of Liberty was immediate and swift. Within the hour, President William Walker was being carried on all major channels across the UCAS.

Sitting behind his desk with a solemn expression, the president spoke of UCAS citizens being held captive in all the breakaway provinces. The rebels, as Walker explained it, were nothing more than terrorists and extremists.

He assured the audience that the new Confederation lacked international legitimacy, and would continue to do so. With that kind of illegitimacy, the renegade provinces could expect no help. Further, President Walker explained that new sanctions would be presented for ratification at the World Summit, targeting an array of commerce and banking activities conducted by the breakaway provinces.

He laid much of the blame for the ongoing hardships in the UCAS on the terrorists controlling the south and midwest. Crime and other disruptions were the bitter fruits of the south's efforts to destabilize the UCAS provinces. As soon as the breakaway provinces were reclaimed, the faster comprehensive order would return.

A master at political theater, President Walker wore a mask of sympathy and injected a tone of regret as he discussed the continued need for a state of martial law in the provinces. He did not discuss why no such state existed in the south, which faced its own waves of crime and instabilities.

At the end of his speech, the President stared straight into the camera and paused. With a hard-edged tone and unblinking eyes, he promised that the UCAS would regain full control.

The broadcast of the president's address concluded and the coverage shifted back to the male and female anchors with the station. Bearing somber expressions, they began discussing the president's words, bringing in a panel of experts to dissect the address and speculate on forthcoming developments.

"Didn't get the memo they are called states now," Gregory remarked, exhibiting a slight grin.

He had little interest in what the contributors had to say. Gregory saw clear enough that full-scale war was coming, sooner than later.

"They've made their intentions obvious enough to us," General Jackson replied in his deep voice. A thoughtful expression resting on his face, he continued staring at the television screen. "We knew they would be coming for all of us at some point, but they've announced it publicly. No mystery about it."

"No, there's definitely no mistaking their purpose or intention," Benjamin said, from where he sat in a chair to the other side of General Jackson. "Walker was pretty straightforward about everything."

Gregory and his brother were all who remained from an earlier meeting of militia leaders and commanders of irregular forces. Whenever possible, General Jackson liked meeting directly with the leaders of the disparate groups, even if they were not official military units of the new Confederation of Free States.

Gregory respected the man immensely for conducting that practice. It sent a strong message to every local citizen militia and irregular volunteer that it really involved an effort by all citizens to defend the newly-defined states. In his eyes, it underscored the ideals in the Charter of Liberty, especially regarding the natural right of individuals to self-defense.

"They got so addicted to undeclared wars, I still find it ironic they've mustered the resolve to formally declare this one," General Jackson commented.

"We committed the most grievous infraction, General Jackson. We held them accountable," Benjamin stated, with a smirk.

"Yes, we did, and we're the ones defending the Grand Charter and what it represented, never forget that," General Jackson replied. "This was a matter of confronting a very dangerous domestic enemy, one that rose right up in our midst and spread like a cancer."

"Yes, and it's an enemy that wants to impose itself on us again," Benjamin said in a more somber air.

"So we need to deliver a strong counter response to that statement," Gregory said firmly, looking towards the general. "One of action, not words. Let them know we aren't going to roll over, and are in it for the long haul. Let them know it will be far too costly for them to prosecute a war against us."

"We have a response readied," General Jackson stated, looking back to Gregory. "We have the assets in place for it too."

Looking towards the general, Gregory raised an eyebrow. It

was a response he had not expected, as the southern and midwestern states had taken up a purely defensive posture all along their lengthy borders. There were skirmishes, raids, and mild incursions all along those boundaries, but nothing resembling a true offensive. The tone of the general's voice testified to something much bigger at hand.

"You look a little surprised, Gregory," General Jackson said, with a bemused chuckle. "But we aren't going to be caught on our heels. We can't afford to be. You know we have no interest in occupying the provinces that chose to remain with the UCAS. But you're right in that we can deliver them a very powerful message about the great costs of war."

"What is this response going to be like?" Benjamin asked, curiosity dancing in his eyes.

"I can't divulge everything to you two, not just yet. There are a few more details to work out, but it will be quite a response," General Jackson replied.

"I sure hope we can be of help to you, General Jackson," Gregory said, showing a trace of eagerness. If a heavy blow could be delivered to the oppressive UCAS regime, a monstrosity that herded so many of its own citizens into detainment camps and had the rest under a choking level of surveillance, then Gregory desired to be a part of it.

"You can definitely be of help," General Jackson answered. "We will need everyone involved for what we intend to do."

"Jack Morgan too?" Gregory queried.

"Most definitely," General Jackson replied. "We can certainly make good use of Jack's boys and girls, and their iron horses. Lots of diversions and feints to carry out."

"It sounds very big," Gregory said. "You've got me curious."

"That's because it is very big, and more than a little brazen," General Jackson said, with a knowing wink. "Trust me, I'll let you know about the details as soon as I can. I'll be meeting with General Barksdale and General Huntington in about an hour. We anticipated correctly what tonight's address was going to be concerned with.

"As always, it has been good visiting with the two of you. It's good for a general to be with men willing to speak frankly, who have good heads on their shoulders."

The big man rose to his feet. His actions were mirrored by a man and woman on his staff, both of whom who were seated a little farther back. At their movements, Gregory and Benjamin also got to their feet, and formal salutes were exchanged before the general departed.

When the general exited, Gregory turned and grinned at his brother. "You are getting those salutes down pretty well. Someone might think you were in the military before all of this fracas."

Benjamin smiled and laughed. "I've always been a quick study. It's gotten me through a few occasions."

"A good trait to have," Gregory remarked. "So what did you think of everything? Both the UCAS announcement and what General Jackson said?"

"Don't know what to think just yet, but the general's got something unusual in mind," Benjamin said. "Where is the enemy going to strike, in your estimation?"

"They are massing in two places that we know of. Out west, and across the river in Losantiville," Gregory said. "Almost ironic, considering we were in Losantiville not too long ago, helping keep a watch and doing some cross-river raiding."

"Two front attack?" Benjamin asked.

"They're not disguising their build-up well, that's for certain," Gregory replied. "But I will go so far as to guess that whatever General Jackson's pondering, it will not involve either front."

"I got that impression too," Benjamin said. "He's doing some out of the box thinking, if I were to hazard a guess."

"Well, we're not going to figure it out tonight," Gregory said, shrugging. "You want to come with me? I need to go check in with the gang."

"I'm gonna stick around here, or maybe go over and get some dinner," Benjamin said. "You go take care of whatever you need to do."

"See you in a bit, Ben," Gregory said, taking leave of his brother.

Gregory made his way out of the tent and started across the grounds of the huge military camp. He slowed his pace, staring down a long line of Lafayette tanks as the brisk evening winds flowed over him. The array of war machines was an impressive sight to behold.

His gaze went a little further, reaching out towards the runway the engineers had recently completed. Drones and other aircraft were already using the new airfield.

As he watched, the roar of an I-16 fighter jet filled his ears as it traveled down the runway and took to the skies. He watched the lights of the fighter grow smaller, as the aircraft ascended into the night.

Gregory found Dante and Consuela playing cards and drinking beers with some of the soldiers in a large tent. From the looks of it, Consuela had faired pretty well in the contest, judging by the pile of cash amassed in front of her.

She cast him a broad grin and a wink. "How are things with you, Greg? Should've stuck around and played some cards."

"And lost what little money I have to you? No thanks," Gregory replied with a chuckle.

"She's good, Greg, real good," Dante said, shaking his head.

"I could've warned you," Greg replied. "But you'd probably still have to learn the hard way. Thick-headed as you are."

"Man, give me some credit," Dante retorted, grinning.

"So what's up with you? Where've you been?" Consuela asked.

"Just hanging out with my brother, and General Jackson," Gregory said.

"He sure does put up with you a lot," Dante said, raising an eyebrow.

"Not sure why he does, but I definitely like what he's about," Gregory said. "He's a good man."

"Any word of what's coming up next? I heard some talk about Walker making an address to the UCAS tonight," Consuela asked. "I didn't want to spoil my evening. Figured I'd get the gist later."

Gregory nodded. "Walker did address the prison nation. And said nothing we didn't know already. They're going to bring a war on us."

"We should hit 'em first then," Dante said at once.

"I think something's brewing in that regard, just don't know the particulars yet," Gregory replied.

"Will it involve us?" Consuela asked.

"General Jackson said so," Gregory replied.

A familiar, tall, wiry figure came into view, hands full with several bottles of beer. Marcus proclaimed, "Got us another round!" He looked over and took notice of Gregory. "Good thing I brought a couple extra, I've got one for you if you want it."

"I'll take it," Gregory said, accepting a cold bottle from Marcus and twisting off the cap. He took a swig. "Now that hits the spot."

"Yes it does," Marcus said, before chugging down about half the contents of a bottle. He smacked his lips and smiled broadly.

Gregory returned the smile and shook his head, and then watched Consuela finish out another round of poker successfully, adding further to her pile of winnings. He caught her eyes for a second and she shot him a triumphant grin.

He took another draught of the beer. It felt so good just to be hanging out with people he considered true friends, even though the circumstances they all faced were growing more dire by the second.

More than ever, Gregory had come to appreciate the idea of savoring each moment with the ones he cared for. Like many soldiers who had endured extended periods of combat, he understood at a painfully intimate level how fast everything could change.

Gregory could look at Consuela, Dante, or Marcus, and know in his heart that he would take a bullet for any one of them. It was a strange thought to ponder, given that he did not know any of them during the time he was leading a reclusive life prior to the outbreak of hostilities.

He hoped they could all make it through the times to come, as a storm of war approached. But he had to accept the cold possibility that few of them, or perhaps even none, would.

Shoving the grave thoughts aside, he brought himself back into the moment as cards were shuffled and another game of poker started up. While too wise to partake in the game, which Consuela would probably win, Gregory looked to the promise of companionship and another cold beer or two.

He did not need anything fancy or complicated. The simple things always brought the most satisfaction. With a relaxed expression, he took another drink and watched his friends while the worries of tomorrow ebbed.

FRIEDRICH

An ocean of light flooded past Friedrich and the others, coursing rapidly towards the jagged western boundary of Purgatarion. Legion upon legion of Avatars proceeded with great haste, with sigil after sigil streaming by in a display staggering to observe.

The air rippled with a dire sense of urgency. Clouds of Gulagar and Gryphons soared overhead towards the boundary. Thousands upon thousands, it appeared as if the entirety of their ranks were emptying out of the Middle Lands.

Periodically, a cluster of Watchers would race through the air, interspersed with the other flying guardians. Friedrich's anxiety rose, knowing that only a matter of extreme importance would draw the Watchers forth.

Looking into the underbelly of the teeming masses of flying beings, Friedrich remembered words spoken after the culmination of his harrowing journey into the Abyss. They had been given to him by a creature who he knew would not utter words idly.

'If you should ever need me again, I will come to you.'

Friedrich knew he could not stand idle when such a climate of emergency swirled all around him. In interior fashion, he called out to the Gryphon. He hoped that his call reached the creature before it departed the Middle Lands.

Along the surface where he stood, waves of Avatars from the east kept flowing by. Something of tremendous magnitude beckoned, taking place beyond the darkness at the edge of the Middle Lands.

"I must go," Friedrich announced to the others standing with him. "I have called for the guardian that bore me into the Abyss when we sought Erishkegal with Enki."

"We all must go," Valaris replied somberly, looking Friedrich in the eye.

"He speaks for all of us," Maroboduus added firmly.

The entire group grew quiet. Without asking them, Friedrich knew they were all calling out to the steeds who had conveyed them into the depths of the dark pit.

"Something terrible has happened," Maroboduus commented, staring out towards the hastening masses of Avatars with a deep frown on his face.

"We cannot stay here," Heinrich interjected. "This is no different than when the Abyss' legions poured into the Middle Lands. We must join you in the fight."

"I have no idea what's happening, or what we may encounter," Friedrich said. "But I do know a lot of souls dwell in the Grey Lands. And I know that's where these forces are heading."

Gryphons began approaching Friedrich's group, one by one. They came from different directions, including one that sped in from the west, where it almost certainly had been part of the contingents heading outward.

Friedrich knew the steed he had summoned at once, when it set its eagle-like claws down upon the surface. The Gryphon stared towards him with a piercing gaze.

'I must keep my oath to you, Precious Soul. But greater danger awaits, if you go onward.'

'It is an attack on the Grey Lands, is it not?' Friedrich asked the creature.

'It is an invasion of the Grey Lands. Not an attack.'

'Then we must go, and see what we can do for the souls there,' Friedrich responded, the grave distinction of an invasion troubling him deeply.

'I will take you there,' the Gryphon responded.

Friedrich looked to his companions, all of whom were climbing up on their steeds.

'We must retrieve our crystal staves first,' Friedrich told the Gryphon, as he got onto its back.

The only relief to be found was that Asa'an had taken Seele for a romp somewhere deeper in the Middle Lands. She had gone into the Abyss with him, but he did not want her to accompany him on the pending journey. She had risked far enough already.

The Gryphon lifted effortlessly from the ground. In moments Friedrich sped across the Middle Lands. Ranks of Avatars continued to flow underneath, and large throngs of winged guardians passed above.

After retrieving their crystal staves, Friedrich's group hastened back westward. There were no more flying contingents of Avatars or guardian creatures to be seen when they arrived at the border area.

The realization did not stop Friedrich, though he had hoped to follow in the wake of Adonai's warriors on the way to the Grey Lands. The last time they had ventured beyond the confines of the Middle Lands, Enki had led them. Now, Friedrich and the others were alone as they flew through the darkness.

A storm of thoughts churned in his mind as they traveled. He had little idea of the threat facing them, other than it was large enough to rouse an entire host from Adonai's realms.

A part of him felt reckless, but he could not remain behind when so many divine creatures placed themselves at risk of the Void. Everyone shared in the struggle against the dark powers of the Abyss.

When the Grey Lands finally came into sight, they appeared like a vast plain set on fire. Friedrich's vision could not reach to either end of the line of defenders, so wide was the front arrayed against the enemy.

A clash of great magnitude well underway, Friedrich's group rushed directly into the midst of the maelstrom. Beyond the line of guardians, Watchers, and Avatars loyal to Adonai, teeming legions of Fallen Avatars and masses of other creatures from the Abyss pressed a tremendous onslaught.

Dread swelled within Friedrich's spirit. He recognized at once the all-out nature of the enemy assault. The infernal hosts had already swept the defenders back to the edge of the Grey Lands, and were marshalling to push Adonai's ranks into the pit beyond. The realization dismayed Friedrich as he gazed upon the relentless assault.

"What can we possibly do in the face of this?" questioned Hans, hovering on a Gryphon to Friedrich's right. His voice thick with uncertainty, he exhibited no small degree of fear. "We'll be swallowed up in that storm."

Friedrich could not argue with his friend's assessment, but he did not reply yet. He eyed the battlefront carefully from the lofty position, having come for a reason that he did not wish to abandon.

Finally, he espied a huge swathe of dark beings gathered behind the fiery line of Adonai's warriors. He knew at once who the darker entities were and why they were being protected.

'Can you gain the help of others of your kind?' Friedrich communicated to his steed. *'Could some be pulled back from the fighting?'*

'It will not be easy,' came the reply from the Gryphon. *'Most of my kind are heavily engaged in the fighting. Your call came to me just in time to come to you, or I would be there now.'*

'Can they be carried to the Middle Lands? The souls who dwell here?' Friedrich asked, looking upon the darker-hued entities shielded by Avatars, Watchers, and other guardian creatures.

'They can. Nothing has ever prevented them from dwelling in the Middle Lands. It is they who have chosen to dwell in the Grey Lands,' the Gryphon responded with a somber edge.

'Can you call to the others of your kind?' Friedrich asked.

'Yes, but it is not certain how many can respond with the battle as it is,' the Gryphon answered.

'Call to your kind, and take me down to where the souls from the Grey Lands are gathered,' Friedich told the creature in the air of a commander. He then called out to his companions, arrayed to the left and right, to fall in behind him.

The Gryphon responded quickly, taking Friedrich into a sharp descent towards the massed souls. Behind Friedrich and his steed, the other Gryphons followed closely in their wake, bringing his companions.

The dark-clad figures backed away quickly when Friedrich and the others landed among them. Over their heads and farther beyond, he could see the wall of Avatars that remained the only thing standing between them and the ravenous hordes of Diabolos.

Friedrich blocked out thoughts of the nearby battle, focusing on his reason for landing. He knew there was little time to act.

"We have called for more steeds, I hope to help you get out of here, to the Middle Lands!" Friedrich called loudly to the crowd of souls.

"Go away!" an emaciated-looking, pale individual shouted angrily at him. "We want nothing of your land! This is where we dwell!"

In light of the circumstances, Friedrich was incredulous at the stark response. His tone reflected his irritation when he spoke again.

"You will not dwell here for much longer, no matter what you want. The hordes that attack now seek to take you captive. So many risk themselves for you now, and many go to the Void this day because of you!"

"Because of us? They wish to hold onto these lands and nothing more," one of the others retorted, in a raspy tone of voice.

"This land is here as a mercy to all of you!" Friedrich snapped back, righteous ire rising within. "The only reason those legions hurried from the White City to the battle here is to save you from the horrors the attackers wish to visit you with. They desire your destruction and your enslavement. They seek to find a way to take you down into the Nether Kingdom as a slave to Diabolos."

As he was speaking, a large number of Gryphons began landing all around the souls. The ashen-looking spirits drew back further, looking highly agitated at the presence of the winged creatures.

"What is this?" shrieked one of the spirits. "Do you seek to take us captive?"

"No. You can stay if you would like," Friedrich said evenly, working to keep his temper from tainting his responses. "You can find out for yourself that what I tell you is true. I offer a choice to those who would listen to me. We will take you from here and return to the Middle Lands, but you must decide quickly. We must leave here! The defense will not hold forever!"

'Something comes, from behind!' the voice of Friedrich's Gryphon sounded in a pressing manner.

Friedrich turned in alarm, seeing numerous Sentinels pouring

over the lip of the cliff-like boundary behind them. The giant spider entities hastily formed up into a line, displaying all variations of their eight-legged kind mixed together.

He heard a distinctive buzzing at that moment, coming from the darkness of the Abyss. If a spirit had blood, his would have felt like ice as he listened to the terrible noise swelling up out of the darkness.

A feeling of dread crept over Friedrich as the sound grew in volume, expanding at a rapid pace as more and more Sentinels joined the thickening defensive line. Some Avatars, mainly contingents of Aishim, along with many Gulagar and Gryphons, added their number to the makeshift position forming up along the rocky edge.

The beings from the Grey Lands screamed fearfully as the space beyond the edge filled abruptly with enormous masses of hideous, insect-like creatures. As the bizarre entities rose into sight, the buzzing soared to a deafening level.

In some ways, the appearance of the things from the darkness resembled giant, winged locusts, each one of them as large as the Gryphon that Friedrich rode upon. Every one of their six legs ended in strange, clawed appendages, like clusters of curving, sharply-honed knife blades.

Their heads took the appearance of misshapen human skulls, elongated in form, with a sharp chin and narrowed crown. Numerous long strands extended outward from their heads, each one resembling a barbed whip.

White flames burned deep within their eye sockets, and their mouths were lined with a combination of lengthy fangs and rows of razor-like teeth. Their bodies exhibited more of the bone-like appearance of their heads, with jagged, uneven surfaces that were the antitheses of elegance or beauty. Behind the creatures trailed long, segmented tails, ending in wicked-looking stingers.

They were demonic entities, fashioned for the sole purpose of destruction. The buzzing continuously surged as masses of the macabre entities swarmed the edges of the Grey Lands.

The fury of their assault horrific to witness, they whipped their long legs about, bringing the knife-like clusters at the far ends to bear upon those they attacked. Tossing their heads to and fro, they unleashed a torrent of biting lashes. Again and again, they stabbed and slashed with their huge stingers.

Many defenders, from Aishim, to Sentinels, Gulagar, Gryphons, and Watchers alike, fell to the Void within the first exchanges of the fighting. Even though a large number of the attackers were also brought down, the losses inflicted upon the locust-host were barely a dent in their overall numbers. The creatures of Adonai fought back with a desperate gravity, using every method at their disposal to blunt the masses of abyssal nightmares.

"We have to punch through this, or everyone here is lost!" Stefan exclaimed, looking forlorn as he watched the intense combat spreading into the far distance.

The predicament facing Friedrich and the others horrid to ponder, the Nether Kindgom's forces loomed to either side of them. He knew he stood within the jaws of a closing, lethal trap.

'Two can ride,' the Gryphon conveyed to Friedrich. *'We will find a way through. We must take to flight now! Whomever would come with us must choose now! We can wait no longer!'*

"Two to every steed!" Friedrich shouted to the spirits, relaying the Gryphon's information. "Those who would go, take a steed now. Or stay and meet your fate! Make your choice now!"

The Gryphons lowered themselves to the ground, wherever they were standing. Though many were tentative, a large number of the dark figures did as they were commanded. With tentative grips, they gained the backs of the winged creatures.

Friedrich looked at the fighting behind him in horror, seeing a mass of the winged nightmares breaking through the defensive line. The Gryphons started taking to flight a moment later. They sped away from the breaks in the line, as the remaining steeds on the ground took wing and followed after.

The multitude lifted sharply upward, and Friedrich could see they were trying to go over the fighting between the locust-things and the defenders. A host of the locust-like beasts rose up to block their path. Friedrich could see that the Gryphons would never pass over them in time, and would be swallowed up within the enemy swarm.

Brilliant light encompassed Friedrich at the forefront of his formation. A trio of huge, fiery bodies rushed by the Gryphon he rode.

They were six-winged Avatars of a high rank, immense in stature and great in power. The three celestial warriors barreled right into the midst of the locust-things.

With whirring blades of fire, the Avatars carved a huge opening for the throng of Gryphons, who angled for the dark portal with all haste. Friedrich watched the locust-things recoil as droves of them were cut down. Yet he also noticed that the area was thickening fast with their presence, as more and more of the beasts rose to aid their companions.

The Gryphons raced through the opening and continued onward at the limits of their speed. The creatures' grating screeches lanced into Friedrich's senses as they passed through their midst.

Seeing the Gryphons escaping, many of the hideous things tried to give chase. Friedrich's spirit tensed at first, but then eased as he noticed the gap growing between the Gryphons and their pursuers.

Looking over his shoulder, Friedrich's spirit sank as he took notice of what happened farther back. The Avatars who had intervened for the Gryphon-mounted spirits were being covered with a multitude of the winged beasts.

Adonai's warriors slashed their great blades like streaks of lightning cleaving through dark clouds, but the assault levied upon them was overwhelming. The outcome of the struggle was terrible to watch. The enemy creatures stabbed, tore, bit, and stung the fiery warriors with a frenzied savagery until there was nothing left to be seen of the courageous celestial warriors.

Sorrow wracked Friedrich's spirit as the mass of Gryphons sped onward, each of the mounts carrying two spirits away from the hellish battle. The trio of Avatars had sacrificed themselves so that imperfect spirits, including Friedrich, could escape an agonizing doom.

He wondered what had happened. Disbelief and confusion churned his thoughts. He could not deny what transpired behind him. The forces of the Abyss were taking over the Grey Lands, overcoming all the defenses of those who served Adonai.

Friedrich never thought such a thing could be possible. The

Grey Lands, though cloaked in shadow and removed from the rest of the Middle Lands, were never supposed to be under the Nether Kingdom's dominion.

It remained a place still warded by the guardian creatures appointed by Adonai. The souls who had chosen to depart the Middle Lands and dwell within the dim environs of the Grey Lands still possessed hope of crossing the gates of the White City, even if most of them failed to recognize that truth.

Friedrich wondered what would happen to the souls who had stubbornly remained behind and rejected the chance to escape. Further, and even more distressing, he wondered whether it was possible that the Middle Lands themselves could fall.

The Nether Kingdom had unleashed power of a kind never anticipated by the Avatars, Watchers, and guardian creatures. Diabolos had gathered tremendous strength in the darkness, preparing horrors in the depths of the Abyss for the servants of Adonai. Nightmares of kinds never before seen were being loosed upon all loyal to the Great Throne.

Assaulted by waves of fear and doubt, Friedrich knew he had to trust in Adonai, no matter how dismaying everything appeared. Whether he fell into the Void or not, the most important thing that he had to hold fast was that he continued doing everything in his power in the service of Adonai.

He could not allow what went beyond his ability or control to consume him. The things that were in the sphere of his influence and ability, he had to attend to with all the strength left in him. In both matters, discernment was necessary, along with trust in Adonai.

After traveling at rapid speeds through a vast stretch of darkness, a bright horizontal glow beckoned to Friedrich from directly ahead. Soon, the multitude of Gryphons drew close enough for him to realize what the extensive line of shimmering, reddish light represented.

Where the outer edge of the Middle Lands appeared at first to be crowned with fire, Friedrich saw that the light indicated immense numbers of Avatars arrayed along the jagged boundary. The towering forms of many powerful Avatars, of the higher orders, could be seen up and down the border, looming above great multitudes of other

Avatar warriors. Friedrich recognized many of the sigils displayed over the various ranks.

The Avatars were part of a great bulwark, drawn up in order and positioned against the fell things of the Abyss. No chances were being taken in regards to the recent assault upon the Grey Lands. If the Enemy intended to carry the attack to the Middle Lands, it would be met with great force.

Friedrich's group soared over the massed Avatars without disturbance, continuing forward into the Middle Lands. The Gryphons kept to a high altitude, curving to the right after crossing over a small range of glistening, sapphire hills.

As beautiful and striking as the landscape below appeared, Friedrich found himself distracted with the inner burdens of what he had just experienced. He kept his eyes fixed forward, trusting that his steed would choose a propitious spot for landing.

After continuing over a great expanse that included silvery plains, crystalline rivers, and rolling, emerald fields, the Gryphons glided downward at last. The creatures alighted in smooth fashion within a broad meadow, filled with light-blue, luminous grasses.

The scene looked particularly surreal to Friedrich under the distressing circumstances. The reigning atmosphere was tranquil, silent, and far removed from the brutal fighting they had barely escaped.

At once, the pairs of riders began disembarking from their Gryphon mounts. The pale souls, draped in their dusky raiment, looked around with expressions of bewilderment and awe. A hush persisted, the refugees of a gloomy, drab realm remaining speechless as they took in the sights of the Middle Lands.

Friedrich could only imagine what the impact was like for each of them. He remembered what a phenomenal contrast it had been between the world of his mortal years and this one.

Having long dwelled within the embrace of darkness, shadow, and storm-ridden skies, the refugees now found themselves within the midst of a luminous, bright, and richly-colorful realm. In both appearance and nature, it bore little resemblance to their former one.

Friedrich felt a light touch upon his shoulder, breaking him out of his observations. He turned to see Silas, Valaris, and Ulrich, who had made their way over to him and were standing at his side. It was Silas' hand that rested on his right shoulder, in a gesture of encouragement and solidarity.

"You did a good thing, Friedrich," Valaris told him, stepping forward and giving him a few firm pats on his other shoulder. "All of these lads here would be in the Void were it not for what you did."

"Thank you for coming with me," Friedrich replied, looking his friend in the eye, knowing that every single one of his greatest friends had risked the Void to accompany him on the desperate mission.

"You do not need to thank me," Valaris replied.

"Valaris is right. We are all in this together no matter what," Silas added.

"Look around you, Friedrich," Ulrich stated, with a large smile. "Sullen though they might be, this great multitude of spirits owes much to you."

"They owe much to Adonai," Friedrich replied, without hesitation. "Not to me. I did only what should have been done."

"But you recognized what had to be done," Valaris said. "You are a leader. You mustered the help that saved them from destruction."

"I just hope they come to a better wisdom here," Ulrich commented. Turning away, he looked around at the few thousand souls who had been spared the unconsciousness of the Void.

"I hope every one of them swiftly finds their way into the White City," Friedrich said, letting his gaze sweep over the rescued masses. He added, "Even if they get there before me. My wish is that all of them are secure in the eternal Home."

"I do think these lads will need some help figuring this place out," Valaris remarked. He then chuckled, and continued, "I suppose I've got longer experience than most of you, save for Maroboduus. That big-hearted, stone-headed lad, he probably remains here just because of me. But know I'll be glad to help in any way I can. I will pass along anything I've learned during my long stay within these lands. Even if I have to thump a few of them on their heads to get them to think straight."

Friedrich laughed at his boisterous friend's words. "Aside from thumping them on the head, that would be a wonderful gift from you. We will have to get them acclimated as best as we can. I suspect this is all a bit of a shock to them."

"To say the least," Silas added, staring out over the refugees. "Especially after all the paranoia and hearsay they were steeped in."

A few of the souls looked in Friedrich's direction. Despite all the beauty surrounding them, and their removal from the greatest danger, some noticeable fear lurked in their expressions. Even now, he could tell that some of them bore mistrust towards their rescuers and environment.

There was no avoiding the truth of the matter, or the considerable challenges that lay ahead. It would be no easy task to befriend and help the souls from the Grey Lands on their path to the White City.

They had hardened themselves to an extreme. Softening things that had long been entrenched would take some considerable effort, both on their part and those who sought to assist.

"We'll get started soon enough with tending to them," Friedrich announced, after an extended pause. He looked to his friends. "For now, I need some time to myself, for just a little while."

It was the only way he could think of to voice the need he felt deep inside. The level of communication between their spirits went far beyond words. The essence he imparted to them embodied his current fatigue, the fears and uncertainties plaguing him, the sorrow weighing his spirit down, and the need to step away from the enormity of everything that was happening. His companions nodded back to him, indicating their understanding.

Friedrich started walking forward at a slow pace, heading west. Passing through a large number of souls from the Grey Lands, he made his way to their farthest edge, the knee-high grasses brushing softly against his legs. In such a tired and mournful state, he took no notice of their glances in his direction, even those who parted way for him. The other souls were like a blur to him. He strode well past the last one of their number until he reached the end of the meadow. After pausing for a moment, he continued.

Beyond the meadow, he moved into an expanse of towering, pillar-like structures of a reflective silver hue. They shimmered magnificently in the light from the kaleidoscopic skies, but Friedrich took no account of their beauty. He kept walking forward, his thoughts far removed from his immediate surroundings.

He continued on through the midst of the lofty formations until he arrived at an open stretch of rocky ground. From there, he saw that only a short distance remained to the end of the Middle Lands; where the rainbow-hued skies culminated, and a maw of pure darkness gaped.

A line of Avatars were gathered there, predominantly the smaller Aishim. The celestial warriors were all oriented towards the darkness, maintaining a vigilant watch.

Friedrich went no further. He stared outward in silence, peering beyond the border. Every part of his spirit longed to see some sign of survivors returning out of the blackness.

He thought of the many thousands he had witnessed, from the legions rushing to the defense of the Grey Lands, to the massive ranks of guardian creatures, Watchers, and Avatars engaged in the battle. His heart grew increasingly heavy as he watched for the faintest flicker of light, but nothing stirred in the black depths before his eyes.

His decisiveness and actions had spared many souls like himself from destruction, but the thought gave him no comfort. He pondered the thousands of divine, majestic beings that had sped without hesitation to protect the souls in the Grey Lands. Every last one of the warriors, whether Avatar, Watcher, or guardian creature, was a blameless spirit who did not merit the awful calamity that befell them.

He thought of the Avatars who had made their escape possible. Friedrich could still see the hordes of abyssal monstrosities clawing, biting, and stabbing the fiery warriors of Adonai, until there was nothing left to be seen of the noble spirits' forms.

He wept for the three great Avatars, thinking of the agony they had suffered, having their spirit-bodies torn apart bit by bit, to the last. There was no doubt in his mind that they knew what was going to happen when they hurled themselves into the swarms of malevolent, winged beasts from the Nether Kingdom.

To his eyes, there looked to be no justice in what had occurred. He wondered how evil could grow and flourish to such a tremendous degree that it now threatened the Middle Lands in a way it never had before.

Creatures of Adonai, many thousands strong, had been overcome and dispatched to the Void. He could see the Sentinels scrambling over the edge of the Grey Lands to form up a line, the legions of Avatars with their bright sigils arrayed against an ocean of adversaries, and Watchers, Gulagar and Gryphons speeding with all haste to engage the nightmares from the depths. Friedrich mourned at the core of his being for all of them, and his spirit grew heavier with the despair creeping into his soul.

He poured out his heart in raw emotion to Adonai, asking when the advancing march of evil and death would be brought to an end. He asked when the glory of life would prevail, to a place where it could never be overcome; when death in all of its forms, including the unconsciousness of the Void, would be crushed forevermore.

It was said that the One so beloved of Adonai, the Liberator, had defeated death. Yet all things in the material world still died, generation after generation, while Avatars and other divine creatures beyond were still falling into the Void by the thousands. Friedrich did not understand how anyone could say death had been defeated when its reach spared no created thing. If anything, death held ultimate dominion everywhere he looked.

For him, the overthrow of death's tremendous power could not come a moment too soon. Death's touch had afflicted him terribly in his mortal years, and during his time of exile in the Middle Lands. His spirit feeling weak and forlorn, Friedrich gazed into the pitch-black darkness beyond the Middle Lands, a lightless gloom undisturbed by so much as a single glint of light.

GREGORY

A stream of thoughts ran through Gregory's mind as the long parade of train cars rumbled through the confines of the dark tunnel. Thousands of militia fighters conveyed to the north, the great movement had been cloaked effectively from enemy eyes.

Intelligence gained from an unanticipated operation in Silver Valley, on the part of a secretive religious order, of all things, had proven to be a gold mine when added to other pieces of intelligence. A much clearer picture of UCAS intentions was forming.

The UCAS was poised to unleash a heavy strike through the West at any hour, with a diversionary posturing around Losantiville to spread the forces of the Confederation thinner. Knowing that the build-up around Losantiville was only a bluff changed defensive strategies considerably, moving up other possibilities.

General Jackson, with the agreement of most of his general staff, believed that the best counter to all of it lay in going on the offensive. Just hours before Gregory had been sent to gather with the militia force and be ferried north, the general had finally shared the plan he had only hinted at before.

Heavy armor and artillery, and other major assets, continued to be shifted west and to Losantiville. As before, the deployments were plain to all eyes, with no effort to disguise the movements, using rail and large convoys of flat-bedded vehicles.

Every effort had been made to make it seem as if all the focus remained on the western border and Losantiville. Both Confederation deployments projected the notion of purely defensive postures, countering the observable movements by the UCAS military.

Meanwhile, the tunnel systems, uncovered when the free provinces learned of the extensive underground facilities built by the UCAS government, were being put to good use. A swiftly-developed plan was implemented.

The tunnels had been collapsed by the UCAS in many places to prevent them from being used by the rebels. Nonetheless, a long stretch reaching to the rebel-held bank of the Columbia River, to the west of the UCAS capital, had been discovered intact.

Dedicated work by engineers and seemingly indefatigable construction crews had gotten the tracks fit for service, using trains similar to those utilized in major airports. An exit had to be created at the far end of the tunnel section, but General Jackson espied a strategic advantage in regards to the unfolding plan.

Large numbers of personnel could be moved close to the river boundary, undetected. From there, they could cross the Columbia River to positions northwest of the capital.

Gregory would be involved in that part of the operation. He just hoped the other elements of the operation were soundly conceived. So many components had to work together in order for the objectives to succeed.

The White Pyramid, the President Abraham Airport, and a potent array of UCAS forces were located on the other side of the Columbia River, across from the areas of the capital containing the Presidential Estate, the various war memorials, and other iconic, historically-rich sites. The White Pyramid and enemy strength on that side of the river worried Gregory. Potent enough to smash a rabble of militia units, it would require a significant effort to hold in check.

When questioned, General Jackson had given Gregory's mind a little ease. The general offered some insight regarding the other aspects of the operation.

A commander fast becoming popular with the free province forces, General Barksdale had been summoned to the region with an airborne division. The division had been quartered at a large airport now being used as an airbase in Leesburg, just under 100 miles south of the UCAS capital.

UCAS intelligence reporting the movement of the division would deem it another deployment countering the western and Losantiville buildups. The Confederation forces were merely preparing to send the division to whichever battlefront needed reinforcement the soonest.

By itself, the airborne division did not posses enough strength to threaten the defenses around the capital. Its nature designed for mobility, the division carried a reserve posture.

The actual purpose for the division's deployment, known only to a select few, was anything but defensive in nature. General Jackson, General Huntington, and General Barksdale had crafted a daring, three-pronged scenario, one that would unfurl when the UCAS moved to launch its major offensive in the west.

The defenses to the west had been placed under the command of General John Ford, a man who General Jackson proclaimed the highest confidence in. General Ford could bend, but not break. Time had to be purchased to allow the greater plan space to develop.

Gregory loved the boldness of the operation from the moment the general briefed him on it. It had not been lost on him that a high degree of trust had been placed in his hands. To be included in the small circle of individuals knowledgeable about the full operational plan was a great honor. It also told him that his own role in the coming operation had an integral, eminent place.

The most-experienced groups of militia fighters from Venorterra and other provinces had been selected to participate in the operation. From all over the Confederation of Free States, militia fighters were expedited to the northernmost region of the rebel-held territory, in the Queenland Province.

In order to avoid tipping off the enemy, the various contingents traveled in small groups, using regular passenger vehicles. To any outside eyes, they looked like nothing more than small convoys of civilians traveling the highways and sticking together for safety. The fact that they carried guns and ammunition was no anomaly. Virtually everyone traveling the roadways for any extended length carried arms.

None of the various militia contingents had an inkling of the summons involving all the others, save for the select few such as Gregory. All of them believed they were just going to be used to reinforce defensive positions in the aftermath of the William Walker speech, regarding the existing state of war between the UCAS and Confederation of Free States.

Slowly, in an array of remote spots, numerous militia encampments of modest sizes became established. No single group of militia fighters reached a size large enough to attract too much attention from enemy spies, drones, or surveillance satellites. There were a few of the latter still maintaining orbit that had not yet been damaged in the torrent of space debris created by the Mandarian attack prior to the taking of Taiyoan.

All of the encampments, from a larger perspective, were situated within an hour drive or less of the tunnel. Once at the tunnel, they could be combined on short notice to form a very large, singular force.

That notice had come, the militia forces had been combined, and Gregory now rode along in the midst of it all. They perched at the cusp of the inventive, grand operation.

"Ready?" Benjamin asked, grinning from where he sat directly across from him.

Gregory smiled back at his brother. He could not help being a little amused. Seeing Benjamin in an army helmet, dressed in combat fatigues with a thicker appearance augmented by plates of body armor, was undeniably an interesting sight. The police officer had definitely become a soldier, transformed right before Gregory's eyes.

"I am, and you look like you are, too," Gregory finally remarked. "I can't deny it."

"I'm liking this new fashion," Benjamin said, chuckling as he glanced down at his outfit.

"You'll get used to it, and tired of it, very quickly," Gregory replied with a wry grin. "Especially lugging a rucksack everywhere. Gets old, trust me."

"Well, here goes nothing then," Benjamin commented, with a smirk. "They're crazy enough to use me, so I might as well look the part."

"They're crazy enough to use militia fighters in an offensive operation," Gregory said. "To most, the strategy is completely insane. To me, it's beyond genius. And to our enemies, it will come as a tremendous surprise."

"Which is what we're after," Benjamin replied, nodding.

The train finally slowed down and drew to a halt. Gregory, Benjamin, and the other occupants disembarked. Side by side, the two brothers marched down to where a huge earthen ramp had been fashioned, leading up to the surface.

He started up the ramp, the latter yawning open into a world gripped in the clutches of war. Gregory lifted his head up as he focused on a number of deep booms in the distance.

The reverberations sounded like elements of an approaching storm, but Gregory knew he heard the thunder of war. The rumbles and thumps reigned in the night as they reached the top of the ramp and came out under the open sky.

"Look at that," Benjamin exclaimed, peering to the north with wide eyes.

For Benjamin the display represented something new. For Gregory, the sight brought back too many memories. Akin to a vicious cascade of lightning, the skies flashed repeatedly on the horizon. He knew immediately what the luminous exhibition indicated.

"They're lighting 'em up," Gregory remarked, staring into the distance. "That's all from our guys. And it's landing right on the heads of their guys."

The attack ferocious in nature, it transpired with a level of intensity greater than anything Gregory had witnessed during his multiple tours of duty overseas. The cascade of resonant booms intertwined with the eerie sounds of blaring claxons blaring, making for a surreal atmosphere.

The dark music heralded destruction and death, things Gregory wished to never encounter again. But he knew he had to continue facing the specter of war, for as long as it took to secure freedom for the sovereign states of the Confederation. The alternative, subjugation by the UCAS, could never be countenanced.

"We're coming in right behind that?" Benjamin asked, an edge of nervousness in his face.

Gregory nodded, hearing the apprehension in his brother's voice. "Best thing to be coming in behind. Believe me, what you see there is getting rid of quite a lot of things that we don't want to run into."

"How can anything survive something like that?" Benjamin said, staring out towards the flashing horizon.

"Believe me, you'd be real surprised," Gregory commented. "We can't let our guard down for a second when we go across."

"I wasn't planning on it," Benjamin replied.

"We do what we came to do, and then we get the hell out of there," Gregory told his brother. "That's how it's done."

"Got it," Benjamin nodded.

Walking away from the top of the ramp, they headed forward with a mass of militia fighters towards the riverbank. A motley fleet of boats teemed within the water, ranging from military-style water vessels to commercial ones.

Everything possible had been scraped up to get the militia fighters across. There was even a pair of old amphibious transports dating back to the Second Great War.

Gregory did not care about the appearance of the vessels. As long as they were operable and could cross the river, they were acceptable to him. He just hoped nothing from the enemy loomed on the opposite bank.

"General Andreas!" exclaimed a military officer as Gregory neared the bustle at the waterline.

Gregory looked to the man striding towards him. A captain by rank, the officer had a determined expression as he saluted Gregory. Still unused to being saluted by higher-ranking officers, Gregory quickly returned the salute and bid the man to be at ease. The quicker they could speak frankly, the better.

"All is ready, your forces can board now, and we'll cross at zero-one-hundred hours," the officer announced. "Scouts on the opposite bank indicate that everything is clear."

"That's the news I was wanting to hear," Gregory responded. "We'd have a pretty hard time making a crossing otherwise. Any word yet on our other friends?"

"General Barksdale's force is on schedule," the officer answered. "And General Huntington is already moving on this side of the bank."

"Then all is in good order, so far," Gregory replied, casting his brother a wink.

Despite the positive gesture, he cradled a little worry, hoping General Huntington executed his part of the plan well. Everything Gregory and General Barksdale did depended on it.

"I'll see you across the river," the captain said.

"See you there," Gregory told the man with an air of confidence, before dismissing him.

If everything went as planned, General Huntington's armor would create enough of a bluff to tie down UCAS forces positioned on the side of the river where the White Pyramid stood. The greater operation had specific goals, but was more of a raid than a true invasion. A little time was all that was needed for success.

"Alright everyone, let's get aboard!" Gregory called out to the fighters all around him. "Time for some sight-seeing in the capital!"

His order disseminated quickly enough as the militia force crowded the shoreline and began boarding the various water vessels. For his part, Gregory asked to be in one of the faster craft and a militia fighter guided him to a twin-engine speed boat.

Gregory told the man piloting it to be sure to take a lead position. If anything lurked on the other bank, on the part of the UCAS, Gregory did not intend to be shielded by the men he intended to lead.

Gregory clapped his brother on the shoulder as Benjamin stood next to him, near the prow of the boat. "Good to have you with me."

"Wouldn't want to be anywhere else," Benjamin replied.

Gregory smiled. "Let's get this done with, then."

He ordered the pilot to maneuver the vessel around to the front of the mass of boats, while the rest of the boarding took place. He could feel the power in the two chugging engines, listening to the low rumble as they moved through the water.

Gregory stared back at the sprawling flotilla and shook his head. The plan both crazy and bold, it would provide the manpower necessary to allow General Barksdale the ability to concentrate his forces in full.

In the background, to the east, the sky continued to flash and boom with a sustained fury. The roar of fighter planes could be heard overhead, and tracers from anti-aircraft guns peppered the sky with ghostly lights.

"Keep softening the bastards up," Gregory whispered, watching the macabre light show on the horizon.

The appointed time finally arrived. The air filled with the sound of engines starting up. Gregory's boat oriented in the direction of the opposite bank, ready for the crossing.

The rush of cold, moist air against his face felt invigorating as the boat accelerated and sped across the river surface. The air erupted with the roar of hundreds upon hundreds of engines, as the unusual armada swept across the river towards the far bank.

Gregory sat near the prow of the vessel, holding onto a rail for stability as the boat skimmed the surface at high speed. He stared towards the dark embankment.

No gunfire opened up at their approach. The scouts had done a thorough job of assessing enemy deployments.

A few minutes later, Gregory stepped out of the boat and onto the shore. He gripped his rifle, looking around at the other vessels coming to a stop.

Militia fighters soon poured onto the shore area. Gregory hustled to coordinate with both militia leaders and the officers from the Confederation forces assisting with their part of the operation. Shouts filled the air as the militia force began to fan out and move farther from the river.

Less than an hour later, Gregory rode in the back of a pickup truck as the militia force pressed into the western side of the capital. He had been ordered to hold a sector containing main roads leading towards the river area, where the makeshift flotilla was operating.

His assignment did not ask him to press an offensive, but to hold the streets, so that Barksdale's troops would have a smooth way out after coming in from the east. Scattered bursts of gunfire indicated a few exchanges with the enemy, but there was no sign of any concerted opposition in the area where the militia deployed.

The best marksmen among the militia force were swiftly located on the rooftops of higher buildings, as fighters flooded the streets below. Machine guns were set up, as were the man-portable weapon systems provided by the Confederation.

A militarized police unit from the capital, complete with a small number of armored vehicles, made an appearance soon after and put up some token resistance. The police were well-armed, with automatic rifles, helmets, and body armor.

The outnumbered unit met with a fearsome barrage. Gregory downed at least three officers with his sniper rifle by the time his fighters destroyed the armored vehicles using the anti-armor weapons provided to his force. Once the vehicles were taken out of action, the remaining enemy melted back into the shadows.

Gregory ordered the marksmen above to vigilance. Using night-vision gear, they were put on watch for any would-be snipers on the part of the bloodied police force.

The streets holding the militia force fell into a deep, eerie silence. The booms and flashes in the distance to the east testified to heavy fighting in other areas, but the local area stayed quiet.

A curious thing began to happen about two hours later. When the first white flag appeared, Gregory's first instinct was that enemy forces were surrendering.

After a brief examination using night-vision capable binoculars, he determined that the ones bearing white flags were civilians. A situation he had not expected then manifested.

A trickle turned into a torrent. Hundreds of unarmed people, including elderly and children, began shuffling down the thoroughfare towards the militia positions.

Before the mass of civilians reached the line held by the militia, Gregory trusted to his instincts, told his men to stand down, and then stepped out into the road. He eyed the man walking in front of the throng, a figure about six feet in height with a thick grey beard, trimmed short.

"We want to be free," the older man stated in a deep-toned voice, before Gregory had a chance to speak. "We live in fear of the government. We live in fear of the gangs running rampant on the streets. This is no place for us any longer."

"I agree," Gregory replied, eyeing two young boys huddled by their mother nearby. "It is no place for any of us."

"We don't believe what the news tells us," the old man said. "We know the Confederation is fighting for its freedom. We'd rather take our chances there."

"What's your name?" Gregory asked him.

"Joseph Johnson, I'm pastor of the Church of the Holy Liberator, about a block from here," the man replied.

"It's nice to meet you, Reverend Johnson, but I wish the circumstances were different," Gregory replied in an amiable fashion. "I am Gregory Andreas. An officer with these forces."

Reverend Johnson nodded. "Pleasure to meet you, Gregory. And glad you are here. Really glad."

Gregory looked over the motley assemblage. There were at least a thousand, and more arrived every minute. In the distance the sky rumbled and lit up with more explosions.

"The police are gone, can't you just let us through?" Reverend Johnson asked, his words taking on a pleading tone. "We'd like to take our chances down south of here."

"Reverend, it is incredibly dangerous right now. You should tell everyone to get back inside," Gregory replied, worried about the growing crowd of civilians in the midst of a contested battle zone. There were no guarantees a counterattack by government forces would not be coming any second. "A full assault is underway, and I have no way of telling you how things are going somewhere else. This area could fall under attack any minute. I'm sorry, it's just too dangerous."

"Dangerous?" Reverend Johnson responded, letting the word linger in the air for a moment. Gregory sensed the rising agitation in the other man, his next words pouring out like water overflowing a dam. "I know you know many dangers as a soldier. I don't have to tell you about dangers in battle. But I'll tell you what dangerous can also be....

"Danger is having your door kicked in during the middle of the night by jack-booted thugs in body armor ... and then being beaten and having your home ransacked, your possessions confiscated, and maybe your dog shot too. All because they got their information wrong ... or were using the excuse of a security emergency ... or were overreacting on some other matter.

"Danger is having your body riddled with volts of electricity ... just because you object to the way you are being talked to or treated by those same kinds of uniformed thugs. Danger is having every phone call you make listened to. Danger is having everywhere you go recorded on video and stored somewhere. Danger is having your wrist scanned, telling them who you are, where you are, at what time, and even what you are buying. Danger is having the means of defending your family taken away from you. Danger is being made to be dependent for what we eat and what kind of health treatments we are allowed and approved to have. Young man, that is also what danger is ... and these people need to be away from it...."

Gregory nodded slowly, understanding every single point the

Reverend made. He could only imagine what a prison life had become for civilians living in UCAS territories, where hysteria, paranoia, and hyper-security thrived. The Reverend had made a case he could not personally argue with.

He thought about the situation facing him as more people kept coming out of buildings and joining the growing crowd on the streets. A great many carried backpacks, luggage, and bags, as if expecting to leave their homes.

He could see the desperation on the faces of the people around the Reverend. It was reflected in the way they clutched their children, and looked towards Gregory.

One of the tasks of the militia force was to escort enemy prisoners, if there were mass surrenders. The people before him were not enemy soldiers, but his forces were capable of channeling a large number of individuals through the streets to where they could be ferried across the river.

Gregory could not find it in their heart to say no to them. They were exercising their free will, just as he had in choosing to fight again. He knew they had been living under a nightmare. If he had lived in the north, he might have found himself in the same situation.

"There are no guarantees, Reverend," Gregory said. "I cannot guarantee safety for anyone with you. We might fall under attack, without warning. And I can't guarantee you anything if we make it to the other side of the river. I can only try to get you there."

"Life never gives guarantees, only Adonai does that," the Reverend responded, with a kind smile. "All I ask is for you to help us, by letting us through so we can take our chances down south."

"Who am I to deny you that, Reverend? We will see you through," Gregory declared, nodding to the man before issuing the command to his subordinates.

"You walk in the light of Adonai, soldier," Reverend Johnson told him. "Thank you. And Bless you."

"Good luck to you and all of the people with you, Reverend," Gregory responded. "Let's get things going, now."

With the help of the people wishing to leave the capital, a large number of cars, pickup trucks, vans, and SUVs were pressed into service. Under the supervision of militia fighters and embedded military officers, the Reverend's people were taken onward, towards the river.

Maintaining his position, Gregory felt powerful emotions watching the display of hope and bravery on the part of each and every man and woman in the departing group. Serenaded by thunderous explosions and the incessant rattle of gunfire, families took leave of their homes and headed towards uncertain futures.

As the civilians were facilitated in their journey, Gregory kept his focus on looking for any signs of counterattacks. Fortunately, his sector of the city remained undisturbed by enemy military or police units.

The militia fighters were anchored in a solid position, with marksmen posted on rooftops all around the area, and anti-armor, man-portable weapon systems deployed on the ground. With the skies clearly under the control of the Confederation, there was little chance of threats from enemy aircraft.

Gregory kept vigil over the evacuating civilians. It would not be long before he expected an appearance from Barksdale's troops. Once that happened, he could look forward to crossing back over the river.

ROBERT JACKSON

A swarm of hunter-drones were released into the night, set free to begin searching for unmanned enemy craft prowling the skies as the ground attack neared. The condensed artillery and missile strike that just concluded had softened up enemy defenses considerably, all along the Columbia River. Self-propelled Guardian Howitzers, Lightning Multiple-rocket Launchers, batteries of non-line of sight artillery, and a range of ground to ground missiles alike had rained down upon identified enemy military positions.

Once known enemy air defense assets had been crippled,

bombers, fighter-bombers, and attack drones sent from multiple airfields were loosed in a torrent of sorties, striking targets all around the capital. The air teemed with booms generated from a host of explosions, often lighting up the sky in such rapid succession that a strobing effect was created.

A few aircraft were lost, but the initial strikes were immensely successful, far exceeding General Jackson's expectations. Only able to scramble a few fighters in response, enemy planes were rapidly driven off or shot down. Air superiority was firmly achieved for the window of time allotted to the operation. That alone gave General Jackson a tremendous advantage.

With air cover established, thousands of militia fighters were brought up from the tunnel and ferried across the Columbia River. The force had been heavily equipped with man-portable systems, ranging from those designed to take out aircraft, to others suited to engage armor. The militia forces had also been provided with a number of light vehicles, including several that had been airlifted in following their crossing.

At the same time that the militia force swarmed the bank to the north and west of the capital, a broad wave of transport aircraft brought Barksdale's Bruisers, as the popular general's airborne division was affectionately known, to the eastern side. The transports were used to deploy a considerable number of light-armored vehicles, of a kind that could be parachuted in alongside the troops.

The role of the militia fighters was two-fold. Their mission had practical elements with definite objectives, but also included another major bluff.

With regard to the mission aspect, the militia force had been tasked with securing the riverfront and routes south of the capital, preparing the way for the eventual withdrawal of Barksdale's troops. Additionally, they were assigned to watch over any prisoners being taken, and serve as their escorts when the planned withdrawal took place.

In terms of subterfuge, the militia force's appearance and movement across the river in great strength had caused critical diversions in UCAS forces, which did not realize they were not formal military units until it was too late. In a brilliant stroke of deception, General Jackson had created an illusion of having more of his military assets engaged in the attack than he actually possessed.

The UCAS had stout military assets in the area. But the combination of assets and the swiftness of the attack took the regime forces by surprise.

A large part of the enemy strength committed early towards the movement of General Huntington's armored force towards the UCAS installations around the White Pyramid. Seeing the UCAS taking the bait, General Jackson knew the mayhem had just begun for the opposing commanders.

A full division alighting to the east of the capital, a division-sized mass of militia fighters pouring into the areas north and west of the capital, and additional armored and mechanized units driving to the fray near the White Pyramid were problematic enough for the enemy. But the deciding factor was the total control of the skies over the capital.

Drones and strike helicopters of the Confederation wreaked havoc upon regime elements trying to evacuate the capital. Fighter jets screamed overhead, maintaining full air superiority.

Then, the development Robert Jackson expected to see unfolded. It was the very reason he had chosen General Barksdale for the operation he had conceived.

Reports began coming in that Barksdale's troops were speeding towards the heart of the UCAS capital, rushing like a tidal wave from the east. Drones and helicopters searched out enemy positions, identifying as many as possible for the ground troops, and often engaging them outright. Without a mandate for occupation, and with specific mission objectives, Barksdale's forces simply bypassed several of the stronger enemy positions.

Chaos pervaded overwhelmed UCAS forces in the path of Barksdale as the night deepened. Morale quickly began to collapse, and most resistance swiftly eroded.

By the time dawn arrived, many smaller units and police contingents began to surrender outright. While realizing they were surrounded and badly outnumbered, they did not likely know that the large force appearing to the west were primarily militia fighters.

The Presidential Estate became overrun later in the morning. Not a moment wasted when Barksdale's troops secured the area, smoke soon billowed into the skies as the grand edifice was burned to the ground.

Watching transmissions of the Presidential Estate being destroyed was like watching something out of a movie for General Jackson. While still strange for the general to accept what was happening before his eyes, and what things had come to, his conviction in the cause he fought for was unwavering and stronger than ever.

The UCAS regime was an enemy that only understood the exercise of power. It had become a corrupted monstrosity with an insatiable hunger for power and the pursuit of power for its own sake. Separate from, and an enemy to, the people, it had become a raging beast, and General Jackson had to stop the rabid thing in its tracks.

At the general's insistence, war memorials and other monuments were left alone for the most part, with the exception of the towering white obelisk named for President Theodore Abraham. The tall, proud structure, carrying the name of a president who had done much to speed the UCAS on its path into tyranny, found itself razed to low stubble within minutes.

Nothing more than a crumpled pile containing chunks of metal, concrete, and debris, the monument's ruins were a more fitting symbol of the truth of things. In the general's eyes, they more accurately represented what had been done to the principles of the Grand Charter by the man it had been named for.

The UCAS forces confronting General Huntington on the other side of the Columbia River were too strong to overcome. Holding their ground, the enemy soon launched a series of counterattacks that pushed General Huntington's forces back along a wide front.

While resounding success like General Barksdale's would have been wonderful, General Jackson was not worried about the setbacks. The intent all along for General Huntington remained in tying up the most powerful elements of the UCAS forces, keeping them from responding to the attacks on the other side of the river.

Nevertheless, one specific target had been earmarked for

destruction within that zone. Following concentrated missile and air strikes, combined with artillery and rocket barrages, the White Pyramid was whittled down until it was a jagged swathe of ruins.

Looking at everything, General Jackson could only hope the blow delivered to the capital was swift and strong enough to gain the free states further international recognition before the full implementation of the plan set forth by the Peace Commission. Once that insidious plan was in motion, it would be increasingly difficult to shore up any international support.

There was little doubt the Peace Commission and other elements at the World Summit were in full disarray with the unexpected assassination of Kaira Antipalos. With the one who had led the Peace Commission and designed the Community Security and Sustainment Plan dead, it was possible a political agreement could be reached.

Levying a spectacular strike upon the capital of the UCAS and destroying many of its iconic symbols of power, General Jackson intended at the very least to drive the enemy to the negotiating table. The assault was a massive roll of the dice, but it was something that had to be attempted. The UCAS enjoyed many advantages that were only starting to come into play, and time was not on the side of the new free states.

GREGORY

The first of General Barksdale's troops had not drawn into sight until dawn transpired and the sun was rising in the embrace of a new morning. The daylight revealed a city that had absorbed a heavy pounding.

Columns of black smoke billowed up all around the capital. The forest of coiling dark pillars reached to the underbelly of the clouds, making it look as if they held up the very sky.

After exchanging passwords to confirm their identities, Gregory smiled at the approach of the first armored vehicles. A sense of relief came over him, as the end of the operation neared.

The militia force began falling back after Barksdale's troops passed through. Reports from scouts keeping an eye on enemy movements indicated no signs of pursuit.

Rumbles in the distance indicated that not all fighting had ceased, though the sounds were too vague for Gregory to ascertain any details. He had no desire to stay and find out what they indicated. All his thoughts were fixed on getting back to a safe haven.

Crossing the river, Gregory eyed a number of Skyhawk and Nemene-class helicopters hovering above, up and down the river. At higher altitudes, many jets and drones streaked across the skies, heading east. The presence of so much air power gave him reassurance. Sorties were continuing to safeguard the river area during the withdrawal.

Stepping onto the shore marking Confederation territory, he turned towards his brother as he stepped off the speed boat. Without saying a word, he gave his younger brother a tight embrace. The mission completed, they were both alive and well.

ARIANNA

The ride back to the military checkpoint went without incident. The trip passed mostly in silence, as driver and passenger alike dwelled within the confines of their own thoughts.

As she drove, Arianna thought of everything that she and her companions had been through since they were allowed through the checkpoint. So much had happened following their encounter of the civilian militia protecting the neighborhood from the encroaching gang terror.

She found that she already missed Wendell, Davis, and many of the other men and women she had met during the time spent in their neighborhood. Arianna hoped they fared well, now that the gang threat had been pushed back. Perhaps with the new weapons and greater numbers of able-bodied men and women from the liberated neighborhood they could hold on until the Confederation military pushed into the area.

Hanging over all of it, like a mass of slate-gray clouds, loomed the death of Kantel. She could feel the sadness in the other An-Ki, but she had no idea what to say to them.

It was hard enough talking to another human in a time of grief, but she did not know where to start with the An-Ki. Arianna found she knew so little about how they dealt with the loss of their loved ones. She was not about to unwittingly transgress by saying the wrong thing.

Arianna felt a sense of relief when the checkpoint and encampment beside it met her sight. She slowed down on her approach, rolling to a stop a short distance from the lowered gate.

One of the soldiers approached as she rolled her window down. "Arianna Darwin?" the soldier asked.

"Yes, that's me," Arianna replied.

"We've been looking for you to arrive," he said.

Arianna nodded, though surprised that the soldier had been told to be looking out for her.

"Captain Johnstone will want to see you now," the soldier announced.

"Good, as we want to see him, and any other officers that might be around," Arianna said. "My uncle has some very important information that needs to be given to them as soon as possible."

The soldier signaled back towards the gate, which began to rise up. He looked back towards Arianna. "Bring your vehicles through, park to the left, and someone will take care of you from there."

Arianna pulled forward, passing slowly by the gate before turning off to the left. Bringing the vehicle to a stop, she shut the engine off and got out of the SUV.

Less than a minute later, a couple of soldiers came and took the group to a large tent where they were promised some hot meals and drinks. Before Arianna and her uncle could partake of the offer, they were led onward, to the tent of Captain Johnstone.

The captain stood inside, as did several other uniformed individuals. Though she could not interpret their insignia, she knew they were all of higher ranks. Their eyes gazed with scrutiny upon the newcomers as Arianna and her uncle were brought before them.

"Welcome back, Arianna. I am very pleased to see that you found your uncle," Captain Johnston said, offering a pleasant smile as he greeted her. "I'm sure it wasn't easy."

"No, definitely not easy, for any of us," Arianna replied, casting a brief glance towards her uncle. She could not even imagine what he had been through, based upon the few things he had shared with her already. The older man had endured nightmares in the depths of the federal base.

"We received word you were coming back this way, and that Benedict was with you," Captain Johnstone said. "We also heard that Benedict had some very important information for us. Some information that could not be delayed."

Part of her was surprised at the revelation, and the other part of her was not. Though the military had not yet pressed into all areas around Coronado, she had no doubts they were keeping as good of an eye as possible on developments.

"Yes, he has a lot to tell you," Arianna told the captain.

"I do. And you will want to pass it along as soon as you can," Benedict added.

"We will not delay you, Benedict. Two generals are here today to hear what you have to say," Captain Johnstone responded.

He turned to indicate a tall, rather thin man of about middle-age standing to his right. Longer of face, the man had piercing eyes set deep in his stern countenance.

"This is General Worthington, who commands the newly-designated Fifth Army that is engaged in liberating the city," Captian Johnston said.

Captain Johnstone then turned towards another middle-aged man to his left. "And this is General Arguello, who is also with the Fifth Army."

General Arguello's thick moustache and pockmarked skin gave him a rougher-edged appearance, but his dark eyes were not unfriendly.

Broader in frame than the other general, he stood a few inches shorter in height.

Arianna's eyes then drifted to the officer standing at the right side of General Arguello. It was all she could do to keep her face straight and show no reaction. The younger officer with short-cropped brown hair had a clean-shaven face, but there was no mistaking his identity.

Whether imagination or not, it seemed as if his eyes exhibited a peculiar blue glow to them for just a second. The corners of his lips turned up ever so slightly, hinting at a grin of familiarity. She had no doubt that the figure was the Avatar Calliel, in an unexpected disguise.

Inside, her heart leapt joyfully and she wanted to shout her elation at seeing Calliel once more. Of all the places she had thought about encountering him, the command tent was far removed from the list.

"It is good to meet you," Benedict said to the generals, nodding his head respectfully towards the men. "I think you will find my information very useful."

"Please proceed," Captain Johnstone invited.

Benedict then briefed the two generals and other officers on what he had discovered in the depths of the UCAS facility. Arianna could see the concern brewing in the eyes of the generals as they learned of the Nephilim and their ability to reproduce.

Of course, Benedict kept the discussion of the Nephilim solidly in the framework of biological experiments and weapons. He said not a single word regarding the supernatural element of their origin.

Added to Benedict's report was the incident with the halted weapons transfer. He described how the event involved the enemy's use of the Nephilim, both in the skies and on the ground.

"Your accounts align very closely with many we have received in recent weeks," General Worthington said in a grave tone when Benedict had finished. "We have also compiled some images of these creatures you speak of. They are being used deep within our territory, and there is little doubt it is at the behest of the enemy."

Relieved to hear the general's response, Arianna had feared that there might be some disbelief or resistance to her uncle's warning. To anyone unfamiliar with the creatures, the tale could seem fantastical.

As the discussion continued, interspersed with some questions, the generals also appeared to appreciate the information regarding the UCAS arming the gangs with advanced weapons. The two generals shared more than one look together as Benedict described the kinds of weaponry that had nearly come into the possession of the gang.

"A convoy is about to be sent east," Captain Johnstone stated, after Benedict completed his discussion with the generals. "The two of you, and all of your companions, will be taken along with it."

"Thank you," Arianna replied. "We really appreciate that."

"Giving you safe passage is the least we can do for you," Captain Johnstone replied. "This information will be very helpful going forward."

"I'm just glad you have it in your possession," Benedict said.

"I wish the both of you a safe return journey," Captain Johnstone said. "May Adonai protect you."

Once dismissed, Arianna and Benedict left the generals and other officers behind in the tent. The soldier who had initially brought them to Captain Johnstone led the two out to where the convoy was being assembled.

She could see at once that it was large and heavily armed, with several types of military vehicles included. No highway brigands would attempt to interfere with a convoy such as the one arrayed before her.

Benedict moved over to join Quinn, Maureen, and the An-Ki, but Arianna stopped as she caught a glimpse of someone very familiar stepping into view near the vehicles. At once, she strode across the open ground towards the Avatar in a military guise.

Walking up to Calliel, she said in a low, terse voice. "Where have you been? I've really needed you for a long time. Maybe a friend of mine wouldn't have died if you came."

Calliel looked back to her, and a glint of sadness shined within his eyes. "I am very sorry, Arianna. I wish I could be near to help at all times, but it is not that way for us. An Avatar must do what is commanded. I have been seeing to a task given to me by those I answer to. It is something that brings me to you and your uncle again, but it is something I could not stray from. No matter how much I wished to go to you."

"I've been looking out for you for a long while," Arianna replied, frowning. "It seemed like you just vanished."

"I know it has taken some time for our paths to come together again," Calliel stated. "But the hour grows late, and all of us are doing everything we can before the abyssal storm breaks upon us."

Arianna nodded quietly, staring at the Avatar. She knew in her heart that Calliel regretted being unable to come to her aid.

Though the loss of Kantel hurt terribly, the death of the An-Ki male was not Calliel's fault. In truth, it was nobody's fault, as Kantel had chosen freely to come along and assist Arianna on the search for her uncle.

About that time, Benedict wandered over to where the two were standing. "I thought I might join the both of you before we leave. Calliel, it is a big surprise seeing you here at this checkpoint. And in a uniform too!" He grinned towards the Avatar.

"I do what I must to complete the tasks given to me," Calliel replied, with a smile.

"Well, you do look the part," Benedict said. "First time I've seen you clean-shaven too!"

Calliel reached up and rubbed the smooth skin on his chin. "It was not by preference. I'd much rather have a beard."

Benedict and Arianna laughed at his response. Her uncle's expression then grew more serious.

"So do you think they'll take my report seriously?" he asked. "After all I've been through, I sure hope so."

Calliel nodded. "I'm sure they will. They've experienced the power of the Nephilim already. They know the creatures are no myth."

"But they are reproducing, Calliel, maybe in great numbers," Benedict said. "I never expected to find that happening."

"They are creatures of flesh," Calliel said. "But it is worrisome, as they grow very fast with a bloodline of Avatars in them."

"Seeing what happened when I was about to be handed over, they're using them in dedicated missions," Benedict said. "They were going to have me taken back by flying ones, and they wiped out all witnesses using another kind on the ground. Thankfully, my niece, her friends, and the An-Ki had other plans for me."

"In time, the Enemy will make their existence known to all," Calliel said. "It is my belief that the Enemy desires to restore the Nephilim to a place of prominence in order to mock the Great Throne."

"That doesn't surprise me at all," Arianna said.

"Then it will be soon, if I'm reading the tea leaves correctly," Benedict said.

"It will, as the hour grows late," Calliel said, looking somber.

"Well, they don't always get their way. They didn't get you," Arianna replied, glancing towards her uncle. "Me and the others made sure of that."

Benedict smiled at her defiant words. "I am most grateful for all of you. And speaking of the others, I think everyone's getting a little restless and ready to get on the road."

Before she could reply, Calliel stated, "Before we attend to the others, there is something that needs to be done first. Now, the both of you, come along with me." The Avatar took a step forward and gestured for them to follow. "I've got something very special to show you on one of these trucks."

The Avatar guided them to the rear of one of the truck and trailer units about to set forth, an HMVS suited for heavy transport. A long, rectangular ISO container rested on the flatbed.

"What do you suppose we have in here?" Calliel asked, grinning as he cast a glance towards the container. "I think you'll be surprised."

"Most everything is a surprise these days," Arianna joked, though she found herself interested in what Calliel had to show them.

Calliel helped Arianna and Benedict climb up onto the bed of the trailer. He unlocked the rear bay doors on the ISO container, swinging one open to allow them access to the interior.

Within the container was a familiar-looking contraption, containing a platform and upper frame comfortably sized for an adult man or woman. A couple of elongated, black cases rested to the side.

Arianna looked upon the equipment in a state of disbelief. It could not be anything other than what she thought it to be. Memories of her uncle's former apartment in Troy, and a momentous night in the midst of an open meadow, floated through her mind in clarity.

To her side, she heard hear uncle say with an air of sheer surprise,

"A gateway device? Right here? Another one exists?"

"It isn't the same as the device you used before," Calliel replied. "This one wasn't built under the guidance of the Abyss. It was fashioned under the guidance of two of my brothers, Nanael and Umabel. This gateway is more powerful than the one you used before."

Floored by the pronouncement, Arianna turned to look towards Calliel. Another device had been created, though this time it did not involve one that had to be confiscated from the enemy like the previous ones.

"What is this one going to be used for, exactly?" Benedict asked the Avatar. "I know it wasn't built for entertainment."

"It is not to be used for going back in time in this world, like the other device," Calliel replied. "This gateway is for going into other worlds."

Arianna and Benedict glanced to each other, and then looked towards the Avatar with looks of astonishment. She did not know what to say in response.

"I see that the idea intrigues you," Calliel replied, with a look of bemusement. "Yes, this is designed for humans. Only one with human free will can make use of this device. Of course, this means that human servants of Diabolos could potentially make use of it, so its nature and existence are kept top secret. But it is time."

"Who?" Arianna finally asked, after Calliel said nothing more.

"Two who already have experience," Calliel said, looking into her eyes.

The implications of the Avatar's words struck her. "Me? Uncle Benedict?" she asked, eyes widening.

Calliel nodded. "Yes, you and your uncle."

"What do you want us to do?" Benedict asked.

Arianna could hear the trepidation underlying his words. The other device had turned their worlds upside down and inside out, resulting in more than one instance of great peril. She could only begin to fathom what a device that was a portal into other entire worlds could lead to.

"I can explain in more detail during the ride back to Venorterra," Calliel said. "We will have a few hours to ourselves, if you would be so kind as to ride along with me."

"Might as well find out what we're in for," Benedict replied with a look of resignation.

Arianna nodded, though she felt an edge of frustration. So soon after finding and rescuing her uncle, they were going to be thrust into yet another task filled with uncertainty.

"The hour grows late. There is no time to spare," Calliel told her gently, in a low voice.

Arianna knew that the Avatar had either read her mind or understood her mood, but she could not disagree with Calliel. Events in the world were unfolding rapidly and spiraling towards some manner of ultimate conclusion. She had to keep moving forward on her path until that moment arrived.

"I understand," she finally replied, looking into the depths of the Avatar's blue eyes. "I'll do whatever needs to be done."

"As we all must do in this final hour," Calliel responded, exhibiting an air of sympathy.

ERISHKEGAL

Erishkegal peered into the rolling cloud masses, rippling with lightning. Far, far above, within realms of undying light, Enki, Inanna, and all of her immortal kind lived with the bounteous Grace of Adonai.

That glorious place seemed so very far away to Erishkegal. Her heart ached with loneliness and a myriad of other burdens, but she knew she had to keeping pressing onward.

Her realm was a hidden refuge, where so many creatures had been spared destruction. A deeper mystery had unfolded with the arrival of human souls, spirits scarred and inflicted with all manner of wounds as they washed up on the shores of Manzazu.

The rate of their arrival clearly had been slowing down, and Erishkegal wondered what that meant. She still had no definitive answers of how they had reached her realm to begin with, but she took them in nonetheless.

Hers was a mission of mercy, whether for the creatures that would have otherwise been destroyed in the Deluge, or human spirits brought in on the sorrowful tides crashing onto the shores of her realm. All were given safe harbor within her dominion.

A vast winged shape approached her august palace, Egalkurzagin, atop the great plateau. The sight of Kur brought a smile to her face. The massive dragon had been her dearest friend throughout the long ages, vigilant in warding the realm and seeing to anything she needed.

She never forgot for a moment that he shared half of his heritage with her. Now, she found herself pondering the fact that the other part of his heritage was shared with the spirits brought to her shores.

"Great Kur, it always brings light to my heart to see you," she addressed the dragon after it landed, a trace of weariness weighing in her voice.

"Erishkegal, my queen, and the queen of all who dwell within Manzazu, it is you who brings me light," Kur responded, gazing down upon her.

"I am but a steward, for Adonai Most High," Erishkegal responded.

Even after the long ages, she found it difficult to be hailed as a queen, but she accepted the honor from Kur and the other inhabitants. She knew it helped them to give special recognition to her, the lone being in all of Manzazu who had known the Heavenly Realms and beheld the Great Throne with her own eyes.

"What brings you to Egalkurzagin?" she asked. "I sense that something troubles you deeply."

"Something is happening in the darkness," Kur replied, with a somber air. "I do not know what it is, but the Galla have drawn back. We have not encountered even one of them during our latest flights."

The Galla, demonic entities from the Ten-Fold Kingdom, were a constant trouble. Traveling in large swarms, they had been one of the principle tasks of Kur and all the flying creatures under the black dragon's authority.

Probing for the whereabouts of anything not under the authority of the Risen Throne, the Galla were both scouts and insatiable killers on behalf of the Master they served. The fact that Kur and all the other winged guardians had not encountered even one of the dark spirits, when they were normally encountered in great throngs and multitudes, stood both anomalous and deeply worrying.

"I feel something within the darkness," Kur continued. "But your deeper knowledge might unveil what it is, if you were to come with me beyond the gates."

Erishkegal shifted form in response to Kur's words. No longer the tall, dark-haired woman of extraordinary beauty that she most often appeared, now she was a fiery, winged creature whose spirit blazed with great intensity. Her luminous blue eyes retained their color, though now they took on the properties of flame.

"I shall go with you," she told the dragon.

Side by side, Erishkegal flew out with Kur towards the seven gates comprising the entrance to Manzazu. The Nephilim giant Neti, guardian of the Seventh Gate, bowed low to her upon their arrival.

From the inside, the gate was a beautiful thing to look upon. Wide golden bands inlaid with sacred glyphs spanned both halves of the gate, placed at several points up the length of its impressive height. The surface itself was dazzling to behold, embedded with an abundance of sapphires, diamonds, and rubies.

She did not need to say a word to Neti. The giant kept his head bowed, his eyes fixed squarely towards the ground as the halves of the gate swung slowly inward.

Erishkegal and Kur passed through the ensuing six great portals in much the same manner, with each gate's guardian exhibiting the deepest respect towards the beloved queen of their realm. At last, she strode out before the final gate, the two halves closing until a solid, obsidian wall, with no trace of the gate itself, loomed behind her.

A number of Kur's fellow winged Anunnaki were arrayed on the rocky surface beyond, dragons and other creatures that could take to flight. They looked towards her expectantly, waiting for some indication of her desire.

"We must go to the barrier," Erishkegal said to Kur and the others.

Ascending, Erishkegal entered the thick gray layer above, which preceded another level filled with churning, flowing lights. Her vision strained as the powerful lights worked to distort her vision and sense of perception. Finally, she entered another dense mass of gray before emerging into sheer darkness.

Kur and the host of flying creatures burst through behind her. Many of the dragons and other winged entities continued forward, spreading out and taking up hovering positions all around the lightless space.

Kur remained near to Erishkegal and turned his extended visage towards her. "Reach into the dark."

Erishkegal cast her Avatar senses forth, searching and extending far from where her form remained suspended in the ebon gloom. Emptiness pervaded a vast expanse of darkness surrounding Manzazu. There was no sign or so much as a trace of a sentient being, not even a primitive creature like a wraith or beastly Galla.

It was as Kur had indicated. Nothing could be found, not a hint, anywhere she probed.

"They have withdrawn," she remarked to Kur, when she was finished with the exercise of her power. She then told the great dragon, "Hold, before we return."

Calling up as much energy as she could muster, she directed her consciousness even farther into the murk. Though she had long-suffered in the depths of the Abyss, protecting and shielding her hidden refuge, her strength had grown far beyond what it had been when she crossed the Veil, while the rains fell in torrents ages ago.

While faint at first, the feeling grew stronger as she honed her focus upon it. Within the darkness coiled a presence, on a scale far beyond her comprehension. She had the distinct sense of something drawing inward, gathering, hastening, and massing within the darkness.

Everything about it made her want to recoil, but she kept her intent steady and discipline stalwart. Whatever was transpiring throughout the darkness, its nature was rooted in the deepest corruption she had ever encountered.

Understanding came to her in that moment. The essence of

a disease far advanced, imperceptible to those it afflicted, permeated the darkness flowing towards the Nether Kingdom. While prideful arrogance prevented any recognition of the lethal malaise on the part of those who advanced it, Erishkegal saw the plague for what it was: Deception, the fruit of the tree of falsehood, manifesting at a level unprecedented.

The One who had fathered it, before time unveiled realms of creation, resided upon a Risen Throne built of the darkest blasphemies, harboring an unquenchable thirst for deicide. A promise inextricably woven into the massing power's fabric strained to be set free for the vilest of harvests. Destruction and desolation of every single thing born of Light loomed nigh, all of it to be perverted into a monstrous Remaking.

Erishkegal had never felt a greater sense of horror than she did when perceiving the malevolent power congregating within the Abyss. The great pit had no end to it. As such, the coalescing power drew upon an infinity of darkness for its sustenance and growth. Diabolos was gathering levels of power she had never thought possible.

A jolt of realization tore through her spirit like lightning. An agony indescribable, the loss of thousands of her kind, and thousands more kindred beings of the heavenly realms, reverberated throughout the core of her spirit.

She sensed that the reach of the Nether Kingdom had drawn very close to the Middle Lands. Diabolos had taken hold of something right on the cusp of the place Adonai had provided for souls not perfected enough to enter the White City.

So many Avatars she had known and longed to see again flashed within her mind. Every one of their images vivid, and every recollection individual, the Avatars were brothers and sisters of a family increasingly torn asunder. Though the Avatars were great in number, Erishkegal cherished each one of them at an intimate level, feeling the pain of every celestial being struck down in a hellish battle far above.

All of them were now consigned to the Void, that terrible place where the light of a living spirit was rendered into misty shadow, removed from all awareness and thought until time itself came to an end. The agony of so much loss and suffering among her brothers and sisters overwhelmed her spirit. Erishkegal loosed a soul-wrenching wail into the Abyss, a swelling cry pouring out a dirge of lamentation, causing Kur to draw farther back from her.

Erishkegal turned towards the greatest of the Anunnaki dwelling within her realm. "The Nether Kingdom gathers its strength. The last hour draws near, and a time of decision is upon us."

Fiery wings outstretched, she glided back into the dense gray of the first layer cloaking Manzazu. Passing into the starry field of lights, and taking no notice of its disorienting properties, she continued through. Flying into the second cloud-like mass, she broke out of the vaporous level a moment later over the arid stretch of ground leading up to the towering, obsidian wall.

When she alighted upon the ground, Erishkegal transformed back into her human-like appearance. Her face held an expression of deep sorrow, both cheeks tear-stained and glistening.

Kur and a great many other Anunnaki landed behind her, though a subdued hush draped over all of them as they eyed their beloved queen. Every one of them sensed the anguish within her, and all were heavy in heart.

Without a word, she stepped slowly towards the high wall. Despair probed for any opening to drive its edge deeper into her spirit. Though feeling drained and weak, she resisted giving in to the pressing feeling.

She knew there would be no time to dwell in her raw sorrows, not a moment to spare for recovery, no matter how much she wished to be by herself in the sanctum within her palace of Egalkurzagin. The Seven Wise Ones who comprised the Tribunal of the Anunnaki had to be summoned without delay.

There were fateful decisions that had to be made, and all available choices would be laden with terrible risks. Erishkegal knew the Abyss would no longer be a place where she could shelter, hide, and protect the ones she had suffered so much for.

Diabolos, the Claimant, was drawing upon all darkness for a great assault. Nothing outside the ramparts of the White City could hope to evade the reach of the Risen Throne any longer.

When the first great gate swung open to allow her through, the guardian assigned to it gazed upon her in dismay and surprise. It had never beheld her so forlorn and distressed.

Graced with a muscular, leonine body, and a majestic set of wings, the massive creature had a human face with all the emotive ability of that race. Its expression reflected the deep anxiety and grief it felt looking upon her in such a state of misery.

Green-specked, golden eyes, with pupils like those of a great cat continued taking in the sight of Manzazu's founder as she walked slowly by. Beholding the visage of sorrow on her face, tears soon fell from the guardian's eyes, wetting the long braids of its beard.

JOVAN

Jovan could not bear to look upon her still body. The fatigue and weakness from a lack of eating and sleep was nothing compared to the void he felt gaping inside. She had come to mean so much to him, and had been revealed to be someone far more incredible than he had ever imagined.

To have it all brought to an end with a brutal thrust from a spear was the height of tragedy. Kaira had become the culmination and embodiment of the Convergence.

Her initiatives and efforts were bringing a fraying world together in unity. She had shown the world the pathway for taking the final steps into a new, unprecedented age.

All of his dreams and hopes had been shattered, and he felt adrift in a sea of nothingness. Tears trickled down his face. Jovan was not one used to feeling such deep emotions. But the sense of loss he felt staring at her inert body on display for the public viewing was indescribable.

Though exhausted beyond measure, he could not find any meaningful sleep since the tragedy occurred, three days prior. Everything had been a blur since, and he had not even bothered to instruct Julianne in regards to ongoing tasks.

The looming funeral stood as something he did not want to think of. Inconsolable as he was, Jovan did not know how he would make it through such a terrible event.

He looked upon Kaira and the tears flowed faster. Lying upon her back, she looked as if she were just sleeping. The area where the spear point had driven through her forehead had been masked to perfection, sparing him a little torment.

The wound had been savage. The examination and autopsy following the murder had produced reports that could not hope to gloss over the horror of the violence inflicted upon Kaira. The entire back of her head had been shattered, and the iron spear had torn through the center of her brain, all the way to the front of her head. Though no consolation could be found for Jovan, he was relieved to hear that she had likely not suffered for even a moment once the weapon had been driven into her skull.

Jovan dropped his eyes to the floor, finding it too difficult to look upon her silent form. He wept uncontrollably, sobbing and not caring who saw his composure breaking down.

Gasps and cries of shock filled the atrium a few seconds later. Jovan did not want to look up, knowing that nothing good could have produced the reaction he heard rippling through the capacious room. Yet he knew he had to, if only to make sure that nobody attempted anything disrespectful to the body of the woman he served with all his soul.

The mistiness of his sore, reddened eyes added to the spark of disbelief as he stared towards the raised slate where Kaira's body lay. Her eyes were open, and her chest raised and lowered with breath as he looked on in stunned awe.

His world spun as Kaira raised herself up into a sitting position. She looked around at the line of people waiting to pay their respects, as if she were doing nothing more than waking from a deep slumber.

A smiled bloomed upon her face, sending an invigorating, lively warmth flooding into the void inside Jovan. Among the crowd there were several others whose expressions mirrored her own. Ethan Forneus, Nathan Focalor, Samel Malkira, and a few others gathered around the dais looked positively exuberant as Kaira swung her legs around and stood on her feet.

The atrium buzzed with excited and fearful voices, but a hush descended upon the audience as Kaira's gaze swept over them. Her eyes sparked with liveliness, and to Jovan's gaze it appeared as if she had a light glow surrounding her body.

He knew he was not dreaming, but he could not explain what he saw before him. Lilith, the Nephilim, and everything he had been exposed to at the highest levels of the Convergence had not prepared him for this astounding moment.

Kaira had been killed before his eyes, in a way that left no possibility of survival. Now, three days after an autopsy in the middle of a visitation period, she had risen back to life. The implications were beyond staggering.

"Why such sorrow?" Kaira asked, her voice carrying strong within the chamber. Her tone had a soothing quality to it. "There is no reason to mourn. This is a cause to celebrate. I have been restored to continue My work and usher in a new age for this suffering world."

She then looked towards a few members of the media who had been allowed privileged access to record images of the visitation. "Your cameras have witnessed for millions this day. Consider this a great gift, one that has been granted each of you. Surely you can show me your appreciation for this gift, and we can have a private moment for those who have come here in person this day?"

The camera operators and photographers all moved at once to cooperate with her request, but looks of bewilderment struck their faces as they turned their attention to their gear. Every one of them clearly found something amiss.

Standing near one of them, Jovan could see that the camera monitor was dark, as was the LED light indicating the device was powered. A puzzled expression on his face, the man quickly changed out the battery, only to find again there was still no power.

"Do not worry yourselves, for when you examine your cameras later you will discover that you have safely recorded what was intended," she said to the anxious-looking media employees.

Slowly, she stepped forward and made her way down the line of people who had come expecting a visitation like any other. She looked each person in the face, smiling, and reaching out to some, to grasp them for a moment on the arm or pat them on the shoulder. Some wept, overcome with emotion, while others stared wide-eyed, looking amazed and joyous.

She continued until she had personally interacted with all in the line and standing about the dais. The last she visited with were those such as Samel Malkira, the highest ranking in the Convergence.

When Jovan's turn arrived, his eyes blurred with tears of rapturous joy as she stood before him, alive once more.

"Take my hands in yours, Jovan," she directed him, in a gentle voice.

He took her hands in his, feeling the soft, warm touch of her skin. "I am no ghost, I am alive, and of flesh," she said, as he looked deep into her eyes.

He had always found her gaze mesmerizing enough, but now it was as if he became engulfed within the look she cast him. The passion he felt towards serving her ignited a fire inside him, resurrecting confidence in the Convergence and the arrival of the new age they worked towards.

"Be at my side, Jovan, for the start of a whole new world," Kaira told him, setting his hands back down at his side and turning towards Ethan Forneus.

When she concluded her visitations, she walked back towards the center of the dais. Turning, her eyes swept across the crowd once more. At last, she addressed the audience.

"My friends, who have worked so hard towards a blessed goal," she stated, her voice rising into a tone of authority. "From here we go forward with all strength. A new world beckons for us all. As death could not stop me, nothing will stop us in our given task.

"A Power beyond this world restored me, and guides us to our full potential. Accept the One who has given Me life, and know the godhead that dwells within each of you."

She turned towards a couple of men standing nearby. One was a priest of the Universalist church, and the other was a Pastor of a large Savioran congregation.

"Come forward," she invited the two men of the clergy.

The pair walked forward to stand together before her. She paused, and her eyes searched the room.

"Come forward," she said, looking deeper into the crowd.

A Davidian rabbi emerged a moment later and continued up to the top of the dais, where he joined the priest and pastor.

Once more, Kaira looked out into the throng of men and women. Her stare fixed upon someone in particular, as she invited, "Come forward".

Several people parted aside to allow a long-bearded man wearing a circular white cap through. Jovan recognized him immediately. He was one of the leading imam's in the Rashidan faith who lived in Yorvik.

The Imam moved up to join the Davidian rabbi, Universalist priest, and Savioran pastor. Kaira looked into the crowd a couple times more, and figures from other world faiths, including the Sindhu and The Triad Gem Path, were added to the group on the dais.

"Could I stand before you now, if I did not have the favor of One with authority over life and death?" she asked them, a warm smile on her face. "Search your hearts, and ask if I speak truth."

Not one of the prominent religious figures uttered a word in dispute. All looked dumbstruck, held in a state of wonder as they gazed back to her.

She looked to the Universalist priest. "All your life you have longed to feel and experience the power of the spiritual. You sank to your knees and prayed so fervently that tears ran down your cheeks the night before you became a priest, under the moonlight in the garden you frequented while in seminary."

The stunned look on the priest's face told Jovan the things described by Kaira had never been shared with anyone. She had pierced his most confidential level, in a way that shook his foundations.

She then turned toward the Davidian rabbi. "And in the silence of your heart, you have longed so deeply to hear the voice of the One with power over creation. This longing has been your companion, all throughout your years, never sated and always thirsting for relief."

One by one, Kaira revealed something intimate and secret

within each of the figures, until all of them beheld her with looks of astonishment. If that was the end of it, Jovan would have found the display beyond incredible, but she was not finished with them.

"Allow me to lay my hands upon you. I shall bestow each of you with the grace of Light, from the One who shows us the true way," Kaira addressed the figures.

All of the assembled clergy nodded their assent to her. With a radiant expression, she set her right palm upon the forehead of the Universalist priest. His eyes widened and his body trembled a moment later.

"Why wear that old, tired symbol, when the living Spirit flows inside of you this very moment? For you are the symbol now, alive and full of Light," Kaira said to the priest in a gentle voice.

Reaching up, he removed the symbol of the Rising Dawn, suspended from a golden chain about his neck. His eyes never leaving Kaira's face, he dropped chain and symbol to the floor, discarded like a piece of trash.

She continued through the others, laying her hands upon each one, producing similar reactions to that of the priest. One by one, each in their own way, they rejected their prior faiths and embraced the path She invited them to walk on.

"Your paths all come together here, where this day you will leave this place in unity, knowing the true way in your hearts and souls," she announced to all gathered in the chamber, when she had finished with the clergy.

Though no prompting of any kind had been given, a strange event occurred, one that reminded Jovan of the night time audience in the lawn before the woodland compound. One by one, the religious leaders dropped to their knees before her. The action spread outward from the dais, with more of the crowd getting down to their knees.

The gesture of obeisance felt natural to Jovan, even desired. He participated along with everyone else who had witnessed the miracle of a resurrection.

Throughout the chamber, within a handful of seconds, titans of business, politics, and the military fell to their knees before Kaira, One who Death itself could claim no dominion over.

THE ABYSS

Teeming legions of Dark Aishim, Fallen Avatars, and infernal creatures of all kinds had drawn up in orderly ranks. Square and rectangular formations arrayed as far as any eye could see heralded a host beyond measure.

The forces of the Nether Kingdom had assembled in the Grey Lands, a place conquered and now fully occupied. Radiant sigils indicating a gathering including many of the most powerful Avatars, of statures reaching all the way to the infernal court, were displayed over the various formations. To all eyes, the sigils shone a little more brightly over the lands wrested from their enemies.

Sigils of Diabolos reigned above all others. Tended by Caim, the great Herald of the Risen Throne, the regal glyphs beamed with a light pure and resplendent. The august servant of Diabolos marched forward behind a pair of titanic Fallen Avatars, passing through an open channel running through the midst of the gathered hosts.

A reverential silence lingered over the multitudes at the display of their Master's sigils. A large procession followed in the wake of the Sigils of Diabolos, featuring many of the greatest authorities of the Nether Kingdom.

Ares kept a pace in back of the one whose appointed hour had come. It was not yet time for the great assault that he deeply hungered for. That command would come soon enough, the way things were proceeding in the material plane.

The world had almost fallen under the full control of the Nether Kingdom. It would not be long before the Veil was pierced, and the Remaking could begin.

Ares had led the conquest and subjugation of the Grey Lands. Though fiercely waged and involving massive forces, that battle stood only a prelude for what was about to come.

Diabolos, the Light Giver, would deliver long-sought vengeance for all those who stood in battle at the Great Schism and fell into the abyssal depths. The Grigori and Erkorenen, made to suffer the terrible Deluge in the world of matter, would also find retribution.

THE UNDYING LIGHT

The august procession reached the forefront of the infernal hosts. Avatars of the highest authority parted to the left and right, taking up places along the facing of the hosts, while Caim and a small escort of Avatars continued forth bearing the Sigils of Diabolos.

Ares drew to a halt just beyond the end of the wide channel. Assembled nearby, the forces of his own realm had been given a place of high honor at the grand ceremony about to transpire.

He gazed at the Avatars taking up places along the front of the hosts. Within all of them, he sensed the ravenous desire to begin the final assault.

The deep hunger for revenge ached without respite in those such as Arioch, one of the nearest to Ares. Arioch's appearance phased between that of a fiery, multi-winged Avatar, and a fearsome, monstrous creature, bat-winged and lion-headed.

Nearby, Xaphan stood within a circle of towering flames, the latter coiling and lashing about. It was no secret to the great Fallen Avatars that Xaphan desired a second opportunity to unleash what had almost come to pass during the outbreak of rebellion in the Great Schism.

Coming over to the side of Diabolos, Xaphan had sought nothing less than to set fire to Adonai's realms. Cast down into the Abyss before the devouring flames could be loosed, Xaphan had focused all energies since upon mastering the fires of vengeance.

Now, the Avatar possessed abilities dwarfing those wielded in that distant age. The infernal maelstrom Xaphan could unleash was awesome to contemplate, especially for one such as Ares, dedicated to the arts of war.

Ares could tell the story of Avatar after Avatar that aligned in essence with the tales of Arioch and Xaphan. All held a similar dynamic in that each had grown far more powerful than they had been at the Great Schism.

A significant number of the more powerful Avatars had become generals in the aftermath of the fall into the Abyss, building legions of Dark Aishim to command in the looming assault. A number had also developed entities unique to their realms across the vast ages, many of the creations in tremendous numbers, all of which would be made use of in the final assault.

Yet Ares stood a general above generals when it came to the mastery of war and the hierarchy established by Diabolos. Ares carried the title Lord of War and his were the armies that would spearhead the attack bringing an end to the hated Enemy.

Ares' ranks were the most prominent of those displayed upon the enormous plain. Teeming legions of Ares' Dark Aishim and formations of other Avatars covered enormous tracts of ground.

In front of his Avatars were the shadowy, winged Makhai, each one of the thousands upon thousands of tall forms wreathed in churning darkness. The black lances of the elite warriors carried upright, the figures billowed with the shrouding dark cloaking their ghastly appearances.

Ares carried a special pride concerning the Makhai, one of the Lord of War's greatest achievements across the ages. The deadly creatures derived their origins from the wickedness given birth in every conflict upon the face of the material world.

Bloodshed, violence, and terror formed their very essence. With their source flowing stronger than ever from a darkening world, their numbers never ceased growing within Ares' realm.

The Makhai had been held back from the taking of the Grey Lands, for Ares had chosen to reserve them in the fullness of their strength for the final assault. Only then would they bare their true forms to the eyes of those they were set loose to destroy.

Sprouted from the teeth of Isemenios, the latest addition to Ares' army stood at the forefront of the infernal ranks, the pointed tip of a great sword. Towering humanoid forms, each possessed a broad pair of leathery wings.

The creatures all had desiccated, sunken skin, drawn tight onto their bodily frames, exposing their bones in a manner bestowing them with a skeletal appearance. Each of the Sons of Ares carried lengthy, double-ended lances, formed of white-hot flame.

Their eyes pits of darkness, cold and merciless, a purified nature reigned within the entities. They had been summoned into being solely to exact vengeance for the deaths of Ares' sons, Ismenios and Kyknos, in the waters sent by the Accursed One.

No grief resided within Ares at the thought of his slain sons. Only rage and a desire for revenge presided; both of which had been made incarnate through the teeth of Ismenios.

The Avatars Phobos and Deimos, the Lord of War's two great lieutenants, stood side by side at the front of the massed Sons of Ares. Each tremendous commanders in their own regard, the pair carried Ares' orders out with unwavering discipline.

Ares' pride swelled further gazing upon the hosts that were his to command. Not only were the legions and ranks of his realm counted in that number, but every last spirit gathered upon the plain. At the declaration of the Shining One, the power of the other generals had been subordinated to Ares for the final assault.

The vast muster on the plain did not represent the entirety of the force under Ares. Multitudes far beyond measure were not even present at the ceremony, but would be summoned forth when the hour of the great assault began. The sands of a sea in the material world could not boast greater numbers than those Ares would soon wield against the Enemy.

Accompanied by the Sigils of Diabolos, Caim and a prominent group of Avatars strode forward, approaching the edge of the Grey Lands. The others drawing to a halt, one among them continued onward, striding to the cusp of the boundary.

Abbadon stood alone before the sprawling darkness beyond. The High Avatar turned to face the herald and the assembled host as the ceremony began.

Caim's voice sounded, carrying far and wide to every last entity within the marshaled host. "The Light Giver, the Shining One, Our Lord and Master of the Ten-Fold Kingdom, grants authority to you, Abbadon, to invoke the Power long-prepared for the final hour. Summon your children from their vigil. There will be no threat from the Enemy during this manifest hour."

Abbadon nodded slowly, turning back toward the boundary with endless darkness gaping just a step further. The Avatar emitted a soaring cry, one building in volume and intensity until it reached a crescendo reverberating all across the gathered hosts.

A deep buzzing began rising from the darkness, swelling rapidly in resonance and magnitude. The Daimonakrida, in immense swarms uncountable, exploded into sight, spiraling upward from beyond the edge of the Grey Lands.

Abaddon's creatures departed their places guarding the border region, where they had clung to the rocky, cliff-like facings; surfaces once covered in webs and patrolled by the Enemy's multi-legged Aracha. Only gossamer wisps and ragged tatters remained of the once-gigantic network of silvery webbing. No longer did the Aracha prowl the nooks, crevices, and ledges, now teeming with Daimonakrida.

Though Ares was the Lord of War, he could not begrudge his admiration for the ingenuity of Abbadon. Loosed from Abbadon's realm, the Daimonakrida proved to be a deadly, unexpected weapon in the assault upon the Grey Lands.

As Ares had envisioned the attack, the Avatars and other creatures of the Enemy found themselves trapped between the jaws of the Nether Kingdom's forces. Once the Daimonakrida horde stormed into the battle, the Enemy's ranks started to crumble.

The Accursed One's forces in the Grey Lands had been destroyed to the last. Out of the great host, only a tiny rabble of Gryphons and humans souls escaped the doom that befell the Enemy's ranks.

"All is coming to pass, as our Lord and Master promised and foretold," Caim stated. "The Remaking draws near. The Enemy will be broken, torn asunder and laid low. Hungers will be sated, and a great inheritance will be given all who serve the Risen Throne."

The resplendent Sigils of Diabolos surged in intensity, casting forth a brilliant light that enveloped Abbadon. The luminance continued flowing steadily from the sigils into the Avatar's form.

Before the vision of all, Abbadon grew in stature and girth. Empowered directly by Diabolos, Abbadon transformed into a spirit rivaling any of the Ten Eminencies of the infernal court. Distinct from any Avatar that Ares had ever beheld in the Ten-Fold Kingdom, the mist-like darkness flowing over Abbadon's form mixed with dynamic streaks of light, resembling crackling rivulets of lightning.

"Call forth the Power!" Caim boomed. The brightness of the sigils ebbed to their original state, and the flow to Abbadon ceased.

Turning, Caim led the solemn procession accompanying the

sigils farther away from Abaddon. At the threshold of the Abyss, the exalted Avatar oriented toward the caliginous depths, gazing downward.

Abaddon's voice rang out, layers of growling thunder speaking the ancient language preceding time itself. Fiery arms spread wide, and six great wings outstretched, Abbadon summoned forth the Power of the Nether Kingdom.

Like fitting a key to a lock, the Fallen Avatar fulfilled the special task given him by Diabolos, opening gateways of power prepared for that precise moment. The power drew upon the infinite darkness of the Abyss, channeling its essence into something of such great might that it promised to shatter the Gates of the White City.

Ares sensed the change in energies at once, weaving through everything around him. The Lord of War marveled at the fundamental shift occurring, most especially the nature of the new influx of power. Something he could never have anticipated was transpiring, a boon of incalculable advantage for the coming assault.

Quietly, Abbadon remained in place, staring into the bottomless pit. Whatever had been unleashed through the invocation surged up from the black depths and took hold all around the vast host.

To the surprise of Ares and all others beholding the proceedings, an astounding phenomenon took place. The darkness beyond the edge of the Grey Lands began filling with a shimmering, spectral light, ascending from far regions well beyond the scope of vision. Though Ares had just begun to fathom the nature of the light, he knew the manifestation held many meanings.

For the enemies of the Nether Kingdom, it stood defiant and boasted the gravest threat, indicating that a decisive hour drew near. For those serving the Risen Throne, it promised fulfillment of long-sought desires, reaching far back in time and space to the moment of the Great Schism.

Merciless, ravenous, and pitiless, the essence of the light proved no mystery. Letting the cold light seep into his gaze, the Lord of War basked in its sepulchral touch, realizing the full nature of the abyssal luminance. Woven into everything Ares had mastered and pursued regarding war, what he now beheld was the Light of Death itself.

THE UNDYING LIGHT

The glimmering light began spreading across the skies of the Grey Lands, overtaking the rolling, thunderous cloud masses. Flowing over the great army and shining upon them, the light conveyed much more than a spectacular visual manifestation. Every single being found their spirit bolstered with increased strength, confidence, and a deepening hunger to destroy all things of the Enemy.

Empowered by the revelation of the light's nature, Ares had never felt a greater sense of resolve. The one shred of doubt that the Lord of War harbored over the long ages concerned the infinite nature of the Accursed One. Within the Light of Death, Diabolos revealed a match for the Enemy's nature.

Derived from the bottomless pit intended to be a place of confinement, desolation, and banishment, the Light of Death harnessed the power of endless darkness, an unlimited source. In direct fashion, Diabolos had found a way to wield the power of Death itself.

As every living thing upon the physical world was subject to that tremendous power, so would every spirit serving the Enemy come to be in the ethereal realms. Unlimited darkness and oblivion would be more than a match for the fragile essence of life reflected in every creature of the Enemy.

Murmuring grew swiftly into a deafening roar, as fervent praise for the Risen Throne broke out among the infernal ranks. From the greatest of Avatars to the lowliest wraith, euphoria of an incredible magnitude took hold of the Nether Kingdom's servants.

The Enemy's promises to the world would be broken asunder. A new order would take its place. The nature of the world, where Death held dominion over every living thing, merely hinted of the things to come in the Remaking.

A profound, irrefutable sign already existed. The Enemy had not truly broken the power of Death in the world of matter, where it continued to claim each and every man, woman, and animal that came into being.

Every last birth of a soul into a body was nothing more than the beginning of an irrevocable slide towards the maw of Death. It had been that way before the Liberator, and continued without blemish after the Liberator's appointed time upon the world.

No matter what had transpired with the Liberator, the fact remained that Death's inescapable hold upon all life continued unabated. The Enemy's promise of a new world of existence, one where there would no longer be any place for Death, would soon be shown to be an abysmal, utter lie; when Diabolos, enthroned in all glory and robed in the unassailable power of Death, seized authority over all creation.

FRIEDRICH

"They've seized the Grey Lands. What do you think they plan on doing now?" Friedrich asked Enki, with no small degree of anxiety.

He had finally located the Avatar close to the boundary of the Middle Lands. Ever since the fall of the Grey Lands, Avatars in great numbers could be found patrolling the border areas. Enki had been no exception, one of many Avatars of great stature engaged in warding the perimeter.

The Avatars were not alone in the endeavor. The Hunt roved along the jagged boundary, as did many other creatures of Adonai. Every effort was being made to shield the inhabitants of the Middle Lands from the threat that had demonstrated its power in overtaking the Grey Lands.

Behind Friedrich, Asa'an and several of his other close companions waited for Enki's response. Like everyone in the Middle Lands, they were all deeply unsettled at the notion that the massed power of Diabolos could draw so close to their borders. None could deny that an entire army loyal to Adonai had been overwhelmed and destroyed.

"The forces of the Adversary plan to wage war upon the Great Throne, as they always have done," Enki stated evenly, staring outward through eyes of fire. "Our enemies gather their strength in the Grey Lands."

"Why not dislodge them from the Grey Lands?" Heinrich asked. "Muster a great force. Take the Grey Lands back from them, and cast them out."

"I do not know the mind of Mikael," Enki replied. "But I have heard nothing yet of such a plan. We have been told to keep a watch on this boundary, and nothing more."

Friedrich perceived a trace of frustration within Enki's words. The Avatar continued quietly gazing westward, peering in the direction of the Grey Lands.

As he looked upon Enki, Friedrich could also sense deep unease within the Avatar. He wondered what troubled his friend.

"What disturbs you?" Friedrich asked, not sure he wanted to know.

"Something I do not like is taking place, not far from here," Enki answered. "It is something in the darkness itself, underneath and within it."

Friedrich peered toward the impenetrable black. Whether the influence of Enki, or some other sense within him, his spirit recoiled from the perception of something greatly amiss.

Nevertheless, his focus remained unwavering, fixed upon the darkness. A quality that had not been there until recently mesmerized him.

Vision remaining locked to the lightless murk, he found a feeling of dread taking hold and overcoming him. The debilitating sensation crept throughout Friedrich's spirit, working a malignant power upon his essence.

The darkness of the Abyss had changed in a fundamental sense. The gloom no longer matched the kind existing ever since his arrival in the Middle Lands. Something profound had happened to the darkness itself, its nature transformed into something unprecedented and foreboding.

Everyone around Friedrich grew silent, their attentions drawn toward the stark vision beyond the Middle Lands. As they watched, a most unexpected sight manifested in the west.

The Exiles stared in growing amazement and great alarm as the horizon filled with a ghostly light. Friedrich recognized the nature of the luminance at once. His spirit took on a deepening chill as he gazed into the abyssal phenomenon; light formed with an eternal essence, undying and everlasting.

The radiance filling his eyes held nothing in common with the Light emitting from within all the beings and things of Adonai's realms, the blessed luminance gracing eternal creatures with a soft, wondrous glow. What Friedrich saw before him was a terrible corruption. Debased and cold, the unholy light reflected the Will of the One who ceaselessly tainted what had once been glorious and without blemish.

Friedrich did not want to know what the powerful manifestation portended. Yet he knew the worst had to be faced. With considerable effort, he turned his gaze from the fell light and looked towards Enki.

"What is the meaning of that light?" he asked in a low voice, a tone filled with apprehension. He could feel the chagrin in the Avatar and, even more troubling, a little shock.

"The Ten-Fold Kingdom rises from the Abyss," Enki stated in a solemn manner. "It claims all darkness to itself. What you see before you is the Light of Death. I did not think such a thing possible. Nonetheless, it rises before us, summoned by the Adversary."

"Rises? Light of Death?" Friedrich asked, not liking the Avatar's severe tone at all. His mind a flurry of questions, he pressed, "How can the Nether Kingdom possibly rise? How can it manifest that light?"

"That light is the sign that Diabolos openly challenges the Great Throne to a final clash, here and upon the world you once knew as your own," Enki informed him. "The Regent of the Nether Kingdom has assumed full power in the material world. The forces prepared by Diabolos for the final assault in the spirit realms are ready. The last phase of a war that began before time is about to unfurl."

Friedrich did not know what to make of the Avatar's words. The loss of the Grey Lands lent considerable weight to the dire tidings, as did the spectral light rising out of the black depths to illuminate the entire western horizon of the Middle Lands.

There was no trace of warmth or beauty within the shimmering wall of light. The Light of Death possessed an icy, detached essence, one devoid of hope and offering no beacon or comfort.

There was no avoiding the truth. The message stood bold

and clear. The Undying Light of Adonai was about to be assailed, the approaching battle heralded with the everlasting, abyssal Light of Death unveiled by Diabolos.

No place existed within the essence of either luminance for the presence of the other. The coming clash promised to culminate a war lasting many ages.

The realization staggering in scope, it took all Friedrich's willpower to hold onto his mental bearings. He looked around at the faces of his friends. He saw their dismay and fear. Friedrich resolved that he would do everything asked of him, on behalf of all those he loved, and also on behalf of the good-hearted souls who were in the deadly path of the looming storm.

"A great task is asked of you in this hour, Precious Soul," Enki stated. The Avatar's words carried a conspicuous air of gravity that brought Friedrich's attention back around. "You have known a task was coming, for Metaraon spoke to you of this already."

Friedrich thought back to the words of Metaraon, who he had encountered while visiting his favorite, wintry region of the Middle Lands with Asa'an and Seele. While a group of child spirits played with Friedrich's companions, the High Avatar had spoken of a time of trial, a journey of worlds to be taken, and a darkness falling over the world Friedrich had once dwelled in. Metaraon had also informed him that he would face a tremendous evil.

"I remember," Friedrich said, nodding, his recollection as vivid as if it had just occurred. "Is the time here for this task?"

"Yes," Enki answered. "The hour has come."

"What is to be asked of me?" Friedrich queried, girding his resolve.

Metaraon had been far from specific regarding the task he would be called to do. Friedrich had wondered often about the enigmatic situation since the encounter and felt relief that he would finally have an answer. Yet under the circumstances, within sight of the Light of Death, it was hard to find any shred of comfort.

"You and another will be called to witness ... in a return to the world you once dwelled in," Enki responded.

"Return?" Friedrich replied, the words sinking into him. Shocked by the revelation, he found it far from anything he had speculated about. "To the physical world? The same one I lived in?"

A torrent of thoughts rushed through his mind. He had imagined his former world to be a thing of the past, forever. In some ways it was, as the world described by Silas, who had lived in the most current age of that world before passing to the Middle Lands, sounded far different than the one Friedrich had experienced. Were he to return to the physical world, he would find himself a foreigner on so many levels.

"Yes," Enki replied. "You will cross the Veil once more and stand in the world that you once dwelled in."

"Of all the Exiles in the Middle Lands, why was I chosen?" Friedrich asked, wrestling with a state of disbelief.

"You have proven yourself on behalf of Avatar and human souls alike," Enki said. "You did not hesitate to enter the Abyss to help me find Erishkegal, just as you did not hesitate to go to the aid of the souls threatened in the Grey Lands. Now, you are called to help Avatars and humans alike, once more, in a perilous hour. You are called to be a witness who denies the power of the Adversary before the entire world; a world held hostage.

"You will face a time of great suffering, but I know you have a heart that can endure and will not waver. A criminal with full guilt must be accused before a judgment. It will be you who accuses the greatest of law breakers, for the greatest of crimes.

"Darkness has become enthroned in the physical world, and this evil must be confronted for what it is. Your witness shall be a warning to those who have failed to see the truth of what is happening in that world."

"And human spirits are being sent for this task? Why not send Avatars, one like you, or Mikael?" Friedrich asked, incredulous that such a weighty matter like this would be entrusted to a mere human soul. Even more so, he found it astounding that at least one human soul to be sent to carry out the task would be an imperfect one like himself, a soul who could not yet pass through the Gates of the White City.

"Adonai has chosen humans for this task, for it is through humanity that the Adversary prevailed in bringing Death to your kind.

It is also through humanity that the Adversary suffered the greatest defeat, one that will resonate in the hour to come. I do not presume to know the mysteries of Adonai, but know that no better choice could have been made."

The words of the Avatar both humbled and daunted Friedrich. His mind swirled with all manner of thoughts and fears. He struggled to envision the mission being asked of him. One aspect about the entire situation vexed him deeply and he could not refrain from questioning Enki.

"Why is Diabolos so powerful? How is all of this even happening, or possible? In the physical world and here?" Friedrich asked, thinking of the dark power he had witnessed in the battle for the Grey Lands, collapsing and overcoming Adonai's servants. "How did Diabolos come into power over the whole world? How did the Grey Lands get taken? How can the Light of Death even persist within view of the Middle Lands?"

"You are speaking of the problem of evil itself," Enki replied. "And the power of evil, something asked by so many humans, in so many ways. It is a question that confounds the greatest of human minds, and even Avatars, but I will try to give you my understanding of it.

"Diabolos seeks to master all things that do not have a place in the Kingdom of Adonai. Of all things that have no place in the Heavenly Realms, the mightiest is Death.

"Diabolos draws upon the power of Death, for it is the greatest and most powerful evil to afflict living beings. It is upon Death that the Adversary built the Nether Kingdom. It is upon Death that Diabolos wields authority over all the governments of the physical world.

"Death is supreme of all evils. All other wickedness is subservient to the power of Death, even Diabolos, though the Adversary is shrouded in arrogance and cannot see this truth.

"Think of disease. It cannot fulfill its evil purpose without that mottled crown of Death. Think of war. Its power is nothing without the touch of Death present within the violence and destruction. Think of famine. Its sting is blunted without the slow agony of the dying. Think of Aging. Its lengthy withering of living beings relies upon that final, triumphant blow provided by Death. Death is paramount to all wickedness and strengthens everything that opposes life.

"Death was the greatest corruption to ever enter the physical world. It was set free when the harmony of creation was broken at the Great Schism. Adonai's Realms, built upon a foundation of life, were then opposed by Diabolos' Realms, built upon a foundation of death; as life itself is opposed by death.

"Ever since has the war of Life and Death raged. Know that Adonai did not seek death for humankind, but humankind became swayed by the seductions of the Adversary, allowing Death's power to come over them in the world of matter. Now, humankind has allowed for darkness enthroned. All the world in imperiled. Only when the power of Death is broken asunder can all be restored."

"Then why does not Adonai break the power of death now?" Friedrich asked, venturing another question that had long frustrated him.

"For everything there is a season, and the gift of Free Will has been given to all souls," Enki said. "Adonai restrains from uprooting all evil to allow souls Free Will to choose the path they wish. Humanity is being allowed to run its full course. But evil cannot be extricated until that happens.

"This is the opposite of Diabolos, who seeks to subjugate every last living being under the authority of the Nether Kingdom. Diabolos does not desire friends, but rather slaves, souls over which the Risen Throne claims all authority.

"This is why one of the names Diabolos is known by is the Claimant. This is why the Nether Kingdom is one where the willpower of weaker souls is devoured by stronger ones, in a malevolent continuum that cannot cease until Diabolos possesses the will of all.

"You can see this reflected in the nature of the physical world, where in violence and death one thing eats another, to be in turn consumed by something else, and on and on. Everything, from the living things too small for a human eye to see, to the greatest living things, consumes life.

"This infection brought into the world by Diabolos is in plain sight, though so few take notice of it. The beauty of nature is a reflection of the Heavenly Realms, but the brutal, pitiless struggle underlying all of it is a reflection of the Nether Kingdom.

"Humankind could have traveled a different path. It is the bitter truth that humankind has so often chosen to listen to the Adversary; in the beginning, and ever since."

The Avatar fell into silence, gazing upon Friedrich. He could sense an undercurrent of condemnation towards humanity within Enki's last words. While they could not be refuted, it remained that the lives and perspectives of Avatars were very different from those of humans.

"It is a hard path, Enki, even for those of us who seek Adonai's realms," Friedrich said, thinking of how difficult his life had been, both in his physical life and his non-physical one. Even though still imperfect, he felt a little defensive regarding the situation faced by souls like himself. "It is so hard to see things clearly, sometimes. I know I have erred in my ways, many times, and I make no excuses for those shortcomings. But it is no easy task to live in the material world.

"We were not born with the vision and understanding afforded the Avatars. We simply had to find our way through the dark valley of the mortal life, plagued by uncertainty, afflictions, misfortunes, and loss."

An unexpected phenomenon then occurred before Friedrich's eyes. The magnificent being standing before him began weeping tears of fire. The whitish tongues of flame fell from Enki's face in a gentle cascade, drifting down slowly to absorb into the surface of the Middle Lands.

"I know, Friedrich. And all Avatars know," Enki told him in a low voice, filled with a strong sense of compassion. "All too well."

Stunned at the rapid development, Friedrich asked, "Why do you weep like this?"

"My spirit aches for all who must take the dark road of the world, a passage through a chasm of shadow," Enki replied, the tear-flames continuing to fall from blazing eyes. "The pain, the sorrow, and the despair that you endure is not lost upon the Avatars. Nor is the injustice inflicted upon so very many of you in a cruel world oppressed by Diabolos.

"Know our burden. You lived but one mortal life, and witnessed the world around you during that time. The Avatars have been made to witness all generations of humankind. We have watched all manner of evil, suffering, and cruelties transpire, again and again.

"Did you think Israfel to be the only one who weeps tears of sorrow over the plight of humankind and lost souls? No, Friedrich, Israfel is not the only one. All Avatars who walk in the Light of Adonai feel this sorrow in the deepest part of their spirit. It is agony of a nature I cannot convey to you."

Friedrich thought of the great Avatar who made a lonely pilgrimage to the edge of the Abyss on a regular basis, peering into the bottomless pit and mourning the souls falling into its depths. He understood now that Enki was no different from Israfel. His Avatar friend endured the same kind of pain.

Friedrich's heart grew heavy at the sight of Enki's sorrow. Grief enveloping him, he could feel the waves of sadness flowing from the Avatar. Friedrich stood in silence, not knowing what to say. To his amazement, tears began falling from his own eyes.

Everything seemed to be going wrong at once, a tinge of despair touching his spirit. He felt that he was no closer to the White City than the day he had arrived.

"Do not despair," Enki said to Friedrich.

"How can I not? With all that is happening? And with all that has happened to so many people," Friedrich replied. "There is just so much pain. In you, in me, in spirits within these realms, in spirits incarnate within the physical world. The pain is everywhere."

"Pain can be washed away in an instant. Though the body vessel perishes in the world of matter, the spirit does not," Enki told him, following several moments of silence.

The fiery tears slowed, and then ceased. The form of the Avatar brightened, the flames comprising its being blazing with greater intensity.

Enki's voice took on a higher strength as he continued. "Take heart, Friedrich, in the trial yet to come. You walk a path calling you to witness before all the power of Death and darkness. Guide your path always by the Undying Light, the Eternal Light over which all the powers of Death and darkness cannot prevail."

Despite the entire horizon being saturated with the unholy light, the despair growing within Friedrich came to an abrupt halt. Cognizance of an unwavering truth defied the spectacular display on the part of the Adversary.

Friedrich found himself heartened. The Undying Light of Adonai dwelled within him, inseparable from everything he was and greater than any weapon that could be given to him.

Looking into Enki's face, Friedrich's voice emerged resolute as he told the Avatar, "Guide me to the place where I am needed."

APPENDIX

ABUNDANT HARVEST VIRUS - developed by Dr. Hadar Tricheur, the virus is known by this name among the people that understand and support its purpose, to effectively decrease the world's population. The virus is eventually named the Thanatos virus in the media and public, to reflect its worldwide manifestation and lethal effect.

ADONAI - the only being possessing the power of primary creation, the ability to call existence out of nothingness, Adonai transcends all time and space. Adonai's Presence has a manifestation on the Great Throne, which is within the heavenly realms, and is attended by the orders of Avatars and all manner of other spirits who have made it into the higher realms.

AISHIM - a special order of Avatars, the Aishim are spirits that were originally mortals, who have been graced with the gift of being an Avatar in the afterworld. Dark Aishim are their counterparts, wicked and malevolent souls that have gained special favor with Diabolos. Entire legions of warriors are formed on both sides out of the Aishim.

AMANZAKO- a Dark Avatar who carries a great amount of rage, making her very unstable, even if she is capable of bestowing great powers on those she favors. She inhabits a powerful realm in the Ten-Fold Kingdom founded by the Dark Avatar Susanoo, where beings such as the Kasha and Namahage dwell.

ANAT - Anat is a Dark Avatar who is one of the consorts of Set. Great in power, she has exacted brutal vengeance on many who have caused harm to figures of the Ten-Fold Kingdom

AN-KI - A shape - shifting race introduced in *The Exodus Gate*, where they take the forms of large, wolfish creatures, able to shift between a 4-legged form and a humanoid, 2-legged form. They were being hunted to extinction in the ancient world, at the time of the Great Flood, by the Nephilim. The Nephilim are referred to by the An-Ki as Night Hunters, due to the latter's tendency to strike unexpectedly out of the darkness.

ANUNNAKI JUDGES - There are seven Nephilim judges on the Tribunal established by Erishkegal in Manzazu, and they are tasked with making judgments on all matters taking place within the underworld realm. The Nephilim existing in Manzazu go by the name of Anunnaki.

ANZU - Lion-headed and eagle-bodied, the Anzu are a form of Nephilim that Friedrich encounters during his visit to Manzazu.

APEP - an exceedingly powerful Dark Avatar, who has few peers in the Ten-Fold Kingdom. Often interacts with Set, who periodically renders tribute to Apep in the form of imprisoned souls.

ARACHA - also called the Edge Dwellers, or the Sentinels, the Aracha are giant spider-like creatures that take a variety of forms, such as the huge Theraph or the rapid Saltic. They ward the boundaries of Purgatarion, and those that are capable of web-spinning have fashioned an enormous network that reaches far down into the bottomless pit.

ARES - A Dark Avatar of great power who draws strength from the very essence of war and violence. Ares realm serves as the outermost boundary of the Ten-Fold Kingdom in the Abyss. Ares realm features a wide array of beings and figures, from the Birds of Ares to the Makhai, all of whom ward the ramparts of Diabolos' infernal kingdom.

ASTARTE – Astarte is a Dark Avatar and consort of Set.

AVATARS - beings comprised of flame-like light, who vary in power and abilities and are grouped into a variety of orders. Once united, there are now two great factions of Avatars. Following the rebellion of Diabolos, a great number went into the Abyss and joined with Diabolos in the building of the Ten-Fold Kingdom. These are known as the Fallen Avatars.

AZAZEL - A powerful Fallen Avatar who was one of the leaders of the effort to take control of the world before the Great Flood. It was Azazel that guided a number of Fallen Avatars into the world, to take on physical forms, and to mate with humans. The offspring of such unions were the Nephilim. Azazel also had a major influence on the development of humans, teaching those that came under his influence the art of weapons and warfare. In the Abyss, he is attended by great numbers of a special kind of Fallen Avatar, called the Seirim.

BABYLON TECHNOLOGIES - A multi-national, hi-tech company with military and civilian divisions, whose headquarters is located in Troy, in the UCAS. The CEO of Babylon Technologies is Dagian Underwood.

CALIFIA PROVINCE - forms most of the west coast of the continental UCAS and is one of its largest provinces.

CALLIEL - an Avatar who becomes involved with Benedict and Arianna in the events of *The Exodus Gate*. He plays a pivotal role in the rescue of the An-Ki, and acts as a guide to both them and the small group of humans that aid them.

CERBERONS - huge, three-headed, dog-like beasts that are spawned from the union of the Fallen Avatars Typhon and Echidna.

CHIMAIRA - another race of offspring from Typhon and Echidna, they are two headed, with one head like that of a lion, and the other of a goat. Their hindquarters are reptilian, including a snake-like tail. They can breathe short jets of fire.

CITY OF ORACLES - has the status of a nation within the World Summit, though it is the seat of the Universalist Church.

CONFEDERATION OF FREE STATES - the new nation formed by the provinces that break away from the UCAS. It's first president is Thomas Locke.

THE CONVERGENCE - a term describing the effort to usher in a new global order, one that will bring about a world-spanning law and economic system. While many groups labor to bring about the Convergence, their visions of it range from purely material perspectives to deeply occult ones. The roots of the Convergence goes back thousands of years, and the process has been meticulously guided by Diabolos and other powerful entities from the Abyss. The manipulation of wars and economies, the creation of crisis, and the response to crisis have been major components of each new step along the road to the achievement of The Convergence.

CORONADO CITY - located at the western edge of the free provinces, Coronado City is a dangerous zone during the events of The Undying Light. The forces of the free provinces have not yet taken control of it, nor has it fallen back to the UCAS government. A powerful street gang with a large number of well-armed fighters has asserted itself in the power vaccum

THE CRAFT - the mystic, occult arts aligned with the will of Diabolos. Only a special few who have pledged their entire beings and souls to Diabolos are given access and revelation pertaining to the Ten-Fold Kingdom, and are able to wield spiritual powers derived from the Abyss. Dagian Underwood is one of the most powerful of those who practice the Craft, but with the granting of such power comes the tether of responsibility, and accountability.

THE CRYSTAL FORESTS OF PURGATARION - immaculate and breathtaking, the Crystal Forests of Purgatarion are where the Exiles can obtain the material they need to fashion hand-wielded weapons that draw off of their own spirit to empower them. As a spirit in Exile cannot draw forth a weapon from their own essence, like the Avatars do when they pull forth fiery blades or spears from their own forms, the Crystal Forests are vital for those Exiles that choose to help defend Purgatarion.

DAIMONAKRIDA - deadly, six-legged creatures that manifest in great swarms. They come from the realm of Abbadon and are unleashed in the events of *The Undying Light.*

DEIMOS - One of two fearsome Dark Avatars who are like lieutenants to Ares, and dwell in his realm.

DEVERS ARMORED FIGHTING VEHICLES - main infantry fighting vehicle of the UCAS military, eventually becoming a part of the military of the Confederation of Free States as well.

DIABOLOS - also referred to as the Shining One, the Light Giver, the Morning Star, and other names, Diabolos is the lord of the Ten-

Fold Kingdom, the greatest power within the Abyss. Diabolos has grown in might ever since leading the first rebellion that began the Great War, and always hungers to be equivalent to Adonai, the only being in existence greater than Diabolos.

DJINN - gargantuan elemental beings that manifest most often as maelstroms of fire. They ward the Void, and take no active part in the Great War. They respond to any disturbance in the Void, such as spirit beings crossing to and from the material planes.

EGALKURZAGIN - This is a great palace complex located within and atop a towering plateau in Manzazu. It contains the Sanctum, which is where Erishkegal can most often be found in her underworld realm.

EMQU - A serpent-headed Anunnaki, one of the seven judges on the Anunnaki Tribunal.

ENYO - One of the several powerful Dark Avatars that dwell in Ares Realm. Enyo is extremely powerful, and is accompanied often by a very fearsome, monstrous demonic entity called Kydoimos.

ETHON - giant eagle-like creatures that are the spawn of Typhon and Echidna. Used both for attack, and to ferry the flightless hellspawn to and from the depths of the Abyss.

EXECUTIVE ORDER 2013 - This is given by UCAS president William Walker, to impose martial law across the country.

FUSION CENTERS - Locations housing personnel and technology for multiple security and surveillance organizations that are part of the UCAS government. They are located all across the country, and they share databases and resources.

GAIA CITY - vast, underground city not far from the Sky Mountains that has been constructed for the elite who are part of the Convergence. There are other such underground facilities throughout the UCAS.

GERYON - brawny and towering in height, the Geryon are offspring of Typhon and Echidna that serve to drive the Orthun into battle, acting like pack-masters. Set upon two thick legs, multiple torsos sprout upward on each Geryon, each torso fitted with powerful arms and a head. The Geryon carry obsidian shields and spear - like weapons that act similar to the crystal weapons carried by the denizens of Purgatarion, in that they draw their force from the spirit of the wielder.

GODRAL - the principle lieutenant to Sargor, Godral is a powerful An-Ki warrior, who is dedicated to his leader and mentor. Godral's Life Mate is Mariassa, and the An-Ki warriors that he is closest to are Kantel and Valia.

GODWINTON - This is the town where Ian, Sheriff Howard, and many others live. It becomes quite a focal point in the *Rising Dawn Saga* for the resistance.

THE GREAT WAR (ALSO KNOWN AT THE FIRST WAR) - This is the war being fought by Diabolos against Adonai, hearkening back to the initial rebellion when a host of Avatars sided with Diabolos.

THE GREY LANDS - A dreary part of the Middle Lands that has broken off, and contains Exiles who are tilting closer and closer to abandoning a path to the White City. It is still warded by Adonai's guardians, but is increasingly infiltrated by the things of the Abyss.

GRYPHONS - creatures of legend in the material world, Gryphons populate the Purgatarion, where they help to protect the Exiles. With the head of eagles, and the bodies of lions, they are swift and powerful.

GUIDED ONES - a term used by those of the Craft to refer to a human who is now a vessel for a Fallen Avatar that is in complete possession of them.

GULAGAR - not unlike a living Gargoyle, these creatures are as still as stone wherever they position themselves throughout Purgatarion, mostly keeping to lofty overlooks. Whenever a creature of the Abyss draws near, they come into full consciousness and motion. Tall, winged, and daunting in appearance, they are one of the strongest guardians for the Exiles.

HERAB-SERAP - A very powerful Avatar, one of the Ten who attend Diabolos at the Risen Throne.

THE HUNT - presided over by the Avatar Arawn, and a penitent, but powerful, human spirit named Mallt, the Hunt consists of a horde of massive hounds that track and pursue anything from the Abyss foolish enough to linger for very long within the boundaries of Purgatarion.

INITIATES OF THE FAITH - humans who have willfully committed themselves to Diabolos. They are very involved in the Convergence, and hold or have been placed in many key positions of authority or responsibility. From special units of soldiers, to officers, to administrators and executives, the Initiates of the Faith see to the things that must be done to clear obstacles and advance the Convergence. Unlike many who work for the Convergence, they understand the true source of the effort.

ISMENIOS - One of the offspring of Ares, whose physical teeth are used to give rise to a new, powerful group of beings, the Sons of Ares.

JEQONADIN - One of the Nephilim, Jeqonadin is the son of the Fallen Avatar Jeqon. Of the Nephilim that share its form, Jeqonadin is the mightiest, and is a relentless hunter of the An-Ki.

KASHA - the Kasha have a cat-like appearance and they navigate the infernal realm they dwell in by means of fiery platforms that fly at great speeds. They are part of the process with the Namahage in the transformation of souls condemned to that realm. The Kasha bring souls to the molten pools for transformation, and then take them away when finished.

KIYOHIMI - with the body of a huge serpent and a beautiful woman's face, Kiyohimi serves as a guardian within the realm of Susanoo, where she directly serves Amanzako. She is as dangerous as her face is comely.

KYDOIMOS - A huge demonic being that dwells in the realm of Areas, and often accompanies the Dark Avatar Enyo.

KYKNOS - One of the offspring of Ares who died when the Great Flood was loosed on the world to destroy the Nephilim. Kyknos always desired to build a temple made out of human skulls, and Ares raised a ghastly temple of skulls in his realm to honor the wish by his son.

LADON - the Ladon are titanic, wingless, dragon - like creatures with as many as a hundred heads. Mainly confined to the Ten-Fold Kingdom, they have not been used in war upon the Middle Lands prior to the events of *The Storm Guardians*.

LA CUCHILLA - a deadly, dangerous street gang that has a strong presence in a multitude of cities all across the UCAS, including the provinces that break away in rebellion. Known for their brutality, one of the objects they are identified with is the machete.

LAFAYETTE TANKS - main battle tank of the UCAS military, eventually becoming the main battle tank of the Confederatio of Free States as well

LIFE MATE - the An-Ki are monogamous creatures that mate for life. The Life Mate is the special male or female that an An-Ki forms a deep bond with. Only with a Life Mate does an An-Ki engage in Life Unions, which take place during one special time of each year, and results in new life. The bonds and commitments of Life Mates , and the connection of those elements to the generation of new life, resonate at very sacred levels with the An-Ki.

LILITH - A Dark Avatar who is one of the Consorts of Sammael. Lilith provides guidance to Jovan Avery, and helps with the progress of the Convergence in the modern age.

LIVING ID - Living ID is a nanoscale implant that is part of a comprehensive personal identity system that was developed by Babylon Technologies to help in the final stages of the Convergence. It ties everything together, from financial transactions, to health care, to personal identity, and with full implementation, no individual can function in society without it.

MADISON- A town in the province of Venorterra larger than

Godwinton, where Seth and others live.

MAKHAI - A formidable group of demonic entities that are in service to Ares in his realm. The Makhai are warriors, and are at the forefront of Ares' best legions.

MANZAZU - the name of Erishkegal's underworld realm.

MIKAEL - the great general of Adonai, Mikael led the legions that hurled Diabolos and his legions out of the heavenly realms following the outbreak of the Great War. It was Mikael that announced the coming of the Deluge to the Fallen Avatars that had become incarnate to give rise to the Nephilim.

MKZS - world-renowned battle rifles designed in Muscovy. They are revered for their dependability and ability to manufacture more easily.

NAMAHAGE - huge, ogre-like creatures that inhabit the infernal realm where Dagian seeks out Amanzako. They tend to the molten pools in that realm, taking condemned souls and transforming them into something more formidable for the war against Adonai.

NAMTAR - Namtar is Erishkegal's vizier, who dwells in Egalkurzagin when not needed at the Anunnaki Tribunal.

NEMEANS - massive lion-like spawn of Typhon and Echidna, these creatures from the Abyss are capable of great speed and punishing attacks, and are often deployed in large numbers.

NEPHILIM - also referred to as the Erkorenen, the Night Hunters, or the Annunaki, they are the offspring of Fallen Avatars and humans, who came into existence during the age prior to the Great Flood. They have a variety of sizes, shapes, and forms, as the blood of the Fallen Avatars expressed itself in the generation of all manner of monstrosities that serve as the basis for most all of the mythical and legendary creatures, in all cultures across the world.

NETI - Neti is the giant Anunnaki that wards the seventh and final gate into Manzazu. Neti is the most formidable and wisest of the gate guardians, and is the final authority on allowing access into Manzazu.

NINGISHZIDA - Ningishzida holds the one of the highest levels of martial authority in Manzazu, and commands its defense and issues of security.

NUMMUS - This is the monetary unit that is planned to replace the UCAS dollar and other currencies, and will serve as a true global currency, though it will not exist in a physical fashion.

THE ORDER – A dedicated order of men that have existed since the Holy Wars, several hundred years ago. They are still called Knights, honoring that legacy, and are involved in active resistance against the forces behind the Convergence.

ORDER OF CHIKARA - an ancient, monastic order fonded in the far east of the world, dediated to the service of the Shining One, Diabolos. Steeped in mystic arts, the monks of this order are capable of great supernatural powers and are one of the strongest groups comprising the Convergence.

ORCAS - elite unit of the UCAS navy, considered to be the best special forces personnel in the entire military.

ORDER OF THE TEMPLE - a centuries-old secret society that is one of several that have come together to advance the Convergence. Members of the Order of the Temple have their own system, signs, and practices, but they have come to work closely with other orders sharing the common cause of bringing about a new global order.

ORIMILI - nation in Aphrike that has been hit especially hard by the Thanatos Virus. It is visited by Kaira in the events of The Undying Light.

PARZILLU - The name of one of the Anunnaki judges of the Anunnaki Tribunal. Parzillu has a fierce leonine countenance.

PEACE COMMISSION (OF THE WORLD SUMMIT) - A very powerful part of the World Summit tasked with facilitating peace among and within nations.

PERIS - a fairy - like race of spirits, who once sided with Diabolos, but have come to reject their ways and seek to gain Adonai's kingdom. They live among the Exiles in the Middle Lands, where they must face their greatest enemies, the bestial Deevs, from time to time. Asa'an, a Peri encountered in *The Exodus Gate*, has a friendship with the Exile Friedrich, and helped him to witness the rare appearance of Quilin within the Middle Lands.

PHOBOS - like Deimos, a Dark Avatar who is a lieutenant to Ares, who dwells in his realm.

PYLONS - Among the Walkers of the Setian Path, focused groups have formed behind the leadership of powerful priests. These groups, called Pylons, tend to explore or focus upon certain specific aspects of the non-physical, and are named according to their special area of emphasis.

PURGATARION - also called the Middle Lands, Purgatarion is where spirits that are not yet pure enough to enter the heavenly realms, but are not wicked enough to fall into the Abyss, take refuge. A variety of guardians have been placed in the Middle Lands to help protect the Exiles, such as Wyverns, Gryphons, the Aracha, the Hunt, the Gulagar, and many more.

QUERAN - the An-Ki leader of one of the three clans that exist after the schism of Sargor's original group that came through the gate. She is supported by a great warrior named Gorthaur.

QILIN - fearsomely powerful creatures of the heavenly realms that diligently protect the pure of spirit. They are encountered in *the Exodus Gate*, accompanying a group of child-spirits being guided by the High Avatar Metaraon

THE REMAKING - The Remaking is the goal of Diabolos, in which all of creation would be reshaped according to the Shining One's will, following the overthrow of Adonai.

REMIEL - One of Adonai's greatest Avatars, one of seven who personally attend the Great Throne.

THE RISEN THRONE - the seat of Diabolos at the 10th level, it represents the genesis of the Ten-Fold Kingdom following the fall from the heavenly realms.

SAMMAEL - one of the greatest of the Fallen Avatars, Sammael has three consorts, Lilith, Namaah, and Agrat Bat Mahlat. Sammael came into the world to subdue it, and prepare the way for the ascension of Diabolos in the time before the Great Flood.

SARGOR - aging leader of the largest faction of An-Ki following the schism in the forest. Sargor is the father of Sarangar, and is supported steadfastly in his leadership by Godral.

SEIRIM - goat-like, demonic creatures that serve the Fallen High Avatar Azazel. They walk upon two legs and have a humanoid body, with a goat's head.

SET - A High Avatar in service to Diabolos. His realm features extraordinary deserts, pyramids, and obelisks, and a special order of priests, the Priests of Set, have been established to administer Set's realm within the Ten Fold Kingdom.

SHIELD MAIDENS OF THE RISING DAWN - Another long-lasting order that has existed for centuries, the Shield Maidens are women who actively fight against the groups involved with the Convergence. Their activities span all spheres, from physical combat, to politics, and economic activity.

SILVER VALLEY - a city of neon, glitter, and entertaintment, Silver Valley is located in the west of the UCAS. Military installations are nearby, and underneath is a tunnel-city formed by the desperate, homeless, and others enduring the economic trials in the UCAS provinces.

SPHINGON - another kind of offspring from Typhon and Echidna, these winged creatures have lion-like bodies with the heads of stunningly beautiful human women, only their jaws are lined with an arsenal of long, spiky teeth.

SOCIETY OF THE RED SHIELD - one of the age - old secret societies that are working towards the attainment of The Convergence. Jovan Avery is a member of this Society, and after reaching its highest level has been introduced to spiritual entities that have given him greatly useful advice and guidance.

SUSANOO - a powerful Fallen Avatar in whose realm Amanzako dwells. Like Amanako, Susanoo harbors a powerful rage that is unpredictable for those who encounter him.

SUSTAINABLE HEALTH AND PROSPERITY INITIATIVE - a comprehensive initiative by the UCAS government that was underway at the time when the southern and midwestern provinces seceded. It is accelerated in the remaining UCAS provinces, bringing tighter control and regulation over individuals and business under the guise of safeguards and sustainability.

THE TEN EMINENCIES - also referred to sometimes as the Grand Council of the 10th Hell, these are Fallen Avatars of great authority, each one empowered by Diabolos over one of the 10 Hells that comprise the Ten-Fold Kingdom.

THE TEN-FOLD KINGDOM - the great Vortex, the realm of Diabolos which is ordered into ten general levels, represented by the Ten Eminencies that attend to Diabolos around the Risen Throne. Each of the ten levels are a Hell each and of themselves, containing innumerable environments and lesser realms.

THANATOS VIRUS - The public/media-given name for the Abundant Harvest Virus that ravages the world unexpectedly.

TROY - the third largest city in the UCAS, where Babylon Technologies is headquartered. Troy is also where Benedict Darwin hosted Sea to Shining Sea, and is also the location of St. Bosco, the Universalist church where Father Brunner and Father Rader are.

URIA - leader of the third faction of An-Ki following the schism of the original clan that came through the gate. Uria's clan is the smallest of the three, and contains no elderly or young, but has some of the most physical, dangerous warriors of the surviving An-Ki.

VERIN - a Fallen Avatar who regrets siding with Diabolos and finds himself an outcast, as it is believe that no Fallen Avatar can ever gain redemption in the heavenly realms. Verin comes to the aid of Skylar on her quest, becoming the most unlikely ally.

THE VOID - the Void is the inner space between the material planes and the non-physical realms. It contains the unconscious spirits that have fallen in conflicts and battles across the ages, and is guarded by the great Djinn, gargantuan elemental beings that manifest most often as maelstroms of fire.

WALKERS OF THE SETIAN PATH - A mystical order dedicated to Set. Set has given power and patronage to this order, revealing hidden arts to those he deems worthy. They are organized into groups called Pylons.

WATCHERS - two groups of Watchers are portrayed in the *Rising Dawn Saga*. The first were servants of Adonai originally, who were assigned to monitor the world. They were seduced into joining with the Fallen Avatars that took on physical bodies and mated with humans to produce the Nephilim. A new order of Watchers was raised up following the great deluge, huge, multi-winged beings, with many eyes, long, extended bodies with four legs, out of which rises a humanoid torso with arms. They are of four general types; echoing the forms of bulls, eagles, lions, and humans.

THE WHITE CITY - a resplendent, pure city with towering ramparts and a great, golden gate that serves as the eastern boundary of Purgatarion. Beyond it are the infinite realms of Adonai, and only a pure soul can approach and pass through the gate. For Exiles, the brightness of it is too dazzling to even gaze upon.

THE WHITE PYRAMID - located in the UCAS capital, the White Pyramid houses the Minstry of Defense.

WORLD SUMMIT - The World Summit is a member - based world body that the advocates of the Convergence would like to evolve into a true world governing authority.

WYVERNS - two-legged, dragon-like creatures, the Wyverns are another race of guardians provided by Adonai to protect the souls dwelling in Purgatarion.

ZEYYA - A female An-Ki who is close to Uria. She harbors a deep hatred of humans and the things of their world.

ABOUT THE AUTHOR

Stephen Zimmer is an award-winning author and filmmaker whose works include cross-genre Rising Dawn Saga, the epic fantasy Fires in Eden series, the Hellscapes short stories, the steampunk Harvey and Solomon Tales, and the sword and sorcery Rayden Valkyrie stories.

Stephen resides in Lexington and can be found at:
www.stephenzimmer.com

You can also follow him on Facebook at:
www.facebook.com/stephenzimmer7

or twitter @sgzimmer

Photography by: Terry Bentley

Transcend Reality!

Check out the following pages
to see more from

All Seventh Star Press titles available in
print and an array of specially priced eBook
formats.

Visit www.seventhstarpress.com for further
information

Connect with Seventh Star Press at
www.seventhstarpress.com
seventhstarpress.blogspot.com
www.facebook.com/seventhstarpress
www.twitter.com/7thstarpress

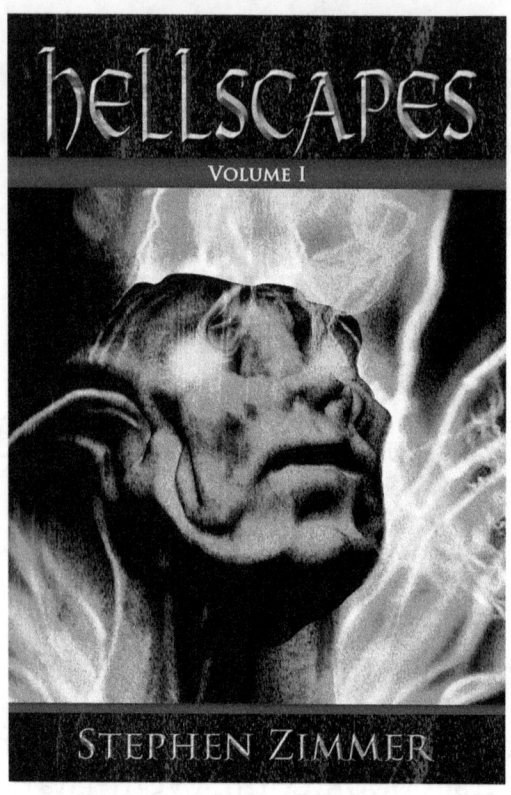

Grand Epic Fantasy from Stephen Zimmer!
Explore the world of Ave in the Fires in Eden Series from
Stephen Zimmer! Epic Fantasy for those who enjoy authors
like George R.R. Martin and Steven Erikson!

Softcover ISBN: 9780982565612

eBook ISBN: 9780982565698

Softcover ISBN: 9780983108627   Softcover ISBN 9781937929855

eBook ISBN: 9780983108610   eBook ISBN 9781937929862

New single author author collections of short
stories from Seventh Star Press!

Now Available!

Have many action-driven fantasy adventures in
the world of Ave in Stephen Zimmer's
Chronicles of Ave, Volume 1.

Softcover: 978-1-937929-30-5
eBook: 978-1-937929-31-2

Devil's Daughter from S.H. Roddey!
Available now as an eBook single!

eBook ISBN: 978-1-941706-07-7

"The Devil is a busy man."

Lydia St. Clair was seventeen when she made her first deal with The Devil. Now twenty-one years old and a professional bounty hunter, Lydia possesses a unique set of skills that make her valuable to Lucifer's grand plans. In the four years since that fateful night she has come full-circle, and now her nemesis has come back to collect on that debt.

Unfortunately for Lydia, He has leverage that will leave her questioning her own humanity.

Begin the Adventures of Blue Shaefer in *Haunting Blue* from R.J. Sullivan!

Softcover ISBN: 978-1-941706-05-3
eBook ISBN: 978-1-941706-06-0

"She's discovered the town's biggest secret ... now there's hell to pay!"

Punk, blue-haired "Blue" Shaefer, is at odds with her workaholic single mother. Raised as a city girl in a suburb of Indianapolis, Blue must abandon the life she knows when her unfeeling mother moves them to a dreadful small town. Blue befriends the only student willing to talk to her: computer nerd "Chip" Farren.

Chip knows the connection between the rickety pirate boat ride at the local amusement park and the missing money from an infamous bank heist the townspeople still talk about. When Blue helps him recover the treasure, they awaken a vengeful ghost who'll stop at nothing--not even murder--to prevent them from exposing the truth behind his evil deeds.

Haunting Blue is Book One of the Adventures of Blue Shaefer

Now available!   A Seventh Star Press Anthology
from editor Michael West!

eBook ISBN: 978-1-937929-69-5
Softcover ISBN: 978-1-937929-60-2

Vampires Don't Sparkle! poses the question: What would
you do if you had unlimited power and eternal life?

Would you...go back to high school? Attend the same classes
year after year, going through the pomp and circumstance
of one graduation after another, until you found the perfect
date to take to prom? Would you...spend your days moping
and brooding, finding your only joy in a game of baseball
on a stormy day? Or would you...do something else?

The authors of this collection have a few ideas; some fanciful,
some humorous, and some as dark as an endless night.

Join us, and discover what it truly means to be "vampyre."

Appalachian Gothic! Jason Sizemore's Irredeemable!
18 Tales of dark fantasy, science fiction, and horror

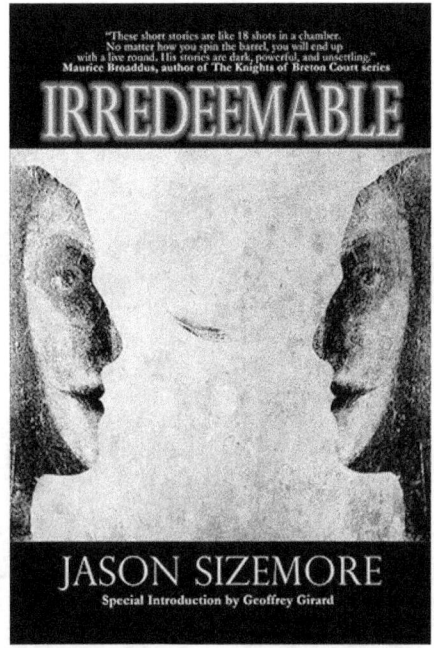

Softcover: 978-1-937929-59-6
eBook: 978-1-937929-68-8

Flowing like mists and shadows through the Appalachian Mountains come 18 tales from the mind of Jason Sizemore. Weaving together elements of southern gothic, science fiction, fantasy, horror, the supernatural, and much more, this diverse collection of short stories brings you an array of characters who must face accountability, responsibility, and, more ominously, retribution.

Whether it is Jack Taylor readying for a macabre, terrifying night in "The Sleeping Quartet," the Wayne brothers and mischief gone badly awry in "Pranks," the title character in "The Dead and Metty Crawford," or the church congregation and their welcoming of a special visitor in "Yellow Warblers," Irredeemable introduces you to a range of ordinary people who come face to face with extraordinary situations.

Whether the undead, aliens, ghosts, or killers of the yakuza, dangers of all kinds lurk within the darkness for those who dare tread upon its ground. Hop aboard and settle in, Irredeemable will take you on an unforgettable ride along a dark speculative fiction road.

Dystoptian Anthology *Perfect Flaw* Now Available!

Softcover ISBN: 978-1-937929-11-4

eBook ISBN: 978-1-937929-13-8

Readers everywhere are invited to experience adventures of a dystopian nature in the anthology Perfect Flaw, from editor Robin Blankenship! Featuring seventeen speculative fiction tales, spanning many genres, Perfect Flaw explores the subject of societies gone wrong. From "utopian" societies masking an underlying controlled state, to stories of people fighting back against repression, in hopes of a better world, the flaws that create a dystopian atmosphere are brought to light. Thought-provoking and entertaining, Perfect Flaw will be a welcome addition to any reader's collection of dystopian literature.

Now Available from Seventh Star Press, the horror stylings of
Michael West
Featuring illustrations and cover art by the award-winning
Matthew Perry!

Trade Paperback ISBN: 9780983740209
eBook ISBN: 9780983740216

Trade Paperback ISBN: 9781937929718
eBook ISBN: 9781937929725

Trade Paperback ISBN: 9781937929954
eBook ISBN:9781937929831

Trade Paperback ISBN: 978-1-937929-18-3
eBook ISBN: 978-1-937929-19-0

A paranormal thrill ride from Eric Garrison! *Four 'Til Late* is Book One of the Road Ghosts Trilogy!

Softcover: 978-1-937929-22-0
eBook: 978-1-937929-23-7

In Four 'Til Late, amateur ghost hunter Brett and his friends Gonzo, Jimbo, and Liz are on a road trip with dangerous detours, dreadful dreams and dire warnings. But that won't keep them from reaching their goal: New Orleans. Along the way they discover that some spirits leave you with more than a hangover and regrets. Can they get there in one piece, or will they be stopped and rest in peace? The bags are packed, the engine's running. Turn up the radio and get moving because the road ghosts are waiting, and it's Four 'Til Late.

Devils in the Darkness, an anthology
from editors Alexander S. Brown and Louise Myers

Softcover: 978-1-937929-54-1
eBook: 978-1-937929-64-0

From the fiery abyss of the underworld comes 20 hellish tales from
the south and southwest. Within these charred pages are stories that
will introduce you to the many demons that stay hidden but are always
nearby...

20 authors provide stories of possessed people, objects, houses,
highways, and the devil's favorite playground - the forest.

Dare to meet Deidless, a demon who is a buyer of souls. Discover
what kind of demons men can summon. Read of battles between good
and evil. Learn of ancient artifacts and stones that crave sacrifice. Finally,
become acquainted with legions of evil.

Again, we invite you, sit back, dim the lights, and prepare yourself
to meet the devils in the darkness.

Southern Haunts: Devils in the Darkness is the next in the exciting
anthology series that began with *Southern Haunts: Spirits That Walk
Among Us.*

Olde School, a new take on the world of fairy tales and folklore from Selah Janel!

Softcover: 978-1-937929-65-7
eBook: 978-1-937929-67-1

Kingdom City has moved into the modern era. Run by a lord mayor and city council (though still under the influence of the High King of The Land), it proudly embraces a blend of progress and tradition. Trolls, ogres, and other Folk walk the streets with humans, but are more likely to be entrepreneurs than cause trouble. Princesses still want to be rescued, but they now frequent online dating services to encourage lords, royals, and politicians to win their favor. The old stories are around, but everyone knows they're just fodder for the next movie franchise. Everyone knows there's no such thing as magic. It's all old superstition and harmless tradition.

Bookish, timid, and more likely to carry a laptop than a weapon, Paddlelump Stonemonger is quickly coming to wish he'd never put a toll bridge over Crescent Ravine. While his success has brought him lots of gold, it's also brought him unwanted attention from the Lord Mayor. Adding to his frustration, Padd's oldest friends give him a hard time when his new maid seems inept at best and conniving at worst. When a shepherd warns Paddlelump of strange noises coming from Thadd Forest, he doesn't think much of it. Unfortunately for him, the history of his land goes back further than anyone can imagine. Before long he'll realize that he should have paid attention to the old tales and carried a club.

Darkness threatens to overwhelm not only Paddlelump, but the entire realm. With a little luck, a strange bird, a feisty waitress, and some sturdy friends, maybe, just maybe, Padd will survive to eat another meal at Trip Trap's diner. It's enough to make the troll want to crawl under his bridge, if he can manage to keep it out of the clutches of greedy politicians.

16 Tales of the Paranormal and Ghostly from editors Alexander S. Brown and J.L. Mulvihill!

Softcover ISBN: 978-1-937929-12-1
eBook ISBN: 978-1-937929-14-5

From the shadowed realms of the paranormal comes 16 chilling tales that dwell in the South and South West. From 16 authors, learn of haunted homes, buildings, landmarks and roads where restless entities from beyond the grave desire acknowledgement amongst the living. Become acquainted with the aftermath of an eclipse that awakens the dead in a Memphis cemetery, see what horrors dwell in the woods at Hell's Gate, learn the dark secrets of Sidney's Cotton, and dare to travel down Ghost Road. These and many other tales are sure to keep you awake as you are introduced to what makes the South and South West so unique.... History and GHOSTS!!!!! So, sit back, dim the lights and prepare yourself to face the spirits that walk among us.

From Bram Stoker Award-winning Editor Michael Knost!

Softcover ISBN:
978-1-937929-61-9
eBook ISBN:
978-1-937929-62-6

Writers Workshop of Science Fiction and Fantasy is a collection of essays and interviews by and with many of the movers-and-shakers in the industry. Each contributor covers the specific element of craft he or she excels in. Expect to find varying perspectives and viewpoints, which is why you many find differing opinions on any particular subject.

This is, after all, a collection of advice from professional storytellers. And no two writers have made it to the stage via the same journey-each has made his or her own path to success. And that's one of the strengths of this book. The reader is afforded the luxury of discovering various approaches and then is allowed to choose what works best for him or her.

Featuring essays and interviews with:
Neil Gaiman, Orson Scott Card, Ursula K. Le Guin, Alan Dean Foster, James Gunn, Tim Powers, Harry Turtledove, Larry Niven, Joe Haldeman, Kevin J. Anderson, Elizabeth Bear, Jay Lake, Nancy Kress, George Zebrowski, Pamela Sargent, Mike Resnick, Ellen Datlow, James Patrick Kelly, Jo Fletcher, Stanley Schmidt, Gordon Van Gelder, Lou Anders, Peter Crowther, Ann VanderMeer, Joh Joseph Adams, Nick Mamatas, Lucy A. Snyder, Alethea Kontis, Nisi Shawl, Jude-Marie Green, Nayad A. Monroe, G. Cameron Fuller, Jackie Gamber, Amanda DeBord, Max Miller, Jason Sizemore.

Urban Fantasy from John F. Allen!
Meet Ivory Blaque!

Softcover: 978-1-937929-16-9
eBook: 978-1-937929-17-6

In The God Killers, the first book of The God Killers Legacy, former professional art thief Ivory Blaque is hired to procure a pair of antique pistols and gets much more than she bargained for when several attempts are made on her life.

Her client turns out to be a shadowy government agent who reveals that she is descended from a race of immortals, and that the pistols are linked to her unique heritage and the special psychic gifts she possesses. He uses the memory of her father to guilt her into working for him.

Ivory eventually gives in to his request, and in return, he presents her with her father's journal, which was written in an unbreakable code. Bishop believes that she is the only one capable of breaking the code and unlocking the plans of the vampire hierarchy. But when the city's top vampire is a sexy incubus with an attraction for her and she's assigned a hot new lycan enforcer to protect her, she finds herself caught between two sets of rock hard abs.

To regain her autonomy, clear her name, unlock the secrets of her past, and protect the lives of those closest to her, Ivory must play along with the forces trying to manipulate her. Ivory's life is rapidly spiraling out of control and headed for an explosive conclusion which she just might not survive.